PENGUIN CLASSICS

NORTH AND SOUTH

ELIZABETH CLEGHORN GASKELL was born in London in 1810, but spent her formative years in Cheshire, Stratford-upon-Avon and the north of England. In 1832 she married the Reverend William Gaskell who became well-known as the minister of the Unitarian Chapel in Manchester's Cross Street. For sixteen years she bore children, worked amongst the poor, travelled and, latterly, began to write. In 1848, *Mary Barton* made her instantly a celebrity. In 1850 Dickens secured her to write for his magazine, *Household Words*, and she contributed fiction for the next thirteen years, notably another industrial novel, *North and South* (1855). In 1850 she met Charlotte Brontë, who became a life-long friend. After Charlotte's death she was chosen by Patrick Brontë to write *The Life of Charlotte Brontë* (1857), a controversial work. Her position as a clergyman's wife and as a successful writer gave her a wide circle of friends both from the professional world of Manchester and from the larger literary world. There is nothing of the amateur about Elizabeth Gaskell. Her output was substantial and wholly professional. As Dickens discovered when he tried to impose his views on her as editor of *Household Words*, she was not to be bullied even by a man as imperious as he was. Her later works, *Sylvia's Lovers* (1863), *Cousin Phillis* (1864) and *Wives and Daughters* (1866), show her still developing in new directions. Elizabeth Gaskell died suddenly in November 1865.

PATRICIA INGHAM is Fellow in English at St Anne's College, Oxford, and Times Lecturer in English Language. She has written extensively on the Victorian novel and on Hardy in particular. Her most recent publications include *Dickens, Women and Language* (1992) and *The Language of Class and Gender: Transformation in the Victorian Novel*. Patricia Ingham is also General Editor of the new Penguin Classics editions of all Thomas Hardy's novels and some of his short stories.

ELIZABETH GASKELL

NORTH AND SOUTH

EDITED WITH AN INTRODUCTION
BY PATRICIA INGHAM

PENGUIN BOOKS

PENGUIN BOOKS

Published by the Penguin Group
Penguin Books Ltd, 80 Strand, London WC2R ORL, England
Penguin Putnam Inc., 375 Hudson Street, New York, New York 10014, USA
Penguin Books Australia Ltd, 250 Camberwell Road, Camberwell, Victoria 3124, Australia
Penguin Books Canada Ltd, 10 Alcorn Avenue, Toronto, Ontario, Canada M4V 3B2
Penguin Books India (P) Ltd, 11 Community Centre, Panchsheel Park, New Delhi – 110 017, India
Penguin Books (NZ) Ltd, Cnr Rosedale and Airborne Roads, Albany, Auckland, New Zealand
Penguin Books (South Africa) (Pty) Ltd, 24 Sturdee Avenue, Rosebank 2196, South Africa

Penguin Books Ltd, Registered Offices: 80 Strand, London WC2R ORL, England

www.penguin.com

First published serialized in *Household Words* 1854–1855
First published in two volumes 1855
This edition published 1995
Reprinted with a new Chronology 2003

14

Introduction and notes copyright © Patricia Ingham, 1995
Chronology copyright © Laura Kranzler 2000
All rights reserved

The moral right of the editor has been asserted

Set in 9.5/11.5 Monophoto Baskerville by Datix International Ltd, Bungay, Suffolk
Printed in England by Clays Ltd, St Ives plc

CONTENTS

BIBLIOGRAPHICAL NOTE

The following is a list of abbreviated titles used in this edition:

Letters: *The Letters of Mrs Gaskell*, ed. J.A.V. Chapple and Arthur Pollard, Manchester University Press, 1966.

Biography: Jenny Uglow, *Elizabeth Gaskell: A Habit of Stories*, London, Faber and Faber, 1993.

CH: *Elizabeth Gaskell: The Critical Heritage*, ed. Angus Easson, London, Routledge, 1991.

CHRONOLOGY

1810   *29 September*: Elizabeth Cleghorn Stevenson born to William
        and Elizabeth Stevenson in Chelsea

1811   *October*: Mother, Elizabeth Stevenson, dies; Elizabeth moves
        to Knutsford, Cheshire, to live with her mother's sister
        Hannah Lumb

1814   William Stevenson marries Catherine Thomson

1821–6 Elizabeth attends Byerley sisters' boarding school (school
        near Warwick, but moves to Avonbank, Stratford-upon-
        Avon in 1824)

1822   Brother, John Stevenson (b. 1799), joins Merchant Navy

1828   John Stevenson disappears on a voyage to India; no defini-
        tive information about his fate

1829   *March*: William Stevenson dies
        Elizabeth stays with uncle in Park Lane, London and visits
        relations, the Turners, at Newcastle upon Tyne

1831   Visits Edinburgh with Ann Turner; has bust sculpted by
        David Dunbar, and her miniature painted by stepmother's
        brother, William John Thomson; visits Ann Turner's sister
        and brother-in-law, Unitarian minister John Robberds, in
        Manchester, where she meets Revd William Gaskell
        (1805–84)

1832   *30 August*: Elizabeth and William marry at St John's Parish
        Church, Knutsford; they honeymoon in North Wales, and
        move to 14 Dover Street, Manchester

1833   *10 July*: Gives birth to stillborn daughter

1834   *12 September*: Gives birth to Marianne

1835   Starts *My Diary* for Marianne

1837   *January*: 'Sketches Among the Poor', No. I, written with
        William, in *Blackwood's Magazine*
        7 February: Gives birth to Margaret Emily (Meta)
        1 May: Hannah Lumb dies

1840   'Clopton Hall' in William Howitt's *Visits to Remarkable Places*

1841   *July*: Gaskells visit Heidelberg

1842   *7 October*: Gives birth to Florence Elizabeth
        Family moves to 121 Upper Rumford Road, Manchester

1844   *23 October*: Gives birth to William

1845   *10 August*: William (son) dies of scarlet fever at Porthmadog, Wales, during family holiday

1846   *3 September*: Gives birth to Julia Bradford

1848   *October*: *Mary Barton* published anonymously; Elizabeth is paid £100 for the copyright by Chapman and Hall

1849   *April–May*: Visits London, meets Charles Dickens and Thomas Carlyle
        June–August: Visits the Lake District, meets William Wordsworth

1850   *June*: Family moves to 42 (later 84) Plymouth Grove, Manchester
        19 August: Meets Charlotte Brontë in Windermere

1851   *June*: 'Disappearances' in *Household Words*; visited by Charlotte Brontë
        July: Visits London and the Great Exhibition
        October: Visits Knutsford
        December–May 1853: *Cranford* in nine instalments in *Household Words*

1852   *December*: 'The Old Nurse's Story' in the Extra Christmas Number of *Household Words*

1853   *January*: *Ruth* published
        April: Charlotte Brontë visits Manchester
        May: Visits Paris
        June: *Cranford* published
        September: Visits Charlotte Brontë at Haworth
        December: 'The Squire's Story' in the Extra Christmas Number of *Household Words*

1854   *January*: Visits Paris with Marianne, meets Madame Mohl
        September–January 1855: *North and South* in *Household Words*

1855   *February–March*: Visits Madame Mohl in Paris with Meta
        June: Asked to write a biography of Charlotte Brontë by Patrick Brontë; *North and South* published

September: *Lizzie Leigh and Other Tales* published

1856 *1 January*: Signs petition to amend the law on married women's property

May: Visits Brussels to conduct research on biography of Brontë

December: 'The Poor Clare' in *Household Words*

1857 *February–May*: Visits Rome, where she meets Charles Norton

March: *The Life of Charlotte Brontë* published, the first book to carry Elizabeth Gaskell's name on the title-page; it was soon followed by a heavily altered third edition.

1858 *January*: 'The Doom of the Griffiths' in *Harper's New Monthly Magazine*

September–December: Visits Heidelberg with Meta and Florence, and visits the Mohls in Paris

1859 *March*: *Round the Sofa and Other Tales* published

Summer: Visits Scotland

October: 'Lois the Witch' in *All the Year Round*

November: Visits Whitby, which provides the setting for *Sylvia's Lovers*

December: 'The Crooked Branch' published in the Extra Christmas Number of *All the Year Round*, as 'The Ghost in the Garden Room'

1860 *February*: 'Curious, if True' in *Cornhill Magazine*

May: *Right at Last and Other Tales* published

July–August: Visits Heidelberg

1861 *January*: 'The Grey Woman' in *All the Year Round*

1862 Visits Paris, Brittany and Normandy to conduct research for articles on French life

1863 *February*: *Sylvia's Lovers* published; Elizabeth is paid £1,000 by Smith, Elder

March–August: Visits France and Italy

1864 *Cousin Phillis* published

August: Visits Switzerland

August–January 1866: *Wives and Daughters* in *Cornhill Magazine*

1865 *March–April*: Visits Paris

CHRONOLOGY

June: Buys The Lawns, Holybourne, Hampshire, as a surprise for William

October: Visits Dieppe; *The Grey Woman and Other Tales* published

12 November: Dies at Holybourne

16 November: Buried at Brook Street Chapel, Knutsford

Cousin Phillis, and Other Tales published

1866 *February: Wives and Daughters: An Every-day Story* published (Elizabeth died without quite completing it)

Laura Kranzler

New readers are advised that this Introduction
makes the details of the plot explicit.

Elizabeth Gaskell's own working title for her novel, first published in Dickens's *Household Words* between September 1854 and January 1855, was 'Margaret Hale'. Under pressure from him it was changed to *North and South*, though it is uncertain who devised the name. As Dickens wrote on 26 July:

North South appears to me to be a better name than Margaret Hale. It implies more, and is expressive of the opposite people brought face to face by the story (*Letters* 7, p.378).[1]

As this comment shows, titles, like headlines, are directives as to how to read what follows: the new version suggests an interpretation in which Margaret Hale's story is secondary to a broader theme of class conflict. Though the usual assumption is that it was not Gaskell herself who thought of the title, it does accurately capture the meaning of the events as she narrates them. On the surface and with the title 'Margaret' or 'Margaret Hale' it is construable as her story – a romantic tale in which, to quote the contemporary *Guardian* reviewer, 'Margaret Hale by her womanly influence is able to calm hatred and real sorrows' (*CH*, 348). This safely categorizes the narrative as belonging to a genre in which class hostility is displaced on to divided lovers whose reconciliation is offered as a figure for class harmony. An example of the type is Charlotte Brontë's *Shirley* (1849), where Robert Moore's harsh treatment of his workers is paralleled by his rejection of Caroline Helstone who, though he loves her, is too poor to be useful to his business prospects. His change of heart and marriage to her coincides with a more paternalistic attitude to his workers and a better, though still autocratic, treatment of them. Happy marriage translates into industrial peace. What the title *North and South* underlines in Gaskell's novel is that in this text the conflict is intractable, not an idea found in Dickens's *Hard Times*. The conflict is not subordinated, as in *Shirley*, but is the central statement about society made by the narrative. And the making of this statement involves a subversive rewriting of the typical middle-class heroine.

'The North' in mid-Victorian fiction is not merely a place but a figure for capitalistic values for which Manchester was often the symbol. These ideas cluster around the perceived virtues of entrepreneurial skill and unremitting self-interest. The latter was famously celebrated as socially and morally valuable in *Self-Help* by Samuel Smiles (1859). He noted approvingly that through its pursuit 'Rising above the heads of the mass there were always to be found a series of individuals distinguished beyond others who commanded the public homage' (chapter 1). The division on to which this society is structured is visible here: the masses as opposed to the successful, whose very success is a demonstration of their superior gifts. Industrial novels were read as necessarily supporting one side or the other. And Gaskell's first condition-of-England narrative, *Mary Barton* (1848), had been thought by some to do 'very great injustice to the employers' (*CH*, 107). She was assumed to have taken the *other* side, to have contested the justice of Smiles's view, and misunderstood and oversympathized with the plight of the workers. She had evidently failed to see that they suffered emiseration in the necessary cause of their masters' profit. 'The South' on the other hand was, in industrial novels, another country: not only physically distant but unrelated. It was merely the natural location of the educated and comfortable middle class. Its exclusion from such texts was a denial of the fact that middle-class status and comfort depended on keeping the social status quo intact and on perpetuating the working class on which commercial success was based.

One attempt had already been made by Charlotte Brontë in *Shirley* to reconsider the relationship between North and South. It flounders into confusion as she first tries to equate the North with Yorkshire working-class virtue and then gives way to the more conventional view of unrelated communities. Gaskell went further than this and alarmed some contemporaries, including a reviewer in *The Leader* in 1855:

as relates to anything special to either the North or the South, or to those two districts in contrast, it is . . . not to mince matters, a failure. We affirm that the Hales, father, mother, and daughter, the Lennoxes; Mr Bell and all that here represents the South, represent simply the well-bred, *unmercantile* middle-classes of England and not any class peculiar to any district or county. While on the other hand, the Thorntons, the Higginses and others, as well as the incidents laid in Milton, are no fair picture of the cotton realms of which Manchester is the metropolis [my emphasis].

(*CH*, 333)

This attempts to blur the discussion of how the 'unmercantile middle-classes'' situation relates to northern industrial misery and to reinscribe industrial society in positive terms as the potent figure of Empire.

What is innovative in *North and South* and presumably the source of this reviewer's discomfort is that in it Gaskell takes a heroine from the 'unmercantile' South – educated, refined, with a taste for virtue, beauty (and comfort) – thrusts her into the ugliness and conflict of the North, and allows her to go native. Usually, as Keating points out, the representative of the South is the middle-class narrator (and an inscribed collusive reader) 'who undertakes a dangerous voyage of discovery into an uncharted working-class world from which he eventually returns with a "fully documented report" of his adventures'.[2] Usually the return is accompanied by some token of improved conditions for the working class implying that all is, will be, or can be well. *North and South* proceeds differently. Margaret Hale, originally the symbol of the South in all its detachment and superiority, is transformed by her life in Milton into a different person both as an individual and as a woman. Her very presence when she returns to the southern luxury of her aunt's house in Harley Street is a denial of middle-class values and the idea of inevitable class separation. She embodies the unbreakable link between southern prosperity and northern misery. She is now both South and North.

Her exile in the North is brought about by her father's defection from the Church of England on conscientious grounds, which causes him to find work in Milton-Northern/Manchester as a private tutor. Margaret's distaste for every aspect of Milton (landscape, manners, smoke, dirt, clothes and wallpaper) reveals values formed in the house of her Aunt Shaw in Harley Street and in the lush countryside of her father's Devonshire living. In the eyes of the local mill-owner, Thornton, she epitomizes the perfect middle-class woman to whom a successful, self-made man like himself can now aspire. Marriage to such a wife would move him into the class which is the natural reward for commercial success. It would take him out of his own apotheosis of working-class domesticity, for his household is 'handsome, ponderous with no sign of feminine habitation'. It has drawing-room furniture (as Margaret snobbishly perceives) 'bagged up with as much care as if the house was to be overwhelmed with lava', 'great alabaster groups ... under their glass shades' and 'smartly-bound' but unread books arranged 'like gaily-coloured spokes of a wheel' (p.112). His own mother's household concerns are cleanliness and ostentation. She is prepared to expend 'care and labour' but not 'to procure ease, to help on habits of tranquil home employment; solely to ornament, and then to preserve ornament from dirt or destruction' (p.112).

By contrast, Margaret produces out of the Hales' poverty pleasing chintz, ornaments of 'trailing ivy', 'pale green birch' and 'copper-coloured beechleaves'. Their drawing-room contains books 'hastily put down' and not cared for 'on account of their binding solely'. Thornton rapturously decodes this elegance and comfort, as 'habitual to the family; and especially of a piece with Margaret'. Angel and domestic heaven are equated as she serves tea:

She looked as if she was ... solely busy with the tea-cups, among which her round ivory hands moved with pretty, noiseless daintiness.

He even reads Margaret in this role as offering a glimpse of her sexuality and its delights:

She had a bracelet on one taper arm, which would fall down over her round wrist ... It seemed as if it fascinated him to see her push it up impatiently, until it tightened her soft flesh; and then to mark the loosening – the fall. (p.80).

But while Thornton is falling for what he perceives to be an icon of middle-class womanhood, he misreads the signs. The comfort and tranquillity of the Hales' drawing-room is a sham. It offers Margaret no support but instead makes inordinate emotional and practical demands on her. Her father does give up a comfortable living because of unexplained 'doubts'. But otherwise he is shown from the start to be (in a conventional sense) 'feminine'. Even his appearance betrays this, especially his face, in which eyelids that are 'large and arched' give to his eyes 'a peculiar languid beauty which was almost feminine' (p.81). Having made his one extreme decision, he cannot carry through its consequences. He is afraid to tell his wife and delegates the task to his daughter in a way that makes it more difficult for both women. It is Margaret who has to manage the practicalities of the move to Milton and her mother's distress. He

cannot speak frankly to his wife, refuses to recognize her fatal illness
and is unable to come to terms with her death:

he uncovered the face, and stroked it gently, making a kind of soft
inarticulate noise, like that of some mother-animal caressing her young
(p.246).

His Oxford friends treat his apostasy with 'something of the protecting kindness which they would have shown to a woman' (p.340). His
timidity, weakness and emotionalism are seen, as critics have noticed,
as undesirable by the narrator. What has not been realized is that
this is not because they are 'feminine' qualities inappropriate in a
man but because they are found in a degree that is excessive in either
sex. Their excess throws the burden of his decisions and his life on to
others, particularly his daughter.

Such burdens are the kind that the stereotypical middle-class
woman of fiction would normally take on willingly and use to perfect
her capacity for self-sacrifice. Margaret copes masterfully and apparently uncritically but is later shown to have felt a sense of extreme
oppression. Nothing breaks her but she feels the injustice of being
denied a life of her own. Hence her 'unwomanly' relief when her
widowed father takes himself off to visit his friend, Bell, in Oxford:

When her father had driven off ... to the railroad, Margaret felt how
great and long had been the pressure on her time and her spirits. It was
astonishing, almost stunning, to feel herself so much at liberty; no one
depending on her for cheering care ... no invalid to plan and think for;
she might be idle, and silent, and forgetful, – and what seemed worth
more than all the other privileges – she might be unhappy if she liked
(p.336).

This is what lies behind the Hales' drawing-room and the conventional façade which Thornton sees as symbolic of a domestic and
sexual heaven. And the family is even more dysfunctional than this:
it conceals the painful secret of an only son, Frederick, in exile for
naval mutiny, and under threat of hanging if he returns. This is
hardly the model patriarchal family which might offer the kind of
pattern for harmonious social relations that some reviewers expected.
It does, however, provide Margaret with a near example of how an
individual may question the established order out of a sense of
burning injustice. It is through affinity with Frederick (whom she
closely resembles physically) that she develops a model for dissent.

Outside the fragile structure that her home represents, Margaret Hale finds herself an alien in Milton. The place destabilizes her sense of class as a constituent of her identity. She arrives believing herself socially superior to all those she finds there. But this is a society unaware of the social hierarchy to which she belonged and from which she is now detached. There is no social group in Milton which shares her tastes, feelings and values. The only options that the northern class system offers are the mill-owning Thorntons' ménage or the workman Higgins's motherless family. Thornton's mother regards her as inferior because her father is only a private tutor and her family is poor. And her lack of status in this place is underlined by Higgins's daughter Bessy, who is dying of an industrial disease. Though dazzled by Margaret's beauty and grace she is surprised at her dining with the 'master' Thornton's family. In the event, since she cannot tolerate the Thorntons' philistinism, Margaret takes refuge with the Higginses. Her social education is instigated by Higgins's refusal of her patronizing offer of a visit. She discovers that for all his poverty and Bessy's attachment to her he will not accept condescension. She can visit them only on terms of equality, after an invitation. And like her, these unpretentious people are looked down on by the Thorntons. So it is with them that she aligns herself, reconciled even to the ugly streets of Milton because of the 'interest they had gained by the simple fact of her having learnt to care for a dweller in them' (p. 100).

This attachment on terms of equality to the working class is bizarre in contemporary terms and still leaves her a social anomaly. It is signalled simply but unambiguously by the ostentatious breaching of a novelistic practice. From early in the nineteenth century there was a clear convention that narrators and other middle-class characters used only 'good' or 'standard' English. Though 'lower-class' characters with suitably high moral standards (like Oliver Twist) may also use it, the reverse move of middle-class speakers into dialect or 'substandard' speech is not made. It is this linguistic apartheid that Margaret Hale symbolically breaches by quite slight 'deviations'. Partly under the influence of her husband, William Gaskell, as he worked on local dialect, Gaskell herself had come to feel that some dialect words had no expressive match in standard English. As she wrote on the subject of Warwickshire words to Walter Savage Landor in May 1854: '... you will remember the country people's use of the word "unked". I can't find any other word to express the exact feeling of strange unusual desolate discomfort, and I sometimes "pother" and "mither" people by using it' (*Letters*, p.292). And she has long been admired for the sensitive handling of dialect, pointed out by Melcher,[3] in which dialectal forms of second personal pronouns are skilfully adapted to status and age as well as degrees of intimacy between speakers.

The significance of Margaret's use of dialect is underlined by a rebuke from her mother which draws attention to it:

'Margaret, don't get to use these horrid Milton words. "Slack of work:" it is a provincialism. What will your aunt Shaw say, if she hears you use it on her return?' (p.233).

Outrageously Margaret claims that the use of Milton words is on a par with her cousin Edith's use of posh military slang, picked up from her officer husband. Mrs Hale is duly shocked by the wilful comparison between 'factory slang' and upper-class affectation. But Margaret insists that 'if I live in a factory town, I must speak factory language when I want it' (p.233). She renames 'slang' as 'language' which she may 'want' (or need). She jokingly offers to teach her mother terms like *knobstick* ('strike-breaker') which Mrs Hale categorizes as 'vulgar'. But Margaret's understanding of the crucial concept of 'vulgarity' has changed; it is the Thorntons' pretensions which are vulgar, not this natural speech. In a further breach of convention the narrator joins Margaret on the wrong side of the class divide by the casual use of a few dialect terms in contexts where the workmen and their families might use them: the wretched Mrs Boucher has an *ill-redd-up* (or 'untidy') house and Margaret is reported as suggesting 'redding up' after Boucher's suicide (p.294). For middle-class speakers to do this is to change the whole orientation of the narrative in relation to class. Usually, as Keating points out, the narrator 'eventually returns'[4] from the dangerous working-class world of industrial society. Margaret, however, crosses the border and does not return; she joins the enemy, though she is still not one of them.

However, she *can* become a Trojan horse in the middle class. In doing so, she finds scope for an unfeminine desire to exert control that is evident to Thornton at their first meeting. Though he was 'in habits of authority himself . . . she seemed to assume some kind of rule over him' (p.63). She is strangely attracted by naked power even when it takes a form she dislikes in the talk of the local mill-owners:

She liked the exultation in the sense of power which these Milton men had. It might be rather rampant in its display ... but still they seemed to defy the old limits of possibility, in a kind of fine intoxication, caused by the recollection of what had been achieved, and what yet should be (p.162).

Margaret is prepared to become accustomed to the strange taste of olives (p.165) that such men represent and to yield like them to the 'fine intoxication' of power in a quite unconventional way. She is scornful of their wives' conversation which takes 'nouns that were signs of things which gave evidence of wealth, – housekeepers, under-gardeners, extent of glass, valuable lace, diamonds, and all such things' and form their 'speech so as to bring them all in, in the prettiest accidental manner possible' (p.166). In her new situation at Milton the only way for her to 'defy the old limits of possibility' for a middle-class woman (a desire later vindicated in her reaction to her widowed father's absence) is to undertake the task that Gaskell claimed for herself in *Mary Barton*: 'to give some utterance to the agony which from time to time convulses this dumb people' – the working class (Preface). Speaking for them, but with all her own middle-class skill, she first battles verbally with Thornton, initiating discussions which debate the question of what the strike, which forms the central event of the plot, means. Their arguments are a debate over the discourses in which contemporary justifications of the existing class structure were coded. Dickens was profoundly uneasy with this discussion, describing it as 'unnecessarily lengthy'.[5]

As a preliminary, Margaret has made Thornton aware of the reductive implications of using the word *hands* for his employees:

'Miss Hale, I know, does not like to hear men called "hands", so I won't use that word, though it comes most readily to my lips as the technical term, whose origin, whatever it was, dates before my time' (p.120).

This disingenuously misses her point, which is to awaken for him the full force of the dead metaphor, all the more a distasteful one to her because now a matter of course. In practice, Thornton secretly agrees with another master, Hamper, who thinks he would survive poverty better than his workers because 'he had head as well as hands, while they had only hands' (p.145).

But Margaret's questioning goes far beyond disliking the use of reductive terms for workers. She problematizes both the contempor-

INTRODUCTION

ary major discourses that justify their emiseration: paternalism and
'the struggle for existence'. She invokes the father–children metaphor,
used by paternalists, grasping that, as J.S. Mill said, 'with paternal
care is connected paternal authority'.[6] If mill-owners are to be
described as, ideally, fathers, then in a patriarchal society they must
be assumed to have absolute authority over their workers. The latter
then pay a high price even if they receive welfare benefits. Margaret,
taught by Higgins, sees this language as a weapon: 'the masters
would like their hands to be merely tall, large children – living in the
present moment – with a blind unreasoning kind of obedience'
(p.119). No one, she adds, not even a workman, remains a child for
ever unless his growth is deliberately stunted by the parent–employer.
Turning the trope against the mill-owners, she deploys it in the
anecdote of a rich father who by keeping his son confined for forty
years turned him into a monster of depravity (and incompetence).
Thornton is driven to defend himself and his authoritarianism on the
grounds that workers *are* by nature 'unfit for independent action', at
least 'during business hours'. This somewhat ludicrously reveals his
illogicality since it is a crude way of detaching 'paternal authority'
from 'paternal care'. Outside business hours, he asserts, 'care' would
be interference with liberty (p.121). Gallagher (1980) argues that
all parties to this discussion discard the idea that industrial society
could be modelled on a patriarchal family because all are aware of
its 'dangers' as well as its 'usefulness'.[7] More exactly, Margaret
dismantles its uses by employers and provokes Thornton into using it
in contradictory ways that reveal how it papers over cracks.

The other emollient explanation of emiseration (and strikes) as
part of the inevitable struggle for existence is also dismantled. It is
Thornton's own preferred metaphor for the way things are, more
suited to his combative nature. He claims to deal with workers' 'tales
of suffering on sound economic principles'. By this he presumably
means that he adopts the classic economists' view that competitive-
ness among entrepreneurs is healthy for the economy and so in the
long run benefits the whole of society. He claims

that, as trade was conducted, there must always be a waxing and
waning of commercial prosperity; and that in the waning a certain
number of masters, as well as of men, must go down into ruin, and be no
more seen among the ranks of the happy and prosperous (p.151).

The narrator's commentary makes clear that Thornton's explanation of economic principles derives its force from a mechanical use of the current metaphor of the 'struggle for existence' (used by Darwin for the title of chapter three of *The Origin of Species*):

He spoke as if this consequence were so entirely logical, that neither employers nor employed had any right to complain if it became their fate: the employer to turn aside from the race he could no longer run, with a bitter sense of incompetency and failure – wounded in the struggle – trampled down by his fellows in their haste to get rich . . . (p.151).

Significantly Thornton considers only the 'intra-species' struggle, prominent in Malthus. Neither here nor in his account of his own energetic rise from poverty does he reflect on the 'inter-species' struggle between class and class, so important to Darwin. That is left to the narrator who, like Margaret, takes the opportunity to draw his conclusion for him:

Of course, speaking so of the fate that, as a master, might be his own . . . he was not likely to have more sympathy with that of workmen, who were passed by in the swift merciless improvement or alteration; who would fain lie down and quietly die out of the world that needed them not (p.152).

It is left also to the female narrator to join in and represent sympathetically 'the hands" reactions: an inability even to rest in their graves 'for the clinging cries of the beloved and helpless they would leave behind'; and a maternal wish that, like the pelican in fables, they could feed their children with their own blood. Such a comment parallels J.S. Mill's cooler statement in his revision of Ricardian economics in 1848:

I confess I am not charmed with the ideal of life held out by those who think that the normal state of human beings is that of struggling to get on; that the trampling, crushing, elbowing, and treading on each other's heels, which form the existing type of social life are the most desirable lot of human kind, or anything but the disagreeable symptoms of one of the phases of industrial progress.[8]

The only connection that Thornton makes between his own and the other class is to offer himself as a role model. As he says earlier, 'one of the great beauties of our system' is that 'a working-man may raise himself into the power and position of a master by his own exertions and behaviour' as he has done (p.84). Since the 'behaviour' referred to is, paradoxically, the very decency, sobriety and dutifulness that he is certain workmen lack, there seems to be little hope for them in his account. This 'answers' with an anecdote Carlyle's question in *Chartism* (1839), 'can the labourer hope to rise to mastership?' It is an answer which represents a widely held view, later crystallized by Samuel Smiles in *Self-Help* (1859). Margaret's response to his Smiles-like eulogy on 'the beauty' of the social system is to demolish it by ironically drawing out its 'logical' implications:

'You consider all who are unsuccessful in raising themselves in the world, from whatever cause, as your enemies, then, if I understand you rightly' (pp.84–5).

When he defends himself as 'honest, punctual, quick, and resolute' with his workers, adding authoritatively 'What the master is, that will the men be', she turns his own argument back on him: 'When I see men violent and obstinate in pursuit of their rights, I may safely infer that the master is the same' (p.123). He attempts a feeble joke to the effect that what the 'rough, heathenish' men of Milton need is not 'rose-water surgery' (of an ineffectual kind) but the savage surgery of a Cromwell from their mill-owner and master. Margaret turns the joke into a weapon by returning to the earlier stage of their argument about paternalism:

'Cromwell is no hero of mine ... But I am trying to reconcile your admiration of despotism with your respect for other men's independence of character' (p.123).

In refusing to accept the usual middle-class explanations of emiseration and strikes, Margaret achieves verbal dominance over Thornton. She transforms the womanly influence referred to by the *Guardian* reviewer. By arguing with him she is, as Pikoulis says, 'staking her claim for identity in a male world',[9] and that turns 'feminine' influence into power. From argument she moves on to attempt control of his actions by driving him to treat his workers as individuals. But this is no longer represented as the universal panacea claimed by paternalists; it is merely what is locally right.

The issue is spelt out through the episode of the attack on Thornton's mill when she coerces him into confronting the strikers face to face. She then exceeds his courage by shielding him physically and taking the only injury. In this way she seizes the central role in a histrionic confrontation. *She* becomes the locus of conflict, a troubling hybrid of south and north, the focus of attention with her 'pale, upturned face ... still and sad as marble', marked by a dramatic 'thread of dark-red blood' (p.178).

At this point issues of class and gender are inextricably entangled. By stepping out of her class to defend the workers and then Thornton, she has stepped out of her gender as conventionally constructed. By becoming an agent in the public sphere and the centre of all eyes she has turned herself into a public woman, an *actress* not an angel, potentially a fallen woman. As one chauvinistic character in a near-contemporary narrative puts it: 'a woman who exhibits herself in any way ... seems little better than a woman of a nameless class',[10] that is, a prostitute. The need to maintain the connection between the public sphere and illicit sexuality is thought plausibly by Harman (1988) to be part of the linguistic mechanism to deny any 'public' career, such as medicine or law, to women.[11] Certainly the sexual nature of the scene, variously interpreted, has been recognized at least since Dodsworth's comments in 1970.[12] In general terms what the scene makes clear is something that the prevailing ideologies insist on for women: the connection between being in the public domain and being recognized as an unwomanly sexual being. As Griselda Pollock (1988) puts it, 'going out in public and the idea of disgrace were closely allied'.[13]

Margaret Hale does far more than merely go out alone in public when she faces the crowd of strikers. So it is assumed generally, and by Thornton's disapproving mother in particular, that he has a duty to make her an 'honest' woman by marrying her. This public perception is internalized by Margaret herself as a sense of sexual guilt. In respect of womanly 'purity', as with her social class, she is a divided self. One side of her denies any sexual motive as she claims that she would have protected any striker in the crowd as readily as Thornton. And yet in looking back on the incident all other circumstances are erased except for the recollection that

a cloud of faces looked up at her, giving her no idea of fierce vivid anger, or of personal danger, but a deep sense of shame that she should thus be the object of universal regard – a sense of shame so acute that ... she would fain have burrowed into the earth to hide herself, and yet she could not escape out of that unwinking glare of many eyes (p.189).

This is her 'womanly' side re-emerging at a moment of crisis.

This horror of being viewed as a public spectacle later translates itself into a sense of sexual sin as (when disturbed by finding her home village changed physically and morally) she imagines herself 'whirled on' through all the phases of her life like sinful lovers in Dante, as if in 'the circle in which the victims of earthly passion eddy continually' (p.390). The reference reveals the other side of herself which knows that she finally protected Thornton from his workers (whose cause she espoused) because she was passionately attracted by him. In denying this she is attempting to obscure a new self-awareness effected by her contact with the crowds of mill-workers in Milton. Their comments on her physical attractiveness first aroused indignation at the offence to her 'delicacy' and later in private some amusement (pp.72–3). Thus was the beginning of an epiphany of which the strike is the climax.

There are two consequences for her divided self in this. One is the displacement of her feelings of sexual guilt on to a lie she told to prevent her brother from capture in England, when he returned to visit their dying mother. This turns into an obsessive desire to 'clear her name' with Thornton by revealing the identity of the man with whom he has seen her alone late at night. The other more significant consequence of the revelation she experiences about her feelings for Thornton is a relentless determination not to let physical attraction give him power over her. Since he too regards her action as compromising, he sees the opportunity to propose marriage. At this she 'shrank and shuddered as under the fascination of some great power, repugnant to her whole previous life' (p.195) of sexless purity. What she most resists is a marriage that will relegate her to a position of mere womanly influence over him. She remembers the 'continued series of opposition' (p.195) in which he earlier showed his contempt for her opinions on life in Milton. Even in the proposal scene he speaks contemptuously of her 'misplaced sympathies' (p.193) with the strikers. He offers her a chance to influence him but what she wants is power. And her desire for power has by now defined a purpose: the politics of gender are to be worked out through the class issue. She will act in defiance of the established order on grounds of the principle revealed to her by her brother Frederick's mutiny against his captain. Loyalty and obedience are virtues when those who wield power are wise and just 'but it is still finer to defy arbitrary power, unjustly and cruelly used – not on behalf of ourselves, but on behalf of others more helpless' (p.109).

This explains a ferocity in the relationship between Margaret and Thornton noticed by Margaret Oliphant (1855) though overlooked by many male reviewers: 'here is love itself, always in a fury, often looking exceedingly like hatred' (*CH*, 346). Their sexual desire is figured as physical violence that parallels their sharp verbal battles. When she refuses to marry him, Thornton feels 'as if Margaret . . . had been a sturdy fish-wife, and given him a sound blow with her fists. He had positive bodily pain' (p.204). Later he feels a desire to strike her in order that 'by some strange overt act of rudeness, he might earn the privilege of telling her the remorse that gnawed at his heart' (p.328). Class struggle has been displaced on to the disharmony between middle-class lovers but this conventional plot is now re-worked. The conflict (or mutiny) is uniquely ferocious in its eroticism; it now clearly reflects the underlying hostility of class relations and it is not smoothly resolved. Margaret only submits to marrying Thornton when she has reduced him to a state in which she can, through her collaborator Higgins, control his actions as an employer. His cast-iron convictions as to the shiftlessness of his employees melt. He not only employs Higgins, though he is a trade unionist, but after discussions with him takes Carlyle's advice (and Margaret's) about creating something more than a 'cash nexus' as a link with his workers. She has in fact returned class conflict to its proper place between employer and employed. The final test of Thornton's new-found virtue comes in economic form when he resists the temptation to speculate with his creditors' money. Ironically this decision proves he was right to think that in this society ruthlessness was the only way to succeed. He loses his mill and is forced to look for work himself, as Higgins was earlier.

Only when she has achieved control over his will in the treatment of his workers can Margaret happily make a rapid sexual submission 'all smash in a moment', as Gaskell wrote in a letter (*Letters*, p.329).

Already before this, after the deaths of her father and Mr Bell, Margaret has returned to London enriched by the latter's legacy. She now perceives middle-class 'unmercantile' life differently. For Milton has made her aware of two things: the previously invisible 'toilers and moilers' who oil the wheels and create the luxurious comfort; and the 'strange unsatisfied vacuum' in her own life. She now always reads Harley Street by contrast with what the narrator calls 'the lurid vividness of life' in Milton (pp.363–4). This gives her a framework for decoding it in a new way. She craves even for talk of the northern town and its inhabitants – 'their energy, their power, their indomitable courage in struggling and fighting' (p.406). She sees the recollections of this as her only defence against becoming 'sleepily deadened into forgetfulness of anything beyond the life which was lapping her round with luxury' (p.364).

Significantly, however, though Margaret's new-found money can return the humiliated Thornton to prosperity, it cannot work the larger miracle of transforming the whole town as Shirley's does for Moore in Brontë's novel. Once more the trope of Frederick's mutiny underpins the narrative. His courageous act did not erase the kind of brutality he was resisting: his fellow mutineers were hanged and he himself was condemned and exiled for ever. Similarly it is stressed that Milton as a whole is unchanged:

Meanwhile, at Milton the chimneys smoked, the ceaseless roar and mighty beat, and dizzying whirl of machinery, struggled and strove perpetually. Senseless and purposeless were wood and iron and steam in their endless labours; but the persistence of their monotonous work was rivalled in tireless endurance by the strong crowds, who, with sense and with purpose, were busy and restless in seeking after – What? (p.408).

The disconcerting syntax of this, switching from statement to question in mid-stream, enacts the inconclusiveness of any attempt to resolve the defects in the social system. What follows dwells on the troubled status quo, as unalterable as the movement and noise of machines:

. . . every man's face was set in lines of eagerness or anxiety; news was sought for with fierce avidity; and men jostled each other aside in the Mart and in the Exchange, as they did in life, in the deep selfishness of competition (p.408).

So the narrative effects no closure. The metonymic argument that the relationship (whatever it is) between Thornton and Higgins can be reproduced until industrial society is entirely at peace is not pursued. Nor does the marriage of Margaret and Thornton figure a way out of the present condition of strife. No answer is ever given to the question that runs through the novel and is the title of chapter XVII, 'What is a strike?' This has now been transformed into another question, 'How can strikes be avoided?' And the answer to that is that, in contemporary society, they cannot. Even Thornton's 'utmost expectation' is that they may not be in his area quite the 'bitter, venomous sources of hatred they have hitherto been' (p.421). Only so much has been achieved and that not for certain. Strikes are not represented as misunderstandings but now exposed as symptoms. And this openness of ending, with all its discomfort, has been brought about by endowing a middle-class woman with the agency and sexuality that throw into question the dominant ideologies of gender and therefore of class. Through effective action in the power politics of gender, Margaret Hale has also made an advance in the power politics of class, moving the discussion of both on to new ground. The text captures the conflicting attitudes to gender and to the gap between rich and poor of which Gaskell wrote in a letter to a woman friend in 1850 about buying a new and better house when so many lived in poverty:

That's the haunting thought to me, at least to one of my 'Mes', for I have a great number, and that's the plague. One of my mes is a true Christian – (only people call her a socialist and communist), another of my mes is a wife and mother . . . Now that's my social self . . . Then I've another self with a full taste for beauty and convenience whh [sic] is pleased on its own account. How am I to reconcile all these warring members? I try to reconcile myself (my first self) by saying it's Wm [sic] who is to decide . . . and his feeling it right ought to be my rule – only that does not quite do. I long (weakly) for the old times when right and wrong did not seem such complicated matters. I am sometimes coward enough to wish we were back in darkness where obedience was the only seen duty of women (*Letters*, p.109).

Patricia Ingham
St Anne's College, Oxford

Acknowledgements

I should like to thank especially Jenny Harrington, Shannon Russell, and the library staff of St Anne's College, Oxford, for all their help. For specific information I am also grateful to Nigel Bowles, Peter Ghosh, Rosemary Kelly and Hazel Rossotti.

Notes

1. G. Storey, K. Tillotson and A. Easson, *The Letters of Charles Dickens*, Oxford, vol.7 (1993), p.378.

2. P.J. Keating, *The Working Classes in Victorian Fiction*, London, Routledge & Kegan Paul, 1971, p.33.

3. G. Melcher, 'Mrs Gaskell and Dialect', *Studies in English Philology, Linguistics and Literature Presented to Alorik Rynell*, ed. M. Ryden and L.A. Björk (Stockholm Studies in English, vol.46, 1978), pp.112–24.

4. Keating, op. cit., p.33.

5. Storey, Tillotson and Easson, op. cit., p.378.

6. J.S. Mill in the *Edinburgh Review*, 1845, vol.81, p.507.

7. C. Gallagher, '*Hard Times* and *North and South*: the Family and Society in two Industrial Novels', *Arizona Quarterly*, vol.36, 1980, pp.70–96.

8. J.S. Mill, *Principles of Political Economy*, 1848, bk.4, chapter 6, section 2.

9. J. Pikoulis, '*North and South*: Varieties of Love and Power', *Yearbook of English Studies*, vol.6, 1976, p.184.

10. G. Jewsbury, *The Half Sisters*, 1848, vol.2, pp.18–19.

11. B.L. Harman, 'In Promiscuous Company: Female Public Appearance in Gaskell's *North and South*', *Victorian Studies*, 1988, vol.31, pp.351–74.

12. M. Dodsworth (ed.), *North and South*, Penguin, 1970, p.18.

13. G. Pollock, *Vision and Difference: Femininity, Feminism and Histories of Art*, London and New York, Routledge, 1988, p.69.

FURTHER READING

Reference

Jeffrey Welch, *Elizabeth Gaskell: An Annotated Bibliography 1929–1975*, New York and London, Garland, 1977.

Robert L. Selig, *Elizabeth Gaskell: A Reference Guide*, Boston, Mass., G.K. Hall, 1977.

Letters and Biography

J.A.V. Chapple and Arthur Pollard (eds.), *The Letters of Mrs Gaskell*, Manchester University Press, 1966. The best introduction to Gaskell's life.

J.A.V. Chapple and J.G. Sharps, *Elizabeth Gaskell: A Portrait in Letters*, Manchester University Press, 1980. A biographical narrative of an unstructured kind, linking a selection of letters.

Jenny Uglow, *Elizabeth Gaskell: A Habit of Stories*, London, Faber and Faber, 1993. Authoritative and detailed.

Winifred Gérin, *Elizabeth Gaskell: A Biography* (Oxford paperback, 1976). Less reliable and less detailed than Uglow.

Literary and Historical Background

David Roberts, *Paternalism in Early Victorian England*, London, Croom Helm, 1979.

Sheila M. Smith, *The Other Nation: The Poor in English Novels of the 1840's and 1850's*, Oxford, Clarendon Press, 1980.

Joseph Kestner, *Protest and Reform: The British Social Narrative by Women 1827–1867*, Madison, University of Wisconsin Press, 1985.

Catherine Gallagher, *The Industrial Reformation of English Fiction: Social Discourse and Narrative Form*, Chicago University Press, 1985.

Barbara Bodenheimer, *The Politics of Story in Victorian Social Fiction*, Ithaca and London, Cornell University Press, 1988.

Contemporary Reviews

Angus Easson (ed.), *Elizabeth Gaskell: The Critical Heritage*, London, Routledge, 1991.

Recent Criticism

BOOKS ON GASKELL

W.A. Clark, *Elizabeth Gaskell and the English Provincial Novel*, London, Methuen, 1975.

Angus Easson, *Elizabeth Gaskell*, London, Routledge & Kegan Paul, 1979.

Deirdre David, *Fictions of Resolution in Three Victorian Novels: North and South, Our Mutual Friend, Daniel Deronda*, London, Macmillan, 1981.

John Lucas, *Elizabeth Gaskell*, Brighton, Harvester, 1982.

Patsy Stoneman, *Elizabeth Gaskell*, Brighton, Harvester, 1987.

ESSAYS AND ARTICLES

There are very large numbers of these. They include (in chronological order):

David Craig, 'Fiction and the Rising Industrial Classes', *Essays in Criticism* 17 (1967), pp.64–74.

Dorothy Collin, 'The Composition of Mrs Gaskell's *North and South*', *Bulletin of the John Rylands Library* 54 (1971), pp.67–93.

John Pikoulis, '*North and South*: Varieties of Love and Power', *Yearbook of English Studies* 6 (1976), pp.176–95.

Stephen Gill, 'Price's Patent Candles: New Light on *North and South*', *Review of English Studies* 27 (1976), pp.313–21.

Nancy F. Cott, 'Passionlessness: A Reinterpretation of Victorian Sexual Ideology', *Signs* 4 (1978), pp.219–36.

Rosemarie Bodenheimer, '*North and South*: a Permanent State of Change', *Nineteenth Century Fiction* 34 (1979), pp.281–301.

Angus Easson, 'Mr Hale's Doubts in *North and South*', *Review of English Studies* 81 (1980), pp.30–40.

Ian Campbell, 'Mrs Gaskell's *North and South* and the Art of the Possible', *Dickens' Studies Annual* 8 (1980), pp.231–50.

Monica C. Fryckstedt, 'The Early Industrial Novel and its Predecessors', *Bulletin of the John Rylands Library* 63 (1980), pp.11–30.

Carol A. Martin, 'No Angel in the House: Victorian Mothers and Daughters in George Eliot and Elizabeth Gaskell', *Midwest Quarterly* 2 (1983), pp.297–314.

Carol A. Martin, 'Gaskell, Darwin and *North and South*', *Studies in the Novel* 15 (1983), pp.91–107.

Carol A. Martin, 'Gaskell's Ghosts: Truth in Disguise', *Studies in the Novel* 21 (Spring 1988), pp.27–40.

No manuscript of *North and South* survives. The novel was first serialized in weekly parts from 2 September 1854 to 27 January 1855 in Dickens's periodical *Household Words*. Thanks partly to miscalculation on his part, Gaskell found herself pressurized to make the work shorter than she intended. What from her viewpoint constituted the worst compression was that made in the last few chapters of the novel.

Consequently for the first (two) volume edition, also published in 1855, the narrative was considerably expanded. The major alterations were to that section of the story in volume 2 which relates to Margaret Hale's emotional development when she returns from the North to Harley Street after her parents' death. These textual changes begin at a point part way through chapter 44 of the serial (twenty-first instalment). The first part of this becomes (with additions) chapter XLIV ('Ease Not Peace'). Quite new were chapter XLV ('Not All a Dream') and chapter XLVI ('Once and Now'). Chapter XLV includes Mr Bell's visit to Margaret in London, his meeting with Henry Lennox and his suggestion to her that they should revisit her father's former living at Helstone. Chapter XLVI describes this visit. Chapter XLVII ('Something Wanting') elaborates on part of the material in chapter 44 of the serial version, including Margaret's wish to visit her brother in Spain. So too does chapter XLVIII ('Ne'er to be Found Again'), which adds Margaret's struggle with her aunt Shaw to visit Mr Bell in Oxford when he becomes ill. The changes to these two chapters underline Margaret's increasing independence, and her ineradicable interest in Milton-Northern and in John Thornton's opinion of her. They also spell out her new and more critical view of Helstone. In the volume editions, Gaskell also added quotations as epigraphs at the beginning of each chapter.

The second edition in volume form, corrected and reset, was published later in 1855. A long descriptive paragraph was added to the end of chapter XLVIII, describing Margaret's thoughts on the night of her return from Oxford after Mr Bell's death. The edition also rightly removed the second occurrence of two paragraphs which appear erroneously in the first edition both in chapter XLIV (original text, volume 2, pp.262–3) and also in chapter XLVII (original text, volume 2, pp.311–13). The repetition is evidently to be accounted for by the insertion of much additional material to the serial version for the volume edition, immediately after their first occurrence. Gaskell then evidently overlooked this earlier use and repeated them at the end of the added material. In the second edition the second of these passages is deleted (see Notes, chapter XLIV, Note 3). There were many other careful corrections. Since this correction appears to be Gaskell's work, I have used the second edition as copy-text and silently removed obvious errors of spelling and omission (*indiviual* to *individual*; *up* to *us*; *quite* to *quiet*; *assared* to *assured*, etc.). Reference to textual changes will also be found in the Notes.

NORTH AND SOUTH.

BY

THE AUTHOR OF "MARY BARTON," "RUTH,"
"CRANFORD," &c.

IN TWO VOLUMES.

LONDON:
CHAPMAN & HALL, 193, PICCADILLY.
1855.

I

CONTENTS

On its first appearance in 'Household Words', this tale was obliged to conform to the conditions imposed by the requirements of a weekly publication, and likewise to confine itself within certain advertised limits, in order that faith might be kept with the public. Although these conditions were made as light as they well could be, the author found it impossible to develope the story in the manner originally intended, and, more especially, was compelled to hurry on events with an improbable rapidity towards the close. In some degree to remedy this obvious defect, various short passages have been inserted, and several new chapters added. With this brief explanation, the tale is commended to the kindness of the reader;

> *'Beseking hym lowly, of mercy and pité,*
> *Of its rude makyng to have compassion.'*

CHAPTER I

'Haste to the Wedding'

Wooed and married and a'[1]

'Edith!' said Margaret, gently, 'Edith!'

But, as Margaret half suspected, Edith had fallen asleep. She lay curled up on the sofa in the back drawing-room in Harley Street, looking very lovely in her white muslin and blue ribbons. If Titania[2] had ever been dressed in white muslin and blue ribbons, and had fallen asleep on a crimson damask sofa in a back drawing-room, Edith might have been taken for her. Margaret was struck afresh by her cousin's beauty. They had grown up together from childhood, and all along Edith had been remarked upon by every one, except Margaret, for her prettiness; but Margaret had never thought about it until the last few days, when the prospect of soon losing her companion seemed to give force to every sweet quality and charm which Edith possessed. They had been talking about wedding dresses, and wedding ceremonies; and Captain Lennox, and what he had told Edith about her future life at Corfu,[3] where his regiment was stationed; and the difficulty of keeping a piano in good tune (a difficulty which Edith seemed to consider as one of the most formidable that could befall her in her married life), and what gowns she should want in the visits to Scotland, which would immediately succeed her marriage; but the whispered tone had latterly become more drowsy; and Margaret, after a pause of a few minutes, found, as she fancied, that in spite of the buzz in the next room, Edith had rolled herself up into a soft ball of muslin and ribbon, and silken curls, and gone off into a peaceful little after-dinner nap.

Margaret had been on the point of telling her cousin of some of the plans and visions which she entertained as to her future life in the country parsonage, where her father and mother lived; and where her bright holidays had always been passed, though for the last ten years her aunt Shaw's house had been considered as her home. But in default of a listener, she had to brood over the change in her life silently as heretofore. It was a happy brooding, although tinged with regret at being separated for an indefinite time from her gentle aunt and dear cousin. As she thought of the delight of filling the important post of only daughter in Helstone parsonage, pieces of the conversation out of the next room came upon her ears. Her aunt Shaw was talking to the five or six ladies who had been dining there, and whose husbands were still in the dining-room. They were the familiar acquaintances of the house; neighbours whom Mrs Shaw called friends, because she happened to dine with them more frequently than with any other people, and because if she or Edith wanted anything from them, or they from her, they did not scruple to make a call at each other's houses before luncheon. These ladies and their husbands were invited, in their capacity of friends, to eat a farewell dinner in honour of Edith's approaching marriage. Edith had rather objected to this arrangement, for Captain Lennox was expected to arrive by a late train this very evening; but, although she was a spoiled child, she was too careless and idle to have a very strong will of her own, and gave way when she found that her mother had absolutely ordered those extra delicacies of the season which are always supposed to be efficacious against immoderate grief at farewell dinners. She contented herself by leaning back in her chair, merely playing with the food on her plate, and looking grave and absent; while all around her were enjoying the mots of Mr Grey, the gentleman who always took the bottom of the table at Mrs Shaw's dinner parties, and asked Edith to give them some music in the drawing-room. Mr Grey was particularly agreeable over this farewell dinner, and the gentlemen staid down stairs[4] longer than usual. It was very well they did – to judge from the fragments of conversation which Margaret overheard.

'I suffered too much myself; not that I was not extremely happy with the poor dear General, but still disparity of age is a drawback; one that I was resolved Edith should not have to encounter. Of course, without any maternal partiality, I foresaw that the dear child was likely to marry early; indeed, I had often said that I was sure she would be married before she was nineteen. I had quite a prophetic feeling when Captain Lennox' – and here the voice dropped into a whisper, but Margaret could easily supply the blank. The course of true love in Edith's case had run remarkably smooth. Mrs Shaw had given way to the presentiment, as she expressed it; and had rather urged on the marriage, although it was below the expectations which many of Edith's acquaintances had formed for her, a young and pretty heiress. But Mrs Shaw said that her only child should marry for love, – and sighed emphatically, as if love had not been her motive for marrying the General. Mrs Shaw enjoyed the romance of the present engagement rather more than her daughter. Not but that Edith was very thoroughly and properly in love; still she would certainly have preferred a good house in Belgravia,[5] to all the picturesqueness of the life which Captain Lennox described at Corfu. The very parts which made Margaret glow as she listened, Edith pretended to shiver and shudder at; partly for the pleasure she had in being coaxed out of her dislike by her fond lover, and partly because anything of a gipsy or make-shift life was really distasteful to her. Yet had any one come with a fine house, and a fine estate, and a fine title to boot, Edith would still have clung to Captain Lennox while the temptation lasted; when it was over, it is possible she might have had little qualms of ill-concealed regret that Captain Lennox could not have united in his person everything that was desirable. In this she was but her mother's child; who after deliberately marrying General Shaw with no warmer feeling than respect for his character and establishment, was constantly, though quietly, bemoaning her hard lot in being united to one whom she could not love.

'I have spared no expense in her trousseau,' were the next words Margaret heard. 'She has all the beautiful Indian shawls and scarfs the General gave to me, but which I shall never wear again.'

'She is a lucky girl,' replied another voice, which Margaret knew to be that of Mrs Gibson, a lady who was taking a double interest in the conversation, from the fact of one of her daughters having been married within the last few weeks. 'Helen had set her heart upon an Indian shawl, but really when I found what an extravagant price was asked, I was obliged to refuse her. She will be quite envious when she hears of Edith having Indian shawls. What kind are they? Delhi? with the lovely little borders?'

Margaret heard her aunt's voice again, but this time it was as if she had raised herself up from her half-recumbent position, and were looking into the more dimly lighted back drawing-room. 'Edith! Edith!' cried she; and then she sank as if wearied by the exertion. Margaret stepped forward.

'Edith is asleep, Aunt Shaw. Is it anything I can do?'

All the ladies said 'Poor child!' on receiving this distressing intelligence about Edith; and the minute lap-dog in Mrs Shaw's arms began to bark, as if excited by the burst of pity.

'Hush, Tiny! you naughty little girl! you will waken your mistress. It was only to ask Edith if she would tell Newton to bring down her shawls: perhaps you would go, Margaret dear?'

Margaret went up into the old nursery at the very top of the house, where Newton was busy getting up some laces which were required for the wedding. While Newton went (not without a muttered grumbling) to undo the shawls, which had already been exhibited four or five times that day, Margaret looked round upon the nursery; the first room in that house with which she had become familiar nine years ago, when she was brought, all untamed from the forest, to share the home, the play, and the lessons of her cousin Edith. She remembered the dark, dim look of the London nursery, presided over by an austere and ceremonious nurse, who was terribly particular about clean hands and torn frocks. She recollected the first tea up there – separate from her father and aunt, who were dining somewhere down below an infinite depth of stairs; for unless she were up in the sky (the child thought), they must be deep down in the bowels of the earth. At home – before she came to live in Harley Street – her mother's dressing-room had been her nursery; and, as they kept early hours in the country parsonage, Margaret had always had her meals with her father and mother. Oh! well did the tall stately girl of eighteen remember the tears shed with such wild passion of grief by the little girl of nine, as she hid her face under the bed-clothes, in that first night; and how she was bidden not to cry by the nurse, because it would disturb Miss Edith; and how she had cried as bitterly, but more quietly, till her newly-seen, grand, pretty aunt had come softly up stairs with Mr Hale to show him his little sleeping daughter. Then the little Margaret had hushed her sobs, and tried to lie quiet as if asleep, for fear of making her father unhappy by her grief, which she dared not express before her aunt, and which she rather thought it was wrong to feel at all after the long hoping, and planning, and contriving they had gone through at home, before her wardrobe could be arranged so as to suit her grander circumstances, and before papa could leave his parish to come up to London, even for a few days.

Now she had got to love the old nursery, though it was but a dismantled place; and she looked all round, with a kind of cat-like regret, at the idea of leaving it for ever in three days.

'Ah Newton!' said she, 'I think we shall all be sorry to leave this dear old room.'

'Indeed, miss, I shan't for one. My eyes are not so good as they were, and the light here is so bad that I can't see to mend laces except just at the window, where there's always a shocking draught – enough to give one one's death of cold.'

'Well, I dare say you will have both good light and plenty of warmth at Naples. You must keep as much of your darning as you can till then. Thank you, Newton, I can take them down – you're busy.'

So Margaret went down laden with shawls,[6] and snuffing up their spicy Eastern smell. Her aunt asked her to stand as a sort of lay figure on which to display them, as Edith was still asleep. No one thought about it; but Margaret's tall, finely made figure, in the black silk dress which she was wearing as mourning for some distant relative of her father's, set off the long beautiful folds of the gorgeous shawls that would have half-smothered Edith. Margaret stood right under the chandelier, quite silent and passive, while her aunt adjusted the draperies. Occasionally, as she was turned round, she caught a glimpse of herself in the mirror over the chimney-piece, and smiled at her own appearance there – the familiar features in the usual garb of a princess. She touched the shawls gently as they hung around her, and took a pleasure in their soft feel and their brilliant colours, and rather liked to be dressed in such splendour – enjoying it much as a child would do, with a quiet pleased smile on her lips. Just then the door opened, and Mr Henry Lennox was suddenly announced. Some of the ladies started back, as if half-ashamed of their feminine interest in dress. Mrs Shaw held out her hand to the new-comer; Margaret stood perfectly still, thinking she might be yet wanted as a sort of block for the shawls; but looking at Mr Lennox with a bright, amused face, as if sure of his sympathy in her sense of the ludicrousness at being thus surprised.

Her aunt was so much absorbed in asking Mr Henry Lennox – who had not been able to come to dinner – all sorts of questions about his brother the bridegroom, his sister the bridesmaid (coming with the Captain from Scotland for the occasion), and various other members of the Lennox family, that Margaret saw she was no more wanted as shawl-bearer, and devoted herself to the amusement of the other visitors, whom her aunt had for the moment forgotten. Almost immediately, Edith came in from the back drawing-room, winking and blinking her eyes at the stronger light, shaking back her slightly-ruffled curls, and altogether looking like the Sleeping Beauty just startled from her dreams. Even in her slumber she had instinctively felt that a Lennox was worth rousing herself for; and she had a multitude of questions to ask about dear Janet, the future, unseen sister-in-law, for whom she professed so much affection, that if

Margaret had not been very proud she might have almost felt jealous of the mushroom rival. As Margaret sank rather more into the background on her aunt's joining the conversation, she saw Henry Lennox directing his look towards a vacant seat near her; and she knew perfectly well that as soon as Edith released him from her questioning, he would take possession of that chair. She had not been quite sure, from her aunt's rather confused account of his engagements, whether he would come that night; it was almost a surprise to see him; and now she was sure of a pleasant evening. He liked and disliked pretty nearly the same things that she did. Margaret's face was lightened up into an honest, open brightness. By-and-by he came. She received him with a smile which had not a tinge of shyness or self-consciousness in it.

'Well, I suppose you are all in the depths of business – ladies' business, I mean. Very different to my business, which is the real true law business. Playing with shawls is very different work to drawing up settlements.'

'Ah, I knew how you would be amused to find us all so occupied in admiring finery. But really Indian shawls are very perfect things of their kind.'

'I have no doubt they are. Their prices are very perfect, too. Nothing wanting.'

The gentlemen came dropping in one by one, and the buzz and noise deepened in tone.

'This is your last dinner-party, is it not? There are no more before Thursday?'

'No. I think after this evening we shall feel at rest, which I am sure I have not done for many weeks; at least, that kind of rest when the hands have nothing more to do, and all the arrangements are complete for an event which must occupy one's head and heart. I shall be glad to have time to think, and I am sure Edith will.'

'I am not so sure about her; but I can fancy that you will. Whenever I have seen you lately, you have been carried away by a whirlwind of some other person's making.'

'Yes,' said Margaret, rather sadly, remembering the never-ending commotion about trifles that had been going on for more than a month past: 'I wonder if a marriage must always be preceded by what you call a whirlwind, or whether in some cases there might not rather be a calm and peaceful time just before it.'

'Cinderella's godmother ordering the trousseau, the wedding-breakfast, writing the notes of invitation, for instance,' said Mr Lennox, laughing.

'But are all these quite necessary troubles?'[7] asked Margaret, looking up straight at him for an answer. A sense of indescribable weariness of all the arrangements for a pretty effect, in which Edith had been busied as supreme authority for the last six weeks, oppressed her just now; and she really wanted some one to help her to a few pleasant, quiet ideas connected with a marriage.

'Oh, of course,' he replied, with a change to gravity in his tone. 'There are forms and ceremonies to be gone through, not so much to satisfy oneself, as to stop the world's mouth, without which stoppage there would be very little satisfaction in life. But how would you have a wedding arranged?'

'Oh, I have never thought much about it; only I should like it to be a very fine summer morning; and I should like to walk to church through the shade of trees; and not to have so many bridesmaids, and to have no wedding-breakfast. I dare say I am resolving against the very things that have given me the most trouble just now.'

'No, I don't think you are. The idea of stately simplicity accords well with your character.'

Margaret did not quite like this speech; she winced away from it more, from remembering former occasions on which he had tried to lead her into a discussion (in which he took the complimentary part) about her own character and ways of going on. She cut his speech rather short by saying:

'It is natural for me to think of Helstone church, and the walk to it, rather than of driving up to a London church in the middle of a paved street.'

'Tell me about Helstone. You have never described it to me. I should like to have some idea of the place you will be living in, when ninety-six Harley Street will be looking dingy and dirty, and dull, and shut up. Is Helstone a village, or a town, in the first place?'

'Oh, only a hamlet; I don't think I could call it a village at all. There is the church and a few houses near it on the green – cottages, rather – with roses growing all over them.'

'And flowering all the year round, especially at Christmas – make your picture complete,' said he.

'No,' replied Margaret, somewhat annoyed, 'I am not making a picture. I am trying to describe Helstone as it really is.[8] You should not have said that.'

'I am penitent,' he answered. 'Only it really sounded like a village in a tale rather than in real life.'

'And so it is,' replied Margaret, eagerly. 'All the other places in England that I have seen seem so hard and prosaic-looking, after the New Forest. Helstone is like a village in a poem – in one of Tennyson's poems. But I won't try and describe it any more. You would only laugh at me if I told you what I think of it – what it really is.'

'Indeed, I would not. But I see you are going to be very resolved. Well, then, tell me that which I should like still better to know: what the parsonage is like.'

'Oh, I can't describe my home. It is home, and I can't put its charm into words.'

'I submit. You are rather severe tonight, Margaret.'

'How?' said she, turning her large soft eyes round full upon him. 'I did not know I was.'

'Why, because I made an unlucky remark, you will neither tell me what Helstone is like, nor will you say anything about your home, though I have told you how much I want to hear about both, the latter especially.'

'But indeed I cannot tell you about my own home. I don't quite think it is a thing to be talked about, unless you knew it.'

'Well, then' – pausing for a moment – 'tell me what you do there. Here you read, or have lessons, or otherwise improve your mind, till the middle of the day; take a walk before lunch, go a drive with your aunt after, and have some kind of engagement in the evening. There, now fill up your day at Helstone. Shall you ride, drive, or walk?'

'Walk, decidedly. We have no horse, not even for papa. He walks to the very extremity of his parish. The walks are so beautiful, it would be a shame to drive – almost a shame to ride.'

'Shall you garden much? That, I believe, is a proper employment for young ladies in the country.'

'I don't know. I am afraid I shan't like such hard work.'

'Archery parties – pic-nics – race-balls – hunt-balls?'

'Oh no!' said she, laughing. 'Papa's living is very small; and even if we were near such things, I doubt if I should go to them.'

'I see, you won't tell me anything. You will only tell me that you are not going to do this and that. Before the vacation ends, I think I shall pay you a call, and see what you really do employ yourself in.'

'I hope you will. Then you will see for yourself how beautiful

Helstone is. Now I must go. Edith is sitting down to play, and I just know enough of music to turn over the leaves for her; and besides, Aunt Shaw won't like us to talk.'

Edith played brilliantly. In the middle of the piece the door half-opened, and Edith saw Captain Lennox hesitating whether to come in. She threw down her music, and rushed out of the room, leaving Margaret standing confused and blushing to explain to the astonished guests what vision had shown itself to cause Edith's sudden flight. Captain Lennox had come earlier than was expected; or was it really so late? They looked at their watches, were duly shocked, and took their leave.

Then Edith came back, glowing with pleasure, half-shyly, half-proudly leading in her tall handsome Captain. His brother shook hands with him, and Mrs Shaw welcomed him in her gentle kindly way, which had always something plaintive in it, arising from the long habit of considering herself a victim to an uncongenial marriage. Now that, the General being gone, she had every good of life, with as few drawbacks as possible, she had been rather perplexed to find an anxiety, if not a sorrow. She had, however, of late settled upon her own health as a source of apprehension; she had a nervous little cough whenever she thought about it; and some complaisant doctor ordered her just what she desired, – a winter in Italy. Mrs Shaw had as strong wishes as most people, but she never liked to do anything from the open and acknowledged motive of her own good will and pleasure; she preferred being compelled to gratify herself by some other person's command or desire. She really did persuade herself that she was submitting to some hard external necessity; and thus she was able to moan and complain in her soft manner, all the time she was in reality doing just what she liked.

It was in this way she began to speak of her own journey to Captain Lennox, who assented, as in duty bound, to all his future mother-in-law said, while his eyes sought Edith, who was busying herself in re-arranging the tea-table, and ordering up all sorts of good things, in spite of his assurances that he had dined within the last two hours.

Mr Henry Lennox stood leaning against the chimney-piece, amused with the family scene. He was close by his handsome brother; he was the plain one in a singularly good-looking family; but his face was intelligent, keen, and mobile; and now and then Margaret wondered what it was that he could be thinking about, while he kept silence, but was evidently observing, with an interest that was slightly sarcastic, all that Edith and she were doing. The sarcastic feeling was called out by Mrs Shaw's conversation with his brother; it was separate from the interest which was excited by what he saw. He thought it a pretty sight to see the two cousins so busy in their little arrangements about the table. Edith chose to do most herself. She was in a humour to enjoy showing her lover how well she could behave as a soldier's wife. She found out that the water in the urn was cold, and ordered up the great kitchen tea-kettle; the only consequence of which was that when she met it at the door, and tried to carry it in, it was too heavy for her, and she came in pouting, with a black mark on her muslin gown, and a little round white hand indented by the handle, which she took to show to Captain Lennox, just like a hurt child, and, of course, the remedy was the same in both cases. Margaret's quickly adjusted spirit-lamp was the most efficacious contrivance, though not so like the gypsy-encampment which Edith, in some of her moods, chose to consider the nearest resemblance to a barrack-life.

After this evening all was bustle till the wedding was over.

CHAPTER II

Roses and Thorns

By the soft green light in the woody glade,[1]
On the banks of moss where thy childhood played;
By the household tree, thro' which thine eye
First looked in love to the summer sky.

MRS HEMANS

Margaret was once more in her morning dress, travelling quietly home with her father, who had come up to assist at the wedding. Her mother had been detained at home by a multitude of half-reasons, none of which anybody fully understood, except Mr Hale, who was perfectly aware that all his arguments in favour of a grey satin gown, which was midway between oldness and newness, had proved unavailing; and that, as he had not the money to equip his wife afresh, from top to toe, she would not show herself at her only sister's only child's wedding. If Mrs Shaw had guessed at the real reason why Mrs Hale did not accompany her husband, she would have showered down gowns upon her; but it was nearly twenty years since Mrs Shaw had been the poor, pretty Miss Beresford, and she had really forgotten all grievances except that of the unhappiness arising from disparity of age in married life, on which she could descant by the half-hour. Dearest Maria had married the man of her heart, only eight years older than herself, with the sweetest temper, and that blue-black hair one so seldom sees. Mr Hale was one of the most delightful preachers she had ever heard, and a perfect model of a parish priest. Perhaps it was not quite a logical deduction from all these premises, but it was still Mrs Shaw's characteristic conclusion, as she thought over her sister's lot: 'Married for love, what can dearest Maria have to wish for in this world?' Mrs Hale, if she spoke truth, might have answered with a ready-made list, 'a silver-gray glacé silk, a white chip bonnet, oh! dozens of things for the wedding, and hundreds of things for the house.'

Margaret only knew that her mother had not found it convenient to come, and she was not sorry to think that their meeting and greeting would take place at Helstone[2] parsonage, rather than, during the confusion of the last two or three days, in the house in Harley Street, where she herself had had to play the part of Figaro,[3] and was wanted everywhere at one and the same time. Her mind and body ached now with the recollection of all she had done and said within the last forty-eight hours. The farewells so hurriedly taken, amongst all the other good-byes, of those she had lived with so long, oppressed her now with a sad regret for the times that were no more; it did not signify what those times had been, they were gone never to return. Margaret's heart felt more heavy than she could ever have thought it possible in going to her own dear home, the place and the life she had longed for for years – at that time of all times for yearning and longing, just before the sharp senses lose their outlines in sleep. She took her mind away with a wrench from the recollection of the past to the bright serene contemplation of the hopeful future. Her eyes began to see, not visions of what had been, but the sight actually before her; her dear father leaning back asleep in the railway carriage. His blue-black hair was grey now, and lay thinly over his brows. The bones of his face were plainly to be seen – too plainly for beauty, if his features had been less finely cut; as it was, they had a grace if not a comeliness of their own. The face was in repose; but it was rather rest after weariness, than the serene calm of the countenance of one who led a placid, contented life. Margaret was painfully struck by the worn, anxious expression; and she went back over the open and avowed circumstances of her father's life, to find the cause for the lines that spoke so plainly of habitual distress and depression.

'Poor Frederick!' thought she, sighing. 'Oh! if Frederick had but been a clergyman, instead of going into the navy, and being lost to us all! I wish I knew all about it. I never understood it from Aunt Shaw; I only knew he could not come back to England because of that terrible affair. Poor dear papa! how sad he looks! I am so glad I am going home, to be at hand to comfort him and mamma.'

She was ready with a bright smile, in which there was not a trace of fatigue, to greet her father when he awakened. He smiled back again, but faintly, as if it were an unusual exertion. His face returned into its lines of habitual anxiety. He had a trick of half-opening his mouth as if to speak, which constantly unsettled the form of the lips, and gave the face an undecided expression. But he had the same large, soft eyes as his daughter, – eyes which moved slowly and almost grandly round in their orbits, and were well veiled by their transparent white eyelids. Margaret was more like him than like her mother. Sometimes people wondered that parents so handsome should have a daughter who was so far from regularly beautiful; not beautiful at all,[4] was occasionally said. Her mouth was wide; no rosebud that could only open just enough to let out a 'yes' and 'no,' and 'an't please you, sir.' But the wide mouth was one soft curve of rich red lips; and the skin, if not white and fair, was of an ivory smoothness and delicacy. If the look on her face was, in general, too dignified and reserved for one so young, now, talking to her father, it was bright as the morning, – full of dimples, and glances that spoke of childish gladness, and boundless hope in the future.

It was the latter part of July when Margaret returned home. The forest trees were all one dark full, dusky green; the fern below them caught all the slanting sunbeams; the weather was sultry and broodingly still. Margaret used to tramp along by her father's side, crushing down the fern with a cruel glee, as she felt it yield under her light foot, and send up the fragrance peculiar to it, – out on the broad commons into the warm scented light, seeing multitudes of wild, free, living creatures, revelling in the sunshine, and the herbs and flowers it called forth. This life – at least these walks – realized all Margaret's anticipations. She took a pride in her forest. Its people were her people. She made hearty friends with them; learned and delighted in using their peculiar words; took up her freedom amongst them; nursed their babies; talked or read with slow distinctness to their old people; carried dainty messes to their sick; resolved before long to teach at the school, where her father went every day as to an appointed task, but she was continually tempted off to go and see some individual friend – man, woman, or child – in some cottage in the green shade of the forest. Her out-of-doors life was perfect. Her indoors life had its drawbacks. With the healthy shame of a child, she blamed herself for her keenness of sight, in perceiving that all was not as it should be there. Her mother – her mother always so kind and tender towards her – seemed now and then so much discontented with their situation; thought that the bishop strangely neglected his episcopal duties, in not giving Mr Hale a better living; and almost reproached her husband because he could not bring himself to say that he wished to leave the parish, and undertake the charge of a larger. He would sigh aloud as he answered, that if he could do what he ought in little Helstone, he should be thankful; but every day he was more overpowered; the world became more bewildering. At each repeated urgency of his wife, that he would put himself in the way of seeking some preferment, Margaret saw that her father shrank more and more; and she strove at such times to reconcile her mother to Helstone. Mrs Hale said that the near neighbourhood of so many trees affected her health; and Margaret would try to tempt her forth on to the beautiful, broad, upland, sun-streaked, cloud-shadowed common; for she was sure that her mother had accustomed herself too much to an in-doors life, seldom extending her walks beyond the church, the school, and the neighbouring cottages. This did good for a time; but when the autumn drew on, and the weather became more changeable, her mother's idea of the unhealthiness of the place increased; and she repined even more frequently that her husband, who was more learned than Mr Hume, a better parish priest than Mr Houldsworth, should not have met with the preferment that these two former neighbours of theirs had done.

This marring of the peace of home, by long hours of discontent, was what Margaret was unprepared for. She knew, and had rather revelled in the idea, that she should have to give up many luxuries, which had only been troubles and trammels to her freedom in Harley Street. Her keen enjoyment of every sensuous pleasure, was balanced finely, if not overbalanced, by her conscious pride in being able to do without them all, if need were. But the cloud never comes in that quarter of the horizon from which we watch for it. There had been slight complaints and passing regrets on her mother's part, over some trifle connected with Helstone, and her father's position there, when Margaret had been spending her holidays at home before; but in the general happiness of the recollection of those times, she had forgotten the small details which were not so pleasant.

In the latter half of September, the autumnal rains and storms came on, and Margaret was obliged to remain more in the house than she had hitherto done. Helstone was at some distance from any neighbours of their own standard of cultivation.

'It is undoubtedly one of the most out-of-the-way places in Eng-land,' said Mrs Hale, in one of her plaintive moods. 'I can't help regretting constantly that papa has really no one to associate with here; he is so thrown away; seeing no one but farmers and labourers from week's end to week's end. If we only lived at the other side of the parish, it would be something; there we should be almost within walking distance of the Stansfields; certainly the Gormans would be within a walk.'

'Gormans,' said Margaret. 'Are those the Gormans who made their fortunes in trade at Southampton? Oh! I'm glad we don't visit them. I don't like shoppy people.[5] I think we are far better off, knowing only cottagers and labourers, and people without pretence.'

'You must not be so fastidious, Margaret, dear!' said her mother, secretly thinking of a young and handsome Mr Gorman whom she had once met at Mr Hume's.

'No! I call mine a very comprehensive taste; I like all people whose occupations have to do with land; I like soldiers and sailors, and the three learned professions, as they call them. I'm sure you don't want me to admire butchers and bakers, and candlestick-makers, do you, mamma?'

'But the Gormans were neither butchers nor bakers, but very respectable coach-builders.'

'Very well. Coach-building is a trade all the same, and I think a much more useless one than that of butchers or bakers. Oh! how tired I used to be of the drives every day in Aunt Shaw's carriage, and how I longed to walk!'

And walk Margaret did, in spite of the weather. She was so happy out of doors, at her father's side, that she almost danced; and with the soft violence of the west wind behind her, as she crossed some heath, she seemed to be borne onwards, as lightly and easily as the fallen leaf that was wafted along by the autumnal breeze. But the evenings were rather difficult to fill up agreeably. Immediately after tea her father withdrew into his small library, and she and her mother were left alone. Mrs Hale had never cared much for books, and had discouraged her husband, very early in their married life, in his desire of reading aloud to her, while she worked. At one time they had tried backgammon as a resource; but as Mr Hale grew to take an increasing interest in his school and his parishioners, he found that the interruptions which arose out of these duties were regarded as hardships by his wife, not to be accepted as the natural conditions of his profession, but to be regretted and struggled against by her as they severally arose. So he withdrew, while the children were yet young, into his library, to spend his evenings (if he were at home), in reading the speculative and metaphysical books which were his delight.

When Margaret had been here before, she had brought down with her a great box of books, recommended by masters or governess, and had found the summer's day all too short to get through the reading she had to do before her return to town. Now there were only the well-bound little-read English Classics, which were weeded out of her father's library to fill up the small book-shelves in the drawing-room. Thomson's Seasons, Hayley's Cowper, Middleton's Cicero,[6] were by far the lightest, newest, and most amusing. The book-shelves did not afford much resource. Margaret told her mother every particular of her London life, to all of which Mrs Hale listened with interest, sometimes amused and questioning, at others a little inclined to compare her sister's circumstances of ease and comfort with the narrower means at Helstone vicarage. On such evenings Margaret was apt to stop talking rather abruptly, and listen to the drip-drip of the rain upon the leads of the little bow-window. Once or twice Margaret found herself mechanically counting the repetition of the monotonous sound, while she wondered if she might venture to put a question on a subject very near to her heart, and ask where Frederick was now; what he was doing; how long it was since they had heard from him. But a consciousness that her mother's delicate health, and positive dislike to Helstone, all dated from the time of the mutiny in which Frederick had been engaged, – the full account of which Margaret had never heard, and which now seemed doomed to be buried in sad oblivion, – made her pause and turn away from the subject each time she approached it. When she was with her mother, her father seemed the best person to apply to for information; and when with him, she thought that she could speak more easily to her mother. Probably there was nothing much to be heard that was new. In one of the letters she had received before leaving Harley Street, her father had told her that they had heard from Frederick; he was still at Rio, and very well in health, and sent his best love to her; which was dry bones, but not the living intelligence she longed for. Frederick was always spoken of, in the rare times when his name was mentioned, as 'Poor Frederick'. His room was kept exactly as he had left it; and was regularly dusted and put into order by Dixon, Mrs Hale's maid, who touched no other part of the household work, but always remembered the day when she had been engaged by Lady Beresford as ladies' maid to Sir John's wards, the pretty Miss Beresfords, the belles of Rutlandshire. Dixon had always considered Mr Hale as the blight which had fallen upon her young lady's prospects in life. If Miss Beresford had not been in such a hurry to marry a poor country clergyman, there was no knowing what she might not have become. But Dixon was too loyal to desert her in her affliction and downfall (alias her married life). She remained with her, and was devoted to her interests; always considering herself as the good and protecting fairy, whose duty it was to baffle the malignant giant, Mr Hale. Master Frederick had been her favourite and pride; and it was with a little softening of her dignified look and manner that she went in weekly to arrange the chamber as carefully as if he might be coming home that very evening.

Margaret could not help believing that there had been some late intelligence of Frederick, unknown to her mother, which was making her father anxious and uneasy. Mrs Hale did not seem to perceive any alteration in her husband's looks or ways. His spirits were always tender and gentle, readily affected by any small piece of intelligence concerning the welfare of others. He would be depressed for many days after witnessing a death-bed, or hearing of any crime. But now Margaret noticed an absence of mind, as if his thoughts were pre-occupied by some subject, the oppression of which could not be relieved by any daily action, such as comforting the survivors, or teaching at the school in hope of lessening the evils in the generation to come. Mr Hale did not go out among his parishioners as much as usual; he was more shut up in his study; was anxious for the village postman, whose summons to the household was a rap on the back-kitchen window-shutter − a signal which at one time had often to be repeated before any one was sufficiently alive to the hour of the day to understand what it was, and attend to him. Now Mr Hale loitered about the garden if the morning was fine, and if not, stood dreamily by the study window until the postman had called, or gone down the lane, giving a half-respectful, half-confidential shake of the head to the parson, who watched him away beyond the sweet-briar hedge, and past the great arbutus, before he turned into the room to begin his day's work, with all the signs of a heavy heart and an occupied mind.

But Margaret was at an age when any apprehension, not absolutely based on a knowledge of facts, is easily banished for a time by a bright sunny day, or some happy outward circumstance. And when the brilliant fourteen fine days of October came on, her cares were all blown away as lightly as thistledown, and she thought of nothing but the glories of the forest. The fern-harvest was over; and now that the rain was gone, many a deep glade was accessible, into which Margaret had only peeped in July and August weather. She had learnt drawing with Edith; and she had sufficiently regretted, during the gloom of the bad weather, her idle revelling in the beauty of the woodlands while it had yet been fine, to make her determined to sketch what she could before winter fairly set in. Accordingly, she was busy preparing her board one morning, when Sarah, the house-maid, threw wide open the drawing-room door, and announced, 'Mr Henry Lennox.'

CHAPTER III

'The More Haste the Worse Speed'

Learn to win a lady's faith[1]
Nobly, as the thing is high;
Bravely, as for life and death –
With a loyal gravity.

Lead her from the festive boards,
Point her to the starry skies,
Guard her, by your truthful words,
Pure from courtship's flatteries.

MRS BROWNING

'Mr Henry Lennox.' Margaret had been thinking of him only a moment before, and remembering his inquiry into her probable occupations at home. It was 'parler du soleil[2] et l'on en voit les rayons;' and the brightness of the sun came over Margaret's face as she put down her board, and went forward to shake hands with him. 'Tell mamma, Sarah,' said she. 'Mamma and I want to ask you so many questions about Edith; I am so much obliged to you for coming.'

'Did not I say that I should?' asked he, in a lower tone than that in which she had spoken.

'But I heard of you so far away in the Highlands that I never thought Hampshire could come in.'

'Oh!' said he, more lightly, 'our young couple were playing such foolish pranks, running all sorts of risks, climbing this mountain, sailing on that lake, that I really thought they needed a Mentor to take care of them. And indeed they did; they were quite beyond my uncle's management, and kept the old gentleman in a panic for sixteen hours out of the twenty-four. Indeed, when I once saw how unfit they were to be trusted alone, I thought it my duty not to leave them till I had seen them safely embarked at Plymouth.'

'Have you been at Plymouth? Oh! Edith never named that. To be sure, she has written in such a hurry lately. Did they really sail on Tuesday?'

'Really sailed, and relieved me from many responsibilities. Edith gave me all sorts of messages for you. I believe I have a little diminutive note somewhere; yes, here it is.'

'Oh! thank you,' exclaimed Margaret; and then, half wishing to read it alone and unwatched, she made the excuse of going to tell her mother again (Sarah surely had made some mistake) that Mr Lennox was there.

When she had left the room, he began in his scrutinizing way to look about him. The little drawing-room was looking its best in the streaming light of the morning sun. The middle window in the bow was opened, and clustering roses and the scarlet honeysuckle came peeping round the corner; the small lawn was gorgeous with verbenas and geraniums of all bright colours. But the very brightness outside made the colours within seem poor and faded. The carpet was far from new; the chintz had been often washed; the whole apartment was smaller and shabbier than he had expected, as back-ground and frame-work for Margaret, herself so queenly. He took up one of the books lying on the table; it was the Paradiso[3] of Dante, in the proper old Italian binding of white vellum and gold; by it lay a dictionary, and some words copied out in Margaret's hand-writing. They were a dull list of words, but somehow he liked looking at them. He put them down with a sigh.

'The living is evidently as small as she said. It seems strange, for the Beresfords belong to a good family.'

Margaret meanwhile had found her mother. It was one of Mrs Hale's fitful days, when everything was a difficulty and a hardship; and Mr Lennox's appearance took this shape, although secretly she felt complimented by his thinking it worth while to call.

'It is most unfortunate! We are dining early today, and having nothing but cold meat, in order that the servants may get on with their ironing; and yet, of course, we must ask him to dinner – Edith's brother-in-law and all. And your papa is in such low spirits this morning about something – I don't know what. I went into the study just now, and he had his face on the table, covering it with his hands. I told him I was sure Helstone air did not agree with him any more than with me, and he suddenly lifted up his head, and begged me not to speak a word more against Helstone, he could not bear it; if there was one place he loved on earth it was Helstone. But I am sure, for all that, it is the damp and relaxing air.'

Margaret had felt as if a thick cloud had come between her and the sun. She had listened patiently, in hopes that it might be some relief to her mother to unburden herself; but now it was time to draw her back to Mr Lennox.

'Papa likes Mr Lennox; they got on together famously at the wedding breakfast. I dare say his coming will do papa good. And never mind the dinner, dear mamma. Cold meat will do capitally for a lunch, which is the light in which Mr Lennox will most likely look upon a two o'clock dinner.'

'But what are we to do with him till then? It is only half-past ten now.'

'I'll ask him to go out sketching with me. I know he draws, and that will take him out of your way, mamma. Only do come in now; he will think it so strange if you don't.'

Mrs Hale took off her black silk apron, and smoothed her face. She looked a very pretty lady-like woman, as she greeted Mr Lennox with the cordiality due to one who was almost a relation. He evidently expected to be asked to spend the day, and accepted the invitation with a glad readiness that made Mrs Hale wish she could add something to the cold beef. He was pleased with everything; delighted with Margaret's idea of going out sketching together; would not have Mr Hale disturbed for the world, with the prospect of so soon meeting him at dinner. Margaret brought out her drawing materials for him to choose from; and after the paper and brushes had been duly selected, the two set out in the merriest spirits in the world.

'Now, please, just stop here for a minute or two,' said Margaret. 'These are the cottages that haunted me so during the rainy fortnight, reproaching me for not having sketched them.'

'Before they tumbled down and were no more seen. Truly, if they are to be sketched – and they are very picturesque – we had better not put it off till next year. But where shall we sit?'

'Oh! you might have come straight from chambers in the Temple, instead of having been two months in the Highlands! Look at this beautiful trunk of a tree, which the wood-cutters have left just in the right place for the light. I will put my plaid over it, and it will be a regular forest throne.'

'With your feet in that puddle for a regal foot-stool! Stay, I will move, and then you can come nearer this way. Who lives in these cottages?'

'They were built by squatters fifty or sixty years ago. One is uninhabited; the foresters are going to take it down, as soon as the old man who lives in the other is dead, poor old fellow! Look – there he is – I must go and speak to him. He is so deaf you will hear all our secrets.'

The old man stood bare-headed in the sun, leaning on his stick at the front of his cottage. His stiff features relaxed into a slow smile as Margaret went up and spoke to him. Mr Lennox hastily introduced the two figures into his sketch,[4] and finished up the landscape with a subordinate reference to them – as Margaret perceived, when the time came for getting up, putting away water, and scraps of paper, and exhibiting to each other their sketches. She laughed and blushed: Mr Lennox watched her countenance.

'Now, I call that treacherous,' said she. 'I little thought you were making old Isaac and me into subjects, when you told me to ask him the history of these cottages.'

'It was irresistible. You can't know how strong a temptation it was. I hardly dare tell you how much I shall like this sketch.'

He was not quite sure whether she heard this latter sentence before she went to the brook to wash her palette. She came back rather flushed, but looking perfectly innocent and unconscious. He was glad of it, for the speech had slipped from him unawares – a rare thing in the case of a man who premeditated his actions so much as Henry Lennox.

The aspect of home was all right and bright when they reached it. The clouds on her mother's brow had cleared off under the propitious influence of a brace of carp, most opportunely presented by a neighbour. Mr Hale had returned from his morning's round, and was awaiting his visitor just outside the wicket gate that led into the garden. He looked a complete gentleman in his rather threadbare coat and well-worn hat. Margaret was proud of her father; she had always a fresh and tender pride in seeing how favourably he impressed every stranger; still her quick eye sought over his face and found there traces of some unusual disturbance, which was only put aside, not cleared away.

Mr Hale asked to look at their sketches.

'I think you have made the tints on the thatch too dark, have you not?' as he returned Margaret's to her, and held out his hand for Mr Lennox's, which was withheld from him one moment, no more.

'No, papa! I don't think I have. The house-leek and stone-crop have grown so much darker in the rain. Is it not like, papa?' said she, peeping over his shoulder, as he looked at the figures in Mr Lennox's drawing.

'Yes, very like. Your figure and way of holding yourself is capital. And it is just poor old Isaac's stiff way of stooping his long rheumatic back. What is this hanging from the branch of the tree? Not a bird's nest, surely.'

'Oh no! that is my bonnet. I never can draw with my bonnet on; it makes my head so hot. I wonder if I could manage figures. There are so many people about here whom I should like to sketch.'

'I should say that a likeness you very much wish to take you would always succeed in,' said Mr Lennox. 'I have great faith in the power of will. I think myself I have succeeded pretty well in yours.' Mr Hale had preceded them into the house, while Margaret was lingering to pluck some roses, with which to adorn her morning gown for dinner.

'A regular London girl would understand the implied meaning of that speech,' thought Mr Lennox. 'She would be up to looking through every speech that a young man made her for the arrière-pensée of a compliment. But I don't believe Margaret, – Stay!' exclaimed he, 'Let me help you;' and he gathered for her some velvety cramoisy roses that were above her reach, and then dividing the spoil he placed two in his button-hole, and sent her in, pleased and happy, to arrange her flowers.

The conversation at dinner flowed on quietly and agreeably. There were plenty of questions to be asked on both sides – the latest intelligence which each could give of Mrs Shaw's movements in Italy to be exchanged; and in the interest of what was said, the unpretending simplicity of the parsonage-ways – above all, in the neighbourhood of Margaret, Mr Lennox forgot the little feeling of disappointment with which he had at first perceived that she had spoken but the simple truth when she had described her father's living as very small.

'Margaret, my child, you might have gathered us some pears for our dessert,' said Mr Hale, as the hospitable luxury of a freshly-decanted bottle of wine was placed on the table.

Mrs Hale was hurried. It seemed as if desserts were impromptu and unusual things at the parsonage; whereas, if Mr Hale would only have looked behind him, he would have seen biscuits and marmalade, and what not, all arranged in formal order on the sideboard. But the idea of pears had taken possession of Mr Hale's mind, and was not to be got rid of.

'There are a few brown beurrés against the south wall which are worth all foreign fruits and preserves. Run, Margaret, and gather us some.'

'I propose that we adjourn into the garden, and eat them there,' said Mr Lennox. 'Nothing is so delicious as to set one's teeth into the crisp, juicy fruit, warm and scented by the sun. The worst is, the wasps are impudent enough to dispute it with one, even at the very crisis and summit of enjoyment.'

He rose, as if to follow Margaret, who had disappeared through the window: he only awaited Mrs Hale's permission. She would rather have wound up the dinner in the proper way, and with all the ceremonies which had gone on so smoothly hitherto, especially as she and Dixon had got out the finger-glasses from the store-room on purpose to be as correct as became General Shaw's widow's sister; but as Mr Hale got up directly, and prepared to accompany his guest, she could only submit.

'I shall arm myself with a knife,' said Mr Hale: 'the days of eating fruit so primitively as you describe are over with me. I must pare it and quarter it before I can enjoy it.'

Margaret made a plate for the pears out of a beet-root leaf, which threw up their brown gold colour admirably. Mr Lennox looked more at her than at the pears; but her father, inclined to cull fastidiously the very zest and perfection of the hour he had stolen from his anxiety, chose daintily the ripest fruit, and sat down on the garden bench to enjoy it at his leisure. Margaret and Mr Lennox strolled along the little terrace walk under the south wall, where the bees still hummed and worked busily in their hives.

'What a perfect life you seem to live here! I have always felt rather contemptuously towards the poets before, with their wishes, "Mine be a cot beside a hill," and that sort of thing:[5] but now I am afraid that the truth is, I have been nothing better than a cockney. Just now I feel as if twenty years' hard study of law would be amply rewarded by one year of such an exquisite serene life as this – such skies!' looking up – 'such crimson and amber foliage, so perfectly motionless as that!' pointing to some of the great forest trees which shut in the garden as if it were a nest.

'You must please to remember that our skies are not always as deep a blue as they are now. We have rain, and our leaves do fall, and get sodden: though I think Helstone is about as perfect a place as any in the world. Recollect how you rather scorned my description of it one evening in Harley Street: "a village in a tale."'

'Scorned, Margaret! That is rather a hard word.'

'Perhaps it is. Only I know I should have liked to have talked to you of what I was very full at the time, and you – what must I call it then? – spoke disrespectfully of Helstone as a mere village in a tale.'

'I will never do so again,' said he warmly. They turned the corner of the walk.

'I could almost wish, Margaret –' he stopped and hesitated. It was so unusual for the fluent lawyer to hesitate that Margaret looked up at him, in a little state of questioning wonder; but in an instant – from what about him she could not tell – she wished herself back with her mother – her father – anywhere away from him, for she was sure he was going to say something to which she should not know what to reply. In another moment the strong pride that was in her came to conquer her sudden agitation, which she hoped he had not perceived. Of course she could answer, and answer the right thing; and it was poor and despicable of her to shrink from hearing any speech, as if she had not power to put an end to it with her high maidenly dignity.

'Margaret,' said he, taking her by surprise, and getting sudden possession of her hand, so that she was forced to stand still and listen, despising herself for the fluttering at her heart all the time; 'Margaret, I wish you did not like Helstone so much – did not seem so perfectly calm and happy here. I have been hoping for these three months past to find you regretting London – and London friends, a little – enough to make you listen more kindly' (for she was quietly, but firmly, striving to extricate her hand from his grasp) 'to one who has not much to offer, it is true – nothing but prospects in the future – but who does love you, Margaret, almost in spite of himself. Margaret, have I startled you too much? Speak!' For he saw her lips quivering almost as if she were going to cry. She made a strong effort to be calm; she would not speak till she had succeeded in mastering her voice, and then she said:

'I was startled. I did not know that you cared for me in that way. I have always thought of you as a friend; and, please, I would rather go on thinking of you so. I don't like to be spoken to as you have been doing. I cannot answer you as you want me to do, and yet I should feel so sorry if I vexed you.'

'Margaret,' said he, looking into her eyes, which met his with their open straight look, expressive of the utmost good faith and reluctance to give pain, 'Do you' – he was going to say – 'love any one else?' But it seemed as if this question would be an insult to the pure serenity of those eyes, 'Forgive me! I have been too abrupt. I am punished. Only let me hope. Give me the poor comfort of telling me you have never seen any one whom you could –' Again a pause. He could not end his sentence. Margaret reproached herself acutely as the cause of his distress.

'Ah! if you had but never got this fancy into your head! It was such a pleasure to think of you as a friend.'

'But I may hope, may I not, Margaret, that some time you will think of me as a lover? Not yet, I see – there is no hurry – but some time –'

She was silent for a minute or two, trying to discover the truth as it was in her own heart, before replying; then she said:

'I have never thought of – you, but as a friend. I like to think of you so; but I am sure I could never think of you as anything else. Pray, let us both forget that all this' ('disagreeable,' she was going to say, but stopped short) 'conversation has taken place.'

He paused before he replied. Then, in his habitual coldness of tone, he answered:

'Of course, as your feelings are so decided, and as this conversation has been so evidently unpleasant to you, it had better not be remembered. That is all very fine in theory, that plan of forgetting whatever is painful, but it will be somewhat difficult for me, at least, to carry it into execution.'

'You are vexed,' said she sadly; 'yet how can I help it?'

She looked so truly grieved as she said this, that he struggled for a moment with his real disappointment, and then answered more cheerfully, but still with a little hardness in his tone:

'You should make allowances for the mortification, not only of a lover, Margaret, but of a man not given to romance in general – prudent, worldly, as some people call me – who has been carried out of his usual habits by the force of a passion – well, we will say no more of that; but in the one outlet which he has formed for the deeper and better feelings of his nature, he meets with rejection and repulse. I shall have to console myself with scorning my own folly. A struggling barrister to think of matrimony!'

Margaret could not answer this. The whole tone of it annoyed her. It seemed to touch on and call out all the points of difference which had often repelled her in him; while yet he was the pleasantest man, the most sympathizing friend, the person of all others who understood her best in Harley Street. She felt a tinge of contempt mingle itself with her pain at having refused him. Her beautiful lip curled in a slight disdain. It was well that, having made the round of the garden, they came suddenly upon Mr Hale, whose whereabouts had been quite forgotten by them. He had not yet finished the pear, which he had delicately peeled in one long strip of silver-paper thinness, and which he was enjoying in a deliberate manner. It was like the story of the eastern king,[6] who dipped his head into a basin of water, at the magician's command, and ere he instantly took it out went through the experience of a lifetime. Margaret felt stunned, and unable to recover her self-possession enough to join in the trivial conversation that ensued between her father and Mr Lennox. She was grave, and little disposed to speak; full of wonder when Mr Lennox would go, and allow her to relax into thought on the events of the last quarter of an hour. He was almost as anxious to take his departure as she was for him to leave; but a few minutes light and careless talking, carried on at whatever effort, was a sacrifice which he owed to his mortified vanity, or his self-respect. He glanced from time to time at her sad and pensive face.

'I am not so indifferent to her as she believes,' thought he to himself. 'I do not give up hope.'

Before a quarter of an hour was over he had fallen into a way of conversing with quiet sarcasm; speaking of life in London and life in the country, as if he were conscious of his second mocking self, and afraid of his own satire. Mr Hale was puzzled. His visitor was a different man to what he had seen him before at the wedding-breakfast, and at dinner today; a lighter, cleverer, more worldly man, and, as such, dissonant to Mr Hale. It was a relief to all three when Mr Lennox said that he must go directly if he meant to catch the five o'clock train. They proceeded to the house to find Mrs Hale, and wish her good-bye. At the last moment, Henry Lennox's real self broke through the crust.

'Margaret, don't despise me; I have a heart, notwithstanding all this good-for-nothing way of talking. As a proof of it, I believe I love you more than ever – if I do not hate you – for the disdain with which you have listened to me during this last half-hour. Good-bye, Margaret – Margaret!'

CHAPTER IV

Doubts and Difficulties

Cast me upon some naked shore,[1]
Where I may tracke
Only the print of some sad wracke,
If thou be there, though the seas roare,
I shall no gentler calm implore.

HABINGTON

He was gone. The house was shut up for the evening. No more deep
blue skies or crimson and amber tints. Margaret went up to dress for
the early tea, finding Dixon in a pretty temper from the interruption
which a visitor had naturally occasioned on a busy day. She showed
it by brushing away viciously at Margaret's hair, under pretence of
being in a great hurry to go to Mrs Hale. Yet, after all, Margaret
had to wait a long time in the drawing-room before her mother came
down. She sat by herself at the fire, with unlighted candles on the
table behind her, thinking over the day, the happy walk, happy
sketching, cheerful pleasant dinner, and the uncomfortable, miserable
walk in the garden.

How different men were to women! Here was she disturbed and
unhappy, because her instinct had made anything but a refusal
impossible; while he, not many minutes after he had met with a
rejection of what ought to have been the deepest, holiest proposal of
his life, could speak as if briefs, success, and all its superficial
consequences of a good house, clever and agreeable society, were the
sole avowed objects of his desires. Oh dear! how she could have loved
him if he had but been different, with a difference which she felt, on
reflection, to be one that went low – deep down. Then she took it
into her head that, after all, his lightness might be but assumed, to
cover a bitterness of disappointment which would have been stamped
on her own heart if she had loved and been rejected.

Her mother came into the room before this whirl of thoughts was
adjusted into anything like order. Margaret had to shake off the
recollections of what had been done and said through the day, and
turn a sympathizing listener to the account of how Dixon had
complained that the ironing-blanket had been burnt again; and how

33

Susan Lightfoot had been seen with artificial flowers in her bonnet, thereby giving evidence of a vain and giddy character. Mr Hale sipped his tea in abstracted silence; Margaret had the responses all to herself. She wondered how her father and mother could be so forgetful, so regardless of their companion through the day, as never to mention his name. She forgot that he had not made them an offer.

After tea Mr Hale got up, and stood with his elbow on the chimney-piece, leaning his head on his hand, musing over something, and from time to time sighing deeply. Mrs Hale went out to consult with Dixon about some winter clothing for the poor. Margaret was preparing her mother's worsted work, and rather shrinking from the thought of the long evening, and wishing bed-time were come that she might go over the events of the day again.

'Margaret!' said Mr Hale, at last, in a sort of sudden desperate way, that made her start. 'Is that tapestry thing of immediate consequence? I mean, can you leave it and come into my study? I want to speak to you about something very serious to us all.'

'Very serious to us all.' Mr Lennox had never had the opportunity of having any private conversation with her father after her refusal, or else that would indeed be a very serious affair. In the first place, Margaret felt guilty and ashamed[2] of having grown so much into a woman as to be thought of in marriage; and secondly, she did not know if her father might not be displeased that she had taken upon herself to decline Mr Lennox's proposal. But she soon felt it was not about anything, which having only lately and suddenly occurred, could have given rise to any complicated thoughts, that her father wished to speak to her. He made her take a chair by him; he stirred the fire, snuffed the candles, and sighed once or twice before he could make up his mind to say – and it came out with a jerk after all – 'Margaret! I am going to leave Helstone.'

'Leave Helstone, papa! But why?'

Mr Hale did not answer for a minute or two. He played with some papers on the table in a nervous and confused manner, opening his lips to speak several times, but closing them again without having the courage to utter a word. Margaret could not bear the sight of the suspense, which was even more distressing to her father than to herself.

'But why, dear papa? Do tell me!'

He looked up at her suddenly, and then said with a slow and enforced calmness:

'Because I must no longer be a minister in the Church of England.'

Margaret had imagined nothing less than that some of the preferments which her mother so much desired had befallen her father at last – something that would force him to leave beautiful, beloved Helstone, and perhaps compel him to go and live in some of the stately and silent Closes which Margaret had seen from time to time in cathedral towns. They were grand and imposing places, but if, to go there, it was necessary to leave Helstone as a home for ever, that would have been a sad, long, lingering pain. But nothing to the shock she received from Mr Hale's last speech. What could he mean? It was all the worse for being so mysterious. The aspect of piteous distress on his face, almost as imploring a merciful and kind judgement from his child, gave her a sudden sickening. Could he have become implicated in anything Frederick had done? Frederick was an outlaw. Had her father, out of a natural love for his son, connived at any –

'Oh! what is it? do speak, papa! tell me all! Why can you no longer be a clergyman? Surely, if the bishop were told all we know about Frederick, and the hard, unjust –'

'It is nothing about Frederick; the bishop would have nothing to do with that. It is all myself. Margaret, I will tell you about it. I will answer any questions this once, but after tonight let us never speak of it again. I can meet the consequences of my painful, miserable doubts; but it is an effort beyond me to speak of what has caused me so much suffering.'

'Doubts, papa! Doubts as to religion?' asked Margaret, more shocked than ever.

'No! not doubts as to religion; not the slightest injury to that.'

He paused. Margaret sighed, as if standing on the verge of some new horror. He began again, speaking rapidly, as if to get over a set task:

'You could not understand it all, if I told you – my anxiety, for years past, to know whether I had any right to hold my living – my efforts to quench my smouldering doubts[3] by the authority of the Church. Oh! Margaret, how I love the holy Church from which I am to be shut out!' He could not go on for a moment or two. Margaret could not tell what to say; it seemed to her as terribly mysterious as if her father were about to turn Mahometan.

'I have been reading today of the two thousand who were ejected[4] from their churches,' – continued Mr Hale, smiling faintly, – 'trying to steal some of their bravery; but it is of no use – no use – I cannot help feeling it acutely.'

'But, papa, have you well considered? Oh! it seems so terrible, so shocking,' said Margaret, suddenly bursting into tears. The one staid foundation of her home, of her idea of her beloved father, seemed reeling and rocking. What could she say? What was to be done? The sight of her distress made Mr Hale nerve himself, in order to try and comfort her. He swallowed down the dry choking sobs which had been heaving up from his heart hitherto, and going to his bookcase he took down a volume, which he had often been reading lately, and from which he thought he had derived strength to enter upon the course in which he was now embarked.

'Listen, dear Margaret,' said he, putting one arm round her waist. She took his hand in hers and grasped it tight, but she could not lift up her head; nor indeed could she attend to what he read, so great was her internal agitation.

'This is the soliloquy of one who was once a clergyman in a country parish, like me; it was written by a Mr Oldfield,[5] minister of Carsington, in Derbyshire, a hundred and sixty years ago, or more. His trials are over. He fought the good fight.' These last two sentences he spoke low, as if to himself. Then he read aloud, –

'When thou canst no longer continue in thy work without dishonour to God, discredit to religion, foregoing thy integrity, wounding conscience, spoiling thy peace, and hazarding the loss of thy salvation; in a word, when the conditions upon which thou must continue (if thou wilt continue) in thy employments are sinful, and unwarranted by the word of God, thou mayest, yea, thou must believe that God will turn thy very silence, suspension, deprivation, and laying aside, to His glory, and the advancement of the Gospel's interest. When God will not use thee in one kind, yet He will in another. A soul that desires to serve and honour Him shall never want opportunity to do it; nor must thou so limit the Holy One of Israel as to think He hath but one way in which He can glorify Himself by thee. He can do it by thy silence as well as by thy preaching; thy laying aside as well as thy continuance in thy work. It is not pretence of doing God the greatest service, or performing the weightiest duty, that will excuse the least sin, though that sin capacitated or gave us the opportunity for doing that duty. Thou wilt have little thanks, O my soul! if, when thou art charged with corrupting God's worship, falsifying thy vows, thou pretendest a necessity for it in order to a continuance in the ministry.'

As he read this, and glanced at much more which he did not read, he gained resolution for himself, and felt as if he too could be brave and firm in doing what he believed to be right; but as he ceased he heard Margaret's low convulsive sob; and his courage sank down under the keen sense of suffering.

'Margaret, dear!' said he, drawing her closer, 'think of the early martyrs; think of the thousands who have suffered.'

'But, father,' said she, suddenly lifting up her flushed, tear-wet face, 'the early martyrs suffered for the truth, while you – oh! dear, dear papa!'

'I suffer for conscience' sake, my child,' said he, with a dignity that was only tremulous from the acute sensitiveness of his character; 'I must do what my conscience bids. I have borne long with self-reproach that would have roused any mind less torpid and cowardly than mine.' He shook his head as he went on. 'Your poor mother's fond wish, gratified at last in the mocking way in which over-fond wishes are too often fulfilled – Sodom apples[6] as they are – has brought on this crisis, for which I ought to be, and I hope I am thankful. It is not a month since the bishop offered me another living; if I had accepted it, I should have had to make a fresh declaration of conformity to the Liturgy at my institution. Margaret, I tried to do it; I tried to content myself with simply refusing the additional preferment, and stopping quietly here, – strangling my conscience now, as I had strained it before. God forgive me!'

He rose and walked up and down the room, speaking low words of self-reproach and humiliation, of which Margaret was thankful to hear but few. At last he said,

'Margaret, I return to the old sad burden: we must leave Helstone.'

'Yes! I see. But when?'

'I have written to the bishop – I dare say I have told you so, but I forget things just now,' said Mr Hale, collapsing into his depressed manner as soon as he came to talk of hard matter-of-fact details, 'informing him of my intention to resign this vicarage. He has been most kind; he has used arguments and expostulations, all in vain – in vain. They are but what I have tried upon myself, without avail. I shall have to take my deed of resignation and wait upon the bishop myself, to bid him farewell. That will be a trial, but worse, far worse, will be the parting from my dear people. There is a curate appointed to read prayers – a Mr Brown. He will come to stay with us tomorrow. Next Sunday I preach my farewell sermon.'

Was it to be so sudden then? thought Margaret; and yet perhaps it was as well. Lingering would only add stings to the pain; it was better to be stunned into numbness by hearing of all these arrangements, which seemed to be nearly completed before she had been told. 'What does mamma say?' asked she, with a deep sigh.

To her surprise, her father began to walk about again before he answered. At length he stopped and replied:

'Margaret, I am a poor coward after all. I cannot bear to give pain. I know so well your mother's married life has not been all she hoped – all she had a right to expect – and this will be such a blow to her, that I have never had the heart, the power to tell her. She must be told though, now,' said he, looking wistfully at his daughter. Margaret was almost overpowered with the idea that her mother knew nothing of it all, and yet the affair was so far advanced!

'Yes, indeed she must,' said Margaret. 'Perhaps, after all, she may not – Oh yes! she will, she must be shocked' – as the force of the blow returned upon herself in trying to realize how another would take it. 'Where are we to go to?' said she at last, struck with a fresh wonder as to their future plans, if plans indeed her father had.

'To Milton-Northern,'⁷ he answered, with a dull indifference, for he had perceived that, although his daughter's love had made her cling to him, and for a moment strive to soothe him with her love, yet the keenness of the pain was as fresh as ever in her mind.

'Milton-Northern! The manufacturing town in Darkshire?'

'Yes,' said he, in the most despondent, indifferent way.

'Why there, papa?' asked she.

'Because there I can earn bread for my family. Because I know no one there, and no one knows Helstone, or can ever talk to me about it.'

'Bread for your family! I thought you and mamma had' – and then she stopped, checking her natural interest regarding their future life, as she saw the gathering gloom on her father's brow. But he, with his quick intuitive sympathy, read in her face, as in a mirror, the reflections of his own moody depression, and turned it off with an effort.

'You shall be told all, Margaret. Only help me to tell your mother. I think I could do anything but that: the idea of her distress turns me sick with dread. If I tell you all, perhaps you could break it to her tomorrow. I am going out for the day, to bid Farmer Dobson and the poor people on Bracy Common good-bye. Would you dislike breaking it to her very much, Margaret?'

Margaret did dislike it, did shrink from it more than from anything she had ever had to do in her life before. She could not speak, all at once. Her father said, 'You dislike it very much, don't you, Margaret?' Then she conquered herself, and said, with a bright strong look on her face:

'It is a painful thing, but it must be done, and I will do it as well as ever I can. You must have many painful things to do.'

Mr Hale shook his head despondingly: he pressed her hand in token of gratitude. Margaret was nearly upset again into a burst of crying. To turn her thoughts, she said: 'Now tell me, papa, what our plans are. You and mamma have some money, independent of the income from the living, have not you? Aunt Shaw has, I know.'

'Yes. I suppose we have about a hundred and seventy pounds a year[8] of our own. Seventy of that has always gone to Frederick, since he has been abroad. I don't know if he wants it all,' he continued in a hesitating manner. 'He must have some pay for serving with the Spanish army.'

'Frederick must not suffer,' said Margaret, decidedly; 'in a foreign country; so unjustly treated by his own. A hundred is left. Could not you, and I, and mamma live on a hundred a year in some very cheap – very quiet part of England? Oh! I think we could.'

'No!' said Mr Hale. 'That would not answer. I must do something. I must make myself busy, to keep off morbid thoughts. Besides, in a country parish I should be so painfully reminded of Helstone, and my duties here. I could not bear it, Margaret. And a hundred a year would go a very little way, after the necessary wants of housekeeping are met, towards providing your mother with all the comforts she has been accustomed to, and ought to have. No: we must go to Milton. That is settled. I can always decide better by myself, and not influenced by those whom I love,' said he as a half apology for having arranged so much before he had told any one of his family of his intentions. 'I cannot stand objections. They make me so undecided.'

Margaret resolved to keep silence. After all, what did it signify where they went, compared to the one terrible change?

Mr Hale continued: 'A few months ago, when my misery of doubt became more than I could bear without speaking, I wrote to Mr Bell – you remember Mr Bell, Margaret?'

'No; I never saw him, I think. But I know who he is. Frederick's godfather – your old tutor at Oxford, don't you mean?'

'Yes. He is a Fellow of Plymouth College there. He is a native of Milton-Northern, I believe. At any rate, he has property there, which has very much increased in value since Milton has become such a large manufacturing town. Well, I had reason to suspect – to imagine – I had better say nothing about it, however. But I felt sure of sympathy from Mr Bell. I don't know that he gave me much strength. He has lived an easy life in his college all his days. But he has been as kind as can be. And it is owing to him we are going to Milton.'

'How?' said Margaret.

'Why, he has tenants, and houses, and mills there; so, though he dislikes the place – too bustling for one of his habits – he is obliged to keep up some sort of connection; and he tells me that he hears there is a good opening for a private tutor there.'

'A private tutor!' said Margaret, looking scornful: 'What in the world do manufacturers want with the classics, or literature, or the accomplishments of a gentleman?'

'Oh,' said her father, 'some of them really seem to be fine fellows, conscious of their own deficiencies, which is more than many a man at Oxford is. Some want resolutely to learn, though they have come to man's estate. Some want their children to be better instructed than they themselves have been. At any rate, there is an opening, as I have said, for a private tutor. Mr Bell has recommended me to a Mr Thornton, a tenant of his, and a very intelligent man, as far as I can judge from his letters. And in Milton, Margaret, I shall find a busy life, if not a happy one, and people and scenes so different that I shall never be reminded of Helstone.'

There was the secret motive, as Margaret knew, from her own feelings. It would be different. Discordant as it was – with almost a detestation for all she had ever heard of the North of England, the manufacturers, the people, the wild and bleak country – there was this one recommendation – it would be different from Helstone, and could never remind them of that beloved place.

'When do we go?' asked Margaret, after a short silence.

'I do not know exactly. I wanted to talk it over with you. You see, your mother knows nothing about it yet: but I think, in a fortnight; – after my deed of resignation is sent in, I shall have no right to remain.'

Margaret was almost stunned.

'In a fortnight!'

'No – no, not exactly to a day. Nothing is fixed,' said her father with anxious hesitation, as he noticed the filmy sorrow that came over her eyes, and the sudden change in her complexion. But she recovered herself immediately.

'Yes, papa, it had better be fixed soon and decidedly, as you say. Only mamma to know nothing about it? It is that that is the great perplexity.'

'Poor Maria!' replied Mr Hale, tenderly. 'Poor, poor Maria! Oh, if I were not married – if I were but myself in the world, how easy it would be! As it is – Margaret, I dare not tell her!'

'No,' said Margaret, sadly, 'I will do it. Give me till tomorrow evening to choose my time. Oh, papa,' cried she, with sudden passionate entreaty, 'say – tell me it is a night-mare – a horrid dream – not the real waking truth! You cannot mean that you are really going to leave the Church – to give up Helstone – to be for ever separate from me, from mamma – led away by some delusion – some temptation! You do not really mean it!'

Mr Hale sat in rigid stillness while she spoke.

Then he looked her in the face, and said in a slow, hoarse, measured way – 'I do mean it, Margaret. You must not deceive yourself into doubting the reality of my words – my fixed intention and resolve.' He looked at her in the same steady, stony manner, for some moments after he had done speaking. She, too, gazed back with pleading eyes before she would believe that it was irrevocable. Then she arose and went, without another word or look, towards the door. As her fingers were on the handle he called her back. He was standing by the fireplace, shrunk and stooping; but as she came near he drew himself up to his full height, and, placing his hands on her head, he said, solemnly:

'The blessing of God be upon thee, my child!'

'And may He restore you to His Church,' responded she, out of the fulness of her heart. The next moment she feared lest this answer to his blessing might be irreverent, wrong – might hurt him as coming from his daughter, and she threw her arms round his neck. He held her to him for a minute or two. She heard him murmur to himself. 'The martyrs and confessors had even more pain to bear – I will not shrink.'

They were startled by hearing Mrs Hale inquiring for her daughter. They started asunder in the full consciousness of all that was before them. Mr Hale hurriedly said – 'Go, Margaret, go. I shall be out all tomorrow. Before night you will have told your mother.'

'Yes,' she replied, and she returned to the drawing-room in a stunned and dizzy state.

CHAPTER V

Decision

I ask Thee for a thoughtful love,[1]
Through constant watching wise,
To meet the glad with joyful smiles,
And to wipe the weeping eyes;
And a heart at leisure from itself
To soothe and sympathize.

ANON

Margaret made a good listener to all her mother's little plans for adding some small comforts to the lot of the poorer parishioners. She could not help listening, though each new project was a stab to her heart. By the time the frost had set in, they should be far away from Helstone. Old Simon's rheumatism might be bad and his eyesight worse; there would be no one to go and read to him, and comfort him with little porringers of broth and good red flannel: or if there was, it would be a stranger, and the old man would watch in vain for her. Mary Domville's little crippled boy would crawl in vain to the door and look for her coming through the forest. These poor friends would never understand why she had forsaken them; and there were many others besides. 'Papa has always spent the income he derived from his living in the parish. I am, perhaps, encroaching upon the next dues, but the winter is likely to be severe, and our poor old people must be helped.'

'Oh, mamma, let us do all we can,' said Margaret, eagerly, not seeing the prudential side of the question, only grasping at the idea that they were rendering such help for the last time; 'we may not be here long.'

'Do you feel ill, my darling?' asked Mrs Hale, anxiously, misunderstanding Margaret's hint of the uncertainty of their stay at Helstone. 'You look pale and tired. It is this soft, damp, unhealthy air.'

'No – no, mamma, it is not that: it is delicious air. It smells of the freshest, purest fragrance, after the smokiness of Harley Street. But I am tired: it surely must be near bedtime.'

'Not far off – it is half-past nine. You had better go to bed at once, dear. Ask Dixon for some gruel. I will come and see you as soon as you are in bed. I am afraid you have taken cold; or the bad air from some of the stagnant ponds –'

'Oh, mamma,' said Margaret, faintly smiling as she kissed her mother, 'I am quite well – don't alarm yourself about me; I am only tired.'

Margaret went upstairs. To soothe her mother's anxiety she submitted to a basin of gruel. She was lying languidly in bed when Mrs Hale came up to make some last inquiries and kiss her before going to her own room for the night. But the instant she heard her mother's door locked, she sprang out of bed, and throwing her dressing-gown on, she began to pace up and down the room, until the creaking of one of the boards reminded her that she must make no noise. She went and curled herself up on the window-seat in the small, deeply-recessed window. That morning when she had looked out her heart had danced at seeing the bright clear lights on the church tower, which foretold a fine and sunny day. This evening – sixteen hours at most had past by – she sat down, too full of sorrow to cry, but with a dull cold pain, which seemed to have pressed the youth and buoyancy out of her heart, never to return. Mr Henry Lennox's visit – his offer – was like a dream, a thing beside her actual life. The hard reality was, that her father had so admitted tempting doubts into his mind as to become a schismatic – an outcast; all the changes consequent upon this grouped themselves around that one great blighting fact.

She looked out upon the dark-gray lines of the church tower, square and straight in the centre of the view, cutting against the deep blue transparent depths beyond, into which she gazed, and felt that she might gaze for ever, seeing at every moment some farther distance, and yet no sign of God![2] It seemed to her at the moment, as if the earth was more utterly desolate than if girt in by an iron dome, behind which there might be the ineffaceable peace and glory of the Almighty: those never-ending depths of space, in their still serenity, were more mocking to her than any material bounds could be – shutting in the cries of earth's sufferers, which now might ascend into that infinite splendour of vastness and be lost – lost for ever, before they reached His throne. In this mood her father came in unheard. The moonlight was strong enough to let him see his daughter in her unusual place and attitude. He came to her and touched her shoulder before she was aware that he was there.

'Margaret, I heard you were up. I could not help coming in to ask you to pray with me – to say the Lord's Prayer; that will do good to both of us.'

Mr Hale and Margaret knelt by the window-seat – he looking up, she bowed down in humble shame. God was there, close around them, hearing her father's whispered words. Her father might be a heretic; but had not she, in her despairing doubts not five minutes before, shown herself a far more utter sceptic? She spoke not a word, but stole to bed after her father had left her, like a child ashamed of its fault. If the world was full of perplexing problems she would trust, and only ask to see the one step needful for the hour. Mr Lennox – his visit, his proposal – the remembrance of which had been so rudely pushed aside by the subsequent events of the day – haunted her dreams[3] that night. He was climbing up some tree of fabulous height to reach the branch whereon was slung her bonnet: he was falling, and she was struggling to save him, but held back by some invisible powerful hand. He was dead. And yet, with a shifting of the scene, she was once more in the Harley Street drawing-room, talking to him as of old, and still with a consciousness all the time that she had seen him killed by that terrible fall.

Miserable, unresting night! Ill preparation for the coming day! She awoke with a start, unrefreshed, and conscious of some reality worse even than her feverish dreams. It all came back upon her; not merely the sorrow, but the terrible discord in the sorrow. Where, to what distance apart, had her father wandered, led by doubts which were to her temptations of the Evil One? She longed to ask, and yet would not have heard for all the world.

The fine crisp morning made her mother feel particularly well and happy at breakfast-time. She talked on, planning village kindnesses, unheeding the silence of her husband and the monosyllabic answers of Margaret. Before the things were cleared away, Mr Hale got up; he leaned one hand on the table, as if to support himself:

'I shall not be at home till evening. I am going to Bracy Common, and will ask Farmer Dobson to give me something for dinner. I shall be back to tea at seven.'

He did not look at either of them, but Margaret knew what he meant. By seven the announcement must be made to her mother. Mr Hale would have delayed making it till half-past six, but Margaret was of different stuff. She could not bear the impending weight on her mind all the day long; better get the worst over; the day would be too short to comfort her mother. But while she stood by the window, thinking how to begin, and waiting for the servant to have left the room, her mother had gone up-stairs to put on her things to go to the school. She came down ready equipped, in a brisker mood than usual.

'Mother, come round the garden with me this morning; just one turn,' said Margaret, putting her arm round Mrs Hale's waist.

They passed through the open window. Mrs Hale spoke — said something — Margaret could not tell what. Her eye caught on a bee entering a deep-belled flower: when that bee flew forth with his spoil she would begin — that should be the sign. Out he came.

'Mamma! Papa is going to leave Helstone!' she blurted forth. 'He's going to leave the Church, and live in Milton-Northern.' There were the three hard facts hardly spoken.

'What makes you say so?' asked Mrs Hale, in a surprised incredulous voice. 'Who has been telling you such nonsense?'

'Papa himself,' said Margaret, longing to say something gentle and consoling, but literally not knowing how. They were close to a garden-bench. Mrs Hale sat down, and began to cry.

'I don't understand you,' she said. 'Either you have made some great mistake, or I don't quite understand you.'

'No, mother, I have made no mistake. Papa has written to the bishop, saying that he has such doubts that he cannot conscientiously remain a priest of the Church of England, and that he must give up Helstone. He has also consulted Mr Bell — Frederick's godfather, you know, mamma; and it is arranged that we go to live in Milton-Northern.' Mrs Hale looked up in Margaret's face all the time she was speaking these words: the shadow on her countenance told that she, at least, believed in the truth of what she said.

'I don't think it can be true,' said Mrs Hale, at length. 'He would surely have told me before it came to this.'

It came strongly upon Margaret's mind that her mother ought to have been told: that whatever her faults of discontent and repining might have been it was an error in her father to have left her to learn his change of opinion, and his approaching change of life, from her better-informed child. Margaret sat down by her mother, and took her unresisting head on her breast, bending her own soft cheeks down caressingly to touch her face.

'Dear, darling mamma! we were so afraid of giving you pain. Papa felt so acutely — you know you are not strong, and there must have been such terrible suspense to go through.'

'When did he tell you, Margaret?'

'Yesterday, only yesterday,' replied Margaret, detecting the jealousy which prompted the inquiry. 'Poor papa!' – trying to divert her mother's thoughts into compassionate sympathy for all her father had gone through. Mrs Hale raised her head.

'What does he mean by having doubts?' she asked. 'Surely, he does not mean that he thinks differently – that he knows better than the Church.'

Margaret shook her head, and the tears came into her eyes, as her mother touched the bare nerve of her own regret.

'Can't the bishop set him right?' asked Mrs Hale, half impatiently.

'I'm afraid not,' said Margaret. 'But I did not ask. I could not bear to hear what he might answer. It is all settled at any rate. He is going to leave Helstone in a fortnight. I am not sure if he did not say he had sent in his deed of resignation.'

'In a fortnight!' exclaimed Mrs Hale. 'I do think this is very strange – not at all right. I call it very unfeeling,' said she, beginning to take relief in tears. 'He has doubts, you say, and gives up his living, and all without consulting me. I dare say, if he had told me his doubts at the first I could have nipped them in the bud.'

Mistaken as Margaret felt her father's conduct to have been, she could not bear to hear it blamed by her mother. She knew that his very reverse had originated in a tenderness for her, which might be cowardly, but was not unfeeling.

'I almost hoped you might have been glad to leave Helstone, mamma,' said she, after a pause. 'You have never been well in this air, you know.'

'You can't think the smoky air of a manufacturing town, all chimneys and dirt like Milton-Northern, would be better than this air, which is pure and sweet, if it is too soft and relaxing. Fancy living in the middle of factories, and factory people! Though, of course, if your father leaves the Church, we shall not be admitted into society anywhere. It will be such a disgrace to us! Poor dear Sir John! It is well he is not alive to see what your father has come to! Every day after dinner, when I was a girl, living with your aunt Shaw, at Beresford Court, Sir John used to give for the first toast – "Church and King, and down with the Rump."'[4]

Margaret was glad that her mother's thoughts were turned away from the fact of her husband's silence to her on the point which must have been so near his heart. Next to the serious vital anxiety as to

46

the nature of her father's doubts, this was the one circumstance of the case that gave Margaret the most pain.

'You know, we have very little society here, mamma. The Gormans, who are our nearest neighbours (to call society – and we hardly ever see them), have been in trade just as much as these Milton-Northern people.'

'Yes,' said Mrs Hale, almost indignantly, 'but at any rate, the Gormans made carriages for half the gentry of the county, and were brought into some kind of intercourse with them; but these factory people, who on earth wears cotton that can afford linen?'

'Well, mamma, I give up the cotton-spinners; I am not standing up for them, any more than for any other trades-people. Only we shall have little enough to do with them.'

'Why on earth has your father fixed on Milton-Northern to live in?'

'Partly,' said Margaret, sighing, 'because it is so very different from Helstone – partly because Mr Bell says there is an opening there for a private tutor.'

'Private tutor in Milton! Why can't he go to Oxford, and be a tutor to gentlemen?'

'You forget, mamma! He is leaving the Church on account of his opinions – his doubts would do him no good at Oxford.'

Mrs Hale was silent for some time, quietly crying. At last she said: –

'And the furniture – How in the world are we to manage the removal? I never removed in my life, and only a fortnight to think about it!'

Margaret was inexpressibly relieved to find that her mother's anxiety and distress was lowered to this point, so insignificant to herself, and on which she could do so much to help. She planned and promised, and led her mother on to arrange fully as much as could be fixed before they knew somewhat more definitively what Mr Hale intended to do. Throughout the day Margaret never left her mother; bending her whole soul to sympathize in all the various turns her feelings took; towards evening especially, as she became more and more anxious that her father should find a soothing welcome home awaiting him, after his return from his day of fatigue and distress. She dwelt upon what he must have borne in secret for long; her mother only replied coldly that he ought to have told her, and that then at any rate he would have had an adviser to give him counsel;

and Margaret turned faint at heart when she heard her father's step in the hall. She dared not go to meet him, and tell him what she had done all day, for fear of her mother's jealous annoyance. She heard him linger, as if awaiting her, or some sign of her; and she dared not stir; she saw by her mother's twitching lips, and changing colour, that she too was aware that her husband had returned. Presently he opened the room-door, and stood there uncertain whether to come in. His face was gray and pale; he had a timid, fearful look in his eyes; something almost pitiful to see in a man's face; but that look of despondent uncertainty, of mental and bodily languor, touched his wife's heart. She went to him, and threw herself on his breast, crying out: –

'Oh! Richard, Richard, you should have told me sooner!'

And then, in tears, Margaret left her, as she rushed up-stairs to throw herself on her bed, and hide her face in the pillows to stifle the hysteric sobs that would force their way at last, after the rigid self-control of the whole day.

How long she lay thus she could not tell. She heard no noise, though the housemaid came in to arrange the room. The affrighted girl stole out again on tip-toe, and went and told Mrs Dixon that Miss Hale was crying as if her heart would break: she was sure she would make herself deadly ill if she went on at that rate. In consequence of this, Margaret felt herself touched, and started up into a sitting posture; she saw the accustomed room, the figure of Dixon in shadow, as the latter stood holding the candle a little behind her, for fear of the effect on Miss Hale's startled eyes, swollen and blinded as they were.

'Oh, Dixon! I did not hear you come into the room!' said Margaret, resuming her trembling self-restraint. 'Is it very late?' continued she, lifting herself languidly off the bed, yet letting her feet touch the ground without fairly standing down, as she shaded her wet ruffled hair off her face, and tried to look as though nothing were the matter; as if she had only been asleep.

'I hardly can tell what time it is,' replied Dixon, in an aggrieved tone of voice. 'Since your mamma told me this terrible news, when I dressed her for tea, I've lost all count of time. I'm sure I don't know what is to become of us all. When Charlotte told me just now you were sobbing, Miss Hale, I thought, no wonder, poor thing! And master thinking of turning Dissenter at his time of life, when, if it is not to be said he's done well in the Church, he's not done badly after all. I had a cousin, miss, who turned Methodist preacher after he was fifty years of age, and a tailor all his life; but then he had never been able to make a pair of trousers to fit, for as long as he had been in the trade, so it was no wonder; but for master! as I said to missus, "What would poor Sir John have said? he never liked your marrying Mr Hale, but if he could have known it would have come to this, he would have sworn worse oaths than ever, if that was possible!"'

Dixon had been so much accustomed to comment upon Mr Hale's proceedings to her mistress (who listened to her, or not, as she was in the humour), that she never noticed Margaret's flashing eye and dilating nostril. To hear her father talked of in this way by a servant to her face!

'Dixon!' she said, in the low tone she always used when much excited, which had a sound in it as of some distant turmoil, or threatening storm breaking far away. 'Dixon! you forget to whom you are speaking.' She stood upright and firm on her feet now, confronting the waiting-maid, and fixing her with her steady discerning eye. 'I am Mr Hale's daughter. Go! You have made a strange mistake, and one that I am sure your own good feeling will make you sorry for when you think about it.'

Dixon hung irresolutely about the room for a minute or two. Margaret repeated, 'You may leave me, Dixon. I wish you to go.' Dixon did not know whether to resent these decided words or to cry; either course would have done with her mistress: but, as she said to herself, 'Miss Margaret has a touch of the old gentleman about her, as well as poor Master Frederick; I wonder where they get it from?' and she, who would have resented such words from any one less haughty and determined in manner, was subdued enough to say, in a half humble, half injured tone:

'Mayn't I unfasten your gown, miss, and do your hair?'

'No! not tonight, thank you.' And Margaret gravely lighted her out of the room, and bolted the door. From henceforth Dixon obeyed and admired Margaret. She said it was because she was so like poor Master Frederick; but the truth was, that Dixon, as do many others, liked to feel herself ruled by a powerful and decided nature.

Margaret needed all Dixon's help in action, and silence in words: for, for some time, the latter thought it her duty to show her sense of affront by saying as little as possible to her young lady; so the energy came out in doing rather than in speaking. A fortnight was a very short time to make arrangements for so serious a removal; as Dixon said, 'Any one but a gentleman – indeed almost any other gentleman –' but catching a look at Margaret's straight, stern brow just here, she coughed the remainder of the sentence away, and meekly took the horehound drop that Margaret offered her, to stop the 'little tickling at my chest, miss.' But almost any one but Mr Hale would have had practical knowledge enough to see, that in so short a time it would be difficult to fix on any house in Milton-Northern, or indeed elsewhere, to which they could remove the furniture that had of necessity to be taken out of Helstone vicarage.

Mrs Hale, overpowered by all the troubles and necessities for immediate household decisions that seemed to come upon her at once, became really ill, and Margaret almost felt it as a relief when her mother fairly took to her bed, and left the management of affairs to her. Dixon, true to her post of body-guard, attended most faithfully to her mistress, and only emerged from Mrs Hale's bedroom to shake her head, and murmur to herself in a manner which Margaret did not choose to hear. For, the one thing clear and straight before her, was the necessity for leaving Helstone. Mr Hale's successor in the living was appointed; and, at any rate, after her father's decision, there must be no lingering now, for his sake, as well as from every other consideration. For he came home every evening more and more depressed, after the necessary leave-taking which he had re-solved to have with every individual parishioner. Margaret, inexperi-enced as she was in all the necessary matter-of-fact business to be got through, did not know to whom to apply for advice. The cook and Charlotte worked away with willing arms and stout hearts at all the moving and packing; and as far as that went, Margaret's admirable sense enabled her to see what was best, and to direct how it should be done. But where were they to go to? In a week they must be gone. Straight to Milton, or where? So many arrangements depended on this decision that Margaret resolved to ask her father one evening, in spite of his evident fatigue and low spirits. He answered:

'My dear! I have really had too much to think about to settle this. What does your mother say? What does she wish? Poor Maria!'

He met with an echo even louder than his sigh. Dixon had just come into the room for another cup of tea for Mrs Hale, and catching Mr Hale's last words, and protected by his presence from Margaret's upbraiding eyes, made bold to say, 'My poor mistress!'

'You don't think her worse today,' said Mr Hale, turning hastily.

'I'm sure I can't say, sir. It's not for me to judge. The illness seems so much more on the mind than on the body.'

Mr Hale looked infinitely distressed.

'You had better take mamma her tea while it is hot, Dixon,' said Margaret, in a tone of quiet authority.

'Oh! I beg your pardon, miss! My thoughts was otherwise occupied in thinking of my poor – of Mrs Hale.'

'Papa!' said Margaret, 'it is this suspense that is bad for you both. Of course, mamma must feel your change of opinions: we can't help that,' she continued, softly; 'but now the course is clear, at least to a certain point. And I think, papa, that I could get mamma to help me in planning, if you could tell me what to plan for. She has never expressed any wish in any way, and only thinks of what can't be helped. Are we to go straight to Milton? Have you taken a house there?'

'No,' he replied. 'I suppose we must go into lodgings, and look about for a house.'

'And pack up the furniture so that it can be left at the railway station, till we have met with one?'

'I suppose so. Do what you think best. Only remember, we shall have much less money to spend.'

They had never had much superfluity, as Margaret knew. She felt that it was a great weight suddenly thrown upon her shoulders. Four months ago, all the decisions she needed to make were what dress she would wear for dinner, and to help Edith to draw out the lists of who should take down whom in the dinner parties at home. Nor was the household in which she lived one that called for much decision. Except in the one grand case of Captain Lennox's offer, everything went on with the regularity of clockwork. Once a year, there was a long discussion between her aunt and Edith as to whether they should go to the Isle of Wight, abroad, or to Scotland; but at such times Margaret herself was secure of drifting, without any exertion of her own, into the quiet harbour of home. Now, since that day when Mr Lennox came, and startled her into a decision, every day brought some question, momentous to her, and to those whom she loved, to be settled.

Her father went up after tea to sit with his wife. Margaret remained alone in the drawing-room. Suddenly she took a candle and went into her father's study for a great atlas, and lugging it back into the drawing-room, she began to pore over the map of England. She was ready to look up brightly when her father came down-stairs.

'I have hit upon such a beautiful plan. Look here – in Darkshire, hardly the breadth of my finger from Milton, is Heston,[5] which I have often heard of from people living in the north as such a pleasant little bathing-place. Now, don't you think we could get mamma there with Dixon, while you and I go and look at houses, and get one all ready for her in Milton? She would get a breath of sea air to set her up for the winter, and be spared all the fatigue, and Dixon would enjoy taking care of her.'

'Is Dixon to go with us?' asked Mr Hale, in a kind of helpless dismay.

'Oh, yes!' said Margaret. 'Dixon quite intends it, and I don't know what mamma would do without her.'

'But we shall have to put up with a very different way of living, I am afraid. Everything is so much dearer in a town. I doubt if Dixon can make herself comfortable. To tell you the truth, Margaret, I sometimes feel as if that woman gave herself airs.'

'To be sure she does, papa,' replied Margaret; 'and if she has to put up with a different style of living, we shall have to put up with her airs, which will be worse. But she really loves us all, and would be miserable to leave us, I am sure – especially in this change; so, for mamma's sake, and for the sake of her faithfulness, I do think she must go.'

'Very well, my dear. Go on. I am resigned. How far is Heston from Milton? The breadth of one of your fingers does not give me a very clear idea of distance.'

'Well, then, I suppose it is thirty miles; that is not much!'

'Not in distance, but in –. Never mind! If you really think it will do your mother good, let it be fixed so.'

This was a great step. Now Margaret could work, and act, and plan in good earnest. And now Mrs Hale could rouse herself from her languor, and forget her real suffering in thinking of the pleasure and the delight of going to the sea-side. Her only regret was that Mr Hale could not be with her all the fortnight she was to be there, as he had been for a whole fortnight once, when they were engaged, and she was staying with Sir John and Lady Beresford at Torquay.

CHAPTER VI

Farewell

Unwatch'd the garden bough shall sway,[1]
The tender blossom flutter down,
Unloved that beech will gather brown,
The maple burn itself away;

Unloved, the sun-flower, shining fair,
Ray round with flames her disk of seed,
And many a rose-carnation feed
With summer spice the humming air;

Till from the garden and the wild
A fresh association blow,
And year by year, the landscape grow
Familiar to the stranger's child;

As year by year the labourer tills
His wonted glebe, or lops the glades;
And year by year our memory fades
From all the circle of the hills.

TENNYSON

The last day came; the house was full of packing-cases, which were being carted off at the front door, to the nearest railway station. Even the pretty lawn at the side of the house was made unsightly and untidy by the straw that had been wafted upon it through the open door and windows. The rooms had a strange echoing sound in them, – and the light came harshly and strongly in through the uncurtained windows, – seeming already unfamiliar and strange. Mrs Hale's dressing-room was left untouched to the last; and there she and Dixon were packing up clothes, and interrupting each other every now and then to exclaim at, and turn over with fond regard, some forgotten treasure, in the shape of some relic of the children while they were yet little. They did not make much progress with their work. Down-stairs, Margaret stood calm and collected, ready to counsel or advise the men who had been called in to help the cook and Charlotte. These two last, crying between whiles, wondered how the young lady could keep up so this last day, and settled it between them that she was not likely to care much for Helstone, having been

53

so long in London. There she stood, very pale and quiet, with her large grave eyes observing everything, – up to every present circumstance, however small. They could not understand how her heart was aching all the time, with a heavy pressure that no sighs could lift off or relieve, and how constant exertion for her perceptive faculties was the only way to keep herself from crying out with pain. Moreover, if she gave way, who was to act? Her father was examining papers, books, registers, what not, in the vestry with the clerk; and when he came in, there were his own books to pack up, which no one but himself could do to his satisfaction. Besides, was Margaret one to give way before strange men, or even household friends like the cook and Charlotte! Not she. But at last the four packers went into the kitchen to their tea; and Margaret moved stiffly and slowly away from the place in the hall where she had been standing so long, out through the bare echoing drawing-room, into the twilight of an early November evening. There was a filmy veil of soft dull mist obscuring, but not hiding, all objects, giving them a lilac hue, for the sun had not yet fully set; a robin was singing, – perhaps, Margaret thought, the very robin that her father had so often talked of as his winter pet, and for which he had made, with his own hands, a kind of robin-house by his study-window. The leaves were more gorgeous than ever; the first touch of frost would lay them all low on the ground. Already one or two kept constantly floating down, amber and golden in the low slanting sun-rays.

Margaret went along the walk under the pear-tree wall. She had never been along it since she paced it at Henry Lennox's side. Here, at this bed of thyme, he began to speak of what she must not think of now. Her eyes were on that late-blowing rose as she was trying to answer; and she had caught the idea of the vivid beauty of the feathery leaves of the carrots in the very middle of his last sentence. Only a fortnight ago! And all so changed! Where was he now? In London, – going through the old round; dining with the old Harley Street set, or with gayer young friends of his own. Even now, while she walked sadly through that damp and drear garden in the dusk, with everything falling and fading, and turning to decay around her, he might be gladly putting away his law-books after a day of satisfactory toil, and freshening himself up, as he had told her he often did, by a run in the Temple Gardens,[2] taking in the while the grand inarticulate mighty roar of tens of thousands of busy men, nigh at hand, but not seen, and catching ever, at his quick turns, glimpses of the lights of the city coming up out of the depths of the river. He had often spoken to Margaret of these hasty walks, snatched in the intervals between study and dinner. At his best times and in his best moods had he spoken of them; and the thought of them had struck upon her fancy. Here there was no sound. The robin had gone away into the vast stillness of night. Now and then, a cottage door in the distance was opened and shut, as if to admit the tired labourer to his home; but that sounded very far away. A stealthy, creeping, cranching sound among the crisp fallen leaves of the forest, beyond the garden, seemed almost close at hand. Margaret knew it was some poacher.[3] Sitting up in her bed-room this past autumn, with the light of her candle extinguished, and purely revelling in the solemn beauty of the heavens and the earth, she had many a time seen the light noiseless leap of the poachers over the garden-fence, their quick tramp across the dewy moonlit lawn, their disappearance in the black still shadow beyond. The wild adventurous freedom of their life had taken her fancy; she felt inclined to wish them success; she had no fear of them. But tonight she was afraid, she knew not why. She heard Charlotte shutting the windows, and fastening up for the night, unconscious that any one had gone out into the garden. A small branch – it might be of rotten wood, or it might be broken by force – came heavily down in the nearest part of the forest; Margaret ran, swift as Camilla,[4] down to the window, and rapped at it with a hurried tremulousness which startled Charlotte within.

'Let me in! Let me in! It is only me, Charlotte!' Her heart did not still its fluttering till she was safe in the drawing-room, with the windows fastened and bolted, and the familiar walls hemming her round, and shutting her in. She had sate down upon a packing-case; cheerless, chill was the dreary and dismantled room – no fire, nor other light, but Charlotte's long unsnuffed candle. Charlotte looked at Margaret with surprise; and Margaret, feeling it rather than seeing it, rose up.

'I was afraid you were shutting me out altogether, Charlotte,' said she, half-smiling. 'And then you would never have heard me in the kitchen, and the doors into the lane and churchyard are locked long ago.'

'Oh, miss, I should have been sure to have missed you soon. The men would have wanted you to tell them how to go on. And I have put tea in master's study, as being the most comfortable room, so to speak.'

'Thank you, Charlotte. You are a kind girl. I shall be sorry to leave you. You must try and write to me, if I can ever give you any little help or good advice. I shall always be glad to get a letter from Helstone, you know. I shall be sure and send you my address when I know it.'

The study was all ready for tea. There was a good blazing fire, and unlighted candles on the table. Margaret sat down on the rug, partly to warm herself, for the dampness of the evening hung about her dress, and overfatigue had made her chilly. She kept herself balanced by clasping her hands together round her knees; her head dropped a little towards her chest; the attitude was one of despondency, whatever her frame of mind might be. But when she heard her father's step on the gravel outside, she started up, and hastily shaking her heavy black hair back, and wiping a few tears away that had come on her cheeks she knew not how, she went out to open the door for him. He showed far more depression than she did. She could hardly get him to talk, although she tried to speak on subjects that would interest him, at the cost of an effort every time which she thought would be her last.

'Have you been a very long walk today?' asked she, on seeing his refusal to touch food of any kind.

'As far as Fordham Beeches. I went to see Widow Maltby: she is sadly grieved at not having wished you good-bye. She says little Susan has kept watch down the lane for days past. – Nay, Margaret, what is the matter, dear?' The thought of the little child watching for her, and continually disappointed – from no forgetfulness on her part, but from sheer inability to leave home – was the last drop in poor Margaret's cup, and she was sobbing away as if her heart would break. Mr Hale was distressingly perplexed. He rose, and walked nervously up and down the room. Margaret tried to check herself, but would not speak until she could do so with firmness. She heard him talking, as if to himself.

'I cannot bear it. I cannot bear to see the sufferings of others. I think I could go through my own with patience. Oh, is there no going back?'

'No, father,' said Margaret, looking straight at him, and speaking low and steadily. 'It is bad to believe you in error. It would be infinitely worse to have known you a hypocrite.' She dropped her voice at the last few words, as if entertaining the idea of hypocrisy for a moment in connection with her father savoured of irreverence.

'Besides,' she went on, 'it is only that I am tired tonight; don't think that I am suffering from what you have done, dear papa. We can't either of us talk about it tonight, I believe,' said she, finding that tears and sobs would come in spite of herself.

'I had better go and take mamma up this cup of tea. She had hers very early, when I was too busy to go to her, and I am sure she will be glad of another now.'

Railroad time inexorably wrenched them away from lovely, beloved Helstone, the next morning. They were gone; they had seen the last of the long low parsonage home, half-covered with China-roses and pyracanthus – more homelike than ever in the morning sun that glittered on its windows, each belonging to some well-loved room. Almost before they had settled themselves into the car, sent from Southampton to fetch them to the station, they were gone away to return no more. A sting at Margaret's heart made her strive to look out to catch the last glimpse of the old church tower at the turn where she knew it might be seen above a wave of the forest trees; but her father remembered this too, and she silently acknowledged his greater right to the one window from which it could be seen. She leant back and shut her eyes, and the tears welled forth, and hung glittering for an instant on the shadowing eyelashes before rolling slowly down her cheeks, and dropping, unheeded, on her dress.

They were to stop in London all night at some quiet hotel. Poor Mrs Hale had cried in her way nearly all day long; and Dixon showed her sorrow by extreme crossness, and a continual irritable attempt to keep her petticoats from even touching the unconscious Mr Hale, whom she regarded as the origin of all this suffering.

They went through the well-known streets, past houses which they had often visited, past shops in which she had lounged, impatient, by her aunt's side, while that lady was making some important and interminable decision – nay, absolutely past acquaintances in the streets; for though the morning had been of an incalculable length to them, and they felt as if it ought long ago to have closed in for the repose of darkness, it was the very busiest time of a London afternoon in November when they arrived there. It was long since Mrs Hale had been in London; and she roused up, almost like a child, to look about her at the different streets, and to gaze after and exclaim at the shops and carriages.

'Oh, there's Harrison's, where I bought so many of my wedding-things. Dear! how altered! They've got immense plate-glass windows, larger than Crawford's in Southampton. Oh, and there, I declare – no, it is not – yes, it is – Margaret, we have just passed Mr Henry Lennox. Where can he be going, among all these shops?'

Margaret started forwards, and as quickly fell back, half-smiling at herself for the sudden motion. They were a hundred yards away by this time; but he seemed like a relic of Helstone – he was associated with a bright morning, an eventful day, and she should have liked to have seen him, without his seeing her, – without the chance of their speaking.

The evening, without employment, passed in a room high up in an hotel, was long and heavy. Mr Hale went out to his bookseller's, and to call on a friend or two. Every one they saw, either in the house or out in the streets, appeared hurrying to some appointment, expected by, or expecting somebody. They alone seemed strange and friendless, and desolate. Yet within a mile, Margaret knew of house after house, where she for her own sake, and her mother for her aunt Shaw's, would be welcomed, if they came in gladness, or even in peace of mind. If they came sorrowing, and wanting sympathy in a complicated trouble like the present, then they would be felt as a shadow in all these houses of intimate acquaintances, not friends. London life is too whirling[5] and full to admit of even an hour of that deep silence of feeling which the friends of Job showed, when 'they sat with him on the ground seven days and seven nights, and none spake a word unto him; for they saw that his grief was very great.'

CHAPTER VII

New Scenes and Faces

Mist clogs the sunshine,[1]
Smoky dwarf houses
Have we round on every side.
MATTHEW ARNOLD

The next afternoon, about twenty miles from Milton-Northern, they entered on the little branch railway that led to Heston. Heston itself was one long straggling street, running parallel to the seashore. It had a character of its own, as different from the little bathing-places in the south of England as they again from those of the continent. To use a Scotch word, every thing looked more 'purposelike.' The country carts had more iron, and less wood and leather about the horse-gear; the people in the streets, although on pleasure bent, had yet a busy mind. The colours looked grayer – more enduring, not so gay and pretty. There were no smock-frocks, even among the country folk; they retarded motion, and were apt to catch on machinery, and so the habit of wearing them had died out. In such towns in the south of England, Margaret had seen the shopmen, when not employed in their business, lounging a little at their doors, enjoying the fresh air, and the look up and down the street. Here, if they had any leisure from customers, they made themselves business in the shop – even, Margaret fancied, to the unnecessary unrolling and re-rolling of ribbons. All these differences struck upon her mind, as she and her mother went out next morning to look for lodgings.

Their two nights at hotels had cost more than Mr Hale had anticipated, and they were glad to take the first clean, cheerful rooms they met with that were at liberty to receive them. There, for the first time for many days, did Margaret feel at rest. There was a dreaminess in the rest, too, which made it still more perfect and luxurious to repose in. The distant sea, lapping the sandy shore with measured sound; the nearer cries of the donkey-boys; the unusual scenes moving before her like pictures, which she cared not in her laziness to have fully explained before they passed away; the stroll down to the beach to breathe the sea-air, soft and warm on that sandy shore even to the end of November; the great long misty sea-line touching the tender-coloured sky; the white sail of a distant boat turning silver in some pale sunbeam: – it seemed as if she could dream her life away in such luxury of pensiveness, in which she made her present all in all, from not daring to think of the past, or wishing to contemplate the future.

But the future must be met, however stern and iron it be. One evening it was arranged that Margaret and her father should go the next day to Milton-Northern, and look out for a house. Mr Hale had received several letters from Mr Bell, and one or two from Mr Thornton, and he was anxious to ascertain at once a good many particulars respecting his position and chances of success there, which he could only do by an interview with the latter gentleman. Margaret knew that they ought to be removing; but she had a repugnance to the idea of a manufacturing town, and believed that her mother was receiving benefit from Heston air, so she would willingly have deferred the expedition to Milton.

For several miles before they reached Milton, they saw a deep lead-coloured cloud hanging over the horizon in the direction in which it lay. It was all the darker from contrast with the pale gray-blue of the wintry sky; for in Heston there had been the earliest signs of frost. Nearer to the town, the air had a faint taste and smell of smoke; perhaps, after all, more a loss of the fragrance of grass and herbage than any positive taste or smell. Quick they were whirled over long, straight, hopeless streets of regularly-built houses, all small and of brick. Here and there a great oblong many-windowed factory stood up, like a hen among her chickens, puffing out black 'unparliamentary' smoke,[2] and sufficiently accounting for the cloud which Margaret had taken to foretell rain. As they drove through the larger and wider streets, from the station to the hotel, they had to stop constantly; great loaded lurries blocked up the not over-wide thoroughfares. Margaret had now and then been into the city in her drives with her aunt. But there the heavy lumbering vehicles seemed various in their purposes and intent; here every van, every wagon and truck, bore cotton, either in the raw shape in bags, or the woven shape in bales of calico. People thronged the footpaths, most of them well-dressed as regarded the material, but with a slovenly looseness which struck Margaret as different from the shabby, threadbare smartness of a similar class in London.

'New Street,' said Mr Hale. 'This, I believe, is the principal street in Milton. Bell has often spoken to me about it. It was the opening of this street from a lane into a great thoroughfare, thirty years ago, which has caused his property to rise so much in value. Mr Thornton's mill must be somewhere not very far off, for he is Mr Bell's tenant. But I fancy he dates from his warehouse.'

'Where is our hotel, papa?'

'Close to the end of this street, I believe. Shall we have lunch before or after we have looked at the houses we marked in the Milton Times?'

'Oh, let us get our work done first.'

'Very well. Then I will only see if there is any note or letter for me from Mr Thornton, who said he would let me know anything he might hear about these houses, and then we will set off. We will keep the cab; it will be safer than losing ourselves, and being too late for the train this afternoon.'

There were no letters awaiting him. They set out on their house-hunting. Thirty pounds a-year was all they could afford to give, but in Hampshire they could have met with a roomy house and pleasant garden for the money. Here, even the necessary accommodation of two sitting-rooms and four bedrooms seemed unattainable. They went through their list, rejecting each as they visited it. Then they looked at each other in dismay.

'We must go back to the second, I think. That one, – in Crampton, don't they call the suburb? There were three sitting-rooms; don't you remember how we laughed at the number compared with the three bed-rooms? But I have planned it all. The front room down-stairs is to be your study and our dining-room (poor papa!), for, you know, we settled mamma is to have as cheerful a sitting-room as we can get; and that front room up-stairs, with the atrocious blue and pink paper and heavy cornice, had really a pretty view over the plain, with a great bend of river, or canal, or whatever it is, down below. Then I could have the little bed-room behind, in that projection at the head of the first flight of stairs – over the kitchen, you know – and you and mamma the room behind the drawing-room, and that closet in the roof will make you a splendid dressing-room.'

'But Dixon, and the girl we are to have to help?'

'Oh, wait a minute. I am overpowered by the discovery of my own genius for management. Dixon is to have – let me see, I had it once – the back sitting-room. I think she will like that. She grumbles so much about the stairs at Heston; and the girl is to have that sloping attic over your room and mamma's. Won't that do?'

'I dare say it will. But the papers. What taste! and the overloading such a house with colour and such heavy cornices!'

'Never mind, papa! Surely, you can charm the landlord into re-papering one or two of the rooms – the drawing-room and your bed-room – for mamma will come most in contact with them; and your bookshelves will hide a great deal of that gaudy pattern in the dining-room.'

'Then you think it the best? If so, I had better go at once and call on this Mr Donkin, to whom the advertisement refers me. I will take you back to the hotel, where you can order lunch, and rest, and by the time it is ready, I shall be with you. I hope I shall be able to get new papers.'

Margaret hoped so too, though she said nothing. She had never come fairly in contact with the taste that loves ornament, however bad, more than the plainness and simplicity which are of themselves the framework of elegance.

Her father took her through the entrance of the hotel, and leaving her at the foot of the staircase, went to the address of the landlord of the house they had fixed upon. Just as Margaret had her hand on the door of their sitting-room, she was followed by a quick-stepping waiter:

'I beg your pardon, ma'am. The gentleman was gone so quickly, I had no time to tell him. Mr Thornton called almost directly after you left; and, as I understood from what the gentleman said, you would be back in an hour, I told him so, and he came again about five minutes ago, and said he would wait for Mr Hale. He is in your room now, ma'am.'

'Thank you. My father will return soon, and then you can tell him.'

Margaret opened the door and went in with the straight, fearless, dignified presence habitual to her. She felt no awkwardness; she had too much the habits of society for that. Here was a person come on business to her father; and, as he was one who had shown himself obliging, she was disposed to treat him with a full measure of civility. Mr Thornton was a good deal more surprised and discomfited than she. Instead of a quiet, middle-aged clergyman, – a young lady came forward with frank dignity, – a young lady of a different type to most of those he was in the habit of seeing. Her dress was very plain: a close straw bonnet of the best material and shape, trimmed with white ribbon; a dark silk gown, without any trimming or flounce; a large Indian shawl, which hung about her in long heavy folds, and which she wore as an empress wears her drapery. He did not understand who she was, as he caught the simple, straight, unabashed look, which showed that his being there was of no concern to the beautiful countenance, and called up no flush of surprise to the pale ivory of the complexion. He had heard that Mr Hale had a daughter, but he had imagined that she was a little girl.

'Mr Thornton, I believe!' said Margaret, after a half-instant's pause, during which his unready words would not come. 'Will you sit down. My father brought me to the door, not a minute ago, but unfortunately he was not told that you were here, and he has gone away on some business. But he will come back almost directly. I am sorry you have had the trouble of calling twice.'

Mr Thornton was in habits of authority himself, but she seemed to assume some kind of rule over him at once. He had been getting impatient at the loss of his time on a market-day, the moment before she appeared, yet now he calmly took a seat at her bidding.

'Do you know where it is that Mr Hale has gone to? Perhaps I might be able to find him.'

'He has gone to a Mr Donkin's in Canute Street. He is the landlord of the house my father wishes to take in Crampton.'

Mr Thornton knew the house. He had seen the advertisement, and been to look at it, in compliance with a request of Mr Bell's that he would assist Mr Hale to the best of his power: and also instigated by his own interest in the case of a clergyman who had given up his living under circumstances such as those of Mr Hale. Mr Thornton had thought that the house in Crampton was really just the thing; but now that he saw Margaret, with her superb ways of moving and looking, he began to feel ashamed of having imagined that it would do very well for the Hales, in spite of a certain vulgarity in it which had struck him at the time of his looking it over.

Margaret could not help her looks; but the short curled upper lip, the round, massive up-turned chin, the manner of carrying her head, her movements, full of a soft feminine defiance, always gave strangers the impression of haughtiness. She was tired now, and would rather have remained silent, and taken the rest her father had planned for her; but, of course, she owed it to herself to be a gentlewoman, and to speak courteously from time to time to this stranger; not over-brushed, nor over polished, it must be confessed, after his rough encounter with Milton streets and crowds. She wished that he would go, as he had once spoken of doing, instead of sitting there, answering with curt sentences all the remarks she made. She had taken off her shawl, and hung it over the back of her chair. She sat facing him and facing the light; her full beauty met his eye; her round white flexile throat rising out of the full, yet lithe figure; her lips, moving so slightly as she spoke, not breaking the cold serene look of her face with any variation from the one lovely haughty curve; her eyes, with their soft gloom, meeting his with quiet maiden freedom. He almost said to himself that he did not like her, before their conversation ended; he tried so to compensate himself for the mortified feeling, that while he looked upon her with an admiration he could not repress, she looked at him with proud indifference, taking him, he thought, for what, in his irritation, he told himself he was – a great rough fellow, with not a grace or a refinement about him. Her quiet coldness of demeanour he interpreted into contemptuousness, and resented it in his heart to the pitch of almost inclining him to get up and go away, and have nothing more to do with these Hales, and their superciliousness.

Just as Margaret had exhausted her last subject of conversation – and yet conversation that could hardly be called which consisted of so few and such short speeches – her father came in, and with his pleasant gentlemanly courteousness of apology, reinstated his name and family in Mr Thornton's good opinion.

Mr Hale and his visitor had a good deal to say respecting their mutual friend, Mr Bell; and Margaret, glad that her part of entertaining the visitor was over, went to the window to try and make herself more familiar with the strange aspect of the street. She got so much absorbed in watching what was going on outside that she hardly heard her father when he spoke to her, and he had to repeat what he said:

'Margaret! the landlord will persist in admiring that hideous paper, and I am afraid we must let it remain.'

'Oh dear! I am sorry!' she replied, and began to turn over in her mind the possibility of hiding part of it, at least, by some of her sketches, but gave up the idea at last, as likely only to make bad worse. Her father, meanwhile, with his kindly country hospitality, was pressing Mr Thornton to stay to luncheon with them. It would have been very inconvenient to him to do so, yet he felt that he should have yielded, if Margaret by word or look had seconded her father's invitation; he was glad she did not, and yet he was irritated at her for not doing it. She gave him a low, grave bow when he left, and he felt more awkward and self-conscious in every limb than he had ever done in all his life before.

'Well, Margaret, now to luncheon, as fast as we can. Have you ordered it?'

'No, papa; that man was here when I came home, and I have never had an opportunity.'

'Then we must take anything we can get. He must have been waiting a long time, I'm afraid.'

'It seemed exceedingly long to me. I was just at the last gasp when you came in. He never went on with any subject, but gave little, short, abrupt answers.'

'Very much to the point though, I should think. He is a clear-headed fellow. He said (did you hear?) that Crampton is on gravelly soil, and by far the most healthy suburb in the neighbourhood of Milton.'

When they returned to Heston, there was the day's account to be given to Mrs Hale, who was full of questions which they answered in the intervals of tea-drinking.

'And what is your correspondent, Mr Thornton, like?'

'Ask Margaret,' said her husband. 'She and he had a long attempt at conversation, while I was away speaking to the landlord.'

'Oh! I hardly know what he is like,' said Margaret, lazily; too tired to tax her powers of description much. And then rousing herself, she said, 'He is a tall, broad-shouldered man, about – how old, papa?'

'I should guess about thirty.'

'About thirty – with a face that is neither exactly plain, nor yet handsome, nothing remarkable – not quite a gentleman,[3] but that was hardly to be expected.'

'Not vulgar or common though,' put in her father, rather jealous of any disparagement of the sole friend he had in Milton.

'Oh no!' said Margaret. 'With such an expression of resolution and power, no face, however plain in feature, could be either vulgar or common. I should not like to have to bargain with him; he looks very inflexible. Altogether a man who seems made for his niche, mamma; sagacious, and strong, as becomes a great tradesman.'

'Don't call the Milton manufacturers tradesmen, Margaret,' said her father. 'They are very different.'

'Are they? I apply the word to all who have something tangible to sell; but if you think the term is not correct, papa, I won't use it. But, oh mamma! speaking of vulgarity and commonness, you must prepare yourself for our drawing-room paper. Pink and blue roses, with yellow leaves! And such a heavy cornice round the room!'

But when they removed to their new house in Milton, the obnoxious papers were gone. The landlord received their thanks very composedly; and let them think, if they liked, that he had relented from his expressed determination not to repaper. There was no particular need to tell them, that what he did not care to do for a Reverend Mr Hale, unknown in Milton, he was only too glad to do at the one short sharp remonstrance of Mr Thornton, the wealthy manufacturer.

CHAPTER VIII

Home Sickness

And it's hame, hame, hame,[1]
Hame fain wad I be.

It needed the pretty light papering of the rooms to reconcile them to Milton. It needed more – more that could not be had. The thick yellow November fogs had come on; and the view of the plain in the valley, made by the sweeping bend of the river, was all shut out when Mrs Hale arrived at her new home.

Margaret and Dixon had been at work for two days, unpacking and arranging, but everything inside the house still looked in disorder; and outside a thick fog crept up to the very windows, and was driven into every open door in choking white wreaths of unwholesome mist.

'Oh, Margaret! are we to live here?' asked Mrs Hale, in blank dismay.

Margaret's heart echoed the dreariness of the tone in which this question was put. She could scarcely command herself enough to say, 'Oh, the fogs in London are sometimes far worse!'

'But then you knew that London itself, and friends lay behind it. Here – well! we are desolate. Oh Dixon, what a place this is!'

'Indeed, ma'am, I'm sure it will be your death before long, and then I know who'll – stay! Miss Hale, that's far too heavy for you to lift.'

'Not at all, thank you, Dixon,' replied Margaret, coldly. 'The best thing we can do for mamma is to get her room quite ready for her to go to bed, while I go and bring her a cup of coffee.'

Mr Hale was equally out of spirits, and equally came upon Margaret for sympathy.

'Margaret, I do believe this is an unhealthy place. Only suppose that your mother's health or yours should suffer. I wish I had gone into some country place in Wales; this is really terrible,' said he, going up to the window.

There was no comfort to be given. They were settled in Milton, and must endure smoke and fogs for a season; indeed, all other life seemed shut out from them by as thick a fog of circumstance. Only the day before, Mr Hale had been reckoning up with dismay how much their removal and fortnight at Heston had cost, and he found it had absorbed nearly all his little stock of ready money. No! here they were, and here they must remain.

At night when Margaret realized this, she felt inclined to sit down in a stupor of despair. The heavy smoky air hung about her bed-room, which occupied the long narrow projection at the back of the house. The window, placed at the side of the oblong, looked to the blank wall of a similar projection, not above ten feet distant. It loomed through the fog like a great barrier to hope. Inside the room everything was in confusion. All their efforts had been directed to make her mother's room comfortable. Margaret sat down on a box, the direction card upon which struck her as having been written at Helstone – beautiful, beloved Helstone! She lost herself in dismal thought: but at last she determined to take her mind away from the present; and suddenly remembered that she had a letter from Edith which she had only half read in the bustle of the morning. It was to tell of their arrival at Corfu; their voyage along the Mediterranean – their music, and dancing on board ship; the gay new life opening upon her; her house with its trellised balcony, and its views over white cliffs and deep blue sea.

Edith wrote fluently and well, if not graphically. She could not only seize the salient and characteristic points of a scene, but she could enumerate enough of indiscriminate particulars for Margaret to make it out for herself. Captain Lennox and another lately married officer shared a villa, high up on the beautiful precipitous rocks overhanging the sea. Their days, late as it was in the year, seemed spent in boating or land pic-nics; all out-of-doors, pleasure-seeking and glad, Edith's life seemed like the deep vault of blue sky above her, free – utterly free from fleck or cloud. Her husband had to attend drill, and she, the most musical officer's wife there, had to copy the new and popular tunes out of the most recent English music, for the benefit of the bandmaster; those seemed their most severe and arduous duties. She expressed an affectionate hope that, if the regiment stopped another year at Corfu, Margaret might come out and pay her a long visit. She asked Margaret if she remembered the day twelve-month on which she, Edith, wrote – how it rained all day long in Harley Street; and how she would not put on her new gown to go to a stupid dinner, and get it all wet and splashed in going to the carriage; and how at that very dinner they had first met Captain Lennox.

Yes! Margaret remembered it well. Edith and Mrs Shaw had gone to dinner. Margaret had joined the party in the evening. The recollection of the plentiful luxury of all the arrangements, the stately handsomeness of the furniture, the size of the house, the peaceful, untroubled ease of the visitors – all came vividly before her, in strange contrast to the present time. The smooth sea of that old life closed up, without a mark left to tell where they had all been. The habitual dinners, the calls, the shopping, the dancing evenings, were all going on, going on for ever, though her Aunt Shaw and Edith were no longer there; and she, of course, was even less missed. She doubted if any one of that old set ever thought of her, except Henry Lennox. He too, she knew, would strive to forget her, because of the pain she had caused him. She had heard him often boast of his power of putting any disagreeable thought far away from him. Then she penetrated farther into what might have been. If she had cared for him as a lover, and had accepted him, and this change in her father's opinions and consequent station had taken place, she could not doubt but that it would have been impatiently received by Mr Lennox. It was a bitter mortification to her in one sense; but she could bear it patiently, because she knew her father's purity of purpose, and that strengthened her to endure his errors, grave and serious though in her estimation they were. But the fact of the world esteeming her father degraded, in its rough wholesale judgement, would have oppressed and irritated Mr Lennox. As she realized what might have been, she grew to be thankful for what was. They were at the lowest now; they could not be worse. Edith's astonishment and her aunt Shaw's dismay would have to be met bravely, when their letters came. So Margaret rose up and began slowly to undress herself, feeling the full luxury of acting leisurely, late as it was, after all the past hurry of the day. She fell asleep, hoping for some brightness, either internal or external. But if she had known how long it would be before the brightness came, her heart would have sunk low down. The time of the year was most unpropitious to health as well as to spirits. Her mother caught a severe cold, and Dixon herself was evidently not well, although Margaret could not insult her more than by trying to save her, or by taking any care of her. They could hear of no girl to assist her; all were at work in the factories; at least, those who applied were well scolded by Dixon, for thinking that such as they could ever be trusted to work in a gentleman's house. So they had to keep a charwoman in almost constant employ. Margaret longed to send for Charlotte; but besides the objection of her being a better servant than they could now afford to keep, the distance was too great.

Mr Hale met with several pupils, recommended to him by Mr Bell, or by the more immediate influence of Mr Thornton. They were mostly of the age when many boys would be still at school, but, according to the prevalent, and apparently well-founded notions of Milton, to make a lad into a good tradesman he must be caught young, and acclimated to the life of the mill, or office, or warehouse. If he were sent to even the Scotch Universities, he came back unsettled for commercial pursuits; how much more so if he went to Oxford or Cambridge, where he could not be entered till he was eighteen? So most of the manufacturers placed their sons in sucking situations[2] at fourteen or fifteen years of age, unsparingly cutting away all off-shoots in the direction of literature or high mental cultivation, in hopes of throwing the whole strength and vigour of the plant into commerce. Still there were some wiser parents; and some young men, who had sense enough to perceive their own deficiencies, and strive to remedy them. Nay, there were a few no longer youths, but men in the prime of life, who had the stern wisdom to acknowledge their own ignorance, and to learn late what they should have learnt early. Mr Thornton was perhaps the oldest of Mr Hale's pupils. He was certainly the favourite. Mr Hale got into the habit of quoting his opinions so frequently, and with such regard, that it became a little domestic joke to wonder what time, during the hour appointed for instruction, could be given to absolute learning, so much of it appeared to have been spent in conversation.

Margaret rather encouraged this light, merry way of viewing her father's acquaintance with Mr Thornton, because she felt that her mother was inclined to look upon this new friendship of her husband's with jealous eyes. As long as his time had been solely occupied with his books and his parishioners, as at Helstone, she had appeared to care little whether she saw much of him or not; but now that he looked eagerly forward to each renewal of his intercourse with Mr Thornton, she seemed hurt and annoyed, as if he were slighting her companionship for the first time. Mr Hale's over-praise had the usual effect of over-praise upon his auditors; they were a little inclined to rebel against Aristides being always called the Just.[3]

After a quiet life in a country parsonage for more than twenty years, there was something dazzling to Mr Hale in the energy which conquered immense difficulties with ease; the power of the machinery of Milton, the power of the men of Milton, impressed him with a sense of grandeur, which he yielded to without caring to inquire into the details of its exercise. But Margaret went less abroad, among machinery and men; saw less of power in its public effect, and, as it happened, she was thrown with one or two of those who, in all measures affecting masses of people, must be acute sufferers for the good of many. The question always is, has everything been done to make the sufferings of these exceptions as small as possible? Or, in the triumph of the crowded procession, have the helpless been trampled on, instead of being gently lifted aside out of the roadway of the conqueror, whom they have no power to accompany on his march?

It fell to Margaret's share to have to look out for a servant to assist Dixon, who had at first undertaken to find just the person she wanted to do all the rough work of the house. But Dixon's ideas of helpful girls were founded on the recollection of tidy elder scholars at Helstone school, who were only too proud to be allowed to come to the parsonage on a busy day, and treated Mrs Dixon with all the respect, and a good deal more of fright, which they paid to Mr and Mrs Hale. Dixon was not unconscious of this awed reverence which was given to her; nor did she dislike it; it flattered her much as Louis the Fourteenth was flattered by his courtiers shading their eyes[4] from the dazzling light of his presence. But nothing short of her faithful love for Mrs Hale could have made her endure the rough independent way in which all the Milton girls, who made application for the servant's place, replied to her inquiries respecting their qualifications. They even went the length of questioning her back again; having doubts and fears of their own, as to the solvency of a family who lived in a house of thirty pounds a-year, and yet gave themselves airs, and kept two servants, one of them so very high and mighty. Mr Hale was no longer looked upon as Vicar of Helstone, but as a man who only spent at a certain rate. Margaret was weary and impatient of the accounts which Dixon perpetually brought to Mrs Hale of the behaviour of these would-be servants. Not but what Margaret was repelled by the rough uncourteous manners of these people; not but what she shrunk with fastidious pride from their hail-fellow accost, and severely resented their unconcealed curiosity as to the means and position of any family who lived in Milton, and yet were not engaged in trade of some kind. But the more Margaret felt impertinence, the more likely she was to be silent on the subject; and, at any rate, if she took upon herself to make inquiry for a servant, she could spare her mother the recital of all her disappointments and fancied or real insults.

Margaret accordingly went up and down to butchers and grocers, seeking for a nonpareil of a girl; and lowering her hopes and expectations every week, as she found the difficulty of meeting with any one in a manufacturing town who did not prefer the better wages and greater independence of working in a mill. It was something of a trial to Margaret to go out by herself in this busy bustling place. Mrs Shaw's ideas of propriety and her own helpless dependence on others, had always made her insist that a footman should accompany Edith and Margaret, if they went beyond Harley Street or the immediate neighbourhood. The limits by which this rule of her aunt's had circumscribed Margaret's independence had been silently rebelled against at the time: and she had doubly enjoyed the free walks and rambles of her forest life, from the contrast which they presented. She went along there with a bounding fearless step, that occasionally broke out into a run, if she were in a hurry, and occasionally was stilled into perfect repose, as she stood listening to, or watching any of the wild creatures who sang in the leafy courts, or glanced out with their keen bright eyes from the low brushwood or tangled furze. It was a trial to come down from such motion or such stillness, only guided by her own sweet will, to the even and decorous pace necessary in streets. But she could have laughed at herself for minding this change, if it had not been accompanied by what was a more serious annoyance.

The side of the town on which Crampton lay was especially a thoroughfare for the factory people. In the back streets around them there were many mills, out of which poured streams of men and women two or three times a day. Until Margaret had learnt the times of their ingress and egress, she was very unfortunate in constantly falling in with them. They came rushing along, with bold, fearless faces, and loud laughs and jests, particularly aimed at all those who appeared to be above them in rank or station. The tones of their unrestrained voices, and their carelessness of all common rules of street politeness, frightened Margaret a little at first. The girls, with their rough, but not unfriendly freedom, would comment on her dress, even touch her shawl or gown to ascertain the exact material; nay, once or twice she was asked questions relative to some article which they particularly admired. There was such a simple reliance on her womanly sympathy with their love of dress, and on her kindliness, that she gladly replied to these inquiries, as soon as she understood them; and half smiled back at their remarks. She did not mind meeting any number of girls, loud spoken and boisterous though they might be. But she alternately dreaded and fired up against the workmen, who commented not on her dress, but on her looks, in the same open fearless manner. She, who had hitherto felt that even the most refined remark on her personal appearance was an impertinence, had to endure undisguised admiration from these outspoken men.[5] But the very out-spokenness marked their innocence of any intention to hurt her delicacy, as she would have perceived if she had been less frightened by the disorderly tumult. Out of her fright came a flash of indignation which made her face scarlet, and her dark eyes gather flame, as she heard some of their speeches. Yet there were other sayings of theirs, which, when she reached the quiet safety of home, amused her even while they irritated her.

For instance, one day, after she had passed a number of men, several of whom had paid her the not unusual compliment of wishing she was their sweetheart, one of the lingerers added, 'Your bonny face, my lass, makes the day look brighter.' And another day, as she was unconsciously smiling at some passing thought, she was addressed by a poorly-dressed, middle-aged workman, with 'You may well smile, my lass; many a one would smile to have such a bonny face.' This man looked so careworn that Margaret could not help giving him an answering smile, glad to think that her looks, such as they were, should have had the power to call up a pleasant thought. He seemed to understand her acknowledging glance, and a silent recognition was established between them whenever the chances of the day brought them across each other's paths. They had never exchanged a word; nothing had been said but that first compliment: yet somehow Margaret looked upon this man with more interest than upon any one else in Milton. Once or twice, on Sundays, she saw him walking with a girl, evidently his daughter, and, if possible, still more unhealthy than he was himself.

One day Margaret and her father had been as far as the fields that lay round the town; it was early spring, and she had gathered some of the hedge and ditch flowers, dog-violets, lesser celandines, and the like, with an unspoken lament in her heart for the sweet profusion of the South. Her father had left her to go into Milton upon some business; and on the road home she met her humble friends. The girl looked wistfully at the flowers, and, acting on a sudden impulse, Margaret offered them to her. Her pale blue eyes lightened up as she took them, and her father spoke for her.

'Thank yo', Miss. Bessy'll think a deal o' them flowers; that hoo will; and I shall think a deal o' yor kindness. Yo're not of this country, I reckon?'

'No!' said Margaret, half sighing. 'I come from the South – from Hampshire,' she continued, a little afraid of wounding his consciousness of ignorance, if she used a name which he did not understand.

'That's beyond London, I reckon? And I come fro' Burnley-ways, and forty mile to th' North. And yet, yo' see, North and South has both met and made kind o' friends in this big smoky place.'

Margaret had slackened her pace to walk alongside of the man and his daughter, whose steps were regulated by the feebleness of the latter. She now spoke to the girl, and there was a sound of tender pity in the tone of her voice as she did so that went right to the heart of the father.

'I'm afraid you are not very strong.'

'No,' said the girl, 'nor never will be.'

'Spring is coming,' said Margaret, as if to suggest pleasant, hopeful thoughts.

'Spring nor summer will do me good,' said the girl quietly.

Margaret looked up at the man, almost expecting some contradiction from him, or at least some remark that would modify his daughter's utter hopelessness. But, instead, he added –

'I'm afeared hoo speaks truth. I'm afeared hoo's too far gone in a waste.'

'I shall have a spring where I'm boun' to, and flowers, and amaranths,[6] and shining robes besides.'

'Poor lass, poor lass!' said her father in a low tone. 'I'm none so sure o' that; but it's a comfort to thee, poor lass, poor lass. Poor father! it'll be soon.'

Margaret was shocked by his words – shocked but not repelled; rather attracted and interested.

'Where do you live? I think we must be neighbours, we meet so often on this road.'

'We put up at nine Frances Street, second turn to th' left at after yo've past th' Goulden Dragon.'

'And your name? I must not forget that.'

'I'm none ashamed o' my name. It's Nicholas Higgins. Hoo's called Bessy Higgins. Whatten yo' asking for?'

Margaret was surprised at this last question, for at Helstone it would have been an understood thing, after the inquiries she had made, that she intended to come and call upon any poor neighbour whose name and habitation she had asked for.

'I thought – I meant to come and see you.' She suddenly felt rather shy of offering the visit, without having any reason to give for her wish to make it, beyond a kindly interest in a stranger. It seemed all at once to take the shape of an impertinence on her part; she read this meaning too in the man's eyes.

'I'm none so fond of having strange folk in my house.' But then relenting, as he saw her heightened colour, he added, 'Yo're a foreigner, as one may say, and maybe don't know many folk here, and yo've given my wench here flowers out of yo'r own hand; – yo' may come if yo' like.'

Margaret was half-amused, half-nettled at this answer. She was not sure if she would go where permission was given so like a favour conferred. But when they came to the turn into Frances Street, the girl stopped a minute, and said,

'Yo'll not forget yo're to come and see us.'

'Aye, aye,' said the father, impatiently, 'hoo'll come. Hoo's a bit set up now, because hoo thinks I might ha' spoken more civilly; but hoo'll think better on it, and come. I can read her proud bonny face like a book. Come along, Bess; there's the mill bell ringing.'

Margaret went home, wondering at her new friends, and smiling at the man's insight into what had been passing in her mind. From that day Milton became a brighter place to her. It was not the long, bleak sunny days of spring, nor yet was it that time was reconciling her to the town of her habitation. It was that in it she had found a human interest.

CHAPTER IX

Dressing for Tea

Let China's earth, enrich'd with colour'd stains,[1]
Pencil'd with gold, and streak'd with azure veins,
The grateful flavour of the Indian leaf,
Or Mocha's sunburnt berry glad receive.

MRS BARBAULD

The day after this meeting with Higgins and his daughter, Mr Hale came upstairs into the little drawing-room at an unusual hour. He went up to different objects in the room, as if examining them, but Margaret saw that it was merely a nervous trick – a way of putting off something he wished, yet feared to say. Out it came at last –

'My dear! I've asked Mr Thornton to come to tea tonight.'

Mrs Hale was leaning back in her easy chair, with her eyes shut, and an expression of pain on her face which had become habitual to her of late. But she roused up into querulousness at this speech of her husband's.

'Mr Thornton! – and tonight! What in the world does the man want to come here for? And Dixon is washing my muslins and laces, and there is no soft water with these horrid east winds, which I suppose we shall have all the year round in Milton.'

'The wind is veering round, my dear,' said Mr Hale, looking out at the smoke, which drifted right from the east, only he did not yet understand the points of the compass, and rather arranged them ad libitum, according to circumstances.

'Don't tell me!' said Mrs Hale, shuddering up, and wrapping her shawl about her still more closely. 'But, east or west wind, I suppose this man comes.'

'Oh, mamma, that shows you never saw Mr Thornton. He looks like a person who would enjoy battling with every adverse thing he could meet with – enemies, winds, or circumstances. The more it rains and blows, the more certain we are to have him. But I'll go and help Dixon. I'm getting to be a famous clear-starcher. And he won't want any amusement beyond talking to papa. Papa, I am really longing to see the Pythias to your Damon.[2] You know I never saw him but once, and then we were so puzzled to know what to say to each other that we did not get on particularly well.'

'I don't know that you would ever like him, or think him agreeable, Margaret. He is not a lady's man.'

Margaret wreathed her throat in a scornful curve.

'I don't particularly admire ladies' men, papa. But Mr Thornton comes here as your friend – as one who has appreciated you' –

'The only person in Milton,' said Mrs Hale.

'So we will give him a welcome, and some cocoa-nut cakes. Dixon will be flattered if we ask her to make some; and I will undertake to iron your caps, mamma.'

Many a time that morning did Margaret wish Mr Thornton far enough away. She had planned other employments for herself: a letter to Edith, a good piece of Dante, a visit to the Higginses. But, instead, she ironed away, listening to Dixon's complaints, and only hoping that by an excess of sympathy she might prevent her from carrying the recital of her sorrows to Mrs Hale. Every now and then, Margaret had to remind herself of her father's regard for Mr Thornton, to subdue the irritation of weariness that was stealing over her, and bringing on one of the bad headaches to which she had lately become liable. She could hardly speak when she sat down at last, and told her mother that she was no longer Peggy the laundry-maid, but Margaret Hale the lady. She meant this speech for a little joke, and was vexed enough with her busy tongue when she found her mother taking it seriously.

'Yes! if any one had told me, when I was Miss Beresford, and one of the belles of the county, that a child of mine would have to stand half a day, in a little poky kitchen, working away like any servant, that we might prepare properly for the reception of a tradesman, and that this tradesman should be the only' –

'Oh, mamma!' said Margaret, lifting herself up, 'don't punish me so for a careless speech. I don't mind ironing, or any kind of work, for you and papa. I am myself a born and bred lady through it all, even though it comes to scouring a floor, or washing dishes. I am tired now, just for a little while; but in half an hour I shall be ready to do the same over again. And as to Mr Thornton's being in trade,[3] why he can't help that now, poor fellow. I don't suppose his education would fit him for much else.' Margaret lifted herself slowly up, and went to her own room; for just now she could not bear much more.

In Mr Thornton's house, at this very same time, a similar, yet different, scene was going on. A large-boned lady, long past middle age, sat at work in a grim handsomely-furnished dining-room. Her features, like her frame, were strong and massive, rather than heavy. Her face moved slowly from one decided expression to another equally decided. There was no great variety in her countenance; but those who looked at it once, generally looked at it again; even the passers-by in the street, half-turned their heads to gaze an instant longer at the firm, severe, dignified woman, who never gave way in street-courtesy, or paused in her straight-onward course to the clearly-defined end which she proposed to herself.

She was handsomely dressed in stout black silk, of which not a thread was worn or discoloured. She was mending a large long table-cloth of the finest texture, holding it up against the light occasionally to discover thin places, which required her delicate care. There was not a book about in the room, with the exception of Matthew Henry's Bible Commentaries,[4] six volumes of which lay in the centre of the massive side-board, flanked by a tea-urn on one side, and a lamp on the other. In some remote apartment, there was exercise upon the piano going on. Some one was practising up a morceau de salon, playing it very rapidly; every third note, on an average, being either indistinct, or wholly missed out, and the loud chords at the end being half of them false, but not the less satisfactory to the performer. Mrs Thornton heard a step, like her own in its decisive character, pass the dining-room door.

'John! Is that you?'

Her son opened the door and showed himself.

'What has brought you home so early? I thought you were going to tea with that friend of Mr Bell's; that Mr Hale.'

'So I am, mother; I am come home to dress!'

'Dress! humph! When I was a girl, young men were satisfied with dressing once in a day. Why should you dress to go and take a cup of tea with an old parson?'

'Mr Hale is a gentleman, and his wife and daughter are ladies.'

'Wife and daughter! Do they teach too? What do they do? You have never mentioned them.'

'No! mother, because I have never seen Mrs Hale; I have only seen Miss Hale for half an hour.'

'Take care you don't get caught by a penniless girl, John.'

'I am not easily caught, mother, as I think you know. But I must not have Miss Hale spoken of in that way, which, you know, is offensive to me. I never was aware of any young lady trying to catch me yet, nor do I believe that any one has ever given themselves that useless trouble.'

Mrs Thornton did not choose to yield the point to her son; or else she had, in general, pride enough for her sex.

'Well! I only say, take care. Perhaps our Milton girls have too much spirit and good feeling to go angling after husbands; but this Miss Hale comes out of the aristocratic counties, where, if all tales be true, rich husbands are reckoned prizes.'

Mr Thornton's brow contracted, and he came a step forward into the room.

'Mother' (with a short scornful laugh), 'you will make me confess. The only time I saw Miss Hale, she treated me with a haughty civility which had a strong flavour of contempt in it. She held herself aloof from me as if she had been a queen, and I her humble, unwashed vassal. Be easy, mother.'

'No! I am not easy, nor content either. What business had she, a renegade clergyman's daughter, to turn up her nose at you! I would dress for none of them – a saucy set! if I were you.' As he was leaving the room, he said: –

'Mr Hale is good, and gentle, and learned. He is not saucy. As for Mrs Hale, I will tell you what she is like tonight, if you care to hear.' He shut the door and was gone.

'Despise my son! treat him as her vassal, indeed! Humph! I should like to know where she could find such another! Boy and man, he's the noblest, stoutest heart I ever knew. I don't care if I am his mother! I can see what's what, and not be blind. I know what Fanny is; and I know what John is. Despise him! I hate her.'

CHAPTER X

Wrought Iron and Gold

We are the trees whom shaking fastens more.[1]
GEORGE HERBERT

Mr Thornton left the house without coming into the dining-room again. He was rather late, and walked rapidly out to Crampton. He was anxious not to slight his new friend by any disrespectful unpunctuality. The church-clock struck half-past seven as he stood at the door awaiting Dixon's slow movements; always doubly tardy when she had to degrade herself by answering the doorbell. He was ushered into the little drawing-room, and kindly greeted by Mr Hale, who led him up to his wife, whose pale face, and shawl-draped figure made a silent excuse for the cold languor of her greeting. Margaret was lighting the lamp when he entered, for the darkness was coming on. The lamp threw a pretty light into the centre of the dusky room, from which, with country habits, they did not exclude the night-skies, and the outer darkness of air. Somehow, that room contrasted itself with the one he had lately left; handsome, ponderous, with no sign of feminine habitation, except in the one spot where his mother sate, and no convenience for any other employment than eating and drinking. To be sure, it was a dining-room; his mother preferred to sit in it; and her will was a household law. But the drawing-room was not like this. It was twice – twenty times as fine; not one quarter as comfortable. Here were no mirrors, not even a scrap of glass to reflect the light, and answer the same purpose as water in a landscape; no gilding; a warm, sober breadth of colouring, well relieved by the dear old Helstone chintz-curtains and chair covers. An open davenport stood in the window opposite the door; in the other there was a stand, with a tall white china vase, from which drooped wreaths of English ivy, pale-green birch, and copper-coloured beech-leaves. Pretty baskets of work stood about in different places: and books, not cared for on account of their binding solely, lay on one table, as if recently put down. Behind the door was another table, decked out for tea, with a white table-cloth, on which flourished the cocoa-nut cakes, and a basket piled with oranges and ruddy American apples, heaped on leaves.

It appeared to Mr Thornton that all these graceful cares were habitual to the family; and especially of a piece with Margaret.[2] She stood by the tea-table in a light-coloured muslin gown, which had a good deal of pink about it. She looked as if she was not attending to the conversation, but solely busy with the tea-cups, among which her round ivory hands moved with pretty, noiseless daintiness. She had a bracelet on one taper arm, which would fall down over her round wrist. Mr Thornton watched the re-placing of this troublesome ornament with far more attention than he listened to her father. It seemed as if it fascinated him to see her push it up impatiently, until it tightened her soft flesh; and then to mark the loosening – the fall. He could almost have exclaimed – 'There it goes, again!' There was so little left to be done after he arrived at the preparation for tea, that he was almost sorry the obligation of eating and drinking came so soon to prevent his watching Margaret. She handed him his cup of tea with the proud air of an unwilling slave; but her eye caught the moment when he was ready for another cup; and he almost longed to ask her to do for him what he saw her compelled to do for her father, who took her little finger and thumb in his masculine hand, and made them serve as sugar-tongs. Mr Thornton saw her beautiful eyes lifted to her father, full of light, half-laughter and half-love, as this bit of pantomime went on between the two, unobserved, as they fancied, by any. Margaret's head still ached, as the paleness of her complexion, and her silence might have testified; but she was resolved to throw herself into the breach, if there was any long untoward pause, rather than that her father's friend, pupil, and guest should have cause to think himself in any way neglected. But the conversation went on; and Margaret drew into a corner, near her mother, with her work, after the tea-things were taken away; and felt that she might let her thoughts roam, without fear of being suddenly wanted to fill up a gap.

Mr Thornton and Mr Hale were both absorbed in the continuation of some subject which had been started at their last meeting. Margaret was recalled to a sense of the present by some trivial, low-spoken remark of her mother's; and on suddenly looking up from her work, her eye was caught by the difference of outward appearance between her father and Mr Thornton, as betokening such distinctly opposite natures. Her father was of slight figure, which made him appear taller than he really was, when not contrasted, as at this time, with the tall, massive frame of another. The lines in her father's face were soft and waving, with a frequent undulating kind of trembling movement passing over them, showing every fluctuating emotion; the eyelids were large and arched, giving to the eyes a peculiar languid beauty which was almost feminine.[3] The brows were finely arched, but were, by the very size of the dreamy lids, raised to a considerable distance from the eyes. Now, in Mr Thornton's face the straight brows fell low over the clear, deep-set earnest eyes, which, without being unpleasantly sharp, seemed intent enough to penetrate into the very heart and core of what he was looking at. The lines in the face were few but firm, as if they were carved in marble, and lay principally about the lips, which were slightly compressed over a set of teeth so faultless and beautiful as to give the effect of sudden sunlight when the rare bright smile, coming in an instant and shining out of the eyes, changed the whole look from the severe and resolved expression of a man ready to do and dare everything, to the keen honest enjoyment of the moment, which is seldom shown so fearlessly and instantaneously except by children. Margaret liked this smile; it was the first thing she had admired in this new friend of her father's; and the opposition of character, shown in all these details of appearance she had just been noticing, seemed to explain the attraction they evidently felt towards each other.

She rearranged her mother's worsted-work,[4] and fell back into her own thoughts – as completely forgotten by Mr Thornton as if she had not been in the room, so thoroughly was he occupied in explaining to Mr Hale the magnificent power, yet delicate adjustment of the might of the steam-hammer, which was recalling to Mr Hale some of the wonderful stories[5] of subservient genii in the Arabian Nights – one moment stretching from earth to sky and filling all the width of the horizon, at the next obediently compressed into a vase small enough to be borne in the hand of a child.

'And this imagination of power, this practical realization of a gigantic thought, came out of one man's brain in our good town. That very man has it within him to mount, step by step, on each wonder he achieves to higher marvels still. And I'll be bound to say, we have many among us who, if he were gone, could spring into the breach and carry on the war which compels, and shall compel, all material power to yield to science.'

'Your boast reminds me of the old lines –[6]

'I've a hundred captains in England,' he said,
'As good as ever was he.'

At her father's quotation Margaret looked suddenly up, with inquiring wonder in her eyes. How in the world had they got from cog-wheels to Chevy Chase.

'It is no boast of mine,' replied Mr Thornton; 'it is plain matter-of-fact. I won't deny that I am proud of belonging to a town – or perhaps I should rather say a district – the necessities of which give birth to such grandeur of conception. I would rather be a man toiling, suffering – nay, failing and successless – here, than lead a dull prosperous life in the old worn grooves of what you call more aristocratic society down in the South, with their slow days of careless ease. One may be clogged with honey and unable to rise and fly.'

'You are mistaken,' said Margaret, roused by the aspersion on her beloved South to a fond vehemence of defence, that brought the colour into her cheeks and the angry tears into her eyes. 'You do not know anything about the South. If there is less adventure or less progress – I suppose I must not say less excitement – from the gambling spirit of trade, which seems requisite to force out these wonderful inventions, there is less suffering also. I see men here going about in the streets who look ground down by some pinching sorrow or care – who are not only sufferers but haters. Now, in the South we have our poor, but there is not that terrible expression in their countenances of a sullen sense of injustice⁷ which I see here. You do not know the South, Mr Thornton,' she concluded, collapsing into a determined silence, and angry with herself for having said so much.

'And may I say you do not know the North?' asked he, with an inexpressible gentleness in his tone, as he saw that he had really hurt her. She continued resolutely silent; yearning after the lovely haunts she had left far away in Hampshire, with a passionate longing that made her feel her voice would be unsteady and trembling if she spoke.

'At any rate, Mr Thornton,' said Mrs Hale, 'you will allow that Milton is a much more smoky, dirty town than you will ever meet with in the South.'

'I'm afraid I must give up its cleanliness,' said Mr Thornton, with the quick gleaming smile. 'But we are bidden by parliament to burn our own smoke; so I suppose, like good little children, we shall do as we are bid – some time.'

'But I think you told me you had altered your chimneys[8] so as to consume the smoke, did you not?' asked Mr Hale.

'Mine were altered by my own will, before parliament meddled with the affair. It was an immediate outlay, but it repays me in the saving of coal. I'm not sure whether I should have done it, if I had waited until the act was passed. At any rate, I should have waited to be informed against and fined, and given all the trouble in yielding that I legally could. But all laws which depend for their enforcement upon informers and fines, become inert from the odiousness of the machinery. I doubt if there has been a chimney in Milton informed against for five years past, although some are constantly sending out one-third of their coal in what is called here unparliamentary smoke.'

'I only know it is impossible to keep the muslin blinds clean here above a week together; and at Helston we have had them up for a month or more, and they have not looked dirty at the end of that time. And as for hands – Margaret, how many times did you say you had washed your hands this morning before twelve o'clock? Three times, was it not?'

'Yes, mamma.'

'You seem to have a strong objection to acts of parliament and all legislation affecting your mode of management down here at Milton,' said Mr Hale.

'Yes, I have; and many others have as well. And with justice, I think. The whole machinery – I don't mean the wood and iron machinery now – of the cotton trade is so new that it is no wonder if it does not work well in every part all at once. Seventy years ago what was it? And now what is it not? Raw, crude materials came together; men of the same level, as regarded education and station, took suddenly the different positions of masters and men, owing to the motherwit, as regarded opportunities and probabilities, which distinguished some, and made them far-seeing as to what great future lay concealed in that rude model of Sir Richard Arkwright's.[9] The rapid development of what might be called a new trade, gave those early masters enormous power of wealth and command. I don't mean merely over the workmen; I mean over purchasers – over the whole world's market. Why, I may give you, as an instance, an advertisement, inserted not fifty years ago in a Milton paper, that so-and-so (one of the half-dozen calico-printers of the time) would close his warehouse at noon each day; therefore, that all purchasers must come before that hour. Fancy a man dictating in this manner the time when he would sell and when he would not sell. Now, I believe, if a good customer chose to come at midnight, I should get up, and stand hat in hand to receive his orders.'

Margaret's lip curled, but somehow she was compelled to listen; she could no longer abstract herself in her own thoughts.

'I only name such things to show what almost unlimited power the manufacturers had about the beginning of this century. The men were rendered dizzy by it. Because a man was successful in his ventures, there was no reason that in all other things his mind should be well-balanced. On the contrary, his sense of justice, and his simplicity, were often utterly smothered under the glut of wealth that came down upon him; and they tell strange tales of the wild extravagance of living indulged in on gala-days by those early cotton-lords. There can be no doubt, too, of the tyranny they exercised over their work-people. You know the proverb, Mr Hale, "Set a beggar on horseback, and he'll ride to the devil," – well, some of these early manufacturers did ride to the devil in a magnificent style – crushing human bone and flesh under their horses' hoofs without remorse. But by-and-by came a re-action; there were more factories, more masters; more men were wanted. The power of masters and men became more evenly balanced; and now the battle is pretty fairly waged between us. We will hardly submit to the decision of an umpire, much less to the interference of a meddler with only a smattering of the knowledge of the real facts of the case, even though that meddler be called the High Court of Parliament.'

'Is there necessity for calling it a battle between the two classes?' asked Mr Hale. 'I know, from your using the term, it is one which gives a true idea of the real state of things to your mind.'

'It is true; and I believe it to be as much a necessity as that prudent wisdom and good conduct are always opposed to, and doing battle with ignorance and improvidence. It is one of the great beauties of our system, that a working-man may raise himself into the power and position of a master[10] by his own exertions and behaviour; that, in fact every one who rules himself to decency and sobriety of conduct, and attention to his duties, comes over to our ranks; it may not be always as a master, but as an overlooker, a cashier, a book-keeper, a clerk, one on the side of authority and order.'

'You consider all who are unsuccessful in raising themselves in the world, from whatever cause, as your enemies, then, if I understand you rightly,' said Margaret, in a clear, cold voice.

'As their own enemies, certainly,' said he, quickly, not a little piqued by the haughty disapproval her form of expression and tone of speaking implied. But, in a moment, his straightforward honesty made him feel that his words were but a poor and quibbling answer to what she had said; and, be she as scornful as she liked, it was a duty he owed to himself to explain, as truly as he could, what he did mean. Yet it was very difficult to separate her interpretation, and keep it distinct from his meaning. He could best have illustrated what he wanted to say by telling them something of his own life; but was it not too personal a subject to speak about to strangers? Still, it was the simple straightforward way of explaining his meaning; so, putting aside the touch of shyness that brought a momentary flush of colour into his dark cheek, he said:

'I am not speaking without book. Sixteen years ago, my father died under very miserable circumstances. I was taken from school, and had to become a man (as well as I could) in a few days. I had such a mother as few are blest with; a woman of strong power, and firm resolve. We went into a small country town, where living was cheaper than in Milton, and where I got employment in a draper's shop (a capital place, by the way, for obtaining a knowledge of goods). Week by week our income came to fifteen shillings, out of which three people had to be kept. My mother managed so that I put by three of these fifteen shillings regularly. This made the beginning; this taught me self-denial. Now that I am able to afford my mother such comforts as her age, rather than her own wish, requires, I thank her silently on each occasion for the early training she gave me. Now when I feel that in my own case it is no good luck, nor merit, nor talent, – but simply the habits of life which taught me to despise indulgences not thoroughly earned, – indeed, never to think twice about them, – I believe that this suffering, which Miss Hale says is impressed on the countenances of the people of Milton, is but the natural punishment of dishonestly-enjoyed pleasure, at some former period of their lives. I do not look on self-indulgent, sensual people as worthy of my hatred; I simply look upon them with contempt for their poorness of character.'

'But you have had the rudiments of a good education,' remarked Mr Hale. 'The quick zest with which you are now reading Homer, shows me that you do not come to it as an unknown book; you have read it before, and are only recalling your old knowledge.'

'That is true, – I had blundered along it at school; I dare say, I was even considered a pretty fair classic[11] in those days, though my Latin and Greek have slipt away from me since. But I ask you, what preparation they were for such a life as I had to lead? None at all. Utterly none at all. On the point of education, any man who can read and write starts fair with me in the amount of really useful knowledge that I had at that time.'

'Well! I don't agree with you. But there I am perhaps somewhat of a pedant. Did not the recollection of the heroic simplicity of the Homeric life nerve you up?'

'Not one bit!' exclaimed Mr Thornton, laughing. 'I was too busy to think about any dead people, with the living pressing alongside of me, neck to neck, in the struggle for bread. Now that I have my mother safe in the quiet peace that becomes her age, and duly rewards her former exertions, I can turn to all that old narration and thoroughly enjoy it.'

'I dare say, my remark came from the professional feeling of there being nothing like leather,' replied Mr Hale.

When Mr Thornton rose up to go away, after shaking hands with Mr and Mrs Hale, he made an advance to Margaret to wish her good-bye in a similar manner. It was the frank familiar custom of the place; but Margaret was not prepared for it. She simply bowed her farewell; although the instant she saw the hand, half put out, quickly drawn back, she was sorry she had not been aware of the intention. Mr Thornton, however, knew nothing of her sorrow, and, drawing himself up to his full height, walked off, muttering as he left the house –

'A more proud, disagreeable girl I never saw. Even her great beauty is blotted out of one's memory by her scornful ways.'

CHAPTER XI

First Impressions

There's iron, they say, in all our blood,
And a grain or two perhaps is good;
But his, he makes me harshly feel,
Has got a little too much of steel.

ANON

'Margaret!' said Mr Hale, as he returned from showing his guest downstairs; 'I could not help watching your face with some anxiety, when Mr Thornton made his confession of having been a shop-boy. I knew it all along from Mr Bell; so I was aware of what was coming; but I half expected to see you get up and leave the room.'

'Oh, papa! you don't mean that you thought me so silly? I really liked that account of himself better than anything else he said. Everything else revolted me, from its hardness; but he spoke about himself so simply – with so little of the pretence that makes the vulgarity of shop-people, and with such tender respect for his mother, that I was less likely to leave the room then than when he was boasting about Milton, as if there was not such another place in the world; or quietly professing to despise people for careless, wasteful improvidence, without ever seeming to think it his duty to try to make them different, – to give them anything of the training which his mother gave him, and to which he evidently owes his position, whatever that may be. No! his statement of having been a shop-boy was the thing I liked best of all.'

'I am surprised at you, Margaret,' said her mother. 'You who were always accusing people of being shoppy at Helstone! I don't think, Mr Hale, you have done quite right in introducing such a person to us without telling us what he had been. I really was very much afraid of showing him how much shocked I was at some parts of what he said. His father "dying in miserable circumstances." Why it might have been in the workhouse.'

'I am not sure if it was not worse than being in the workhouse,' replied her husband. 'I heard a good deal of his previous life from Mr Bell before we came here; and as he has told you a part, I will fill up what he left out. His father speculated wildly, failed, and then killed himself, because he could not bear the disgrace. All his former friends shrunk from the disclosures that had to be made of his dishonest gambling – wild, hopeless struggles, made with other people's money, to regain his own moderate portion of wealth. No one came forwards to help the mother and this boy. There was another child, I believe, a girl; too young to earn money, but of course she had to be kept. At least, no friend came forwards immediately, and Mrs Thornton is not one, I fancy, to wait till tardy kindness comes to find her out. So they left Milton. I knew he had gone into a shop, and that his earnings, with some fragment of property secured to his mother, had been made to keep them for a long time. Mr Bell said they absolutely lived upon water-porridge for years – how, he did not know; but long after the creditors had given up hope of any payment of old Mr Thornton's debts (if, indeed, they ever had hoped at all about it, after his suicide,) this young man returned to Milton, and went quietly round to each creditor, paying him the first instalment of the money owing to him. No noise – no gathering together of creditors – it was done very silently and quietly, but all was paid at last; helped on materially by the circumstance of one of the creditors, a crabbed old fellow (Mr Bell says), taking in Mr Thornton as a kind of partner.'

'That really is fine,' said Margaret. 'What a pity such a nature should be tainted by his position as a Milton manufacturer.'

'How tainted?' asked her father.

'Oh, papa, by that testing everything by the standard of wealth. When he spoke of the mechanical powers, he evidently looked upon them only as new ways of extending trade and making money. And the poor men around him – they were poor because they were vicious – out of the pale of his sympathies because they had not his iron nature, and the capabilities that it gives him for being rich.'

'Not vicious; he never said that. Improvident and self-indulgent were his words.'

Margaret was collecting her mother's working materials, and preparing to go to bed. Just as she was leaving the room, she hesitated – she was inclined to make an acknowledgement which she thought would please her father, but which to be full and true must include a little annoyance. However, out it came.

'Papa, I do think Mr Thornton a very remarkable man; but personally I don't like him at all.'

'And I do!' said her father laughing. 'Personally, as you call it, and all. I don't set him up for a hero, or anything of that kind. But good night, child. Your mother looks sadly tired tonight, Margaret.'

Margaret had noticed her mother's jaded appearance with anxiety for some time past, and this remark of her father's sent her up to bed with a dim fear lying like a weight on her heart. The life in Milton was so different from what Mrs Hale had been accustomed to live in Helstone, in and out perpetually into the fresh and open air; the air itself was so different, deprived of all revivifying principle as it seemed to be here; the domestic worries pressed so very closely, and in so new and sordid a form, upon all the women in the family, that there was good reason to fear that her mother's health might be becoming seriously affected. There were several other signs of something wrong about Mrs Hale. She and Dixon held mysterious consultations in her bedroom, from which Dixon would come out crying and cross, as was her custom when any distress of her mistress called upon her sympathy. Once Margaret had gone into the chamber soon after Dixon left it, and found her mother on her knees, and as Margaret stole out she caught a few words, which were evidently a prayer for strength and patience to endure severe bodily suffering. Margaret yearned to re-unite the bond of intimate confidence which had been broken by her long residence at her aunt Shaw's, and strove by gentle caresses and softened words to creep into the warmest place in her mother's heart. But though she received caresses and fond words back again, in such profusion as would have gladdened her formerly, yet she felt that there was a secret withheld from her, and she believed it bore serious reference to her mother's health. She lay awake very long this night, planning how to lessen the evil influence of their Milton life on her mother. A servant to give Dixon permanent assistance should be got, if she gave up her whole time to the search; and then, at any rate, her mother might have all the personal attention she required, and had been accustomed to her whole life.

Visiting register offices, seeing all manner of unlikely people, and very few in the least likely, absorbed Margaret's time and thoughts for several days. One afternoon she met Bessy Higgins in the street, and stopped to speak to her.

'Well, Bessy, how are you? Better, I hope, now the wind has changed.'

'Better and not better, if yo' know what that means.'

'Not exactly,' replied Margaret, smiling.

'I'm better in not being torn to pieces by coughing o' nights, but I'm weary and tired o' Milton, and longing to get away to the land o' Beulah;[1] and when I think I'm farther and farther off, my heart sinks, and I'm no better; I'm worse.'

Margaret turned round to walk alongside of the girl in her feeble progress homeward. But for a minute or two she did not speak. At last she said in a low voice,

'Bessy, do you wish to die?' For she shrank from death herself, with all the clinging to life so natural to the young and healthy.

Bessy was silent in her turn for a minute or two. Then she replied,

'If yo'd led the life I have, and getten as weary of it as I have, and thought at times, "maybe it'll last for fifty or sixty years – it does wi' some," – and got dizzy and dazed, and sick, as each of them sixty years seemed to spin about me, and mock me with its length of hours and minutes, and endless bits o' time – oh, wench! I tell thee thou'd been glad enough when th' doctor said he feared thou'd never see another winter.'

'Why, Bessy, what kind of a life has yours been?'

'Nought worse than many others, I reckon. Only I fretted again it, and they didn't.'

'But what was it? You know, I'm a stranger here, so perhaps I'm not so quick at understanding what you mean as if I'd lived all my life at Milton.'

'If yo'd ha' come to our house when yo' said yo' would, I could maybe ha' told you. But father says yo're just like th' rest on 'em; it's out o' sight out o' mind wi' you.'

'I don't know who the rest are; and I've been very busy; and, to tell the truth, I had forgotten my promise –'

'Yo' offered it! we asked none of it.'

'I had forgotten what I said for the time,' continued Margaret quietly. 'I should have thought of it again when I was less busy. May I go with you now?'

Bessy gave a quick glance at Margaret's face, to see if the wish expressed was really felt. The sharpness in her eye turned to a wistful longing as she met Margaret's soft and friendly gaze.

'I ha' none so many to care for me; if yo' care yo' may come.'

So they walked on together in silence. As they turned up into a small court, opening out of a squalid street, Bessy said,

'Yo'll not be daunted if father's at home, and speaks a bit gruffish at first. He took a mind to ye, yo' see, and he thought a deal o' your coming to see us; and just because he liked yo' he were vexed and put about.'

'Don't fear, Bessy.'

But Nicholas was not at home when they entered. A great slatternly girl, not so old as Bessy, but taller and stronger, was busy at the wash-tub, knocking about the furniture in a rough capable way, but altogether making so much noise that Margaret shrunk, out of sympathy with poor Bessy, who had sat down on the first chair, as if completely tired out with her walk. Margaret asked the sister for a cup of water, and while she ran to fetch it (knocking down the fire-irons, and tumbling over a chair in her way), she unloosed Bessy's bonnet strings, to relieve her catching breath.

'Do you think such a life as this is worth caring for?' gasped Bessy, at last. Margaret did not speak, but held the water to her lips. Bessy took a long and feverish draught, and then fell back and shut her eyes. Margaret heard her murmur to herself: 'They shall hunger no more, neither thirst any more; neither shall the sun light on them, nor any heat.'

Margaret bent over and said, 'Bessy, don't be impatient with your life, whatever it is – or may have been. Remember who gave it you, and made it what it is!'

She was startled by hearing Nicholas speak behind her; he had come in without her noticing him.

'Now, I'll not have my wench preached to. She's bad enough as it is, with her dreams and her methodee fancies, and her visions of cities with goulden gates and precious stones. But if it amuses her I let it abe, but I'm none going to have more stuff poured into her.'

'But surely,' said Margaret, facing round, 'you believe in what I said, that God gave her life, and ordered what kind of life it was to be?'

'I believe what I see, and no more. That's what I believe, young woman. I don't believe all I hear – no! not by a big deal. I did hear a young lass make an ado about knowing where we lived, and coming to see us. And my wench here thought a deal about it, and flushed up many a time, when hoo little knew as I was looking at her, at the sound of a strange step. But hoo's come at last, – and hoo's welcome, as long as hoo'll keep from preaching on what hoo knows nought about.'

Bessy had been watching Margaret's face; she half sate up to speak now, laying her hand on Margaret's arm with a gesture of entreaty.

'Don't be vexed wi' him – there's many a one thinks like him; many and many a one here. If yo' could hear them speak, yo'd not be shocked at him; he's a rare good man, is father – but oh!' said she, falling back in despair, 'what he says at times makes me long to die more than ever, for I want to know so many things, and am so tossed about wi' wonder.'

'Poor wench – poor old wench, – I'm loth to vex thee, I am; but a man mun speak out for the truth, and when I see the world going all wrong at this time o' day, bothering itself wi' things it knows nought about, and leaving undone all the things that lie in disorder close at its hand – why, I say, leave a' this talk about religion alone, and set to work on what yo' see and know. That's my creed. It's simple, and not far to fetch, nor hard to work.'

But the girl only pleaded the more with Margaret.

'Don't think hardly on him – he's a good man, he is. I sometimes think I shall be moped wi' sorrow even in the City of God, if father is not there.' The feverish colour came into her cheek, and the feverish flame into her eye. 'But you will be there, father! you shall! Oh! my heart!' She put her hand to it, and became ghastly pale.

Margaret held her in her arms, and put the weary head to rest upon her bosom. She lifted the thin soft hair from off the temples, and bathed them with water. Nicholas understood all her signs for different articles with the quickness of love, and even the round-eyed sister moved with laborious gentleness at Margaret's 'hush!' Presently the spasm that fore-shadowed death had passed away, and Bessy roused herself and said, –

'I'll go to bed, – it's best place; but,' catching at Margaret's gown, 'yo'll come again, – I know yo' will – but just say it!'

'I will come tomorrow,' said Margaret.

Bessy leant back against her father, who prepared to carry her upstairs; but as Margaret rose to go, he struggled to say something: 'I could wish there were a God, if it were only to ask him to bless thee.'

Margaret went away very sad and thoughtful.

She was late for tea at home. At Helstone unpunctuality at meal-times was a great fault in her mother's eyes; but now this, as well as many other little irregularities, seemed to have lost their power of irritation, and Margaret almost longed for the old complainings.

'Have you met with a servant, dear?'

'No, mamma; that Anne Buckley would never have done.'

'Suppose I try,' said Mr Hale. 'Everybody else has had their turn at this great difficulty. Now let me try. I may be the Cinderella to put on the slipper after all.'

Margaret could hardly smile at this little joke, so oppressed was she by her visit to the Higginses.

'What would you do, papa? How would you set about it?'

'Why, I would apply to some good house-mother to recommend me one known to herself or her servants.'

'Very good. But we must first catch our house-mother.'

'You have caught her. Or rather she is coming into the snare, and you will catch her tomorrow, if you're skilful.'

'What do you mean, Mr Hale?' asked his wife, her curiosity aroused.

'Why, my paragon pupil (as Margaret calls him), has told me that his mother intends to call on Mrs and Miss Hale tomorrow.'

'Mrs Thornton!' exclaimed Mrs Hale.

'The mother of whom he spoke to us?' said Margaret.

'Mrs Thornton; the only mother he has, I believe,' said Mr Hale quietly.

'I shall like to see her. She must be an uncommon person,' her mother added. 'Perhaps she may have a relation who might suit us, and be glad of our place. She sounded to be such a careful economical person, that I should like any one out of the same family.'

'My dear,' said Mr Hale alarmed. 'Pray don't go off on that idea. I fancy Mrs Thornton is as haughty and proud in her way, as our little Margaret here is in hers, and that she completely ignores that old time of trial, and poverty, and economy, of which he speaks so openly. I am sure, at any rate, she would not like strangers to know anything about it.'

'Take notice that is not my kind of haughtiness, papa, if I have any at all; which I don't agree to, though you're always accusing me of it.'

'I don't know positively that it is hers either; but from little things I have gathered from him, I fancy so.'

They cared too little to ask in what manner her son had spoken about her. Margaret only wanted to know if she must stay in to receive this call, as it would prevent her going to see how Bessy was, until late in the day, since the early morning was always occupied in household affairs; and then she recollected that her mother must not be left to have the whole weight of entertaining her visitor.

CHAPTER XII

Morning Calls

Well – I suppose we must.[1]
FRIENDS IN COUNCIL

Mr Thornton had had some difficulty in working up his mother to the desired point of civility. She did not often make calls; and when she did, it was in heavy state that she went through her duties. Her son had given her a carriage; but she refused to let him keep horses for it; they were hired for the solemn occasions, when she paid morning or evening visits. She had had horses for three days, not a fortnight before, and had comfortably 'killed off'[2] all her acquaintances, who might now put themselves to trouble and expense in their turn. Yet Crampton was too far off for her to walk; and she had repeatedly questioned her son as to whether his wish that she should call on the Hales was strong enough to bear the expense of cab-hire. She would have been thankful if it had not; for, as she said, 'she saw no use in making up friendships and intimacies with all the teachers and masters in Milton; why, he would be wanting her to call on Fanny's dancing-master's wife, the next thing!'

'And so I would, mother, if Mr Mason and his wife were friendless in a strange place, like the Hales.'

'Oh! you need not speak so hastily. I am going tomorrow. I only wanted you exactly to understand about it.'

'If you are going tomorrow, I shall order horses.'

'Nonsense, John. One would think you were made of money.'

'Not quite, yet. But about the horses I'm determined. The last time you were out in a cab, you came home with a headache from the jolting.'

'I never complained of it, I'm sure.'

'No! My mother is not given to complaints,' said he, a little proudly. 'But so much the more I have to watch over you. Now, as for Fanny there, a little hardship would do her good.'

'She is not made of the same stuff as you are, John. She could not bear it.'

Mrs Thornton was silent after this; for her last words bore relation to a subject which mortified her. She had an unconscious contempt for a weak character; and Fanny was weak in the very points in which her mother and brother were strong. Mrs Thornton was not a woman much given to reasoning; her quick judgment and firm resolution served her in good stead of any long arguments and discussions with herself; she felt instinctively that nothing could strengthen Fanny to endure hardships patiently, or face difficulties bravely; and though she winced as she made this acknowledgment to herself about her daughter, it only gave her a kind of pitying tenderness of manner towards her; much of the same description of demeanour with which mothers are wont to treat their weak and sickly children. A stranger, a careless observer might have considered that Mrs Thornton's manner to her children betokened far more love to Fanny than to John. But such a one would have been deeply mistaken. The very daringness with which mother and son spoke out unpalatable truths, the one to the other, showed a reliance on the firm centre of each other's souls; which the uneasy tenderness of Mrs Thornton's manner to her daughter, the shame with which she thought to hide the poverty of her child in all the grand qualities which she herself possessed unconsciously, and which she set so high a value upon in others – this shame, I say, betrayed the want of a secure resting-place for her affection. She never called her son by any name but John; 'love,' and 'dear,' and such like terms, were reserved for Fanny. But her heart gave thanks for him day and night; and she walked proudly among women for his sake.

'Fanny dear! I shall have horses to the carriage today, to go and call on these Hales. Should not you go and see nurse? It's in the same direction, and she's always so glad to see you. You could go on there while I am at Mrs Hale's.'

'Oh! mamma, it's such a long way, and I am so tired.'

'With what?' asked Mrs Thornton, her brow slightly contracting.

'I don't know – the weather, I think. It is so relaxing. Couldn't you bring nurse here, mamma? The carriage could fetch her, and she could spend the rest of the day here, which I know she would like.'

Mrs Thornton did not speak; but she laid her work on the table, and seemed to think.

'It will be a long way for her to walk back at night!' she remarked, at last.

'Oh, but I will send her home in a cab. I never thought of her walking.'

At this point, Mr Thornton came in, just before going to the mill.

'Mother! I need hardly say, that if there is any little thing that could serve Mrs Hale as an invalid, you will offer it, I'm sure.'

'If I can find it out, I will. But I have never been ill myself, so I am not much up to invalids' fancies.'

'Well! here is Fanny, then, who is seldom without an ailment. She will be able to suggest something, perhaps – won't you, Fan?'

'I have not always an ailment,' said Fanny, pettishly; 'and I am not going with mamma. I have a headache today, and I shan't go out.'

Mr Thornton looked annoyed. His mother's eyes were bent on her work, at which she was now stitching away busily.

'Fanny! I wish you to go,' said he, authoritatively. 'It will do you good, instead of harm. You will oblige me by going, without my saying anything more about it.'

He went abruptly out of the room after saying this.

If he had staid a minute longer, Fanny would have cried at his tone of command, even when he used the words, 'You will oblige me.' As it was, she grumbled.

'John always speaks as if I fancied I was ill, and I am sure I never do fancy any such thing. Who are these Hales that he makes such a fuss about?'

'Fanny, don't speak so of your brother. He has good reasons of some kind or other, or he would not wish us to go. Make haste and put your things on.'

But the little altercation between her son and her daughter did not incline Mrs Thornton more favourably towards 'these Hales.' Her jealous heart repeated her daughter's question, 'Who are they, that he is so anxious we should pay them all this attention?' It came up like a burden to a song, long after Fanny had forgotten all about it in the pleasant excitement of seeing the effect of a new bonnet in the looking-glass.

Mrs Thornton was shy. It was only of late years that she had had leisure enough in her life to go into society; and as society she did not enjoy it. As dinner-giving, and as criticizing other people's dinners, she took satisfaction in it. But this going to make acquaintance with strangers was a very different thing. She was ill at ease, and looked more than usually stern and forbidding as she entered the Hales' little drawing-room.

Margaret was busy embroidering a small piece of cambric for some little article of dress for Edith's expected baby – 'Flimsy, useless work,'[3] as Mrs Thornton observed to herself. She liked Mrs Hale's double-knitting far better; that was sensible of its kind. The room altogether was full of knick-knacks, which must take a long time to dust; and time to people of limited income was money.

She made all these reflections as she was talking in her stately way to Mrs Hale, and uttering all the stereotyped commonplaces that most people can find to say with their senses blindfolded. Mrs Hale was making rather more exertion in her answers, captivated by some real old lace which Mrs Thornton wore; 'lace,' as she afterwards observed to Dixon, 'of that old English point which has not been made for this seventy years, and which cannot be bought. It must have been an heir-loom, and shows that she had ancestors.' So the owner of the ancestral lace became worthy of something more than the languid exertion to be agreeable to a visitor, by which Mrs Hale's efforts at conversation would have been otherwise bounded. And presently, Margaret, racking her brain to talk to Fanny, heard her mother and Mrs Thornton plunge into the interminable subject of servants.

'I suppose you are not musical,' said Fanny, 'as I see no piano.'

'I am fond of hearing good music; I cannot play well myself; and papa and mamma don't care much about it; so we sold our old piano when we came here.'

'I wonder how you can exist without one. It almost seems to me a necessary of life.'

'Fifteen shillings a week, and three saved out of them!' thought Margaret to herself. 'But she must have been very young. She probably has forgotten her own personal experience. But she must know of those days.' Margaret's manner had an extra tinge of coldness in it when she next spoke.

'You have good concerts here, I believe.'

'Oh, yes! Delicious! Too crowded, that is the worst. The directors admit so indiscriminately. But one is sure to hear the newest music there. I always have a large order to give to Johnson's, the day after a concert.'

'Do you like new music simply for its newness, then?'

'Oh; one knows it is the fashion in London, or else the singers would not bring it down here. You have been in London, of course.'

'Yes,' said Margaret, 'I have lived there for several years.'

'Oh! London and the Alhambra are the two places I long to see!'

'London and the Alhambra!'

'Yes! ever since I read the Tales of the Alhambra.[4] Don't you know them?'

'I don't think I do. But surely, it is a very easy journey to London.'

'Yes; but somehow,' said Fanny, lowering her voice, 'mamma has never been to London herself, and can't understand my longing. She is very proud of Milton; dirty, smoky place, as I feel it to be. I believe she admires it the more for those very qualities.'

'If it has been Mrs Thornton's home for some years, I can well understand her loving it,' said Margaret, in her clear bell-like voice.

'What are you saying about me, Miss Hale? May I inquire?'

Margaret had not the words ready for an answer to this question, which took her a little by surprise, so Miss Thornton replied:

'Oh, mamma! we are only trying to account for your being so fond of Milton.'

'Thank you,' said Mrs Thornton. 'I do not feel that my very natural liking for the place where I was born and brought up, – and which has since been my residence for some years, requires any accounting for.'

Margaret was vexed. As Fanny had put it, it did seem as if they had been impertinently discussing Mrs Thornton's feelings; but she also rose up against that lady's manner of showing that she was offended.

Mrs Thornton went on after a moment's pause:

'Do you know anything of Milton, Miss Hale? Have you seen any of our factories? our magnificent warehouses?'

'No!' said Margaret. 'I have not seen anything of that description as yet.'

Then she felt that, by concealing her utter indifference to all such places, she was hardly speaking with truth; so she went on:

'I dare say, papa would have taken me before now if I had cared. But I really do not find much pleasure in going over manufactories.'

'They are very curious places,' said Mrs Hale, 'but there is so much noise and dirt always. I remember once going in a lilac silk to see candles made, and my gown was utterly ruined.'

'Very probably,' said Mrs Thornton, in a short displeased manner. 'I merely thought, that as strangers newly come to reside in a town which has risen to eminence in the country, from the character and progress of its peculiar business, you might have cared to visit some of the places where it is carried on; places unique in the kingdom, I am informed. If Miss Hale changes her mind and condescends to be curious as to the manufactures of Milton, I can only say I shall be glad to procure her admission to print-works, or reed-making, or the more simple operations of spinning carried on in my son's mill. Every improvement of machinery is, I believe, to be seen there, in its highest perfection.'

'I am so glad you don't like mills and manufactories, and all those kind of things,' said Fanny, in a half-whisper, as she rose to accompany her mother, who was taking leave of Mrs Hale with rustling dignity.

'I think I should like to know all about them, if I were you,' replied Margaret quietly.

'Fanny!' said her mother, as they drove away, 'we will be civil to these Hales: but don't form one of your hasty friendships with the daughter. She will do you no good, I see. The mother looks very ill, and seems a nice, quiet kind of person.'

'I don't want to form any friendship with Miss Hale, mamma,' said Fanny, pouting. 'I thought I was doing my duty by talking to her, and trying to amuse her.'

'Well! at any rate John must be satisfied now.'

CHAPTER XIII

A Soft Breeze in a Sultry Place

That doubt and trouble, fear and pain,[1]
And anguish, all, are shadows vain,
That death itself shall not remain;

That weary deserts we may tread,
A dreary labyrinth may thread,
Thro' dark ways underground be led;

Yet, if we will one Guide obey,
The dreariest path, the darkest way
Shall issue out in heavenly day;

And we, on divers shores now cast,
Shall meet, our perilous voyage past,
All in our Father's house at last!

R. C. TRENCH

Margaret flew up stairs as soon as their visitors were gone, and put on her bonnet and shawl, to run and inquire how Bessy Higgins was, and sit with her as long as she could before dinner. As she went along the crowded narrow streets, she felt how much of interest they had gained by the simple fact of her having learnt to care for a dweller in them.

Mary Higgins, the slatternly younger sister, had endeavoured as well as she could to tidy up the house for the expected visit. There had been rough-stoning done in the middle of the floor, while the flags under the chairs and table and round the walls retained their dark unwashed appearance. Although the day was hot, there burnt a large fire in the grate, making the whole place feel like an oven. Margaret did not understand that the lavishness of coals was a sign of hospitable welcome to her on Mary's part, and thought that perhaps the oppressive heat was necessary for Bessy. Bessy herself lay on a squab, or short sofa, placed under the window. She was very much more feeble than on the previous day, and tired with raising herself at every step to look out and see if it was Margaret coming. And now that Margaret was there, and had taken a chair by her, Bessy lay back silent, and content to look at Margaret's face, and touch her articles of dress, with a childish admiration of their fineness of texture.

'I never knew why folk in the Bible cared for soft raiment afore. But it must be nice to go dressed as yo' do. It's different fro' common. Most fine folk tire my eyes out wi' their colours; but some-how yours rest me. Where did ye get this frock?'

'In London,' said Margaret, much amused.

'London! Have yo' been in London?'

'Yes! I lived there for some years. But my home was in a forest; in the country.'

'Tell me about it,' said Bessy. 'I like to hear speak of the country, and trees, and such like things.' She leant back, and shut her eyes, and crossed her hands over her breast, lying at perfect rest, as if to receive all the ideas Margaret could suggest.

Margaret had never spoken of Helstone since she left it, except just naming the place incidentally. She saw it in dreams more vivid than life, and as she fell away to slumber at nights her memory wandered in all its pleasant places. But her heart was opened to this girl: 'Oh, Bessy, I loved the home we have left so dearly! I wish you could see it. I cannot tell you half its beauty. There are great trees standing all about it, with their branches stretching long and level, and making a deep shade of rest even at noonday. And yet, though every leaf may seem still, there is a continual rushing sound of movement all around – not close at hand. Then sometimes the turf is as soft and fine as velvet; and sometimes quite lush with the perpetual moisture of a little, hidden, tinkling brook near at hand. And then in other parts there are billowy ferns – whole stretches of fern; some in the green shadow; some with long streaks of golden sunlight lying on them – just like the sea.'

'I have never seen the sea,' murmured Bessy. 'But go on.'

'Then, here and there, there are wide commons, high up as if above the very tops of the trees –'

'I'm glad of that. I felt smothered like down below. When I have gone for an out, I've always wanted to get high up and see far away, and take a deep breath o' fulness in that air. I get smothered enough in Milton, and I think the sound yo' speak of among the trees, going on for ever and ever, would send me dazed; it's that made my head ache so in the mill. Now on these commons I reckon there is but little noise?'

'No,' said Margaret; 'nothing but here and there a lark high in the air. Sometimes I used to hear a farmer speaking sharp and loud to his servants; but it was so far away that it only reminded me pleasantly that other people were hard at work in some distant place, while I just sat on the heather and did nothing.'

'I used to think once that if I could have a day of doing nothing, to rest me – a day in some quiet place like that yo' speak on – it would maybe set me up. But now I've had many days o' idleness, and I'm just as weary o' them as I was o' my work. Sometimes I'm so tired out I think I cannot enjoy heaven without a piece of rest first. I'm rather afeard o' going straight there without getting a good sleep in the grave to set me up.'

'Don't be afraid, Bessy,' said Margaret, laying her hand on the girl's; 'God can give you more perfect rest than even idleness on earth, or the dead sleep of the grave can do.'

Bessy moved uneasily; then she said:

'I wish father would not speak as he does. He means well, as I told yo' yesterday, and tell yo' again and again. But yo' see, though I don't believe him a bit by day, yet by night – when I'm in a fever, half-asleep and half-awake – it comes back upon me – oh! so bad! And I think, if this should be th' end of all, and if all I've been born for is just to work my heart and my life away, and to sicken i' this dree place, wi' them mill-noises in my ears for ever, until I could scream out for them to stop, and let me have a little piece o' quiet – and wi' the fluff filling my lungs, until I thirst to death for one long deep breath o' the clear air yo' speak on – and my mother gone, and I never able to tell her again how I loved her, and o' all my troubles – I think if this life is th' end, and that there's no God to wipe away all tears from all eyes – yo' wench, yo'!' said she, sitting up, and clutching violently, almost fiercely, at Margaret's hand, 'I could go mad, and kill yo', I could.' She fell back completely worn out with her passion. Margaret knelt down by her.

'Bessy – we have a Father in Heaven.'

'I know it! I know it,' moaned she, turning her head uneasily from side to side. 'I'm very wicked. I've spoken very wickedly. Oh! don't be frightened by me and never come again. I would not harm a hair of your head. And,' opening her eyes, and looking earnestly at Margaret, 'I believe, perhaps, more than yo' do o' what's to come. I read the book o' Revelations until I know it off by heart, and I never doubt when I'm waking, and in my senses, of all the glory I'm to come to.'

'Don't let us talk of what fancies come into your head when you are feverish. I would rather hear something about what you used to do when you were well.'

'I think I was well when mother died, but I have never been rightly strong sin' somewhere about that time. I began to work in a carding-room soon after, and the fluff got into my lungs, and poisoned me.'[2]

'Fluff?' said Margaret, inquiringly.

'Fluff,' repeated Bessy. 'Little bits, as fly off fro' the cotton, when they're carding it, and fill the air till it looks all fine white dust. They say it winds round the lungs, and tightens them up. Anyhow, there's many a one as works in a carding-room, that falls into a waste, coughing and spitting blood, because they're just poisoned by the fluff.'

'But can't it be helped?' asked Margaret.

'I dunno. Some folk have a great wheel at one end o' their carding-rooms to make a draught, and carry off th' dust; but that wheel costs a deal o' money – five or six hundred pound, maybe, and brings in no profit; so it's but a few of th' masters as will put 'em up; and I've heard tell o' men who didn't like working in places where there was a wheel, because they said as how it made 'em hungry, after they'd been long used to swallowing fluff, to go without it, and that their wage ought to be raised if they were to work in such places. So between masters and men th' wheels fall through. I know I wish there'd been a wheel in our place, though.'

'Did not your father know about it?' asked Margaret.

'Yes! and he were sorry. But our factory were a good one on the whole; and a steady likely set o' people; and father was afeard of letting me go to a strange place, for though yo' would na think it now, many a one then used to call me a gradely lass enough. And I did na like to be reckoned nesh and soft, and Mary's schooling were to be kept up, mother said, and father he were always liking to buy books, and go to lectures o' one kind or another – all which took money – so I just worked on till I shall ne'er get the whirr out o' my ears, or the fluff out o' my throat i' this world. That's all.'

'How old are you?' asked Margaret.

'Nineteen, come July.'

'And I too am nineteen.' She thought, more sorrowfully than Bessy did, of the contrast between them. She could not speak for a moment or two for the emotion she was trying to keep down.

'About Mary,' said Bessy. 'I wanted to ask yo' to be a friend to her. She's seventeen, but she's th' last on us. And I don't want her to go to th' mill, and yet I dunno what she's fit for.'

'She could not do' – Margaret glanced unconsciously at the uncleaned corners of the room – 'She could hardly undertake a servant's place, could she? We have an old faithful servant, almost a friend, who wants help, but who is very particular; and it would not be right to plague her with giving her any assistance that would really be an annoyance and an irritation.'

'No, I see. I reckon yo're right. Our Mary's a good wench; but who has she had to teach her what to do about a house? No mother, and me at the mill till I were good for nothing but scolding her for doing badly what I didn't know how to do a bit. But I wish she could ha' lived wi' yo', for all that.'

'But even though she may not be exactly fitted to come and live with us as a servant – and I don't know about that – I will always try and be a friend to her for your sake, Bessy. And now I must go. I will come again as soon as I can; but if it should not be tomorrow, or the next day, or even a week or a fortnight hence, don't think I've forgotten you. I may be busy.'

'I'll know yo' won't forget me again. I'll not mistrust yo' no more. But remember, in a week or a fortnight I may be dead and buried!'

'I'll come as soon as I can, Bessy,' said Margaret, squeezing her hand tight. 'But you'll let me know if you are worse.'

'Ay, that will I,' said Bessy, returning the pressure.

From that day forwards Mrs Hale became more and more of a suffering invalid. It was now drawing near to the anniversary of Edith's marriage, and looking back upon the year's accumulated heap of troubles, Margaret wondered how they had been borne. If she could have anticipated them, how she would have shrunk away and hid herself from the coming time! And yet day by day had, of itself, and by itself, been very endurable – small, keen, bright little spots of positive enjoyment having come sparkling into the very middle of sorrows. A year ago, or when she first went to Helstone, and first became silently conscious of the querulousness in her mother's temper, she would have groaned bitterly over the idea of a long illness to be borne in a strange, desolate, noisy, busy place, with diminished comforts on every side of the home life. But with the increase of serious and just ground of complaint, a new kind of patience had sprung up in her mother's mind. She was gentle and quiet in intense bodily suffering, almost in proportion as she had been restless and depressed when there had been no real cause for grief. Mr Hale was in exactly that stage of apprehension which, in men of his stamp, takes the shape of wilful blindness. He was more irritated than Margaret had ever known him at his daughter's expressed anxiety.

'Indeed, Margaret, you are growing fanciful! God knows I should be the first to take the alarm if your mother were really ill; we always saw when she had her headaches at Helstone, even without her telling us. She looks quite pale and white when she is ill; and now she has a bright healthy colour in her cheeks, just as she used to have when I first knew her.'

'But, papa,' said Margaret, with hesitation, 'do you know, I think that is the flush of pain.'

'Nonsense, Margaret. I tell you, you are too fanciful. You are the person not well, I think. Send for the doctor tomorrow for yourself; and then, if it will make your mind easier, he can see your mother.'

'Thank you, dear papa. It will make me happier, indeed.' And she went up to him to kiss him. But he pushed her away – gently enough, but still as if she had suggested unpleasant ideas, which he should be glad to get rid of as readily as he could of her presence. He walked uneasily up and down the room.

'Poor Maria!' said he, half soliloquizing, 'I wish one could do right without sacrificing others. I shall hate this town, and myself too, if she – Pray, Margaret, does your mother often talk to you of the old places: of Helstone, I mean?'

'No, papa,' said Margaret, sadly.

'Then, you see, she can't be fretting after them, eh? It has always been a comfort to me to think that your mother was so simple and open that I knew every little grievance she had. She never would conceal anything seriously affecting her health from me; would she, eh, Margaret? I am quite sure she would not. So don't let me hear of these foolish morbid ideas. Come, give me a kiss, and run off to bed.'

But she heard him pacing about (racooning, as she and Edith used to call it) long after her slow and languid undressing was finished – long after she began to listen as she lay in bed.

CHAPTER XIV

The Meeting

I was used
To sleep at nights as sweetly as a child, – [1]
Now if the wind blew rough, it made me start,
And think of my poor boy tossing about
Upon the roaring seas. And then I seemed
To feel that it was hard to take him from me
For such a little fault.

SOUTHEY

It was a comfort to Margaret about this time, to find that her mother drew more tenderly and intimately towards her than she had ever done since the days of her childhood. She took her to her heart as a confidential friend – the post Margaret had always longed to fill, and had envied Dixon for being preferred to. Margaret took pains to respond to every call made upon her for sympathy – and they were many – even when they bore relation to trifles, which she would no more have noticed or regarded herself than the elephant would perceive the little pin at his feet, which yet he lifts carefully up at the bidding of his keeper. All unconsciously Margaret drew near to a reward.

One evening, Mr Hale being absent, her mother began to talk to her about her brother Frederick, the very subject on which Margaret had longed to ask questions, and almost the only one on which her timidity overcame her natural openness. The more she wanted to hear about him, the less likely she was to speak.

'Oh, Margaret, it was so windy last night! It came howling down the chimney in our room! I could not sleep. I never can when there is such a terrible wind. I got into a wakeful habit when poor Frederick was at sea; and now, even if I don't waken all at once, I dream of him[2] in some stormy sea, with great, clear, glass-green walls of waves on either side his ship, but far higher than her very masts, curling over her with that cruel, terrible white foam, like some gigantic crested serpent. It is an old dream, but it always comes back on windy nights, till I am thankful to waken, sitting straight and stiff up in bed with my terror. Poor Frederick! He is on land now, so wind can do him no harm. Though I did think it might shake down some of those tall chimneys.'

'Where is Frederick now, mamma? Our letters are directed to the care of Messrs Barbour, at Cadiz, I know; but where is he himself?'

'I can't remember the name of the place, but he is not called Hale; you must remember that, Margaret. Notice the F.D. in every corner of the letters. He has taken the name of Dickenson. I wanted him to have been called Beresford, to which he had a kind of right, but your father thought he had better not. He might be recognized, you know, if he were called by my name.'

'Mamma,' said Margaret, 'I was at Aunt Shaw's when it all happened; and I suppose I was not old enough to be told plainly about it. But I should like to know now, if I may – if it does not give you too much pain to speak about it.'

'Pain! No,' replied Mrs Hale, her cheek flushing. 'Yet it is pain to think that perhaps I may never see my darling boy again. Or else he did right, Margaret. They may say what they like, but I have his own letters to show, and I'll believe him, though he is my son, sooner than any court-martial on earth. Go to my little japan cabinet, dear, and in the second left-hand drawer you will find a packet of letters.'

Margaret went. There were the yellow, sea-stained letters, with the peculiar fragrance which ocean letters have. Margaret carried them back to her mother, who untied the silken string with trembling fingers, and, examining their dates, she gave them to Margaret to read, making her hurried, anxious remarks on their contents, almost before her daughter could have understood what they were.'

'You see, Margaret, how from the very first he disliked Captain Reid. He was second lieutenant in the ship – the Orion – in which Frederick sailed the very first time. Poor little fellow, how well he looked in his midshipman's dress, with his dirk in his hand, cutting open all the newspapers with it as if it were a paper-knife! But this Mr Reid, as he was then, seemed to take a dislike to Frederick from the very beginning. And then – stay! these are the letters he wrote on board the Russell. When he was appointed to her, and found his old enemy Captain Reid in command, he did mean to bear all his tyranny patiently. Look! this is the letter. Just read it, Margaret. Where is it he says – Stop – "my father may rely upon me, that I will bear with all proper patience everything that one officer and gentleman can take from another. But from my former knowledge of my present captain, I confess I look forward with apprehension to a long course of tyranny on board the Russell." You see, he promises to bear patiently, and I am sure he did, for he was the sweetest-tempered boy, when he was not vexed, that could possibly be. Is that the letter in which he speaks of Captain Reid's impatience with the men, for not going through the ship's manœuvres as quickly as the Avenger? You see, he says that they had many new hands on board the Russell, while the Avenger had been nearly three years on the station, with nothing to do but to keep slavers off, and work her men, till they ran up and down the rigging like rats or monkeys.'

Margaret slowly read the letter, half illegible through the fading of the ink. It might be – it probably was – a statement of Captain Reid's imperiousness in trifles, very much exaggerated by the narra-tor, who had written it while fresh and warm from the scene of altercation. Some sailors being aloft in the main-topsail rigging, the captain had ordered them to race down, threatening the hindmost with the cat-of-nine-tails. He who was the farthest on the spar, feeling the impossibility of passing his companions, and yet passion-ately dreading the disgrace of the flogging, threw himself desperately down to catch a rope considerably lower, failed, and fell sense-less on deck. He only survived for a few hours afterwards, and the indignation of the ship's crew was at boiling point when young Hale wrote.

'But we did not receive this letter till long, long after we heard of the mutiny. Poor Fred! I dare say it was a comfort to him to write it, even though he could not have known how to send it, poor fellow! And then we saw a report in the papers – that's to say, long before Fred's letter reached us – of an atrocious mutiny having broken out on board the Russell, and that the mutineers had remained in possession of the ship, which had gone off, it was supposed, to be a pirate; and that Captain Reid was sent adrift in a boat with some men – officers or something – whose names were all given, for they were picked up by a West-Indian steamer. Oh, Margaret! how your father and I turned sick over that list, when there was no name of Frederick Hale. We thought it must be some mistake; for poor Fred was such a fine fellow, only perhaps rather too passionate; and we hoped that the name of Carr, which was in the list, was a misprint for that of Hale – newspapers are so careless. And towards post-time the next day, papa set off to walk to Southampton to get the papers; and I could not stop at home, so I went to meet him. He was very late – much later than I thought he would have been; and I sat down under the hedge to wait for him. He came at last, his arms hanging loose down, his head sunk, and walking heavily along, as if every step was a labour and a trouble. Margaret, I see him now.'

'Don't go on, mamma. I can understand it all,' said Margaret, leaning up caressingly against her mother's side, and kissing her hand.

'No, you can't Margaret. No one can who did not see him then. I could hardly lift myself up to go and meet him – everything seemed so to reel around me all at once. And when I got to him, he did not speak, or seem surprised to see me there, more than three miles from home, beside the Oldham beech-tree; but he put my arm in his, and kept stroking my hand, as if he wanted to soothe me to be very quiet under some great heavy blow; and when I trembled so all over that I could not speak, he took me in his arms, and stooped down his head on mine, and began to shake and to cry in a strange muffled, groaning voice, till I, for very fright, stood quite still, and only begged him to tell me what he had heard. And then, with his hand jerking, as if some one else moved it against his will, he gave me a wicked newspaper to read, calling our Frederick a "traitor of the blackest dye," "a base, ungrateful disgrace to his profession." Oh! I cannot tell what bad words they did not use. I took the paper in my hands as soon as I had read it – I tore it up to little bits – I tore it –

Oh! I believe, Margaret, I tore it with my teeth. I did not cry. I could not. My cheeks were as hot as fire, and my very eyes burnt in my head. I saw your father looking grave at me. I said it was a lie, and so it was. Months after, this letter came, and you see what provocation Frederick had. It was not for himself, or his own injuries, he rebelled; but he would speak his mind to Captain Reid, and so it went on from bad to worse; and you see, most of the sailors stuck by Frederick.

'I think, Margaret,' she continued, after a pause, in a weak, trembling, exhausted voice, 'I am glad of it – I am prouder of Frederick standing up against injustice, than if he had been simply a good officer.'

'I am sure I am,' said Margaret, in a firm, decided tone. 'Loyalty and obedience to wisdom and justice are fine; but it is still finer to defy arbitrary power,[3] unjustly and cruelly used – not on behalf of ourselves, but on behalf of others more helpless.'

'For all that, I wish I could see Frederick once more – just once. He was my first baby, Margaret.' Mrs Hale spoke wistfully, and almost as if apologizing for the yearning, craving wish, as though it were a depreciation of her remaining child. But such an idea never crossed Margaret's mind. She was thinking how her mother's desire could be fulfilled.

'It is six or seven years ago – would they still prosecute him, mother? If he came and stood his trial, what would be the punishment? Surely, he might bring evidence of his great provocation.'

'It would do no good,' replied Mrs Hale. 'Some of the sailors who accompanied Frederick were taken, and there was a court-martial held on them on board the Amicia; I believed all they said in their defence, poor fellows, because it just agreed with Frederick's story – but it was of no use, –' and for the first time during the conversation Mrs Hale began to cry; yet something possessed Margaret to force the information she foresaw, yet dreaded, from her mother.

'What happened to them, mamma?' asked she.

'They were hung at the yard-arm,' said Mrs Hale, solemnly. 'And the worst was that the court, in condemning them to death, said they had suffered themselves to be led astray from their duty by their superior officers.'

They were silent for a long time.

'And Frederick was in South America for several years, was he not?'

'Yes. And now he is in Spain. At Cadiz, or somewhere near it. If he comes to England he will be hung. I shall never see his face again – for if he comes to England he will be hung.'

There was no comfort to be given. Mrs Hale turned her face to the wall, and lay perfectly still in her mother's despair. Nothing could be said to console her. She took her hand out of Margaret's with a little impatient movement, as if she would fain be left alone with the recollection of her son. When Mr Hale came in, Margaret went out, oppressed with gloom, and seeing no promise of brightness on any side of the horizon.

CHAPTER XV

Masters and Men

Thought fights with thought; out springs a spark of truth[1]
From the collision of the sword and shield.

W.S. LANDOR

'Margaret,' said her father, the next day, 'we must return Mrs Thornton's call. Your mother is not very well, and thinks she cannot walk so far; but you and I will go this afternoon.'

As they went, Mr Hale began about his wife's health, with a kind of veiled anxiety, which Margaret was glad to see awakened at last.

'Did you consult the doctor, Margaret? Did you send for him?'

'No, papa, you spoke of his coming to see me. Now I was well. But if I only knew of some good doctor, I would go this afternoon, and ask him to come, for I am sure mamma is seriously indisposed.'

She put the truth thus plainly and strongly because her father had so completely shut his mind against the idea, when she had last named her fears. But now the case was changed. He answered in a despondent tone:

'Do you think she has any hidden complaint? Do you think she is really very ill? Has Dixon said anything? Oh, Margaret! I am haunted by the fear that our coming to Milton has killed her. My poor Maria!'

'Oh, papa! don't imagine such things,' said Margaret, shocked. 'She is not well, that is all. Many a one is not well for a time; and with good advice gets better and stronger than ever.'

'But has Dixon said anything about her?'

'No! You know Dixon enjoys making a mystery out of trifles; and she has been a little mysterious about mamma's health, which has alarmed me rather, that is all. Without any reason, I dare say. You know, papa, you said the other day I was getting fanciful.'

'I hope and trust you are. But don't think of what I said then. I like you to be fanciful about your mother's health. Don't be afraid of telling me your fancies. I like to hear them, though, I dare say, I spoke as if I was annoyed. But we will ask Mrs Thornton if she can tell us of a good doctor. We won't throw away our money on any but some one first-rate. Stay, we turn up this street.'

The street did not look as if it could contain any house large enough for Mrs Thornton's habitation. Her son's presence never gave any impression as to the kind of house he lived in; but, unconsciously, Margaret had imagined that tall, massive, hand-somely dressed Mrs Thornton must live in a house of the same character as herself. Now Marlborough Street consisted of long rows of small houses, with a blank wall here and there; at least that was all they could see from the point at which they entered it.

'He told me he lived in Marlborough Street, I'm sure,' said Mr Hale, with a much perplexed air.

'Perhaps it is one of the economies he still practises, to live in a very small house. But here are plenty of people about; let me ask.'

She accordingly inquired of a passer-by, and was informed that Mr Thornton lived close to the mill, and had the factory lodge-door pointed out to her, at the end of the long dead wall they had noticed.

The lodge-door was like a common garden-door; on one side of it were great closed gates for the ingress and egress of lurries and wagons. The lodge-keeper admitted them into a great oblong yard, on one side of which were offices for the transaction of business; on the opposite, an immense many-windowed mill, whence proceeded the continual clank of machinery and the long groaning roar of the steam-engine, enough to deafen those who lived within the enclosure. Opposite to the wall, along which the street ran, on one of the narrow sides of the oblong, was a handsome stone-coped house, – blackened, to be sure, by the smoke, but with paint, windows, and steps kept scrupulously clean. It was evidently a house which had been built some fifty or sixty years. The stone facings – the long, narrow windows, and the number of them – the flights of steps up to the front door, ascending from either side, and guarded by railing – all witnessed to its age. Margaret only wondered why people who could afford to live in so good a house, and keep it in such perfect order, did not prefer a much smaller dwelling in the country, or even some suburb; not in the continual whirl and din of the factory. Her unaccustomed ears could hardly catch her father's voice, as they stood on the steps awaiting the opening of the door. The yard, too, with the great doors in the dead wall as a boundary, was but a dismal look-out for the sitting-rooms of the house – as Margaret found when they had mounted the old-fashioned stairs, and been ushered into the drawing-room, the three windows of which went over the front door and the room on the right-hand side of the entrance. There was no one in the drawing-room. It seemed as though no one had been in it since the day when the furniture was bagged up with as much care as if the house was to be overwhelmed with lava, and discovered a thousand years hence. The walls were pink and gold: the pattern on the carpet represented bunches of flowers on a light ground, but it was carefully covered up in the centre by a linen drugget, glazed and colourless. The window-curtains were lace; each chair and sofa had its own particular veil of netting, or knitting. Great alabaster groups occupied every flat surface, safe from dust under their glass shades. In the middle of the room, right under the bagged-up chandelier, was a large circular table, with smartly-bound books arranged at regular intervals round the circumference of its polished surface, like gaily-coloured spokes of a wheel. Everything reflected light, nothing absorbed it. The whole room had a painfully spotted, spangled, speckled look about it, which impressed Margaret so unpleasantly that she was hardly conscious of the peculiar cleanliness required to keep everything so white and pure in such an atmosphere, or of the trouble that must be willingly expended to secure that effect of icy, snowy discomfort. Wherever she looked there was evidence of care and labour, but not care and labour to procure ease, to help on habits of tranquil home employment; solely to ornament, and then to preserve ornament from dirt or destruction.

They had leisure to observe, and to speak to each other, in low voices, before Mrs Thornton appeared. They were talking of what all the world might hear: but it is a common effect of such a room as this to make people speak low, as if unwilling to awaken the unused echoes.

At last Mrs Thornton came in, rustling in handsome black silk, as was her wont; her muslins and laces rivalling, not excelling, the pure whiteness of the muslins and netting of the room. Margaret explained how it was that her mother could not accompany them to return Mrs Thornton's call; but in her anxiety not to bring back her father's fears too vividly, she gave but a bungling account, and left the impression on Mrs Thornton's mind that Mrs Hale's was some temporary or fanciful fine-ladyish indisposition, which might have been put aside had there been a strong enough motive; or that if it was too severe to allow her to come out that day, the call might have been deferred. Remembering, too, the horses to her carriage, hired for her own visit to the Hales, and how Fanny had been ordered to go by Mr Thornton, in order to pay every respect to them, Mrs Thornton drew up slightly offended, and gave Margaret no sympathy – indeed, hardly any credit for the statement of her mother's indisposition.

'How is Mr Thornton?' asked Mr Hale. 'I was afraid he was not well, from his hurried note yesterday.'

'My son is rarely ill; and when he is, he never speaks about it, or makes it an excuse for not doing anything. He told me he could not get leisure to read with you last night, sir. He regretted it, I am sure; he values the hours spent with you.'

'I am sure they are equally agreeable to me,' said Mr Hale. 'It makes me feel young again to see his enjoyment and appreciation of all that is fine in classical literature.'

'I have no doubt the classics are very desirable for people who have leisure. But, I confess, it was against my judgment that my son renewed his study of them. The time and place in which he lives, seem to me to require all his energy and attention. Classics may do very well[2] for men who loiter away their lives in the country or in colleges; but Milton men ought to have their thoughts and powers absorbed in the work of today. At least, that is my opinion.' This last clause she gave out with 'the pride that apes humility.'[3]

'But, surely, if the mind is too long directed to one object only, it will get stiff and rigid, and unable to take in many interests,' said Margaret.

'I do not quite understand what you mean by a mind getting stiff and rigid. Nor do I admire those whirligig characters that are full of this thing today, to be utterly forgetful of it in their new interest tomorrow. Having many interests does not suit the life of a Milton manufacturer. It is, or ought to be, enough for him to have one great desire, and to bring all the purposes of his life to bear on the fulfilment of that.'

'And that is –?' asked Mr Hale.

Her sallow cheek flushed, and her eye lightened, as she answered:

'To hold and maintain a high, honourable place among the merchants of his country – the men of his town. Such a place my son has earned for himself. Go where you will – I don't say in England only, but in Europe – the name of John Thornton of Milton is known and respected amongst all men of business. Of course, it is unknown in the fashionable circles,' she continued, scornfully. 'Idle gentlemen and ladies are not likely to know much of a Milton manufacturer, unless he gets into parliament, or marries a lord's daughter.'

Both Mr Hale and Margaret had an uneasy, ludicrous consciousness that they had never heard of this great name, until Mr Bell had written them word that Mr Thornton would be a good friend to have in Milton. The proud mother's world was not their world of Harley Street gentilities on the one hand, or country clergymen and Hampshire squires on the other. Margaret's face, in spite of all her endeavours to keep it simply listening in its expression, told the sensitive Mrs Thornton this feeling of hers.

'You think you never heard of this wonderful son of mine, Miss Hale. You think I'm an old woman whose ideas are bounded by Milton, and whose own crow is the whitest ever seen.'

'No,' said Margaret, with some spirit. 'It may be true, that I was thinking I had hardly heard Mr Thornton's name before I came to Milton. But since I have come here, I have heard enough to make me respect and admire him, and to feel how much justice and truth there is in what you have said of him.'

'Who spoke to you of him?' asked Mrs Thornton, a little mollified, yet jealous lest any one else's words should not have done him full justice.

Margaret hesitated before she replied. She did not like this authoritative questioning. Mr Hale came in, as he thought, to the rescue.

'It was what Mr Thornton said himself, that made us know the kind of man he was. Was it not, Margaret?'

Mrs Thornton drew herself up, and said –

'My son is not the one to tell of his own doings. May I again ask you, Miss Hale, from whose account you formed your favourable opinion of him? A mother is curious and greedy of commendation of her children, you know.'

Margaret replied, 'It was as much from what Mr Thornton withheld of that which we had been told of his previous life by Mr Bell, – it was more that than what he said, that made us all feel what reason you have to be proud of him.'

'Mr Bell! What can he know of John? He, living a lazy life in a drowsy college. But I'm obliged to you, Miss Hale. Many a missy young lady[4] would have shrunk from giving an old woman the pleasure of hearing that her son was well spoken of.'

'Why?' asked Margaret, looking straight at Mrs Thornton, in bewilderment.

'Why! because I suppose they might have consciences that told them how surely they were making the old mother into an advocate for them, in case they had any plans on the son's heart.'

She smiled a grim smile, for she had been pleased by Margaret's frankness; and perhaps she felt that she had been asking questions too much as if she had a right to catechize. Margaret laughed outright at the notion presented to her; laughed so merrily that it grated on Mrs Thornton's ear, as if the words that called forth that laugh, must have been utterly and entirely ludicrous.

Margaret stopped her merriment as soon as she saw Mrs Thornton's annoyed look.

'I beg your pardon, madam. But I really am very much obliged to you for exonerating me from making any plans on Mr Thornton's heart.'

'Young ladies have, before now,' said Mrs Thornton, stiffly.

'I hope Miss Thornton is well,' put in Mr Hale, desirous of changing the current of the conversation.

'She is as well as she ever is. She is not strong,' replied Mrs Thornton, shortly.

'And Mr Thornton? I suppose I may hope to see him on Thursday?'

'I cannot answer for my son's engagements. There is some uncomfortable work going on in the town; a threatening of a strike. If so, his experience and judgment will make him much consulted by his friends. But I should think he could come on Thursday. At any rate, I am sure he will let you know if he cannot.'

'A strike!' asked Margaret. 'What for? What are they going to strike for?'[5]

'For the mastership and ownership of other people's property,' said Mrs Thornton, with a fierce snort. 'That is what they always strike for. If my son's work-people strike, I will only say they are a pack of ungrateful hounds. But I have no doubt they will.'

'They are wanting higher wages, I suppose?' asked Mr Hale.

'That is the face of the thing. But the truth is, they want to be masters, and make the masters into slaves on their own ground. They are always trying at it; they always have it in their minds; and every five or six years, there comes a struggle between masters and men. They'll find themselves mistaken this time, I fancy, – a little out of their reckoning. If they turn out, they mayn't find it so easy to go in again. I believe, the masters have a thing or two in their heads which will teach the men not to strike again in a hurry, if they try it this time.'

'Does it not make the town very rough?' asked Margaret.

'Of course it does. But surely you are not a coward, are you? Milton is not the place for cowards. I have known the time when I have had to thread my way through a crowd of white, angry men, all swearing they would have Makinson's blood as soon as he ventured to show his nose out of his factory; and he, knowing nothing of it, some one had to go and tell him, or he was a dead man; and it needed to be a woman, – so I went. And when I had got in, I could not get out. It was as much as my life was worth. So I went up to the roof, where there were stones piled ready to drop on the heads of the crowd, if they tried to force the factory doors. And I would have lifted those heavy stones, and dropped them with as good an aim as the best man there, but that I fainted with the heat I had gone through. If you live in Milton, you must learn to have a brave heart, Miss Hale.'

'I would do my best,' said Margaret rather pale. 'I do not know whether I am brave or not till I am tried; but I am afraid I should be a coward.'

'South country people are often frightened by what our Darkshire men and women only call living and struggling. But when you've been ten years among a people who are always owing their betters a grudge, and only waiting for an opportunity to pay it off, you'll know whether you are a coward or not; take my word for it.'

Mr Thornton came that evening to Mr Hale's. He was shown up into the drawing-room, where Mr Hale was reading aloud to his wife and daughter.

'I am come partly to bring you a note from my mother, and partly to apologize for not keeping to my time yesterday. The note contains the address you asked for; Dr Donaldson.'

'Thank you!' said Margaret, hastily, holding out her hand to take the note, for she did not wish her mother to hear that they had been making any inquiry about a doctor. She was pleased that Mr Thornton seemed immediately to understand her feeling; he gave her the note without another word of explanation.

Mr Hale began to talk about the strike. Mr Thornton's face assumed a likeness to his mother's worst expression, which immediately repelled the watching Margaret.

'Yes; the fools will have a strike. Let them. It suits us well enough. But we gave them a chance. They think trade is flourishing as it was last year. We see the storm on the horizon and draw in our sails. But because we don't explain our reasons,[6] they won't believe we're acting reasonably. We must give them line and letter for the way we choose to spend or save our money. Henderson tried a dodge with his men, out at Ashley, and failed. He rather wanted a strike; it would have suited his book well enough. So when the men came to ask for the five per cent they are claiming, he told 'em he'd think about it, and give them his answer on the pay day; knowing all the while what his answer would be, of course, but thinking he'd strengthen their conceit of their own way. However, they were too deep for him, and heard something about the bad prospects of trade. So in they came on the Friday, and drew back their claim, and now he's obliged to go on working. But we Milton masters have today sent in our decision. We won't advance a penny. We tell them we may have to lower wages; but can't afford to raise. So here we stand, waiting for their next attack.'

'And what will that be?' asked Mr Hale.

'I conjecture, a simultaneous strike. You will see Milton without smoke in a few days, I imagine, Miss Hale.'

'But why,' asked she, 'could you not explain what good reason you have for expecting a bad trade? I don't know whether I use the right words, but you will understand what I mean.'

'Do you give your servants reasons for your expenditure, or your economy in the use of your own money? We, the owners of capital, have a right to choose what we will do with it.'

'A human right,' said Margaret, very low.

'I beg your pardon, I did not hear what you said.'

'I would rather not repeat it,' said she; 'it related to a feeling which I do not think you would share.'

'Won't you try me?' pleaded he; his thoughts suddenly bent upon learning what she had said. She was displeased with his pertinacity, but did not choose to affix too much importance to her words.

'I said you had a human right. I meant that there seemed no reason but religious ones, why you should not do what you like with your own.'

'I know we differ in our religious opinions; but don't you give me credit for having some, though not the same as yours?'

He was speaking in a subdued voice, as if to her alone. She did not wish to be so exclusively addressed. She replied out in her usual tone:

'I do not think that I have any occasion to consider your special religious opinions in the affair. All I meant to say is, that there is no human law to prevent the employers from utterly wasting or throwing away all their money, if they choose; but that there are passages in the Bible which would rather imply – to me at least – that they neglected their duty as stewards if they did so. However, I know so little about strikes, and rate of wages, and capital, and labour, that I had better not talk to a political economist like you.'[7]

'Nay, the more reason,' said he, eagerly. 'I shall only be too glad to explain to you all that may seem anomalous or mysterious to a stranger; especially at a time like this, when our doings are sure to be canvassed by every scribbler who can hold a pen.'

'Thank you,' she answered, coldly. 'Of course, I shall apply to my father in the first instance for any information he can give me, if I get puzzled with living here amongst this strange society.'

'You think it strange. Why?'

'I don't know – I suppose because, on the very face of it, I see two classes dependent on each other in every possible way, yet each evidently regarding the interests of the other as opposed to their own; I never lived in a place before where there were two sets of people always running each other down.'

'Who have you heard running the masters down? I don't ask who you have heard abusing the men; for I see you persist in misunderstanding what I said the other day. But who have you heard abusing the masters?'

Margaret reddened; then smiled as she said,

'I am not fond of being catechized. I refuse to answer your

question. Besides, it has nothing to do with the fact. You must take my word for it, that I have heard some people, or, it may be, only some one of the workpeople, speak as though it were the interest of the employers to keep them from acquiring money – that it would make them too independent if they had a sum in the savings' bank.'

'I dare say it was that man Higgins who told you all this,' said Mrs Hale. Mr Thornton did not appear to hear what Margaret evidently did not wish him to know. But he caught it, nevertheless.

'I heard, moreover, that it was considered to the advantage of the masters to have ignorant workmen – not hedge-lawyers, as Captain Lennox used to call those men in his company who questioned and would know the reason for every order.'

This latter part of her sentence she addressed rather to her father than to Mr Thornton. Who is Captain Lennox? asked Mr Thornton of himself, with a strange kind of displeasure, that prevented him for the moment from replying to her! Her father took up the conversation.

'You never were fond of schools, Margaret, or you would have seen and known before this, how much is being done for education in Milton.'

'No!' said she, with sudden meekness. 'I know I do not care enough about schools. But the knowledge and the ignorance of which I was speaking, did not relate to reading and writing, – the teaching or information one can give to a child. I am sure, that what was meant was ignorance of the wisdom that shall guide men and women. I hardly know what that is. But he – that is, my informant – spoke as if the masters would like their hands to be merely tall, large children – living in the present moment – with a blind unreasoning kind of obedience.'

'In short, Miss Hale, it is very evident that your informant found a pretty ready listener to all the slander he chose to utter against the masters,' said Mr Thornton, in an offended tone.

Margaret did not reply. She was displeased at the personal character Mr Thornton affixed to what she had said.

Mr Hale spoke next:

'I must confess that, although I have not become so intimately acquainted with any workmen as Margaret has, I am very much struck by the antagonism between the employer and the employed, on the very surface of things. I even gather this impression from what you yourself have from time to time said.'

Mr Thornton paused awhile before he spoke. Margaret had just left the room, and he was vexed at the state of feeling between himself and her. However, the little annoyance, by making him cooler and more thoughtful, gave a greater dignity to what he said:

'My theory is, that my interests are identical with those of my workpeople[8] and vice-versa. Miss Hale, I know, does not like to hear men called "hands," so I won't use that word, though it comes most readily to my lips as the technical term, whose origin, whatever it was, dates before my time. On some future day – in some millennium – in Utopia, this unity may be brought into practice – just as I can fancy a republic the most perfect form of government.'

'We will read Plato's Republic as soon as we have finished Homer.'

'Well, in the Platonic year,[9] it may fall out that we are all – men, women, and children – fit for a republic: but give me a constitutional monarchy in our present state of morals and intelligence. In our infancy we require a wise despotism to govern us. Indeed, long past infancy, children and young people are the happiest under the unfailing laws of a discreet, firm authority. I agree with Miss Hale so far as to consider our people in the condition of children, while I deny that we, the masters, have anything to do with the making or keeping them so. I maintain that despotism is the best kind of government for them; so that in the hours in which I come in contact with them I must necessarily be an autocrat. I will use my best discretion – from no humbug or philanthropic feeling, of which we have had rather too much in the North – to make wise laws and come to just decisions in the conduct of my business – laws and decisions which work for my own good in the first instance – for theirs in the second; but I will neither be forced to give my reasons, nor flinch from what I have once declared to be my resolution. Let them turn out! I shall suffer as well as they: but at the end they will find I have not bated nor altered one jot.'

Margaret had re-entered the room and was sitting at her work; but she did not speak. Mr Hale answered –

'I dare say I am talking in great ignorance; but from the little I know, I should say that the masses were already passing rapidly into the troublesome stage which intervenes between childhood and manhood, in the life of the multitude as well as that of the individual. Now, the error which many parents commit in the treatment of the individual at this time is, insisting on the same unreasoning obedience as when all he had to do in the way of duty was, to obey the simple laws of "Come when you're called," and "Do as you're bid!" But a wise parent humours the desire for independent action, so as to become the friend and adviser when his absolute rule shall cease. If I get wrong in my reasoning, recollect, it is you who adopted the analogy.'

'Very lately,' said Margaret, 'I heard a story of what happened in Nuremberg only three or four years ago. A rich man there lived alone in one of the immense mansions which were formerly both dwellings and warehouses. It was reported that he had a child, but no one knew of it for certain. For forty years this rumour kept rising and falling – never utterly dying away. After his death it was found to be true. He had a son – an overgrown man with the unexercised intellect of a child, whom he had kept up in that strange way, in order to save him from temptation and error. But, of course, when this great old child was turned loose into the world, every bad counsellor had power over him. He did not know good from evil. His father had made the blunder of bringing him up in ignorance and taking it for innocence; and after fourteen months of riotous living, the city authorities had to take charge of him, in order to save him from starvation. He could not even use words effectively enough to be a successful beggar.'

'I used the comparison (suggested by Miss Hale) of the position of the master to that of a parent; so I ought not to complain of your turning the simile into a weapon against me. But, Mr Hale, when you are setting up a wise parent as a model for us, you said he humoured his children in their desire for independent action. Now certainly, the time is not come for the hands to have any independent action during business hours; I hardly know what you would mean by it then. And I say, that the masters would be trenching on the independence of their hands, in a way that I, for one, should not feel justified in doing, if we interfered too much with the life they lead out of the mills. Because they labour ten hours a-day for us, I do not see that we have any right to impose leading-strings upon them for the rest of their time.[10] I value my own independence so highly that I can fancy no degradation greater than that of having another man perpetually directing and advising and lecturing me, or even planning too closely in any way about my actions. He might be the wisest of men, or the most powerful – I should equally rebel and resent his interference. I imagine this is a stronger feeling in the North of England than in the South.'

'I beg your pardon, but is not that because there has been none of the equality of friendship between the adviser and advised classes? Because every man has had to stand in an unchristian and isolated position, apart from and jealous of his brother-man: constantly afraid of his rights being trenched upon?'

'I only state the fact. I am sorry to say, I have an appointment at eight o'clock, and I must just take facts as I find them tonight, without trying to account for them; which, indeed, would make no difference in determining how to act as things stand – the facts must be granted.'

'But,' said Margaret in a low voice, 'it seems to me that it makes all the difference in the world –' Her father made a sign to her to be silent, and allow Mr Thornton to finish what he had to say. He was already standing up and preparing to go.

'You must grant me this one point. Given a strong feeling of independence in every Darkshire man, have I any right to obtrude my views, of the manner in which he shall act, upon another (hating it as I should do most vehemently myself), merely because he has labour to sell, and I capital to buy?'

'Not in the least,' said Margaret, determined just to say this one thing; 'not in the least because of your labour and capital positions, whatever they are, but because you are a man, dealing with a set of men over whom you have, whether you reject the use of it or not, immense power; just because your lives and your welfare are so constantly and intimately interwoven. God has made us so that we must be mutually dependent. We may ignore our own dependence, or refuse to acknowledge that others depend upon us in more respects than the payment of weekly wages; but the thing must be, nevertheless. Neither you nor any other master can help yourselves. The most proudly independent man depends on those around him for their insensible influence on his character – his life. And the most isolated of all your Darkshire Egos has dependants clinging to him on all sides; he cannot shake them off, any more than the great rock he resembles can shake off –'

'Pray don't go into similes, Margaret; you have led us off once already,' said her father, smiling, yet uneasy at the thought that they were detaining Mr Thornton against his will, which was a mistake; for he rather liked it, as long as Margaret would talk, although what she said only irritated him.

'Just tell me, Miss Hale, are you yourself ever influenced – no, that is not a fair way of putting it; – but if you are ever conscious of being influenced by others, and not by circumstances, have those others been working directly or indirectly? Have they been labouring to exhort, to enjoin, to act rightly for the sake of example, or have they been simple, true men, taking up their duty, and doing it unflinchingly, without a thought of how their actions were to make this man industrious, that man saving? Why, if I were a workman, I should be twenty times more impressed by the knowledge that my master was honest, punctual, quick, resolute in all his doings (and hands are keener spies even than valets), than by any amount of interference, however kindly meant, with my ways of going on out of work-hours. I do not choose to think too closely on what I am myself; but, I believe, I rely on the straightforward honesty of my hands, and the open nature of their opposition, in contra-distinction to the way in which the turn-out will be managed in some mills, just because they know I scorn to take a single dishonourable advantage, or do an underhand thing myself. It goes farther than a whole course of lectures on 'Honesty is the Best Policy' – life diluted into words. No, no! What the master is, that will the men be, without over-much taking thought on his part.'

'That is a great admission,' said Margaret, laughing. 'When I see men violent and obstinate in pursuit of their rights, I may safely infer that the master is the same; that he is a little ignorant of that spirit which suffereth long,[11] and is kind, and seeketh not her own.'

'You are just like all strangers who don't understand the working of our system, Miss Hale,' said he, hastily. 'You suppose that our men are puppets of dough, ready to be moulded into any amiable form we please. You forget we have only to do with them for less than a third of their lives; and you seem not to perceive that the duties of a manufacturer are far larger and wider than those merely of an employer of labour; we have a wide commercial character to maintain, which makes us into the great pioneers of civilization.'

'It strikes me,' said Mr Hale, smiling, 'that you might pioneer a little at home. They are a rough, heathenish set of fellows, these Milton men of yours.'

'They are that,' replied Mr Thornton. 'Rose-water surgery[12] won't do for them. Cromwell[13] would have made a capital mill-owner, Miss Hale. I wish we had him to put down this strike for us.'

'Cromwell is no hero of mine,' said she, coldly. 'But I am trying to reconcile your admiration of despotism with your respect for other men's independence of character.'

He reddened at her tone. 'I choose to be the unquestioned and irresponsible master of my hands. During the hours that they labour for me. But those hours past, our relation ceases; and then comes in the same respect for their independence that I myself exact.'

He did not speak again for a minute, he was too much vexed. But he shook it off, and bade Mr and Mrs Hale good night. Then, drawing near to Margaret, he said in a lower voice –

'I spoke hastily to you once this evening, and am afraid, rather rudely. But you know I am but an uncouth Milton manufacturer; will you forgive me?'

'Certainly,' said she, smiling up in his face, the expression of which was somewhat anxious and oppressed, and hardly cleared away as he met her sweet funny countenance, out of which all the north-wind effect of their discussion had entirely vanished. But she did not put out her hand to him, and again he felt the omission, and set it down to pride.

CHAPTER XVI

The Shadow of Death

Trust in that veilèd hand, which leads
None by the path that he would go;
And always be for change prepared,
For the world's law is ebb and flow.
FROM THE ARABIC

The next afternoon Dr Donaldson came to pay his first visit to Mrs Hale. The mystery that Margaret hoped their late habits of intimacy had broken through, was resumed. She was excluded from the room, while Dixon was admitted. Margaret was not a ready lover, but where she loved she loved passionately, and with no small degree of jealousy.

She went into her mother's bed-room, just behind the drawing-room, and paced it up and down, while awaiting the doctor's coming out. Every now and then she stopped to listen; she fancied she heard a moan. She clenched her hands tight, and held her breath. She was sure she heard a moan. Then all was still for a few minutes more; and then there was the moving of chairs, the raised voices, all the little disturbances of leave-taking.

When she heard the door open, she went quickly out of the bed-room.

'My father is from home, Dr Donaldson; he has to attend a pupil at this hour. May I trouble you to come into his room down stairs?'

She saw, and triumphed over all the obstacles which Dixon threw in her way; assuming her rightful position as daughter of the house in something of the spirit of the Elder Brother,[1] which quelled the old servant's officiousness very effectually. Margaret's conscious assumption of this unusual dignity of demeanour towards Dixon, gave her an instant's amusement in the midst of her anxiety. She knew, from the surprised expression on Dixon's face, how ridiculously grand she herself must be looking; and the idea carried her down stairs into the room; it gave her that length of oblivion from the keen sharpness of the recollection of the actual business in hand. Now, that came back, and seemed to take away her breath. It was a moment or two before she could utter a word.

But she spoke with an air of command, as she asked: –

'What is the matter with mamma? You will oblige me by telling the simple truth.' Then, seeing a slight hesitation on the doctor's part, she added –

'I am the only child she has – here, I mean. My father is not sufficiently alarmed, I fear; and, therefore, if there is any serious apprehension, it must be broken to him gently. I can do this. I can nurse my mother. Pray, speak, sir; to see your face, and not be able to read it, gives me a worse dread than I trust any words of yours will justify.'

'My dear young lady, your mother seems to have a most attentive and efficient servant, who is more like her friend –'

'I am her daughter, sir.'

'But when I tell you she expressly desired that you might not be told –'

'I am not good or patient enough to submit to the prohibition. Besides, I am sure you are too wise – too experienced to have promised to keep the secret.'

'Well,' said he, half-smiling, though sadly enough, 'there you are right. I did not promise. In fact, I fear, the secret will be known soon enough without my revealing it.'

He paused. Margaret went very white, and compressed her lips a little more. Otherwise not a feature moved. With the quick insight into character, without which no medical man can rise to the eminence of Dr Donaldson, he saw that she would exact the full truth; that she would know if one iota was withheld; and that the withholding would be torture more acute than the knowledge of it. He spoke two short sentences in a low voice, watching her all the time; for the pupils of her eyes dilated into a black horror, and the whiteness of her complexion became livid. He ceased speaking. He waited for that look to go off, – for her gasping breath to come. Then she said: –

'I thank you most truly, sir, for your confidence. That dread has haunted me for many weeks. It is a true, real agony. My poor, poor mother!' her lips began to quiver, and he let her have the relief of tears, sure of her power of self-control to check them.

A few tears – those were all she shed, before she recollected the many questions she longed to ask.

'Will there be much suffering?'

He shook his head. 'That we cannot tell. It depends on constitution; on a thousand things. But the late discoveries of medical science have given us large power of alleviation.'

'My father!' said Margaret, trembling all over.

'I do not know Mr Hale. I mean it is difficult to give advice. But I should say, bear on, with the knowledge you have forced me to give you so abruptly, till the fact which I could not withhold has become in some degree familiar to you, so that you may, without too great an effort, be able to give what comfort you can to your father. Before then, – my visits, which, of course, I shall repeat from time to time, although I fear I can do nothing but alleviate, – a thousand little circumstances will have occurred to awaken his alarm, to deepen it – so that he will be all the better prepared. – Nay, my dear young lady – nay, my dear – I saw Mr Thornton, and I honour your father for the sacrifice he has made, however mistaken I may believe him to be. – Well, this once, if it will please you, my dear. Only remember, when I come again, I come as a friend. And you must learn to look upon me as such, because seeing each other – getting to know each other at such times as these, is worth years of morning calls.'

Margaret could not speak for crying: but she wrung his hand at parting.

'That's what I call a fine girl!' thought Dr Donaldson, when he was seated in his carriage, and had time to examine his ringed hand, which had slightly suffered from her pressure. 'Who would have thought that little hand could have given such a squeeze? But the bones were well put together, and that gives immense power. What a queen she is! With her head thrown back at first, to force me into speaking the truth; and then bent so eagerly forward to listen. Poor thing! I must see she does not overstrain herself. Though it's astonishing how much those thorough-bred creatures can do and suffer. That girl's game to the back-bone. Another, who had gone that deadly colour, could never have come round without either fainting or hysterics. But she wouldn't do either – not she! And the very force of her will brought her round. Such a girl as that would win my heart, if I were thirty years younger. It's too late now. Ah! here we are at the Archers'.' So out he jumped, with thought, wisdom, experience, sympathy, and ready to attend to the calls made upon them by this family, just as if there were none other in the world.

Meanwhile, Margaret had returned into her father's study for a moment, to recover strength before going upstairs into her mother's presence.

'Oh, my God, my God! but this is terrible. How shall I bear it? Such a deadly disease! no hope! Oh, mamma, mamma, I wish I had never gone to aunt Shaw's, and been all those precious years away from you! Poor mamma! how much she must have borne! Oh, I pray thee, my God, that her sufferings may not be too acute, too dreadful. How shall I bear to see them? How can I bear papa's agony? He must not be told yet; not all at once. It would kill him. But I won't lose another moment of my own dear, precious mother.'

She ran upstairs. Dixon was not in the room. Mrs Hale lay back in an easy chair, with a soft white shawl wrapped around her, and a becoming cap put on, in expectation of the doctor's visit. Her face had a little faint colour in it, and the very exhaustion after the examination gave it a peaceful look. Margaret was surprised to see her look so calm.

'Why, Margaret, how strange you look! What is the matter?' And then, as the idea stole into her mind of what was indeed the real state of the case, she added, as if a little displeased: 'you have not been seeing Dr Donaldson, and asking him any questions – have you, child?' Margaret did not reply – only looked wistfully towards her. Mrs Hale became more displeased. 'He would not, surely, break his word to me, and –'

'Oh yes, mamma, he did. I made him. It was I – blame me.' She knelt down by her mother's side, and caught her hand – she would not let it go, though Mrs Hale tried to pull it away. She kept kissing it, and the hot tears she shed bathed it.

'Margaret, it was very wrong of you. You knew I did not wish you to know.' But, as if tired with the contest, she left her hand in Margaret's clasp, and by-and-by she returned the pressure faintly. That encouraged Margaret to speak.

'Oh, mamma! let me be your nurse. I will learn anything Dixon can teach me. But you know I am your child, and I do think I have a right to do everything for you.'

'You don't know what you are asking,' said Mrs Hale, with a shudder.

'Yes, I do. I know a great deal more than you are aware of. Let me be your nurse. Let me try, at any rate. No one has ever, shall ever try so hard as I will do. It will be such a comfort, mamma.'

'My poor child! Well, you shall try. Do you know, Margaret, Dixon and I thought you would quite shrink from me if you knew –'

'Dixon thought!' said Margaret, her lip curling. 'Dixon could not give me credit for enough true love – for as much as herself! She thought, I suppose, that I was one of those poor sickly women who like to lie on rose leaves, and be fanned all day. Don't let Dixon's fancies come any more between you and me, mamma. Don't please!' implored she.

'Don't be angry with Dixon,' said Mrs Hale, anxiously. Margaret recovered herself.

'No! I won't. I will try and be humble, and learn her ways, if you will only let me do all I can for you. Let me be in the first place, mother – I am greedy of that. I used to fancy you would forget me while I was away at aunt Shaw's, and cry myself to sleep at nights with that notion in my head.'

'And I used to think, how will Margaret bear our makeshift poverty after the thorough comfort and luxury in Harley Street, till I have many a time been more ashamed of your seeing our contrivances at Helstone than of any stranger finding them out.'

'Oh, mamma! and I did so enjoy them. They were so much more amusing than all the jog-trot Harley Street ways. The wardrobe shelf with handles, that served as a supper-tray on grand occasions! And the old tea-chests stuffed and covered for ottomans! I think what you call the makeshift contrivances at dear Helstone were a charming part of the life there.'

'I shall never see Helstone again, Margaret,' said Mrs Hale, the tears welling up into her eyes. Margaret could not reply. Mrs Hale went on. 'While I was there, I was for ever wanting to leave it. Every place seemed pleasanter. And now I shall die far away from it. I am rightly punished.'

'You must not talk so,' said Margaret, impatiently. 'He said you might live for years. Oh, mother! we will have you back at Helstone yet.'

'No, never! That I must take as a just penance. But, Margaret – Frederick!'

At the mention of that one word, she suddenly cried out loud, as in some sharp agony. It seemed as if the thought of him upset all her composure, destroyed the calm, overcame the exhaustion. Wild passionate cry succeeded to cry – 'Frederick! Frederick! Come to me. I am dying. Little first-born child, come to me once again!'

She was in violent hysterics. Margaret went and called Dixon in terror. Dixon came in a huff, and accused Margaret of having over-excited her mother. Margaret bore all meekly, only trusting that her father might not return. In spite of her alarm, which was even greater than the occasion warranted, she obeyed all Dixon's directions promptly and well, without a word of self-justification. By so doing she mollified her accuser. They put her mother to bed, and Margaret sate by her till she fell asleep, and afterwards till Dixon beckoned her out of the room, and, with a sour face, as if doing something against the grain, she bade her drink a cup of coffee which she had prepared for her in the drawing-room, and stood over her in a commanding attitude as she did so.

'You shouldn't have been so curious, Miss, and then you wouldn't have needed to fret before your time. It would have come soon enough. And now, I suppose, you'll tell master, and a pretty household I shall have of you!'

'No, Dixon,' said Margaret, sorrowfully, 'I will not tell papa. He could not bear it as I can.' And by way of proving how well she bore it, she burst into tears.

'Ay! I knew how it would be. Now you'll waken your mamma, just after she's gone to sleep so quietly. Miss Margaret my dear, I've had to keep it down this many a week; and though I don't pretend I can love her as you do, yet I loved her better than any other man, woman, or child – no one but Master Frederick ever came near her in my mind. Ever since Lady Beresford's maid first took me in to see her dressed out in white crape, and corn-ears, and scarlet poppies, and I ran a needle down into my finger, and broke it in, and she tore up her worked pocket-handkerchief, after they'd cut it out, and came in to wet the bandages again with lotion when she returned from the ball – where she'd been the prettiest young lady of all – I've never loved any one like her. I little thought then that I should live to see her brought so low. I don't mean no reproach to nobody. Many a one calls you pretty and handsome, and what not. Even in this smoky place, enough to blind one's eyes, the owls can see that. But you'll never be like your mother for beauty – never; not if you live to be a hundred.'

'Mamma is very pretty still. Poor mamma!'

'Now don't ye set off again, or I shall give way at last' (whimpering). 'You'll never stand master's coming home, and questioning, at this rate. Go out and take a walk, and come in something like. Many's the time I've longed to walk it off – the thought of what was the matter with her, and how it must all end.'

'Oh, Dixon!' said Margaret, 'how often I've been cross with you, not knowing what a terrible secret you had to bear!'

'Bless you, child! I like to see you showing a bit of a spirit. It's the good old Beresford blood. Why, the last Sir John but two shot his steward down, there where he stood, for just telling him that he'd racked the tenants, and he'd racked the tenants till he could get no more money off them than he could get skin off a flint.'

'Well, Dixon, I won't shoot you, and I'll try not to be cross again.'

'You never have. If I've said it at times, it has always been to myself, just in private, by way of making a little agreeable conversation, for there's no one here fit to talk to. And when you fire up, you're the very image of Master Frederick. I could find in my heart to put you in a passion any day, just to see his stormy look coming like a great cloud over your face. But now you go out, Miss. I'll watch over missus; and as for master, his books are company enough for him, if he should come in.'

'I will go,' said Margaret. She hung about Dixon for a minute or so, as if afraid and irresolute; then suddenly kissing her, she went quickly out of the room.

'Bless her!' said Dixon. 'She's as sweet as a nut. There are three people I love; it's missus, Master Frederick, and her. Just them three. That's all. The rest be hanged, for I don't know what they're in the world for. Master was born, I suppose, for to marry missus. If I thought he loved her properly, I might get to love him in time. But he should ha' made a deal more on her, and not been always reading, reading, thinking, thinking. See what it has brought him to! Many a one who never reads nor thinks either, gets to be Rector, and Dean, and what not; and I dare say master might, if he'd just minded missus, and let the weary reading and thinking alone. – There she goes' (looking out of the window as she heard the front door shut). 'Poor young lady! her clothes look shabby to what they did when she came to Helstone a year ago. Then she hadn't so much as a darned stocking or a cleaned pair of gloves in all her wardrobe. And now –!'

CHAPTER XVII

What is a Strike?

There are briars besetting every path,[1]
Which call for patient care;
There is a cross in every lot,
And an earnest need for prayer.

ANON

Margaret went out heavily and unwillingly enough. But the length of a street – yes, the air of a Milton Street – cheered her young blood before she reached her first turning. Her step grew lighter, her lip redder. She began to take notice, instead of having her thoughts turned so exclusively inward. She saw unusual loiterers in the streets: men with their hands in their pockets sauntering along; loud-laughing and loud-spoken girls clustered together, apparently excited to high spirits, and a boisterous independence of temper and behaviour. The more ill-looking of the men – the discreditable minority – hung about on the steps of the beer-houses and gin-shops, smoking, and commenting pretty freely on every passer-by. Margaret disliked the prospect of the long walk through these streets, before she came to the fields which she had planned to reach. Instead, she would go and see Bessy Higgins. It would not be so refreshing as a quiet country walk, but still it would perhaps be doing the kinder thing.

Nicholas Higgins was sitting by the fire smoking, as she went in. Bessy was rocking herself on the other side.

Nicholas took the pipe out of his mouth, and standing up, pushed his chair towards Margaret; he leant against the chimney-piece in a lounging attitude, while she asked Bessy how she was.

'Hoo's rather down i' th' mouth in regard to spirits, but hoo's better in health. Hoo doesn't like this strike. Hoo's a deal too much set on peace and quietness at any price.'

'This is th' third strike I've seen,' said she, sighing, as if that was answer and explanation enough.

'Well, third time pays for all. See if we don't dang th' masters this time. See if they don't come, and beg us to come, back at our own price. That's all. We've missed it afore time, I grant yo'; but this time we'n laid our plans desperate deep.'

'Why do you strike?'[2] asked Margaret. 'Striking is leaving off work till you get your own rate of wages, is it not? You must not wonder at my ignorance; where I come from I never heard of a strike.'

'I wish I were there,' said Bessy, wearily. 'But it's not for me to get sick and tired o' strikes. This is the last I'll see. Before it's ended I shall be in the Great City – the Holy Jerusalem.'

'Hoo's so full of th' life to come, hoo cannot think of th' present. Now I, yo' see, am bound to do the best I can here. I think a bird i' th' hand is worth two i' th' bush. So them's the different views we take on th' strike question.'

'But,' said Margaret, 'if the people struck, as you call it, where I come from, as they are mostly all field labourers, the seed would not be sown, the hay got in, the corn reaped.'

'Well?' said he. He had resumed his pipe, and put his 'well' in the form of an interrogation.

'Why,' she went on, 'what would become of the farmers?'

He puffed away. 'I reckon they'd have either to give up their farms, or to give fair rate of wage.'

'Suppose they could not, or would not do the last; they could not give up their farms all in a minute, however much they might wish to do so; but they would have no hay, nor corn to sell that year; and where would the money come from to pay the labourers' wages the next?'

Still puffing away. At last he said:

'I know nought of your ways down South. I have heerd they're a pack of spiritless, down-trodden men; welly clemmed to death; too much dazed wi' clemming to know when they're put upon. Now, it's not so here. We known when we're put upon; and we'en too much blood in us to stand it. We just take our hands fro' our looms, and say, "Yo' may clem us, but yo'll not put upon us, my masters!" and be danged to 'em, they shan't this time!'

'I wish I lived down South,' said Bessy.

'There's a deal to bear there,' said Margaret. 'There are sorrows to bear everywhere. There is very hard bodily labour to be gone through, with very little food to give strength.'

'But it's out of doors,' said Bessy. 'And away from the endless, endless noise, and sickening heat.'

'It's sometimes in heavy rain, and sometimes in bitter cold. A young person can stand it; but an old man gets racked with rheumatism, and bent and withered before his time; yet he must just work on the same, or else go to the workhouse.'

'I thought yo' were so taken wi' the ways of the South country.'

'So I am,' said Margaret, smiling a little, as she found herself thus caught. 'I only mean, Bessy, there's good and bad in everything in this world; and as you felt the bad up here, I thought it was but fair you should know the bad down there.'

'And yo' say they never strike down there?' asked Nicholas, abruptly.

'No!' said Margaret; 'I think they have too much sense.'

'An' I think,' replied he, dashing the ashes out of his pipe with so much vehemence that it broke, 'it's not that they've too much sense, but that they've too little spirit.'

'O, father!' said Bessy, 'what have ye gained by striking? Think of that first strike when mother died – how we all had to clem – you the worst of all; and yet many a one went in every week at the same wage, till all were gone in that there was work for; and some went beggars all their lives at after.'

'Ay,' said he. 'That there strike was badly managed. Folk got into th' management of it, as were either fools or not true men. Yo'll see, it'll be different this time.'

'But all this time you've not told me what you're striking for,' said Margaret, again.

'Why, yo' see, there's five or six masters who have set themselves again paying the wages they've been paying these two years past, and flourishing upon, and getting richer upon. And now they come to us, and say we're to take less. And we won't. We'll just clem them to death first; and see who'll work for 'em then. They'll have killed the goose that laid 'em the golden eggs, I reckon.'

'And so you plan dying, in order to be revenged upon them!'

'No,' said he, 'I dunnot. I just look forward to the chance of dying at my post sooner than yield. That's what folk call fine and honourable in a soldier, and why not in a poor weaver-chap?'

'But,' said Margaret, 'a soldier dies in the cause of the Nation – in the cause of others.'

He laughed grimly. 'My lass,' said he, 'yo're but a young wench, but don't yo' think I can keep three people – that's Bessy, and Mary, and me – on sixteen shilling a week? Dun yo' think it's for mysel' I'm striking work at this time? It's just as much in the cause of others as yon soldier – only m'appen, the cause he dies for is just that of somebody he never clapt eyes on, nor heerd on all his born days, while I take up John Boucher's cause, as lives next door but one, wi' a sickly wife, and eight childer, none on 'em factory age;[3] and I don't take up his cause only, though he's a poor good-for-nought, as can only manage two looms at a time, but I take up th' cause o' justice. Why are we to have less wage now, I ask, than two year ago?'

'Don't ask me,' said Margaret; 'I am very ignorant. Ask some of your masters. Surely they will give you a reason for it. It is not merely an arbitrary decision of theirs, come to without reason.'

'Yo're just a foreigner, and nothing more,' said he, contemptuously. 'Much yo' know about it. Ask th' masters! They'd tell us to mind our own business, and they'd mind theirs. Our business being, yo' understand, to take the bated wage, and be thankful; and their business to bate us down to clemming point, to swell their profits. That's what it is.'

'But,' said Margaret, determined not to give way, although she saw she was irritating him, 'the state of trade may be such as not to enable them to give you the same remuneration.'

'State o' trade! That's just a piece o' masters' humbug. It's rate o' wages I was talking of. Th' masters keep th' state o' trade in their own hands; and just walk it forward like a black bug-a-boo, to frighten naughty children with into being good. I'll tell yo' it's their part, – their cue, as some folks call it, – to beat us down, to swell their fortunes; and it's ours to stand up and fight hard, – not for ourselves alone, but for them round about us – for justice and fair play. We help to make their profits, and we ought to help spend 'em. It's not that we want their brass so much this time, as we've done many a time afore. We 'n getten money laid by; and we're resolved to stand and fall together; not a man on us will go in for less wage than th' Union says is our due. So I say, "hooray for the strike," and let Thornton, and Slickson, and Hamper, and their set look to it!'

'Thornton!' said Margaret. 'Mr Thornton of Marlborough Street?'

'Aye! Thornton o' Marlborough Mill, as we call him.'

'He is one of the masters you are striving with, is he not? What sort of a master is he?'

'Did yo' ever see a bulldog? Set a bulldog on hind legs, and dress him up in coat and breeches, and yo'n just getten John Thornton.'

'Nay,' said Margaret, laughing, 'I deny that. Mr Thornton is plain enough, but he's not like a bulldog, with its short broad nose, and snarling upper lip.'

'No! not in look, I grant yo'. But let John Thornton get hold on a notion, and he'll stick to it like a bulldog; yo' might pull him away wi' a pitchfork ere he'd leave go. He's worth fighting wi', is John Thornton. As for Slickson, I take it, some o' these days he'll wheedle his men back wi' fair promises; that they'll just get cheated out of as soon as they're in his power again. He'll work his fines well out on 'em, I'll warrant. He's as slippery as an eel, he is. He's like a cat, – as sleek, and cunning, and fierce. It'll never be an honest up and down fight wi' him, as it will be wi' Thornton. Thornton's as dour as a door-nail; an obstinate chap, every inch on him, – th' oud bulldog!'

'Poor Bessy!' said Margaret, turning round to her. 'You sigh over it all. You don't like struggling and fighting as your father does, do you?'

'No!' said she, heavily. 'I'm sick on it. I could have wished to have had other talk about me in my latter days, than just the clashing and clanging and clattering that has wearied a' my life long, about work and wages, and masters, and hands, and knobsticks.'

'Poor wench! latter days be farred! Thou'rt looking a sight better already for a little stir and change. Beside, I shall be a deal here to make it more lively for thee.'

'Tobacco-smoke chokes me!' said she, querulously.

'Then I'll never smoke no more i' th' house!' he replied, tenderly. 'But why didst thou not tell me afore, thou foolish wench?'

She did not speak for a while, and then so low that only Margaret heard her:

'I reckon, he'll want a' the comfort he can get out o' either pipe or drink afore he's done.'

Her father went out of doors, evidently to finish his pipe.

Bessy said passionately,

'Now am not I a fool, – am I not, Miss? – there, I knew I ought for to keep father at home, and away fro' the folk that are always ready for to tempt a man, in time o' strike, to go drink,[4] – and there my tongue must needs quarrel with this pipe o' his'n, – and he'll go off, I know he will, – as often as he wants to smoke – and nobody knows where it'll end. I wish I'd letten myself be choked first.'

'But does your father drink?' asked Margaret.

'No – not to say drink,' replied she, still in the same wild excited tone. 'But what win ye have? There are days wi' you, as wi' other folk, I suppose, when yo' get up and go through th' hours, just longing for a bit of a change – a bit of a fillip, as it were. I know I ha' gone and bought a four-pounder out o' another baker's shop to common on such days, just because I sickened at the thought of going on for ever wi' the same sight in my eyes, and the same sound in my ears, and the same taste i' my mouth, and the same thought (or no thought, for that matter) in my head, day after day, for ever. I've longed for to be a man to go spreeing, even if it were only a tramp to some new place in search o' work. And father – all men – have it stronger in 'em than me to get tired o' sameness and work for ever. And what is 'em to do? It's little blame to them if they do go into th' gin-shop for to make their blood flow quicker, and more lively, and see things they never see at no other time – pictures, and looking-glass, and such like. But father never was a drunkard, though maybe, he's got worse for drink, now and then. Only yo' see,' and now her voice took a mournful, pleading tone, 'at times o' strike there's much to knock a man down, for all they start so hopefully; and where's the comfort to come fro'? He'll get angry and mad – they all do – and then they get tired out wi' being angry and mad, and maybe ha' done things in their passion they'd be glad to forget. Bless yo'r sweet pitiful face! but yo' dunnot know what a strike is yet.'

'Come, Bessy,' said Margaret. 'I won't say you're exaggerating, because I don't know enough about it: but, perhaps, as you're not well, you're only looking on one side, and there is another and a brighter to be looked to.'

'It's all well enough for yo' to say so, who have lived in pleasant green places all your life long, and never known want or care, or wickedness either, for that matter.'

'Take care,' said Margaret, her cheek flushing, and her eye lightening, 'how you judge, Bessy. I shall go home to my mother, who is so ill – so ill, Bessy, that there's no outlet but death for her out of the prison of her great suffering; and yet I must speak cheerfully to my father, who has no notion of her real state, and to whom the knowledge must come gradually. The only person – the only one who could sympathize with me and help me – whose presence could comfort my mother more than any other earthly thing – is falsely accused – would run the risk of death, if he came to see his dying mother. This I tell you – only you, Bessy. You must not mention it. No other person in Milton – hardly any other person in England knows. Have I not care? Do I not know anxiety, though I go about well-dressed, and have food enough? Oh, Bessy, God is just, and our lots are well portioned out by Him, although none but He knows the bitterness of our souls.'

'I ask your pardon,' replied Bessy, humbly. 'Sometimes, when I've thought o' my life, and the little pleasure I've had in it, I've believed that, maybe, I was one of those doomed to die by the falling of a star from heaven; "And the name of the star is called Wormwood;[5] and the third part of the waters became wormwood; and men died of the waters, because they were made bitter." One can bear pain and sorrow better if one thinks it has been prophesied long before for one: somehow, then it seems as if my pain was needed for the fulfilment; otherways it seems all sent for nothing.'

'Nay, Bessy – think!' said Margaret. 'God does not willingly afflict. Don't dwell so much on the prophecies, but read the clearer parts of the Bible.'

'I dare say it would be wiser; but where would I hear such grand words of promise – hear tell o' anything so far different fro' this dreary world, and this town above a', as in Revelations? Many's the time I've repeated the verses in the seventh chapter[6] to myself, just for the sound. It's as good as an organ, and as different from every day, too. No, I cannot give up Revelations. It gives me more comfort than any other book i' the Bible.'

'Let me come and read you some of my favourite chapters.'

'Ay,' said she, greedily, 'come. Father will maybe hear yo.' He's deaved wi' my talking; he says it's all nought to do with the things o' today, and that's his business.'

'Where is your sister?'

'Gone fustian-cutting.[7] I were loth to let her go; but somehow we must live; and th' Union can't afford us much.'

'Now I must go. You have done me good, Bessy.'

'I done you good!'

'Yes. I came here very sad, and rather too apt to think my own cause for grief was the only one in the world. And now I hear how you have had to bear for years, and that makes me stronger.'

'Bless yo'! I thought a' the good-doing was on the side of gentlefolk. I shall get proud if I think I can do good to yo'.'

'You won't do it if you think about it. But you'll only puzzle yourself if you do, that's one comfort.'

'Yo're not like no one I ever seed. I dunno what to make of yo'.'

'Nor I of myself. Good-bye!'

Bessy stilled her rocking to gaze after her.

'I wonder if there are many folk like her down South. She's like a breath of country air, somehow. She freshens me up above a bit. Who'd ha' thought that face – as bright and as strong as the angel I dream of – could have known the sorrow she speaks on? I wonder how she'll sin. All on us must sin. I think a deal on her, for sure. But father does the like, I see. And Mary even. It's not often hoo's stirred up to notice much.'

CHAPTER XVIII

Likes and Dislikes

My heart revolts within me, and two voices[1]
Make themselves audible within my bosom.
WALLENSTEIN

On Margaret's return home she found two letters on the table: one was a note for her mother, – the other, which had come by the post, was evidently from her Aunt Shaw – covered with foreign postmarks – thin, silvery, and rustling. She took up the other, and was examining it, when her father came in suddenly:

'So your mother is tired, and gone to bed early! I'm afraid, such a thundery day was not the best in the world for the doctor to see her. What did he say? Dixon tells me he spoke to you about her.'

Margaret hesitated. Her father's looks became more grave and anxious:

'He does not think her seriously ill?'

'Not at present; she needs care, he says: he was very kind, and said he would call again, and see how his medicines worked.'

'Only care – he did not recommend change of air? – he did not say this smoky town was doing her any harm, did he, Margaret?'

'No! not a word,' she replied, gravely. 'He was anxious, I think.'

'Doctors have that anxious manner; it's professional,' said he.

Margaret saw, in her father's nervous ways, that the first impression of possible danger was made upon his mind, in spite of all his making light of what she told him. He could not forget the subject, – could not pass from it to other things; he kept recurring to it through the evening, with an unwillingness to receive even the slightest unfavourable idea, which made Margaret inexpressibly sad.

'This letter is from Aunt Shaw, papa. She has got to Naples, and finds it too hot, so she has taken apartments at Sorrento. But I don't think she likes Italy.'

'He did not say anything about diet, did he?'

'It was to be nourishing, and digestible. Mamma's appetite is pretty good, I think.'

'Yes! and that makes it all the more strange he should have thought of speaking about diet.'

'I asked him, papa.' Another pause. Then Margaret went on: 'Aunt Shaw says, she has sent me some coral ornaments, papa; but,' added Margaret, half-smiling, 'she is afraid the Milton Dissenters won't appreciate them. She has got all her ideas of Dissenters from the Quakers, has not she?'

'If ever you hear or notice that your mother wishes for anything, be sure you let me know. I am so afraid she does not tell me always what she would like. Pray, see after that girl Mrs Thornton named. If we had a good, efficient house-servant, Dixon could be constantly with her, and I'd answer for it we'd soon set her up amongst us, if care will do it. She's been very much tired of late, with the hot weather, and the difficulty of getting a servant. A little rest will put her quite to rights – eh, Margaret?'

'I hope so,' said Margaret, – but so sadly, that her father took notice of it. He pinched her cheek.

'Come; if you look so pale as this, I must rouge you up a little. Take care of yourself, child, or you'll be wanting the doctor next.'

But he could not settle to anything that evening. He was continually going backwards and forwards, on laborious tiptoe; to see if his wife was still asleep. Margaret's heart ached at his restlessness – his trying to stifle and strangle the hideous fear that was looming out of the dark places of his heart.

He came back at last, somewhat comforted.

'She's awake now, Margaret. She quite smiled as she saw me standing by her. Just her old smile. And she says she feels refreshed, and ready for tea. Where's the note for her? She wants to see it. I'll read it to her while you make tea.'

The note proved to be a formal invitation from Mrs Thornton, to Mr, Mrs, and Miss Hale to dinner, on the twenty-first instant. Margaret was surprised to find an acceptance contemplated, after all she had learnt of sad probabilities during the day. But so it was. The idea of her husband's and daughter's going to this dinner had quite captivated Mrs Hale's fancy, even before Margaret had heard the contents of the note. It was an event to diversify the monotony of the invalid's life; and she clung to the idea of their going, with even fretful pertinacity, when Margaret objected.

'Nay, Margaret! if she wishes it, I'm sure we'll both go willingly. She never would wish it unless she felt herself really stronger – really better than we thought she was, eh, Margaret?' said Mr Hale, anxiously, as she prepared to write the note of acceptance, the next day.

'Eh! Margaret?' questioned he, with a nervous motion of his hands. It seemed cruel to refuse him the comfort he craved for. And besides, his passionate refusal to admit the existence of fear, almost inspired Margaret herself with hope.

'I do think she is better since last night,' said she. 'Her eyes look brighter, and her complexion clearer.'

'God bless you,' said her father earnestly. 'But is it true? Yesterday was so sultry. Every one felt ill. It was a most unlucky day for Dr Donaldson to see her on.'

So he went away to his day's duties, now increased by the preparation of some lectures he had promised to deliver to the working people at a neighbouring Lyceum.[2] He had chosen Ecclesiastical Architecture as his subject, rather more in accordance with his own taste and knowledge than as falling in with the character of the place or the desire for particular kinds of information among those to whom he was to lecture. And the institution itself, being in debt, was only too glad to get a gratis course from an educated and accomplished man like Mr Hale, let the subject be what it might.

'Well, mother,' asked Mr Thornton that night, 'who have accepted your invitations for the twenty-first?'

'Fanny, where are the notes? The Slicksons accept, Collingbrooks accept, Stephenses accept, Browns decline. Hales – father and daughter come, – mother too great an invalid – Macphersons come, and Mr Horsfall, and Mr Young. I was thinking of asking the Porters, as the Browns can't come.'

'Very good. Do you know, I'm really afraid Mrs Hale is very far from well, from what Dr Donaldson says.'

'It's strange of them to accept a dinner-invitation if she's very ill,' said Fanny.

'I didn't say very ill,' said her brother, rather sharply. 'I only said very far from well. They may not know it either.' And then he suddenly remembered that, from what Dr Donaldson had told him, Margaret, at any rate, must be aware of the exact state of the case.

'Very probably they are quite aware of what you said yesterday, John – of the great advantage it would be to them – to Mr Hale, I mean, to be introduced to such people as the Stephenses and the Collingbrooks.'

'I'm sure that motive would not influence them. No! I think I understand how it is.'

'John!' said Fanny, laughing in her little, weak, nervous way. 'How you profess to understand these Hales, and how you never will allow that we can know anything about them. Are they really so very different to most people one meets with?'

She did not mean to vex him; but if she had intended it, she could not have done it more thoroughly. He chafed in silence, however, not deigning to reply to her question.

'They do not seem to me out of the common way,' said Mrs Thornton. 'He appears a worthy kind of man enough; rather too simple for trade – so it's perhaps as well he should have been a clergyman first, and now a teacher. She's a bit of a fine lady, with her invalidism; and as for the girl – she's the only one who puzzles me when I think about her – which I don't often do. She seems to have a great notion of giving herself airs; and I can't make out why. I could almost fancy she thinks herself too good for her company at times. And yet they're not rich; from all I can hear they never have been.'

'And she's not accomplished, mamma. She can't play.'

'Go on, Fanny. What else does she want to bring her up to your standard?'

'Nay! John,' said his mother, 'that speech of Fanny's did no harm. I myself heard Miss Hale say she could not play. If you would let us alone, we could perhaps like her, and see her merits.'

'I'm sure I never could!' murmured Fanny, protected by her mother. Mr Thornton heard, but did not care to reply. He was walking up and down the dining-room, wishing that his mother would order candles, and allow him to set to work at either reading or writing, and so put a stop to the conversation. But he never thought of interfering in any of the small domestic regulations that Mrs Thornton observed, in habitual remembrance of her old economies.

'Mother,' said he, stopping, and bravely speaking out the truth, 'I wish you would like Miss Hale.'

'Why?' asked she, startled by his earnest, yet tender manner. 'You're never thinking of marrying her? – a girl without a penny.'

'She would never have me,' said he, with a short laugh.

'No, I don't think she would,' answered his mother. 'She laughed in my face, when I praised her for speaking out something Mr Bell had said in your favour. I liked the girl for doing it so frankly, for it made me sure she had no thought of you; and the next minute she vexed me so by seeming to think – Well, never mind! Only you're right in saying she's too good an opinion of herself to think of you. The saucy jade! I should like to know where she'd find a better!'

If these words hurt her son, the dusky light prevented him from betraying any emotion. In a minute he came up quite cheerfully to his mother, and putting one hand lightly on her shoulder, said:

'Well, as I'm just as much convinced of the truth of what you have been saying as you can be; and as I have no thought or expectation of ever asking her to be my wife, you'll believe me for the future that I'm quite disinterested in speaking about her. I foresee trouble for that girl – perhaps want of motherly care – and I only wish you to be ready to be a friend to her, in case she needs one. Now, Fanny,' said he, 'I trust you have delicacy enough to understand, that it is as great an injury to Miss Hale as to me – in fact, she would think it a greater – to suppose that I have any reason, more than I now give, for begging you and my mother to show her every kindly attention.'

'I cannot forgive her her pride,' said his mother; 'I will befriend her, if there is need, for your asking, John. I would befriend Jezebel herself if you asked me. But this girl, who turns up her nose at us all – who turns up her nose at you –'

'Nay, mother; I have never yet put myself, and I mean never to put myself, within reach of her contempt.'

'Contempt, indeed!' – (One of Mrs Thornton's expressive snorts.) – 'Don't go on speaking of Miss Hale, John, if I've to be kind to her. When I'm with her, I don't know if I like or dislike her most; but when I think of her, and hear you talk of her, I hate her. I can see she's given herself airs to you as well as if you'd told me out.'

'And if she has,' said he – and then he paused for a moment – then went on: 'I'm not a lad, to be cowed by a proud look from a woman, or to care for her misunderstanding me and my position. I can laugh at it!'

'To be sure! and at her too, with her fine notions and haughty tosses!'

'I only wonder why you talk so much about her, then,' said Fanny. 'I'm sure, I'm tired enough of the subject.'

'Well!' said her brother, with a shade of bitterness. 'Suppose we find some more agreeable subject. What do you say to a strike, by way of something pleasant to talk about?'

'Have the hands actually turned out?' asked Mrs Thornton, with vivid interest.

'Hamper's men are actually out. Mine are working out their week, through fear of being prosecuted for breach of contract. I'd have had every one of them up and punished for it that left his work before his time was out.'

'The law expenses would have been more than the hands themselves were worth – a set of ungrateful naughts!' said his mother.

'To be sure. But I'd have shown them how I keep my word, and how I mean them to keep theirs. They know me by this time. Slickson's men are off – pretty certain he won't spend money in getting them punished. We're in for a turn-out, mother.'

'I hope there are not many orders in hand?'

'Of course there are. They know that well enough. But they don't quite understand all, though they think they do.'

'What do you mean, John?'

Candles had been brought, and Fanny had taken up her interminable piece of worsted-work, over which she was yawning; throwing herself back in her chair, from time to time, to gaze at vacancy, and think of nothing at her ease.

'Why,' said he, 'the Americans are getting their yarns so into the general market,[3] that our only chance is producing them at a lower rate. If we can't, we may shut up shop at once, and hands and masters go alike on tramp. Yet these fools go back to the prices paid three years ago – nay, some of their leaders quote Dickinson's prices now – though they know as well as we do that, what with fines pressed out of their wages as no honourable man would extort them, and other ways which I for one would scorn to use, the real rate of wage paid at Dickinson's is less than at ours. Upon my word, mother, I wish the old combination-laws[4] were in force. It is too bad to find out that fools – ignorant wayward men like these – just by uniting their weak silly heads, are to rule over the fortunes of those who bring all the wisdom that knowledge and experience, and often painful thought and anxiety, can give. The next thing will be – indeed, we're all but come to it now – that we shall have to go and ask – stand hat in hand – and humbly ask the secretary of the Spinners' Union to be so kind as to furnish us with labour at their own price. That's what they want – they, who haven't the sense to see that, if we don't get a fair share of the profits to compensate us for our wear and tear here in England, we can move off to some other country; and that, what with home and foreign competition, we are none of us likely to make above a fair share, and may be thankful enough if we can get that, in an average number of years.'

'Can't you get hands from Ireland? I wouldn't keep these fellows a day. I'd teach them that I was master, and could employ what servants I liked.'

'Yes! to be sure, I can; and I will, too, if they go on long. It will be trouble and expense, and I fear there will be some danger; but I will do it, rather than give in.'

'If there is to be all this extra expense, I'm sorry we're giving a dinner just now.'

'So am I, – not because of the expense, but because I shall have much to think about, and many unexpected calls on my time. But we must have had Mr Horsfall, and he does not stay in Milton long. And as for the others, we owe them dinners, and it's all one trouble.'

He kept on with his restless walk – not speaking any more, but drawing a deep breath from time to time, as if endeavouring to throw off some annoying thought. Fanny asked her mother numerous small questions, all having nothing to do with the subject, which a wiser person would have perceived was occupying her attention. Consequently, she received many short answers. She was not sorry when, at ten o'clock, the servants filed in to prayers. These her mother always read, – first reading a chapter. They were now working steadily through the Old Testament. When prayers were ended, and his mother had wished him good-night, with that long steady look of hers which conveyed no expression of the tenderness that was in her heart, but yet had the intensity of a blessing, Mr Thornton continued his walk. All his business plans had received a check, a sudden pull-up, from this approaching turn-out. The fore-thought of many anxious hours was thrown away, utterly wasted by their insane folly, which would injure themselves even more than him, though no one could set any limit to the mischief they were doing. And these were the men who thought themselves fitted to direct the masters in the disposal of their capital! Hamper had said, only this very day, that if he were ruined by the strike, he would start life again, comforted by the conviction that those who brought it on were in a worse predicament than he himself, – for he had head as well as hands, while they had only hands; and if they drove away their market, they could not follow it, nor turn to anything else. But this thought was no consolation to Mr Thornton. It might be that revenge gave him no pleasure; it might be that he valued the position he had earned with the sweat of his brow, so much that he keenly felt its being endangered by the ignorance or folly of others, – so keenly that he had no thoughts to spare for what would be the consequences of their conduct to themselves. He paced up and down, setting his teeth a little now and then. At last it struck two. The candles were flickering in their sockets. He lighted his own, muttering to himself:

'Once for all, they shall know whom they have got to deal with. I can give them a fortnight, – no more. If they don't see their madness before the end of that time, I must have hands from Ireland. I believe it's Slickson's doing, confound him and his dodges! He thought he was overstocked; so he seemed to yield at first, when the deputation came to him, – and of course, he only confirmed them in their folly, as he meant to do. That's where it spread from.'

CHAPTER XIX

Angel Visits

As angels in some brighter dreams[1]
  Call to the soul when man doth sleep,
So some strange thoughts transcend our wonted themes,
  And into glory peep.

HENRY VAUGHAN

Mrs Hale was curiously amused and interested by the idea of the Thornton dinner-party. She kept wondering about the details, with something of the simplicity of a little child, who wants to have all its anticipated pleasures described beforehand. But the monotonous life led by invalids often makes them like children, inasmuch as they have neither of them any sense of proportion in events, and seem each to believe that the walls and curtains which shut in their world, and shut out everything else, must of necessity be larger than anything hidden beyond. Besides, Mrs Hale had had her vanities as a girl; had perhaps unduly felt their mortification when she became a poor clergyman's wife; – they had been smothered and kept down; but they were not extinct; and she liked to think of seeing Margaret dressed for a party, and discussed what she should wear, with an unsettled anxiety that amused Margaret, who had been more accustomed to society in her one year in Harley Street than her mother in five and twenty years of Helstone.

'Then you think you shall wear your white silk. Are you sure it will fit? It's nearly a year since Edith was married!'

'Oh yes, mamma! Mrs Murray made it, and it's sure to be right; it may be a straw's breadth shorter or longer-waisted, according to my having grown fat or thin. But I don't think I've altered in the least.'

'Hadn't you better let Dixon see it? It may have gone yellow with lying by.'

'If you like, mamma. But if the worst comes to the worst, I've a very nice pink gauze which aunt Shaw gave me, only two or three months before Edith was married. That can't have gone yellow.'

'No! but it may have faded.'

'Well! then I've a green silk. I feel more as if it was the embarrassment of riches.'

'I wish I knew what you ought to wear,' said Mrs Hale, nervously.

Margaret's manner changed instantly. 'Shall I go and put them on one after another, mamma, and then you could see which you liked best?'

'But – yes! perhaps that will be best.'

So off Margaret went. She was very much inclined to play some pranks when she was dressed up at such an unusual hour; to make her rich white silk balloon out into a cheese, to retreat backwards from her mother as if she were the queen; but when she found that these freaks of hers were regarded as interruptions to the serious business, and as such annoyed her mother, she became grave and sedate. What had possessed the world (her world) to fidget so about her dress, she could not understand; but that very afternoon, on naming her engagement to Bessy Higgins (apropos of the servant that Mrs Thornton had promised to inquire about), Bessy quite roused up at the intelligence.

'Dear! and are you going to dine at Thornton's at Marlborough Mills?'

'Yes, Bessy. Why are you so surprised?'

'Oh, I dunno. But they visit wi' a' th' first folk in Milton.'

'And you don't think we're quite the first folk in Milton, eh, Bessy?'

Bessy's cheeks flushed a little at her thought being thus easily read.

'Well,' said she, 'yo' see, they thinken a deal o' money here; and I reckon yo've not getten much.'

'No,' said Margaret, 'that's very true. But we are educated people, and have lived amongst educated people. Is there anything so wonderful, in our being asked out to dinner by a man who owns himself inferior to my father by coming to him to be instructed? I don't mean to blame Mr Thornton. Few drapers' assistants, as he was once, could have made themselves what he is.'

'But can yo' give dinners back, in yo're small house? Thornton's house is three times as big.'

'Well, I think we could manage to give Mr Thornton a dinner back, as you call it. Perhaps not in such a large room, nor with so many people. But I don't think we've thought about it at all in that way.'

'I never thought yo'd be dining with Thorntons,'[2] repeated Bessy. 'Why, the mayor hissel' dines there; and the members of Parliament and all.'

'I think I could support the honour of meeting the mayor of Milton.'

'But them ladies dress so grand!' said Bessy, with an anxious look at Margaret's print gown, which her Milton eyes appraised at sevenpence a yard.

Margaret's face dimpled up into a merry laugh. 'Thank you, Bessy, for thinking so kindly about my looking nice among all the smart people. But I've plenty of grand gowns, – a week ago, I should have said they were far too grand for anything I should ever want again. But as I'm to dine at Mr Thornton's, and perhaps to meet the mayor, I shall put on my very best gown, you may be sure.'

'What win yo' wear?' asked Bessy, somewhat relieved.

'White silk,' said Margaret. 'A gown I had for a cousin's wedding, a year ago.'

'That'll do!' said Bessy, falling back in her chair. 'I should be loth to have yo' looked down upon.'

'Oh! I'll be fine enough, if that will save me from being looked down upon in Milton.'

'I wish I could see you dressed up,' said Bessy. 'I reckon yo're not what folk would ca' pretty; yo've not red and white enough for that. But dun yo' know, I ha' dreamt of yo', long afore ever I seed yo'.'

'Nonsense, Bessy!'

'Ay, but I did. Yo'r very face, – looking wi' yo'r clear steadfast eyes out o' th' darkness, wi' yo'r hair blown off from yo'r brow, and going out like rays round yo'r forehead, which was just as smooth and as straight as it is now, – and yo' always came to give me strength, which I seemed to gather out o' yo'r deep comforting eyes, – and yo' were drest in shining raiment – just as yo'r going to be drest. So, yo' see, it was yo'!'

'Nay, Bessy,' said Margaret, gently, 'it was but a dream.'

'And why might na I dream a dream in my affliction as well as others? Did not many a one i' the Bible? Ay, and see visions too! Why, even my father thinks a deal o' dreams! I tell yo' again, I saw yo' as plainly, coming swiftly towards me, wi' yo'r hair blown back wi' the very swiftness o' the motion, just like the way it grows, a little standing off like; and the white shining dress on yo've getten to wear. Let me come and see yo' in it. I want to see yo' and touch yo' as in very deed yo' were in my dream.'

'My dear Bessy, it is quite a fancy of yours.'

'Fancy or no fancy, – yo've come, as I knew yo' would, when I saw yo'r movement in my dream, – and when yo're here about me, I reckon I feel easier in my mind, and comforted, just as a fire comforts one on a dree day. Yo' said it were on th' twenty-first; please God, I'll come and see yo'.'

'Oh Bessy! you may come and welcome; but don't talk so – it really makes me sorry. It does indeed.'

'Then I'll keep it to mysel', if I bite my tongue out. Not but what it's true for all that.'

Margaret was silent. At last she said,

'Let us talk about it sometimes, if you think it true. But not now. Tell me, has your father turned out?'

'Ay!' said Bessy, heavily – in a manner very different from that she had spoken in but a minute or two before. 'He and many another, – all Hamper's men, – and many a one besides. Th' women are as bad as th' men, in their savageness, this time. Food is high, – and they mun have food for their childer, I reckon. Suppose Thorntons sent 'em their dinner out, – th' same money, spent on potatoes and meal, would keep many a crying babby quiet, and hush up its mother's heart for a bit!'

'Don't speak so!' said Margaret. 'You'll make me feel wicked and guilty in going to this dinner.'

'No!' said Bessy. 'Some's pre-elected to sumptuous feasts, and purple and fine linen, – may be yo're one on 'em. Others toil and moil all their lives long – and the very dogs are not pitiful in our days, as they were in the days of Lazarus.[3] But if yo' ask me to cool yo'r tongue wi' th' tip of my finger, I'll come across the great gulf to yo' just for th' thought o' what yo've been to me here.'

'Bessy! you're very feverish! I can tell it in the touch of your hand, as well as in what you're saying. It won't be division enough, in that awful day, that some of us have been beggars here, and some of us have been rich, – we shall not be judged by that poor accident, but by our faithful following of Christ.'

Margaret got up, and found some water: and soaking her pocket-handkerchief in it, she laid the cool wetness on Bessy's forehead, and began to chafe the stone-cold feet. Bessy shut her eyes, and allowed herself to be soothed. At last she said.

'Yo'd ha' been deaved out o' yo'r five wits, as well as me, if yo'd had one body after another, coming in to ask for father, and staying to tell me each one their tale. Some spoke o' deadly hatred, and made my blood run cold wi' the terrible things they said o' th' masters, – but more, being women, kept plaining, plaining (wi' the tears running down their cheeks, and never wiped away, nor heeded), of the price o' meat, and how their childer could na sleep at nights for th' hunger.'

'And do they think the strike will mend this?' asked Margaret.

'They say so,' replied Bessy. 'They do say trade has been good for long, and the masters has made no end o' money; how much father doesn't know, but, in course, th' Union does; and, as is natural, they wanten their share o' th' profits, now that food is getting dear; and th' Union says they'll not be doing their duty if they don't make the masters give 'em their share. But masters has getten th' upper hand somehow; and I'm feared they'll keep it now and evermore. It's like th' great battle o' Armageddon,⁴ the way they keep on, grinning and fighting at each other, till even while they fight, they are picked off into the pit.'

Just then Nicholas Higgins came in. He caught his daughter's last words.

'Ay! and I'll fight on too; and I'll get it this time. It'll not take long for to make 'em give in, for they've getten a pretty lot of orders, all under contract; and they'll soon find out they'd better give us our five per cent than lose the profit they'll gain; let alone the fine for not fulfilling the contract. Aha, my masters! I know who'll win.'

Margaret fancied from his manner that he must have been drinking, not so much from what he said, as from the excited way in which he spoke; and she was rather confirmed in this idea by the evident anxiety Bessy showed to hasten her departure. Bessy said to her, –

'The twenty-first – that's Thursday week. I may come and see yo' dressed for Thornton's, I reckon. What time is yo'r dinner?'

Before Margaret could answer, Higgins broke out,

'Thornton's! Ar' t' going to dine at Thornton's? Ask him to give yo' a bumper to the success of his orders. By th' twenty-first, I reckon, he'll be pottered in his brains how to get 'em done in time. Tell him, there's seven hundred 'll come marching into Marlborough Mills, the morning after he gives the five per cent, and will help him through his contract in no time. You'll have 'em all there. My master, Hamper. He's one o' th' oud-fashioned sort. Ne'er meets a man bout an oath or a curse; I should think he were going to die if he spoke me civil; but arter all, his bark's waur than his bite, and yo' may tell him one o' his turn-outs said so, if yo' like. Eh! but yo'll have a lot of prize mill-owners at Thornton's! I should like to get speech o' them, when they're a bit inclined to sit still after dinner, and could na run for the life on 'em. I'd tell 'em my mind. I'd speak up again th' hard way they're driving on us!'

'Good-bye!' said Margaret, hastily. 'Good-bye, Bessy! I shall look to see you on the twenty-first, if you're well enough.'

The medicines and treatment which Dr Donaldson had ordered for Mrs Hale, did her so much good at first that not only she herself, but Margaret, began to hope that he might have been mistaken, and that she could recover permanently. As for Mr Hale, although he had never had an idea of the serious nature of their apprehensions, he triumphed over their fears with an evident relief, which proved how much his glimpse into the nature of them had affected him. Only Dixon croaked for ever into Margaret's ear. However, Margaret defied the raven, and would hope.

They needed this gleam of brightness in-doors, for out-of-doors, even to their uninstructed eyes, there was a gloomy brooding appearance of discontent. Mr Hale had his own acquaintances among the working men, and was depressed with their earnestly-told tales of suffering and long-endurance. They would have scorned to speak of what they had to bear to any one who might, from his position, have understood it without their words. But here was this man, from a distant county, who was perplexed by the workings of the system into the midst of which he was thrown, and each was eager to make him a judge, and to bring witness of his own causes for irritation. Then Mr Hale brought all his budget of grievances, and laid it before Mr Thornton, for him, with his experience as a master, to arrange them, and explain their origin; which he always did, on sound economical principles; showing that, as trade was conducted, there must always be a waxing and waning of commercial prosperity;[5] and that in the waning a certain number of masters, as well as of men, must go down into ruin, and be no more seen among the ranks of the happy and prosperous. He spoke as if this consequence were so entirely logical, that neither employers nor employed had any right to complain if it became their fate: the employer to turn aside from the race he could no longer run, with a bitter sense of incompetency and failure – wounded in the struggle – trampled down by his fellows in their haste to get rich – slighted where he once was honoured – humbly asking for, instead of bestowing, employment with a lordly hand. Of course, speaking so of the fate that, as a master, might be his own in the fluctuations of commerce, he was not likely to have more sympathy with that of the workmen, who were passed by in the swift merciless improvement or alteration; who would fain lie down and quietly die out of the world that needed them not, but felt as if they could never rest in their graves for the clinging cries of the beloved and helpless they would leave behind; who envied the power of the wild bird, that can feed her young with her very heart's blood. Margaret's whole soul rose up against him while he reasoned in this way – as if commerce were everything and humanity nothing. She could hardly thank him for the individual kindness, which brought him that very evening to offer her – for the delicacy which made him understand that he must offer her privately – every convenience for illness that his own wealth or his mother's foresight had caused them to accumulate in their household, and which, as he learnt from Dr Donaldson, Mrs Hale might possibly require. His presence, after the way he had spoken – his bringing before her the doom, which she was vainly trying to persuade herself might yet be averted from her mother – all conspired to set Margaret's teeth on edge, as she looked at him, and listened to him. What business had he to be the only person, except Dr Donaldson and Dixon, admitted to the awful secret, which she held shut up in the most dark and sacred recess of her heart – not daring to look at it, unless she invoked heavenly strength to bear the sight – that, some day soon, she should cry aloud for her mother, and no answer would come out of the blank, dumb darkness? Yet he knew all. She saw it in his pitying eyes. She heard it in his grave and tremulous voice. How reconcile those eyes, that voice, with the hard-reasoning, dry, merciless way in which he laid down axioms of trade, and serenely followed them out to their full consequences? The discord jarred upon her inexpressibly. The more because of the gathering woe of which she heard from Bessy. To be sure, Nicholas Higgins, the father, spoke differently. He had been appointed a committee-man, and said that he knew secrets of which the exoteric knew nothing. He said this more expressly and particularly, on the very day before Mrs Thornton's dinner-party, when Margaret, going in to speak to Bessy, found him arguing the point with Boucher, the neighbour of whom she had frequently heard mention, as by turns exciting Higgins's compassion, as an unskilful workman with a large family depending upon him for support, and at other times enraging his more energetic and sanguine neighbour by his want of what the latter called spirit. It was very evident that

Higgins was in a passion when Margaret entered. Boucher stood, with both hands on the rather high mantelpiece, swaying himself a little on the support which his arms, thus placed, gave him, and looking wildly into the fire, with a kind of despair that irritated Higgins, even while it went to his heart. Bessy was rocking herself violently backwards and forwards, as was her wont (Margaret knew by this time) when she was agitated. Her sister Mary was tying on her bonnet (in great clumsy bows, as suited her great clumsy fingers), to go to her fustian-cutting, blubbering out loud the while, and evidently longing to be away from a scene that distressed her.

Margaret came in upon this scene. She stood for a moment at the door – then, her finger on her lips, she stole to a seat on the squab near Bessy. Nicholas saw her come in, and greeted her with a gruff, but not unfriendly nod. Mary hurried out of the house, catching gladly at the open door, and crying aloud when she got away from her father's presence. It was only John Boucher that took no notice whatever who came in and who went out.

'It's no use, Higgins. Hoo cannot live long a' this'n. Hoo's just sinking away – not for want o' meat hersel' – but because hoo cannot stand th' sight o' the little ones clemming. Ay, clemming! Five shilling a week may do well enough for thee, wi' but two mouths to fill, and one on 'em a wench who can welly earn her own meat. But it's clemming to us. An' I tell thee plain – if hoo dies, as I'm 'feard hoo will afore we've getten th' five per cent, I'll fling th' money back i' th' master's face, and say, "Be domned to yo'; be domned to th' whole cruel world o' yo'; that could na leave me th' best wife that ever bore childer to a man!" An' look thee, lad, I'll hate thee, and th' whole pack o' th' Union. Ay, an' chase yo' through heaven wi my hatred, – I will, lad! I will, – if yo're leading me astray i' this matter. Thou saidst, Nicholas, on Wednesday sennight – and it's now Tuesday i' th' second week – that afore a fortnight we'd ha' the masters coming a-begging to us to take back our work, at our own wage – and time's nearly up, – and there's our lile Jack lying a-bed, too weak to cry, but just every now and then sobbing up his heart for want o' food, – our lile Jack, I tell thee, lad! Hoo's never looked up sin' he were born, and hoo loves him as if he were her very life, – as he is, – for I reckon he'll ha' cost me that precious price, – our lile Jack, who wakened me each morn wi' putting his sweet little lips to my great rough fou' face, a-seeking a smooth place to kiss, – an' he lies clemming.' Here the deep sobs choked the poor man, and Nicholas looked up, with eyes brimful of tears, to Margaret, before he could gain courage to speak.

'Hou'd up, man. Thy lile Jack shall na' clem. I ha' getten brass, and we'll go buy the chap a sup o' milk an' a good four-pounder this very minute. What's mine's thine, sure enough, i' thou'st i' want. Only, dunnot lose heart, man!' continued he, as he fumbled in a tea-pot for what money he had. 'I lay yo' my heart and soul we'll win for a' this: it's but bearing on one more week, and yo' just see th' way th' masters 'll come round, praying on us to come back to our mills. An' th' Union – that's to say, I – will take care yo've enough for th' childer and th' missus. So dunnot turn faint-heart, and go to th' tyrants a-seeking work.'

The man turned round at these words, turned round a face so white, and gaunt, and tear-furrowed, and hopeless, that its very calm forced Margaret to weep.

'Yo' know well, that a worser tyrant than e'er th' masters were says. "Clem to death, and see 'em a' clem to death, ere yo' dare go again th' Union." Yo' know it well, Nicholas, for a' yo're one on 'em. Yo' may be kind hearts, each separate; but once banded together, yo've no more pity for a man than a wild hunger-maddened wolf.'

Nicholas had his hand on the lock of the door – he stopped and turned round on Boucher, close following:

'So help me God! man alive – if I think not I'm doing best for thee, and for all on us. If I'm going wrong when I think I'm going right, it's their sin, who ha' left me where I am, in my ignorance. I ha' thought till my brains ached. – Beli' me, John, I have. An' I say again, there's no help for us but having faith i' th' Union. They'll win the day, see if they dunnot!'

Not one word had Margaret or Bessy spoken. They had hardly uttered the sighing, that the eyes of each called to the other to bring up from the depths of her heart. At last Bessy said,

'I never thought to hear father call on God again. But yo' heard him say, "So help me God!"'

'Yes!' said Margaret. 'Let me bring you what money I can spare, – let me bring you a little food for that poor man's children. Don't let them know it comes from any one but your father. It will be but little.'

Bessy lay back without taking any notice of what Margaret said. She did not cry – she only quivered up her breath.

'My heart's drained dry o' tears,' she said. 'Boucher's been in these days past, a telling me of his fears and his troubles. He's but a weak kind o' chap, I know, but he's a man for a' that; and tho' I've been angry, many a time afore now, wi' him an' his wife, as knew no more nor him how to manage, yet, yo' see, all folks isn't wise, yet God lets 'em live – ay, an' gives 'em some one to love, and be loved by, just as good as Solomon.[6] An', if sorrow comes to them they love, it hurts 'em as sore as e'er it did Solomon. I can't make it out. Perhaps it's as well such a one as Boucher has th' Union to see after him. But I'd just like for to see th' men as make th' Union, and put 'em one by one face to face wi' Boucher. I reckon, if they heard him, they'd tell him (if I cotched 'em one by one), he might go back and get what he could for his work, even if it weren't so much as they ordered.'

Margaret sat utterly silent. How was she ever to go away into comfort and forget that man's voice, with the tone of unutterable agony, telling more by far than his words of what he had to suffer? She took out her purse; she had not much in it of what she could call her own, but what she had she put into Bessy's hand without speaking.

'Thank yo'. There's many on 'em gets no more, and is not so bad off, – leastways does not show it as he does. But father won't let 'em want, now he knows. Yo' see, Boucher's been pulled down wi' his childer, – and her being so cranky, and a' they could pawn has gone this last twelvemonth. Yo're not to think we'd ha' letten 'em clem, for all we're a bit pressed oursel'; if neighbours doesn't see after neighbours, I dunno who will.' Bessy seemed almost afraid lest Margaret should think they had not the will, and, to a certain degree, the power of helping one whom she evidently regarded as having a claim upon them. 'Besides,' she went on, 'father is sure and positive the masters must give in within these next few days, – that they canna hould on much longer. But I thank yo' all the same, – I thank yo' for mysel', as much as for Boucher, for it just makes my heart warm to yo' more and more.'

Bessy seemed much quieter today, but fearfully languid and exhausted. As she finished speaking, she looked so faint and weary that Margaret became alarmed.

'It's nout,' said Bessy. 'It's not death yet. I had a fearfu' night wi' dreams – or somewhat like dreams, for I were wide awake – and I'm all in a swounding daze today, – only yon poor chap made me alive again. No! it's not death yet, but death is not far off. Ay! Cover me

155

up, and I'll may be sleep, if th' cough will let me. Good night – good afternoon, m'appen I should say – but th' light is dim an' misty today.'

CHAPTER XX

Men and Gentlemen

Old and young, boy, let 'em all eat, I have it;[1]
Let 'em have ten tire of teeth a-piece, I care not.
ROLLO, DUKE OF NORMANDY

Margaret went home so painfully occupied with what she had heard and seen that she hardly knew how to rouse herself up to the duties which awaited her; the necessity for keeping up a constant flow of cheerful conversation for her mother, who, now that she was unable to go out, always looked to Margaret's return from the shortest walk as bringing in some news.

'And can your factory friend come on Thursday to see you dressed?'

'She was so ill I never thought of asking her,' said Margaret, dolefully.

'Dear! Everybody is ill now, I think,' said Mrs Hale, with a little of the jealousy which one invalid is apt to feel of another. 'But it must be very sad to be ill in one of those little back streets.' (Her kindly nature prevailing, and the old Helstone habits of thought returning.) 'It's bad enough here. What could you do for her, Margaret? Mr Thornton has sent me some of his old port wine since you went out. Would a bottle of that do her good, think you?'

'No, mamma! I don't believe they are very poor, – at least, they don't speak as if they were; and, at any rate, Bessy's illness is consumption – she won't want wine. Perhaps, I might take her a little preserve, made of our dear Helstone fruit. No! there's another family to whom I should like to give – Oh mamma, mamma! how am I to dress up in my finery, and go off and away to smart parties, after the sorrow I have seen today?' exclaimed Margaret, bursting the bounds she had preordained for herself before she came in, and telling her mother of what she had seen and heard at Higgins's cottage.

It distressed Mrs Hale excessively. It made her restlessly irritated till she could do something. She directed Margaret to pack up a basket in the very drawing-room, to be sent there and then to the family; and was almost angry with her for saying, that it would not signify if it did not go till morning, as she knew Higgins had provided for their immediate wants, and she herself had left money with Bessy. Mrs Hale called her unfeeling for saying this; and never gave herself breathing-time till the basket was sent out of the house. Then she said:

'After all, we may have been doing wrong. It was only the last time Mr Thornton was here that he said, those were no true friends who helped to prolong the struggle by assisting the turn-outs. And this Boucher man was a turn-out,[2] was he not?'

The question was referred to Mr Hale by his wife, when he came up-stairs, fresh from giving a lesson to Mr Thornton, which had ended in conversation, as was their wont. Margaret did not care if their gifts had prolonged the strike; she did not think far enough for that, in her present excited state.

Mr Hale listened, and tried to be as calm as a judge; he recalled all that had seemed so clear not half-an-hour before, as it came out of Mr Thornton's lips; and then he made an unsatisfactory compromise. His wife and daughter had not only done quite right in this instance, but he did not see for a moment how they could have done otherwise. Nevertheless, as a general rule, it was very true what Mr Thornton said, that as the strike, if prolonged, must end in the masters' bringing hands from a distance (if, indeed, the final result were not, as it had often been before, the invention of some machine which would diminish the need of hands at all), why, it was clear enough that the kindest thing was to refuse all help which might bolster them up in their folly. But, as to this Boucher, he would go and see him the first thing in the morning, and try and find out what could be done for him.

Mr Hale went the next morning, as he proposed. He did not find Boucher at home, but he had a long talk with his wife; promised to ask for an Infirmary order[3] for her; and, seeing the plenty provided by Mrs Hale, and somewhat lavishly used by the children, who were masters down-stairs in their father's absence, he came back with a more consoling and cheerful account than Margaret had dared to hope for; indeed, what she had said the night before had prepared her father for so much worse a state of things that, by a re-action of his imagination, he described all as better than it really was.

'But I will go again, and see the man himself,' said Mr Hale. 'I hardly know as yet how to compare one of these houses with our Helstone cottages. I see furniture here which our labourers would never have thought of buying, and food commonly used which they would consider luxuries; yet for these very families there seems no other resource, now that their weekly wages are stopped, but the pawn-shop. One had need to learn a different language, and measure by a different standard, up here in Milton.'

Bessy, too, was rather better this day. Still she was so weak that she seemed to have entirely forgotten her wish to see Margaret dressed – if, indeed, that had not been the feverish desire of a half-delirious state.

Margaret could not help comparing this strange dressing of hers, to go where she did not care to be – her heart heavy with various anxieties – with the old, merry, girlish toilettes that she and Edith had performed scarcely more than a year ago. Her only pleasure now in decking herself out was in thinking that her mother would take delight in seeing her dressed. She blushed when Dixon, throwing the drawing-room door open, made an appeal for admiration.

'Miss Hale looks well, ma'am, – doesn't she? Mrs Shaw's coral couldn't have come in better. It just gives the right touch of colour, ma'am. Otherwise, Miss Margaret, you would have been too pale.'

Margaret's black hair was too thick to be plaited; it needed rather to be twisted round and round, and have its fine silkiness compressed into massive coils, that encircled her head like a crown, and then were gathered into a large spiral knot behind. She kept its weight together by two large coral pins, like small arrows for length. Her white silk sleeves were looped up with strings of the same material, and on her neck, just below the base of her curved and milk-white throat, there lay heavy coral beads.

'Oh, Margaret! how I should like to be going with you to one of the old Barrington assemblies, – taking you as Lady Beresford used to take me.'

Margaret kissed her mother for this little burst of maternal vanity; but she could hardly smile at it, she felt so much out of spirits.

'I would rather stay at home with you, – much rather, mamma.'

'Nonsense, darling! Be sure you notice the dinner well. I shall like to hear how they manage these things in Milton. Particularly the second course, dear. Look what they have instead of game.'

Mrs Hale would have been more than interested, – she would

have been astonished, if she had seen the sumptuousness of the dinner-table and its appointments. Margaret, with her London culti-vated taste, felt the number of delicacies to be oppressive; one half of the quantity would have been enough, and the effect lighter and more elegant. But it was one of Mrs Thornton's rigorous laws of hospitality, that of each separate dainty enough should be provided for all the guests to partake, if they felt inclined. Careless to abstemi-ousness in her daily habits, it was part of her pride to set a feast before such of her guests as cared for it. Her son shared this feeling. He had never known – though he might have imagined, and had the capability to relish – any kind of society but that which depended on an exchange of superb meals: and even now, though he was denying himself the personal expenditure of an unnecessary sixpence, and had more than once regretted that the invitations for this dinner had been sent out, still, as it was to be, he was glad to see the old magnificence of preparation.

Margaret and her father were the first to arrive. Mr Hale was anxiously punctual to the time specified. There was no one up-stairs in the drawing-room but Mrs Thornton and Fanny. Every cover was taken off, and the apartment blazed forth in yellow silk damask and a brilliantly-flowered carpet. Every corner seemed filled up with ornament, until it became a weariness to the eye,[4] and presented a strange contrast to the bald ugliness of the look-out into the great mill-yard, where wide folding gates were thrown open for the admis-sion of carriages. The mill loomed high on the left-hand side of the windows, casting a shadow down from its many stories, which darkened the summer evening before its time.

'My son was engaged up to the last moment on business. He will be here directly, Mr Hale. May I beg you to take a seat?'

Mr Hale was standing at one of the windows as Mrs Thornton spoke. He turned away, saying,

'Don't you find such close neighbourhood to the mill rather unpleasant at times?'

She drew herself up:

'Never. I am not become so fine as to desire to forget the source of my son's wealth and power. Besides, there is not such another factory in Milton. One room alone is two hundred and twenty square yards.'

'I meant that the smoke and the noise – the constant going out and coming in of the work-people, might be annoying!'

'I agree with you, Mr Hale!' said Fanny. 'There is a continual smell of steam, and oily machinery – and the noise is perfectly deafening.'

'I have heard noise that was called music far more deafening. The engine-room is at the street-end of the factory; we hardly hear it, except in summer weather, when all the windows are open; and as for the continual murmur of the work-people, it disturbs me no more than the humming of a hive of bees. If I think of it at all, I connect it with my son, and feel how all belongs to him, and that his is the head that directs it. Just now, there are no sounds to come from the mill; the hands have been ungrateful enough to turn out, as perhaps you have heard. But the very business (of which I spoke, when you entered), had reference to the steps he is going to take to make them learn their place.' The expression on her face, always stern, deepened into dark anger, as she said this. Nor did it clear away when Mr Thornton entered the room; for she saw, in an instant, the weight of care and anxiety which he could not shake off, although his guests received from him a greeting that appeared both cheerful and cordial. He shook hands with Margaret. He knew it was the first time their hands had met, though she was perfectly unconscious of the fact. He inquired after Mrs Hale, and heard Mr Hale's sanguine, hopeful account; and glancing at Margaret, to understand how far she agreed with her father, he saw that no dissenting shadow crossed her face. And as he looked with this intention, he was struck anew with her great beauty. He had never seen her in such dress before; and yet now it appeared as if such elegance of attire was so befitting her noble figure and lofty serenity of countenance, that she ought to go always thus apparelled. She was talking to Fanny; about what, he could not hear; but he saw his sister's restless way of continually arranging some part of her gown, her wandering eyes, now glancing here, now there, but without any purpose in her observation; and he contrasted them uneasily with the large soft eyes that looked forth steadily at one object, as if from out their light beamed some gentle influence of repose: the curving lines of the red lips, just parted in the interest of listening to what her companion said – the head a little bent forwards, so as to make a long sweeping line from the summit, where the light caught on the glossy raven hair, to the smooth ivory tip of the shoulder; the round white arms, and taper hands, laid lightly across each other, but perfectly motionless in their pretty attitude. Mr Thornton sighed as he took in all this with one of his sudden comprehensive glances. And then he turned his back to the young ladies, and threw himself, with an effort, but with all his heart and soul, into a conversation with Mr Hale.

More people came – more and more. Fanny left Margaret's side, and helped her mother to receive her guests. Mr Thornton felt that in this influx no one was speaking to Margaret, and was restless under this apparent neglect. But he never went near her himself; he did not look at her. Only, he knew what she was doing – or not doing – better than he knew the movements of any one else in the room. Margaret was so unconscious of herself, and so much amused by watching other people, that she never thought whether she was left unnoticed or not. Somebody took her down to dinner; she did not catch the name; nor did he seem much inclined to talk to her. There was a very animated conversation going on among the gentlemen; the ladies, for the most part, were silent, employing themselves in taking notes of the dinner and criticizing each other's dresses. Margaret caught the clue to the general conversation, grew interested and listened attentively. Mr Horsfall, the stranger, whose visit to the town was the original germ of the party, was asking questions relative to the trade and manufactures of the place; and the rest of the gentlemen – all Milton men, – were giving him answers and explanations. Some dispute arose, which was warmly contested; it was referred to Mr Thornton, who had hardly spoken before; but who now gave an opinion, the grounds of which were so clearly stated that even the opponents yielded. Margaret's attention was thus called to her host; his whole manner, as master of the house, and entertainer of his friends, was so straightforward, yet simple and modest, as to be thoroughly dignified. Margaret thought she had never seen him to so much advantage. When he had come to their house, there had been always something, either of over-eagerness or of that kind of vexed annoyance which seemed ready to pre-suppose that he was unjustly judged, and yet felt too proud to try and make himself better understood. But now, among his fellows, there was no uncertainty as to his position. He was regarded by them as a man of great force of character; of power in many ways. There was no need to struggle for their respect. He had it, and he knew it; and the security of this gave a fine grand quietness to his voice and ways, which Margaret had missed before.

He was not in the habit of talking to ladies; and what he did say was a little formal. To Margaret herself he hardly spoke at all. She was surprised to think how much she enjoyed this dinner. She knew enough now to understand many local interests – nay, even some of the technical words employed by the eager millowners. She silently took a very decided part in the question they were discussing. At any rate they talked in desperate earnest, – not in the used-up style that wearied her so in the old London parties. She wondered that with all this dwelling on the manufactures and trade of the place, no allusion was made to the strike then pending. She did not yet know how coolly such things were taken by the masters, as having only one possible end. To be sure, the men were cutting their own throats, as they had done many a time before; but if they would be fools, and put themselves into the hands of a rascally set of paid delegates,[5] they must take the consequence. One or two thought Thornton looked out of spirits; and, of course, he must lose by this turn-out. But it was an accident that might happen to themselves any day; and Thornton was as good to manage a strike as any one; for he was as iron a chap as any in Milton. The hands had mistaken their man in trying that dodge on him. And they chuckled inwardly at the idea of the workmen's discomfiture and defeat, in their attempt to alter one iota of what Thornton had decreed.

It was rather dull for Margaret after dinner. She was glad when the gentlemen came, not merely because she caught her father's eye to brighten her sleepiness up; but because she could listen to something larger and grander than the petty interests which the ladies had been talking about. She liked the exultation in the sense of power which these Milton men had. It might be rather rampant in its display, and savour of boasting; but still they seemed to defy the old limits of possibility, in a kind of fine intoxication, caused by the recollection of what had been achieved, and what yet should be. If in her cooler moments she might not approve of their spirit in all things, still there was much to admire in their forgetfulness of themselves and the present, in their anticipated triumphs over all inanimate matter at some future time which none of them should live to see. She was rather startled when Mr Thornton spoke to her, close at her elbow:

'I could see you were on our side in our discussion at dinner, – were you not, Miss Hale?'

'Certainly. But then I know so little about it. I was surprised, however, to find from what Mr Horsfall said, that there were others who thought in so diametrically opposite a manner, as the Mr Morison he spoke about. He cannot be a gentleman – is he?'

'I am not quite the person to decide on another's gentlemanliness,[6] Miss Hale. I mean, I don't quite understand your application of the word. But I should say that this Morison is no true man. I don't know who he is; I merely judge him from Mr Horsfall's account.'

'I suspect my "gentleman" includes your "true man."'

'And a great deal more, you would imply. I differ from you. A man is to me a higher and a completer being than a gentleman.'

'What do you mean?' asked Margaret. 'We must understand the words differently.'

'I take it that "gentleman" is a term that only describes a person in his relation to others; but when we speak of him as "a man," we consider him not merely with regard to his fellow-men, but in relation to himself, – to life – to time – to eternity. A cast-away lonely as Robinson Crusoe[7] – a prisoner immured in a dungeon for life – nay, even a saint in Patmos,[8] has his endurance, his strength, his faith, best described by being spoken of as "a man." I am rather weary of this word "gentlemanly," which seems to me to be often inappropriately used, and often, too, with such exaggerated distortion of meaning, while the full simplicity of the noun "man," and the adjective "manly" are unacknowledged – that I am induced to class it with the cant of the day.'

Margaret thought a moment, – but before she could speak her slow conviction, he was called away by some of the eager manufacturers, whose speeches she could not hear, though she could guess at their import by the short clear answers Mr Thornton gave, which came steady and firm as the boom of a distant minute gun. They were evidently talking of the turn-out, and suggesting what course had best be pursued. She heard Mr Thornton say:

'That has been done.' Then came a hurried murmur, in which two or three joined.

'All those arrangements have been made.'

Some doubts were implied, some difficulties named by Mr Slickson, who took hold of Mr Thornton's arm, the better to impress his words. Mr Thornton moved slightly away, lifted his eyebrows a very little, and then replied:

'I take the risk. You need not join in it unless you choose.' Still some more fears were urged.

'I'm not afraid of anything so dastardly as incendiarism. We are open enemies; and I can protect myself from any violence that I apprehend. And I will assuredly protect all others who come to me for work. They know my determination by this time, as well and as fully as you do.'

Mr Horsfall took him a little on one side, as Margaret conjectured, to ask him some other question about the strike; but, in truth, it was to inquire who she herself was – so quiet, so stately, and so beautiful.

'A Milton lady?' asked he, as the name was given.

'No! from the south of England – Hampshire, I believe,' was the cold, indifferent answer.

Mrs Slickson was catechizing Fanny on the same subject.

'Who is that fine distinguished-looking girl? A sister of Mr Horsfall's?'

'Oh dear, no! That is Mr Hale, her father, talking now to Mr Stephens. He gives lessons; that is to say, he reads with young men. My brother John goes to him twice a week, and so he begged mamma to ask them here, in hopes of getting him known. I believe, we have some of their prospectuses, if you would like to have one.'

'Mr Thornton! Does he really find time to read with a tutor, in the midst of all his business, – and this abominable strike in hand as well?'

Fanny was not sure, from Mrs Slickson's manner, whether she ought to be proud or ashamed of her brother's conduct; and, like all people who try and take other people's 'ought' for the rule of their feelings, she was inclined to blush for any singularity of action. Her shame was interrupted by the dispersion of the guests.

CHAPTER XXI

The Dark Night

On earth is known to none[1]
The smile that is not sister to a tear.

ELLIOTT

Margaret and her father walked home. The night was fine, the streets clean, and with her pretty white silk, like Leezie Lindsay's gown[2] o' green satin, in the ballad, 'kilted up to her knee,' she was off with her father – ready to dance along with the excitement of the cool, fresh night air.

'I rather think Thornton is not quite easy in his mind about this strike. He seemed very anxious tonight.'

'I should wonder if he were not. But he spoke with his usual coolness to the others, when they suggested different things, just before we came away.'

'So he did after dinner as well. It would take a good deal to stir him from his cool manner of speaking; but his face strikes me as anxious.'

'I should be, if I were he. He must know of the growing anger and hardly smothered hatred of his workpeople, who all look upon him as what the Bible calls a "hard man," – not so much unjust as unfeeling; clear in judgment, standing upon his "rights" as no human being ought to stand, considering what we and all our petty rights are in the sight of the Almighty. I am glad you think he looks anxious. When I remember Boucher's half mad words and ways, I cannot bear to think how coolly Mr Thornton spoke.'

'In the first place, I am not so convinced as you are about that man Boucher's utter distress; for the moment, he was badly off, I don't doubt. But there is always a mysterious supply of money from these Unions; and, from what you said, it was evident the man was of a passionate, demonstrative nature, and gave strong expression to all he felt.'

'Oh, papa!'

'Well! I only want you to do justice to Mr Thornton, who is, I suspect, of an exactly opposite nature, – a man who is far too proud to show his feelings. Just the character I should have thought beforehand, you would have admired, Margaret.'

'So I do, – so I should; but I don't feel quite so sure as you do of the existence of those feelings. He is a man of great strength of character, – of unusual intellect, considering the few advantages he has had.'

'Not so few. He has led a practical life from a very early age; has been called upon to exercise judgment and self-control. All that develops one part of the intellect. To be sure, he needs some of the knowledge of the past, which gives the truest basis for conjecture as to the future; but he knows this need, – he perceives it, and that is something. You are quite prejudiced against Mr Thornton, Margaret.'

'He is the first specimen of a manufacturer – of a person engaged in trade – that I had ever the opportunity of studying, papa. He is my first olive:[3] let me make a face while I swallow it. I know he is good of his kind, and by and by I shall like the kind. I rather think I am already beginning to do so. I was very much interested by what the gentlemen were talking about, although I did not understand half of it. I was quite sorry when Miss Thornton came to take me to the other end of the room, saying she was sure I should be uncomfortable at being the only lady among so many gentlemen. I had never thought about it, I was so busy listening; and the ladies were so dull, papa – oh, so dull! Yet I think it was clever too. It reminded me of our old game of having each so many nouns to introduce into a sentence.'

'What do you mean, child?' asked Mr Hale.

'Why, they took nouns that were signs of things which gave evidence of wealth, – housekeepers, under-gardeners, extent of glass, valuable lace, diamonds, and all such things; and each one formed her speech so as to bring them all in, in the prettiest accidental manner possible.'

'You will be as proud of your one servant when you get her, if all is true about her that Mrs Thornton says.'

'To be sure, I shall. I felt like a great hypocrite tonight, sitting there in my white silk gown, with my idle hands before me, when I remembered all the good, thorough, house-work they had done today. They took me for a fine lady, I'm sure.'

'Even I was mistaken enough to think you looked like a lady, my dear,' said Mr Hale, quietly smiling.

But smiles were changed to white and trembling looks, when they saw Dixon's face, as she opened the door.

'Oh, master! – Oh, Miss Margaret! Thank God you are come! Dr Donaldson is here. The servant next door went for him, for the charwoman is gone home. She's better now; but, oh, sir! I thought she'd have died an hour ago.'

Mr Hale caught Margaret's arm to steady himself from falling. He looked at her face, and saw an expression upon it of surprise and extremest sorrow, but not the agony of terror that contracted his own unprepared heart. She knew more than he did, and yet she listened with that hopeless expression of awed apprehension.

'Oh! I should not have left her – wicked daughter that I am!' moaned forth Margaret, as she supported her trembling father's hasty steps upstairs. Dr Donaldson met them on the landing.

'She is better now,' he whispered. 'The opiate has taken effect. The spasms were very bad: no wonder they frightened your maid; but she'll rally this time.'

'This time! Let me go to her!' Half an hour ago, Mr Hale was a middle-aged man; now his sight was dim, his senses wavering, his walk tottering, as if he were seventy years of age.

Dr Donaldson took his arm, and led him into the bed-room. Margaret followed close. There lay her mother, with an unmistake-able look on her face. She might be better now; she was sleeping, but Death had signed her for his own, and it was clear that ere long he would return to take possession. Mr Hale looked at her for some time without a word. Then he began to shake all over, and, turning away from Dr Donaldson's anxious care, he groped to find the door; he could not see it, although several candles, brought in the sudden affright, were burning and flaring there. He staggered into the drawing-room, and felt about for a chair. Dr Donaldson wheeled one to him, and placed him in it. He felt his pulse.

'Speak to him, Miss Hale. We must rouse him.'

'Papa!' said Margaret, with a crying voice that was wild with pain. 'Papa! Speak to me!' The speculation came again into his eyes, and he made a great effort.

'Margaret, did you know of this? Oh, it was cruel of you!'

'No, sir, it was not cruel!' replied Dr Donaldson, with quick decision. 'Miss Hale acted under my directions. There may have been a mistake, but it was not cruel. Your wife will be a different creature tomorrow, I trust. She has had spasms, as I anticipated, though I did not tell Miss Hale of my apprehensions. She has taken the opiate I brought with me; she will have a good long sleep; and tomorrow, that look which has alarmed you so much will have passed away.'

'But not the disease?'

Dr Donaldson glanced at Margaret. Her bent head, her face raised with no appeal for a temporary reprieve, showed that quick observer of human nature that she thought it better that the whole truth should be told.

'Not the disease. We cannot touch the disease, with all our poor vaunted skill. We can only delay its progress – alleviate the pain it causes. Be a man, sir – a Christian. Have faith in the immortality of the soul, which no pain, no mortal disease, can assail or touch!'

But all the reply he got, was in the choked words, 'You have never been married, Dr Donaldson; you do not know what it is,' and in the deep, manly sobs, which went through the stillness of the night like heavy pulses of agony.

Margaret knelt by him, caressing him with tearful caresses. No one, not even Dr Donaldson, knew how the time went by. Mr Hale was the first to dare to speak of the necessities of the present moment.

'What must we do?' asked he. 'Tell us both. Margaret is my staff – my right hand.'

Dr Donaldson gave his clear, sensible directions. No fear for to-night – nay, even peace for tomorrow, and for many days yet. But no enduring hope of recovery. He advised Mr Hale to go to bed, and leave only one to watch the slumber, which he hoped would be undisturbed. He promised to come again early in the morning. And with a warm and kindly shake of the hand, he left them.

They spoke but few words; they were too much exhausted by their terror to do more than decide upon the immediate course of action. Mr Hale was resolved to sit up through the night, and all that Margaret could do was to prevail upon him to rest on the drawing-room sofa. Dixon stoutly and bluntly refused to go to bed; and, as for Margaret, it was simply impossible that she should leave her mother, let all the doctors in the world speak of 'husbanding resources,' and 'one watcher only being required.' So, Dixon sat, and stared, and winked, and drooped, and picked herself up again with a jerk, and finally gave up the battle, and fairly snored. Margaret had taken off her gown and tossed it aside with a sort of impatient disgust, and put on her dressing-gown. She felt as if she never could sleep again; as if her whole senses were acutely vital, and all endued with double keenness, for the purposes of watching. Every sight and sound – nay, even every thought, touched some nerve to the very quick. For more than two hours, she heard her father's restless movements in the next room. He came perpetually to the door of her mother's chamber, pausing there to listen, till she, not hearing his close unseen presence, went and opened it to tell him how all went on, in reply to the questions his baked lips could hardly form. At last, he, too, fell asleep, and all the house was still. Margaret sate behind the curtain thinking. Far away in time, far away in space, seemed all the interests of past days. Not more than thirty-six hours ago, she cared for Bessy Higgins and her father, and her heart was wrung for Boucher; now, that was all like a dreaming memory of some former life; – everything that had passed out of doors seemed dissevered from her mother, and therefore unreal. Even Harley Street appeared more distinct; there she remembered, as if it were yesterday, how she had pleased herself with tracing out her mother's features in her

Aunt Shaw's face, – and how letters had come, making her dwell on the thoughts of home with all the longing of love. Helstone, itself, was in the dim past. The dull gray days of the preceding winter and spring, so uneventless and monotonous, seemed more associated with what she cared for now above all price. She would fain have caught at the skirts of that departing time, and prayed it to return, and give her back what she had too little valued while it was yet in her possession. What a vain show Life seemed! How unsubstantial, and flickering, and flitting! It was as if from some aerial belfry, high up above the stir and jar of the earth, there was a bell continually tolling, 'All are shadows! – all are passing! – all is past!' And when the morning dawned, cool and gray, like many a happier morning before – when Margaret looked one by one at the sleepers, it seemed as if the terrible night were unreal as a dream; it, too, was a shadow. It, too, was past.

Mrs Hale herself was not aware when she awoke, how ill she had been the night before. She was rather surprised at Dr Donaldson's early visit, and perplexed by the anxious faces of husband and child. She consented to remain in bed that day, saying she certainly was tired; but, the next, she insisted on getting up; and Dr Donaldson gave his consent to her returning into the drawing-room. She was restless and uncomfortable in every position, and before night she became very feverish. Mr Hale was utterly listless, and incapable of deciding on anything.

'What can we do to spare mamma such another night?' asked Margaret on the third day.

'It is, to a certain degree, the reaction after the powerful opiates I have been obliged to use. It is more painful for you to see than for her to bear, I believe. But, I think, if we could get a water-bed it might be a good thing. Not but what she will be better tomorrow; pretty much like herself as she was before this attack. Still, I should like her to have a water-bed.[4] Mrs Thornton has one, I know. I'll try and call there this afternoon. Stay,' said he, his eye catching on Margaret's face, blanched with watching in a sick room, 'I'm not sure whether I can go; I've a long round to take. It would do you no harm to have a brisk walk to Marlborough Street, and ask Mrs Thornton if she can spare it.'

'Certainly,' said Margaret. 'I could go while mamma is asleep this afternoon. I'm sure Mrs Thornton would lend it to us.'

Dr Donaldson's experience told them rightly. Mrs Hale seemed to shake off the consequences of her attack, and looked brighter and better this afternoon than Margaret had ever hoped to see her again. Her daughter left her after dinner, sitting in her easy chair, with her hand lying in her husband's, who looked more worn and suffering than she by far. Still he could smile now – rather slowly, rather faintly, it is true; but a day or two before, Margaret never thought to see him smile again.

It was about two miles from their house in Crampton Crescent to Marlborough Street. It was too hot to walk very quickly. An August sun beat straight down into the street at three o'clock in the afternoon. Margaret went along, without noticing anything very different from usual in the first mile and a half of her journey; she was absorbed in her own thoughts, and had learnt by this time to thread her way through the irregular stream of human beings that flowed through Milton streets. But, by and by, she was struck with an unusual heaving among the mass of people in the crowded road on which she was entering. They did not appear to be moving on, so much as talking, and listening, and buzzing with excitement, without much stirring from the spot where they might happen to be. Still, as they made way for her, and, wrapt up in the purpose of her errand, and the necessities that suggested it, she was less quick of observation than she might have been, if her mind had been at ease; she had got into Marlborough Street before the full conviction forced itself upon her, that there was a restless, oppressive sense of irritation abroad among the people; a thunderous atmosphere, morally as well as physically, around her. From every narrow lane opening out on Marlborough Street came up a low distant roar, as of myriads of fierce indignant voices. The inhabitants of each poor squalid dwelling were gathered round the doors and windows, if indeed they were not actually standing in the middle of the narrow ways – all with looks intent towards one point. Marlborough Street itself was the focus of all those human eyes, that betrayed intensest interest of various kinds; some fierce with anger, some lowering with relentless threats, some dilated with fear, or imploring entreaty; and, as Margaret reached the small side entrance by the folding doors in the great dead wall of Marlborough mill-yard, and waited the porter's answer to the bell, she looked round and heard the first long far-off roll of the tempest; – saw the first slow-surging wave of the dark crowd come, with its threatening crest, tumble over, and retreat, at the far end of the street, which a moment ago, seemed so full of repressed noise, but which now was ominously still; all these circumstances forced themselves on Margaret's notice, but did not sink down into her pre-occupied heart. She did not know what they meant – what was their deep significance; while she did know, did feel the keen sharp pressure of the knife that was soon to stab her through and through by leaving her motherless. She was trying to realize that, in order that, when it came, she might be ready to comfort her father.

The porter opened the door cautiously, not nearly wide enough to admit her.

'It's you, is it, ma'am?' said he, drawing a long breath, and widening the entrance, but still not opening it fully. Margaret went in. He hastily bolted it behind her.

'Th' folk are all coming up here I reckon?' asked he.

'I don't know. Something unusual seemed going on; but this street is quite empty, I think.'

She went across the yard and up the steps to the house door. There was no near sound, – no steam-engine at work with beat and pant, – no click of machinery, or mingling and clashing of many sharp voices; but far away, the ominous gathering roar, deep-clamouring.

<h2 style="text-align:center">CHAPTER XXII</h2>

<h1 style="text-align:center">A Blow and Its Consequences</h1>

But work grew scarce, while bread grew dear,[1]
And wages lessened, too;
For Irish hordes were bidders here,
Our half-paid work to do.

CORN LAW RHYMES

Margaret was shown into the drawing-room. It had returned into its normal state of bag and covering. The windows were half open because of the heat, and the Venetian blinds covered the glass, – so that a gray grim light, reflected from the pavement below, threw all the shadows wrong, and combined with the green-tinged upper light to make even Margaret's own face, as she caught it in the mirrors, look ghastly and wan. She sat and waited; no one came. Every now and then, the wind seemed to bear the distant multitudinous sound nearer; and yet there was no wind! It died away into profound stillness between whiles.

Fanny came in at last.

'Mamma will come directly, Miss Hale. She desired me to apologize to you as it is. Perhaps you know my brother has imported hands from Ireland,[2] and it has irritated the Milton people excessively – as if he hadn't a right to get labour where he could; and the stupid wretches here wouldn't work for him; and now they've frightened these poor Irish starvelings so with their threats, that we daren't let them out. You may see them huddled in that top room in the mill, – and they're to sleep there, to keep them safe from those brutes, who will neither work nor let them work. And mamma is seeing about their food, and John is speaking to them, for some of the women are crying to go back. Ah! here's mamma!'

Mrs Thornton came in with a look of black sternness on her face, which made Margaret feel she had arrived at a bad time to trouble her with her request. However, it was only in compliance with Mrs Thornton's expressed desire, that she would ask for whatever they might want in the progress of her mother's illness. Mrs Thornton's brow contracted, and her mouth grew set, while Margaret spoke with gentle modesty of her mother's restlessness, and Dr Donaldson's wish that she should have the relief of a water-bed. She ceased. Mrs Thornton did not reply immediately. Then she started up and exclaimed –

'They're at the gates! Call John, Fanny, – call him in from the mill! They're at the gates! They'll batter them in! Call John, I say!'

And simultaneously, the gathering tramp – to which she had been listening, instead of heeding Margaret's words – was heard just right outside the wall, and an increasing din of angry voices raged behind the wooden barrier, which shook as if the unseen maddened crowd made battering-rams of their bodies, and retreated a short space only to come with more united steady impetus against it, till their great beats made the strong gates quiver, like reeds before the wind.

The women gathered round the windows, fascinated to look on the scene which terrified them. Mrs Thornton, the women-servants, Margaret, – all were there. Fanny had returned, screaming upstairs as if pursued at every step, and had thrown herself in hysterical sobbing on the sofa. Mrs Thornton watched for her son, who was still in the mill. He came out, looked up at them – the pale cluster of faces – and smiled good courage to them, before he locked the factory-door. Then he called to one of the women to come down and undo his own door, which Fanny had fastened behind her in her mad flight. Mrs Thornton herself went. And the sound of his well-known and commanding voice, seemed to have been like the taste of blood to the infuriated multitude outside. Hitherto they had been voiceless, wordless, needing all their breath for their hard-labouring efforts to break down the gates. But now, hearing him speak inside, they set up such a fierce unearthly groan, that even Mrs Thornton was white with fear as she preceded him into the room. He came in a little flushed, but his eyes gleaming, as in answer to the trumpet call of danger, and with a proud look of defiance on his face, that made him a noble, if not a handsome man. Margaret had always dreaded lest her courage should fail her in any emergency, and she should be proved to be, what she dreaded lest she was – a coward. But now, in this real great time of reasonable fear and nearness of terror, she forgot herself, and felt only an intense sympathy – intense to painfulness – in the interests of the moment.

Mr Thornton came frankly forwards:

'I'm sorry, Miss Hale, you have visited us at this unfortunate moment, when, I fear, you may be involved in whatever risk we have to bear. Mother! hadn't you better go into the back rooms? I'm not sure whether they may not have made their way from Pinner's Lane into the stable-yard; but if not, you will be safer there than here. Go Jane!' continued he, addressing the upper-servant. And she went, followed by the others.

'I stop here!' said his mother. 'Where you are, there I stay.' And indeed, retreat into the back rooms was of no avail; the crowd had surrounded the outbuildings at the rear, and were sending forth their awful threatening roar behind. The servants retreated into the garrets, with many a cry and shriek. Mr Thornton smiled scornfully as he heard them. He glanced at Margaret, standing all by herself at the window nearest the factory. Her eyes glittered, her colour was deepened on cheek and lip. As if she felt his look, she turned to him and asked a question that had been for some time in her mind:

'Where are the poor imported work-people? In the factory there?'

'Yes! I left them cowered up in a small room, at the head of a back flight of stairs; bidding them run all risks, and escape down there, if they heard any attack made on the mill-doors. But it is not them – it is me they want.'

'When can the soldiers be here?' asked his mother, in a low but not unsteady voice.

He took out his watch with the same measured composure with which he did everything. He made some little calculation:

'Supposing Williams got straight off when I told him, and hadn't to dodge about amongst them – it must be twenty minutes yet.'

'Twenty minutes!' said his mother, for the first time showing her terror in the tones of her voice.

'Shut down the windows instantly, mother,' exclaimed he: 'the gates won't bear such another shock. Shut down that window, Miss Hale.'

Margaret shut down her window, and then went to assist Mrs Thornton's trembling fingers.

From some cause or other, there was a pause of several minutes in the unseen street. Mrs Thornton looked with wild anxiety at her son's countenance, as if to gain the interpretation of the sudden stillness from him. His face was set into rigid lines of contemptuous defiance; neither hope nor fear could be read there.

Fanny raised herself up:

'Are they gone?' asked she, in a whisper.

'Gone!' replied he. 'Listen!'

She did listen; they all could hear the one great straining breath; the creak of wood slowly yielding; the wrench of iron; the mighty fall of the ponderous gates. Fanny stood up tottering – made a step or two towards her mother, and fell forwards into her arms in a fainting fit. Mrs Thornton lifted her up with a strength that was as much that of the will as of the body, and carried her away.

'Thank God!' said Mr Thornton, as he watched her out. 'Had you not better go upstairs, Miss Hale?'

Margaret's lips formed a 'No!' – but he could not hear her speak, for the tramp of innumerable steps right under the very wall of the house, and the fierce growl of low deep angry voices that had a ferocious murmur of satisfaction in them, more dreadful than their baffled cries not many minutes before.

'Never mind!' said he, thinking to encourage her. 'I am very sorry you should have been entrapped into all this alarm; but it cannot last long now; a few minutes more, and the soldiers will be here.'

'Oh, God!' cried Margaret, suddenly; 'there is Boucher. I know his face, though he is livid with rage, – he is fighting to get to the front – look! look!'

'Who is Boucher?' asked Mr Thornton, coolly, and coming close to the window to discover the man in whom Margaret took such an interest. As soon as they saw Mr Thornton, they set up a yell, – to call it not human is nothing, – it was as the demoniac desire of some terrible wild beast for the food that is withheld from his ravening. Even he drew back for a moment, dismayed at the intensity of hatred he had provoked.

'Let them yell!' said he. 'In five minutes more –. I only hope my poor Irishmen are not terrified out of their wits by such a fiendlike noise. Keep up your courage for five minutes, Miss Hale.'

'Don't be afraid for me,' she said hastily. 'But what in five minutes? Can you do nothing to soothe these poor creatures? It is awful to see them.'

'The soldiers will be here directly, and that will bring them to reason.'

'To reason!' said Margaret quickly. 'What kind of reason?'

'The only reason that does with men that make themselves into wild beasts. By heaven! they've turned to the mill-door!'

'Mr Thornton,' said Margaret, shaking all over with her passion, 'go down this instant, if you are not a coward. Go down and face them like a man. Save these poor strangers, whom you have decoyed here. Speak to your workmen as if they were human beings. Speak to them kindly. Don't let the soldiers come in and cut down poor creatures who are driven mad. I see one there who is. If you have any courage or noble quality in you, go out and speak to them, man to man.'

He turned and looked at her while she spoke. A dark cloud came over his face while he listened. He set his teeth as he heard her words.

'I will go. Perhaps I may ask you to accompany me downstairs, and bar the door behind me; my mother and sister will need that protection.'

'Oh! Mr Thornton! I do not know – I may be wrong – only –'

But he was gone; he was downstairs in the hall; he had unbarred the front door; all she could do, was to follow him quickly, and fasten it behind him, and clamber up the stairs again with a sick heart and a dizzy head. Again she took her place by the farthest window. He was on the steps below; she saw that by the direction of a thousand angry eyes; but she could neither see nor hear anything save the savage satisfaction of the rolling angry murmur. She threw the window wide open. Many in the crowd were mere boys; cruel and thoughtless, – cruel because they were thoughtless; some were men, gaunt as wolves, and mad for prey. She knew how it was; they were like Boucher, – with starving children at home – relying on ultimate success in their efforts to get higher wages, and enraged beyond measure at discovering that Irishmen were to be brought in to rob their little ones of bread. Margaret knew it all; she read it in Boucher's face, forlornly desperate and livid with rage. If Mr Thornton would but say something to them – let them hear his voice only – it seemed as if it would be better than this wild beating and raging against the stony silence that vouchsafed them no word, even of anger or reproach. But perhaps he was speaking now; there was a momentary hush of their noise, inarticulate as that of a troop of animals. She tore her bonnet off; and bent forwards to hear. She could only see; for if Mr Thornton had indeed made the attempt to speak, the momentary instinct to listen to him was past and gone, and the people were raging worse than ever. He stood with his arms folded; still as a statue; his face pale with repressed excitement. They were trying to intimidate him – to make him flinch; each was urging the other on to some immediate act of personal violence. Margaret felt intuitively, that in an instant all would be uproar; the first touch would cause an explosion, in which, among such hundreds of infuriated men and reckless boys, even Mr Thornton's life would be unsafe, – that in another instant the stormy passions would have passed their bounds, and swept away all barriers of reason, or apprehension of consequence. Even while she looked, she saw lads in the background stooping to take off their heavy wooden clogs – the readiest missile they could find; she saw it was the spark to the gunpowder, and, with a cry, which no one heard, she rushed out of the room, down stairs, – she had lifted the great iron bar of the door with an imperious force – had thrown the door open wide – and was there, in face of that angry sea of men,[3] her eyes smiting them with flaming arrows of reproach. The clogs were arrested in the hands that held them – the countenances, so fell not a moment before, now looked irresolute, and as if asking what this meant. For she stood between them and their enemy. She could not speak, but held out her arms towards them till she could recover breath.

'Oh, do not use violence! He is one man, and you are many;' but her words died away, for there was no tone in her voice; it was but a hoarse whisper. Mr Thornton stood a little on one side; he had moved away from behind her, as if jealous of anything that should come between him and danger.

'Go!' said she, once more (and now her voice was like a cry). 'The soldiers are sent for – are coming. Go peaceably. Go away. You shall have relief from your complaints, whatever they are.'

'Shall them Irish blackguards be packed back again?' asked one from out the crowd, with fierce threatening in his voice.

'Never, for your bidding!' exclaimed Mr Thornton. And instantly the storm broke. The hootings rose and filled the air – but Margaret did not hear them. Her eye was on the group of lads who had armed themselves with their clogs some time before. She saw their gesture – she knew its meaning, – she read their aim. Another moment, and Mr Thornton might be smitten down, – he whom she had urged and goaded to come to this perilous place. She only thought how she could save him. She threw her arms around him; she made her body into a shield from the fierce people beyond. Still, with his arms folded, he shook her off.

'Go away,' said he, in his deep voice. 'This is no place for you.'

'It is!' said she. 'You did not see what I saw.' If she thought her sex would be a protection, – if, with shrinking eyes she had turned away from the terrible anger of these men, in any hope that ere she looked again they would have paused and reflected, and slunk away, and vanished, she was wrong. Their reckless passion had carried them too far to stop – at least had carried some of them too far; for it is always the savage lads, with their love of cruel excitement, who head the riot – reckless to what bloodshed it may lead. A clog whizzed through the air. Margaret's fascinated eyes watched its progress; it missed its aim, and she turned sick with affright, but changed not her position, only hid her face on Mr Thornton's arm. Then she turned and spoke again:

'For God's sake! do not damage your cause by this violence. You do not know what you are doing.' She strove to make her words distinct.

A sharp pebble flew by her, grazing forehead and cheek, and drawing a blinding sheet of light before her eyes. She lay like one dead on Mr Thornton's shoulder. Then he unfolded his arms, and held her encircled in one for an instant:

'You do well!' said he. 'You come to oust the innocent stranger. You fall – you hundreds – on one man; and when a woman comes before you, to ask you for your own sakes to be reasonable creatures, your cowardly wrath falls upon her! You do well!' They were silent while he spoke. They were watching, open-eyed and open-mouthed, the thread of dark-red blood which wakened them up from their trance of passion. Those nearest the gate stole out ashamed; there was a movement through all the crowd – a retreating movement. Only one voice cried out:

'Th' stone were meant for thee; but thou wert sheltered behind a woman!'

Mr Thornton quivered with rage. The blood-flowing had made Margaret conscious – dimly, vaguely, conscious. He placed her gently on the door-step; her head leaning against the frame.

'Can you rest there?' he asked. But without waiting for her answer, he went slowly down the steps right into the middle of the crowd. 'Now kill me, if it is your brutal will. There is no woman to shield me here. You may beat me to death – you will never move me from what I have determined upon – not you!' He stood amongst them, with his arms folded, in precisely the same attitude as he had been in on the steps.

But the retrograde movement towards the gate had begun – as unreasoningly, perhaps as blindly, as the simultaneous anger. Or, perhaps, the idea of the approach of the soldiers, and the sight of that pale, upturned face, with closed eyes, still and sad as marble, though the tears welled out of the long entanglement of eyelashes, and dropped down; and, heavier, slower plash than even tears, came the drip of blood from her wound. Even the most desperate – Boucher himself – drew back, faltered away, scowled, and finally went off, muttering curses on the master, who stood in his unchanging attitude, looking after their retreat with defiant eyes. The moment that retreat had changed into a flight (as it was sure from its very character to do), he darted up the steps to Margaret.

She tried to rise without his help.

'It is nothing,' she said, with a sickly smile. 'The skin is grazed, and I was stunned at the moment. Oh, I am so thankful they are gone!' And she cried without restraint.

He could not sympathize with her. His anger had not abated; it was rather rising the more as his sense of immediate danger was passing away. The distant clank of the soldiers was heard; just five minutes too late to make this vanished mob feel the power of authority and order. He hoped they would see the troops, and be quelled by the thought of their narrow escape. While these thoughts crossed his mind, Margaret clung to the doorpost to steady herself: but a film came over her eyes – he was only just in time to catch her. 'Mother – mother!' cried he; 'Come down – they are gone, and Miss Hale is hurt!' He bore her into the dining-room, and laid her on the sofa there; laid her down softly, and looking on her pure white face, the sense of what she was to him came upon him so keenly that he spoke it out in his pain:

'Oh, my Margaret – my Margaret! no one can tell what you are to me! Dead – cold as you lie there, you are the only woman I ever loved! Oh, Margaret – Margaret!'

Inarticulately as he spoke, kneeling by her, and rather moaning than saying the words, he started up, ashamed of himself, as his mother came in. She saw nothing, but her son a little paler, a little sterner than usual.

'Miss Hale is hurt, mother. A stone has grazed her temple. She has lost a good deal of blood, I'm afraid.'

'She looks very seriously hurt, – I could almost fancy her dead,' said Mrs Thornton, a good deal alarmed.

'It is only a fainting-fit. She has spoken to me since.' But all the blood in his body seemed to rush inwards to his heart as he spoke, and he absolutely trembled.

'Go and call Jane, – she can find me the things I want; and do you go to your Irish people, who are crying and shouting as if they were mad with fright.'

He went. He went away as if weights were tied to every limb that bore him from her. He called Jane; he called his sister. She should have all womanly care, all gentle tendance. But every pulse beat in him as he remembered how she had come down and placed herself in foremost danger, – could it be to save him? At the time, he had pushed her aside, and spoken gruffly; he had seen nothing but the unnecessary danger she had placed herself in. He went to his Irish people, with every nerve in his body thrilling at the thought of her, and found it difficult to understand enough of what they were saying to soothe and comfort away their fears. There, they declared, they would not stop; they claimed to be sent back.

And so he had to think, and talk, and reason.

Mrs Thornton bathed Margaret's temples with eau de Cologne. As the spirit touched the wound, which till then neither Mrs Thornton nor Jane had perceived, Margaret opened her eyes; but it was evident she did not know where she was, nor who they were. The dark circles deepened, the lips quivered and contracted, and she became insensible once more.

'She has had a terrible blow,' said Mrs Thornton. 'Is there any one who will go for a doctor?'

'Not me, ma'am, if you please,' said Jane, shrinking back. 'Them rabble may be all about; I don't think the cut is so deep, ma'am, as it looks.'

'I will not run the chance. She was hurt in our house. If you are a coward, Jane, I am not. I will go.'

'Pray, ma'am, let me send one of the police. There's ever so many come up, and soldiers too.'

'And yet you're afraid to go; I will not have their time taken up with our errands. They'll have enough to do to catch some of the mob. You will not be afraid to stop in this house,' she asked contemptuously, 'and go on bathing Miss Hale's forehead, shall you? I shall not be ten minutes away.'

'Couldn't Hannah go, ma'am?'

'Why Hannah? Why any but you? No, Jane, if you don't go, I do.'

Mrs Thornton went first to the room in which she had left Fanny stretched on the bed. She started up as her mother entered.

'Oh, mamma, how you terrified me! I thought you were a man that had got into the house.'

'Nonsense! The men are all gone away. There are soldiers all round the place, seeking for their work now it is too late. Miss Hale is lying on the dining-room sofa badly hurt. I am going for the doctor.'

'Oh! don't, mamma! they'll murder you.' She clung to her mother's gown. Mrs Thornton wrenched it away with no gentle hand.

'Find me some one else to go; but that girl must not bleed to death.'

'Bleed! oh, how horrid! How has she got hurt?'

'I don't know, – I have no time to ask. Go down to her, Fanny, and do try to make yourself of use. Jane is with her; and I trust it looks worse than it is. Jane has refused to leave the house, cowardly woman! And I won't put myself in the way of any more refusals from my servants, so I am going myself.'

'Oh, dear, dear!' said Fanny, crying, and preparing to go down rather than be left alone, with the thought of wounds and bloodshed in the very house.

'Oh, Jane!' said she, creeping into the dining-room, 'what is the matter? How white she looks! How did she get hurt? Did they throw stones into the drawing-room?'

Margaret did indeed look white and wan, although her senses were beginning to return to her. But the sickly daze of the swoon made her still miserably faint. She was conscious of movement around her, and of refreshment from the eau de Cologne, and a craving for the bathing to go on without intermission; but when they stopped to talk, she could no more have opened her eyes, or spoken to ask for more bathing, than the people who lie in death-like trance can move, or utter sound, to arrest the awful preparations for their burial, while they are yet fully aware, not merely of the actions of those around them, but of the idea that is the motive for such actions.

Jane paused in her bathing, to reply to Miss Thornton's question.

'She'd have been safe enough, miss, if she'd stayed in the drawing-room, or come up to us; we were in the front garret, and could see it all, out of harm's way.'

'Where was she, then?' said Fanny, drawing nearer by slow degrees, as she became accustomed to the sight of Margaret's pale face.

'Just before the front door – with master!' said Jane, significantly.

'With John! with my brother! How did she get there?'

'Nay, miss, that's not for me to say,' answered Jane, with a slight toss of her head. 'Sarah did' –

'Sarah what?' said Fanny, with impatient curiosity.

Jane resumed her bathing, as if what Sarah did or said was not exactly the thing she liked to repeat.

'Sarah what?' asked Fanny, sharply. 'Don't speak in these half sentences, or I can't understand you.'

'Well, miss, since you will have it – Sarah, you see, was in the best place for seeing, being at the right-hand window; and she says, and said at the very time too, that she saw Miss Hale with her arms about master's neck, hugging him before all the people.'

'I don't believe it,' said Fanny. 'I know she cares for my brother; any one can see that; and I dare say, she'd give her eyes if he'd marry her, – which he never will, I can tell her. But I don't believe she'd be so bold and forward as to put her arms round his neck.'

'Poor young lady! she's paid for it dearly if she did. It's my belief, that the blow has given her such an ascendency of blood to the head as she'll never get the better from. She looks like a corpse now.'

'Oh, I wish mamma would come!' said Fanny, wringing her hands. 'I never was in the room with a dead person before.'

'Stay, miss! She's not dead: her eye-lids are quivering, and here's wet tears a-coming down her cheeks. Speak to her, Miss Fanny!'

'Are you better now?' asked Fanny, in a quavering voice.

No answer; no sign of recognition; but a faint pink colour returned to her lips, although the rest of her face was ashen pale.

Mrs Thornton came hurriedly in, with the nearest surgeon she could find.

'How is she? Are you better, my dear?' as Margaret opened her filmy eyes, and gazed dreamily at her. 'Here is Mr Lowe come to see you.'

Mrs Thornton spoke loudly and distinctly, as to a deaf person. Margaret tried to rise, and drew her ruffled, luxuriant hair instinctively over the cut.

'I am better now,' said she, in a very low, faint voice. 'I was a little sick.'

She let him take her hand and feel her pulse. The bright colour came for a moment into her face, when he asked to examine the wound in her forehead; and she glanced up at Jane, as if shrinking from her inspection more than from the doctor's.

'It is not much, I think. I am better now. I must go home.'

'Not until I have applied some strips of plaster, and you have rested a little.'

She sat down hastily, without another word, and allowed it to be bound up.

'Now, if you please,' said she, 'I must go. Mamma will not see it, I think. It is under the hair, is it not?'

'Quite; no one could tell.'

'But you must not go,' said Mrs Thornton, impatiently. 'You are not fit to go.'

'I must,' said Margaret, decidedly. 'Think of mamma. If they should hear – Besides I must go,' said she, vehemently. 'I cannot stay here. May I ask for a cab?'

'You are quite flushed and feverish,' observed Mr Lowe.

'It is only with being here, when I do so want to go. The air – getting away, would do me more good than anything,' pleaded she.

'I really believe it is as she says,' Mr Lowe replied. 'If her mother is so ill as you told me on the way here, it may be very serious if she hears of this riot, and does not see her daughter back at the time she expects. The injury is not deep. I will fetch a cab, if your servants are still afraid to go out.'

'Oh, thank you!' said Margaret. 'It will do me more good than anything. It is the air of this room that makes me feel so miserable.'

She leant back on the sofa, and closed her eyes. Fanny beckoned her mother out of the room, and told her something that made her equally anxious with Margaret for the departure of the latter. Not that she fully believed Fanny's statement; but she credited enough to make her manner to Margaret appear very much constrained at wishing her good-bye.

Mr Lowe returned in the cab.

'If you will allow me, I will see you home, Miss Hale. The streets are not very quiet yet.'

Margaret's thoughts were quite alive enough to the present to make her desirous of getting rid of both Mr Lowe and the cab before she reached Crampton Crescent, for fear of alarming her father and mother. Beyond that one aim she would not look. That ugly dream of insolent words spoken about herself, could never be forgotten – but could be put aside till she was stronger – for, oh! she was very weak; and her mind sought for some present fact to steady itself upon, and keep it from utterly losing consciousness in another hideous, sickly swoon.

CHAPTER XXIII

Mistakes

Which when his mother saw, she in her mind[1]
Was troubled sore, ne wist well what to ween.
SPENSER

Margaret had not been gone five minutes when Mr Thornton came in, his face all a-glow.

'I could not come sooner: the superintendent would – Where is she?' He looked round the dining-room, and then almost fiercely at his mother, who was quietly re-arranging the disturbed furniture, and did not instantly reply. 'Where is Miss Hale?' asked he again.

'Gone home,' said she, rather shortly.

'Gone home!'

'Yes. She was a great deal better. Indeed, I don't believe it was so very much of a hurt; only some people faint at the least thing.'

'I am sorry she is gone home,' said he, walking uneasily about. 'She could not have been fit for it.'

'She said she was; and Mr Lowe said she was. I went for him myself.'

'Thank you, mother.' He stopped, and partly held out his hand to give her a grateful shake. But she did not notice the movement.

'What have you done with your Irish people?'

'Sent to the Dragon for a good meal for them, poor wretches. And then, luckily, I caught Father Grady, and I've asked him in to speak to them, and dissuade them from going off in a body. How did Miss Hale go home? I'm sure she could not walk.'

'She had a cab. Everything was done properly, even to the paying. Let us talk of something else. She has caused disturbance enough.'

'I don't know where I should have been but for her.'

'Are you become so helpless as to have to be defended by a girl?' asked Mrs Thornton, scornfully.

He reddened. 'Not many girls would have taken the blows on herself which were meant for me; – meant with right down goodwill, too.'

'A girl in love will do a good deal,' replied Mrs Thornton, shortly.

'Mother!' He made a step forwards; stood still; heaved with passion.

She was a little startled at the evident force he used to keep himself calm. She was not sure of the nature of the emotions she had provoked. It was only their violence that was clear. Was it anger? His eyes glowed, his figure was dilated, his breath came thick and fast. It was a mixture of joy, of anger, of pride, of glad surprise, of panting doubt; but she could not read it. Still it made her uneasy, – as the presence of all strong feeling, of which the cause is not fully understood or sympathized in, always has this effect. She went to the side-board, opened a drawer, and took out a duster, which she kept there for any occasional purpose. She had seen a drop of eau de Cologne on the polished arm of the sofa, and instinctively sought to wipe it off. But she kept her back turned to her son much longer than was necessary; and when she spoke, her voice seemed unusual and constrained.

'You have taken some steps about the rioters, I suppose? You don't apprehend any more violence, do you? Where were the police? Never at hand when they're wanted!'

'On the contrary, I saw three or four of them, when the gates gave way, struggling and beating about in fine fashion; and more came running up just when the yard was clearing. I might have given some of the fellows in charge then, if I had had my wits about me. But there will be no difficulty, plenty of people can identify them.'

'But won't they come back tonight?'

'I'm going to see about a sufficient guard for the premises. I have appointed to meet Captain Hanbury in half an hour at the station.'

'You must have some tea first.'

'Tea! Yes, I suppose I must. It's half-past six, and I may be out for some time. Don't sit up for me, mother.'

'You expect me to go to bed before I have seen you safe, do you?'

'Well, perhaps not.' He hesitated for a moment. 'But if I've time, I shall go round by Crampton, after I've arranged with the police and seen Hamper and Clarkson.' Their eyes met; they looked at each other intently for a minute. Then she asked:

'Why are you going round by Crampton?'

'To ask after Miss Hale.'

'I will send. Williams must take the water-bed she came to ask for. He shall inquire how she is.'

'I must go myself.'

'Not merely to ask how Miss Hale is?'

'No, not merely for that. I want to thank her for the way in which she stood between me and the mob.'

'What made you go down at all? It was putting your head into the lion's mouth!'

He glanced sharply at her; saw that she did not know what had passed between him and Margaret in the drawing-room; and replied by another question:

'Shall you be afraid to be left without me, until I can get some of the police; or had we better send Williams for them now, and they could be here by the time we have done tea? There's no time to be lost. I must be off in a quarter of an hour.'

Mrs Thornton left the room. Her servants wondered at her directions, usually so sharply-cut and decided, now confused and uncertain. Mr Thornton remained in the dining-room, trying to think of the business he had to do at the police-office, and in reality thinking of Margaret. Everything seemed dim and vague beyond – behind –

besides the touch of her arms round his neck – the soft clinging which made the dark colour come and go in his cheek as he thought of it.

The tea would have been very silent, but for Fanny's perpetual description of her own feelings; how she had been alarmed – and then thought they were gone – and then felt sick and faint and trembling in every limb.

'There, that's enough,' said her brother, rising from the table. 'The reality was enough for me.' He was going to leave the room, when his mother stopped him with her hand upon his arm.

'You will come back here before you go to the Hales',' said she, in a low, anxious voice.

'I know what I know,' said Fanny to herself.

'Why? Will it be too late to disturb them?'

'John, come back to me for this one evening. It will be late for Mrs Hale. But that is not it. Tomorrow, you will – Come back tonight, John!' She had seldom pleaded with her son at all – she was too proud for that: but she had never pleaded in vain.

'I will return straight here after I have done my business. You will be sure to inquire after them? – after her?'

Mrs Thornton was by no means a talkative companion to Fanny, nor yet a good listener while her son was absent. But on his return, her eyes and ears were keen to see and to listen to all the details which he could give, as to the steps he had taken to secure himself, and those whom he chose to employ, from any repetition of the day's outrages. He clearly saw his object. Punishment and suffering, were the natural consequences to those who had taken part in the riot. All that was necessary, in order that property should be protected, and that the will of the proprietor might cut to his end, clean and sharp as a sword.

'Mother! You know what I have got to say to Miss Hale, tomorrow?'

The question came upon her suddenly, during a pause in which she, at least, had forgotten Margaret.

She looked up at him.

'Yes! I do. You can hardly do otherwise.'

'Do otherwise! I don't understand you.'

'I mean that, after allowing her feelings so to overcome her, I consider you bound in honour –'

'Bound in honour,' said he, scornfully. 'I'm afraid honour has nothing to do with it. "Her feelings overcome her!" What feelings do you mean?'

'Nay, John, there is no need to be angry. Did she not rush down, and cling to you to save you from danger?'

'She did!' said he. 'But, mother,' continued he, stopping short in his walk right in front of her, 'I dare not hope. I never was faint-hearted before; but I cannot believe such a creature cares for me.'

'Don't be foolish, John. Such a creature! Why, she might be a duke's daughter, to hear you speak. And what proof more would you have, I wonder, of her caring for you? I can believe she has had a struggle with her aristocratic way of viewing things; but I like her the better for seeing clearly at last. It is a good deal for me to say,' said Mrs Thornton, smiling slowly, while the tears stood in her eyes; 'for after tonight, I stand second. It was to have you to myself, all to myself, a few hours longer, that I begged you not to go till tomorrow!'

'Dearest mother!' (Still love is selfish, and in an instant he reverted to his own hopes and fears in a way that drew the cold creeping shadow over Mrs Thornton's heart.) 'But I know she does not care for me. I shall put myself at her feet – I must. If it were but one chance in a thousand – or a million – I should do it.'

'Don't fear!' said his mother, crushing down her own personal mortification at the little notice he had taken of the rare ebullition of her maternal feelings – of the pang of jealousy that betrayed the intensity of her disregarded love. 'Don't be afraid,' she said, coldly. 'As far as love may go she may be worthy of you. It must have taken a good deal to overcome her pride. Don't be afraid, John,' said she, kissing him, as she wished him good-night. And she went slowly and majestically out of the room. But when she got into her own, she locked the door, and sate down to cry unwonted tears.

Margaret entered the room (where her father and mother still sat, holding low conversation together), looking very pale and white. She came close up to them before she could trust herself to speak.

'Mrs Thornton will send the water-bed, mamma.'

'Dear, how tired you look! Is it very hot, Margaret?'

'Very hot, and the streets are rather rough with the strike.'

Margaret's colour came back vivid and bright as ever; but it faded away instantly.

'Here has been a message from Bessy Higgins, asking you to go to her,' said Mrs Hale. 'But I'm sure you look too tired.'

'Yes!' said Margaret. 'I am tired, I cannot go.'

She was very silent and trembling while she made tea. She was thankful to see her father so much occupied with her mother as not to notice her looks. Even after her mother went to bed, he was not content to be absent from her, but undertook to read her to sleep. Margaret was alone.

'Now I will think of it – now I will remember it all. I could not before – I dared not.' She sat still in her chair, her hands clasped on her knees, her lips compressed, her eyes fixed as one who sees a vision. She drew a deep breath.

'I, who hate scenes – I, who have despised people for showing emotion – who have thought them wanting in self-control – I went down and must needs throw myself into the mêlée, like a romantic fool! Did I do any good? They would have gone away without me, I dare say.' But this was over-leaping the rational conclusion, – as in an instant her well-poised judgment felt. 'No, perhaps, they would not. I did some good. But what possessed me to defend that man as if he were a helpless child! Ah!' said she, clenching her hands together, 'it is no wonder those people thought I was in love with him, after disgracing myself in that way. I in love – and with him too!' Her pale cheeks suddenly became one flame of fire; and she covered her face with her hands. When she took them away, her palms were wet with scalding tears.

'Oh how low I am fallen that they should say that of me! I could not have been so brave for any one else, just because he was so utterly indifferent to me – if, indeed, I do not positively dislike him. It made me the more anxious that there should be fair play on each side; and I could see what fair play was. It was not fair,' said she, vehemently, 'that he should stand there – sheltered, awaiting the soldiers, who might catch those poor maddened creatures as in a trap – without an effort on his part, to bring them to reason. And it was worse than unfair for them to set on him as they threatened. I would do it again, let who will say what they like of me. If I saved one blow, one cruel, angry action that might otherwise have been committed, I did a woman's work. Let them insult my maiden pride as they will – I walk pure before God!'

She looked up, and a noble peace seemed to descend and calm her face, till it was 'stiller than chiselled marble.'[2]

Dixon came in:

'If you please, Miss Margaret, here's the water-bed from Mrs Thornton's. It's too late for tonight, I'm afraid, for missus is nearly asleep: but it will do nicely for tomorrow.'

'Very,' said Margaret. 'You must send our best thanks.'

Dixon left the room for a moment.

'If you please, Miss Margaret, he says he's to ask particular how you are. I think he must mean missus; but he says his last words were, to ask how Miss Hale was.'

'Me!' said Margaret, drawing herself up. 'I am quite well. Tell him I am perfectly well.' But her complexion was as deadly white as her handkerchief; and her head ached intensely.

Mr Hale now came in. He had left his sleeping wife; and wanted, as Margaret saw, to be amused and interested by something that she was to tell him. With sweet patience did she bear her pain, without a word of complaint; and rummaged up numberless small subjects for conversation – all except the riot, and that she never named once. It turned her sick to think of it.

'Good-night, Margaret. I have every chance of a good night myself, and you are looking very pale with your watching. I shall call Dixon if your mother needs anything. Do you go to bed and sleep like a top; for I'm sure you need it, poor child!'

'Good-night, papa.'

She let her colour go – the forced smile fade away – the eyes grow dull with heavy pain. She released her strong will from its laborious task. Till morning she might feel ill and weary.

She lay down and never stirred. To move hand or foot, or even so much as one finger, would have been an exertion beyond the powers of either volition or motion. She was so tired, so stunned, that she thought she never slept at all; her feverish thoughts passed and repassed the boundary between sleeping and waking, and kept their own miserable identity. She could not be alone, prostrate, powerless as she was, – a cloud of faces looked up at her, giving her no idea of fierce vivid anger, or of personal danger, but a deep sense of shame that she should thus be the object of universal regard – a sense of shame so acute that it seemed as if she would fain have burrowed into the earth to hide herself, and yet she could not escape out of that unwinking glare of many eyes.

CHAPTER XXIV

Mistakes Cleared Up

Your beauty was the first that won the place,[1]
And scal'd the walls of my undaunted heart,
Which, captive now, pines in a caitive case,
Unkindly met with rigour for desert; –
Yet not the less your servant shall abide,
In spite of rude repulse or silent pride.

WILLIAM FOWLER

The next morning, Margaret dragged herself up, thankful that the night was over, – unrefreshed, yet rested. All had gone well through the house; her mother had only wakened once. A little breeze was stirring in the hot air, and though there were no trees to show the playful tossing movement caused by the wind among the leaves, Margaret knew how, somewhere or another, by wayside, in copses, or in thick green woods, there was a pleasant, murmuring dancing sound, – a rushing and falling noise, the very thought of which was an echo of distant gladness in her heart.

She sat at her work in Mrs Hale's room. As soon as that forenoon slumber was over, she would help her mother to dress; after dinner, she would go and see Bessy Higgins. She would banish all recollection of the Thornton family, – no need to think of them till they absolutely stood before her in flesh and blood. But, of course, the effort not to think of them brought them only the more strongly before her; and from time to time, the hot flush came over her pale face, sweeping it into colour, as a sunbeam from between watery clouds comes swiftly moving over the sea.

Dixon opened the door very softly, and stole on tiptoe up to Margaret, sitting by the shaded window.

'Mr Thornton, Miss Margaret. He is in the drawing-room.'

Margaret dropped her sewing.

'Did he ask for me? Isn't papa come in?'

'He asked for you, miss; and master is out.'

'Very well, I will come,' said Margaret, quietly. But she lingered strangely.

Mr Thornton stood by one of the windows, with his back to the door, apparently absorbed in watching something in the street. But, in truth, he was afraid of himself. His heart beat thick at the thought of her coming. He could not forget the touch of her arms around his neck, impatiently felt as it had been at the time; but now the recollection of her clinging defence of him, seemed to thrill him through and through, – to melt away every resolution, all power of self-control, as if it were wax before a fire. He dreaded lest he should go forwards to meet her, with his arms held out in mute entreaty that she would come and nestle there, as she had done, all unheeded, the day before, but never unheeded again. His heart throbbed loud and quick. Strong man as he was, he trembled at the anticipation of what he had to say, and how it might be received. She might droop, and flush, and flutter to his arms, as to her natural home and resting-place. One moment, he glowed with impatience at the thought that she might do this, – the next, he feared a passionate rejection, the very idea of which withered up his future with so deadly a blight that he refused to think of it. He was startled by the sense of the presence of some one else in the room. He turned round. She had come in so gently, that he had never heard her; the street noises had been more distinct to his inattentive ear than her slow movements, in her soft muslin gown.

She stood by the table, not offering to sit down. Her eyelids were dropped half over her eyes; her teeth were shut, not compressed; her lips were just parted over them, allowing the white line to be seen between their curve. Her slow deep breathings dilated her thin and beautiful nostrils; it was the only motion visible on her countenance. The fine-grained skin, the oval cheek, the rich outline of her mouth, its corners deep set in dimples, – were all wan and pale today; the loss of their usual natural healthy colour being made more evident by the heavy shadow of the dark hair, brought down upon the temples, to hide all sign of the blow she had received. Her head, for all its drooping eyes, was thrown a little back, in the old proud attitude. Her long arms hung motionless by her sides. Altogether she looked like some prisoner, falsely accused of a crime that she loathed and despised, and from which she was too indignant to justify herself.

Mr Thornton made a hasty step or two forwards; recovered himself, and went with quiet firmness to the door (which she had left open), and shut it. Then he came back, and stood opposite to her for a moment, receiving the general impression of her beautiful presence, before he dared to disturb it, perhaps to repel it, by what he had to say.

'Miss Hale, I was very ungrateful yesterday –'

'You had nothing to be grateful for,' said she, raising her eyes, and looking full and straight at him. 'You mean, I suppose, that you believe you ought to thank me for what I did.' In spite of herself – in defiance of her anger – the thick blushes came all over her face, and burnt into her very eyes; which fell not nevertheless from their grave and steady look. 'It was only a natural instinct; any woman would have done just the same. We all feel the sanctity of our sex as a high privilege when we see danger.[2] I ought rather,' said she, hastily, 'to apologize to you, for having said thoughtless words which sent you down into the danger.'

'It was not your words; it was the truth they conveyed, pungently as it was expressed. But you shall not drive me off upon that, and so escape the expression of my deep gratitude, my –' he was on the verge now; he would not speak in the haste of his hot passion; he would weigh each word. He would; and his will was triumphant. He stopped in mid career.

'I do not try to escape from anything,' said she. 'I simply say, that you owe me no gratitude; and I may add, that any expression of it will be painful to me, because I do not feel that I deserve it. Still, if it will relieve you from even a fancied obligation, speak on.'

'I do not want to be relieved from any obligation,' said he, goaded by her calm manner. 'Fancied, or not fancied – I question not myself to know which – I choose to believe that I owe my very life to you – ay – smile, and think it an exaggeration if you will. I believe it, because it adds a value to that life to think – oh, Miss Hale!' continued he, lowering his voice to such a tender intensity of passion that she shivered and trembled before him, 'to think circumstance so wrought, that whenever I exult in existence henceforward, I may say to myself, "All this gladness in life, all honest pride in doing my work in the world, all this keen sense of being, I owe to her!" And it doubles the gladness, it makes the pride glow, it sharpens the sense of existence till I hardly know if it is pain or pleasure, to think that I owe it to one – nay, you must, you shall hear' – said he, stepping forwards with stern determination – 'to one whom I love, as I do not believe man ever loved woman before.' He held her hand tight in his. He panted as he listened for what should come. He threw the hand away with indignation, as he heard her icy tone; for icy it was, though the words came faltering out, as if she knew not where to find them.

'Your way of speaking shocks me. It is blasphemous. I cannot help it, if that is my first feeling. It might not be so, I dare say, if I understood the kind of feeling you describe. I do not want to vex you; and besides, we must speak gently, for mamma is asleep; but your whole manner offends me –'

'How!' exclaimed he. 'Offends you! I am indeed most unfortunate.'

'Yes!' said she, with recovered dignity. 'I do feel offended; and, I think, justly. You seem to fancy that my conduct of yesterday' – again the deep carnation blush, but this time with eyes kindling with indignation rather than shame – 'was a personal act between you and me; and that you may come and thank me for it, instead of perceiving, as a gentleman would – yes! a gentleman,' she repeated in allusion to their former conversation about that word, 'that any woman, worthy of the name of woman, would come forward to shield, with her reverenced helplessness, a man in danger from the violence of numbers.'

'And the gentleman thus rescued is forbidden the relief of thanks!' he broke in contemptuously. 'I am a man. I claim the right of expressing my feelings.'

'And I yielded to the right; simply saying that you gave me pain by insisting upon it,' she replied, proudly. 'But you seem to have imagined, that I was not merely guided by womanly instinct, but' – and here the passionate tears (kept down for long – struggled with vehemently) came up into her eyes, and choked her voice – 'but that I was prompted by some particular feeling for you – you! Why, there was not a man – not a poor desperate man in all that crowd – for whom I had not more sympathy – for whom I should not have done what little I could more heartily.'

'You may speak on, Miss Hale. I am aware of all these misplaced sympathies of yours. I now believe that it was only your innate sense of oppression – (yes; I, though a master, may be oppressed) – that made you act so nobly as you did. I know you despise me; allow me to say, it is because you do not understand me.'

'I do not care to understand,' she replied, taking hold of the table to steady herself; for she thought him cruel – as, indeed, he was – and she was weak with her indignation.

'No, I see you do not. You are unfair and unjust.'

Margaret compressed her lips. She would not speak in answer to such accusations. But, for all that – for all his savage words, he could have thrown himself at her feet, and kissed the hem of her garment. She did not speak; she did not move. The tears of wounded pride fell hot and fast. He waited awhile, longing for her to say something, even a taunt, to which he might reply. But she was silent. He took up his hat.

'One word more. You look as if you thought it tainted you to be loved by me. You cannot avoid it. Nay, I, if I would, cannot cleanse you from it. But I would not, if I could. I have never loved any woman before: my life has been too busy, my thoughts too much absorbed with other things. Now I love, and will love. But do not be afraid of too much expression on my part.'

'I am not afraid,' she replied, lifting herself straight up. 'No one yet has ever dared to be impertinent to me, and no one ever shall. But, Mr Thornton, you have been very kind to my father,' said she, changing her whole tone and bearing to a most womanly softness. 'Don't let us go on making each other angry. Pray don't!' He took no notice of her words: he occupied himself in smoothing the nap of his hat with his coat-sleeve, for half a minute or so; and then, rejecting her offered hand, and making as if he did not see her grave look of regret, he turned abruptly away, and left the room. Margaret caught one glance at his face before he went.

When he was gone, she thought she had seen the gleam of unshed tears in his eyes; and that turned her proud dislike into something different and kinder, if nearly as painful – self-reproach for having caused such mortification to any one.

'But how could I help it?' asked she of herself. 'I never liked him. I was civil; but I took no trouble to conceal my indifference. Indeed, I never thought about myself or him, so my manners must have shown the truth. All that yesterday, he might mistake. But that is his fault, not mine. I would do it again, if need were, though it does lead me into all this shame and trouble.'

CHAPTER XXV

Frederick

Revenge may have her own;[1]
Roused discipline aloud proclaims their cause,
And injured navies urge their broken laws.

BYRON

Margaret began to wonder whether all offers were as unexpected beforehand, – as distressing at the time of their occurrence, as the two she had had. An involuntary comparison between Mr Lennox and Mr Thornton arose in her mind. She had been sorry, that an expression of any other feeling than friendship had been lured out by circumstances from Henry Lennox. That regret was the predominant feeling, on the first occasion of her receiving a proposal. She had not felt so stunned – so impressed as she did now, when echoes of Mr Thornton's voice yet lingered about the room. In Lennox's case, he seemed for a moment to have slid over the boundary between friendship and love; and the instant afterwards, to regret it nearly as much as she did, although for different reasons. In Mr Thornton's case, as far as Margaret knew, there was no intervening stage of friendship. Their intercourse had been one continued series of opposition. Their opinions clashed; and indeed, she had never perceived that he had cared for her opinions, as belonging to her, the individual. As far as they defied his rock-like power of character, his passion-strength, he seemed to throw them off from him with contempt, until she felt the weariness of the exertion of making useless protests; and now, he had come, in this strange wild passionate way, to make known his love! For, although at first it had struck her, that his offer was forced and goaded out of him by sharp compassion for the exposure she had made of herself, – which he, like others, might misunderstand – yet, even before he left the room, – and certainly, not five minutes after, the clear conviction dawned upon her, shined bright upon her, that he did love her; that he had loved her; that he would love her. And she shrank and shuddered as under the fascination of some great power, repugnant to her whole previous life. She crept away, and hid from his idea. But it was of no use. To parody a line out of Fairfax's Tasso[2]

His strong idea wandered through her thought.

She disliked him the more for having mastered her inner will. How dared he say that he would love her still, even though she shook him off with contempt? She wished she had spoken more – stronger. Sharp, decisive speeches came thronging into her mind, now that it was too late to utter them. The deep impression made by the interview, was like that of a horror in a dream; that will not leave the room although we waken up, and rub our eyes, and force a stiff rigid smile upon our lips. It is there – there, cowering and jibbering, with fixed ghastly eyes, in some corner of the chamber, listening to hear whether we dare to breathe of its presence to any one. And we dare not; poor cowards that we are!

And so she shuddered away from the threat of his enduring love. What did he mean? Had she not the power to daunt him? She would see. It was more daring than became a man to threaten her so. Did he ground it upon the miserable yesterday? If need were, she would do the same tomorrow, – by a crippled beggar, willingly and gladly, – but by him, she would do it, just as bravely, in spite of his deductions, and the cold slime of women's impertinence. She did it because it was right, and simple, and true to save where she could save; even to try to save. 'Fais ce que dois, advienne que pourra.'

Hitherto she had not stirred from where he had left her; no outward circumstances had roused her out of the trance of thought in which she had been plunged by his last words, and by the look of his deep intent passionate eyes, as their flames had made her own fall before them. She went to the window, and threw it open, to dispel the oppression which hung around her. Then she went and opened the door, with a sort of impetuous wish to shake off the recollection of the past hour in the company of others, or in active exertion. But all was profoundly hushed in the noonday stillness of a house, where an invalid catches the unrefreshing sleep that is denied to the night-hours. Margaret would not be alone. What should she do? 'Go and see Bessy Higgins, of course,' thought she, as the recollection of the message sent the night before flashed into her mind. And away she went.

When she got there, she found Bessy lying on the settle, moved close to the fire, though the day was sultry and oppressive. She was laid down quite flat, as if resting languidly after some paroxysm of pain. Margaret felt sure she ought to have the greater freedom of breathing which a more sitting posture would procure; and, without a word, she raised her up, and so arranged the pillows, that Bessy was more at ease, though very languid.

'I thought I should na' ha' seen yo' again,' said she, at last, looking wistfully in Margaret's face.

'I'm afraid you're much worse. But I could not have come yesterday, my mother was so ill – for many reasons,' said Margaret, colouring.

'Yo'd m'appen think I went beyond my place in sending Mary for yo'. But the wranglin' and the loud voices had just torn me to pieces, and I thought when father left, oh! if I could just hear her voice, reading me some words o' peace and promise, I could die away into the silence and rest o' God, just as a baby is hushed up to sleep by its mother's lullaby.'

'Shall I read you a chapter, now?'

'Ay, do! M'appen I shan't listen to th' sense, at first; it will seem far away – but when yo' come to words I like – to th' comforting texts – it'll seem close in my ear, and going through me as it were.'

Margaret began. Bessy tossed to and fro. If, by an effort, she attended for one moment, it seemed as though she were convulsed into double restlessness the next. At last, she burst out: 'Don't go on reading. It's no use. I'm blaspheming all the time in my mind, wi' thinking angrily on what canna be helped. – Yo'd hear of th' riot, m'appen, yesterday at Marlborough Mills? Thornton's factory, yo' know.'

'Your father was not there, was he?' said Margaret, colouring deeply.

'Not he. He'd ha' given his right hand if it had never come to pass. It's that that's fretting me. He's fairly knocked down in his mind by it. It's no use telling him, fools will always break out o' bounds. Yo' never saw a man so down-hearted as he is.'

'But why?' asked Margaret. 'I don't understand.'

'Why yo' see, he's a committee-man on this special strike. Th' Union appointed him because, though I say it as shouldn't say it, he's reckoned a deep chap, and true to th' back-bone. And he and t'other committee-men laid their plans. They were to hou'd together through thick and thin; what the major part thought, t'others were to think, whether they would or no. And above all there was to be no going again the law of the land. Folk would go with them if they saw them striving and starving wi' dumb patience; but if there was once any noise o' fighting and struggling – even wi' knobsticks – all was up, as they knew by th' experience of many, and many a time before. They would try and get speech o' th' knobsticks, and coax 'em, and reason wi' 'em, and m'appen warn 'em off; but whatever came, the Committee charged all members o' th' Union to lie down and die, if need were, without striking a blow; and then they reckoned they were sure o' carrying th' public with them. And beside all that, Committee knew they were right in their demand, and they didn't want to have right all mixed up wi' wrong, till folk can't separate it, no more nor I can th' physic-powder from th' jelly yo' gave me to mix it in; jelly is much the biggest, but powder tastes it all through. Well, I've told yo' at length about this'n, but I'm tired out. Yo' just think for yo'rsel, what it mun be for father to have a' his work undone, and by such a fool as Boucher, who must needs go right again the orders of Committee, and ruin th' strike just as bad as if he meant to be a Judas. Eh! but father giv'd it him last night! He went so far as to say, he'd go and tell police where they might find th' ringleader o' th' riot; he'd give him up to th' mill-owners to do what they would wi' him. He'd show the world that th' real leaders o' the strike were not such as Boucher, but steady thoughtful men; good hands, and good citizens, who were friendly to law and judgment, and would uphold order; who only wanted their right wage, and wouldn't work, even though they starved, till they got 'em; but who would ne'er injure property or life. For,' dropping her voice, 'they do say, that Boucher threw a stone at Thornton's sister, that welly killed her.'

'That's not true,' said Margaret. 'It was not Boucher that threw the stone' – she went first red, then white.

'You'd be there then, were yo'?' asked Bessy languidly: for indeed she had spoken with many pauses, as if speech was unusually difficult to her.

'Yes. Never mind. Go on. Only it was not Boucher that threw the stone. But what did he answer to your father?'

'He did na' speak words. He were all in such a tremble wi' spent passion, I could na' bear to look at him. I heard his breath coming quick, and at one time I thought he were sobbing. But when father said he'd give him up to police, he gave a great cry, and struck father on th' face wi' his closed fist, and he off like lightning. Father were stunned wi' the blow at first, for all Boucher were weak wi' passion and wi' clemming. He sat down a bit, and put his hand afore his eyes; and then made for th' door. I dunno' where I got strength, but I threw mysel' off th' settle and clung to him. "Father, father!" said I. "Thou'll never go peach on that poor clemmed man. I'll never leave go on thee, till thou sayst thou wunnot." "Dunnot be a fool," says he, "words come readier than deeds to most men. I never thought o' telling th' police on him; though by G –, he deserves it, and I should na' ha' minded if some one else had done the dirty work, and got him clapped up. But now he has strucken me, I could do it less nor ever, for it would be getting other men to take up my quarrel. But if ever he gets well o'er this clemming, and is in good condition, he and I'll have an up and down fight, purring an' a', and I'll see what I can do for him." And so father shook me off, – for indeed, I was low and faint enough, and his face was all clay white, where it weren't bloody, and turned me sick to look at. And I know not if I slept or waked, or were in a dead swoon, till Mary come in; and I told her to fetch yo' to me. And now dunnot talk to me, but just read out th' chapter. I'm easier in my mind for having spit it out; but I want some thoughts of the world that's far away to take the weary taste of it out o' my mouth. Read me – not a sermon chapter, but a story chapter; they've pictures in them, which I see when my eyes are shut. Read about the New Heavens, and the New Earth;[3] and m'appen I'll forget this.'

Margaret read in her soft low voice. Though Bessy's eyes were shut, she was listening for some time, for the moisture of tears gathered heavy on her eyelashes. At last she slept; with many starts, and muttered pleadings. Margaret covered her up, and left her, for she had an uneasy consciousness that she might be wanted at home, and yet, until now, it seemed cruel to leave the dying girl.

Mrs Hale was in the drawing-room on her daughter's return. It was one of her better days, and she was full of praises of the water-bed. It had been more like the beds at Sir John Beresford's than anything she had slept on since. She did not know how it was, but people seemed to have lost the art of making the same kind of beds as they used to do in her youth. One would think it was easy enough; there was the same kind of feathers to be had, and yet somehow, till this last night she did not know when she had had a good sound resting sleep.

Mr Hale suggested, that something of the merits of the feather-beds of former days might be attributed to the activity of youth, which gave a relish to rest; but this idea was not kindly received by his wife.

'No, indeed, Mr Hale, it was those beds at Sir John's. Now, Margaret, you're young enough, and go about in the day; are the beds comfortable? I appeal to you. Do they give you a feeling of perfect repose when you lie down upon them: or rather, don't you toss about, and try in vain to find an easy position, and waken in the morning as tired as when you went to bed?'

Margaret laughed. 'To tell the truth, mamma, I've never thought about my bed at all, what kind it is. I'm so sleepy at night, that if I only lie down anywhere, I nap off directly. So I don't think I'm a competent witness. But then, you know, I never had the opportunity of trying Sir John Beresford's beds. I never was at Oxenham.'

'Were not you? Oh, no! to be sure. It was poor darling Fred I took with me, I remember. I only went to Oxenham once after I was married, – to your Aunt Shaw's wedding; and poor little Fred was the baby then. And I know Dixon did not like changing from lady's maid to nurse, and I was afraid that if I took her near her old home, and amongst her own people, she might want to leave me. But poor baby was taken ill at Oxenham, with his teething; and, what with my being a great deal with Anna just before her marriage, and not being very strong myself, Dixon had more of the charge of him than she ever had before; and it made her so fond of him, and she was so proud when he would turn away from every one and cling to her, that I don't believe she ever thought of leaving me again; though it was very different from what she'd been accustomed to. Poor Fred! Every body loved him. He was born with the gift of winning hearts. It makes me think very badly of Captain Reid when I know that he disliked my own dear boy. I think it a certain proof he had a bad heart. Ah! Your poor father, Margaret. He has left the room. He can't bear to hear Fred spoken of.'

'I love to hear about him, mamma. Tell me all you like; you never can tell me too much. Tell me what he was like as a baby.'

'Why, Margaret, you must not be hurt, but he was much prettier than you were. I remember, when I first saw you in Dixon's arms, I said, "Dear, what an ugly little thing!" And she said, "It's not every child that's like Master Fred, bless him!" Dear! how well I remember it. Then I could have had Fred in my arms every minute of the day, and his cot was close by my bed; and now, now – Margaret – I don't know where my boy is, and sometimes I think I shall never see him again.'

Margaret sat down by her mother's sofa on a little stool, and softly took hold of her hand, caressing it and kissing it, as if to comfort. Mrs Hale cried without restraint. At last, she sat straight, stiff up on the sofa, and turning round to her daughter, she said with tearful, almost solemn earnestness, 'Margaret, if I can get better, – if God lets me have a chance of recovery, it must be through seeing my son Frederick once more. It will waken up all the poor springs of health left in me.'

She paused, and seemed to try and gather strength for something more yet to be said. Her voice was choked as she went on – was quavering as with the contemplation of some strange, yet closely-present idea.

'And, Margaret, if I am to die – if I am one of those appointed to die before many weeks are over – I must see my child first. I cannot think how it must be managed; but I charge you, Margaret, as you yourself hope for comfort in your last illness, bring him to me that I may bless him. Only for five minutes, Margaret. There could be no danger in five minutes. Oh, Margaret, let me see him before I die!'

Margaret did not think of anything that might be utterly unreasonable in this speech: we do not look for reason or logic in the passionate entreaties of those who are sick unto death; we are stung with the recollection of a thousand slighted opportunities of fulfilling the wishes of those who will soon pass away from among us: and do they ask us for the future happiness of our lives, we lay it at their feet, and will it away from us. But this wish of Mrs Hale's was so natural, so just, so right to both parties, that Margaret felt as if, on Frederick's account as well as on her mother's, she ought to overlook all intermediate chances of danger, and pledge herself to do everything in her power for its realization. The large, pleading, dilated eyes were fixed upon her wistfully, steady in their gaze, though the poor white lips quivered like those of a child. Margaret gently rose up and stood opposite to her frail mother; so that she might gather the secure fulfilment of her wish from the calm steadiness of her daughter's face.

'Mamma, I will write tonight, and tell Frederick what you say. I am as sure that he will come directly to us, as I am sure of my life. Be easy, mamma, you shall see him as far as anything earthly can be promised.'

'You will write tonight? Oh, Margaret! the post goes out at five – you will write by it, won't you? I have so few hours left – I feel, dear, as if I should not recover, though sometimes your father over-persuades me into hoping; you will write directly, won't you? Don't lose a single post; for just by that very post I may miss him.'

'But, mamma, papa is out.'

'Papa is out! and what then? Do you mean that he would deny me this last wish, Margaret? Why, I should not be ill – be dying – if he had not taken me away from Helstone, to this unhealthy, smoky, sunless place.'

'Oh, mamma!' said Margaret.

'Yes; it is so, indeed. He knows it himself; he has said so many a time. He would do anything for me; you don't mean he would refuse me this last wish – prayer, if you will. And, indeed, Margaret, the longing to see Frederick stands between me and God. I cannot pray till I have this one thing; indeed, I cannot. Don't lose time, dear, dear Margaret. Write by this very next post. Then he may be here – here in twenty-two days! For he is sure to come. No cords or chains can keep him. In twenty-two days I shall see my boy.' She fell back, and for a short time she took no notice of the fact that Margaret sat motionless, her hand shading her eyes.

'You are not writing!' said her mother at last. 'Bring me some pens and paper; I will try and write myself.' She sat up, trembling all over with feverish eagerness. Margaret took her hand down and looked at her mother sadly.

'Only wait till papa comes in. Let us ask him how best to do it.'

'You promised, Margaret, not a quarter of an hour ago; – you said he should come.'

'And so he shall, mamma; don't cry, my own dear mother. I'll write here, now, – you shall see me write, – and it shall go by this very post; and if papa thinks fit, he can write again when he comes in, – it is only a day's delay. Oh, mamma, don't cry so pitifully, – it cuts me to the heart.'

Mrs Hale could not stop her tears; they came hysterically; and, in truth, she made no effort to control them, but rather called up all the pictures of the happy past, and the probable future – painting the scene when she should lie a corpse, with the son she had longed to see in life weeping over her, and she unconscious of his presence – till she was melted by self-pity into a state of sobbing and exhaustion that made Margaret's heart ache. But at last she was calm, and greedily watched her daughter, as she began her letter; wrote it with swift urgent entreaty; sealed it up hurriedly, for fear her mother should ask to see it: and then, to make security most sure, at Mrs Hale's own bidding, took it herself to the post-office. She was coming home when her father overtook her.

'And where have you been, my pretty maid?' asked he.

'To the post-office, – with a letter; a letter to Frederick. Oh, papa, perhaps I have done wrong: but mamma was seized with such a passionate yearning to see him – she said it would make her well again, – and then she said that she must see him before she died, – I cannot tell you how urgent she was! Did I do wrong?'

Mr Hale did not reply at first. Then he said:

'You should have waited till I came in, Margaret.'

'I tried to persuade her –' and then she was silent.

'I don't know,' said Mr Hale, after a pause. 'She ought to see him if she wishes it so much, for I believe it would do her much more good than all the doctor's medicine, – and, perhaps, set her up altogether! but the danger to him, I'm afraid, is very great.'

'All these years since the mutiny, papa?'

'Yes; it is necessary, of course, for government to take very stringent measures for the repression of offences against authority, more particularly in the navy, where a commanding officer needs to be surrounded in his men's eyes with a vivid consciousness of all the power there is at home to back him, and take up his cause, and avenge any injuries offered to him, if need be. Ah! it's no matter to them how far their authorities have tyrannized, – galled hasty tempers to madness, – or, if that can be any excuse afterwards, it is never allowed for in the first instance; they spare no expense, they send out ships, – they scour the seas to lay hold of the offenders, – the lapse of years does not wash out the memory of the offence, – it is a fresh and vivid crime on the Admiralty books till it is blotted out by blood.'

'Oh, papa, what have I done! And yet it seemed so right at the time. I'm sure Frederick himself would run the risk.'

'So he would; so he should! Nay, Margaret, I'm glad it is done, though I durst not have done it myself.[4] I'm thankful it is as it is; I should have hesitated till, perhaps, it might have been too late to do any good. Dear Margaret, you have done what is right about it; and the end is beyond our control.'

It was all very well; but her father's account of the relentless manner in which mutinies were punished made Margaret shiver and creep. If she had decoyed her brother home to blot out the memory of his error by his blood! She saw her father's anxiety lay deeper than the source of his latter cheering words. She took his arm and walked home pensively and wearily by his side.

CHAPTER XXVI

Mother and Son

I have found that holy place of rest[1]
Still changeless.

MRS HEMANS

When Mr Thornton had left the house that morning he was almost blinded by his baffled passion. He was as dizzy as if Margaret, instead of looking, and speaking, and moving like a tender graceful woman, had been a sturdy fish-wife, and given him a sound blow with her fists. He had positive bodily pain, – a violent headache, and a throbbing intermittent pulse. He could not bear the noise, the garish light, the continued rumble and movement of the street. He called himself a fool for suffering so; and yet he could not, at the moment, recollect the cause of his suffering, and whether it was adequate to the consequences it had produced. It would have been a relief to him, if he could have sat down and cried on a door-step by a little child, who was raging and storming, through his passionate tears, at some injury he had received. He said to himself, that he hated Margaret, but a wild, sharp sensation of love cleft his dull, thunderous feeling like lightning, even as he shaped the words expressive of hatred. His greatest comfort was in hugging his torment; and in feeling, as he had indeed said to her, that though she might despise him, condemn him, treat him with her proud sovereign indifference, he did not change one whit. She could not make him change. He loved her, and would love her; and defy her, and this miserable bodily pain.

He stood still for a moment, to make this resolution firm and clear. There was an omnibus passing – going into the country; the conductor thought he was wishing for a place, and stopped near the pavement. It was too much trouble to apologize and explain; so he mounted upon it, and was borne away, – past long rows of houses – then past detached villas with trim gardens, till they came to real country hedge-rows, and, by-and-by, to a small country town. Then every body got down; and so did Mr Thornton, and because they walked away he did so too. He went into the fields, walking briskly, because the sharp motion relieved his mind. He could remember all about it now; the pitiful figure he must have cut; the absurd way in which he had gone and done the very thing he had so often agreed with himself in thinking would be the most foolish thing in the world; and had met with exactly the consequences which, in these wise moods, he had always foretold were certain to follow, if he ever did make such a fool of himself. Was he bewitched by those beautiful eyes, that soft, half-open, sighing mouth which lay so close upon his shoulder only yesterday? He could not even shake off the recollection that she had been there; that her arms had been round him, once – if never again. He only caught glimpses of her; he did not understand her altogether. At one time she was so brave, and at another so timid; now so tender, and then so haughty and regal-proud. And then he thought over every time. he had ever seen her once again, by way of finally forgetting her. He saw her in every dress, in every mood, and did not know which became her best. Even this morning, how magnificent she had looked, – her eyes flashing out upon him at the idea that, because she had shared his danger yesterday, she had cared for him the least!

If Mr Thornton was a fool in the morning, as he assured himself at least twenty times he was, he did not grow much wiser in the afternoon. All that he gained in return for his sixpenny omnibus ride, was a more vivid conviction that there never was, never could be, any one like Margaret; that she did not love him and never would; but that she – no! nor the whole world – should never hinder him from loving her. And so he returned to the little market-place, and remounted the omnibus to return to Milton.

It was late in the afternoon when he was set down, near his warehouse. The accustomed places brought back the accustomed habits and trains of thought. He knew how much he had to do – more than his usual work, owing to the commotion of the day before. He had to see his brother magistrates; he had to complete the arrangements, only half made in the morning, for the comfort and safety of his newly imported Irish hands; he had to secure them from all chance of communication with the discontented work-people of Milton. Last of all, he had to go home and encounter his mother.

Mrs Thornton had sat in the dining-room all day, every moment expecting the news of her son's acceptance by Miss Hale. She had braced herself up many and many a time, at some sudden noise in the house; had caught up the half-dropped work, and begun to ply her needle diligently, though through dimmed spectacles, and with an unsteady hand! and many times had the door opened, and some indifferent person entered on some insignificant errand. Then her rigid face unstiffened from its grey frost-bound expression, and the features dropped into the relaxed look of despondency, so unusual to their sternness. She wrenched herself away from the contemplation of all the dreary changes that would be brought about to herself by her son's marriage; she forced her thoughts into the accustomed house-hold grooves. The newly-married couple-to-be would need fresh household stocks of linen; and Mrs Thornton had clothes-basket upon clothes-basket, full of table-cloths and napkins, brought in, and began to reckon up the store. There was some confusion between what was hers, and consequently marked G.H.T. (for George and Hannah Thornton), and what was her son's – bought with his money, marked with his initials. Some of those marked G.H.T. were Dutch damask of the old kind, exquisitely fine; none were like them now. Mrs Thornton stood looking at them long, – they had been her pride when she was first married. Then she knit her brows, and pinched and compressed her lips tight, and carefully unpicked the GH. She went so far as to search for the Turkey-red marking-thread to put in the new initials; but it was all used, – and she had no heart to send for any more just yet. So she looked fixedly at vacancy; a series of visions passing before her, in all of which her son was the principal, the sole object, – her son, her pride, her property. Still he did not come. Doubtless he was with Miss Hale. The new love was displacing her already from her place as first in his heart. A terrible pain – a pang of vain jealousy – shot through her: she hardly knew whether it was more physical or mental; but it forced her to sit down. In a moment, she was up again as straight as ever, – a grim smile upon her face for the first time that day, ready for the door opening, and the rejoicing triumphant one, who should never know the sore regret his mother felt at his marriage. In all this, there was little thought enough of the future daughter-in-law as an individual. She was to be John's wife. To take Mrs Thornton's place as mistress of the house, was only one of the rich consequences which decked out the supreme glory; all household plenty and comfort, all purple and fine linen, honour, love, obedience, troops of friends, would all come as naturally as jewels on a king's robe, and be as little thought of for their separate value. To be chosen by John, would separate a kitchen-wench from the rest of the world. And Miss Hale was not so bad. If she had been a Milton lass, Mrs Thornton would have positively liked her. She was pungent, and had taste, and spirit, and flavour in her. True, she was sadly prejudiced, and very ignorant; but that was to be expected from her southern breeding. A strange sort of mortified comparison of Fanny with her, went on in Mrs Thornton's mind; and for once she spoke harshly to her daughter; abused her roundly; and then, as if by way of penance, she took up Henry's Commentaries, and tried to fix her attention on it, instead of pursuing the employment she took pride and pleasure in, and continuing her inspection of the table-linen.

His step at last! She heard him, even while she thought she was finishing a sentence; while her eye did pass over it, and her memory could mechanically have repeated it word for word, she heard him come in at the hall-door. Her quickened sense could interpret every sound of motion: now he was at the hat-stand – now at the very room-door. Why did he pause? Let her know the worst.

Yet her head was down over the book; she did not look up. He came close to the table, and stood still there, waiting till she should have finished the paragraph which apparently absorbed her. By an effort she looked up. 'Well, John?'

He knew what that little speech meant. But he had steeled himself. He longed to reply with a jest; the bitterness of his heart could have uttered one, but his mother deserved better of him. He came round behind her, so that she could not see his looks, and, bending back her gray, stony face, he kissed it, murmuring:

'No one loves me, – no one cares for me, but you, mother.'

He turned away and stood leaning his head against the mantel-piece, tears forcing themselves into his manly eyes. She stood up, – she tottered. For the first time in her life, the strong woman tottered. She put her hands on his shoulders; she was a tall woman. She looked into his face; she made him look at her.

'Mother's love is given by God, John. It holds fast for ever and ever. A girl's love is like a puff of smoke, – it changes with every wind. And she would not have you, my own lad, would not she?' She set her teeth; she showed them like a dog for the whole length of her mouth. He shook his head.

'I am not fit for her, mother; I knew I was not.'

She ground out words between her closed teeth. He could not hear what she said; but the look in her eyes interpreted it to be a curse, – if not as coarsely worded, as fell in intent as ever was uttered. And yet her heart leapt up light, to know he was her own again.

'Mother!' said he, hurriedly, 'I cannot hear a word against her. Spare me, – spare me! I am very weak in my sore heart; – I love her yet; I love her more than ever.'

'And I hate her,' said Mrs Thornton, in a low fierce voice. 'I tried not to hate her, when she stood between you and me, because, – I said to myself, – she will make him happy; and I would give my heart's blood to do that. But now, I hate her for your misery's sake. Yes, John, it's no use hiding up your aching heart from me. I am the mother that bore you, and your sorrow is my agony; and if you don't hate her, I do.'

'Then, mother, you make me love her more. She is unjustly treated by you, and I must make the balance even. But why do we talk of love or hatred? She does not care for me, and that is enough, – too much. Let us never name the subject again. It is the only thing you can do for me in the matter. Let us never name her.'

'With all my heart. I only wish that she, and all belonging to her, were swept back to the place they came from.'

He stood still, gazing into the fire for a minute or two longer. Her dry dim eyes filled with unwonted tears as she looked at him; but she seemed just as grim and quiet as usual when he next spoke.

'Warrants are out against three men for conspiracy, mother. The riot yesterday helped to knock up the strike.'

And Margaret's name was no more mentioned between Mrs Thornton and her son. They fell back into their usual mode of talk, – about facts, not opinions, far less feelings. Their voices and tones were calm and cold; a stranger might have gone away and thought that he had never seen such frigid indifference of demeanour between such near relations.

CHAPTER XXVII

Fruit-piece

For never any thing can be amiss[1]
When simpleness and duty tender it.
MIDSUMMER NIGHT'S DREAM

Mr Thornton went straight and clear into all the interests of the
following day. There was a slight demand for finished goods; and as
it affected his branch of the trade, he took advantage of it, and drove
hard bargains. He was sharp to the hour at the meeting of his
brother magistrates, – giving them the best assistance of his strong
sense, and his power of seeing consequences at a glance, and so
coming to a·rapid decision. Older men, men of long standing in the
town, men of far greater wealth – realized and turned into land,
while his was all floating capital, engaged in his trade – looked to
him for prompt, ready wisdom. He was the one deputed to see and
arrange with the police – to lead in all the requisite steps. And he
cared for their unconscious deference no more than for the soft west
wind, that scarcely made the smoke from the great tall chimneys
swerve in its straight upward course. He was not aware of the silent
respect paid to him. If it had been otherwise, he would have felt it as
an obstacle in his progress to the object he had in view. As it was, he
looked to the speedy accomplishment of that alone. It was his
mother's greedy ears that sucked in, from the womenkind of these
magistrates and wealthy men, how highly Mr This or Mr That
thought of Mr Thornton; that if he had not been there, things would
have gone on very differently, – very badly, indeed. He swept off his
business right and left that day. It seemed as though his deep
mortification of yesterday, and the stunned purposeless course of the
hours afterwards, had cleared away all the mists from his intellect.
He felt his power and revelled in it. He could almost defy his heart.
If he had known it, he could have sang the song of the miller[2] who
lived by the river Dee: –

I care for nobody –
Nobody cares for me.

The evidence against Boucher, and other ring-leaders of the riot, was taken before him; that against the three others, for conspiracy, failed. But he sternly charged the police to be on the watch; for the swift right arm of the law should be in readiness to strike, as soon as they could prove a fault. And then he left the hot reeking room in the borough court, and went out into the fresher, but still sultry street. It seemed as though he gave way all at once; he was so languid that he could not control his thoughts; they would wander to her; they would bring back the scene, – not of his repulse and rejection the day before, but the looks, the actions of the day before that. He went along the crowded streets mechanically, winding in and out among the people, but never seeing them, – almost sick with longing for that one half-hour – that one brief space of time when she clung to him, and her heart beat against his – to come once again.

'Why, Mr Thornton! you're cutting me very coolly, I must say. And how is Mrs Thornton? Brave weather this! We doctors don't like it, I can tell you!'

'I beg your pardon, Dr Donaldson. I really didn't see you. My mother's quite well, thank you. It is a fine day, and good for the harvest, I hope. If the wheat is well got in, we shall have a brisk trade next year, whatever you doctors have.'

'Ay, ay. Each man for himself. Your bad weather, and your bad times, are my good ones. When trade is bad, there's more undermining of health, and preparation for death, going on among you Milton men than you're aware of.'

'Not with me, Doctor. I'm made of iron. The news of the worst bad debt I ever had, never made my pulse vary. This strike, which affects me more than any one else in Milton, – more than Hamper, – never comes near my appetite. You must go elsewhere for a patient, Doctor.'

'By the way, you've recommended me a good patient, poor lady! Not to go on talking in this heartless way, I seriously believe that Mrs Hale – that lady in Crampton, you know – hasn't many weeks to live. I never had any hope of cure, as I think I told you; but I've been seeing her today, and I think very badly of her.'

Mr Thornton was silent. The vaunted steadiness of pulse failed him for an instant.

'Can I do anything, Doctor?' he asked, in an altered voice. 'You know – you would see, that money is not very plentiful; are there any comforts or dainties she ought to have?'

'No,' replied the Doctor, shaking his head. 'She craves for fruit, – she has a constant fever on her; but jargonelle pears will do as well as anything, and there are quantities of them in the market.'

'You will tell me, if there is anything I can do, I'm sure,' replied Mr Thornton. 'I rely upon you.'

'Oh! never fear! I'll not spare your purse, – I know it's deep enough. I wish you'd give me carte-blanche for all my patients, and all their wants.'

But Mr Thornton had no general benevolence,[3] – no universal philanthropy; few even would have given him credit for strong affections. But he went straight to the first fruit-shop in Milton, and chose out the bunch of purple grapes with the most delicate bloom upon them, – the richest-coloured peaches, – the freshest vine-leaves. They were packed into a basket, and the shopman awaited the answer to his inquiry, 'Where shall we send them to, sir?'

There was no reply. 'To Marlborough Mills, I suppose, sir?'

'No!' Mr Thornton said. 'Give the basket to me, – I'll take it.'

It took up both his hands to carry it; and he had to pass through the busiest part of the town for feminine shopping. Many a young lady of his acquaintance turned to look after him, and thought it strange to see him occupied just like a porter or an errand-boy.

He was thinking, 'I will not be daunted from doing as I choose by the thought of her. I like to take this fruit to the poor mother, and it is simply right that I should. She shall never scorn me out of doing what I please. A pretty joke, indeed, if, for fear of a haughty girl, I failed in doing a kindness to a man I liked! I do it for Mr Hale; I do it in defiance of her.'

He went at an unusual pace, and was soon at Crampton. He went upstairs two steps at a time, and entered the drawing-room before Dixon could announce him, – his face flushed, his eyes shining with kindly earnestness. Mrs Hale lay on the sofa, heated with fever. Mr Hale was reading aloud. Margaret was working on a low stool by her mother's side. Her heart fluttered, if his did not, at this interview. But he took no notice of her, – hardly of Mr Hale himself; he went up straight with his basket to Mrs Hale, and said, in that subdued and gentle tone, which is so touching when used by a robust man in full health, speaking to a feeble invalid, –

'I met Dr Donaldson, ma'am, and as he said fruit would be good for you, I have taken the liberty – the great liberty – of bringing you some that seemed to me fine.' Mrs Hale was excessively surprised;

excessively pleased; quite in a tremble of eagerness. Mr Hale with fewer words expressed a deeper gratitude.

'Fetch a plate, Margaret – a basket – anything.' Margaret stood up by the table, half afraid of moving or making any noise to arouse Mr Thornton into a consciousness of her being in the room. She thought it would be so awkward for both to be brought into conscious collision; and fancied that, from her being on a low seat at first, and now standing behind her father, he had overlooked her in his haste. As if he did not feel the consciousness of her presence all over, though his eyes had never rested on her!

'I must go,' said he, 'I cannot stay. If you will forgive this liberty, – my rough ways, – too abrupt, I fear – but I will be more gentle next time. You will allow me the pleasure of bringing you some fruit again, if I should see any that is tempting. Good afternoon, Mr Hale. Good-bye, ma'am.'

He was gone. Not one word: not one look to Margaret. She believed that he had not seen her. She went for a plate in silence, and lifted the fruit out tenderly, with the points of her delicate taper fingers. It was good of him to bring it; and after yesterday too!

'Oh! it is so delicious!' said Mrs Hale, in a feeble voice. 'How kind of him to think of me! Margaret love, only taste these grapes! Was it not good of him?'

'Yes!' said Margaret, quietly.

'Margaret!' said Mrs Hale, rather querulously, 'you won't like anything Mr Thornton does. I never saw anybody so prejudiced.'

Mr Hale had been peeling a peach for his wife; and, cutting off a small piece for himself, he said –

'If I had any prejudices, the gift of such delicious fruit as this would melt them all away. I have not tasted such fruit – no! not even in Hampshire – since I was a boy; and to boys, I fancy, all fruit is good. I remember eating sloes and crabs with a relish. Do you remember the matted-up currant bushes, Margaret, at the corner of the west-wall in the garden at home?'

Did she not? Did she not remember every weather-stain on the old-stone wall; the grey and yellow lichens that marked it like a map; the little crane's-bill that grew in the crevices? She had been shaken by the events of the last two days; her whole life just now was a strain upon her fortitude; and, somehow, these careless words of her father's, touching on the remembrance of the sunny times of old, made her start up, and, dropping her sewing on the ground, she went hastily out of the room into her own little chamber. She had hardly given way to the first choking sob, when she became aware of Dixon standing at her drawers, and evidently searching for something.

'Bless me, miss! How you startled me! Missus is not worse, is she? Is anything the matter?'

'No, nothing. Only I'm silly, Dixon, and want a glass of water. What are you looking for? I keep my muslins in that drawer.'

Dixon did not speak, but went on rummaging. The scent of lavender came out and perfumed the room.

At last Dixon found what she wanted; what it was Margaret could not see. Dixon faced round, and spoke to her:

'Now, I don't like telling you what I wanted, because you've fretting enough to go through, and I know you'll fret about this. I meant to have kept it from you till night, may be, or such times as that.'

'What is the matter? Pray tell me, Dixon, at once.'

'That young woman you go to see – Higgins, I mean.'

'Well?'

'Well! she died this morning, and her sister is here – come to beg a strange thing. It seems, the young woman who died had a fancy for being buried in something of yours, and so the sister's come to ask for it, – and I was looking for a night-cap that wasn't too good to give away.'

'Oh! let me find one,' said Margaret, in the midst of her tears. 'Poor Bessy! I never thought I should not see her again.'

'Why, that's another thing. This girl down-stairs wanted me to ask you, if you would like to see her.'

'But she's dead!' said Margaret, turning a little pale. 'I never saw a dead person. No! I would rather not.'

'I should never have asked you, if you hadn't come in. I told her you wouldn't.'

'I will go down and speak to her,' said Margaret, afraid lest Dixon's harshness of manner might wound the poor girl. So, taking the cap in her hand, she went to the kitchen. Mary's face was all swollen with crying, and she burst out afresh when she saw Margaret.

'Oh, ma'am, she loved yo', she loved yo', she did indeed!' And for a long time, Margaret could not get her to say anything more than this. At last, her sympathy, and Dixon's scolding, forced out a few facts. Nicholas Higgins had gone out in the morning, leaving Bessy as well as on the day before. But in an hour she was taken worse; some neighbour ran to the room where Mary was working; they did not know where to find her father; Mary had only come in a few minutes before she died.

'It were a day or two ago she axed to be buried in somewhat o' yourn. She were never tired o' talking o' yo'. She used to say yo' were the prettiest thing she'd ever clapped eyes on. She loved yo' dearly. Her last words were, "Give her my affectionate respects; and keep father fro' drink." Yo'll come and see her, ma'am. She would ha' thought it a great compliment, I know.'

Margaret shrank a little from answering.

'Yes, perhaps I may. Yes, I will. I'll come before tea. But where's your father, Mary?'

Mary shook her head, and stood up to be going.

'Miss Hale,' said Dixon, in a low voice, 'where's the use o' your going to see the poor thing laid out? I'd never say a word against it, if it could do the girl any good; and I wouldn't mind a bit going myself, if that would satisfy her. They've just a notion, these common folks, of its being a respect to the departed. Here,' said she, turning sharply round, 'I'll come and see your sister. Miss Hale is busy, and she can't come, or else she would.'

The girl looked wistfully at Margaret. Dixon's coming might be a compliment, but it was not the same thing to the poor sister, who had had her little pangs of jealousy, during Bessy's lifetime, at the intimacy between her and the young lady.

'No, Dixon!' said Margaret with decision. 'I will go. Mary, you shall see me this afternoon.' And for fear of her own cowardice, she went away, in order to take from herself any chance of changing her determination.

CHAPTER XXVIII

Comfort in Sorrow

Through cross to crown! – And though thy spirit's life[1]
Trials untold assail with giant strength,
Good cheer! good cheer! Soon ends the bitter strife,
And thou shalt reign in peace with Christ at length.

ROSEGARTEN

Ay sooth, we feel too strong in weal, to need Thee on that road;[2]
But woe being come, the soul is dumb, that crieth not on 'God'.

MRS BROWNING

That afternoon she walked swiftly to the Higgins's house. Mary was looking out for her, with a half-distrustful face. Margaret smiled into her eyes to re-assure her. They passed quickly through the house-place, upstairs, and into the quiet presence of the dead. Then Margaret was glad that she had come. The face, often so weary with pain, so restless with troublous thoughts, had now the faint soft smile of eternal rest upon it. The slow tears gathered into Margaret's eyes, but a deep calm entered into her soul. And that was death! It looked more peaceful than life. All beautiful scriptures[3] came into her mind. 'They rest from their labours.' 'The weary are at rest.' 'He giveth His beloved sleep.'

Slowly, slowly Margaret turned away from the bed. Mary was humbly sobbing in the back-ground. They went down stairs without a word.

Resting his hand upon the house-table, Nicholas Higgins stood in the midst of the floor; his great eyes startled open by the news he had heard, as he came along the court, from many busy tongues. His eyes were dry and fierce; studying the reality of her death; bringing himself to understand that her place should know her no more. For she had been sickly, dying so long, that he had persuaded himself she would not die; that she would 'pull through.'

Margaret felt as if she had no business to be there, familiarly acquainting herself with the surroundings of death which he, the father, had only just learnt. There had been a pause of an instant on the steep crooked stair, when she first saw him; but now she tried to steal past his abstracted gaze, and to leave him in the solemn circle of his household misery.

215

Mary sat down on the first chair she came to, and throwing her apron over her head, began to cry.

The noise appeared to rouse him. He took sudden hold of Margaret's arm, and held her till he could gather words to speak. His throat seemed dry; they came up thick, and choked, and hoarse:

'Were yo' with her? Did yo' see her die?'

'No!' replied Margaret, standing still with the utmost patience, now she found herself perceived. It was some time before he spoke again, but he kept his hold on her arm.

'All men must die,' said he at last, with a strange sort of gravity, which first suggested to Margaret the idea that he had been drinking – not enough to intoxicate himself, but enough to make his thoughts bewildered. 'But she were younger than me.' Still he pondered over the event, not looking at Margaret, though he grasped her tight. Suddenly, he looked up at her with a wild searching inquiry in his glance. 'Yo're sure and certain she's dead – not in a dwam, a faint? – she's been so before, often.'

'She is dead,' replied Margaret. She felt no fear in speaking to him, though he hurt her arm with his gripe, and wild gleams came across the stupidity of his eyes.

'She is dead!' she said.

He looked at her still with that searching look, which seemed to fade out of his eyes as he gazed. Then he suddenly let go his hold of Margaret, and, throwing his body half across the table, he shook it and every piece of furniture in the room, with his violent sobs. Mary came trembling towards him.

'Get thee gone! – get thee gone!' he cried striking wildly and blindly at her. 'What do I care for thee?' Margaret took her hand, and held it softly in hers. He tore his hair, he beat his head against the hard wood, then he lay exhausted and stupid. Still his daughter and Margaret did not move. Mary trembled from head to foot.

At last – it might have been a quarter of an hour, it might have been an hour – he lifted himself up. His eyes were swollen and bloodshot, and he seemed to have forgotten that any one was by; he scowled at the watchers when he saw them. He shook himself heavily, gave them one more sullen look, spoke never a word, but made for the door.

'Oh, father, father!' said Mary, throwing herself upon his arm, – 'not tonight! Any night but tonight. Oh, help me! he's going out to drink again! Father, I'll not leave yo'. Yo' may strike, but I'll not leave yo'. She told me last of all to keep yo' fro' drink!'

But Margaret stood in the doorway, silent yet commanding. He looked up at her defyingly.

'It's my own house. Stand out o' the way, wench, or I'll make yo'!' He had shaken off Mary with violence; he looked ready to strike Margaret. But she never moved a feature – never took her deep, serious eyes off him. He stared back on her with gloomy fierceness. If she had stirred hand or foot, he would have thrust her aside with even more violence than he had used to his own daughter, whose face was bleeding from her fall against a chair.

'What are yo' looking at me in that way for?' asked he at last, daunted and awed by her severe calm. 'If yo' think for to keep me from going what gait I choose, because she loved yo' – and in my own house, too, where I never asked yo' to come, yo're mista'en. It's very hard upon a man that he can't go to the only comfort left.'

Margaret felt that he acknowledged her power. What could she do next? He had seated himself on a chair, close to the door; half-conquered, half-resenting; intending to go out as soon as she left her position, but unwilling to use the violence he had threatened not five minutes before. Margaret laid her hand on his arm.

'Come with me,' she said. 'Come and see her!'

The voice in which she spoke was very low and solemn; but there was no fear or doubt expressed in it, either of him or of his compliance. He sullenly rose up. He stood uncertain, with dogged irresolution upon his face. She waited him there; quietly and patiently waited for his time to move. He had a strange pleasure in making her wait; but at last he moved towards the stairs.

She and he stood by the corpse.

'Her last words to Mary were, "Keep my father fro' drink."'

'It canna hurt her now,' muttered he. 'Nought can hurt her now.' Then, raising his voice to a wailing cry, he went on: 'We may quarrel and fall out – we may make peace and be friends – we may clem to skin and bone – and nought o' all our griefs will ever touch her more. Hoo's had her portion on 'em. What wi' hard work first, and sickness at last, hoo's led the life of a dog. And to die without knowing one good piece o' rejoicing in all her days! Nay, wench, whatever hoo said, hoo can know nought about it now, and I mun ha' a sup o' drink just to steady me again sorrow.'

'No,' said Margaret, softening with his softened manner. 'You shall not. If her life has been what you say, at any rate she did not fear death as some do. Oh, you should have heard her speak of the life to come – the life hidden with God, that she is now gone to.'

He shook his head, glancing sideways up at Margaret as he did so. His pale, haggard face struck her painfully.

'You are sorely tired. Where have you been all day – not at work?'

'Not at work, sure enough,' said he, with a short, grim laugh. 'Not at what you call work. I were at the Committee, till I were sickened out wi' trying to make fools hear reason. I were fetched to Boucher's wife afore seven this morning. She's bed-fast, but she were raving and raging to know where her dunder-headed brute of a chap was, as if I'd to keep him – as if he were fit to be ruled by me. The d–d fool, who has put his foot in all our plans! And I've walked my feet sore wi' going about for to see men who wouldn't be seen, now the law is raised again us. And I were sore-hearted, too, which is worse than sore-footed; and if I did see a friend who ossed to treat me, I never knew hoo lay a-dying here. Bess, lass, thou'd believe me, thou wouldst – wouldstn't thou?' turning to the poor dumb form with wild appeal.

'I am sure,' said Margaret, 'I am sure you did not know: it was quite sudden. But now, you see, it would be different; you do know; you do see her lying there; you hear what she said with her last breath. You will not go?'

No answer. In fact, where was he to look for comfort?

'Come home with me,' said she at last, with a bold venture, half trembling at her own proposal as she made it. 'At least you shall have some comfortable food, which I'm sure you need.'

'Yo'r father's a parson?' asked he, with a sudden turn in his ideas.

'He was,' said Margaret, shortly.

'I'll go and take a dish o' tea with him, since yo've asked me. I've many a thing I often wished to say to a parson, and I'm not particular as to whether he's preaching now, or not.'

Margaret was perplexed; his drinking tea with her father, who would be totally unprepared for his visitor – her mother so ill – seemed utterly out of the question; and yet if she drew back now, it would be worse than ever – sure to drive him to the gin-shop. She thought that if she could only get him to their own house, it was so great a step gained that she would trust to the chapter of accidents for the next.

'Goodbye, ou'd wench! We've parted company at last, we have! But thou'st been a blessin' to thy father ever sin' thou wert born.

Bless thy white lips, lass, – they've a smile on 'em now! and I'm glad to see it once again, though I'm lone and forlorn for evermore.'

He stooped down and fondly kissed his daughter; covered up her face, and turned to follow Margaret. She had hastily gone down stairs to tell Mary of the arrangement; to say it was the only way she could think of to keep him from the gin-palace;[4] to urge Mary to come too, for her heart smote her at the idea of leaving the poor affectionate girl alone. But Mary had friends among the neighbours, she said, who would come in and sit a bit with her; it was all right; but father –

He was there by them as she would have spoken more. He had shaken off his emotion, as if he was ashamed of having ever given way to it; and had even o'erleaped himself so much that he assumed a sort of bitter mirth, like the crackling of thorns under a pot.

'I'm going to take my tea wi' her father, I am!'

But he slouched his cap low down over his brow as he went out into the street, and looked neither to the right nor to the left, while he tramped along by Margaret's side; he feared being upset by the words, still more the looks, of sympathizing neighbours. So he and Margaret walked in silence.

As he got near the street in which he knew she lived, he looked down at his clothes, his hands, and shoes.

'I should m'appen ha' cleaned mysel', first?'

It certainly would have been desirable, but Margaret assured him he should be allowed to go into the yard, and have soap and towel provided; she could not let him slip out of her hands just then.

While he followed the house-servant along the passage, and through the kitchen, stepping cautiously on every dark mark in the pattern of the oil-cloth, in order to conceal his dirty foot-prints, Margaret ran upstairs. She met Dixon on the landing.

'How is mamma? – where is papa?'

Missus was tired, and gone into her own room. She had wanted to go to bed, but Dixon had persuaded her to lie down on the sofa, and have her tea brought to her there; it would be better than getting restless by being too long in bed.

So far, so good. But where was Mr Hale? In the drawing-room. Margaret went in half breathless with the hurried story she had to tell. Of course, she told it incompletely; and her father was rather 'taken aback' by the idea of the drunken weaver awaiting him in his quiet study, with whom he was expected to drink tea, and on whose behalf Margaret was anxiously pleading. The meek, kind-hearted Mr Hale would have readily tried to console him in his grief, but, unluckily, the point Margaret dwelt upon most forcibly was the fact of his having been drinking, and her having brought him home with her as a last expedient to keep him from the gin-shop. One little event had come out of another so naturally that Margaret was hardly conscious of what she had done, till she saw the slight look of repugnance on her father's face.

'Oh, papa! he really is a man you will not dislike – if you won't be shocked to begin with.'

'But, Margaret, to bring a drunken man home – and your mother so ill!'

Margaret's countenance fell. 'I am sorry, papa. He is very quiet – he is not tipsy at all. He was only rather strange at first, but that might be the shock of poor Bessy's death.' Margaret's eyes filled with tears. Mr Hale took hold of her sweet pleading face in both his hands, and kissed her forehead.

'It is all right, dear. I'll go and make him as comfortable as I can, and do you attend to your mother. Only, if you can come in and make a third in the study, I shall be glad.'

'Oh, yes – thank you.' But as Mr Hale was leaving the room, she ran after him:

'Papa – you must not wonder at what he says: he's an – I mean he does not believe in much of what we do.'

'Oh dear! a drunken infidel weaver!' said Mr Hale to himself, in dismay. But to Margaret he only said, 'If your mother goes to sleep, be sure you come directly.'

Margaret went into her mother's room. Mrs Hale lifted herself up from a doze.

'When did you write to Frederick, Margaret? Yesterday, or the day before?'

'Yesterday, mamma.'

'Yesterday. And the letter went?'

'Yes. I took it myself.'

'Oh, Margaret, I'm so afraid of his coming! If he should be recognized! If he should be taken! If he should be executed, after all these years that he has kept away and lived in safety! I keep falling asleep and dreaming that he is caught and being tried.'

'Oh, mamma, don't be afraid. There will be some risk no doubt; but we will lessen it as much as ever we can. And it is so little! Now, if we were at Helstone, there would be twenty – a hundred times as much. There, everybody would remember him; and if there was a stranger known to be in the house, they would be sure to guess it was Frederick; while here, nobody knows or cares for us enough to notice what we do. Dixon will keep the door like a dragon – won't you, Dixon – while he is here?'

'They'll be clever if they come in past me!' said Dixon, showing her teeth at the bare idea.

'And he need not go out, except in the dusk, poor fellow!'

'Poor fellow!' echoed Mrs Hale. 'But I almost wish you had not written. Would it be too late to stop him if you wrote again, Margaret?'

'I'm afraid it would, mamma,' said Margaret, remembering the urgency with which she had entreated him to come directly, if he wished to see his mother alive.

'I always dislike that doing things in such a hurry,' said Mrs Hale.

Margaret was silent.

'Come now, ma'am,' said Dixon, with a kind of cheerful authority, 'you know seeing Master Frederick is just the very thing of all others you're longing for. And I'm glad Miss Margaret wrote off straight, without shilly-shallying. I've had a great mind to do it myself. And we'll keep him snug, depend upon it. There's only Martha in the house that would not do a good deal to save him on a pinch; and I've been thinking she might go and see her mother just at that very time. She's been saying once or twice she should like to go, for her mother has had a stroke since she came here; only she didn't like to ask. But I'll see about her being safe off, as soon as we know when he comes, God bless him! So take your tea, ma'am, in comfort, and trust to me.'

Mrs Hale did trust in Dixon more than in Margaret. Dixon's words quieted her for the time. Margaret poured out the tea in silence, trying to think of something agreeable to say; but her thoughts made answer something like Daniel O'Rourke,[5] when the man-in-the-moon asked him to get off his reaping-hook. 'The more you ax us, the more we won't stir.' The more she tried to think of something – anything besides the danger to which Frederick would be exposed – the more closely her imagination clung to the unfortunate idea presented to her. Her mother prattled with Dixon, and seemed to have utterly forgotten the possibility of Frederick being tried and executed – utterly forgotten that at her wish, if by

Margaret's deed, he was summoned into this danger. Her mother was one of those who throw out terrible possibilities, miserable probabilities, unfortunate chances of all kinds, as a rocket throws out sparks; but if the sparks light on some combustible matter, they smoulder first, and burst out into a frightful flame at last. Margaret was glad when, her filial duties gently and carefully performed, she could go down into the study. She wondered how her father and Higgins had got on.

In the first place, the decorous, kind-hearted, simple, old-fashioned gentleman, had unconsciously called out, by his own refinement and courteousness of manner, all the latent courtesy in the other.

Mr Hale treated all his fellow-creatures alike: it never entered into his head to make any difference because of their rank. He placed a chair for Nicholas; stood up till he, at Mr Hale's request, took a seat; and called him, invariably, 'Mr Higgins,' instead of the curt 'Nicholas' or 'Higgins,' to which the 'drunken infidel weaver' had been accustomed. But Nicholas was neither an habitual drunkard nor a thorough infidel. He drank to drown care, as he would have himself expressed it: and he was infidel so far as he had never yet found any form of faith to which he could attach himself, heart and soul.

Margaret was a little surprised, and very much pleased, when she found her father and Higgins in earnest conversation – each speaking with gentle politeness to the other, however their opinions might clash. Nicholas – clean, tidied (if only at the pump-trough), and quiet spoken – was a new creature to her, who had only seen him in the rough independence of his own hearthstone. He had 'slicked' his hair down with the fresh water; he had adjusted his neck-handkerchief, and borrowed an odd candle-end to polish his clogs with; and there he sat, enforcing some opinion on her father, with a strong Darkshire accent, it is true, but with a lowered voice, and a good, earnest composure on his face. Her father, too, was interested in what his companion was saying. He looked round as she came in, smiled, and quietly gave her his chair, and then sat down afresh as quickly as possible, and with a little bow of apology to his guest for the interruption. Higgins nodded to her as a sign of greeting; and she softly adjusted her working materials on the table, and prepared to listen.

'As I was a-sayin, sir, I reckon yo'd not ha' much belief in yo' if yo' lived here, – if yo'd been bred here. I ax your pardon if I use wrong words; but what I mean by belief just now, is a-thinking on sayings and maxims and promises made by folk yo' never saw, about the things and the life yo' never saw, nor no one else. Now, yo' say these are true things, and true sayings, and a true life. I just say, where's the proof? There's many and many a one wiser, and scores better learned than I am around me, – folk who've had time to think on these things, – while my time has had to be gi'en up to getting my bread. Well, I sees these people. Their lives is pretty much open to me. They're real folk. They don't believe i' the Bible, – not they. They may say they do, for form's sake; but Lord, sir, d'ye think their first cry i' th' morning is, "What shall I do to get hold on eternal life?"[6] or "What shall I do to fill my purse this blessed day? Where shall I go? What bargains shall I strike?" The purse and the gold and the notes is real things; things as can be felt and touched; them's realities; and eternal life is all a talk, very fit for – I ax your pardon, sir; yo'r a parson out o' work, I believe. Well! I'll never speak disrespectful of a man in the same fix as I'm in mysel'. But I'll just ax yo' another question, sir, and I dunnot want yo' to answer it, only to put in yo'r pipe, and smoke it, afore yo' go for to set down us, who only believe in what we see, as fools and noddies. If salvation, and life to come, and what not, was true – not in men's words, but in men's hearts' core – dun yo' not think they'd din us wi' it as they do wi' political 'conomy? There're mighty anxious to come round us wi' that piece o' wisdom; but t'other would be a greater convarsion, if it were true.'

'But the masters have nothing to do with your religion. All that they are connected with you in is trade, – so they think, – and all that it concerns them, therefore, to rectify your opinions in is the science of trade.'

'I'm glad, sir,' said Higgins, with a curious wink of his eye, 'that yo' put in, "so they think." I'd ha' thought yo' a hypocrite, I'm afeard, if yo' hadn't, for all yo'r a parson, or rayther because yo'r a parson. Yo' see, if yo'd spoken o' religion as a thing that, if it was true, it didn't concern all men to press on all men's attention, above everything else in this 'varsal earth, I should ha' thought yo' a knave for to be a parson; and I'd rather think yo' a fool than a knave. No offence, I hope, sir.'

'None at all. You consider me mistaken, and I consider you far more fatally mistaken. I don't expect to convince you in a day, – not in one conversation; but let us know each other, and speak freely to each other about these things, and the truth will prevail. I should not believe in God if I did not believe that. Mr Higgins, I trust, whatever else you have given up, you believe' – (Mr Hale's voice dropped low in reverence) – 'you believe in Him.'

Nicholas Higgins suddenly stood straight, stiff up. Margaret started to her feet, – for she thought, by the working of his face, he was going into convulsions. Mr Hale looked at her dismayed. At last Higgins found words:

'Man! I could fell yo' to the ground for tempting me. Whatten business have yo' to try me wi' your doubts? Think o' her lying theere, after the life hoo's led; and think then how yo'd deny me the one sole comfort left – that there is a God, and that He set her her life. I dunnot believe she'll ever live again,' said he, sitting down, and drearily going on, as if to the unsympathizing fire. 'I dunnot believe in any other life than this, in which she dreed such trouble, and had such never-ending care; and I cannot bear to think it were all a set o' chances, that might ha' been altered wi' a breath o' wind. There's many a time when I've thought I didna believe in God, but I've never put it fair out before me in words, as many men do. I may ha' laughed at those who did, to brave it out like – but I have looked round at after, to see if He heard me, if so be there was a He; but today, when I'm left desolate, I wunnot listen to yo' wi' yo'r questions, and yo'r doubts. There's but one thing steady and quiet i' all this reeling world, and, reason or no reason, I'll cling to that. It's a' very well for happy folk' –

Margaret touched his arm very softly. She had not spoken before, nor had he heard her rise.

'Nicholas, we do not want to reason; you misunderstand my father. We do not reason – we believe; and so do you. It is the one sole comfort in such times.'

He turned round and caught her hand. 'Ay! it is, it is' – (brushing away the tears with the back of his hand). – 'But yo' know, she's lying dead at home; and I'm welly dazed wi' sorrow, and at times I hardly know what I'm saying. It's as if speeches folk ha' made – clever and smart things as I've thought at the time – come up now my heart's welly brossen. Th' strike's failed as well; dun yo' know that, miss? I were coming whoam to ask her, like a beggar as I am, for a bit o' comfort i' that trouble; and I were knocked down by one who told me she were dead – just dead. That were all; but that were enough for me.'

Mr Hale blew his nose, and got up to snuff the candles in order to conceal his emotion. 'He's not an infidel, Margaret; how could you say so?' muttered he reproachfully. 'I've a good mind to read him the fourteenth chapter of Job.'[7]

'Not yet, papa, I think. Perhaps not at all. Let us ask him about the strike, and give him all the sympathy he needs, and hoped to have from poor Bessy.'

So they questioned and listened. The workmen's calculations were based (like too many of the masters') on false premises. They reckoned on their fellow-men as if they possessed the calculable powers of machines, no more, no less; no allowance for human passions getting the better of reason, as in the case of Boucher and the rioters; and believing that the representations of their injuries would have the same effect on strangers far away, as the injuries (fancied or real) had upon themselves. They were consequently surprised and indignant at the poor Irish, who had allowed themselves to be imported and brought over to take their places. This indignation was tempered, in some degree, by contempt for 'them Irishers,' and by pleasure at the idea of the bungling way in which they would set to work, and perplex their new masters with their ignorance and stupidity, strange exaggerated stories of which were already spreading through the town. But the most cruel cut of all was that of the Milton workmen, who had defied and disobeyed the commands of the Union to keep the peace, whatever came; who had originated discord in the camp, and spread the panic of the law being arrayed against them.

'And so the strike is at an end,' said Margaret.

'Ay, miss. It's save as save can. Th' factory doors will need open wide tomorrow to let in all who'll be axing for work; if it's only just to show they'd nought to do wi' a measure, which if we'd been made o' th' right stuff would ha' brought wages up to a point they'n not been at this ten year.'

'You'll get work, shan't you?' asked Margaret. 'You're a famous workman, are not you?'

'Hamper'll let me work at his mill, when he cuts off his right hand – not before, and not after,' said Nicholas, quietly. Margaret was silenced and sad.

'About the wages,' said Mr Hale. 'You'll not be offended, but I think you made some sad mistakes. I should like to read you some remarks in a book I have.' He got up and went to his book-shelves.

'Yo' needn't trouble yoursel', sir,' said Nicholas. 'Their book-stuff goes in at one ear and out at t'other. I can make nought on't. Afore

Hamper and me had this split, th' overlooker telled him I were
stirring up the men to ask for higher wages; and Hamper met me one
day in th' yard. He'd a thin book i' his hand, and says he, "Higgins,
I'm told you're one of those damned fools that think you can get
higher wages for asking for 'em; ay, and keep 'em up too, when
you've forced 'em up. Now, I'll give yo' a chance and try if yo've
any sense in yo'. Here's a book written by a friend o' mine, and if
yo'll read it yo'll see how wages find their own level,[8] without either
masters or men having aught to do with them; except the men cut
their own throats wi' striking, like the confounded noodles they are."
Well, now, sir, I put it to yo', being a parson, and having been in th'
preaching line, and having had to try and bring folk o'er to what yo'
thought was a right way o' thinking – did yo' begin by calling 'em
fools and such like, or didn't yo' rayther give 'em some kind words at
first, to make 'em ready for to listen and be convinced, if they could;
and in yo'r preaching, did yo' stop every now and then, and say, half
to them and half to yo'rsel', "But yo're such a pack o' fools, that I've
a strong notion it's no use my trying to put sense into yo'?" I were
not i' th' best state, I'll own, for taking in what Hamper's friend had
to say – I were so vexed at the way it were put to me; – but I
thought, "Come, I'll see what these chaps has got to say, and try if
it's them or me as is th' noodle." So I took th' book and tugged at it;
but, Lord bless yo', it went on about capital and labour, and labour
and capital, till it fair sent me off to sleep. I ne'er could rightly fix i'
my mind which was which; and it spoke on 'em as if they was
vartues or vices; and what I wanted for to know were the rights o'
men, whether they were rich or poor – so be they only were men.'

'But for all that,' said Mr Hale, 'and granting to the full the
offensiveness, the folly, the unchristianness of Mr Hamper's way of
speaking to you in recommending his friend's book, yet if it told you
what he said it did, that wages find their own level, and that the
most successful strike can only force them up for a moment, to sink in
far greater proportion afterwards, in consequence of that very strike,
the book would have told you the truth.'

'Well, sir,' said Higgins, rather doggedly; 'it might, or it might
not. There's two opinions go to settling that point. But suppose it
was truth double strong, it were no truth to me if I couldna take it
in. I daresay there's truth in yon Latin book on your shelves; but it's
gibberish and not truth to me, unless I know the meaning o' the
words. If yo', sir, or any other knowledgeable, patient man come to

me, and says he'll larn me what the words mean, and not blow me up if I'm a bit stupid, or forget how one thing hangs on another – why, in time I may get to see the truth of it; or I may not. I'll not be bound to say I shall end in thinking the same as any man. And I'm not one who think truth can be shaped out in words, all neat and clean, as th' men at th' foundry cut out sheet-iron. Same bones won't go down wi' every one. It'll stick here i' this man's throat, and there i' t'other's. Let alone that, when down, it may be too strong for this one, too weak for that. Folk who sets up to doctor th' world wi' their truth, mun suit different for different minds; and be a bit tender in th' way of giving it too, or th' poor sick fools may spit it out i' their faces. Now Hamper first gi'es me a box on my ear, and then he throws his big bolus at me, and says he reckons it'll do me no good, I'm such a fool, but there it is.'

'I wish some of the kindest and wisest of the masters would meet some of you men, and have a good talk on these things; it would, surely, be the best way of getting over your difficulties, which, I do believe, arise from your ignorance – excuse me, Mr Higgins – on subjects which it is for the mutual interest of both masters and men should be well understood by both. I wonder' – (half to his daughter), 'if Mr Thornton might not be induced to do such a thing?'

'Remember, papa,' said she in a very low voice, 'what he said one day – about governments, you know.' She was unwilling to make any clearer allusion to the conversation they had held on the mode of governing work-people – by giving men intelligence enough to rule themselves, or by a wise despotism on the part of the master – for she saw that Higgins had caught Mr Thornton's name, if not the whole of the speech: indeed, he began to speak of him.

'Thornton! He's the chap as wrote off at once for these Irishers; and led to th' riot that ruined th' strike. Even Hamper wi' all his bullying, would ha' waited a while – but it's a word and a blow wi' Thornton. And, now, when th' Union would ha' thanked him for following up th' chase after Boucher, and them chaps as went right again our commands, it's Thornton who steps forrard and coolly says that, as th' strike's at an end, he, as party injured, doesn't want to press the charge again the rioters. I thought he'd had more pluck. I thought he'd ha' carried his point, and had his revenge in an open way; but says he (one in court told me his very words) "they are well known; they will find the natural punishment of their conduct, in the difficulty they will meet wi' in getting employment. That will be severe enough." I only wish they'd cotched Boucher, and had him up before Hamper. I see th' oud tiger setting on him! would he ha' let him off? Not he!'

'Mr Thornton was right,' said Margaret. 'You are angry against Boucher, Nicholas; or else you would be the first to see, that where the natural punishment would be severe enough for the offence, any farther punishment would be something like revenge.'

'My daughter is no great friend of Mr Thornton's,' said Mr Hale, smiling at Margaret; while she, as red as any carnation, began to work with double diligence, 'but I believe what she says is the truth. I like him for it.'

'Well, sir, this strike has been a weary piece of business to me; and yo'll not wonder if I'm a bit put out wi' seeing it fail, just for a few men who would na suffer in silence, and hou'd out, brave and firm.'

'You forget!' said Margaret. 'I don't know much of Boucher; but the only time I saw him it was not his own sufferings he spoke of, but those of his sick wife – his little children.'

'True! but he were not made of iron himsel'. He'd ha' cried out for his own sorrows, next. He were not one to bear.'

'How came he into the Union?' asked Margaret innocently. 'You don't seem to have much respect for him; nor gained much good from having him in.'

Higgins's brow clouded. He was silent for a minute or two. Then he said, shortly enough:

'It's not for me to speak o' th' Union. What they does, they does. Them that is of a trade mun hang together; and if they're not willing to take their chance along wi' th' rest, th' Union has ways and means.'

Mr Hale saw that Higgins was vexed at the turn the conversation had taken, and was silent. Not so Margaret, though she saw Higgins's feeling as clearly as he did. By instinct she felt, that if he could but be brought to express himself in plain words, something clear would be gained on which to argue for the right and the just.

'And what are the Union's ways and means?'

He looked up at her, as if on the point of dogged resistance to her wish for information. But her calm face, fixed on his, patient and trustful, compelled him to answer.

'Well! If a man doesn't belong to th' Union, them as works next looms has orders not to speak to him – if he's sorry or ill it's a' the same; he's out o' bounds; he's none o' us; he comes among us, he works among us, but he's none o' us. I' some places them's fined who speaks to him.[9] Yo' try that, miss; try living a year or two among them as looks away if yo' look at 'em; try working within two yards o' crowds o' men, who, yo' know, have a grinding grudge at yo' in their hearts – to whom if yo' say yo'r glad, not an eye brightens, nor a lip moves, – to whom if your heart's heavy, yo' can never say nought, because they'll ne'er take notice on your sighs or sad looks (and a man's no man who'll groan out loud 'bout folk asking him what's the matter?) – just yo' try that, miss – ten hours for three hundred days, and yo'll know a bit what th' Union is.'

'Why!' said Margaret, 'what tyranny this is! Nay, Higgins, I don't care one straw for your anger. I know you can't be angry with me if you would, and I must tell you the truth: that I never read, in all the history I have read, of a more slow, lingering torture than this. And you belong to the Union! And you talk of the tyranny of the masters!'

'Nay,' said Higgins, 'yo' may say what yo' like! The dead stand between yo' and every angry word o' mine. D' ye think I forget who's lying *there*, and how hoo loved yo'? And it's th' masters as has made us sin, if th' Union is a sin. Not this generation maybe, but their fathers. Their fathers ground our fathers to the very dust; ground us to powder! Parson! I reckon, I've heerd my mother read out a text, "The fathers have eaten sour grapes and th' children's teeth are set on edge."[10] It's so wi' them. In those days of sore oppression th' Unions began; it were a necessity. It's a necessity now, according to me. It's a withstanding of injustice, past, present, or to come. It may be like war; along wi' it come crimes; but I think it were a greater crime to let it alone. Our only chance is binding men together in one common interest; and if some are cowards and some are fools, they mun come along and join the great march, whose only strength is in numbers.'

'Oh!' said Mr Hale, sighing, 'your Union in itself would be beautiful, glorious, – it would be Christianity itself – if it were but for an end which affected the good of all, instead of that of merely one class as opposed to another.'

'I reckon it's time for me to be going, sir,' said Higgins, as the clock struck ten.

'Home?' said Margaret very softly. He understood her, and took her offered hand. 'Home, miss. Yo' may trust me, tho' I am one o' th' Union.'

'I do trust you most thoroughly, Nicholas.'

'Stay!' said Mr Hale, hurrying to the bookshelves. 'Mr Higgins! I'm sure you'll join us in family prayer?'

Higgins looked at Margaret, doubtfully. Her grave sweet eyes met his; there was no compulsion, only deep interest in them. He did not speak, but he kept his place.

Margaret the Churchwoman, her father the Dissenter, Higgins the Infidel, knelt down together. It did them no harm.

CHAPTER XXIX

A Ray of Sunshine

Some wishes crossed my mind and dimly cheered it,[1]
And one or two poor melancholy pleasures,
Each in the pale unwarming light of hope,
Silvering its flimsy wing, flew silent by –
Moths in the moonbeam!

COLERIDGE

The next morning brought Margaret a letter from Edith. It was affectionate and inconsequent like the writer. But the affection was charming to Margaret's own affectionate nature; and she had grown up with the inconsequence, so she did not perceive it. It was as follows: –

'Oh, Margaret, it is worth a journey from England to see my boy! He is a superb little fellow, especially in his caps, and most especially in the one you sent him, you good, dainty-fingered, persevering little lady! Having made all the mothers here envious, I want to show him to somebody new, and hear a fresh set of admiring expressions; perhaps, that's all the reason; perhaps it is not, – nay, possibly, there is just a little cousinly love mixed with it; but I do want you so much to come here, Margaret! I'm sure it would be the very best thing for Aunt Hale's health; everybody here is young and well, and our skies are always blue, and our sun always shines, and the band plays deliciously from morning till night; and, to come back to the burden of my ditty, my baby always smiles. I am constantly wanting you to draw him for me, Margaret. It does not signify what he is doing; that

very thing is prettiest, gracefulest, best. I think I love him a great deal
better than my husband, who is getting stout and grumpy, – what he
calls "busy." No! he is not. He has just come in with news of such a
charming pic-nic, given by the officers of the Hazard, at anchor in the
bay below. Because he has brought in such a pleasant piece of news, I
retract all I said just now. Did not somebody burn his hand[2] for
having said or done something he was sorry for? Well, I can't burn
mine, because it would hurt me, and the scar would be ugly; but I'll
retract all I said as fast as I can. Cosmo is quite as great a darling as
baby, and not a bit stout, and as ungrumpy as ever husband was;
only, sometimes he is very, very busy. I may say that without leze-
wifely duty – where was I? – I had something very particular to say, I
know, once. Oh, it is this – Dearest Margaret! – you must come and
see me; it would do Aunt Hale good, as I said before. Get the doctor
to order it for her. Tell him that it's the smoke of Milton that does her
harm. I have no doubt it is that, really. Three months (you must not
come for less) of this delicious climate – all sunshine, and grapes as
common as blackberries, would quite cure her. I don't ask my uncle'
– (Here the letter became more constrained, and better written; Mr
Hale was in the corner, like a naughty child, for having given up his
living.) – 'because, I dare say, he disapproves of war, and soldiers,
and bands of music; at least, I know that many Dissenters are
members of the Peace Society,[3] and I am afraid he would not like to
come; but, if he would, dear, pray say that Cosmo[4] and I will do our
best to make him happy; and I'll hide up Cosmo's red coat and
sword, and make the band play all sorts of grave, solemn things; or, if
they do play pomps and vanities, it shall be in double slow time. Dear
Margaret, if he would like to accompany you and Aunt Hale, we will
try and make it pleasant, though I'm rather afraid of any one who
has done something for conscience' sake. You never did, I hope. Tell
Aunt Hale not to bring many warm clothes, though I'm afraid it will
be late in the year before you can come. But you have no idea of the
heat here! I tried to wear my great beauty Indian shawl at a picnic. I
kept myself up with proverbs as long as I could; "Pride must abide,"
– and such wholesome pieces of pith; but it was of no use. I was like
mamma's little dog Tiny with an elephant's trappings on – smothered,
hidden, killed with my finery; so I made it into a capital carpet for us
all to sit down upon. Here's this boy of mine, Margaret, – if you don't
pack up your things as soon as you get this letter, and come straight
off to see him, I shall think you're descended from King Herod!'[5]

Margaret did long for a day of Edith's life – her freedom from care, her cheerful home, her sunny skies. If a wish could have transported her, she would have gone off; just for one day. She yearned for the strength which such a change would give, – even for a few hours to be in the midst of that bright life, and to feel young again. Not yet twenty! and she had had to bear up against such hard pressure that she felt quite old. That was her first feeling after reading Edith's letter. Then she read it again, and, forgetting herself, was amused at its likeness to Edith's self, and was laughing merrily over it when Mrs Hale came into the drawing-room, leaning on Dixon's arm. Margaret flew to adjust the pillows. Her mother seemed more than usually feeble.

'What were you laughing at, Margaret?' asked she, as soon as she had recovered from the exertion of settling herself on the sofa.

'A letter I have had this morning from Edith. Shall I read it you, mamma?'

She read it aloud, and for a time it seemed to interest her mother, who kept wondering what name Edith had given to her boy, and suggesting all probable names, and all possible reasons why each and all of these names should be given. Into the very midst of these wonders Mr Thornton came, bringing another offering of fruit for Mrs Hale. He could not – say rather, he would not – deny himself the chance of the pleasure of seeing Margaret. He had no end in this but the present gratification. It was the sturdy wilfulness of a man usually most reasonable and self-controlled. He entered the room, taking in at a glance the fact of Margaret's presence; but after the first cold distant bow, he never seemed to let his eyes fall on her again. He only stayed to present his peaches – to speak some gentle kindly words – and then his cold offended eyes met Margaret's with a grave farewell, as he left the room. She sat down silent and pale.

'Do you know, Margaret, I really begin quite to like Mr Thornton.'

No answer at first. Then Margaret forced out an icy 'Do you?'

'Yes! I think he is really getting quite polished in his manners.'

Margaret's voice was more in order now. She replied,

'He is very kind and attentive, – there is no doubt of that.'

'I wonder Mrs Thornton never calls. She must know I am ill, because of the water-bed.'

'I dare say she hears how you are from her son.'

'Still, I should like to see her. You have so few friends here, Margaret.'

Margaret felt what was in her mother's thoughts, – a tender craving to bespeak the kindness of some woman towards the daughter that might be so soon left motherless. But she could not speak.

'Do you think,' said Mrs Hale, after a pause, 'that you could go and ask Mrs Thornton to come and see me? Only once, – I don't want to be troublesome.'

'I will do anything, if you wish it, mamma, – but if – but when Frederick comes –'

'Ah, to be sure! we must keep our doors shut, – we must let no one in. I hardly know whether I dare wish him to come or not. Sometimes I think I would rather not. Sometimes I have such frightful dreams about him.'

'Oh, mamma! we'll take good care. I will put my arm in the bolt[6] sooner than he should come to the slightest harm. Trust the care of him to me, mamma. I will watch over him like a lioness over her young.'

'When can we hear from him?'

'Not for a week yet, certainly, – perhaps more.'

'We must send Martha away in good time. It would never do to have her here when he comes, and then send her off in a hurry.'

'Dixon is sure to remind us of that. I was thinking that, if we wanted any help in the house while he is here, we could perhaps get Mary Higgins. She is very slack of work, and is a good girl, and would take pains to do her best, I am sure, and would sleep at home, and need never come upstairs, so as to know who is in the house.'

'As you please. As Dixon pleases. But, Margaret, don't get to use these horrid Milton words.[7] "Slack of work:" it is a provincialism. What will your aunt Shaw say, if she hears you use it on her return?'

'Oh, mamma! don't try and make a bugbear of aunt Shaw,' said Margaret, laughing. 'Edith picked up all sorts of military slang[8] from Captain Lennox, and aunt Shaw never took any notice of it.'

'But yours is factory slang.'

'And if I live in a factory town, I must speak factory language when I want it. Why, mamma, I could astonish you with a great many words you never heard in your life. I don't believe you know what a knobstick is.'

'Not I, child. I only know it has a very vulgar sound; and I don't want to hear you using it.'

'Very well, dearest mother, I won't. Only I shall have to use a whole explanatory sentence instead.'

'I don't like this Milton,' said Mrs Hale. 'Edith is right enough in saying it's the smoke that has made me so ill.'

Margaret started up as her mother said this. Her father had just entered the room, and she was most anxious that the faint impression she had seen on his mind that the Milton air had injured her mother's health, should not be deepened, – should not receive any confirmation. She could not tell whether he had heard what Mrs Hale had said or not; but she began speaking hurriedly of other things, unaware that Mr Thornton was following him.

'Mamma is accusing me of having picked up a great deal of vulgarity since we came to Milton.'

The 'vulgarity' Margaret spoke of, referred purely to the use of local words, and the expression arose out of the conversation they had just been holding. But Mr Thornton's brow darkened; and Margaret suddenly felt how her speech might be misunderstood by him; so, in the natural sweet desire to avoid giving unnecessary pain, she forced herself to go forwards with a little greeting, and continue what she was saying, addressing herself to him expressly.

'Now, Mr Thornton, though "knobstick" has not a very pretty sound, is it not expressive? Could I do without it, in speaking of the thing it represents? If using local words is vulgar, I was very vulgar in the Forest,[9] – was I not, mamma?'

It was unusual with Margaret to obtrude her own subject of conversation on others; but, in this case, she was so anxious to prevent Mr Thornton from feeling annoyance at the words he had accidentally overheard, that it was not until she had done speaking that she coloured all over with consciousness, more especially as Mr Thornton seemed hardly to understand the exact gist or bearing of what she was saying, but passed her by, with a cold reserve of ceremonious movement, to speak to Mrs Hale.

The sight of him reminded her of the wish to see his mother, and commend Margaret to her care. Margaret, sitting in burning silence, vexed and ashamed of her difficulty in keeping her right place, and her calm unconsciousness of heart, when Mr Thornton was by, heard her mother's slow entreaty that Mrs Thornton would come and see her; see her soon; tomorrow, if it were possible. Mr Thornton promised that she should – conversed a little, and then took his leave; and Margaret's movements and voice seemed at once released from some invisible chains. He never looked at her; and yet, the careful avoidance of his eyes betokened that in some way he knew exactly where, if they fell by chance, they would rest on her. If she spoke, he gave no sign of attention, and yet his next speech to any one else was modified by what she had said; sometimes there was an express answer to what she had remarked, but given to another person as though unsuggested by her. It was not the bad manners of ignorance: it was the wilful bad manners arising from deep offence. It was wilful at the time; repented of afterwards. But no deep plan, no careful cunning could have stood him in such good stead. Margaret thought about him more than she had ever done before; not with any tinge of what is called love, but with regret that she had wounded him so deeply, – and with a gentle, patient striving to return to their former position of antagonistic friendship; for a friend's position was what she found that he had held in her regard, as well as in that of the rest of the family. There was a pretty humility in her behaviour to him, as if mutely apologizing for the over-strong words which were the reaction from the deeds of the day of the riot.

But he resented those words bitterly. They rung in his ears; and he was proud of the sense of justice which made him go on in every kindness he could offer to her parents. He exulted in the power he showed in compelling himself to face her, whenever he could think of any action which might give her father or mother pleasure. He thought that he disliked seeing one who had mortified him so keenly; but he was mistaken. It was a stinging pleasure to be in the room with her, and feel her presence. But he was no great analyser of his own motives, and was mistaken, as I have said.

CHAPTER XXX

Home at Last

The saddest birds a season find to sing.[1]
SOUTHWELL

Never to fold the robe o'er secret pain,[2]
Never, weighed down by memory's clouds again,
To bow thy head! Thou art gone home!
MRS HEMANS

Mrs Thornton came to see Mrs Hale the next morning. She was much worse. One of those sudden changes – those great visible strides towards death, had been taken in the night, and her own family were startled by the gray sunken look her features had assumed in that one twelve hours of suffering. Mrs Thornton – who had not seen her for weeks – was softened all at once. She had come because her son asked it from her as a personal favour, but with all the proud bitter feelings of her nature in arms against that family of which Margaret formed one. She doubted the reality of Mrs Hale's illness; she doubted any want beyond a momentary fancy on that lady's part, which should take her out of her previously settled course of employment for the day. She told her son that she wished they had never come near the place; that he had never got acquainted with them; that there had been no such useless languages as Latin and Greek ever invented. He bore all this pretty silently; but when she had ended her invective against the dead languages, he quietly returned to the short, curt, decided expression of his wish that she should go and see Mrs Hale at the time appointed, as most likely to be convenient to the invalid. Mrs Thornton submitted with as bad a grace as she could to her son's desire, all the time liking him the better for having it; and exaggerating in her own mind the same notion that he had of extraordinary goodness on his part in so perseveringly keeping up with the Hales.

His goodness verging on weakness (as all the softer virtues did in her mind), and her own contempt for Mr and Mrs Hale, and positive dislike to Margaret, were the ideas which occupied Mrs Thornton, till she was struck into nothingness before the dark shadow of the wings of the angel of death. There lay Mrs Hale – a mother like herself – a much younger woman than she was, – on the bed from which there was no sign of hope that she might ever rise again. No more variety of light and shade for her in that darkened room; no power of action, scarcely change of movement; faint alternations of whispered sound and studious silence; and yet that monotonous life seemed almost too much! When Mrs Thornton, strong and prosperous with life, came in, Mrs Hale lay still, although from the look on her face she was evidently conscious of who it was. But she did not even open her eyes for a minute or two. The heavy moisture of tears stood on the eyelashes before she looked up; then with her hand groping feebly over the bed-clothes, for the touch of Mrs Thornton's large firm fingers, she said, scarcely above her breath – Mrs Thornton had to stoop from her erectness to listen, –

'Margaret – you have a daughter – my sister is in Italy. My child will be without a mother; – in a strange place, – if I die – will you' –[3]

And her filmy wandering eyes fixed themselves with an intensity of wistfulness on Mrs Thornton's face. For a minute, there was no change in its rigidness; it was stern and unmoved; – nay, but that the eyes of the sick woman were growing dim with the slow-gathering tears, she might have seen a dark cloud cross the cold features. And it was no thought of her son, or of her living daughter Fanny, that stirred her heart at last; but a sudden remembrance, suggested by something in the arrangement of the room, – of a little daughter – dead in infancy – long years ago – that, like a sudden sunbeam, melted the icy crust, behind which there was a real tender woman.

'You wish me to be a friend to Miss Hale,' said Mrs Thornton, in her measured voice, that would not soften with her heart, but came out distinct and clear.

Mrs Hale, her eyes still fixed on Mrs Thornton's face, pressed the hand that lay below hers on the coverlet. She could not speak. Mrs Thornton sighed, 'I will be a true friend, if circumstances require it. Not a tender friend. That I cannot be,' – ('to her,' she was on the point of adding, but she relented at the sight of that poor, anxious face.) – 'It is not my nature to show affection even where I feel it, nor do I volunteer advice in general. Still, at your request, – if it will be any comfort to you, I will promise you.' Then came a pause. Mrs Thornton was too conscientious to promise what she did not mean to perform; and to perform anything in the way of kindness on behalf of Margaret, more disliked at this moment than ever, was difficult; almost impossible.

'I promise,' said she, with grave severity; which, after all, inspired the dying woman with faith as in something more stable than life itself, – flickering, flitting, wavering life! 'I promise that in any difficulty in which Miss Hale' –

'Call her Margaret!' gasped Mrs Hale.

'In which she comes to me for help, I will help her with every power I have, as if she were my own daughter. I also promise that if ever I see her doing what I think is wrong' –

'But Margaret never does wrong – not wilfully wrong,' pleaded Mrs Hale. Mrs Thornton went on as before; as if she had not heard:

'If ever I see her doing what I believe to be wrong – such wrong not touching me or mine, in which case I might be supposed to have an interested motive – I will tell her of it, faithfully and plainly, as I should wish my own daughter to be told.'

There was a long pause. Mrs Hale felt that this promise did not

include all; and yet it was much. It had reservations in it which she
did not understand; but then she was weak, dizzy, and tired. Mrs
Thornton was reviewing all the probable cases in which she had
pledged herself to act. She had a fierce pleasure in the idea of telling
Margaret unwelcome truths, in the shape of performance of duty.
Mrs Hale began to speak:

'I thank you. I pray God to bless you. I shall never see you again
in this world. But my last words are, I thank you for your promise of
kindness to my child.'

'Not kindness!' testified Mrs Thornton, ungraciously truthful to
the last. But having eased her conscience by saying these words, she
was not sorry that they were not heard. She pressed Mrs Hale's soft
languid hand; and rose up and went her way out of the house
without seeing a creature.

During the time that Mrs Thornton was having this interview
with Mrs Hale, Margaret and Dixon were laying their heads together, and consulting how they should keep Frederick's coming a
profound secret to all out of the house. A letter from him might now
be expected any day; and he would assuredly follow quickly on its
heels. Martha must be sent away on her holiday; Dixon must keep
stern guard on the front door, only admitting the few visitors that
ever came to the house into Mr Hale's room down-stairs – Mrs
Hale's extreme illness giving her a good excuse for this. If Mary
Higgins was required as a help to Dixon in the kitchen, she was to
hear and see as little of Frederick as possible; and he was, if necessary,
to be spoken of to her under the name of Mr Dickinson. But her
sluggish and incurious nature was the greatest safeguard of all.

They resolved that Martha should leave them that very afternoon
for this visit to her mother. Margaret wished that she had been sent
away on the previous day, as she fancied it might be thought strange
to give a servant a holiday when her mistress's state required so
much attendance.

Poor Margaret! All that afternoon she had to act the part of a
Roman daughter,[4] and give strength out of her own scanty stock to
her father. Mr Hale would hope, would not despair, between the
attacks of his wife's malady; he buoyed himself up in every respite
from her pain, and believed that it was the beginning of ultimate
recovery. And so, when the paroxysms came on, each more severe
than the last, they were fresh agonies, and greater disappointments
to him. This afternoon, he sat in the drawing-room, unable to bear

the solitude of his study, or to employ himself in any way. He buried his head in his arms, which lay folded on the table. Margaret's heart ached to see him; yet, as he did not speak, she did not like to volunteer any attempt at comfort. Martha was gone. Dixon sat with Mrs Hale while she slept. The house was very still and quiet, and darkness came on, without any movement to procure candles. Margaret sat at the window, looking out at the lamps and the street, but seeing nothing, – only alive to her father's heavy sighs. She did not like to go down for lights, lest the tacit restraint of her presence being withdrawn, he might give way to more violent emotion, without her being at hand to comfort him. Yet she was just thinking that she ought to go and see after the well-doing of the kitchen fire, which there was nobody but herself to attend to, when she heard the muffled door-bell ring with so violent a pull, that the wires jingled all through the house, though the positive sound was not great. She started up, passed her father, who had never moved at the veiled, dull sound, – returned, and kissed him tenderly. And still he never moved, nor took any notice of her fond embrace. Then she went down softly, through the dark, to the door. Dixon would have put the chain on before she opened it, but Margaret had not a thought of fear in her pre-occupied mind. A man's tall figure stood between her and the luminous street. He was looking away; but at the sound of the latch he turned quickly round.

'Is this Mr Hale's?' said he, in a clear, full, delicate voice.

Margaret trembled all over; at first she did not answer. In a moment she sighed out,

'Frederick!' and stretched out both her hands to catch his, and draw him in.

'Oh, Margaret!' said he, holding her off by her shoulders, after they had kissed each other, as if even in that darkness he could see her face, and read in its expression a quicker answer to his question than words could give, –

'My mother! is she alive?'

'Yes, she is alive, dear, dear brother! She – as ill as she can be she is; but alive! She is alive!'

'Thank God!' said he.

'Papa is utterly prostrate with this great grief.'

'You expect me, don't you?'

'No, we have had no letter.'

'Then I have come before it. But my mother knows I am coming?'

'Oh! we all knew you would come. But wait a little! Step in here. Give me your hand. What is this? Oh! your carpet-bag. Dixon has shut the shutters; but this is papa's study, and I can take you to a chair to rest yourself for a few minutes; while I go and tell him.'

She groped her way to the taper and the lucifer matches. She suddenly felt shy, when the little feeble light made them visible. All she could see was, that her brother's face was unusually dark in complexion, and she caught the stealthy look of a pair of remarkably long-cut blue eyes, that suddenly twinkled up with a droll consciousness of their mutual purpose of inspecting each other. But though the brother and sister had an instant of sympathy in their reciprocal glances, they did not exchange a word; only, Margaret felt sure that she should like her brother as a companion as much as she already loved him as a near relation. Her heart was wonderfully lighter as she went up-stairs; the sorrow was no less in reality, but it became less oppressive from having some one in precisely the same relation to it as that in which she stood. Not her father's desponding attitude had power to damp her now. He lay across the table, helpless as ever; but she had the spell by which to rouse him. She used it perhaps too violently in her own great relief.

'Papa,' said she, throwing her arms fondly round his neck; pulling his weary head up in fact with her gentle violence, till it rested in her arms, and she could look into his eyes, and let them gain strength and assurance from hers.

'Papa! guess who is here!'

He looked at her; she saw the idea of the truth glimmer into their filmy sadness, and be dismissed thence as a wild imagination.

He threw himself forward, and hid his face once more in his stretched-out arms, resting upon the table as heretofore. She heard him whisper; she bent tenderly down to listen. 'I don't know. Don't tell me it is Frederick – not Frederick. I cannot bear it, – I am too weak. And his mother is dying!'

He began to cry and wail like a child. It was so different to all which Margaret had hoped and expected, that she turned sick with disappointment, and was silent for an instant. Then she spoke again – very differently – not so exultingly, far more tenderly and carefully.

'Papa, it is Frederick! Think of mamma, how glad she will be! And oh, for her sake, how glad we ought to be! For his sake, too, – our poor, poor boy!'

Her father did not change his attitude, but he seemed to be trying to understand the fact.

'Where is he?' asked he at last, his face still hidden in his prostrate arms.

'In your study, quite alone. I lighted the taper, and ran up to tell you. He is quite alone, and will be wondering why –'

'I will go to him,' broke in her father; and he lifted himself up and leant on her arm as on that of a guide.

Margaret led him to the study door, but her spirits were so agitated that she felt she could not bear to see the meeting. She turned away, and ran upstairs, and cried most heartily. It was the first time she had dared to allow herself this relief for days. The strain had been terrible, as she now felt. But Frederick was come! He, the one precious brother, was there, safe, amongst them again! She could hardly believe it. She stopped her crying, and opened her bedroom door. She heard no sound of voices, and almost feared she might have dreamt. She went down-stairs, and listened at the study door. She heard the buzz of voices; and that was enough. She went into the kitchen, and stirred up the fire, and lighted the house, and prepared for the wanderer's refreshment. How fortunate it was that her mother slept! She knew that she did, from the candle-lighter thrust through the keyhole of her bedroom door. The traveller could be refreshed and bright, and the first excitement of the meeting with his father all be over, before her mother became aware of anything unusual.

When all was ready, Margaret opened the study door, and went in like a serving-maiden, with a heavy tray held in her extended arms. She was proud of serving Frederick. But he, when he saw her, sprang up in a minute, and relieved her of her burden. It was a type, a sign, of all the coming relief which his presence would bring. The brother and sister arranged the table together, saying little, but their hands touching, and their eyes speaking the natural language of expression, so intelligible to those of the same blood. The fire had gone out; and Margaret applied herself to light it, for the evenings had begun to be chilly: and yet it was desirable to make all noises as distant as possible from Mrs Hale's room.

'Dixon says it is a gift to light a fire; not an art to be acquired.'

'Poeta nascitur, non fit,'[5] murmured Mr Hale; and Margaret was glad to hear a quotation once more, however languidly given.

'Dear old Dixon! How we shall kiss each other!' said Frederick. 'She used to kiss me, and then look in my face to be sure I was the right person, and then set to again! But, Margaret, what a bungler you are! I never saw such a little awkward, good-for-nothing pair of hands. Run away, and wash them, ready to cut bread-and-butter for me, and leave the fire. I'll manage it. Lighting fires is one of my natural accomplishments.'

So Margaret went away; and returned; and passed in and out of the room, in a glad restlessness that could not be satisfied with sitting still. The more wants Frederick had, the better she was pleased; and he understood all this by instinct. It was a joy snatched in the house of mourning, and the zest of it was all the more pungent, because they knew in the depths of their hearts what irremediable sorrow awaited them.

In the middle, they heard Dixon's foot on the stairs. Mr Hale started from his languid posture in his great arm-chair, from which he had been watching his children in a dreamy way, as if they were acting some drama of happiness, which it was pretty to look at, but which was distinct from reality, and in which he had no part. He stood up, and faced the door, showing such a strange, sudden anxiety to conceal Frederick from the sight of any person entering, even though it were the faithful Dixon, that a shiver came over Margaret's heart: it reminded her of the new fear in their lives. She caught at Frederick's arm, and clutched it tight, while a stern thought compressed her brows, and caused her to set her teeth. And yet they knew it was only Dixon's measured tread. They heard her walk the length of the passage, – into the kitchen. Margaret rose up.

'I will go to her, and tell her. And I shall hear how mamma is.' Mrs Hale was awake. She rambled at first; but after they had given her some tea she was refreshed, though not disposed to talk. It was better that the night should pass over before she was told of her son's arrival. Dr Donaldson's appointed visit would bring nervous excitement enough for the evening; and he might tell them how to prepare her for seeing Frederick. He was there, in the house; could be summoned at any moment.

Margaret could not sit still. It was a relief to her to aid Dixon in all her preparations for 'Master Frederick.' It seemed as though she never could be tired again. Each glimpse into the room where he sate by his father, conversing with him, about, she knew not what, nor cared to know, – was increase of strength to her. Her own time for talking and hearing would come at last, and she was too certain of this to feel in a hurry to grasp it now. She took in his appearance and liked it. He had delicate features, redeemed from effeminacy by the swarthiness of his complexion, and his quick intensity of expression. His eyes were generally merry-looking, but at times they and his mouth so suddenly changed, and gave her such an idea of latent passion, that it almost made her afraid. But this look was only for an instant; and had in it no doggedness, no vindictiveness; it was rather the instantaneous ferocity of expression that comes over the countenances of all natives of wild or southern countries – a ferocity which enhances the charm of the childlike softness into which such a look may melt away. Margaret might fear the violence of the impulsive nature thus occasionally betrayed, but there was nothing in it to make her distrust, or recoil in the least, from the new-found brother. On the contrary, all their intercourse was peculiarly charming to her from the very first. She knew then how much responsibility she had had to bear, from the exquisite sensation of relief which she felt in Frederick's presence. He understood his father and mother – their characters and their weaknesses, and went along with a careless freedom, which was yet most delicately careful not to hurt or wound any of their feelings. He seemed to know instinctively when a little of the natural brilliancy of his manner and conversation would not jar on the deep depression of his father, or might relieve his mother's pain. Whenever it would have been out of tune, and out of time, his patient devotion and watchfulness came into play, and made him an admirable nurse. Then Margaret was almost touched into tears by the allusions which he often made to their childish days in the New Forest; he had never forgotten her – or Helstone either – all the time he had been roaming among distant countries and foreign people. She might talk to him of the old spot,. and never fear tiring him. She had been afraid of him before he came, even while she had longed for his coming; seven or eight years had, she felt, produced such great changes in herself that, forgetting how much of the original Margaret was left, she had reasoned that if her tastes and feelings had so materially altered, even in her stay-at-home life, his wild career, with which she was but imperfectly acquainted, must have almost substituted another Frederick for the tall stripling in his middy's uniform, whom she remembered looking up to with such admiring awe. But in their absence they had grown nearer to each other in age, as well as in many other things. And so it was that the weight, this sorrowful time, was lightened to Margaret. Other light than that of Frederick's presence she had none. For a few hours, the mother rallied on seeing her son. She sate with his hand in hers; she

243

would not part with it even while she slept; and Margaret had to feed him like a baby, rather than that he should disturb her mother by removing a finger. Mrs Hale wakened while they were thus engaged; she slowly moved her head round on the pillow, and smiled at her children, as she understood what they were doing, and why it was done.

'I am very selfish,' said she; 'but it will not be for long.' Frederick bent down and kissed the feeble hand that imprisoned his.

This state of tranquillity could not endure for many days, nor perhaps for many hours; so Dr Donaldson assured Margaret. After the kind doctor had gone away, she stole down to Frederick, who, during the visit, had been adjured to remain quietly concealed in the back parlour, usually Dixon's bedroom, but now given up to him.

Margaret told him what Dr Donaldson said.

'I don't believe it,' he exclaimed. 'She is very ill; she may be dangerously ill, and in immediate danger, too; but I can't imagine that she could be as she is, if she were on the point of death. Margaret! she should have some other advice – some London doctor. Have you never thought of that?'

'Yes,' said Margaret, 'more than once. But I don't believe it would do any good. And, you know, we have not the money to bring any great London surgeon down, and I am sure Dr Donaldson is only second in skill to the very best, – if, indeed, he is to them.'

Frederick began to walk up and down the room impatiently.

'I have credit in Cadiz,' said he, 'but none here, owing to this wretched change of name. Why did my father leave Helstone? That was the blunder.'

'It was no blunder,' said Margaret gloomily. 'And above all possible chances, avoid letting papa hear anything like what you have just been saying. I can see that he is tormenting himself already with the idea that mamma would never have been ill if we had stayed at Helstone, and you don't know papa's agonizing power of self-reproach!'

Frederick walked away as if he were on the quarter-deck. At last he stopped right opposite to Margaret, and looked at her drooping and desponding attitude for an instant.

'My little Margaret!' said he, caressing her. 'Let us hope as long as we can. Poor little woman! what! is this face all wet with tears? I will hope. I will, in spite of a thousand doctors. Bear up, Margaret, and be brave enough to hope!'

Margaret choked in trying to speak, and when she did it was very low.

'I must try to be meek enough to trust. Oh, Frederick! mamma was getting to love me so! And I was getting to understand her. And now comes death to snap us asunder!'

'Come, come, come! Let us go up-stairs, and do something, rather than waste time that may be so precious. Thinking has, many a time, made me sad, darling; but doing never did in all my life. My theory is a sort of parody on the maxim of "Get money, my son, honestly if you can; but get money." My precept is, "Do something, my sister, do good if you can; but, at any rate, do something."'

'Not excluding mischief,' said Margaret, smiling faintly through her tears.

'By no means. What I do exclude is the remorse afterwards. Blot your misdeeds out (if you are particularly conscientious), by a good deed, as soon as you can; just as we did a correct sum at school on the slate, where an incorrect one was only half rubbed out. It was better than wetting our sponge with our tears; both less loss of time where tears had to be waited for, and a better effect at last.'

If Margaret thought Frederick's theory rather a rough one at first, she saw how he worked it out into continual production of kindness in fact. After a bad night with his mother (for he insisted on taking his turn as a sitter-up) he was busy next morning before breakfast, contriving a leg-rest for Dixon, who was beginning to feel the fatigues of watching. At breakfast-time, he interested Mr Hale with vivid, graphic, rattling accounts of the wild life he had led in Mexico, South America, and elsewhere. Margaret would have given up the effort in despair to rouse Mr Hale out of his dejection; it would even have affected herself and rendered her incapable of talking at all. But Fred, true to his theory, did something perpetually; and talking was the only thing to be done, besides eating, at breakfast.

Before the night of that day, Dr Donaldson's opinion was proved to be too well founded. Convulsions came on; and when they ceased, Mrs Hale was unconscious. Her husband might lie by her shaking the bed with his sobs; her son's strong arms might lift her tenderly up into a comfortable position; her daughter's hands might bathe her face; but she knew them not. She would never recognize them again, till they met in Heaven.

Before the morning came all was over.

Then Margaret rose from her trembling and despondency, and became as a strong angel of comfort to her father and brother. For Frederick had broken down now, and all his theories were of no use to him. He cried so violently when shut up alone in his little room at night, that Margaret and Dixon came down in affright to warn him to be quiet: for the house partitions were but thin, and the next-door neighbours might easily hear his youthful passionate sobs, so different from the slower trembling agony of after-life, when we become inured to grief, and dare not be rebellious against the inexorable doom, knowing who it is that decrees.

Margaret sate with her father in the room with the dead. If he had cried, she would have been thankful. But he sate by the bed quite quietly; only, from time to time, he uncovered the face, and stroked it gently, making a kind of soft inarticulate noise, like that of some mother-animal[6] caressing her young. He took no notice of Margaret's presence. Once or twice she came up to kiss him; and he submitted to it, giving her a little push away when she had done, as if her affection disturbed him from his absorption in the dead. He started when he heard Frederick's cries, and shook his head: – 'Poor boy! poor boy!' he said, and took no more notice. Margaret's heart ached within her. She could not think of her own loss in thinking of her father's case. The night was wearing away, and the day was at hand, when, without a word of preparation, Margaret's voice broke upon the stillness of the room, with a clearness of sound that startled even herself: 'Let not your heart be troubled,' it said; and she went steadily on through all that chapter of unspeakable consolation.[7]

CHAPTER XXXI

'Should Auld Acquaintance be Forgot?'

Show not that manner, and these features all,[1]
The serpent's cunning, and the sinner's fall?

CRABBE

The chill, shivery October morning came; not the October morning of the country, with soft, silvery mists, clearing off before the sunbeams that bring out all the gorgeous beauty of colouring, but the October morning of Milton, whose silver mists were heavy fogs, and where the sun could only show long dusky streets when he did break through and shine. Margaret went languidly about, assisting Dixon in her task of arranging the house. Her eyes were continually blinded by tears, but she had no time to give way to regular crying. The father and brother depended upon her; while they were giving way to grief, she must be working, planning, considering. Even the necessary arrangements for the funeral seemed to devolve upon her.

When the fire was bright and crackling – when everything was ready for breakfast, and the tea-kettle was singing away, Margaret gave a last look round the room before going to summon Mr Hale and Frederick. She wanted everything to look as cheerful as possible; and yet, when it did so, the contrast between it and her own thoughts forced her into sudden weeping. She was kneeling by the sofa, hiding her face in the cushions that no one might hear her cry, when she was touched on the shoulder by Dixon.

'Come, Miss Hale – come, my dear! You must not give way, or where shall we all be? There is not another person in the house fit to give a direction of any kind, and there is so much to be done. There's who's to manage the funeral; and who's to come to it; and where it's to be; and all to be settled: and Master Frederick's like one crazed with crying, and master never was a good one for settling; and, poor gentleman, he goes about now as if he was lost. It's bad enough, my dear, I know; but death comes to us all; and you're well off never to have lost any friend till now.'

Perhaps so. But this seemed a loss by itself; not to bear comparison with any other event in the world. Margaret did not take any comfort from what Dixon said, but the unusual tenderness of the prim old servant's manner touched her to the heart; and, more from a desire to show her gratitude for this than for any other reason, she roused herself up, and smiled in answer to Dixon's anxious look at her; and went to tell her father and brother that breakfast was ready.

Mr Hale came – as if in a dream, or rather with the unconscious motion of a sleep-walker, whose eyes and mind perceive other things than what are present. Frederick came briskly in, with a forced cheerfulness, grasped her hand, looked into her eyes, and burst into tears. She had to try and think of little nothings to say all breakfast-time, in order to prevent the recurrence of her companions' thoughts too strongly to the last meal they had taken together, when there had been a continual strained listening for some sound or signal from the sick-room.

After breakfast, she resolved to speak to her father, about the funeral. He shook his head, and assented to all she proposed, though many of her propositions absolutely contradicted one another. Margaret gained no real decision from him; and was leaving the room languidly, to have a consultation with Dixon, when Mr Hale motioned her back to his side.

'Ask Mr Bell,' said he in a hollow voice.

'Mr Bell!' said she, a little surprised. 'Mr Bell of Oxford?'

'Mr Bell,' he repeated. 'Yes. He was my groom's-man.'

Margaret understood the association.

'I will write today,' said she. He sank again into listlessness. All morning she toiled on, longing for rest, but in a continual whirl of melancholy business.

Towards evening, Dixon said to her:

'I've done it, miss. I was really afraid for master, that he'd have a stroke with grief. He's been all this day with poor missus; and when I've listened at the door, I've heard him talking to her, and talking to her, as if she was alive. When I went in he would be quite quiet, but all in a maze like. So I thought to myself, he ought to be roused; and if it gives him a shock at first, it will, maybe, be the better afterwards. So I've been and told him, that I don't think it's safe for Master Frederick to be here. And I don't. It was only on Tuesday, when I was out, that I met a Southampton man – the first I've seen since I came to Milton; they don't make their way much up here, I think. Well, it was young Leonards, old Leonards the draper's son, as great a scamp as ever lived – who plagued his father almost to death, and then ran off to sea. I never could abide him. He was in the Orion at the same time as Master Frederick, I know; though I don't recollect if he was there at the mutiny.'

'Did he know you?' said Margaret, eagerly.

'Why, that's the worst of it. I don't believe he would have known me but for my being such a fool as to call out his name. He were a Southampton man, in a strange place, or else I should never have been so ready to call cousins with him, a nasty, good-for-nothing fellow. Says he, "Miss Dixon! who would ha' thought of seeing you here? But perhaps I mistake, and you're Miss Dixon no longer?" So I told him he might still address me as an unmarried lady, though if I hadn't been so particular, I'd had good chances of matrimony. He was polite enough: "He couldn't look at me and doubt me." But I were not to be caught with such chaff from such a fellow as him, and so I told him; and, by way of being even, I asked him after his father (who I knew had turned him out of doors), as if they was the best friends as ever was. So then, to spite me – for you see we were getting savage, for all we were so civil to each other – he began to inquire after Master Frederick, and said, what a scrape he'd got into (as if Master Frederick's scrapes would ever wash George Leonards' white, or make 'em look otherwise than nasty, dirty black), and how he'd be hung for mutiny if ever he were caught, and how a hundred pound reward had been offered for catching him, and what a disgrace he had been to his family – all to spite me, you see, my dear, because before now I've helped old Mr Leonards to give George a good rating, down in Southampton. So I said, there were other families as I knew, who had far more cause to blush for their sons, and to be thankful if they could think they were earning an honest living far away from home. To which he made answer, like the impudent chap he is, that he were in a confidential situation, and if I knew of any young man who had been so unfortunate as to lead vicious courses, and wanted to turn steady, he'd have no objection to lend him his patronage. He, indeed! Why, he'd corrupt a saint. I've not felt so bad myself for years as when I were standing talking to him the other day. I could have cried to think I couldn't spite him better, for he kept smiling in my face, as if he took all my compliments for earnest; and I couldn't see that he minded what I said in the least, while I was mad with all his speeches.'

'But you did not tell him anything about us – about Frederick?'

'Not I,' said Dixon. 'He had never the grace to ask where I was staying; and I shouldn't have told him if he had asked. Nor did I ask him what his precious situation was. He was waiting for a bus, and just then it drove up, and he hailed it. But, to plague me to the last, he turned back before he got in, and said, "If you can help me to trap Lieutenant Hale, Miss Dixon, we'll go partners in the reward. I know you'd like to be my partner, now wouldn't you? Don't be shy, but say yes." And he jumped on the bus, and I saw his ugly face leering at me with a wicked smile to think how he'd had the last word of plaguing.'

Margaret was made very uncomfortable by this account of Dixon's.

'Have you told Frederick?' asked she.

'No,' said Dixon. 'I were uneasy in my mind at knowing that bad Leonards was in town; but there was so much else to think about that I did not dwell on it at all. But when I saw master sitting so stiff, and with his eyes so glazed and sad, I thought it might rouse him to have to think of Master Frederick's safety a bit. So I told him all, though I blushed to say how a young man had been speaking to me. And it has done master good. And if we're to keep Master Frederick in hiding, he would have to go, poor fellow, before Mr Bell came.'

'Oh, I'm not afraid of Mr Bell; but I am afraid of this Leonards. I must tell Frederick. What did Leonards look like?'

'A bad-looking fellow, I can assure you, miss. Whiskers such as I should be ashamed to wear – they are so red. And for all he said he'd got a confidential situation, he was dressed in fustian just like a working-man.'

It was evident that Frederick must go. Go, too, when he had so completely vaulted into his place in the family, and promised to be such a stay and staff to his father and sister. Go, when his cares for the living mother, and sorrow for the dead, seemed to make him one of those peculiar people who are bound to us by a fellow-love for them that are taken away. Just as Margaret was thinking all this, sitting over the drawing-room fire – her father restless and uneasy under the pressure of this newly-aroused fear, of which he had not as yet spoken – Frederick came in, his brightness dimmed, but the extreme violence of his grief passed away. He came up to Margaret, and kissed her forehead.

'How wan you look, Margaret!' said he in a low voice. 'You have been thinking of everybody, and no one has thought of you. Lie on this sofa – there is nothing for you to do.'

'That is the worst,' said Margaret, in a sad whisper. But she went and lay down, and her brother covered her feet with a shawl, and then sate on the ground by her side; and the two began to talk in a subdued tone.

Margaret told him all that Dixon had related of her interview with young Leonards. Frederick's lips closed with a long whew of dismay.

'I should just like to have it out with that young fellow. A worse sailor was never on board ship – nor a much worse man either. I declare, Margaret – you know the circumstances of the whole affair?'

'Yes, mamma told me.'

'Well, when all the sailors who were good for anything were indignant with our captain, this fellow, to curry favour – pah! And to think of his being here! Oh, if he'd a notion I was within twenty miles of him, he'd ferret me out to pay off old grudges. I'd rather anybody had the hundred pounds they think I am worth than that rascal. What a pity poor old Dixon could not be persuaded to give me up, and make a provision for her old age!'

'Oh, Frederick, hush! Don't talk so.'

Mr Hale came towards them, eager and trembling. He had overheard what they were saying. He took Frederick's hand in both of his:

'My boy, you must go. It is very bad – but I see you must. You have done all you could – you have been a comfort to her.'

'Oh, papa, must he go?' said Margaret, pleading against her own conviction of necessity.

'I declare, I've a good mind to face it out, and stand my trial. If I could only pick up my evidence! I cannot endure the thought of being in the power of such a blackguard as Leonards. I could almost have enjoyed – in other circumstances – this stolen visit: it has had all the charm which the Frenchwoman attributed to forbidden pleasures.'

'One of the earliest things I can remember,' said Margaret, 'was your being in some great disgrace, Fred, for stealing apples. We had plenty of our own – trees loaded with them; but some one had told you that stolen fruit tasted sweetest, which you took au pied de la lettre, and off you went a-robbing. You have not changed your feelings much since then.'

'Yes – you must go,' repeated Mr Hale, answering Margaret's question, which she had asked some time ago. His thoughts were fixed on one subject, and it was an effort to him to follow the zigzag remarks of his children – an effort which he did not make.

Margaret and Frederick looked at each other. That quick momentary sympathy would be theirs no longer if he went away. So much was understood through eyes that could not be put into words. Both coursed the same thought till it was lost in sadness. Frederick shook it off first:

'Do you know, Margaret, I was very nearly giving both Dixon and myself a good fright this afternoon. I was in my bedroom; I had heard a ring at the front door, but I thought the ringer must have done his business and gone away long ago; so I was on the point of making my appearance in the passage, when, as I opened my room door, I saw Dixon coming downstairs; and she frowned and kicked me into hiding again. I kept the door open, and heard a message given to some man that was in my father's study, and that then went away. Who could it have been? Some of the shopmen?'

'Very likely,' said Margaret, indifferently. 'There was a little quiet man who came up for orders about two o'clock.'

'But this was not a little man – a great powerful fellow; and it was past four when he was here.'

'It was Mr Thornton,' said Mr Hale. They were glad to have drawn him into the conversation.

'Mr Thornton!' said Margaret, a little surprised. 'I thought –'

'Well, little one, what did you think?' asked Frederick, as she did not finish her sentence.

'Oh, only,' said she, reddening and looking straight at him, 'I fancied you meant some one of a different class, not a gentleman; somebody come on an errand.'

'He looked like some one of that kind,' said Frederick, carelessly. 'I took him for a shopman, and he turns out a manufacturer.'

Margaret was silent. She remembered how at first, before she knew his character, she had spoken, and thought of him just as Frederick was doing. It was but a natural impression that was made upon him, and yet she was a little annoyed by it. She was unwilling to speak; she wanted to make Frederick understand what kind of person Mr Thornton was – but she was tongue-tied.

Mr Hale went on. 'He came to offer any assistance in his power, I believe. But I could not see him. I told Dixon to ask him if he would like to see you – I think I asked her to find you, and you would go to him. I don't know what I said.'

'He has been a very agreeable acquaintance, has he not?' asked Frederick, throwing the question like a ball for any one to catch who chose.

'A very kind friend,' said Margaret, when her father did not answer.

Frederick was silent for a time. At last he spoke:

'Margaret, it is painful to think I can never thank those who have shown you kindness. Your acquaintances and mine must be separate. Unless, indeed, I run the chances of a court-martial, or unless you and my father would come to Spain.' He threw out this last suggestion as a kind of feeler; and then suddenly made the plunge. 'You don't know how I wish you would. I have a good position – the chance of a better,' continued he, reddening like a girl. 'That Dolores Barbour that I was telling you of, Margaret – I only wish you knew her; I am sure you would like – no, love is the right word, like is so poor – you would love her, father, if you knew her. She is not eighteen; but if she is in the same mind another year, she is to be my wife. Mr Barbour won't let us call it an engagement. But if you would come, you would find friends everywhere, besides Dolores. Think of it, father. Margaret, be on my side.'

'No – no more removals for me,' said Mr Hale. 'One removal has cost me my wife. No more removals in this life. She will be here; and here will I stay out my appointed time.'

'Oh, Frederick,' said Margaret, 'tell us more about her. I never thought of this; but I am so glad. You will have some one to love and care for you out there. Tell us all about it.'

'In the first place, she is a Roman Catholic. That's the only objection I anticipated. But my father's change of opinion – nay, Margaret, don't sigh.'

Margaret had reason to sigh a little more before the conversation ended. Frederick himself was Roman Catholic[2] in fact, though not in profession as yet. This was, then, the reason why his sympathy in her extreme distress at her father's leaving the Church had been so faintly expressed in his letters. She had thought it was the carelessness of a sailor; but the truth was, that even then he was himself inclined to give up the form of religion into which he had been baptized, only that his opinions were tending in exactly the opposite direction to those of his father. How much love had to do with this change not even Frederick himself could have told. Margaret gave up talking about this branch of the subject at last; and, returning to the fact of the engagement, she began to consider it in some fresh light:

'But for her sake, Fred, you surely will try and clear yourself of the exaggerated charges brought against you, even if the charge of mutiny itself be true. If there were to be a court-martial, and you could find your witnesses, you might, at any rate, show how your disobedience to authority was because that authority was unworthily exercised.'

Mr Hale roused himself up to listen to his son's answer.

'In the first place, Margaret, who is to hunt up my witnesses? All of them are sailors, drafted off to other ships, except those whose evidence would go for very little, as they took part, or sympathized in the affair. In the next place, allow me to tell you, you don't know what a court-martial is, and consider it as an assembly where justice is administered, instead of what it really is – a court where authority weighs nine-tenths in the balance, and evidence forms only the other tenth. In such cases, evidence itself can hardly escape being influenced by the prestige of authority.'

'But is it not worth trying, to see how much evidence might be discovered and arrayed on your behalf? At present, all those who knew you formerly, believe you guilty without any shadow of excuse. You have never tried to justify yourself, and we have never known where to seek for proofs of your justification. Now, for Miss Barbour's sake, make your conduct as clear as you can in the eye of the world. She may not care for it; she has, I am sure, that trust in you that we all have; but you ought not to let her ally herself to one under such a serious charge, without showing the world exactly how it is you stand. You disobeyed authority – that was bad; but to have stood by, without word or act, while the authority was brutally used, would have been infinitely worse. People know what you did; but not the motives that elevate it out of a crime into an heroic protection of the weak. For Dolores' sake, they ought to know.'

'But how must I make them know? I am not sufficiently sure of the purity and justice of those who would be my judges, to give myself up to a court-martial, even if I could bring a whole array of truth speaking witnesses. I can't send a bellman about, to cry aloud and proclaim in the streets what you are pleased to call my heroism. No one would read a pamphlet of self-justification so long after the deed, even if I put one out.'

'Will you consult a lawyer as to your chances of exculpation?' asked Margaret, looking up, and turning very red.

'I must first catch my lawyer, and have a look at him, and see how I like him, before I make him into my confidant. Many a briefless barrister might twist his conscience into thinking, that he could earn a hundred pounds very easily by doing a good action – in giving me, a criminal, up to justice.'

'Nonsense, Frederick! – because I know a lawyer on whose honour I can rely; of whose cleverness in his profession people speak very highly; and who would, I think, take a good deal of trouble for any of – of Aunt Shaw's relations. Mr Henry Lennox, papa.'

'I think it is a good idea,' said Mr Hale. 'But don't propose anything which will detain Frederick in England. Don't, for your mother's sake.'

'You could go to London tomorrow evening by a night-train,' continued Margaret, warming up into her plan. 'He must go tomorrow, I'm afraid, papa,' said she, tenderly; 'we fixed that, because of Mr Bell, and Dixon's disagreeable acquaintance.'

'Yes; I must go tomorrow,' said Frederick decidedly.

Mr Hale groaned. 'I can't bear to part with you, and yet I am miserable with anxiety as long as you stop here.'

'Well then,' said Margaret, 'listen to my plan. He gets to London on Friday morning. I will – you might – no! it would be better for me to give him a note to Mr Lennox. You will find him at his chambers in the Temple.'

'I will write down a list of all the names I can remember on board the Orion. I could leave it with him to ferret them out. He is Edith's husband's brother, isn't he? I remember your naming him in your letters. I have money in Barbour's hands. I can pay a pretty long bill, if there is any chance of success. Money, dear father, that I had meant for a different purpose; so I shall only consider it as borrowed from you and Margaret.'

'Don't do that,' said Margaret. 'You won't risk it if you do. And it will be a risk; only it is worth trying. You can sail from London as well as from Liverpool?'

'To be sure, little goose. Wherever I feel water heaving under a plank, there I feel at home. I'll pick up some craft or other to take me off, never fear. I won't stay twenty-four hours in London, away from you on the one hand, and from somebody else on the other.'

It was rather a comfort to Margaret that Frederick took it into his head to look over her shoulder as she wrote to Mr Lennox. If she had not been thus compelled to write steadily and concisely on, she might have hesitated over many a word, and been puzzled to choose between many an expression, in the awkwardness of being the first to resume the intercourse of which the concluding event had been so unpleasant to both sides. However, the note was taken from her before she had even had time to look it over, and treasured up in a pocket-book, out of which fell a long lock of black hair, the sight of which caused Frederick's eyes to glow with pleasure.

'Now you would like to see that, wouldn't you?' said he. 'No! you must wait till you see her herself. She is too perfect to be known by fragments. No mean brick shall be a specimen of the building of my palace.'

CHAPTER XXXII

Mischances

*What! remain to be
Denounced – dragged, it may be, in chains.*[1]

WERNER

All the next day they sate together – they three. Mr Hale hardly ever spoke but when his children asked him questions, and forced him, as it were, into the present. Frederick's grief was no more to be seen or heard; the first paroxysm had passed over, and now he was ashamed of having been so battered down by emotion; and though his sorrow for the loss of his mother was a deep real feeling, and would last out his life, it was never to be spoken of again. Margaret, not so passionate at first, was more suffering now. At times she cried a good deal; and her manner, even when speaking on indifferent things, had a mournful tenderness about it, which was deepened whenever her looks fell on Frederick, and she thought of his rapidly approaching departure. She was glad he was going, on her father's account, however much she might grieve over it on her own. The anxious terror in which Mr Hale lived lest his son should be detected and captured, far out-weighed the pleasure he derived from his presence. The nervousness had increased since Mrs Hale's death, probably because he dwelt upon it more exclusively. He started at every unusual sound; and was never comfortable unless Frederick sate out of the immediate view of any one entering the room. Towards evening he said:

'You will go with Frederick to the station, Margaret? I shall want to know he is safely off. You will bring me word that he is clear of Milton, at any rate?'

'Certainly,' said Margaret. 'I shall like it, if you won't be lonely without me, papa.'

'No, no! I should always be fancying some one had known him, and that he had been stopped, unless you could tell me you had seen him off. And go to the Outwood station. It is quite as near, and not so many people about. Take a cab there. There is less risk of his being seen. What time is your train, Fred?'

'Ten minutes past six; very nearly dark. So what will you do, Margaret?'

256

'Oh, I can manage. I am getting very brave and very hard. It is a well-lighted road all the way home, if it should be dark. But I was out last week much later.'

Margaret was thankful when the parting was over – the parting from the dead mother and the living father. She hurried Frederick into the cab, in order to shorten a scene which she saw was so bitterly painful to her father, who would accompany his son as he took his last look at his mother. Partly in consequence of this, and partly owing to one of the very common mistakes in the 'Railway Guide' as to the times when trains arrive at the smaller stations, they found, on reaching Outwood, that they had nearly twenty minutes to spare. The booking-office was not open, so they could not even take the ticket. They accordingly went down the flight of steps that led to the level of the ground below the railway. There was a broad cinder-path diagonally crossing a field which lay along-side of the carriage-road, and they went there to walk backwards and forwards for the few minutes they had to spare.

Margaret's hand lay in Frederick's arm. He took hold of it affectionately.

'Margaret! I am going to consult Mr Lennox as to the chance of exculpating myself, so that I may return to England whenever I choose, more for your sake than for the sake of any one else. I can't bear to think of your lonely position if anything should happen to my father. He looks sadly changed – terribly shaken. I wish you could get him to think of the Cadiz plan, for many reasons. What could you do if he were taken away? You have no friend near. We are curiously bare of relations.'

Margaret could hardly keep from crying at the tender anxiety with which Frederick was bringing before her an event which she herself felt was not very improbable, so severely had the cares of the last few months told upon Mr Hale. But she tried to rally as she said:

'There have been such strange unexpected changes in my life during these last two years, that I feel more than ever that it is not worth while to calculate too closely what I should do if any future event took place. I try to think only upon the present.' She paused; they were standing still for a moment, close on the field side of the stile leading into the road; the setting sun fell on their faces. Frederick held her hand in his, and looked with wistful anxiety into her face, reading there more care and trouble than she would betray by words. She went on:

'We shall write often to one another, and I will promise – for I see it will set your mind at ease – to tell you every worry I have. Papa is' – she started a little, a hardly visible start – but Frederick felt the sudden motion of the hand he held, and turned his full face to the road, along which a horseman was slowly riding, just passing the very stile where they stood. Margaret bowed; her bow was stiffly returned.

'Who is that?' said Frederick, almost before he was out of hearing.

Margaret was a little drooping, a little flushed, as she replied: 'Mr Thornton; you saw him before, you know.'

'Only his back. He is an unprepossessing-looking fellow. What a scowl he has!'

'Something has happened to vex him,' said Margaret, apologetically. 'You would not have thought him unprepossessing if you had seen him with mamma.'

'I fancy it must be time to go and take my ticket. If I had known how dark it would be, we wouldn't have sent back the cab, Margaret.'

'Oh, don't fidget about that. I can take a cab here, if I like; or go back by the rail-road, when I should have shops and people and lamps all the way from the Milton station-house. Don't think of me; take care of yourself. I am sick with the thought that Leonards may be in the same train with you. Look well into the carriage before you get in.'

They went back to the station. Margaret insisted upon going into the full light of the flaring gas inside to take the ticket. Some idle-looking young men were lounging about with the station-master. Margaret thought she had seen the face of one of them before, and returned him a proud look of offended dignity for his somewhat impertinent stare of undisguised admiration. She went hastily to her brother, who was standing outside, and took hold of his arm. 'Have you got your bag? Let us walk about here on the platform,' said she, a little flurried at the idea of so soon being left alone, and her bravery oozing out rather faster than she liked to acknowledge even to herself. She heard a step following them along the flags; it stopped when they stopped, looking out along the line and hearing the whizz of the coming train. They did not speak; their hearts were too full. Another moment, and the train would be here; a minute more, and he would be gone. Margaret almost repented the urgency with which she had entreated him to go to London; it was throwing more chances of detection in his way. If he had sailed for Spain by Liverpool, he might have been off in two or three hours.

Frederick turned round, right facing the lamp, where the gas darted up in vivid anticipation of the train. A man in the dress of a railway porter started forward; a bad-looking man, who seemed to have drunk himself into a state of brutality, although his senses were in perfect order.

'By your leave, miss!' said he, pushing Margaret rudely on one side, and seizing Frederick by the collar.

'Your name is Hale, I believe?'

In an instant – how, Margaret did not see, for everything danced before her eyes – but by some sleight of wrestling,[2] Frederick had tripped him up, and he fell from the height of three or four feet, which the platform was elevated above the space of soft ground, by the side of the railroad. There he lay.

'Run, run!' gasped Margaret. 'The train is here. It was Leonards, was it? oh, run! I will carry your bag.' And she took him by the arm to push him along with all her feeble force. A door was opened in a carriage – he jumped in; and as he leant out to say, 'God bless you, Margaret!' the train rushed past her; and she was left standing alone. She was so terribly sick and faint that she was thankful to be able to turn into the ladies' waiting-room, and sit down for an instant. At first she could do nothing but gasp for breath. It was such a hurry; such a sickening alarm; such a near chance. If the train had not been there at the moment, the man would have jumped up again and called for assistance to arrest him. She wondered if the man had got up: she tried to remember if she had seen him move; she wondered if he could have been seriously hurt. She ventured out; the platform was all alight, but still quite deserted; she went to the end, and looked over, somewhat fearfully. No one was there; and then she was glad she had made herself go, and inspect, for otherwise terrible thoughts would have haunted her dreams. And even as it was, she was so trembling and affrighted that she felt she could not walk home along the road, which did indeed seem lonely and dark, as she gazed down upon it from the blaze of the station. She would wait till the down train passed and take her seat in it. But what if Leonards recognized her as Frederick's companion! She peered about, before venturing into the booking-office to take her ticket. There were only some railway officials standing about; and talking loud to one another.

'So Leonards has been drinking again!' said one, seemingly in authority. 'He'll need all his boasted influence to keep his place this time.'

'Where is he?' asked another, while Margaret, her back towards them, was counting her change with trembling fingers, not daring to turn round until she heard the answer to this question.

'I don't know. He came in not five minutes ago, with some long story or other about a fall he'd had, swearing awfully; and wanted to borrow some money from me to go to London by the next up-train. He made all sorts of tipsy promises, but I'd something else to do than listen to him; I told him to go about his business; and he went off at the front door.'

'He's at the nearest vaults, I'll be bound,' said the first speaker. 'Your money would have gone there too, if you'd been such a fool as to lend it.'

'Catch me! I knew better what his London meant. Why, he has never paid me off that five shillings' – and so they went on.

And now all Margaret's anxiety was for the train to come. She hid herself once more in the ladies' waiting-room, and fancied every noise was Leonards' step – every loud and boisterous voice was his. But no one came near her until the train drew up; when she was civilly helped into a carriage by a porter, into whose face she durst not look till they were in motion, and then she saw that it was not Leonards'.

CHAPTER XXXIII

Peace

Sleep on, my love, in thy cold bed,[1]
Never to be disquieted!
My last Good Night – thou wilt not wake
Till I thy fate shall overtake.

DR KING

Home seemed unnaturally quiet after all this terror and noisy commo-. tion. Her father had seen all due preparation made for her refreshment on her return; and then sate down again in his accustomed chair, to fall into one of his sad waking dreams. Dixon had got Mary Higgins to scold and direct in the kitchen; and her scolding was not the less energetic because it was delivered in an angry whisper; for, speaking above her breath she would have thought irreverent, as long as there was any one dead lying in the house. Margaret had resolved not to mention the crowning and closing affright to her father. There was no use in speaking about it; it had ended well; the only thing to be feared was lest Leonards should in some way borrow money enough to effect his purpose of following Frederick to London, and hunting him out there. But there were immense chances against the success of any such plan; and Margaret determined not to torment herself by thinking of what she could do nothing to prevent. Frederick would be as much on his guard as she could put him; and in a day or two at most he would be safely out of England.

'I suppose we shall hear from Mr Bell tomorrow,' said Margaret.

'Yes,' replied her father. 'I suppose so.'

'If he can come, he will be here tomorrow evening, I should think.'

'If he cannot come, I shall ask Mr Thornton to go with me to the funeral. I cannot go alone. I should break down utterly.'

'Don't ask Mr Thornton, papa. Let me go with you,' said Margaret, impetuously.

'You! My dear, women do not generally go.'[2]

'No: because they can't control themselves. Women of our class don't go, because they have no power over their emotions, and yet are ashamed of showing them. Poor women go, and don't care if they are seen overwhelmed with grief. But I promise you, papa, that if you will let me go, I will be no trouble. Don't have a stranger, and leave me out. Dear papa! if Mr Bell cannot come, I shall go. I won't urge my wish against your will, if he does.'

Mr Bell could not come. He had the gout. It was a most affectionate letter, and expressed great and true regret for his inability to attend. He hoped to come and pay them a visit soon, if they would have him; his Milton property required some looking after, and his agent had written to him to say that his presence was absolutely necessary; or else he had avoided coming near Milton as long as he could, and now the only thing that would reconcile him to this necessary visit was the idea that he should see, and might possibly be able to comfort his old friend.

Margaret had all the difficulty in the world to persuade her father not to invite Mr Thornton. She had an indescribable repugnance to this step being taken. The night before the funeral, came a stately note from Mrs Thornton to Miss Hale, saying that, at her son's desire, their carriage should attend the funeral, if it would not be disagreeable to the family. Margaret tossed the note to her father.

'Oh, don't let us have these forms,' said she. 'Let us go alone – you and me, papa. They don't care for us, or else he would have offered to go himself, and not have proposed this sending an empty carriage.'

'I thought you were so extremely averse to his going, Margaret,' said Mr Hale in some surprise.

'And so I am. I don't want him to come at all; and I should especially dislike the idea of our asking him. But this seems such a mockery of mourning that I did not expect it from him.' She startled her father by bursting into tears. She had been so subdued in her grief, so thoughtful for others, so gentle and patient in all things, that he could not understand her impatient ways tonight; she seemed agitated and restless; and at all the tenderness which her father in his turn now lavished upon her, she only cried the more.

She passed so bad a night that she was ill prepared for the additional anxiety caused by a letter received from Frederick. Mr Lennox was out of town; his clerk said that he would return by the following Tuesday at the latest; that he might possibly be at home on Monday. Consequently, after some consideration, Frederick had determined upon remaining in London a day or two longer. He had thought of coming down to Milton again; the temptation had been very strong; but the idea of Mr Bell domesticated in his father's house, and the alarm he had received at the last moment at the railway station, had made him resolve to stay in London. Margaret might be assured he would take every precaution against being tracked by Leonards. Margaret was thankful that she received this letter while her father was absent in her mother's room. If he had been present, he would have expected her to read it aloud to him, and it would have raised in him a state of nervous alarm which she would have found it impossible to soothe away. There was not merely the fact, which disturbed her excessively, of Frederick's detention in London, but there were allusions to the recognition at the last moment at Milton, and the possibility of a pursuit, which made her blood run cold; and how then would it have affected her father? Many a time did Margaret repent of having suggested and urged on the plan of consulting Mr Lennox. At the moment, it had seemed as if it would occasion so little delay – add so little to the apparently small chances of detection; and yet everything that had since occurred had tended to make it so undesirable. Margaret battled hard against this regret of hers for what could not now be helped; this self-reproach for having said what had at the time appeared to be wise, but which after events were proving to have been so foolish. But her father was in too depressed a state of mind and body to struggle healthily; he would succumb to all these causes for morbid regret over what could not be recalled. Margaret summoned up all her forces to her aid. Her father seemed to have forgotten that they had any reason to expect a letter from Frederick that morning. He was absorbed in one idea – that the last visible token of the presence of his wife was to be carried away from him, and hidden from his sight. He trembled pitifully as the undertaker's man was arranging his crape draperies around him. He looked wistfully at Margaret; and, when released, he tottered towards her, murmuring, 'Pray for me, Margaret. I have no strength left in me. I cannot pray. I give her up because I must. I try to bear it: indeed I do. I know it is God's will. But I cannot see why she died. Pray for me, Margaret, that I may have faith to pray. It is a great strait, my child.'

Margaret sat by him in the coach, almost supporting him in her arms; and repeating all the noble verses of holy comfort, or texts expressive of faithful resignation, that she could remember. Her voice never faltered; and she herself gained strength by doing this. Her father's lips moved after her, repeating the well-known texts as her words suggested them; it was terrible to see the patient struggling effort to obtain the resignation which he had not strength to take into his heart as a part of himself.

Margaret's fortitude nearly gave way as Dixon, with a slight motion of her hand, directed her notice to Nicholas Higgins and his daughter, standing a little aloof, but deeply attentive to the ceremonial. Nicholas wore his usual fustian clothes, but had a bit of black stuff sewn round his hat – a mark of mourning which he had never shown to his daughter Bessy's memory. But Mr Hale saw nothing. He went on repeating to himself, mechanically as it were, all the funeral service as it was read by the officiating clergyman; he sighed twice or thrice when all was ended; and then, putting his hand on Margaret's arm, he mutely entreated to be led away, as if he were blind, and she his faithful guide.

Dixon sobbed aloud; she covered her face with her handkerchief, and was so absorbed in her own grief, that she did not perceive that the crowd, attracted on such occasions, was dispersing, till she was spoken to by some one close at hand. It was Mr Thornton. He had been present all the time, standing, with bent head, behind a group of people, so that, in fact, no one had recognized him.

'I beg your pardon, – but, can you tell me how Mr Hale is? And Miss Hale, too? I should like to know how they both are.'

'Of course, sir. They are much as is to be expected. Master is terribly broke down. Miss Hale bears up better than likely.'

Mr Thornton would rather have heard that she was suffering the natural sorrow. In the first place, there was selfishness enough in him to have taken pleasure in the idea that his great love might come in to comfort and console her; much the same kind of strange passionate pleasure which comes stinging through a mother's heart, when her drooping infant nestles close to her, and is dependent upon her for everything. But this delicious vision of what might have been – in which, in spite of all Margaret's repulse, he would have indulged only a few days ago – was miserably disturbed by the recollection of what he had seen near the Outwood station. 'Miserably disturbed!' that is not strong enough. He was haunted by the remembrance of the handsome young man, with whom she stood in an attitude of such familiar confidence; and the remembrance shot through him like an agony, till it made him clench his hands tight in order to subdue the pain. At that late hour, so far from home! It took a great moral effort to galvanize his trust[3] – erewhile so perfect – in Margaret's pure and exquisite maidenliness, into life; as soon as the effort ceased, his trust dropped down dead and powerless: and all sorts of wild fancies chased each other like dreams through his mind. Here was a little piece of miserable, gnawing confirmation. 'She bore up better than likely' under this grief. She had then some hope to look to, so bright than even in her affectionate nature it could come in to lighten the dark hours of a daughter newly made motherless. Yes! he knew how she would love. He had not loved her without gaining that instinctive knowledge of what capabilities were in her. Her soul would walk in glorious sunlight if any man was worthy, by his power of loving, to win back her love. Even in her mourning she would rest with a peaceful faith upon his sympathy. His sympathy! Whose? That other man's. And that it was another was enough to make Mr Thornton's pale grave face grow doubly wan and stern at Dixon's answer.

'I suppose I may call,' said he coldly. 'On Mr Hale, I mean. He will perhaps admit me after tomorrow or so.'

He spoke as if the answer were a matter of indifference to him. But it was not so. For all his pain, he longed to see the author of it. Although he hated Margaret at times, when he thought of that gentle familiar attitude and all the attendant circumstances, he had a restless desire to renew her picture in his mind – a longing for the very atmosphere she breathed. He was in the Charybdis of passion[4], and must perforce circle and circle ever nearer round the fatal centre.

'I dare say, sir, master will see you. He was very sorry to have to deny you the other day; but circumstances was not agreeable just then.'

For some reason or other, Dixon never named this interview that she had had with Mr Thornton to Margaret. It might have been mere chance, but so it was that Margaret never heard that he had attended her poor mother's funeral.

CHAPTER XXXIV

False and True

Truth will fail thee never, never![1]
Though thy bark be tempest-driven,
Though each plank be rent and riven,
Truth will bear thee on for ever!

ANON

The 'bearing up better than likely' was a terrible strain upon Margaret. Sometimes she thought she must give way, and cry out with pain, as the sudden sharp thought came across her, even during her apparently cheerful conversations with her father, that she had no longer a mother. About Frederick, too, there was great uneasiness. The Sunday post[2] intervened, and interfered with their London letters, and on Tuesday Margaret was surprised and disheartened to find that there was still no letter. She was quite in the dark as to his plans, and her father was miserable at all this uncertainty. It broke in upon his lately acquired habit of sitting still in one easy chair for half a day together. He kept pacing up and down the room; then out of it; and she heard him upon the landing opening and shutting the

bed-room doors, without any apparent object. She tried to tranquil-
lize him by reading aloud; but it was evident he could not listen for
long together. How thankful she was then, that she had kept to
herself the additional cause for anxiety produced by their encounter
with Leonards. She was thankful to hear Mr Thornton announced.
His visit would force her father's thoughts into another channel.

He came up straight to her father, whose hands he took and
wrung without a word – holding them in his for a minute or two,
during which time his face, his eyes, his look, told of more sympathy
than could be put into words. Then he turned to Margaret. Not
'better than likely' did she look. Her stately beauty was dimmed with
much watching and with many tears. The expression on her countenance was of gentle patient sadness – nay of positive present suffering.
He had not meant to greet her otherwise than with his late studied
coldness of demeanour; but he could not help going up to her, as she
stood a little aside, rendered timid by the uncertainty of his manner
of late, and saying the few necessary common-place words in so
tender a voice, that her eyes filled with tears, and she turned away to
hide her emotion. She took her work and sate down very quiet and
silent. Mr Thornton's heart beat quick and strong, and for the time
he utterly forgot the Outwood lane. He tried to talk to Mr Hale: and
– his presence always a certain kind of pleasure to Mr Hale, as his
power and decision made him, and his opinions, a safe, sure port –
was unusually agreeable to her father, as Margaret saw.

Presently Dixon came to the door and said, 'Miss Hale, you are
wanted.'

Dixon's manner was so flurried that Margaret turned sick at
heart. Something had happened to Fred. She had no doubt of that.
It was well that her father and Mr Thornton were so much occupied
by their conversation.

'What is it, Dixon?' asked Margaret, the moment she had shut the
drawing-room door.

'Come this way, miss,' said Dixon, opening the door of what had
been Mrs Hale's bed-chamber, now Margaret's, for her father refused
to sleep there again after his wife's death. 'It's nothing, miss,' said
Dixon, choking a little. 'Only a police-inspector. He wants to see
you, miss. But I dare say, it's about nothing at all.'

'Did he name –' asked Margaret, almost inaudibly.

'No, miss; he named nothing. He only asked if you lived here, and
if he could speak to you. Martha went to the door, and let him in;

she has shown him into master's study. I went to him myself, to try if that would do; but no – it's you, miss, he wants.'

Margaret did not speak again till her hand was on the lock of the study door. Here she turned round and said, 'Take care papa does not come down. Mr Thornton is with him now.'

The inspector was almost daunted by the haughtiness of her manner as she entered. There was something of indignation expressed in her countenance, but so kept down and controlled, that it gave her a superb air of disdain. There was no surprise, no curiosity. She stood awaiting the opening of his business there. Not a question did she ask.

'I beg your pardon, ma'am, but my duty obliges me to ask you a few plain questions. A man has died at the Infirmary, in consequence of a fall, received at Outwood station, between the hours of five and six on Thursday evening, the twenty-sixth instant. At the time, this fall did not seem of much consequence; but it was rendered fatal, the doctors say, by the presence of some internal complaint, and the man's own habit of drinking.'

The large dark eyes, gazing straight into the inspector's face, dilated a little. Otherwise there was no motion perceptible to his experienced observation. Her lips swelled out into a richer curve than ordinary, owing to the enforced tension of the muscles, but he did not know what was their usual appearance, so as to recognize the unwonted sullen defiance of the firm sweeping lines. She never blenched or trembled. She fixed him with her eye. Now – as he paused before going on, she said, almost as if she would encourage him in telling his tale – 'Well – go on!'

'It is supposed that an inquest will have to be held; there is some slight evidence to prove that the blow, or push, or scuffle that caused the fall, was provoked by this poor fellow's half-tipsy impertinence to a young lady, walking with the man who pushed the deceased over the edge of the platform. This much was observed by some one on the platform, who, however, thought no more about the matter, as the blow seemed of slight consequence. There is also some reason to identify the lady with yourself; in which case –'

'I was not there,' said Margaret, still keeping her expressionless eyes fixed on his face, with the unconscious look of a sleep-walker.

The inspector bowed but did not speak. The lady standing before him showed no emotion, no fluttering fear, no anxiety, no desire to end the interview. The information he had received was very vague;

one of the porters, rushing out to be in readiness for the train, had seen a scuffle, at the other end of the platform, between Leonards and a gentleman accompanied by a lady, but heard no noise; and before the train had got to its full speed after starting, he had been almost knocked down by the headlong run of the enraged half intoxicated Leonards, swearing and cursing awfully. He had not thought any more about it, till his evidence was routed out by the inspector, who, on making some farther inquiry at the railroad station, had heard from the station-master that a young lady and gentleman had been there about that hour – the lady remarkably handsome – and said, by some grocer's assistant present at the time, to be a Miss Hale, living at Crampton, whose family dealt at his shop. There was no certainty that the one lady and gentleman were identical with the other pair, but there was great probability. Leonards himself had gone, half-mad with rage and pain, to the nearest gin-palace for comfort; and his tipsy words had not been attended to by the busy waiters there; they, however, remembered his starting up and cursing himself for not having sooner thought of the electric telegraph, for some purpose unknown; and they believed that he left with the idea of going there. On his way, overcome by pain or drink, he had lain down in the road, where the police had found him and taken him to the Infirmary: there he had never recovered sufficient consciousness to give any distinct account of his fall, although once or twice he had had glimmerings of sense sufficient to make the authorities send for the nearest magistrate, in hopes that he might be able to take down the dying man's deposition of the cause of his death. But when the magistrate had come, he was rambling about being at sea, and mixing up names of captains and lieutenants in an indistinct manner with those of his fellow porters at the railway; and his last words were a curse on the 'Cornish trick'[3] which had, he said, made him a hundred pounds poorer than he ought to have been. The inspector ran all this over in his mind – the vagueness of the evidence to prove that Margaret had been at the station – the unflinching, calm denial which she gave to such a supposition. She stood awaiting his next word with a composure that appeared supreme.

'Then, madam, I have your denial that you were the lady accompanying the gentleman who struck the blow, or gave the push, which caused the death of this poor man?'

A quick, sharp pain went through Margaret's brain. 'Oh God!

that I knew Frederick were safe!' A deep observer of human countenances might have seen the momentary agony shoot out of her great
gloomy eyes, like the torture of some creature brought to bay. But
the inspector though a very keen, was not a very deep observer. He
was a little struck, notwithstanding, by the form of the answer,
which sounded like a mechanical repetition of her first reply – not
changed and modified in shape so as to meet his last question.

'I was not there,' said she, slowly and heavily. And all this time
she never closed her eyes, or ceased from that glassy, dream-like
stare. His quick suspicions were aroused by this dull echo of her
former denial. It was as if she had forced herself to one untruth, and
had been stunned out of all power of varying it.

He put up his book of notes in a very deliberate manner. Then he
looked up; she had not moved any more than if she had been some
great Egyptian statue.

'I hope you will not think me impertinent when I say, that I may
have to call on you again. I may have to summon you to appear on
the inquest, and prove an alibi, if my witnesses' (it was but one who
had recognized her) 'persist in deposing to your presence at the
unfortunate event.' He looked at her sharply. She was still perfectly
quiet – no change of colour, or darker shadow of guilt, on her proud
face. He thought to have seen her wince: he did not know Margaret
Hale. He was a little abashed by her regal composure. It must have
been a mistake of identity. He went on:

'It is very unlikely, ma'am, that I shall have to do anything of the
kind. I hope you will excuse me for doing what is only my duty,
although it may appear impertinent.'

Margaret bowed her head as he went towards the door. Her lips
were stiff and dry. She could not speak even the common words of
farewell. But suddenly she walked forwards, and opened the study
door, and preceded him to the door of the house, which she threw
wide open for his exit. She kept her eyes upon him in the same dull,
fixed manner, until he was fairly out of the house. She shut the door,
and went half-way into the study; then turned back, as if moved by
some passionate impulse, and locked the door inside.

Then she went into the study, paused – tottered forward – paused
again – swayed for an instant where she stood, and fell prone on the
floor in a dead swoon.

CHAPTER XXXV

Expiation

There's nought so finely spun
But it cometh to the sun.

Mr Thornton sate on and on. He felt that his company gave pleasure to Mr Hale; and was touched by the half-spoken wishful entreaty that he would remain a little longer – the plaintive 'Don't go yet,' which his poor friend put forth from time to time. He wondered Margaret did not return; but it was with no view of seeing her that he lingered. For the hour – and in the presence of one who was so thoroughly feeling the nothingness of earth – he was reasonable and self-controlled. He was deeply interested in all her father said

Of death, and of the heavy lull,
And of the brain that has grown dull.

It was curious how the presence of Mr Thornton had power over Mr Hale to make him unlock the secret thoughts which he kept shut up even from Margaret. Whether it was that her sympathy would be so keen, and show itself in so lively a manner, that he was afraid of the reaction upon himself, or whether it was that to his speculative mind all kinds of doubts presented themselves at such a time, pleading and crying aloud to be resolved into certainties, and that he knew she would have shrunk from the expression of any such doubts – nay, from him himself as capable of conceiving them – whatever was the reason, he could unburden himself better to Mr Thornton than to her of all the thoughts and fancies and fears that had been frost-bound in his brain till now. Mr Thornton said very little; but every sentence he uttered added to Mr Hale's reliance and regard for him. Was it that he paused in the expression of some remembered agony, Mr Thornton's two or three words would complete the sentence, and show how deeply its meaning was entered into. Was it a doubt – a fear – a wandering uncertainty seeking rest, but finding none – so tear-blinded were its eyes – Mr Thornton, instead of being shocked, seemed to have passed through that very stage of thought himself, and could suggest where the exact ray of light was to be found, which should make the dark places plain. Man of action as he was, busy in the world's great battle, there was a deeper religion binding him to God in his heart, in spite of his strong wilfulness, through all his mistakes, than Mr Hale had ever dreamed. They never spoke of such things again, as it happened; but this one conversation made them peculiar people to each other; knit them together, in a way which no loose indiscriminate talking about sacred things can ever accomplish. When all are admitted, how can there be a Holy of Holies?

And all this while, Margaret lay as still and white as death on the study floor! She had sunk under her burden. It had been heavy in weight and long carried; and she had been very meek and patient, till all at once her faith had given way, and she had groped in vain for help! There was a pitiful contraction of suffering upon her beautiful brows, although there was no other sign of consciousness remaining. The mouth – a little while ago, so sullenly projected in defiance – was relaxed and livid.

> '*E par che de la sua labbia si mova*[1]
> *Uno spirto soave e pien d'amore,*
> *Chi va dicendo a l'anima: sospira!*'

The first symptom of returning life was a quivering about the lips – a little mute soundless attempt at speech; but the eyes were still closed; and the quivering sank into stillness. Then, feebly leaning on her arms for an instant to steady herself, Margaret gathered herself up, and rose. Her comb had fallen out of her hair; and with an intuitive desire to efface the traces of weakness, and bring herself into order again, she sought for it, although from time to time, in the course of the search, she had to sit down and recover strength. Her head drooped forwards – her hands meekly laid one upon the other – she tried to recall the force of her temptation, by endeavouring to remember the details which had thrown her into such deadly fright; but she could not. She only understood two facts – that Frederick had been in danger of being pursued and detected in London, as not only guilty of manslaughter, but as the more unpardonable leader of the mutiny, and that she had lied to save him. There was one comfort; her lie had saved him, if only by gaining some additional time. If the inspector came again tomorrow, after she had received the letter she longed for to assure her of her brother's safety, she would brave shame, and stand in her bitter penance – she, the lofty Margaret – acknowledging before a crowded justice-room, if need were, that she had been as 'a dog, and done this thing.'² But if he came before she heard from Frederick; if he returned, as he had half threatened, in a few hours, why! she would tell that lie again; though how the words would come out, after all this terrible pause for reflection and self-reproach, without betraying her falsehood, she did not know, she could not tell. But her repetition of it would gain time – time for Frederick.

She was roused by Dixon's entrance into the room; she had just been letting out Mr Thornton.

He had hardly gone ten steps in the street, before a passing omnibus stopped close by him, and a man got down, and came up to him, touching his hat as he did so. It was the police-inspector.

Mr Thornton had obtained for him his first situation in the police, and had heard from time to time of the progress of his protégé, but they had not often met, and at first Mr Thornton did not remember him.

'My name is Watson – George Watson, sir, that you got –'

'Ah, yes! I recollect. Why you are getting on famously, I hear.'

'Yes, sir. I ought to thank you, sir. But it is on a little matter of business I made so bold as to speak to you now. I believe you were the magistrate who attended to take down the deposition of a poor man who died in the Infirmary last night.'

'Yes,' replied Mr Thornton. 'I went and heard some kind of a rambling statement, which the clerk said was of no great use. I'm afraid he was but a drunken fellow, though there is no doubt he came to his death by violence at last. One of my mother's servants was engaged to him, I believe, and she is in great distress today. What about him?'

'Why, sir, his death is oddly mixed up with somebody in the house I saw you coming out of just now; it was a Mr Hale's, I believe.'

'Yes!' said Mr Thornton, turning sharp round and looking into the inspector's face with sudden interest. 'What about it?'

'Why, sir, it seems to me that I have got a pretty distinct chain of evidence, inculpating a gentleman who was walking with Miss Hale that night at the Outwood station, as the man who struck or pushed Leonards off the platform and so caused his death. But the young lady denies that she was there at the time.'

'Miss Hale denies she was there!' repeated Mr Thornton, in an altered voice. 'Tell me, what evening was it? What time?'

'About six o'clock, on the evening of Thursday, the twenty-sixth.'

They walked on, side by side, in silence for a minute or two. The inspector was the first to speak.

'You see, sir, there is like to be a coroner's inquest; and I've got a young man who is pretty positive, – at least he was at first; – since he has heard of the young lady's denial, he says he should not like to swear; but still he's pretty positive that he saw Miss Hale at the station, walking about with a gentleman, not five minutes before the time, when one of the porters saw a scuffle, which he set down to some of Leonards' impudence – but which led to the fall which caused his death. And seeing you come out of the very house, sir, I thought I might make bold to ask if – you see, it's always awkward having to do with cases of disputed identity, and one doesn't like to doubt the word of a respectable young woman unless one has strong proof to the contrary.'

'And she denied having been at the station that evening!' repeated Mr Thornton, in a low, brooding tone.

'Yes, sir, twice over, as distinct as could be. I told her I should call again, but seeing you just as I was on my way back from questioning the young man who said it was her, I thought I would ask your advice, both as the magistrate who saw Leonards on his death-bed, and as the gentleman who got me my berth in the force.'

'You were quite right,' said Mr Thornton. 'Don't take any steps till you have seen me again.'

'The young lady will expect me to call, from what I said.'

'I only want to delay you an hour. It's now three. Come to my warehouse at four.'

'Very well, sir!'

And they parted company. Mr Thornton hurried to his warehouse, and, sternly forbidding his clerks to allow any one to interrupt him, he went his way to his own private room, and locked the door. Then he indulged himself in the torture of thinking it all over, and realizing every detail. How could he have lulled himself into the unsuspicious calm in which her tearful image had mirrored itself not two hours before, till he had weakly pitied her and yearned towards her, and forgotten the savage, distrustful jealousy with which the sight of her – and that unknown to him – at such an hour – in such a place – had inspired him! How could one so pure have stooped from her decorous and noble manner of bearing! But was it decorous – was it? He hated himself for the idea that forced itself upon him, just for an instant – no more – and yet, while it was present, thrilled him

273

with its old potency of attraction towards her image. And then this falsehood – how terrible must be some dread of shame to be revealed – for, after all, the provocation given by such a man as Leonards was, when excited by drinking, might, in all probability, be more than enough to justify any one who came forward to state the circumstances openly and without reserve! How creeping and deadly that fear which could bow down the truthful Margaret to falsehood! He could almost pity her. What would be the end of it? She could not have considered all she was entering upon; if there was an inquest and the young man came forward. Suddenly he started up. There should be no inquest. He would save Margaret. He would take the responsibility of preventing the inquest, the issue of which, from the uncertainty of the medical testimony (which he had vaguely heard the night before, from the surgeon in attendance), could be but doubtful; the doctors had discovered an internal disease far advanced, and sure to prove fatal; they had stated that death might have been accelerated by the fall, or by the subsequent drinking and exposure to cold. If he had but known how Margaret would have become involved in the affair – if he had but foreseen that she would have stained her whiteness by a falsehood, he could have saved her by a word; for the question, of inquest or no inquest, had hung trembling in the balance only the night before. Miss Hale might love another – was indifferent and contemptuous to him – but he would yet do her faithful acts of service of which she should never know. He might despise her, but the woman whom he had once loved should be kept from shame; and shame it would be to pledge herself to a lie in a public court, or otherwise to stand and acknowledge her reason for desiring darkness rather than light.

Very gray and stern did Mr Thornton look, as he passed out through his wondering clerks. He was away about half an hour; and scarcely less stern did he look when he returned, although his errand had been successful.

He wrote two lines on a slip of paper, put it in an envelope, and sealed it up. This he gave to one of the clerks, saying: –

'I appointed Watson – he who was a packer in the warehouse, and who went into the police – to call on me at four o'clock. I have just met with a gentleman from Liverpool who wishes to see me before he leaves town. Take care to give this note to Watson when he calls.'

The note contained these words:

'There will be no inquest.[3] Medical evidence not sufficient to justify it. Take no further steps. I have not seen the coroner; but I will take the responsibility.'

'Well,' thought Watson, 'it relieves me from an awkward job. None of my witnesses seemed certain of anything except the young woman. She was clear and distinct enough; the porter at the railroad had seen a scuffle; or when he found it was likely to bring him in as a witness, then it might not have been a scuffle, only a little larking, and Leonards might have jumped off the platform himself; – he would not stick firm to anything. And Jennings, the grocer's shopman, – well, he was not quite so bad, but I doubt if I could have got him up to an oath after he heard that Miss Hale flatly denied it. It would have been a troublesome job and no satisfaction. And now I must go and tell them they won't be wanted.'

He accordingly presented himself again at Mr Hale's that evening. Her father and Dixon would fain have persuaded Margaret to go to bed; but they, neither of them, knew the reason for her low continued refusals to do so. Dixon had learnt part of the truth – but only part. Margaret would not tell any human being of what she had said, and she did not reveal the fatal termination to Leonards' fall from the platform. So Dixon's curiosity combined with her allegiance to urge Margaret to go to rest, which her appearance, as she lay on the sofa, showed but too clearly that she required. She did not speak except when spoken to; she tried to smile back in reply to her father's anxious looks and words of tender enquiry; but, instead of a smile, the wan lips resolved themselves into a sigh. He was so miserably uneasy that, at last, she consented to go into her own room, and prepare for going to bed. She was indeed inclined to give up the idea that the inspector would call again that night, as it was already past nine o'clock.

She stood by her father, holding on to the back of his chair.

'You will go to bed soon, papa, won't you? Don't sit up alone!'

What his answer was she did not hear; the words were lost in the far smaller point of sound that magnified itself to her fears, and filled her brain. There was a low ring at the door-bell.

She kissed her father and glided down stairs, with a rapidity of motion of which no one would have thought her capable, who had seen her, the minute before. She put aside Dixon.

'Don't come; I will open the door. I know it is him – I can – I must manage it all myself.'

'As you please, miss!' said Dixon testily; but in a moment afterwards, she added, 'But you're not fit for it. You are more dead than alive.'

'Am I?' said Margaret, turning round and showing her eyes all aglow with strange fire, her cheeks flushed, though her lips were baked and livid still.

She opened the door to the Inspector, and preceded him into the study. She placed the candle on the table, and snuffed it carefully, before she turned round and faced him.

'You are late!' said she. 'Well?' She held her breath for the answer.

'I'm sorry to have given any unnecessary trouble, ma'am; for, after all, they've given up all thoughts of holding an inquest. I have had other work to do and other people to see, or I should have been here before now.'

'Then it is ended,' said Margaret. 'There is to be no further enquiry.'

'I believe I've got Mr Thornton's note about me,' said the Inspector, fumbling in his pocket-book.

'Mr Thornton's!' said Margaret.

'Yes! he's a magistrate – ah! here it is.' She could not see to read it – no, not although she was close to the candle. The words swam before her. But she held it in her hand, and looked at it as if she were intently studying it.

'I'm sure, ma'am, it's a great weight off my mind; for the evidence was so uncertain, you see, that the man had received any blow at all, – and if any question of identity came in, it so complicated the case, as I told Mr Thornton –'

'Mr Thornton!' said Margaret, again.

'I met him this morning, just as he was coming out of this house, and, as he's an old friend of mine, besides being the magistrate who saw Leonards last night, I made bold to tell him of my difficulty.'

Margaret sighed deeply. She did not want to hear any more; she was afraid alike of what she had heard, and of what she might hear. She wished that the man would go. She forced herself to speak.

'Thank you for calling. It is very late. I dare say it is past ten o'clock. Oh! here is the note!' she continued, suddenly interpreting the meaning of the hand held out to receive it. He was putting it up, when she said, 'I think it is a cramped, dazzling sort of writing. I could not read it; will you just read it to me?'

He read it aloud to her.

'Thank you. You told Mr Thornton that I was not there?'

'Oh, of course, ma'am. I'm sorry now that I acted upon information, which seems to have been so erroneous. At first the young man was so positive; and now he says that he doubted all along, and hopes that his mistake won't have occasioned you such annoyance as to lose their shop your custom. Good night, ma'am.'

'Good night.' She rang the bell for Dixon to show him out. As Dixon returned up the passage Margaret passed her swiftly.

'It is all right!' said she, without looking at Dixon; and before the woman could follow her with further questions she had sped upstairs, and entered her bed-chamber, and bolted her door.

She threw herself, dressed as she was, upon her bed. She was too much exhausted to think. Half an hour or more elapsed before the cramped nature of her position, and the chilliness, supervening upon great fatigue, had the power to rouse her numbed faculties. Then she began to recall, to combine, to wonder. The first idea that presented itself to her was, that all this sickening alarm on Frederick's behalf was over; that the strain was past. The next was a wish to remember every word of the Inspector's which related to Mr Thornton. When had he seen him? What had he said? What had Mr Thornton done? What were the exact words of his note? And until she could recollect, even to the placing or omitting an article, the very expressions which he had used in the note, her mind refused to go with its progress. But the next conviction she came to was clear enough; – Mr Thornton had seen her close to Outwood station on the fatal Thursday night, and had been told of her denial that she was there. She stood as a liar in his eyes. She was a liar. But she had no thought of penitence before God; nothing but chaos and night surrounded the one lurid fact that, in Mr Thornton's eyes, she was degraded. She cared not to think, even to herself, of how much of excuse she might plead. That had nothing to do with Mr Thornton; she never dreamed that he, or any one else, could find cause for suspicion in what was so natural as her accompanying her brother; but what was really false and wrong was known to him, and he had a right to judge her. 'Oh, Frederick! Frederick!' she cried, 'what have I not sacrificed for you!' Even when she fell asleep her thoughts were compelled to travel the same circle, only with exaggerated and monstrous circumstances of pain.

When she awoke a new idea flashed upon her with all the brightness of the morning. Mr Thornton had learnt her falsehood before he went to the coroner; that suggested the thought, that he had possibly been influenced so to do with a view of sparing her the repetition of her denial. But she pushed this notion on one side with the sick wilfulness of a child. If it were so, she felt no gratitude to him, as it only showed her how keenly he must have seen that she was disgraced already, before he took such unwonted pains to spare her any further trial of truthfulness, which had already failed so signally. She would have gone through the whole – she would have perjured herself to save Frederick, rather – far rather – than Mr Thornton should have had the knowledge that prompted him to interfere to save her. What ill-fate brought him in contact with the Inspector? What made him be the very magistrate sent for to receive Leonards' deposition? What had Leonards said? How much of it was intelligible to Mr Thornton, who might already, for aught she knew, be aware of the old accusation against Frederick, through their mutual friend, Mr Bell? If so, he had striven to save the son, who came in defiance of the law to attend his mother's death-bed. And under this idea she could feel grateful – not yet, if ever she should, if his interference had been prompted by contempt. Oh! had any one such just cause to feel contempt for her? Mr Thornton, above all people, on whom she had looked down from her imaginary heights till now! She suddenly found herself at his feet, and was strangely distressed at her fall. She shrank from following out the premises to their conclusion, and so acknowledging to herself how much she valued his respect and good opinion. Whenever this idea presented itself to her at the end of a long avenue of thoughts, she turned away from following that path – she would not believe in it.

It was later than she fancied, for in the agitation of the previous night, she had forgotten to wind up her watch; and Mr Hale had given especial orders that she was not to be disturbed by the usual awakening. By and by the door opened cautiously, and Dixon put her head in. Perceiving that Margaret was awake, she came forwards with a letter.

'Here's something to do you good, miss. A letter from Master Frederick.'

'Thank you, Dixon. How late it is!'

She spoke very languidly, and suffered Dixon to lay it on the counterpane before her, without putting out a hand to take it.

'You want your breakfast, I'm sure. I will bring it you in a minute. Master has got the tray all ready, I know.'

Margaret did not reply; she let her go; she felt that she must be alone before she could open that letter. She opened it at last. The first thing that caught her eye was the date two days earlier than she received it. He had then written when he had promised, and their alarm might have been spared. But she would read the letter and see. It was hasty enough, but perfectly satisfactory. He had seen Henry Lennox, who knew enough of the case to shake his head over it, in the first instance, and tell him he had done a very daring thing in returning to England, with such an accusation, backed by such powerful influence, hanging over him. But when they had come to talk it over, Mr Lennox had acknowledged that there might be some chance of his acquittal, if he could but prove his statements by credible witnesses – that in such case it might be worth while to stand his trial, otherwise it would be a great risk. He would examine – he would take every pains. 'It struck me,' said Frederick, 'that your introduction, little sister of mine, went a long way. Is it so? He made many inquiries, I can assure you. He seemed a sharp, intelligent fellow, and in good practice too, to judge from the signs of business and the number of clerks about him. But these may be only lawyer's dodges. I have just caught a packet on the point of sailing – I am off in five minutes. I may have to come back to England again on this business, so keep my visit secret. I shall send my father some rare old sherry, such as you cannot buy in England, – (such stuff as I've got in the bottle before me)! He needs something of the kind – my dear love to him – God bless him. I'm sure – here's my cab. P.S. – What an escape that was! Take care you don't breathe of my having been – not even to the Shaws.'

Margaret turned to the envelope; it was marked 'Too late.' The letter had probably been trusted to some careless waiter, who had forgotten to post it. Oh! what slight cobwebs of chances stand between us and Temptation! Frederick had been safe, and out of England twenty, nay, thirty hours ago; and it was only about seventeen hours since she had told a falsehood to baffle pursuit, which even then would have been vain. How faithless she had been! Where now was her proud motto, 'Fais ce que dois, advienne que pourra?' If she had but dared to bravely tell the truth as regarded herself, defying them to find out what she refused to tell concerning another, how light of heart she would now have felt! Not humbled before God, as having failed in trust towards Him; not degraded and abased in Mr Thornton's sight. She caught herself up at this with a miserable tremor; here was she classing his low opinion of her alongside with the displeasure of God. How was it that he haunted her imagination so persistently? What could it be? Why did she care for what he thought, in spite of all her pride; in spite of herself? She believed that she could have borne the sense of Almighty displeasure, because He knew all, and could read her penitence, and hear her cries for help in time to come. But Mr Thornton – why did she tremble, and hide her face in the pillow? What strong feeling had overtaken her at last?

She sprang out of bed and prayed long and earnestly. It soothed and comforted her so to open her heart. But as soon as she reviewed her position she found the sting was still there; that she was not good enough, nor pure enough to be indifferent to the lowered opinion of a fellow creature; that the thought of how he must be looking upon her with contempt, stood between her and her sense of wrong-doing. She took her letter in to her father as soon as she was dressed. There was so slight an allusion to their alarm at the railroad station, that Mr Hale passed over it without paying any attention to it. Indeed, beyond the mere fact of Frederick having sailed undiscovered and unsuspected, he did not gather much from the letter at the time, he was so uneasy about Margaret's pallid looks. She seemed continually on the point of weeping.

'You are sadly overdone, Margaret. It is no wonder. But you must let me nurse you now.'

He made her lie down on the sofa, and went for a shawl to cover her with. His tenderness released her tears; and she cried bitterly.

'Poor child! – poor child!' said he, looking fondly at her, as she lay with her face to the wall, shaking with her sobs. After a while they ceased, and she began to wonder whether she durst give herself the relief of telling her father of all her trouble. But there were more reasons against it than for it. The only one for it was the relief to herself; and against it was the thought that it would add materially to her father's nervousness, if it were indeed necessary for Frederick to come to England again; that he would dwell on the circumstance of his son's having caused the death of a man, however unwittingly and unwillingly; that this knowledge would perpetually recur to trouble him, in various shapes of exaggeration and distortion from the simple truth. And about her own great fault – he would be distressed beyond measure at her want of courage and faith, yet perpetually troubled to make excuses for her. Formerly Margaret would have come to him as priest as well as father, to tell him of her temptation and her sin; but latterly they had not spoken much on such subjects; and she knew not how, in his change of opinions, he would reply if the depth of her soul called unto his. No; she would keep her secret, and bear the burden alone. Alone she would go before God, and cry for His absolution. Alone she would endure her disgraced position in the opinion of Mr Thornton. She was unspeakably touched by the tender efforts of her father to think of cheerful subjects on which to talk, and so to take her thoughts away from dwelling on all that had happened of late. It was some months since he had been so talkative as he was this day. He would not let her sit up, and offended Dixon desperately by insisting on waiting upon her himself.

At last she smiled; a poor, weak little smile; but it gave him the truest pleasure.

'It seems strange[4] to think, that what gives us most hope for the future should be called Dolores,' said Margaret. The remark was more in character with her father than with her usual self; but today they seemed to have changed natures.

'Her mother was a Spaniard, I believe: that accounts for her religion. Her father was a stiff Presbyterian when I knew him. But it is a very soft and pretty name.'

'How young she is! – younger by fourteen months than I am. Just the age that Edith was when she was engaged to Captain Lennox. Papa, we will go and see them in Spain.'

He shook his head. But he said, 'If you wish it, Margaret. Only let us come back here. It would seem unfair – unkind to your mother, who always, I'm afraid, disliked Milton so much, if we left it now she is lying here, and cannot go with us. No, dear; you shall go and see them, and bring me back a report of my Spanish daughter.'

'No, papa, I won't go without you. Who is to take care of you when I am gone?'

'I should like to know which of us is taking care of the other. But if you went, I should persuade Mr Thornton to let me give him double lessons. We would work up the classics famously. That would be a perpetual interest. You might go on, and see Edith at Corfu, if you liked.'

Margaret did not speak all at once. Then she said rather gravely: 'Thank you, papa. But I don't want to go. We will hope that Mr Lennox will manage so well, that Frederick may bring Dolores to see us when they are married. And as for Edith, the regiment won't remain much longer in Corfu. Perhaps we shall see both of them here before another year is out.'

Mr Hale's cheerful subjects had come to an end. Some painful recollection had stolen across his mind, and driven him into silence. By-and-by Margaret said:

'Papa – did you see Nicholas Higgins at the funeral? He was there, and Mary too. Poor fellow! it was his way of showing sympathy. He has a good warm heart under his bluff abrupt ways.'

'I am sure of it,' replied Mr Hale. 'I saw it all along, even while you tried to persuade me that he was all sorts of bad things. We will go and see them tomorrow, if you are strong enough to walk so far.'

'Oh yes. I want to see them. We did not pay Mary – or rather she refused to take it, Dixon says. We will go so as to catch him just after his dinner, and before he goes to his work.'

Towards evening Mr Hale said:

'I half expected Mr Thornton would have called. He spoke of a book yesterday which he had, and which I wanted to see. He said he would try and bring it today.'

Margaret sighed. She knew he would not come. He would be too delicate to run the chance of meeting her, while her shame must be so fresh in his memory. The very mention of his name renewed her trouble, and produced a relapse into the feeling of depressed, pre-occupied exhaustion. She gave way to listless languor. Suddenly it struck her that this was a strange manner to show her patience, or to reward her father for his watchful care of her all through the day. She sate up and offered to read aloud. His eyes were failing, and he gladly accepted her proposal. She read well: she gave the due emphasis; but had any one asked her, when she had ended, the meaning of what she had been reading, she could not have told. She was smitten with a feeling of ingratitude to Mr Thornton, inasmuch as, in the morning, she had refused to accept the kindness he had shown her in making further inquiry from the medical men, so as to obviate any inquest being held. Oh! she was grateful! She had been cowardly and false, and had shown her cowardliness and falsehood in action that could not be recalled; but she was not ungrateful. It sent a glow to her heart, to know how she could feel towards one who had reason to despise her. His cause for contempt was so just, that she should have respected him less if she had thought he did not feel contempt. It was a pleasure to feel how thoroughly she respected him. He could not prevent her doing that; it was the one comfort in all this misery.

Late in the evening, the expected book arrived, 'with Mr Thornton's kind regards, and wishes to know how Mr Hale is.'

'Say that I am much better, Dixon, but that Miss Hale –'

'No, papa,' said Margaret, eagerly – 'don't say anything about me. He does not ask.'

'My dear child, how you are shivering!' said her father, a few minutes afterwards. 'You must go to bed directly. You have turned quite pale!'

Margaret did not refuse to go, though she was loth to leave her father alone. She needed the relief of solitude after a day of busy thinking, and busier repenting.

But she seemed much as usual the next day; the lingering gravity and sadness, and the occasional absence of mind, were not unnatural symptoms in the early days of grief. And almost in proportion to her re-establishment in health, was her father's relapse into his abstracted musing upon the wife he had lost, and the past era in his life that was closed to him for ever.

CHAPTER XXXVI

Union Not Always Strength

The steps of the bearers, heavy and slow,[1]
The sobs of the mourners, deep and low.
SHELLEY

At the time arranged the previous day, they set out on their walk to see Nicholas Higgins and his daughter. They both were reminded of their recent loss, by a strange kind of shyness in their new habiliments, and in the fact that it was the first time, for many weeks, that they had deliberately gone out together. They drew very close to each other in unspoken sympathy.

Nicholas was sitting by the fire-side in his accustomed corner: but he had not his accustomed pipe. He was leaning his head upon his hand, his arm resting on his knee. He did not get up when he saw them, though Margaret could read the welcome in his eye.

'Sit ye down, sit ye down. Fire's welly out,' said he, giving it a vigorous poke, as if to turn attention away from himself. He was rather disorderly, to be sure, with a black unshaven beard of several days' growth, making his pale face look yet paler, and a jacket which would have been all the better for patching.

'We thought we should have a good chance of finding you, just after dinner-time,' said Margaret.

'We have had our sorrow too, since we saw you,' said Mr Hale.

'Ay, ay. Sorrows is more plentiful than dinners just now; I reckon, my dinner hour stretches all o'er the day; yo're pretty sure of finding me.'

'Are you out of work?' asked Margaret.

'Ay,' he replied shortly. Then, after a moment's silence, he added, looking up for the first time: 'I'm not wanting brass. Dunno yo' think it. Bess, poor lass, had a little stock under her pillow, ready to slip into my hand, last moment, and Mary is fustian-cutting. But I'm out o' work a' the same.'

'We owe Mary some money,' said Mr Hale, before Margaret's sharp pressure on his arm could arrest the words.

'If hoo takes it, I'll turn her out o' doors. I'll bide inside these four walls, and she'll bide out. That's a'.'

'But we owe her many thanks for her kind service,' began Mr Hale again.

'I ne'er thanked yo'r daughter theer for her deeds o' love to my poor wench. I ne'er could find th' words. I'se have to begin and try now, if yo' start making an ado about what little Mary could sarve yo'.'

'Is it because of the strike you're out of work?' asked Margaret gently.

'Strike's ended. It's o'er for this time. I'm out o' work because I ne'er asked for it. And I ne'er asked for it, because good words is scarce, and bad words is plentiful.'

He was in a mood to take a surly pleasure in giving answers that were like riddles. But Margaret saw that he would like to be asked for the explanation.

'And good words are –?'

'Asking for work. I reckon them's almost the best words that men can say. "Gi' me work" means "and I'll do it like a man." Them's good words.'

'And bad words are refusing you work when you ask for it.'

'Ay. Bad words is saying "Aha, my fine chap! Yo've been true to yo'r order, and I'll be true to mine. Yo' did the best yo' could for them as wanted help; that's yo'r way of being true to yo'r kind; and I'll be true to mine. Yo've been a poor fool, as knowed no better nor be a true faithful fool. So go and be d–d to yo'. There's no work for yo' here." Them's bad words. I'm not a fool; and if I was, folk ought to ha' taught me how to be wise after their fashion. I could mappen ha' learnt, if any one had tried to teach me.'

'Would it not be worth while,' said Mr Hale, 'to ask your old master if he would take you back again? It might be a poor chance, but it would be a chance.'

He looked up again, with a sharp glance at the questioner; and then tittered a low and bitter laugh.

'Measter! if it's no offence, I'll ask yo' a question or two in my turn.'

'You're quite welcome,' said Mr Hale.

'I reckon yo'n some way of earning your bread. Folk seldom lives i' Milton just for pleasure, if they can live anywhere else.'

'You are quite right. I have some independent property, but my intention in settling in Milton was to become a private tutor.'

'To teach folk. Well! I reckon they pay yo' for teaching them, dunnot they?'

'Yes,' replied Mr Hale, smiling. 'I teach in order to get paid.'

'And them that pays yo', dun they tell yo' whatten to do, or whatten not to do wi' the money they gives you in just payment for your pains – in fair exchange like?'

'No; to be sure not!'

'They dunnot say, "Yo' may have a brother, or a friend as dear as a brother, who wants this here brass for a purpose both yo' and he think right; but yo' mun promise not give it to him. Yo' may see a good use, as yo' think, to put yo'r money to; but we don't think it good, and so if yo' spend it a-thatens we'll just leave off dealing with yo'." They dunnot say that, dun they?'

'No: to be sure not!'

'Would yo' stand it if they did?'

'It would be some very hard pressure that would make me even think of submitting to such dictation.'

'There's not the pressure on all the broad earth that would make me,' said Nicholas Higgins. 'Now yo've got it. Yo've hit the bull's eye. Hampers – that's where I worked – makes their men pledge 'emselves they'll not give a penny to help th' Union or keep turn-outs fro' clemming. They may pledge and make pledge,' continued he, scornfully; 'they nobbut make liars and hypocrites. And that's a less sin, to my mind, to making men's hearts so hard that they'll not do a kindness to them as needs it, or help on the right and just cause, though it goes again the strong hand. But I'll ne'er forswear mysel' for a' the work the king could gi'e me. I'm a member o' the Union; and I think it's the only thing to do the workman any good. And I've been a turn-out, and known what it were to clem; so if I get a shilling, sixpence shall go to them if they axe it from me. Consequence is, I dunnot see where I'm to get a shilling.'

'Is that rule about not contributing to the Union in force at all the mills?' asked Margaret.

'I cannot say. It's a new regulation at ourn; and I reckon they'll find that they cannot stick to it. But it's in force now. By-and-by they'll find out, tyrants makes liars.'

There was a little pause. Margaret was hesitating whether she should say what was in her mind; she was unwilling to irritate one who was already gloomy and despondent enough. At last out it came. But in her soft tones, and with her reluctant manner, showing that she was unwilling to say anything unpleasant, it did not seem to annoy Higgins, only to perplex him.

'Do you remember poor Boucher saying that the Union was a tyrant? I think he said it was the worst tyrant of all. And I remember at the time I agreed with him.'

It was a long while before he spoke. He was resting his head on his two hands, and looking down into the fire, so she could not read the expression on his face.

'I'll not deny but what th' Union finds it necessary to force a man into his own good. I'll speak truth. A man leads a dree life who's not i' th' Union. But once i' th' Union, his interests are taken care on better nor he could do it for himsel', or by himsel', for that matter. It's the only way working men can get their rights, by all joining together. More the members, more chance for each one separate man having justice done him. Government takes care o' fools and madmen; and if any man is inclined to do himsel' or his neighbour a hurt, it puts a bit of a check on him, whether he likes it or no. That's all we do i' th' Union. We can't clap folk into prison; but we can make a man's life so heavy to be borne, that he's obliged to come in, and be wise and helpful in spite of himself. Boucher were a fool all along, and ne'er a worse fool than at th' last.'

'He did you harm?' asked Margaret.

'Ay, that did he. We had public opinion on our side, till he and his sort began rioting and breaking laws. It were all o'er wi' the strike then.'

'Then would it not have been far better to have left him alone, and not forced him to join the Union? He did you no good; and you drove him mad.'

'Margaret,' said her father, in a low and warning tone, for he saw the cloud gathering on Higgins's face.

'I like her,' said Higgins, suddenly. 'Hoo speaks plain out what's in her mind. Hoo doesn't comprehend th' Union for all that. It's a great power: it's our only power. I ha' read a bit o' poetry about a plough going o'er a daisy, as made tears come into my eyes, afore I'd other cause for crying. But the chap ne'er stopped driving the plough, I'se warrant, for all he were pitiful about the daisy. He'd too much mother wit for that. Th' Union's the plough making ready the land for harvest-time. Such as Boucher – 'twould be settin' him up too much to liken him to a daisy; he's liker a weed lounging over the ground – mun just make up their mind to be put out o' the way. I'm sore vexed wi' him just now. So, mappen, I dunnot speak him fair. I could go o'er him wi' a plough mysel', wi' a' the pleasure in life.'

'Why? What has he been doing? Anything fresh?'

'Ay, to be sure. He's ne'er out o' mischief, that man. First of a' he must go raging like a mad fool, and kick up yon riot. Then he'd to go into hiding, where he'd been yet, if Thornton had followed him out as I'd hoped he would ha' done. But Thornton, having got his own purpose, didn't care to go on wi' the prosecution for the riot. So Boucher slunk back again to his house. He ne'er showed himsel' abroad for a day or two. He had that grace. And then, where think ye that he went? Why, to Hampers'. Damn him! He went wi' his mealy-mouthed face, that turns me sick to look at, a-asking for work, though he knowed well enough the new rule, o' pledging themselves to give nought to th' Unions; nought to help the starving turn-out! Why he'd a clemmed to death, if th' Union had na' helped him in his pinch. There he went, ossing to promise aught, and pledge himsel' to aught – to tell a' he know'd on our proceedings, the good-for-nothing Judas! But I'll say this for Hamper, and thank him for it at my dying day, he drove Boucher away, and would na listen to him – ne'er a word – though folk standing by, says the traitor cried like a babby!'

'Oh! how shocking! how pitiful!' exclaimed Margaret. 'Higgins, I don't know you today. Don't you see how you've made Boucher what he is, by driving him into the Union against his will – without his heart going with it. You have made him what he is!'

Made him what he is! What was he?

Gathering, gathering along the narrow street, came a hollow, measured sound; now forcing itself on their attention. Many voices were hushed and low: many steps were heard, not moving onwards, at least not with any rapidity or steadiness of motion, but as if circling round one spot. Yes, there was one distinct, slow tramp of feet, which made itself a clear path through the air, and reached their ears; the measured laboured walk of men carrying a heavy burden. They were all drawn towards the house-door by some irresistible impulse; impelled thither – not by a poor curiosity, but as if by some solemn blast.

Six men walked in the middle of the road, three of them being policemen. They carried a door, taken off its hinges, upon their shoulders, on which lay some dead human creature; and from each side of the door there were constant droppings. All the street turned out to see, and, seeing, to accompany the procession, each one questioning the bearers, who answered almost reluctantly at last, so often had they told the tale.

'We found him i' th' brook in the field beyond there.'

'Th' brook! – why there's not water enough to drown him!'

'He was a determined chap. He lay with his face downwards. He was sick enough o' living, choose what cause he had for it.'

Higgins crept up to Margaret's side, and said in a weak piping kind of voice: 'It's not John Boucher? He had na spunk enough. Sure! It's not John Boucher! Why, they are a' looking this way! Listen! I've a singing in my head, and I cannot hear.'

They put the door down carefully upon the stones, and all might see the poor drowned wretch – his glassy eyes, one half open, staring right upwards to the sky. Owing to the position in which he had been found lying, his face was swollen and discoloured; besides, his skin was stained by the water in the brook, which had been used for dyeing purposes. The fore part of his head was bald; but the hair grew thin and long behind, and every separate lock was a conduit for water. Through all these disfigurements, Margaret recognized John Boucher. It seemed to her so sacrilegious to be peering into that poor distorted, agonized face, that, by a flash of instinct, she went forwards and softly covered the dead man's countenance with her handkerchief. The eyes that saw her do this followed her, as she turned away from her pious office, and were thus led to the place where Nicholas Higgins stood, like one rooted to the spot. The men spoke together, and then one of them came up to Higgins, who would have fain shrunk back into his house.

'Higgins, thou knowed him! Thou mun go tell the wife. Do it gently, man, but do it quick, for we canna leave him here long.'

'I canna go,' said Higgins. 'Dunnot ask me. I canna face her.'

'Thou knows her best,' said the man. 'We'n done a deal in bringing him here – thou take thy share.'

'I canna do it,' said Higgins. 'I'm welly felled wi' seeing him. We wasn't friends; and now he's dead.'

'Well, if thou wunnot thou wunnot. Some one mun, though. It's a dree task; but it's a chance, every minute, as she doesn't hear on it in some rougher way nor a person going to make her let on by degrees, as it were.'

'Papa, do you go,' said Margaret, in a low voice.

'If I could – if I had time to think of what I had better say; but all at once –' Margaret saw that her father was indeed unable. He was trembling from head to foot.

'I will go,' said she.

'Bless yo', miss, it will be a kind act; for she's been but a sickly sort of body, I hear, and few hereabouts know much on her.'

Margaret knocked at the closed door; but there was such a noise, as of many little ill-ordered children, that she could hear no reply; indeed, she doubted if she was heard, and as every moment of delay made her recoil from her task more and more, she opened the door and went in, shutting it after her, and even, unseen to the woman, fastening the bolt.

Mrs Boucher was sitting in a rocking-chair, on the other side of the ill-redd-up fireplace; it looked as if the house had been untouched for days by any effort at cleanliness.

Margaret said something, she hardly knew what, her throat and mouth were so dry, and the children's noise completely prevented her from being heard. She tried again.

'How are you, Mrs Boucher? But very poorly, I'm afraid.'

'I've no chance o' being well,' said she querulously. 'I'm left alone to manage these childer, and nought for to give 'em for to keep 'em quiet. John should na ha' left me, and me so poorly.'

'How long is it since he went away?'

'Four days sin'. No one would give him work here, and he'd to go on tramp toward Greenfield. But he might ha' been back afore this, or sent me some word if he'd gotten work. He might –'

'Oh, don't blame him,' said Margaret. 'He felt it deeply, I'm sure –'

'Willto' hold thy din, and let me hear the lady speak!' addressing herself, in no very gentle voice, to a little urchin of about a year old. She apologetically continued to Margaret, 'He's always mithering me for "daddy" and "butty;" and I ha' no butties to give him, and daddy's away, and forgotten us a', I think. He's his father's darling, he is,' said she, with a sudden turn of mood, and, dragging the child up to her knee, she began kissing it fondly.

Margaret laid her hand on the woman's arm to arrest her attention. Their eyes met.

'Poor little fellow!' said Margaret, slowly; 'he *was* his father's darling.'

'He *is* his father's darling,' said the woman, rising hastily, and standing face to face with Margaret. Neither of them spoke for a moment or two. Then Mrs Boucher began in a low, growling tone, gathering in wildness as she went on: 'He *is* his father's darling, I say. Poor folk can love their childer as well as rich. Why dunno yo' speak? Why dun yo' stare at me wi' your great pitiful eyes? Where's John?' Weak as she was, she shook Margaret to force out an answer. 'Oh, my God!' said she, understanding the meaning of that tearful look. She sank back into the chair. Margaret took up the child and put him into her arms.

'He loved him,' said she.

'Ay,' said the woman, shaking her head, 'he loved us a'. We had some one to love us once. It's a long time ago; but when he were in life and with us, he did love us, he did. He loved this babby mappen the best on us; but he loved me and I loved him, though I was calling him five minutes agone. Are yo' sure he's dead?' said she, trying to get up. 'If it's only that he's ill and like to die, they may bring him round yet. I'm but an ailing creature mysel' – I've been ailing this long time.'

'But he is dead – he is drowned!'

'Folk are brought round after they're dead-drowned. Whatten was I thinking of, to sit still when I should be stirring mysel'? Here, whisth thee, child – whisth thee! tak' this, tak' aught to play wi', but dunnot cry while my heart's breaking! Oh, where is my strength gone to? Oh, John – husband!'

Margaret saved her from falling by catching her in her arms. She sate down in the rocking-chair, and held the woman upon her knees, her head lying on Margaret's shoulder. The other children, clustered together in affright, began to understand the mystery of the scene; but the ideas came slowly, for their brains were dull and languid of perception. They set up such a cry of despair as they guessed the truth, that Margaret knew not how to bear it. Johnny's cry was loudest of them all, though he knew not why he cried, poor little fellow.

The mother quivered as she lay in Margaret's arms. Margaret heard a noise at the door.

'Open it. Open it quick,' said she to the eldest child. 'It's bolted; make no noise – be very still. Oh, papa, let them go upstairs very softly and carefully, and perhaps she will not hear them. She has fainted – that's all.'

'It's as well for her, poor creature,' said a woman, following in the wake of the bearers of the dead. 'But yo're not fit to hold her. Stay, I'll run fetch a pillow, and we'll let her down easy on the floor.'

This helpful neighbour was a great relief to Margaret; she was evidently a stranger to the house, a new comer in the district, indeed; but she was so kind and thoughtful that Margaret felt she was no longer needed; and that it would be better, perhaps, to set an example of clearing the house, which was filled with idle, if sympathizing gazers.

She looked round for Nicholas Higgins. He was not there. So she spoke to the woman who had taken the lead in placing Mrs Boucher on the floor.

'Can you give all these people a hint that they had better leave in quietness? So that when she comes round, she should only find one or two that she knows about her. Papa, will you speak to the men, and get them to go away? She cannot breathe, poor thing, with this crowd about her.'

Margaret was kneeling down by Mrs Boucher and bathing her face with vinegar; but in a few minutes she was surprised at the gush of fresh air. She looked round, and saw a smile pass between her father and the woman.

'What is it?' asked she.

'Only our good friend here,' replied her father, 'hit on a capital expedient for clearing the place.'

'I bid 'em begone, and each take a child with 'em, and to mind that they were orphans, and their mother a widow. It was who could do most, and the childer are sure of a bellyfull today, and of kindness too. Does hoo know how he died?'

'No,' said Margaret; 'I could not tell her all at once.'

'Hoo mun be told because of th' Inquest. See! Hoo's coming round; shall you or I do it? or mappen your father would be best?'

'No; you, you,' said Margaret.

They awaited her perfect recovery in silence. Then the neighbour woman sat down on the floor, and took Mrs Boucher's head and shoulders on her lap.

'Neighbour,' said she, 'your man is dead. Guess yo' how he died?'

'He were drowned,' said Mrs Boucher, feebly, beginning to cry for the first time, at this rough probing of her sorrows.

'He were found drowned. He were coming home very hopeless o' aught on earth. He thought God could na be harder than men; mappen not so hard; mappen as tender as a mother; mappen tenderer. I'm not saying he did right, and I'm not saying he did wrong. All I say is, may neither me nor mine ever have his sore heart, or we may do like things.'

'He has left me alone wi' a' these children!' moaned the widow, less distressed at the manner of the death than Margaret expected; but it was of a piece with her helpless character to feel his loss as principally affecting herself and her children.

'Not alone,' said Mr Hale, solemnly. 'Who is with you? Who will take up your cause?' The widow opened her eyes wide, and looked at the new speaker, of whose presence she had not been aware till then.

'Who has promised to be a father to the fatherless?' continued he.

'But I've getten six children, sir, and the eldest not eight years of age. I'm not meaning for to doubt His power, sir, – only it needs a deal o' trust;' and she began to cry afresh.

'Hoo'll be better able to talk tomorrow, sir,' said the neighbour. 'Best comfort now would be the feel of a child at her heart. I'm sorry they took the babby.'

'I'll go for it,' said Margaret. And in a few minutes she returned, carrying Johnnie, his face all smeared with eating, and his hands loaded with treasures in the shape of shells, and bits of crystal, and the head of a plaster figure. She placed him in his mother's arms.

'There!' said the woman, 'now you go. They'll cry together, and comfort together, better nor any one but a child can do. I'll stop with her as long as I'm needed, and if yo' come tomorrow, yo' can have a deal o' wise talk with her, that she's not up to today.'

As Margaret and her father went slowly up the street, she paused at Higgins's closed door.

'Shall we go in?' asked her father. 'I was thinking of him too.'

They knocked. There was no answer, so they tried the door. It was bolted, but they thought they heard him moving within.

'Nicholas!' said Margaret. There was no answer, and they might have gone away, believing the house to be empty, if there had not been some accidental fall, as of a book, within.

'Nicholas!' said Margaret again. 'It is only us. Won't you let us come in?'

'No,' said he. 'I spoke as plain as I could, 'bout using words, when I bolted th' door. Let me be, this day.'

Mr Hale would have urged their desire, but Margaret placed her finger on his lips.

'I don't wonder at it,' said she. 'I myself long to be alone. It seems the only thing to do one good after a day like this.'

CHAPTER XXXVII

Looking South

A spade! a rake! a hoe![1]
A pickaxe or a bill:
A hook to reap, or a scythe to mow,
A flail, or what ye will –
And here's a ready hand
To ply the needful tool,
And skill'd enough, by lessons rough,
In Labour's rugged school.

HOOD

Higgins's door was locked the next day, when they went to pay their call on the widow Boucher: but they learnt this time from an officious neighbour, that he was really from home. He had, however, been in to see Mrs Boucher, before starting on his day's business, whatever that was. It was but an unsatisfactory visit to Mrs Boucher; she considered herself as an ill-used woman by her poor husband's suicide; and there was quite germ of truth enough in this idea to make it a very difficult one to refute. Still, it was unsatisfactory to see how completely her thoughts were turned upon herself and her own position, and this selfishness extended even to her relations with her children, whom she considered as incumbrances, even in the very midst of her somewhat animal affection for them. Margaret tried to make acquaintances with one or two of them, while her father strove to raise the widow's thoughts into some higher channel than that of mere helpless querulousness. She found that the children were truer and simpler mourners than the widow. Daddy had been a kind daddy to them; each could tell, in their eager stammering way, of some tenderness shown, some indulgence granted by the lost father.

'Is yon thing upstairs really him? it doesna look like him. I'm feared on it, and I never was feared o' daddy.'

Margaret's heart bled to hear that the mother, in her selfish requirement of sympathy, had taken her children upstairs to see their disfigured father. It was intermingling the coarseness of horror with the profoundness of natural grief. She tried to turn their thoughts in some other direction; on what they could do for mother; on what – for this was a more efficacious way of putting it – what father would have wished them to do. Margaret was more successful than Mr Hale in her efforts. The children seeing their little duties lie in action close around them, began to try each one to do something that she suggested towards redding up[2] the slatternly room. But her father set too high a standard, and too abstract a view, before the indolent invalid. She could not rouse her torpid mind into any vivid imagination of what her husband's misery might have been before he had resorted to the last terrible step; she could only look upon it as it affected herself; she could not enter into the enduring mercy of the God who had not specially interposed to prevent the water from drowning her prostrate husband; and although she was secretly blaming her husband for having fallen into such drear despair, and denying that he had any excuse for his last rash act, she was inveterate in her abuse of all who could by any possibility be supposed to have driven him to such desperation. The masters – Mr Thornton in particular, whose mill had been attacked by Boucher, and who, after the warrant had been issued for his apprehension on the charge of rioting, had caused it to be withdrawn, – the Union, of which Higgins was the representative to the poor woman, – the children so numerous, so hungry, and so noisy – all made up one great army of personal enemies, whose fault it was that she was now a helpless widow.

Margaret heard enough of this unreasonableness to dishearten her; and when they came away she found it impossible to cheer her father.

'It is the town life,' said she. 'Their nerves are quickened by the haste and bustle and speed of everything around them, to say nothing of the confinement in these pent-up houses, which of itself is enough to induce depression and worry of spirits. Now in the country, people live so much more out of doors, even children, and even in the winter.'

'But people must live in towns. And in the country some get such stagnant habits of mind that they are almost fatalists.'

'Yes; I acknowledge that. I suppose each mode of life produces its own trials and its own temptations. The dweller in towns must find it as difficult to be patient and calm, as the country-bred man must find it to be active, and equal to unwonted emergencies. Both must find it hard to realize a future of any kind; the one because the present is so living and hurrying and close around him; the other because his life tempts him to revel in the mere sense of animal existence, not knowing of, and consequently not caring for any pungency of pleasure for the attainment of which he can plan, and deny himself and look forward.'

'And thus both the necessity for engrossment, and the stupid content in the present, produce the same effects. But this poor Mrs Boucher! how little we can do for her.'

'And yet we dare not leave her without our efforts, although they may seem so useless. Oh papa! it's a hard world to live in!'

'So it is, my child. We feel it so just now, at any rate; but we have been very happy, even in the midst of our sorrow. What a pleasure Frederick's visit was!'

'Yes, that it was,' said Margaret, brightly. 'It was such a charming, snatched, forbidden thing.' But she suddenly stopped speaking. She had spoiled the remembrance of Frederick's visit to herself by her own cowardice. Of all faults the one she most despised in others was the want of bravery; the meanness of heart which leads to untruth. And here had she been guilty of it! Then came the thought of Mr Thornton's cognisance of her falsehood. She wondered if she should have minded detection half so much from any one else. She tried herself in imagination with her Aunt Shaw and Edith; with her father; with Captain and Mr Lennox; with Frederick. The thought of the last knowing what she had done, even in his own behalf, was the most painful, for the brother and sister were in the first flush of their mutual regard and love; but even any fall in Frederick's opinion was as nothing to the shame, the shrinking shame she felt at the thought of meeting Mr Thornton again. And yet she longed to see him, to get it over; to understand where she stood in his opinion. Her cheeks burnt as she recollected how proudly she had implied an objection to trade (in the early days of their acquaintance), because it too often led to the deceit of passing off inferior for superior goods, in the one branch; of assuming credit for wealth and resources not possessed, in the other. She remembered Mr Thornton's look of calm disdain, as in few words he gave her to understand that, in the great scheme of commerce, all dishonourable ways of acting were sure to prove injurious in the long run, and that, testing such actions simply according to the poor standard of success, there was folly and not wisdom in all such, and every kind of deceit in trade, as well as in other things. She remembered – she, then strong in her own un-tempted truth – asking him, if he did not think that buying in the cheapest and selling in the dearest market proved some want of the transparent justice which is so intimately connected with the idea of truth: and she had used the word chivalric – and her father had corrected her with the higher word, Christian; and so drawn the argument upon himself, while she sat silent by with a slight feeling of contempt.

No more contempt for her! – no more talk about the chivalric! Henceforward she must feel humiliated and disgraced in his sight. But when should she see him? Her heart leaped up in apprehension at every ring of the door-bell; and yet when it fell down to calmness, she felt strangely saddened and sick at heart at each disappointment. It was very evident that her father expected to see him, and was surprised that he did not come. The truth was, that there were points in their conversation the other night on which they had no time then to enlarge; but it had been understood that if possible on the succeeding evening – if not then, at least the very first evening that Mr Thornton could command, – they should meet for further discussion. Mr Hale had looked forward to this meeting ever since they had parted. He had not yet resumed the instruction to his pupils, which he had relinquished at the commencement of his wife's more serious illness, so he had fewer occupations than usual; and the great interest of the last day or so (Boucher's suicide) had driven him back with more eagerness than ever upon his speculations. He was restless all evening. He kept saying, 'I quite expected to have seen Mr Thornton. I think the messenger who brought the book last night must have had some note, and forgot to deliver it. Do you think there has been any message left today?'

'I will go and inquire, papa,' said Margaret, after the changes on these sentences had been rung once or twice. 'Stay, there's a ring!' She sate down instantly, and bent her head attentively over her work. She heard a step on the stairs, but it was only one, and she knew it was Dixon's. She lifted up her head and sighed, and believed she felt glad.

'It's that Higgins, sir. He wants to see you, or else Miss Hale. Or it might be Miss Hale first, and then you, sir; for he's in a strange kind of way.'

'He had better come up here, Dixon; and then he can see us both, and choose which he likes for his listener.'

'Oh! very well, sir. I've no wish to hear what he's got to say, I'm sure; only, if you could see his shoes, I'm sure you'd say the kitchen was the fitter place.'

'He can wipe them, I suppose,' said Mr Hale. So Dixon flung off, to bid him walk upstairs. She was a little mollified, however, when he looked at his feet with a hesitating air; and then, sitting down on the bottom stair, he took off the offending shoes, and without a word walked upstairs.

'Sarvant, sir!' said he, slicking his hair down when he came into the room: 'If hoo'l excuse me (looking at Margaret) for being i' my stockings; I'se been tramping a' day, and streets is none o' th' cleanest.'

Margaret thought that fatigue might account for the change in his manner, for he was unusually quiet and subdued; and he had evidently some difficulty in saying what he came to say.

Mr Hale's ever-ready sympathy with anything of shyness or hesitation, or want of self-possession, made him come to his aid.

'We shall have tea up directly, and then you'll take a cup with us, Mr Higgins. I am sure you are tired, if you've been out much this wet relaxing day. Margaret, my dear, can't you hasten tea?'

Margaret could only hasten tea by taking the preparation of it into her own hands, and so offending Dixon, who was emerging out of her sorrow for her late mistress into a very touchy, irritable state. But Martha, like all who came in contact with Margaret – even Dixon herself, in the long run – felt it a pleasure and an honour to forward any of her wishes; and her readiness, and Margaret's sweet forbearance, soon made Dixon ashamed of herself.

'Why master and you must always be asking the lower classes upstairs, since we came to Milton, I cannot understand. Folk at

Helstone were never brought higher than the kitchen; and I've let one or two of them know before now that they might think it an honour to be even there.'

Higgins found it easier to unburden himself to one than to two. After Margaret left the room, he went to the door and assured himself that it was shut. Then he came and stood close to Mr Hale.

'Master,' said he, 'yo'd not guess easy what I've been tramping after today. Special if yo' remember my manner o' talk yesterday. I've been a seeking work. I have,' said he. 'I said to mysel', I'd keep a civil tongue in my head, let who would say what 'em would. I'd set my teeth into my tongue sooner nor speak i' haste. For that man's sake – yo' understand,' jerking his thumb back in some unknown direction.

'No, I don't,' said Mr Hale, seeing he waited for some kind of assent, and completely bewildered as to who 'that man' could be.

'That chap as lies theer,' said he, with another jerk. 'Him as went and drowned himself, poor chap! I did na' think he'd got it in him to lie still and let th' water creep o'er him till he died. Boucher, yo' know.'

'Yes, I know now,' said Mr Hale. 'Go back to what you were saying: you'd not speak in haste –'

'For his sake. Yet not for his sake; for where'er he is, and whate'er, he'll ne'er know other clemming or cold again; but for the wife's sake, and the bits o' childer.'

'God bless you!' said Mr Hale, starting up; then, calming down, he said breathlessly, 'What do you mean? Tell me out.'

'I have told yo',' said Higgins, a little surprised at Mr Hale's agitation. 'I would na ask for work for mysel'; but them's left as a charge on me. I reckon, I would ha guided Boucher to a better end; but I set him off o' th' road, and so I mun answer for him.'

Mr Hale got hold of Higgins's hand and shook it heartily, without speaking. Higgins looked awkward and ashamed.

'Theer, theer, master! Theer's ne'er a man, to call a man, amongst us, but what would do th' same; ay, and better too; for, belie' me, Is'e ne'er got a stroke o' work, nor yet a sight of any. For all I telled Hamper that, let alone his pledge – which I would not sign – no, I could na, not e'en for this – he'd ne'er ha' such a worker on his mill as I would be – he'd ha' none o' me – no more would none o' th' others. I'm a poor black feckless sheep – childer may clem for aught I can do, unless, parson, yo'd help me?'

'Help you! How? I would do anything, – but what can I do?'

'Miss there' – for Margaret had re-entered the room, and stood silent, listening – 'has often talked grand o' the South, and the ways down there. Now I dunnot know how far off it is, but I've been thinking if I could get 'em down theer, where food is cheap and wages good, and all the folk, rich and poor, master and man, friendly like; yo' could, may be, help me to work. I'm not forty-five, and I've a deal o' strength in me, measter.'

'But what kind of work could you do, my man?'

'Well, I reckon I could spade a bit –'

'And for that,' said Margaret, stepping forwards, 'for anything you could do, Higgins, with the best will in the world, you would, may be, get nine shillings a week; may be ten, at the outside. Food is much the same as here, except that you might have a little garden –'

'The childer could work at that,' said he. 'I'm sick o' Milton anyways, and Milton is sick o' me.'

'You must not go to the South,' said Margaret, 'for all that. You could not stand it. You would have to be out all weathers. It would kill you with rheumatism. The mere bodily work at your time of life would break you down. The fare is far different to what you have been accustomed to.'

'I'se nought particular about my meat,' said he, as if offended.

'But you've reckoned on having butcher's meat once a day,[3] if you're in work; pay for that out of your ten shillings, and keep those poor children if you can. I owe it to you – since it's my way of talking that has set you off on this idea – to put it all clear before you. You would not bear the dulness of the life; you don't know what it is; it would eat you away like rust. Those that have lived there all their lives, are used to soaking in the stagnant waters. They labour on,[4] from day to day, in the great solitude of steaming fields – never speaking or lifting up their poor, bent, downcast heads. The hard spade-work robs their brain of life; the sameness of their toil deadens their imagination; they don't care to meet to talk over thoughts and speculations, even of the weakest, wildest kind, after their work is done; they go home brutishly tired, poor creatures! caring for nothing but food and rest. You could not stir them up into any companionship, which you get in a town as plentiful as the air you breathe, whether it be good or bad – and that I don't know; but I do know, that you of all men are not one to bear a life among such labourers. What would be peace to them, would be eternal fretting to you. Think no more of it, Nicholas, I beg. Besides, you could never pay to get mother and children all there – that's one good thing.'

'I've reckoned for that. One house mun do for us a', and the furniture o' t'other would go a good way. And men theer mun have their families to keep – mappen six or seven childer. God help 'em!' said he, more convinced by his own presentation of the facts than by all Margaret had said, and suddenly renouncing the idea, which had but recently formed itself in a brain worn out by the day's fatigue and anxiety. 'God help 'em! North an' South have each getten their own troubles. If work's sure and steady theer, labour's paid at starvation prices; while here we'n rucks o' money coming in one quarter, and ne'er a farthing th' next. For sure, th' world is in a confusion[5] that passes me or any other man to understand; it needs fettling, and who's to fettle it, if it's as yon folks say, and there's nought but what we see?'

Mr Hale was busy cutting bread and butter; Margaret was glad of this, for she saw that Higgins was better left to himself: that if her father began to speak ever so mildly on the subject of Higgins's thoughts, the latter would consider himself challenged to an argument, and would feel himself bound to maintain his own ground. She and her father kept up an indifferent conversation until Higgins, scarcely aware whether he ate or not, had made a very substantial meal. Then he pushed his chair away from the table, and tried to take an interest in what they were saying; but it was of no use; and he fell back into dreamy gloom. Suddenly, Margaret said (she had been thinking of it for some time, but the words had stuck in her throat), 'Higgins, have you been to Marlborough Mills to seek for work?'

'Thornton's?' asked he. 'Ay, I've been at Thornton's.'

'And what did he say?'

'Such a chap as me is not like to see the measter. Th' o'erlooker bid me go and be d–d.'

'I wish you had seen Mr Thornton,' said Mr Hale. 'He might not have given you work, but he would not have used such language.'

'As to th' language, I'm welly used to it; it dunnot matter to me. I'm not nesh mysel' when I'm put out. It were th' fact that I were na wanted theer, no more nor ony other place, as I minded.'

'But I wish you had seen Mr Thornton,' repeated Margaret. 'Would you go again – it's a good deal to ask, I know – but would you go tomorrow and try him? I should be so glad if you would.'

'I'm afraid it would be of no use,' said Mr Hale, in a low voice. 'It would be better to let me speak to him.' Margaret still looked at Higgins for his answer. Those grave soft eyes of hers were difficult to resist. He gave a great sigh.

'It would tax my pride above a bit; if it were for mysel', I could stand a deal o' clemming first; I'd sooner knock him down than ask a favour from him. I'd a deal sooner be flogged mysel'; but yo're not a common wench, axing yo'r pardon, nor yet have yo' common ways about yo'. I'll e'en make a wry face, and go at it tomorrow. Dunna yo' think that he'll do it. That man has it in him to be burnt at the stake afore he'll give in. I do it for yo'r sake, Miss Hale, and it's first time in my life as e'er I give way to a woman. Neither my wife nor Bess could e'er say that much again me.'

'All the more do I thank you,' said Margaret, smiling. 'Though I don't believe you: I believe you have just given way to wife and daughter as much as most men.'

'And as to Mr Thornton,' said Mr Hale, 'I'll give you a note to him, which, I think I may venture to say, will ensure you a hearing.'

'I thank yo' kindly, sir, but I'd as lief stand on my own bottom. I dunnot stomach the notion of having favour curried for me, by one as doesn't know the ins and outs of the quarrel. Meddling 'twixt master and man is liker meddling 'twixt husband and wife than aught else: it takes a deal o' wisdom for to do ony good. I'll stand guard at the lodge door. I'll stand there fro' six in the morning till I get speech on him. But I'd liefer sweep th' streets, if paupers had na' got hold on that work. Dunna yo' hope, miss. There'll be more chance o' getting milk out of a flint. I wish yo' a very good night, and many thanks to yo'.'

'You'll find your shoes by the kitchen fire; I took them there to dry,' said Margaret.

He turned round and looked at her steadily, and then he brushed his lean hand across his eyes and went his way.

'How proud that man is!' said her father, who was a little annoyed at the manner in which Higgins had declined his intercession with Mr Thornton.

'He is,' said Margaret; 'but what grand makings of a man there are in him, pride and all.'

'It's amusing to see how he evidently respects the part in Mr Thornton's character which is like his own.'

'There's granite in all these northern people, papa, is there not?'

'There was none in poor Boucher, I'm afraid; none in his wife either.'

'I should guess from their tones that they had Irish blood in them. I wonder what success he'll have tomorrow. If he and Mr Thornton would speak out together as man to man – if Higgins would forget that Mr Thornton was a master, and speak to him as he does to us – and if Mr Thornton would be patient enough to listen to him with his human heart, not with his master's ears –'

'You are getting to do Mr Thornton justice at last, Margaret,' said her father, pinching her ear.

Margaret had a strange choking at her heart, which made her unable to answer. 'Oh!' thought she, 'I wish I were a man, that I could go and force him to express his disapprobation, and tell him honestly that I knew I deserved it. It seems hard to lose him as a friend just when I had begun to feel his value. How tender he was with dear mamma! If it were only for her sake, I wish he would come, and then at least I should know how much I was abased in his eyes.'

CHAPTER XXXVIII

Promises Fulfilled

Then proudly, proudly up she rose,
Tho' the tear was in her e'e,
'Whate'er ye say, think what ye may,
Ye's get na word frae me!'
SCOTCH BALLAD

It was not merely that Margaret was known to Mr Thornton to have spoken falsely, – though she imagined that for this reason only was she so turned in his opinion, – but that this falsehood of hers bore a distinct reference in his mind to some other lover. He could not forget the fond and earnest look that had passed between her and some other man – the attitude of familiar confidence, if not of positive endearment. The thought of this perpetually stung him; it was a picture before his eyes, wherever he went and whatever he was doing. In addition to this (and he ground his teeth as he remembered it), was the hour, dusky twilight; the place, so far away from home, and comparatively unfrequented. His nobler self had said at first, that all this last might be accidental, innocent, justifiable; but once allow her right to love and be beloved (and had he any reason to deny her right? – had not her words been severely explicit when she cast his love away from her?), she might easily have been beguiled into a longer walk, on to a later hour than she had anticipated. But that falsehood! which showed a fatal consciousness of something wrong, and to be concealed, which was unlike her. He did her that justice, though all the time it would have been a relief to believe her utterly unworthy of his esteem. It was this that made the misery – that he passionately loved her, and thought her, even with all her faults, more lovely and more excellent than any other woman; yet he deemed her so attached to some other man, so led away by her affection for him, as to violate her truthful nature. The very falsehood that stained her, was a proof how blindly she loved another – this dark, slight, elegant, handsome man – while he himself was rough, and stern, and strongly made. He lashed himself into an agony of fierce jealousy. He thought of that look, that attitude! – how he would have laid his life at her feet for such tender glances, such fond detention! He mocked at himself for having valued the mechanical way in which she had protected him from the fury of the mob; now he had seen how soft and bewitching she looked when with a man she really loved. He remembered, point by point, the sharpness of her words – 'There was not a man in all that crowd for whom she would not have done as much, far more readily than for him.' He shared with the mob, in her desire of averting bloodshed from them; but this man, this hidden lover, shared with nobody; he had looks, words, hand-cleavings, lies, concealment, all to himself.

Mr Thornton was conscious that he had never been so irritable as he was now, in all his life long; he felt inclined to give a short abrupt answer, more like a bark than a speech, to every one that asked him a question; and this consciousness hurt his pride: he had always piqued himself on his self-control, and control himself he would. So the manner was subdued to a quiet deliberation, but the matter was even harder and sterner than common. He was more than usually silent at home; employing his evenings in a continual pace backwards and forwards, which would have annoyed his mother exceedingly if it had been practised by any one else; and did not tend to promote any forbearance on her part even to this beloved son.

'Can you stop – can you sit down for a moment? I have something to say to you, if you would give up that everlasting walk, walk, walk.'

He sat down instantly, on a chair against the wall.

'I want to speak to you about Betsy. She says she must leave us; that her lover's death has so affected her spirits she can't give her heart to her work.'

'Very well. I suppose other cooks are to be met with.'

'That's so like a man. It's not merely the cooking, it is that she knows all the ways of the house. Besides, she tells me something about your friend Miss Hale.'

'Miss Hale is no friend of mine. Mr Hale is my friend.'

'I am glad to hear you say so, for if she had been your friend, what Betsy says would have annoyed you.'

'Let me hear it,' said he, with the extreme quietness of manner he had been assuming for the last few days.

'Betsy says, that the night on which her lover – I forget his name – for she always calls him "he" –'

'Leonards.'

'The night on which Leonards was last seen at the station – when he was last seen on duty, in fact – Miss Hale was there, walking about with a young man who, Betsy believes, killed Leonards by some blow or push.'

'Leonards was not killed by any blow or push.'

'How do you know?'

'Because I distinctly put the question to the surgeon of the Infirmary. He told me there was an internal disease of long standing, caused by Leonards' habit of drinking to excess; that the fact of his becoming rapidly worse while in a state of intoxication, settled the question as to whether the last fatal attack was caused by excess of drinking, or the fall.'

'The fall! What fall?'

'Caused by the blow or push of which Betsy speaks.'

'Then there was a blow or push?'

'I believe so.'

'And who did it?'

'As there was no inquest, in consequence of the doctor's opinion, I cannot tell you.'

'But Miss Hale was there?'

No answer.

'She will have to bear it, if I speak in her dead mother's name.'

'Well!' said he, breaking away, 'don't tell me any more about it. I cannot endure to think of it. It will be better that you should speak to her any way, than that she should not be spoken to at all. – Oh! that look of love!' continued he, between his teeth, as he bolted himself into his own private room. 'And that cursed lie; which showed some terrible shame in the background, to be kept from the light in which I thought she lived perpetually! Oh, Margaret, Margaret! Mother, how you have tortured me! Oh! Margaret, could you not have loved me? I am but uncouth and hard, but I would never have led you into any falsehood for me.'

The more Mrs Thornton thought over what her son had said, in pleading for a merciful judgment for Margaret's indiscretion, the more bitterly she felt inclined towards her. She took a savage pleasure in the idea of 'speaking her mind' to her, in the guise of a fulfilment of a duty. She enjoyed the thought of showing herself untouched by the 'glamour,' which she was well aware Margaret had the power of throwing over many people. She snorted scornfully over the picture of the beauty of her victim; her jet black hair, her clear smooth skin, her lucid eyes would not help to save her one word of the just and stern reproach which Mrs Thornton spent half the night in preparing to her mind.

'Is Miss Hale within?' She knew she was, for she had seen her at the window, and she had her feet inside the little hall before Martha had half answered her question.

Margaret was sitting alone, writing to Edith, and giving her many particulars of her mother's last days. It was a softening employment, and she had to brush away the unbidden tears as Mrs Thornton was announced.

She was so gentle and ladylike in her mode of reception that her visitor was somewhat daunted; and it became impossible to utter the speech, so easy of arrangement with no one to address it to. Margaret's low rich voice was softer than usual; her manner more gracious, because in her heart she was feeling very grateful to Mrs Thornton for the courteous attention of her call. She exerted herself to find subjects of interest for conversation; praised Martha, the servant whom Mrs Thornton had found for them; had asked Edith for a little Greek air, about which she had spoken to Miss Thornton. Mrs Thornton was fairly discomfited. Her sharp Damascus blade seemed out of place, and useless among rose-leaves. She was silent, because she was trying to task herself up to her duty. At last, she stung herself into its performance by a suspicion which, in spite of all probability, she allowed to cross her mind, that all this sweetness was put on with a view of propitiating Mr Thornton; that, somehow, the other attachment had fallen through, and that it suited Miss Hale's purpose to recall her rejected lover. Poor Margaret! there was perhaps so much truth in the suspicion as this: that Mrs Thornton was the mother of one whose regard she valued, and feared to have lost; and this thought unconsciously added to her natural desire of pleasing one who was showing her kindness by her visit. Mrs Thornton stood up to go, but yet she seemed to have something more to say. She cleared her throat and began:

'Miss Hale, I have a duty to perform. I promised your poor mother that, as far as my poor judgment went, I would not allow you to act in any way wrongly, or (she softened her speech down a little here) inadvertently, without remonstrating; at least, without offering advice, whether you took it or not.'

Margaret stood before her, blushing like any culprit, with her eyes dilating as she gazed at Mrs Thornton. She thought she had come to speak to her about the falsehood she had told – that Mr Thornton had employed her to explain the danger she had exposed herself to, of being confuted in full court! and although her heart sank to think he had not rather chosen to come himself, and upbraid her, and receive her penitence, and restore her again to his good opinion, yet she was too much humbled not to bear any blame on this subject patiently and meekly.

Mrs Thornton went on:

'At first, when I heard from one of my servants, that you had been seen walking about with a gentleman, so far from home as the Outwood station, at such a time of the evening, I could hardly believe it. But my son, I am sorry to say, confirmed her story. It was indiscreet, to say the least; many a young woman has lost her character before now –'

Margaret's eyes flashed fire. This was a new idea – this was too insulting. If Mrs Thornton had spoken to her about the lie she had told, well and good – she would have owned it, and humiliated herself. But to interfere with her conduct – to speak of her character! she – Mrs Thornton, a mere stranger – it was too impertinent! She would not answer her – not one word. Mrs Thornton saw the battle-spirit in Margaret's eyes, and it called up her combativeness also.

'For your mother's sake, I have thought it right to warn you against such improprieties; they must degrade you in the long run in the estimation of the world, even if in fact they do not lead you to positive harm.'

'For my mother's sake,' said Margaret, in a tearful voice, 'I will bear much; but I cannot bear everything. She never meant me to be exposed to insult, I am sure.'

'Insult, Miss Hale!'

'Yes, madam,' said Margaret more steadily, 'it is insult. What do you know of me that should lead you to suspect – Oh!' said she, breaking down, and covering her face with her hands – 'I know now, Mr Thornton has told you –'

'No, Miss Hale,' said Mrs Thornton, her truthfulness causing her to arrest the confession Margaret was on the point of making, though her curiosity was itching to hear it. 'Stop. Mr Thornton has told me nothing. You do not know my son. You are not worthy to know him. He said this. Listen, young lady, that you may understand, if you can, what sort of a man you rejected. This Milton manufacturer, his great tender heart scorned as it was scorned, said to me only last night, "Go to her. I have good reason to know that she is in some strait, arising out of some attachment; and she needs womanly counsel." I believe those were his very words. Farther than that – beyond admitting the fact of your being at the Outwood station with a gentleman, on the evening of the twenty-sixth – he has said nothing – not one word against you. If he has knowledge of anything which should make you sob so, he keeps it to himself.'

Margaret's face was still hidden in her hands, the fingers of which were wet with tears, Mrs Thornton was a little mollified.

'Come, Miss Hale. There may be circumstances, I'll allow, that, if explained, may take off from the seeming impropriety.'

Still no answer. Margaret was considering what to say; she wished to stand well with Mrs Thornton; and yet she could not, might not, give any explanation. Mrs Thornton grew impatient.

'I shall be sorry to break off an acquaintance; but for Fanny's sake – as I told my son, if Fanny had done so we should consider it a great disgrace – and Fanny might be led away –'

'I can give you no explanation,' said Margaret, in a low voice. 'I have done wrong, but not in the way you think or know about. I think Mr Thornton judges me more mercifully than you;' – she had hard work to keep herself from choking with her tears – 'but, I believe, madam, you mean to do rightly.'

'Thank you,' said Mrs Thornton, drawing herself up; 'I was not aware that my meaning was doubted. It is the last time I shall interfere. I was unwilling to consent to do it, when your mother asked me. I had not approved of my son's attachment to you, while I only suspected it. You did not appear to me worthy of him. But when you compromised yourself as you did at the time of the riot, and exposed yourself to the comments of servants and workpeople, I felt it was no longer right to set myself against my son's wish of proposing to you – a wish, by the way, which he had always denied entertaining until the day of the riot.' Margaret winced, and drew in her breath with a long, hissing sound; of which, however, Mrs Thornton took no notice. 'He came; you had apparently changed your mind. I told my son yesterday, that I thought it possible, short as was the interval, you might have heard or learnt something of this other lover –'

'What must you think of me, madam?' asked Margaret, throwing her head back with proud disdain, till her throat curved outwards like a swan's. 'You can say nothing more, Mrs Thornton. I decline every attempt to justify myself for anything. You must allow me to leave the room.'

And she swept out of it with the noiseless grace of an offended princess. Mrs Thornton had quite enough of natural humour to make her feel the ludicrousness of the position in which she was left. There was nothing for it but to show herself out. She was not particularly annoyed at Margaret's way of behaving. She did not care enough for her for that. She had taken Mrs Thornton's remonstrance to the full as keenly to heart as that lady expected; and Margaret's passion at once mollified her visitor, far more than any silence or reserve could have done. It showed the effect of her words. 'My young lady,' thought Mrs Thornton to herself; 'you've a pretty good temper of your own. If John and you had come together, he would have had to keep a tight hand over you, to make you know your place. But I don't think you will go a-walking again with your beau, at such an hour of the day, in a hurry. You've too much pride and spirit in you for that. I like to see a girl fly out at the notion of being talked about. It shows they're neither giddy, nor bold by nature. As for that girl, she might be bold, but she'd never be giddy. I'll do her that justice. Now as to Fanny, she'd be giddy, and not bold. She's no courage in her, poor thing!'

Mr Thornton was not spending the morning so satisfactorily as his mother. She, at any rate, was fulfilling her determined purpose. He was trying to understand where he stood; what damage the strike had done him. A good deal of his capital was locked up in new and expensive machinery; and he had also bought cotton largely, with a view to some great orders which he had in hand. The strike had thrown him terribly behindhand, as to the completion of these orders. Even with his own accustomed and skilled workpeople, he would have had some difficulty in fulfilling his engagements; as it was, the incompetence of the Irish hands, who had to be trained to their work, at a time requiring unusual activity, was a daily annoyance.

It was not a favourable hour for Higgins to make his request. But he had promised Margaret to do it at any cost. So, though every moment added to his repugnance, his pride, and his sullenness of temper, he stood leaning against the dead wall, hour after hour, first on one leg, then on the other. At last the latch was sharply lifted, and out came Mr Thornton.

'I want for to speak to yo', sir.'

'Can't stay now, my man. I'm too late as it is.'

'Well, sir, I reckon I can wait till yo' come back.'

Mr Thornton was half way down the street. Higgins sighed. But it was no use. To catch him in the street was his only chance of seeing 'the measter;' if he had rung the lodge bell, or even gone up to the house to ask for him, he would have been referred to the overlooker. So he stood still again, vouchsafing no answer, but a short nod of recognition to the few men who knew and spoke to him, as the crowd drove out of the millyard at dinner-time, and scowling with all his might at the Irish 'knobsticks' who had just been imported. At last Mr Thornton returned.

'What! you there still!'

'Ay, sir. I mun speak to yo'.'

'Come in here, then. Stay, we'll go across the yard; the men are not come back, and we shall have it to ourselves. These good people, I see, are at dinner;' said he, closing the door of the porter's lodge.

He stopped to speak to the overlooker. The latter said in a low tone:

'I suppose you know, sir, that that man is Higgins, one of the leaders of the Union; he that made that speech in Hurstfield.'

'No, I didn't,' said Mr Thornton, looking around sharply at his follower. Higgins was known to him by name as a turbulent spirit.

'Come along,' said he, and his tone was rougher than before. 'It is men such as this,' thought he, 'who interrupt commerce and injure the very town they live in: mere demagogues, lovers of power, at whatever cost to others.'

'Well, sir! what do you want with me?' said Mr Thornton, facing round at him, as soon as they were in the counting-house of the mill.

'My name is Higgins' –

'I know that,' broke in Mr Thornton. 'What do you want, Mr Higgins? That's the question.'

'I want work.'

'Work! You're a pretty chap to come asking me for work. You don't want impudence, that's very clear.'

'I've getten enemies and backbiters, like my betters; but I ne'er heerd o' ony of them calling me o'er modest,' said Higgins. His blood was a little roused by Mr Thornton's manner, more than by his words.

Mr Thornton saw a letter addressed to himself on the table. He took it up and read it through. At the end, he looked up and said, 'What are you waiting for?'

'An answer to the question I axed.'

'I gave it you before. Don't waste any more of your time.'

'Yo' made a remark, sir, on my impudence: but I were taught that it was manners to say either "yes" or "no," when I were axed a civil question. I should be thankfu' to yo' if yo' give me work. Hamper will speak to my being a good hand.'

'I've a notion you'd better not send me to Hamper to ask for a character, my man. I might hear more than you'd like.'

'I'd take th' risk. Worst they could say of me is, that I did what I thought best, even to my own wrong.'

'You'd better go and try them, then, and see whether they'll give you work. I've turned off upwards of a hundred of my best hands, for no other fault than following you and such as you; and d'ye think I'll take you on? I might as well put a fire-brand into the midst of the cotton-waste.'

Higgins turned away; then the recollection of Boucher came over him, and he faced round with the greatest concession he could persuade himself to make.

'I'd promise yo', measter, I'd not speak a word as could do harm, if so be yo' did right by us; and I'd promise more: I'd promise that when I seed yo' going wrong, and acting unfair, I'd speak to yo' in private first; and that would be a fair warning. If yo' and I did na agree in our opinion o' your conduct, yo' might turn me off at an hour's notice.'

'Upon my word, you don't think small beer of yourself! Hamper has had a loss of you. How came he to let you and your wisdom go?'

'Well, we parted wi' mutual dissatisfaction. I wouldn't gi'e the pledge they were asking; and they wouldn't have me at no rate. So I'm free to make another engagement; and as I said before, though I should na' say it, I'm a good hand, measter, and a steady man – specially when I can keep fro' drink; and that I shall do now, if I ne'er did afore.'

'That you may have more money laid up for another strike, I suppose?'

'No! I'd be thankful if I was free to do that; it's for to keep th' widow and childer of a man who was drove mad by them knobsticks o' yourn; put out of his place by a Paddy[1] that did na know weft fro' warp.'

'Well! you'd better turn to something else, if you've any such good intention in your head. I shouldn't advise you to stay in Milton: you're too well known here.'

'If it were summer,' said Higgins, 'I'd take to Paddy's work, and go as a navvy, or haymaking, or summut, and ne'er see Milton again. But it's winter, and th' childer will clem.'

'A pretty navvy you'd make! why, you couldn't do half a day's work at digging against an Irishman.'

'I'd only charge half-a-day for th' twelve hours, if I could only do half-a-day's work in th' time. Yo're not knowing of any place, where they could gi' me a trial, away fro' the mills, if I'm such a firebrand? I'd take any wage they thought I was worth, for the sake of those childer.'

'Don't you see what you would be? You'd be a knobstick. You'd be taking less wages than the other labourers – all for the sake of another man's children. Think how you'd abuse any poor fellow who was willing to take what he could get to keep his own children. You and your Union would soon be down upon him. No! no! if it's only for the recollection of the way in which you've used the poor knobsticks before now, I say No! to your question. I'll not give you work. I won't say, I don't believe your pretext for coming and asking for work; I know nothing about it. It may be true, or it may not. It's a very unlikely story, at any rate. Let me pass. I'll not give you work. There's your answer.'

'I hear, sir. I would na ha' troubled yo', but that I were bid to come, by one as seemed to think yo'd getten some soft place in yo'r heart. Hoo were mistook, and I were misled. But I'm not the first man as is misled by a woman.'

'Tell her to mind her own business the next time, instead of taking up your time and mine too. I believe women are at the bottom of every plague in this world. Be off with you.'

'I'm obleeged to yo' for a' yo'r kindness, measter, and most of a' for yo'r civil way o' saying good-bye.'

Mr Thornton did not deign a reply. But, looking out of the window a minute after, he was struck with the lean, bent figure going out of the yard: the heavy walk was in strange contrast with the resolute, clear determination of the man to speak to him. He crossed to the porter's lodge:

'How long has that man Higgins been waiting to speak to me?'

'He was outside the gate before eight o'clock, sir. I think he's been there ever since.'

'And it is now –?'

'Just one, sir.'

'Five hours,' thought Mr Thornton: 'it's a long time for a man to wait, doing nothing but first hoping and then fearing.'

CHAPTER XXXIX

Making Friends

Nay, I have done; you get no more of me:[1]
And I am glad, yea glad with all my heart,
That thus so clearly I myself am free.

DRAYTON

Margaret shut herself up in her own room, after she had quitted Mrs Thornton. She began to walk backwards and forwards, in her old habitual way of showing agitation; but, then, remembering that in that slightly-built house every step was heard from one room to another, she sate down until she heard Mrs Thornton go safely out of the house. She forced herself to recollect all the conversation that had passed between them; speech by speech she compelled her

314

memory to go through with it. At the end, she rose up, and said to herself, in a melancholy tone:

'At any rate, her words do not touch me; they fall off from me; for I am innocent of all the motives she attributes to me. But still, it is hard to think that any one – any woman – can believe all this of another so easily. It is hard and sad. Where I have done wrong she does not accuse me – she does not know. He never told her: I might have known he would not!'

She lifted up her head, as if she took pride in any delicacy of feeling which Mr Thornton had shown. Then, as a new thought came across her, she pressed her hands tightly together:

'He, too, must take poor Frederick for some lover.' (She blushed as the word passed through her mind.) 'I see it now. It is not merely that he knows of my falsehood, but he believes that some one else cares for me; and that I – Oh dear! – oh dear! what shall I do? What do I mean? Why do I care what he thinks, beyond the mere loss of his good opinion as regards my telling the truth or not? I cannot tell. But I am very miserable! Oh, how unhappy this last year has been! I have passed out of childhood into old age. I have had no youth – no womanhood; the hopes of womanhood have closed for me – for I shall never marry; and I anticipate cares and sorrows just as if I were an old woman, and with the same fearful spirit. I am weary² of this continual call upon me for strength. I could bear up for papa; because that is a natural, pious duty. And I think I could bear up against – at any rate, I could have the energy to resent, Mrs Thornton's unjust, impertinent suspicions. But it is hard to feel how completely he must misunderstand me. What has happened to make me so morbid today? I do not know. I only know I cannot help it. I must give way sometimes. No, I will not, though,' said she, springing to her feet. 'I will not – I *will* not think of myself and my own position. I won't examine into my own feelings. It would be of no use now. Some time, if I live to be an old woman, I may sit over the fire, and, looking into the embers, see the life that might have been.'

All this time, she was hastily putting on her things to go out, only stopping from time to time to wipe her eyes, with an impatience of gesture at the tears that would come, in spite of all her bravery.

'I dare say, there's many a woman makes as sad a mistake as I have done, and only finds it out too late. And how proudly and impertinently I spoke to him that day! But I did not know then. It has come upon me little by little, and I don't know where it began.

315

Now I won't give way. I shall find it difficult to behave in the same way to him, with this miserable consciousness upon me; but I will be very calm and very quiet, and say very little. But, to be sure, I may not see him; he keeps out of our way evidently. That would be worse than all. And yet no wonder that he avoids me, believing what he must about me.'

She went out, going rapidly towards the country, and trying to drown reflection by swiftness of motion.

As she stood on the door-step, at her return, her father came up:

'Good girl!' said he. 'You've been to Mrs Boucher's. I was just meaning to go there, if I had time, before dinner.'

'No, papa; I have not,' said Margaret, reddening, 'I never thought about her. But I will go directly after dinner; I will go while you are taking your nap.'

Accordingly Margaret went. Mrs Boucher was very ill; really ill – not merely ailing. The kind and sensible neighbour, who had come in the other day, seemed to have taken charge of everything. Some of the children were gone to the neighbours. Mary Higgins had come for the three youngest at dinner-time; and since then Nicholas had gone for the doctor. He had not come as yet; Mrs Boucher was dying; and there was nothing to do but to wait. Margaret thought that she should like to know his opinion, and that she could not do better than go and see the Higginses in the meantime. She might then possibly hear whether Nicholas had been able to make his application to Mr Thornton.

She found Nicholas busily engaged in making a penny spin on the dresser, for the amusement of three little children, who were clinging to him in a fearless manner. He, as well as they, was smiling at a good long spin; and Margaret thought, that the happy look of interest in his occupation was a good sign. When the penny stopped spinning, 'lile Johnnie' began to cry.

'Come to me,' said Margaret, taking him off the dresser, and holding him in her arms; she held her watch to his ear, while she asked Nicholas if he had seen Mr Thornton.

The look on his face changed instantly.

'Ay!' said he. 'I've seen and heerd too much on him.'

'He refused you, then?' said Margaret, sorrowfully.

'To be sure. I knew he'd do it all along. It's no good expecting marcy at the hands o' them measters. Yo're a stranger and a foreigner, and aren't likely to know their ways; but I knowed it.'

'I am sorry I asked you. Was he angry? He did not speak to you as Hamper did, did he?'

'He weren't o'er-civil!' said Nicholas, spinning the penny again, as much for his own amusement as for that of the children. 'Never yo' fret, I'm only where I was. I'll go on tramp tomorrow. I gave him as good as I got. I told him, I'd not that good opinion on him that I'd ha' come a second time of mysel'; but yo'd advised me for to come, and I were beholden to yo'.'

'You told him I sent you?'

'I dunno' if I ca'd yo' by your name. I dunnot think I did. I said, a woman who knew no better had advised me for to come and see if there was a soft place in his heart.'

'And he –?' asked Margaret.

'Said I were to tell yo' to mind yo'r own business. – That's the longest spin yet, my lads. – And them's civil words to what he used to me. But ne'er mind. We're but where we was; and I'll break stones on th' road afore I let these little uns clem.'

Margaret put the struggling Johnnie out of her arms, back into his former place on the dresser.

'I am sorry I asked you to go to Mr Thornton's. I am disappointed in him.'

There was a slight noise behind her. Both she and Nicholas turned round at the same moment, and there stood Mr Thornton, with a look of displeased surprise upon his face. Obeying her swift impulse, Margaret passed out before him, saying not a word, only bowing low to hide the sudden paleness that she felt had come over her face. He bent equally low in return, and then closed the door after her. As she hurried to Mrs Boucher's, she heard the clang, and it seemed to fill up the measure of her mortification. He too was annoyed to find her there. He had tenderness in his heart – 'a soft place,' as Nicholas Higgins called it; but he had some pride in concealing it; he kept it very sacred and safe, and was jealous of every circumstance that tried to gain admission. But if he dreaded exposure of his tenderness, he was equally desirous that all men should recognize his justice; and he felt that he had been unjust, in giving so scornful a hearing to any one who had waited, with humble patience, for five hours, to speak to him. That the man had spoken saucily to him when he had the opportunity, was nothing to Mr Thornton. He rather liked him for it; and he was conscious of his own irritability of temper at the time, which probably made them both quits. It was the five hours of waiting that struck Mr Thornton. He had not five hours to spare himself; but one hour – two hours, of his hard penetrating intellectual, as well as bodily labour, did he give up to going about collecting evidence as to the truth of Higgins's story, the nature of his character, the tenor of his life. He tried not to be, but was convinced that all that Higgins had said was true. And then the conviction went in, as if by some spell, and touched the latent tenderness of his heart; the patience of the man, the simple generosity of the motive (for he had learnt about the quarrel between Boucher and Higgins), made him forget entirely the mere reasonings of justice, and overleap them by a diviner instinct. He came to tell Higgins he would give him work; and he was more annoyed to find Margaret there than by hearing her last words; for then he understood that she was the woman who had urged Higgins to come to him; and he dreaded the admission of any thought of her, as a motive to what he was doing solely because it was right.

'So that was the lady you spoke of as a woman?' said he indignantly to Higgins. 'You might have told me who she was.'

'And then, maybe, yo'd ha' spoken of her more civil than yo' did; yo'd getten a mother who might ha' kept yo'r tongue in check when yo' were talking o' women being at the root o' all the plagues.'

'Of course you told that to Miss Hale?'

'In coorse I did. Leastways, I reckon I did. I telled her she weren't to meddle again in aught that concerned yo'.'

'Whose children are those – yours?' Mr Thornton had a pretty good notion whose they were, from what he had heard; but he felt awkward in turning the conversation round from this unpromising beginning.

'They're not mine, and they are mine.'

'They are the children you spoke of to me this morning?'

'When yo' said,' replied Higgins, turning round, with ill-smothered fierceness, 'that my story might be true or might not, but it were a very unlikely one. Measter, I've not forgotten.'

Mr Thornton was silent for a moment; then he said: 'No more have I. I remember what I said. I spoke to you about these children in a way I had no business to do. I did not believe you. I could not have taken care of another man's children myself, if he had acted towards me as I hear Boucher did towards you. But I know now that you spoke truth. I beg your pardon.'

Higgins did not turn round, or immediately respond to this. But when he did speak, it was in a softened tone, although the words were gruff enough.

'Yo've no business to go prying into what happened between Boucher and me. He's dead, and I'm sorry. That's enough.'

'So it is. Will you take work with me? That's what I came to ask.'

Higgins's obstinacy wavered, recovered strength, and stood firm. He would not speak. Mr Thornton would not ask again. Higgins's eye fell on the children.

'Yo've called me impudent, and a liar, and a mischief-maker, and yo' might ha' said wi' some truth, as I were now and then given to drink. An' I ha' called you a tyrant, an' an oud bull-dog, and a hard, cruel master; that's where it stands. But for th' childer. Measter, do yo' think we can e'er get on together?'

'Well!' said Mr Thornton, half-laughing, 'it was not my proposal that we should go together. But there's one comfort, on your own showing. We neither of us can think much worse of the other than we do now.'

'That's true,' said Higgins, reflectively. 'I've been thinking, ever sin' I saw you, what a marcy it were yo' did na take me on, for that I ne'er saw a man whom I could less abide. But that's maybe been a hasty judgment; and work's work to such as me. So, measter, I'll come; and what's more, I thank yo'; and that's a deal fro' me,' said he, more frankly, suddenly turning round and facing Mr Thornton fully for the first time.

'And this is a deal from me,' said Mr Thornton, giving Higgins's hand a good grip. 'Now mind you come sharp to your time,' continued he, resuming the master. 'I'll have no laggards at my mill. What fines we have, we keep pretty sharply. And the first time I catch you making mischief, off you go. So now you know where you are.'

'Yo' spoke of my wisdom this morning. I reckon I may bring it wi' me; or would yo' rayther have me 'bout my brains?'

''Bout your brains if you use them for meddling with my business; with your brains if you can keep them to your own.'

'I shall need a deal o' brains to settle where my business ends and yo'rs begins.'

'Your business has not begun yet, and mine stands still for me. So good afternoon.'

Just before Mr Thornton came up to Mrs Boucher's door, Margaret came out of it. She did not see him; and he followed her for several yards, admiring her light and easy walk, and her tall and graceful figure. But, suddenly, this simple emotion of pleasure was tainted, poisoned by jealousy. He wished to overtake her, and speak to her, to see how she would receive him, now she must know he was aware of some other attachment. He wished too, but of this wish he was rather ashamed, that she should know that he had justified her wisdom in sending Higgins to him to ask for work, and had repented him of his morning's decision. He came up to her. She started.

'Allow me to say, Miss Hale, that you were rather premature in expressing your disappointment. I have taken Higgins on.'

'I am glad of it,' said she, coldly.

'He tells me, he repeated to you, what I said this morning about –' Mr Thornton hesitated. Margaret took it up:

'About women not meddling. You had a perfect right to express your opinion, which was a very correct one, I have no doubt. But,' she went on a little more eagerly, 'Higgins did not quite tell you the exact truth.' The word 'truth,' reminded her of her own untruth, and she stopped short, feeling exceedingly uncomfortable.

Mr Thornton at first was puzzled to account for her silence; and then he remembered the lie she had told, and all that was foregone. 'The exact truth!' said he. 'Very few people do speak the exact truth. I have given up hoping for it. Miss Hale, have you no explanation to give me? You must perceive what I cannot but think.'

Margaret was silent. She was wondering whether an explanation of any kind would be consistent with her loyalty to Frederick.

'Nay,' said he, 'I will ask no farther. I may be putting temptation in your way. At present, believe me, your secret is safe with me. But you run great risks, allow me to say, in being so indiscreet. I am now only speaking as a friend of your father's: if I had any other thought or hope, of course that is at an end. I am quite disinterested.'

'I am aware of that,' said Margaret, forcing herself to speak in an indifferent, careless way. 'I am aware of what I must appear to you, but the secret is another person's, and I cannot explain it without doing him harm.'

'I have not the slightest wish to pry into the gentleman's secrets,' he said, with growing anger. 'My own interest in you is – simply that of a friend. You may not believe me, Miss Hale, but it is – in spite of the persecution I'm afraid I threatened you with at one time – but that is all given up; all passed away. You believe me, Miss Hale?'

'Yes,' said Margaret, quietly and sadly.

'Then, really, I don't see any occasion for us to go on walking together. I thought, perhaps you might have had something to say, but I see we are nothing to each other. If you're quite convinced, that any foolish passion on my part is entirely over, I will wish you good afternoon.' He walked off very hastily.

'What can he mean?' thought Margaret – 'what could he mean by speaking so, as if I were always thinking that he cared for me, when I know he does not; he cannot. His mother will have said all those cruel things about me to him. But I won't care for him. I surely am mistress enough of myself to control this wild, strange, miserable feeling, which tempted me even to betray my own dear Frederick, so that I might but regain his good opinion – the good opinion of a man who takes such pains to tell me that I am nothing to him. Come! poor little heart! be cheery and brave. We'll be a great deal to one another, if we are thrown off and left desolate.'

Her father was almost startled by her merriment this afternoon. She talked incessantly, and forced her natural humour to an unusual pitch; and if there was a tinge of bitterness in much of what she said; if her accounts of the old Harley Street set were a little sarcastic, her father could not bear to check her, as he would have done at another time – for he was glad to see her shake off her cares. In the middle of the evening, she was called down to speak to Mary Higgins; and when she came back, Mr Hale imagined that he saw traces of tears on her cheeks. But that could not be, for she brought good news – that Higgins had got work at Mr Thornton's mill. Her spirits were damped, at any rate, and she found it very difficult to go on talking at all, much more in the wild way that she had done. For some days her spirits varied strangely; and her father was beginning to be anxious about her, when news arrived from one or two quarters that promised some change and variety for her. Mr Hale received a letter from Mr Bell, in which that gentleman volunteered a visit to them; and Mr Hale imagined that the promised society of his old Oxford friend would give as agreeable a turn to Margaret's ideas as it did to his own. Margaret tried to take an interest in what pleased her father; but she was too languid to care about any Mr Bell, even though he were twenty times her godfather. She was more roused by a letter from Edith, full of sympathy about her aunt's death; full of details about herself, her husband, and child; and at the end saying, that as the climate did not suit the baby, and as Mrs Shaw was talking of returning to England, she thought it probable that Captain

Lennox might sell out, and that they might all go and live again in the old Harley Street house; which, however, would seem very incomplete without Margaret. Margaret yearned after that old house, and the placid tranquillity of that old well-ordered, monotonous life. She had found it occasionally tiresome while it lasted; but since then she had been buffeted about, and felt so exhausted by this recent struggle with herself, that she thought that even stagnation would be a rest and a refreshment. So she began to look towards a long visit to the Lennoxes, on their return to England, as to a point – no, not of hope – but of leisure, in which she could regain her power and command over herself. At present it seemed to her as if all subjects tended towards Mr Thornton; as if she could not forget him with all her endeavours. If she went to see the Higginses, she heard of him there; her father had resumed their readings together, and quoted his opinions perpetually; even Mr Bell's visit brought his tenant's name upon the tapis; for he wrote word that he believed he must be occupied some great part of his time with Mr Thornton, as a new lease was in preparation, and the terms of it must be agreed upon.

CHAPTER XL

Out of Tune

I have no wrong, where I can claim no right,[1]
Naught ta'en me fro, where I have nothing had,
Yet of my woe I cannot so be quite;
Namely, since that another may be glad
With that, that thus in sorrow makes me sad.

WYATT

Margaret had not expected much pleasure to herself from Mr Bell's visit – she had only looked forward to it on her father's account, but when her godfather came, she at once fell into the most natural position of friendship in the world. He said she had no merit in being what she was, a girl so entirely after his own heart; it was an hereditary power which she had, to walk in and take possession of his regard; while she, in reply, gave him much credit for being so fresh and young under his Fellow's cap and gown.

'Fresh and young in warmth and kindness, I mean. I'm afraid I must own, that I think your opinions are the oldest and mustiest I have met with this long time.'

'Hear this daughter of yours, Hale! Her residence in Milton has quite corrupted her. She's a democrat, a red republican, a member of the Peace Society, a socialist –'

'Papa, it's all because I'm standing up for the progress of commerce. Mr Bell would have had it keep still at exchanging wild-beast skins for acorns.'

'No, no. I'd dig the ground and grow potatoes. And I'd shave the wild-beast skins and make the wool into broad cloth. Don't exaggerate, missy. But I'm tired of this bustle. Everybody rushing over everybody, in their hurry to get rich.'

'It is not every one who can sit comfortably in a set of college rooms, and let his riches grow without any exertion of his own. No doubt there is many a man here who would be thankful if his property would increase as yours has done, without his taking any trouble about it,' said Mr Hale.

'I don't believe they would. It's the bustle and the struggle they like. As for sitting still, and learning from the past, or shaping out the future by faithful work done in a prophetic spirit – Why! Pooh! I don't believe there's a man in Milton who knows how to sit still; and it is a great art.'

'Milton people, I suspect, think Oxford men don't know how to move. It would be a very good thing if they mixed a little more.'

'It might be good for the Miltoners. Many things might be good for them which would be very disagreeable for other people.'

'Are you not a Milton man yourself?' asked Margaret. 'I should have thought you would have been proud of your town.'

'I confess, I don't see what there is to be proud of. If you'll only come to Oxford, Margaret, I will show you a place to glory in.'

'Well!' said Mr Hale, 'Mr Thornton is coming to drink tea with us tonight, and he is as proud of Milton as you of Oxford. You two must try and make each other a little more liberal-minded.'

'I don't want to be more liberal-minded, thank you,' said Mr Bell.

'Is Mr Thornton coming to tea, papa?' asked Margaret in a low voice.

'Either to tea or soon after. He could not tell. He told us not to wait.'

Mr Thornton had determined that he would make no inquiry of

his mother as to how far she had put her project into execution of speaking to Margaret about the impropriety of her conduct. He felt pretty sure that, if this interview took place, his mother's account of what passed at it would only annoy and chagrin him, though he would all the time be aware of the colouring which it received by passing through her mind. He shrank from hearing Margaret's very name mentioned; he, while he blamed her – while he was jealous of her – while he renounced her – he loved her sorely, in spite of himself. He dreamt of her; he dreamt she came dancing towards him with outspread arms, and with a lightness and gaiety which made him loathe her, even while it allured him. But the impression of this figure of Margaret – with all Margaret's character taken out of it, as completely as if some evil spirit had got possession of her form – was so deeply stamped upon his imagination, that when he wakened he felt hardly able to separate the Una from the Duessa;[2] and the dislike he had to the latter seemed to envelop and disfigure the former. Yet he was too proud to acknowledge his weakness by avoiding the sight of her. He would neither seek an opportunity of being in her company nor avoid it. To convince himself of his power of self-control, he lingered over every piece of business this afternoon; he forced every movement into unnatural slowness and deliberation; and it was consequently past eight o'clock before he reached Mr Hale's. Then there were business arrangements to be transacted in the study with Mr Bell; and the latter kept on, sitting over the fire, and talking wearily, long after all business was transacted, and when they might just as well have gone upstairs. But Mr Thornton would not say a word about moving their quarters; he chafed and chafed, and thought Mr Bell a most prosy companion; while Mr Bell returned the compliment in secret, by considering Mr Thornton about as brusque and curt a fellow as he had ever met with, and terribly gone off both in intelligence and manner. At last, some slight noise in the room above suggested the desirableness of moving there. They found Margaret with a letter open before her, eagerly discussing its contents with her father. On the entrance of the gentlemen, it was immediately put aside; but Mr Thornton's eager senses caught some few words of Mr Hale's to Mr Bell.

'A letter from Henry Lennox. It makes Margaret very hopeful.'

Mr Bell nodded. Margaret was red as a rose when Mr Thornton looked at her. He had the greatest mind in the world to get up and go out of the room that very instant, and never set foot in the house again.

'We were thinking,' said Mr Hale, 'that you and Mr Thornton

had taken Margaret's advice, and were each trying to convert the other, you were so long in the study.'

'And you thought there would be nothing left of us but an opinion, like the Kilkenny cat's[3] tail. Pray whose opinion did you think would have the most obstinate vitality?'

Mr Thornton had not a notion what they were talking about, and disdained to inquire. Mr Hale politely enlightened him.

'Mr Thornton, we were accusing Mr Bell this morning of a kind of Oxonian mediæval bigotry against his native town; and we – Margaret, I believe – suggested that it would do him good to associate a little with Milton manufacturers.'

'I beg your pardon. Margaret thought it would do the Milton manufacturers good to associate a little more with Oxford men. Now wasn't it so, Margaret?'

'I believe I thought it would do both good to see a little more of the other, – I did not know it was my idea any more than papa's.'

'And so you see, Mr Thornton, we ought to have been improving each other down stairs, instead of talking over vanished families of Smiths and Harrisons. However, I am willing to do my part now. I wonder when you Milton men intend to live.[4] All your lives seem to be spent in gathering together the materials for life.'

'By living, I suppose you mean enjoyment.'

'Yes, enjoyment, – I don't specify of what, because I trust we should both consider mere pleasure as very poor enjoyment.'

'I would rather have the nature of the enjoyment defined.'

'Well! enjoyment of leisure – enjoyment of the power and influence which money gives. You are all striving for money. What do you want it for?'

Mr Thornton was silent. Then he said, 'I really don't know. But money is not what I strive for.'

'What then?'

'It is a home question. I shall have to lay myself open to such a catechist, and I am not sure that I am prepared to do it.'

'No!' said Mr Hale; 'don't let us be personal in our catechism. You are neither of you representative men; you are each of you too individual for that.'

'I am not sure whether to consider that as a compliment or not. I should like to be the representative of Oxford, with its beauty and its learning, and its proud old history. What do you say, Margaret; ought I to be flattered?'

'I don't know Oxford. But there is a difference between being the representative of a city and the representative man of its inhabitants.'

'Very true, Miss Margaret. Now I remember, you were against me this morning, and were quite Miltonian and manufacturing in your preferences.' Margaret saw the quick glance of surprise that Mr Thornton gave her, and she was annoyed at the construction which he might put on this speech of Mr Bell's. Mr Bell went on –

'Ah! I wish I could show you our High Street – our Radcliffe Square. I am leaving out our colleges, just as I give Mr Thornton leave to omit his factories in speaking of the charms of Milton. I have a right to abuse my birth-place. Remember I am a Milton man.'

Mr Thornton was annoyed more than he ought to have been at all that Mr Bell was saying. He was not in a mood for joking. At another time, he could have enjoyed Mr Bell's half testy condemnation of a town where the life was so at variance with every habit he had formed; but now, he was galled enough to attempt to defend what was never meant to be seriously attacked.

'I don't set up Milton as a model of a town.'

'Not in architecture?' slyly asked Mr Bell.

'No! we've been too busy to attend to mere outward appearances.'

'Don't say *mere* outward appearances,' said Mr Hale, gently. 'They impress us all, from childhood upward – every day of our life.'

'Wait a little while,' said Mr Thornton. 'Remember, we are of a different race from the Greeks,[5] to whom beauty was everything, and to whom Mr Bell might speak of a life of leisure and serene enjoyment, much of which entered in through their outward senses. I don't mean to despise them, any more than I would ape them. But I belong to Teutonic blood; it is little mingled in this part of England to what it is in others; we retain much of their language; we retain more of their spirit; we do not look upon life as a time for enjoyment, but as a time for action and exertion. Our glory and our beauty arise out of our inward strength, which makes us victorious over material resistance, and over greater difficulties still. We are Teutonic up here in Darkshire in another way. We hate to have laws made for us at a distance. We wish people would allow us to right ourselves, instead of continually meddling, with their imperfect legislation. We stand up for self-government, and oppose centralization.'

'In short, you would like the Heptarchy[6] back again. Well, at any rate, I revoke what I said this morning – that you Milton people did not reverence the past. You are regular worshippers of Thor.'

'If we do not reverence the past as you do in Oxford, it is because we want something which can apply to the present more directly. It is fine when the study of the past leads to a prophecy of the future. But to men groping in new circumstances, it would be finer if the words of experience could direct us how to act in what concerns us most intimately and immediately; which is full of difficulties that must be encountered; and upon the mode in which they are met and conquered – not merely pushed aside for the time – depends our future. Out of the wisdom of the past, help us over the present. But no! People can speak of Utopia much more easily than of the next day's duty; and yet when that duty is all done by others, who so ready to cry, "Fie, for shame!"'

'And all this time I don't see what you are talking about. Would you Milton men condescend to send up your today's difficulty to Oxford? You have not tried us yet.'

Mr Thornton laughed outright at this. 'I believe I was talking with reference to a good deal that has been troubling us of late; I was thinking of the strikes we have gone through, which are troublesome and injurious things enough, as I am finding to my cost. And yet this last strike, under which I am smarting, has been respectable.'

'A respectable strike!' said Mr Bell. 'That sounds as if you were far gone in the worship of Thor.'

Margaret felt, rather than saw, that Mr Thornton was chagrined by the repeated turning into jest of what he was feeling as very serious. She tried to change the conversation from a subject about which one party cared little, while, to the other, it was deeply, because personally, interesting. She forced herself to say something.

'Edith says she finds the printed calicoes in Corfu better and cheaper than in London.'

'Does she?' said her father. 'I think that must be one of Edith's exaggerations. Are you sure of it, Margaret?'

'I am sure she says so, papa.'

'Then I am sure of the fact,' said Mr Bell. 'Margaret, I go so far in my idea of your truthfulness, that it shall cover your cousin's character. I don't believe a cousin of yours could exaggerate.'

'Is Miss Hale so remarkable for truth?' said Mr Thornton, bitterly. The moment he had done so, he could have bitten his tongue out. What was he? And why should he stab her with her shame in this way? How evil he was tonight; possessed by ill-humour at being detained so long from her; irritated by the mention of some name, because he thought it belonged to a more successful lover; now ill-tempered because he had been unable to cope, with a light heart, against one who was trying, by gay and careless speeches, to make the evening pass pleasantly away, – the kind old friend to all parties, whose manner by this time might be well known to Mr Thornton, who had been acquainted with him for many years. And then to speak to Margaret as he had done! She did not get up and leave the room, as she had done in former days, when his abruptness or his temper had annoyed her. She sat quite still, after the first momentary glance of grieved surprise, that made her eyes look like some child's who has met with an unexpected rebuff; they slowly dilated into mournful, reproachful sadness; and then they fell, and she bent over her work, and did not speak again. But he could not help looking at her, and he saw a sigh tremble over her body, as if she quivered in some unwonted chill. He felt as the mother would have done, in the midst of 'her rocking it, and rating it,'[8] had she been called away before her slow confiding smile, implying perfect trust in mother's love, had proved the renewing of its love. He gave short sharp answers; he was uneasy and cross, unable to discern between jest and earnest; anxious only for a look, a word of hers, before which to prostrate himself in penitent humility. But she neither looked nor spoke. Her round taper fingers flew in and out of her sewing, as steadily and swiftly as if that were the business of her life. She could not care for him, he thought, or else the passionate fervour of his wish would have forced her to raise those eyes, if but for an instant, to read the late repentance in his. He could have struck her before he left, in order that by some strange overt act of rudeness, he might earn the privilege of telling her the remorse that gnawed at his heart. It was well that the long walk in the open air wound up this evening for him. It sobered him back into grave resolution, that henceforth he would see as little of her as possible, – since the very sight of that face and form, the very sounds of that voice (like the soft winds of pure melody) had such power to move him from his balance. Well! He had known what love was – a sharp pang, a fierce experience, in the midst of whose flames he was struggling! but, through that furnace he would fight his way out into the serenity of middle age, – all the richer and more human for having known this great passion.

When he had somewhat abruptly left the room, Margaret rose from her seat, and began silently to fold up her work. The long seams were heavy, and had an unusual weight for her languid arms.

The round lines on her face took a lengthened, straighter form, and her whole appearance was that of one who had gone through a day of great fatigue. As the three prepared for bed, Mr Bell muttered forth a little condemnation of Mr Thornton.

'I never saw a fellow so spoiled by success. He can't bear a word; a jest of any kind. Everything seems to touch on the soreness of his high dignity. Formerly, he was as simple and noble as the open day; you could not offend him, because he had no vanity.'

'He is not vain now,' said Margaret, turning round from the table, and speaking with quiet distinctness. 'Tonight he has not been like himself. Something must have annoyed him before he came here.'

Mr Bell gave her one of his sharp glances from above his spectacles. She stood it quite calmly; but, after she had left the room, he suddenly asked, –

'Hale! did it ever strike you that Thornton and your daughter have what the French call a tendresse for each other?'

'Never!' said Mr Hale, first startled and then flurried by the new idea. 'No, I am sure you are wrong. I am almost certain you are mistaken. If there is anything, it is all on Mr Thornton's side. Poor fellow! I hope and trust he is not thinking of her, for I am sure she would not have him.'

'Well! I'm a bachelor, and have steered clear of love affairs all my life; so perhaps my opinion is not worth having. Or else I should say there were very pretty symptoms about her!'

'Then I am sure you are wrong,' said Mr Hale. 'He may care for her, though she really has been almost rude to him at times. But she! – why, Margaret would never think of him, I'm sure! Such a thing has never entered her head.'

'Entering her heart would do. But I merely threw out a suggestion of what might be. I dare say I was wrong. And whether I was wrong or right, I'm very sleepy; so, having disturbed your night's rest (as I can see) with my untimely fancies, I'll betake myself with an easy mind to my own.'

But Mr Hale resolved that he would not be disturbed by any such nonsensical idea; so he lay awake, determining not to think about it.

Mr Bell took his leave the next day, bidding Margaret look to him as one who had a right to help and protect her in all her troubles, of whatever nature they might be. To Mr Hale he said, –

'That Margaret of yours has gone deep into my heart. Take care of her, for she is a very precious creature, – a great deal too good for

329

Milton, – only fit for Oxford, in fact. The town, I mean; not the men. I can't match her yet. When I can, I shall bring my young man to stand side by side with your young woman, just as the genie in the Arabian Nights[9] brought Prince Caralmazan to match with the fairy's Princess Badoura.'

'I beg you'll do no such thing. Remember the misfortunes that ensued; and besides, I can't spare Margaret.'

'No; on second thoughts, we'll have her to nurse us ten years hence, when we shall be two cross old invalids. Seriously, Hale! I wish you'd leave Milton; which is a most unsuitable place for you, though it was my recommendation in the first instance. If you would, I'd swallow my shadows of doubts, and take a college living; and you and Margaret should come and live at the parsonage – you to be a sort of lay curate, and take the unwashed off my hands; and she to be our housekeeper – the village Lady Bountiful – by day; and read us to sleep in the evenings. I could be very happy in such a life. What do you think of it?'

'Never!' said Mr Hale, decidedly. 'My one great change has been made and my price of suffering paid. Here I stay out my life; and here will I be buried, and lost in the crowd.'

'I don't give up my plan yet. Only I won't bait you with it any more just now. Where's the Pearl?[10] Come, Margaret, give me a farewell kiss; and remember, my dear, where you may find a true friend, as far as his capability goes. You are my child, Margaret. Remember that, and God bless you!'

So they fell back into the monotony of the quiet life they would henceforth lead. There was no invalid to hope and fear about; even the Higginses – so long a vivid interest – seemed to have receded from any need of immediate thought. The Boucher children, left motherless orphans, claimed what of Margaret's care she could bestow; and she went pretty often to see Mary Higgins, who had charge of them. The two families were living in one house: the elder children were at humble schools, the younger ones were tended, in Mary's absence at her work, by the kind neighbour whose good sense had struck Margaret at the time of Boucher's death. Of course she was paid for her trouble; and indeed, in all his little plans and arrangements for these orphan children, Nicholas showed a sober judgment, and regulated method of thinking, which were at variance with his former more eccentric jerks of action. He was so steady at his work, that Margaret did not often see him during these winter months; but when she did, she saw that he winced away from any reference to the father of those children, whom he had so fully and heartily taken under his care. He did not speak easily of Mr Thornton.

'To tell the truth,' said he, 'he fairly bamboozles me. He's two chaps. One chap I knowed of old as were measter all o'er. T'other chap hasn't an ounce of measter's flesh about him. How them two chaps is bound up in one body, is a craddy for me to find out. I'll not be beat by it, though. Meanwhile he comes here pretty often; that's how I know the chap that's a man, not a measter. And I reckon he's taken aback by me pretty much as I am by him; for he sits and listens and stares, as if I were some strange beast newly caught in some of the zones. But I'm none daunted. It would take a deal to daunt me in my own house, as he sees. And I tell him some of my mind that I reckon he'd ha' been the better of hearing when he were a younger man.'

'And does he not answer you?' asked Mr Hale.

'Well! I'll not say th' advantage is all on his side, for all I take credit for improving him above a bit. Sometimes he says a rough thing or two, which is not agreeable to look at at first, but has a queer smack o' truth in it when yo' come to chew it. He'll be coming tonight, I reckon, about them childer's schooling. He's not satisfied wi' the make of it, and wants for t' examine 'em.'

'What are they' – began Mr Hale; but Margaret, touching his arm, showed him her watch.

'It is nearly seven,' she said. 'The evenings are getting longer now. Come, papa.' She did not breathe freely till they were some distance from the house. Then, as she became more calm, she wished that she had not been in so great a hurry; for, somehow, they saw Mr Thornton but very seldom now; and he might have come to see Higgins, and for the old friendship's sake she should like to have seen him tonight.

Yes! he came very seldom, even for the dull cold purpose of lessons. Mr Hale was disappointed in his pupil's lukewarmness about Greek literature, which had but a short time ago so great an interest for him. And now it often happened that a hurried note from Mr Thornton would arrive, just at the last moment, saying that he was so much engaged that he could not come to read with Mr Hale that evening. And though other pupils had taken more than his place as to time, no one was like his first scholar in Mr Hale's heart. He was depressed and sad at this partial cessation of an intercourse which had become dear to him; and he used to sit pondering over the reason that could have occasioned this change.

He startled Margaret, one evening as she sat at her work, by suddenly asking:

'Margaret! had you ever any reason for thinking that Mr Thornton cared for you?'

He almost blushed as he put this question; but Mr Bell's scouted idea recurred to him, and the words were out of his mouth before he well knew what he was about.

Margaret did not answer immediately; but by the bent drooping of her head, he guessed what her reply would be.

'Yes; I believe – oh papa, I should have told you.' And she dropped her work, and hid her face in her hands.

'No, dear; don't think that I am impertinently curious. I am sure you would have told me if you had felt that you could return his regard. Did he speak to you about it?'

No answer at first; but by-and-by a little gentle reluctant 'Yes.'

'And you refused him?'

A long sigh; a more helpless, nerveless attitude, and another 'Yes.' But before her father could speak, Margaret lifted up her face, rosy with some beautiful shame, and, fixing her eyes upon him, said:

'Now, papa, I have told you this, and I cannot tell you more; and then the whole thing is so painful to me; every word and action connected with it is so unspeakably bitter, that I cannot bear to think of it. Oh, papa, I am sorry to have lost you this friend, but I could not help it – but oh! I am very sorry.' She sate down on the ground, and laid her head on his knees.

'I too, am sorry, my dear. Mr Bell quite startled me when he said, some idea of the kind –'

'Mr Bell! Oh, did Mr Bell see it?'

'A little; but he took it into his head that you – how shall I say it? – that you were not ungraciously disposed towards Mr Thornton. I knew that could never be. I hoped the whole thing was but an imagination; but I knew too well what your real feelings were to suppose that you could ever like Mr Thornton in that way. But I am very sorry.'

They were very quiet and still for some minutes. But, on stroking her cheek in a caressing way soon after, he was almost shocked to find her face wet with tears. As he touched her, she sprang up, and smiling with forced brightness, began to talk of the Lennoxes with such a vehement desire to turn the conversation, that Mr Hale was too tender-hearted to try to force it back into the old channel.

'Tomorrow – yes, tomorrow they will be back in Harley Street. Oh, how strange it will be! I wonder what room they will make into the nursery? Aunt Shaw will be happy with the baby. Fancy Edith a mamma! And Captain Lennox – I wonder what he will do with himself now he has sold out!'

'I'll tell you what,' said her father anxious to indulge her in this fresh subject of interest, 'I think I must spare you for a fortnight just to run up to town and see the travellers. You could learn more, by half an hour's conversation with Mr Henry Lennox, about Frederick's chances, than in a dozen of these letters of his; so it would, in fact, be uniting business with pleasure.'

'No, papa, you cannot spare me, and what's more, I won't be spared.' Then, after a pause, she added: 'I am losing hope sadly about Frederick; he is letting us down gently, but I can see that Mr Lennox himself has no hope of hunting up the witnesses under years and years of time. No,' said she, 'that bubble was very pretty, and very dear to our hearts; but it has burst like many another; and we must console ourselves with being glad that Frederick is so happy, and with being a great deal to each other. So, don't offend me by talking of being able to spare me, papa, for I assure you you can't.'

But the idea of a change took root and germinated in Margaret's heart, although not in the way in which her father proposed it at first. She began to consider how desirable something of the kind would be to her father, whose spirits, always feeble, now became too frequently depressed, and whose health, though he never complained, had been seriously affected by his wife's illness and death. There were the regular hours of reading with his pupils, but that all giving and no receiving could no longer be called companionship, as in the old days when Mr Thornton came to study under him. Margaret was conscious of the want under which he was suffering, unknown to himself; the want of a man's intercourse with men. At Helstone there had been perpetual occasions for an interchange of visits with neighbouring clergymen; and the poor labourers in the fields, or leisurely tramping home at eve, or tending their cattle in the forest, were always at liberty to speak or be spoken to. But in Milton every one was too busy for quiet speech, or any ripened intercourse of thought; what they said was about business, very present and actual; and when the tension of mind relating to their daily affairs was over, they sunk into fallow rest until next morning. The workman was not to be found after the day's work was done; he had gone away to some lecture, or some club, or some beer-shop, according to his degree of character. Mr Hale thought of trying to deliver a course of lectures at some of the institutions, but he contemplated doing this so much as an effort of duty, and with so little of the genial impulse of love towards his work and its end, that Margaret was sure that it would not be well done until he could look upon it with some kind of zest.

CHAPTER XLI

The Journey's End

I see my way as birds their trackless way —[1]
I shall arrive! what time, what circuit first,
I ask not: but unless God send his hail
Or blinding fire-balls, sleet, or stifling snow,
In some time — his good time — I shall arrive;
He guides me and the bird. In His good time!
BROWNING'S PARACELSUS

So the winter was getting on, and the days were beginning to lengthen, without bringing with them any of the brightness of hope which usually accompanies the rays of a February sun. Mrs Thornton had of course entirely ceased to come to the house. Mr Thornton came occasionally, but his visits were addressed to her father, and were confined to the study. Mr Hale spoke of him as always the same; indeed, the very rarity of their intercourse seemed to make Mr Hale set only the higher value on it. And from what Margaret could gather of what Mr Thornton had said, there was nothing in the cessation of his visits which could arise from any umbrage or vexation. His business affairs had become complicated during the strike, and required closer attention than he had given to them last winter. Nay, Margaret could even discover that he spoke from time to time of her, and always, as far as she could learn, in the same calm friendly way, never avoiding and never seeking any mention of her name.

She was not in spirits to raise her father's tone of mind. The dreary peacefulness of the present time had been preceded by so long a period of anxiety and care – even intermixed with storms – that her mind had lost its elasticity. She tried to find herself occupation in teaching the two younger Boucher children, and worked hard at goodness; hard, I say most truly, for her heart seemed dead to the end of all her efforts; and though she made them punctually and painfully, yet she stood as far off as ever from any cheerfulness; her life seemed still bleak and dreary. The only thing she did well, was what she did out of unconscious piety, the silent comforting and consoling of her father. Not a mood of his but what found a ready sympathizer in Margaret; not a wish of his that she did not strive to forecast, and to fulfil. They were quiet wishes to be sure, and hardly named without hesitation and apology. All the more complete and beautiful was her meek spirit of obedience. March brought the news of Frederick's marriage. He and Dolores wrote; she in Spanish–English, as was but natural, and he with little turns and inversions of words which proved how far the idioms of his bride's country were infecting him.

On the receipt of Henry Lennox's letter, announcing how little hope there was of his ever clearing himself at a court-martial, in the absence of the missing witnesses, Frederick had written to Margaret a pretty vehement letter, containing his renunciation of England[2] as his country; he wished he could unnative himself, and declared that he would not take his pardon if it were offered him, nor live in the country if he had permission to do so. All of which made Margaret cry sorely, so unnatural did it seem to her at the first opening; but on consideration, she saw rather in such expression the poignancy of the disappointment which had thus crushed his hopes; and she felt that there was nothing for it but patience. In the next letter, Frederick spoke so joyfully of the future that he had no thought for the past; and Margaret found a use in herself for the patience she had been craving for him. She would have to be patient. But the pretty, timid, girlish letters of Dolores were beginning to have a charm for both Margaret and her father. The young Spaniard was so evidently anxious to make a favourable impression upon her lover's English relations, that her feminine care peeped out at every erasure; and the letters announcing the marriage, were accompanied by a splendid black lace mantilla, chosen by Dolores herself for her unseen sister-in-law, whom Frederick had represented as a paragon of beauty, wisdom and virtue. Frederick's worldly position was raised by this marriage on to as high a level as they could desire. Barbour and Co.

was one of the most extensive Spanish houses, and into it he was received as a junior partner. Margaret smiled a little, and then sighed as she remembered afresh her old tirades against trade. Here was her preux chevalier of a brother turned merchant, trader! But then she rebelled against herself, and protested silently against the confusion implied between a Spanish merchant and a Milton mill-owner. Well! trade or no trade, Frederick was very, very happy. Dolores must be charming, and the mantilla was exquisite! And then she returned to the present life.

Her father had occasionally experienced a difficulty in breathing this spring, which had for the time distressed him exceedingly. Margaret was less alarmed, as this difficulty went off completely in the intervals; but she still was so desirous of his shaking off the liability altogether, as to make her very urgent that he should accept Mr Bell's invitation to visit him at Oxford this April. Mr Bell's invitation included Margaret. Nay more, he wrote a special letter commanding her to come; but she felt as if it would be a greater relief to her to remain quietly at home, entirely free from any responsibility whatever, and so to rest her mind and heart in a manner which she had not been able to do for more than two years past.

When her father had driven off on his way to the railroad, Margaret felt how great and long had been the pressure on her time and her spirits. It was astonishing, almost stunning, to feel herself so much at liberty; no one depending on her for cheering care, if not for positive happiness; no invalid to plan and think for; she might be idle, and silent, and forgetful, – and what seemed worth more than all the other privileges – she might be unhappy if she liked. For months past, all her own personal cares and troubles had had to be stuffed away into a dark cupboard; but now she had leisure to take them out, and mourn over them, and study their nature, and seek the true method of subduing them into the elements of peace. All these weeks she had been conscious of their existence in a dull kind of way, though they were hidden out of sight. Now, once for all she would consider them, and appoint to each of them its right work in her life. So she sat almost motionless for hours in the drawing-room, going over the bitterness of every remembrance with an unwincing resolution. Only once she cried aloud, at the stinging thought of the faithlessness which gave birth to that abasing falsehood.

She now would not even acknowledge the force of the temptation;

her plans for Frederick had all failed, and the temptation lay there a dead mockery, – a mockery which had never had life in it; the lie had been so despicably foolish, seen by the light of the ensuing events, and faith in the power of truth so infinitely the greater wisdom!

In her nervous agitation, she unconsciously opened a book of her father's that lay upon the table, – the words that caught her eye in it, seemed almost made for her present state of acute self-abasement: –

Je ne voudrois[3] pas reprendre mon cœur en ceste sorte: meurs de honte, aveugle, impudent, traistre et desloyal à ton Dieu, et sembables choses; mais je voudrois le corriger par voye de compassion. Or sus, mon pauvre cœur, nous voilà tombez dans la fosse, laquelle nous avions tant resolu d'eschapper. Ah! relevons-nous, et quittons-là pour jamais, reclamons la misericorde de Dieu, et esperons en elle qu'elle nous assistera pour desormais estre plus fermes; et remettons-nous au chemin de l'humilité. Courage, soyons meshuy sur nos gardes, Dieu nous aydera.

'The way of humility. Ah,' thought Margaret, 'that is what I have missed! But courage, little heart. We will turn back, and by God's help we may find the lost path.'

So she rose up, and determined at once to set to on some work which should take her out of herself. To begin with she called in Martha, as she passed the drawing-room door in going upstairs, and tried to find out what was below the grave, respectful, servant-like manner, which crusted over her individual character with an obedience that was almost mechanical. She found it difficult to induce Martha to speak of any of her personal interests; but at last she touched the right chord, in naming Mrs Thornton. Martha's whole face brightened, and, on a little encouragement, out came a long story, of how her father had been in early life connected with Mrs Thornton's husband – nay, had even been in a position to show him some kindness; what, Martha hardly knew, for it had happened when she was quite a little child; and circumstances had intervened to separate the two families until Martha was nearly grown up, when, her father having sunk lower and lower from his original occupation as clerk in a warehouse, and her mother being dead, she and her sister, to use Martha's own expression, would have been 'lost' but for Mrs Thornton; who sought them out, and thought for them, and cared for them.

'I had had the fever, and was but delicate; and Mrs Thornton, and Mr Thornton too, they never rested till they had nursed me up in their own house, and sent me to the sea and all. The doctors said the fever was catching, but they cared none for that – only Miss Fanny, and she went a-visiting these folk that she is going to marry into. So, though she was afraid at the time, it has all ended well.'

'Miss Fanny going to be married!' exclaimed Margaret.

'Yes; and to a rich gentleman, too, only he's a deal older than she is. His name is Watson; and his mills are somewhere out beyond Hayleigh; it's a very good marriage, for all he's got such grey hair.'

At this piece of information, Margaret was silent long enough for Martha to recover her propriety, and, with it, her habitual shortness of answer. She swept up the hearth, asked at what time she should prepare tea, and quitted the room with the same wooden face with which she had entered it. Margaret had to pull herself up from indulging a bad trick, which she had lately fallen into, of trying to imagine how every event that she heard of in relation to Mr Thornton would affect him: whether he would like it or dislike it.

The next day she had the little Boucher children for their lessons, and took a long walk, and ended by a visit to Mary Higgins. Somewhat to Margaret's surprise, she found Nicholas already come home from his work; the lengthening light had deceived her as to the lateness of the evening. He too seemed, by his manners, to have entered a little more on the way of humility; he was quieter, and less self-asserting.

'So th' oud gentleman's away on his travels, is he?' said he. 'Little 'uns told me so. Eh! but the're sharp 'uns, they are; I a'most think they beat my own wenches for sharpness, though mappen it's wrong to say so, and one on 'em in her grave. There's summut in th' weather, I reckon, as sets folk a-wandering. My measter, him at th' shop yonder, is spinning about th' world somewhere.'

'Is that the reason you're so soon at home tonight?' asked Margaret innocently.

'Thou know'st nought about it, that's all,' said he, contemptuously. 'I'm not one wi' two faces – one for my measter, and t'other for his back. I counted a' th' clocks in the town striking afore I'd leave my work. No! yon Thornton's good enough for to fight wi', but too good for to be cheated. It were you as getten me the place, and I thank yo' for it. Thornton's is not a bad mill, as times go. Stand down, lad, and say yo'r pretty hymn to Miss Marget. That's right; steady on thy legs, and right arm out as straight as a skewer. One to stop, two to stay, three mak' ready, and four away!'

The little fellow repeated a Methodist hymn, far above his comprehension in point of language, but of which the swinging rhythm had caught his ear, and which he repeated with all the developed cadence of a member of parliament. When Margaret had duly applauded, Nicholas called for another, and yet another, much to her surprise, as she found him thus oddly and unconsciously led to take an interest in the sacred things which he had formerly scouted.

It was past the usual tea-time when she reached home; but she had the comfort of feeling that no one had been kept waiting for her; and of thinking her own thoughts while she rested, instead of anxiously watching another person to learn whether to be grave or gay. After tea she resolved to examine a large packet of letters, and pick out those that were to be destroyed.

Among them she came to four or five of Mr Henry Lennox's, relating to Frederick's affairs; and she carefully read them over again, with the sole intention, when she began, to ascertain exactly on how fine a chance the justification of her brother hung. But when she had finished the last, and weighed the pros and cons, the little personal revelation of character contained in them forced itself on her notice. It was evident enough, from the stiffness of the wording, that Mr Lennox had never forgotten his relation to her in any interest he might feel in the subject of the correspondence. They were clever letters; Margaret saw that in a twinkling; but she missed out of them all hearty and genial atmosphere. They were to be preserved, however, as valuable; so she laid them carefully on one side. When this little piece of business was ended, she fell into a reverie; and the thought of her absent father ran strangely in Margaret's head this night. She almost blamed herself for having felt her solitude (and consequently his absence) as a relief; but these two days had set her up afresh, with new strength and brighter hope. Plans which had lately appeared to her in the guise of tasks, now appeared like pleasures. The morbid scales had fallen from her eyes, and she saw her position and her work more truly. If only Mr Thornton would restore her the lost friendship, – nay, if he would only come from time to time to cheer her father as in former days, – though she should never see him, she felt as if the course of her future life, though not brilliant in prospect, might lie clear and even before her. She sighed as she rose up to go to bed. In spite of the 'One step's enough for me,' – in spite of the one plain duty of devotion to her father, – there lay at her heart an anxiety and a pang of sorrow.

And Mr Hale thought of Margaret, that April evening, just as strangely and as persistently as she was thinking of him. He had been fatigued by going about among his old friends and old familiar places. He had had exaggerated ideas of the change which his altered opinions might make in his friends' reception of him; but although some of them might have felt shocked or grieved or indignant at his falling off in the abstract, as soon as they saw the face of the man whom they had once loved, they forgot his opinions in himself; or only remembered them enough to give an additional tender gravity to their manner. For Mr Hale had not been known to many; he had belonged to one of the smaller colleges, and had always been shy and reserved; but those who in youth had cared to penetrate to the delicacy of thought and feeling that lay below his silence and indecision, took him to their hearts, with something of the protecting kindness which they would have shown to a woman.[4] And the renewal of this kindliness, after the lapse of years, and an interval of so much change, overpowered him more than any roughness or expression of disapproval could have done.

'I'm afraid we've done too much,' said Mr Bell. 'You're suffering now from having lived so long in that Milton air.'

'I am tired,' said Mr Hale. 'But it is not Milton air. I'm fifty-five years of age, and that little fact of itself accounts for any loss of strength.'

'Nonsense! I'm upwards of sixty, and feel no loss of strength, either bodily or mental. Don't let me hear you talking so. Fifty-five! why, you're quite a young man.'

Mr Hale shook his head. 'These last few years!' said he. But after a minute's pause, he raised himself from his half recumbent position, in one of Mr Bell's luxurious easy-chairs, and said with a kind of trembling earnestness:

'Bell! you're not to think, that if I could have foreseen all that would come of my change of opinion, and my resignation of my living – no! not even if I could have known how *she* would have suffered, – that I would undo it – the act of open acknowledgment that I no longer held the same faith as the church in which I was a priest. As I think now, even if I could have foreseen that cruellest martyrdom of suffering, through the sufferings of one whom I loved, I would have done just the same as far as that step of openly leaving the church went. I might have done differently, and acted more wisely, in all that I subsequently did for my family. But I don't think God endued me with over-much wisdom or strength,' he added, falling back into his old position.

Mr Bell blew his nose ostentatiously before answering. Then he said:

'He gave you strength to do what your conscience told you was right; and I don't see that we need any higher or holier strength than that; or wisdom either. I know I have not that much; and yet men set me down in their fool's books as a wise man; an independent character; strong-minded, and all that cant. The veriest idiot who obeys his own simple law of right, if it be but in wiping his shoes on a door-mat, is wiser and stronger than I. But what gulls men are!'

There was a pause. Mr Hale spoke first, in continuation of his thought.

'About Margaret.'

'Well! about Margaret. What then?'

'If I die —'

'Nonsense!'

'What will become of her — I often think? I suppose the Lennoxes will ask her to live with them. I try to think they will. Her aunt Shaw loved her well in her own quiet way; but she forgets to love the absent.'

'A very common fault. What sort of people are the Lennoxes?'

'He, handsome, fluent, and agreeable. Edith, a sweet little spoiled beauty. Margaret loves her with all her heart, and Edith with as much of her heart as she can spare.'

'Now, Hale; you know that girl of yours has got pretty nearly all my heart. I told you that before. Of course, as your daughter, as my god-daughter, I took great interest in her before I saw her the last time. But this visit that I paid to you at Milton made me her slave. I went, a willing old victim, following the car of the conqueror. For, indeed, she looks as grand and serene as one who has struggled, and may be struggling, and yet has the victory secure in sight. Yes, in spite of all her present anxieties, that was the look on her face. And so, all I have is at her service, if she needs it; and will be hers, whether she will or no, when I die. Moreover, I myself, will be her preux chevalier, sixty and gouty though I be. Seriously, old friend, your daughter shall be my principal charge in life, and all the help that either my wit or my wisdom or my willing heart can give, shall be hers. I don't choose her out as a subject for fretting. Something, I know of old, you must have to worry yourself about, or you wouldn't be happy. But you're going to outlive me by many a long year. You, spare, thin men are always tempting and always cheating Death! It's the stout, florid fellows like me, that always go off first.'

If Mr Bell had had a prophetic eye he might have seen the torch all but inverted and the angel with the grave and composed face[5] standing very nigh, beckoning to his friend. That night Mr Hale laid his head down on the pillow on which it never more should stir with life. The servant who entered his room in the morning, received no answer to his speech; drew near the bed, and saw the calm, beautiful face lying white and cold under the ineffaceable seal of death. The attitude was exquisitely easy; there had been no pain — no struggle. The action of the heart must have ceased as he lay down.

Mr Bell was stunned by the shock; and only recovered when the time came for being angry at every suggestion of his man's.

'A coroner's inquest? Pooh. You don't think I poisoned him! Dr Forbes says it is just the natural end of a heart complaint. Poor old Hale! You wore out that tender heart of yours before its time. Poor old friend! how he talked of his — Wallis, pack up a carpet-bag for me in five minutes. Here have I been talking. Pack it up, I say. I must go to Milton by the next train.'

The bag was packed, the cab ordered, the railway reached, in twenty minutes from the moment of this decision. The London train whizzed by, drew back some yards, and in Mr Bell was hurried by the impatient guard. He threw himself back in his seat, to try, with closed eyes, to understand how one in life yesterday could be dead today; and shortly tears stole out between his grizzled eye-lashes, at the feeling of which he opened his keen eyes, and looked as severely cheerful as his set determination could make him. He was not going to blubber before a set of strangers. Not he!

There was no set of strangers, only one sitting far from him on the same side. By and by Mr Bell peered at him, to discover what manner of man it was that might have been observing his emotion; and behind the great sheet of the outspread 'Times,' he recognized Mr Thornton.

'Why, Thornton! is that you?' said he, removing hastily to a closer proximity. He shook Mr Thornton vehemently by the hand, until the gripe ended in a sudden relaxation, for the hand was wanted to wipe away tears. He had last seen Mr Thornton in his friend Hale's company.

'I'm going to Milton, bound on a melancholy errand. Going to break to Hale's daughter the news of his sudden death!'

'Death! Mr Hale dead!'

'Ay; I keep saying it to myself, "Hale is dead!" but it doesn't make it any the more real. Hale is dead for all that. He went to bed well, to all appearance, last night, and was quite cold this morning when my servant went to call him.'

'Where? I don't understand!'

'At Oxford. He came to stay with me; hadn't been in Oxford this seventeen years – and this is the end of it.'

Not one word was spoken for above a quarter of an hour. Then Mr Thornton said:

'And she!' and stopped full short.

'Margaret you mean. Yes! I am going to tell her. Poor fellow! how full his thoughts were of her all last night! Good God! Last night only. And how immeasurably distant he is now! But I take Margaret as my child for his sake. I said last night I would take her for her own sake. Well, I take her for both.'

Mr Thornton made one or two fruitless attempts to speak, before he could get out the words:

'What will become of her!'

'I rather fancy there will be two people waiting for her: myself for one. I would take a live dragon into my house to live, if, by hiring such a chaperon, and setting up an establishment of my own, I could make my old age happy with having Margaret for a daughter. But there are those Lennoxes!'

'Who are they?' asked Mr Thornton with trembling interest.

'Oh, smart London people, who very likely will think they've the best right to her. Captain Lennox married her cousin – the girl she was brought up with. Good enough people, I dare say. And there's her aunt, Mrs Shaw. There might be a way open, perhaps, by my offering to marry that worthy lady! but that would be quite a pis aller. And then there's that brother!'

'What brother? A brother of her aunt's?'

'No, no; a clever Lennox, (the captain's a fool, you must understand); a young barrister, who will be setting his cap at Margaret. I know he has had her in his mind this five years or more: one of his chums told me as much; and he was only kept back by her want of fortune. Now that will be done away with.'

'How?' asked Mr Thornton, too earnestly curious to be aware of the impertinence of his question.

'Why, she'll have my money at my death. And if this Henry Lennox is half good enough for her, and she likes him – well! I might find another way of getting a home through a marriage. I'm dreadfully afraid of being tempted, at an unguarded moment, by the aunt.'

Neither Mr Bell nor Mr Thornton was in a laughing humour; so the oddity of any of the speeches which the former made was unnoticed by them. Mr Bell whistled, without emitting any sound beyond a long hissing breath; changed his seat, without finding comfort or rest; while Mr Thornton sat immoveably still, his eyes fixed on one spot in the newspaper, which he had taken up in order to give himself leisure to think.

'Where have you been?' asked Mr Bell, at length.

'To Havre. Trying to detect the secret of the great rise in the price of cotton.'

'Ugh! Cotton, and speculations, and smoke, well-cleansed and well-cared-for machinery, and unwashed and neglected hands. Poor old Hale! Poor old Hale! If you could have known the change which it was to him from Helstone. Do you know the New Forest at all?'

'Yes.' (Very shortly.)

'Then you can fancy the difference between it and Milton. What part were you in? Were you ever at Helstone? a little picturesque village, like some in the Odenwald?[6] You know Helstone?'

'I have seen it. It was a great change to leave it and come to Milton.'

He took up his newspaper with a determined air, as if resolved to avoid further conversation; and Mr Bell was fain to resort to his former occupation of trying to find out how he could best break the news to Margaret.

She was at an up-stairs window; she saw him alight; she guessed the truth with an instinctive flash. She stood in the middle of the drawing-room, as if arrested in her first impulse to rush down-stairs, and as if by the same restraining thought she had been turned to stone; so white and immoveable was she.

'Oh! don't tell me! I know it from your face! You would have sent – you would not have left him – if he were alive! Oh papa, papa!'

CHAPTER XLII

Alone! Alone!

When some beloved voice that was to you[1]
Both sound and sweetness, faileth suddenly,
And silence, against which you dare not cry,
Aches round you like a strong disease and new –
What hope? what help? what music will undo
That silence to your sense?

MRS BROWNING

The shock had been great. Margaret fell into a state of prostration, which did not show itself in sobs and tears, or even find the relief of words. She lay on the sofa, with her eyes shut, never speaking but when spoken to, and then replying in whispers. Mr Bell was perplexed. He dared not leave her; he dared not ask her to accompany him back to Oxford, which had been one of the plans he had formed on the journey to Milton, her physical exhaustion was evidently too complete for her to undertake any such fatigue – putting the sight that she would have to encounter out of the question. Mr Bell sate over the fire, considering what he had better do. Margaret lay motionless, and almost breathless by him. He would not leave her, even for the dinner which Dixon had prepared for him down-stairs, and, with sobbing hospitality, would fain have tempted him to eat. He had a plateful of something brought up to him. In general, he was particular and dainty enough, and knew well each shade of flavour in his food, but now the devilled chicken tasted like sawdust. He minced up some of the fowl for Margaret, and peppered and salted it well; but when Dixon, following his directions, tried to feed her, the languid shake of head, proved that in such a state as Margaret was in, food would only choke, not nourish her.

Mr Bell gave a great sigh; lifted up his stout old limbs (stiff with travelling) from their easy position, and followed Dixon out of the room.

'I can't leave her. I must write to them at Oxford, to see that the preparations are made: they can be getting on with these till I arrive. Can't Mrs Lennox come to her? I'll write and tell her she must. The girl must have some woman-friend about her, if only to talk her into a good fit of crying.'

Dixon was crying – enough for two; but, after wiping her eyes and steadying her voice, she managed to tell Mr Bell, that Mrs Lennox was too near her confinement to be able to undertake any journey at present.

'Well! I suppose we must have Mrs Shaw; she's come back to England, isn't she?'

'Yes, sir, she's come back; but I don't think she will like to leave Mrs Lennox at such an interesting time,' said Dixon, who did not much approve of a stranger entering the household, to share with her in her ruling care of Margaret.

'Interesting time be –' Mr Bell restricted himself to coughing over the end of his sentence. 'She could be content to be at Venice or Naples, or some of those Popish places, at the last "interesting time," which took place in Corfu, I think. And what does that little prosperous woman's "interesting time" signify, in comparison with that poor creature there, – that helpless, homeless, friendless, Margaret – lying as still on that sofa as if it were an altar-tomb, and she the stone statue on it. I tell you, Mrs Shaw shall come. See that a room, or whatever she wants, is got ready for her by tomorrow night. I'll take care she comes.'

Accordingly Mr Bell wrote a letter, which Mrs Shaw declared, with many tears, to be so like one of the dear general's when he was going to have a fit of the gout, that she should always value and preserve it. If he had given her the option, by requesting or urging her, as if a refusal were possible, she might not have come – true and sincere as was her sympathy with Margaret. It needed the sharp uncourteous command to make her conquer her vis inertiæ,[2] and allow herself to be packed by her maid, after the latter had completed the boxes. Edith, all cap, shawls, and tears, came out to the top of the stairs, as Captain Lennox was taking her mother down to the carriage:

'Don't forget, mamma: Margaret must come and live with us. Sholto[3] will go to Oxford on Wednesday, and you must send word by Mr Bell to him when we're to expect you. And if you want Sholto, he can go on from Oxford to Milton. Don't forget, mamma; you are to bring back Margaret.'

Edith re-entered the drawing-room. Mr Henry Lennox was there, cutting open the pages of a new Review. Without lifting his head, he said, 'If you don't like Sholto to be so long absent from you, Edith, I hope you will let me go down to Milton, and give what assistance I can.'

'Oh, thank you,' said Edith, 'I dare say old Mr Bell will do everything he can, and more help may not be needed. Only one does not look for much savoir-faire from a resident Fellow. Dear, darling Margaret! won't it be nice to have her here, again? You were both great allies, years ago.'

'Were we?' asked he indifferently, with an appearance of being interested in a passage in the Review.

'Well, perhaps not – I forget. I was so full of Sholto. But doesn't it fall out well, that if my uncle was to die, it should be just now, when we are come home, and settled in the old house, and quite ready to receive Margaret? Poor thing! what a change it will be to her from Milton! I'll have new chintz for her bedroom, and make it look new and bright, and cheer her up a little.'

In the same spirit of kindness, Mrs Shaw journeyed to Milton, occasionally dreading the first meeting, and wondering how it would be got over; but more frequently planning how soon she could get Margaret away from 'that horrid place,' and back into the pleasant comforts of Harley Street.

'Oh dear!' she said to her maid; 'look at those chimneys! My poor sister Hale! I don't think I could have rested at Naples, if I had known what it was! I must have come and fetched her and Margaret away.' And to herself she acknowledged, that she had always thought her brother-in-law rather a weak man, but never so weak as now, when she saw for what a place he had exchanged the lovely Helstone home.

Margaret had remained in the same state; white, motionless, speechless, tearless. They had told her that her Aunt Shaw was coming; but she had not expressed either surprise or pleasure, or dislike to the idea. Mr Bell, whose appetite had returned, and who appreciated Dixon's endeavours to gratify it, in vain urged upon her to taste some sweetbreads stewed with oysters; she shook her head with the same quiet obstinacy as on the previous day; and he was obliged to console himself for her rejection, by eating them all himself. But Margaret was the first to hear the stopping of the cab that brought her aunt from the railway station. Her eyelids quivered, her lips coloured and trembled. Mr Bell went down to meet Mrs Shaw; and when they came up. Margaret was standing, trying to steady her dizzy self; and when she saw her aunt, she went forward to the arms open to receive her, and first found the passionate relief of tears on her aunt's shoulder. All thoughts of quiet habitual love, of tenderness for years, of relationship to the dead, – all that inexplicable likeness in look, tone, and gesture, that seem to belong to one family, and which reminded Margaret so forcibly at this moment of her mother, – came in to melt and soften her numbed heart into the overflow of warm tears.

Mr Bell stole out of the room, and went down into the study, where he ordered a fire, and tried to divert his thoughts by taking down and examining the different books. Each volume brought a remembrance or a suggestion of his dead friend. It might be a change of employment from his two days' work of watching Margaret, but it was no change of thought. He was glad to catch the sound of Mr Thornton's voice, making enquiry at the door. Dixon was rather cavalierly dismissing him; for with the appearance of Mrs Shaw's maid, came visions of former grandeur of the Beresford blood, of the 'station' (so she was pleased to term it) from which her young lady had been ousted, and to which she was now, please God, to be restored. These visions, which she had been dwelling on with complacency in her conversation with Mrs Shaw's maid (skilfully eliciting meanwhile all the circumstances of state and consequence connected with the Harley Street establishment, for the edification of the listening Martha), made Dixon rather inclined to be supercilious in her treatment of any inhabitant of Milton; so, though she always stood rather in awe of Mr Thornton, she was as curt as she durst be in telling him that he could see none of the inmates of the house that night. It was rather uncomfortable to be contradicted in her statement by Mr Bell's opening the study-door, and calling out:

'Thornton! is that you? Come in for a minute or two; I want to speak to you.' So Mr Thornton went into the study, and Dixon had to retreat into the kitchen, and reinstate herself in her own esteem by a prodigious story of Sir John Beresford's coach and six, when he was high sheriff.

'I don't know what I wanted to say to you after all. Only it's dull enough to sit in a room where everything speaks to you of a dead friend. Yet Margaret and her aunt must have the drawing-room to themselves!'

'Is Mrs – is her aunt come?' asked Mr Thornton.

'Come? Yes! maid and all. One would have thought she might have come by herself at such a time! And now I shall have to turn out and find my way to the Clarendon.'

'You must not go to the Clarendon. We have five or six empty bed-rooms at home.'

'Well aired?'

'I think you may trust my mother for that.'

'Then I'll only run up-stairs and wish that wan girl good-night, and make my bow to her aunt, and go off with you straight.'

Mr Bell was some time up-stairs. Mr Thornton began to think it long, for he was full of business, and had hardly been able to spare the time for running up to Crampton, and enquiring how Miss Hale was.

When they had set out upon their walk, Mr Bell said:

'I was kept by those women in the drawing-room. Mrs Shaw is anxious to get home − on account of her daughter, she says − and wants Margaret to go off with her at once. Now she is no more fit for travelling than I am for flying. Besides, she says, and very justly, that she has friends she must see − that she must wish good-bye to several people; and then her aunt worried her about old claims, and was she forgetful of old friends? And she said with a great burst of crying, she should be glad enough to go from a place where she had suffered so much. Now I must return to Oxford tomorrow, and I don't know on which side of the scale to throw in my voice.'

He paused, as if asking a question; but he received no answer from his companion, the echo of whose thoughts kept repeating −

'Where she had suffered so much.' Alas! and that was the way in which this eighteen months in Milton − to him so unspeakably precious, down to its very bitterness, which was worth all the rest of life's sweetness − would be remembered. Neither loss of father, nor loss of mother, dear as she was to Mr Thornton, could have poisoned the remembrance of the weeks, the days, the hours, when a walk of two miles, every step of which was pleasant, as it brought him nearer and nearer to her, took him to her sweet presence − every step of which was rich, as each recurring moment that bore him away from her made him recall some fresh grace in her demeanour, or pleasant pungency in her character. Yes! whatever had happened to him, external to his relation to her, he could never have spoken of that time, when he could have seen her every day − when he had her within his grasp, as it were − as a time of suffering. It had been a royal time of luxury to him, with all its stings and contumelies, compared to the poverty that crept round and clipped the anticipation of the future down to sordid fact, and life without an atmosphere of either hope or fear.

Mrs Thornton and Fanny were in the dining-room; the latter in a flutter of small exultation, as the maid held up one glossy material after another, to try the effect of the wedding-dresses by candlelight. Her mother really tried to sympathize with her, but could not. Neither taste nor dress were in her line of subjects, and she heartily wished that Fanny had accepted her brother's offer of having the wedding clothes provided by some first-rate London dressmaker, without the endless, troublesome discussions, and unsettled wavering, that arose out of Fanny's desire to choose and superintend everything herself. Mr Thornton was only too glad to mark his grateful approbation of any sensible man, who could be captivated by Fanny's second-rate airs and graces, by giving her ample means for providing herself with the finery, which certainly rivalled, if it did not exceed, the lover in her estimation. When her brother and Mr Bell came in, Fanny blushed and simpered, and fluttered over the signs of her employment, in a way which could not have failed to draw attention from any one else but Mr Bell. If he thought about her and her silks and satins at all, it was to compare her and them with the pale sorrow he had left behind him, sitting motionless, with bent head and folded hands, in a room where the stillness was so great that you might almost fancy the rush in your straining ears was occasioned by the spirits of the dead, yet hovering round their beloved. For, when Mr Bell had first gone up-stairs, Mrs Shaw lay asleep on the sofa; and no sound broke the silence.

Mrs Thornton gave Mr Bell her formal, hospitable welcome. She was never so gracious as when receiving her son's friends in her son's house; and the more unexpected they were the more honour to her admirable housekeeping preparations for comfort.

'How is Miss Hale?' she asked.

'About as broken down by this last stroke as she can be.'

'I am sure it is very well for her that she has such a friend as you.'

'I wish I were her only friend, madam. I daresay it sounds very brutal; but here have I been displaced, and turned out of my post of comforter and adviser by a fine lady aunt; and there are cousins and what not claiming her in London, as if she were a lap-dog belonging to them. And she is too weak and miserable to have a will of her own.'

'She must indeed be weak,' said Mrs Thornton, with an implied meaning which her son understood well. 'But where,' continued Mrs Thornton, 'have these relations been all this time that Miss Hale has appeared almost friendless, and has certainly had a good deal of anxiety to bear?' But she did not feel interest enough in the answer to her question to wait for it. She left the room to make her household arrangements.

'They have been living abroad. They have some kind of claim upon her. I will do them that justice. The aunt brought her up, and she and the cousin have been like sisters. The thing vexing me, you see, is that I wanted to take her for a child of my own; and I am jealous of these people, who don't seem to value the privilege of their right. Now it would be different if Frederick claimed her.'

'Frederick!' exclaimed Mr Thornton. 'Who is he? What right −?' He stopped short in his vehement question.

'Frederick,' said Mr Bell in surprise. 'Why don't you know? He's her brother. Have you not heard −'

'I never heard his name before. Where is he? Who is he?'

'Surely I told you about him, when the family first came to Milton − the son who was concerned in that mutiny.'

'I never heard of him till this moment. Where does he live?'

'In Spain. He's liable to be arrested the moment he sets foot on English ground. Poor fellow! he will grieve at not being able to attend his father's funeral. We must be content with Captain Lennox; for I don't know of any other relation to summon.'

'I hope I may be allowed to go?'

'Certainly; thankfully. You're a good fellow, after all, Thornton. Hale liked you. He spoke to me, only the other day, about you at Oxford. He regretted he had seen so little of you lately. I am obliged to you for wishing to show him respect.'

'But about Frederick. Does he never come to England?'

'Never.'

'He was not over here about the time of Mrs Hale's death?'

'No. Why, I was here then. I hadn't seen Hale for years and years: and, if you remember, I came − No, it was some time after that that I came. But poor Frederick Hale was not here then. What made you think he was?'

'I saw a young man walking with Miss Hale one day,' replied Mr Thornton, 'and I think it was about that time.'

'Oh, that would be this young Lennox, the Captain's brother. He's a lawyer, and they were in pretty constant correspondence with him; and I remember Mr Hale told me he thought he would come down. Do you know,' said Mr Bell, wheeling round, and shutting one eye, the better to bring the forces of the other to bear with keen scrutiny on Mr Thornton's face, 'that I once fancied you had a little tenderness for Margaret?'

No answer. No change of countenance.

'And so did poor Hale. Not at first, and not till I had put it into his head.'

'I admired Miss Hale. Every one must do so. She is a beautiful creature,' said Mr Thornton, driven to bay by Mr Bell's pertinacious questioning.

'Is that all! You can speak of her in that measured way, as simply a "beautiful creature" – only something to catch the eye. I did hope you had had nobleness enough in you to make you pay her the homage of the heart. Though I believe – in fact I know, she would have rejected you, still to have loved her without return would have lifted you higher than all those, be they who they may, that have never known her to love. "Beautiful creature" indeed! Do you speak of her as you would of a horse or a dog?'

Mr Thornton's eyes glowed like red embers.

'Mr Bell,' said he, 'before you speak so, you should remember that all men are not as free to express what they feel as you are. Let us talk of something else.' For though his heart leaped up, as at a trumpet-call, to every word that Mr Bell had said, and though he knew that what he had said would henceforward bind the thought of the old Oxford Fellow closely up with the most precious things of his heart, yet he would not be forced into any expression of what he felt towards Margaret. He was no mocking-bird of praise, to try because another extolled what he reverenced and passionately loved, to outdo him in laudation. So he turned to some of the dry matters of business that lay between Mr Bell and him, as landlord and tenant.

'What is that heap of brick and mortar we came against in the yard? Any repairs wanted?'

'No, none, thank you.'

'Are you building on your own account? If you are, I'm very much obliged to you.'

'I'm building a dining-room – for the men I mean – the hands.'

'I thought you were hard to please, if this room wasn't good enough to satisfy you, a bachelor.'

'I've got acquainted with a strange kind of chap, and I put one or two children in whom he is interested to school. So, as I happened to be passing near his house one day, I just went there about some trifling payment to be made; and I saw such a miserable black frizzle of a dinner – a greasy cinder of meat, as first set me a-thinking. But it was not till provisions grew so high this winter that I bethought me how, by buying things wholesale, and cooking a good quantity of provisions together, much money might be saved, and much comfort gained. So I spoke to my friend – or my enemy – the man I told you of – and he found fault with every detail of my plan; and in consequence I laid it aside, both as impracticable, and also because if I forced it into operation I should be interfering with the independence of my men; when, suddenly, this Higgins came to me and graciously signified his approval of a scheme so nearly the same as mine, that I might fairly have claimed it; and, moreover, the approval of several of his fellow-workmen, to whom he had spoken. I was a little "riled," I confess, by his manner, and thought of throwing the whole thing overboard to sink or swim. But it seemed childish to relinquish a plan which I had once thought wise and well-laid, just because I myself did not receive all the honour and consequence due to the originator. So I coolly took the part assigned to me, which is something like that of steward to a club. I buy in the provisions wholesale, and provide a fitting matron or cook.'

'I hope you give satisfaction in your new capacity. Are you a good judge of potatoes and onions? But I suppose Mrs Thornton assists you in your marketing.'

'Not a bit,' replied Mr Thornton. 'She disapproves of the whole plan, and now we never mention it to each other. But I manage pretty well, getting in great stocks from Liverpool, and being served in butcher's meat by our own family butcher. I can assure you, the hot dinners the matron turns out are by no means to be despised.'

'Do you taste each dish as it goes in, in virtue of your office? I hope you have a white wand.'

'I was very scrupulous, at first, in confining myself to the mere purchasing part, and even in that I rather obeyed the men's orders, conveyed through the housekeeper, than went by my own judgment. At one time, the beef was too large, at another the mutton was not fat enough. I think they saw how careful I was to leave them free, and not to intrude my own ideas upon them; so, one day, two or three of the men – my friend Higgins among them – asked me if I would not come in and take a snack. It was a very busy day, but I saw that the men would be hurt if, after making the advance, I didn't meet them half-way, so I went in, and I never made a better dinner in my life. I told them (my next neighbours I mean, for I'm no speech-maker) how much I'd enjoyed it; and for some time, whenever that especial dinner recurred in their dietary, I was sure to be met by these men, with a "Master, there's hot-pot for dinner today, win yo' come?" If they had not asked me, I would no more have intruded on them than I'd have gone to the mess at the barracks without invitation.'

'I should think you were rather a restraint on your hosts' conversation. They can't abuse the masters while you're there. I suspect they take it out on non-hot-pot days.'

'Well! hitherto we've steered clear of all vexed questions. But if any of the old disputes came up again, I would certainly speak out my mind next hot-pot day. But you are hardly acquainted with our Darkshire fellows, for all you're a Darkshire man yourself. They have such a sense of humour, and such a racy mode of expression! I am getting really to know some of them now, and they talk pretty freely before me.'

'Nothing like the act of eating for equalizing men. Dying is nothing to it. The philosopher dies sententiously – the pharisee ostentatiously – the simple-hearted humbly – the poor idiot blindly, as the sparrow falls to the ground,[4] the philosopher and idiot, publican and pharisee, all eat after the same fashion – given an equally good digestion. There's theory for theory for you!'

'Indeed I have no theory; I hate theories.'

'I beg your pardon. To show my penitence, will you accept a ten pound note towards your marketing, and give the poor fellows a feast?'

'Thank you; but I'd rather not. They pay me rent for the oven and cooking-places at the back of the mill: and will have to pay more for the new dining-room. I don't want it to fall into a charity. I don't want donations. Once let in the principle, and I should have people going, and talking, and spoiling the simplicity of the whole thing.'

'People will talk about any new plan. You can't help that.'

'My enemies, if I have any, may make a philanthropic fuss about this dinner-scheme; but you are a friend, and I expect you will pay my experiment the respect of silence. It is but a new broom at present, and sweeps clean enough. But by-and-by we shall meet with plenty of stumbling-blocks, no doubt.'

CHAPTER XLIII

Margaret's Flittin'

The meanest thing to which we bid adieu,[1]
Loses its meanness in the parting hour.

ELLIOTT

Mrs Shaw took as vehement a dislike as it was possible for one of her gentle nature to do, against Milton. It was noisy, and smoky, and the poor people whom she saw in the streets were dirty, and the rich ladies over-dressed, and not a man that she saw, high or low, had his clothes made to fit him. She was sure Margaret would never regain her lost strength while she stayed in Milton; and she herself was afraid of one of her old attacks of the nerves. Margaret must return with her, and that quickly. This, if not the exact force of her words, was at any rate the spirit of what she urged on Margaret, till the latter, weak, weary, and broken-spirited, yielded a reluctant promise that, as soon as Wednesday was over, she would prepare to accompany her aunt back to town, leaving Dixon in charge of all the arrangements for paying bills, disposing of furniture, and shutting up the house. Before that Wednesday – that mournful Wednesday, when Mr Hale was to be interred, far away from either of the homes he had known in life, and far away from the wife who lay lonely among strangers (and this last was Margaret's great trouble, for she thought that if she had not given way to that overwhelming stupor during the first sad days, she could have arranged things otherwise) – before that Wednesday, Margaret received a letter from Mr Bell.

MY DEAR MARGARET: – I did mean to have returned to Milton on Thursday, but unluckily it turns out to be one of the rare occasions when we, Plymouth Fellows, are called upon to perform any kind of duty, and I must not be absent from my post. Captain Lennox and Mr Thornton are here. The former seems a smart, well-meaning man; and has proposed to go over to Milton, and assist you in any search for the will; of course there is none, or you would have found it by this time, if you followed my directions. Then the Captain declares he must take you and his mother-in-law home; and, in his wife's present state, I don't see how you can expect him to remain away longer than Friday. However, that

355

Dixon of yours is trusty; and can hold her, or your own, till I come. I will put matters into the hands of my Milton attorney if there is no will; for I doubt this smart captain is no great man of business. Nevertheless, his moustachios are splendid. There will have to be a sale, so select what things you wish reserved. Or you can send a list afterwards. Now two things more, and I have done. You know, or if you don't, your poor father did, that you are to have my money and goods when I die. Not that I mean to die yet; but I name this just to explain what is coming. These Lennoxes seem very fond of you now; and perhaps may continue to be; perhaps not. So it is best to start with a formal agreement; namely, that you are to pay them two hundred and fifty pounds a year, as long as you and they find it pleasant to live together. (This, of course, includes Dixon; mind you don't be cajoled into paying any more for her.) Then you won't be thrown adrift, if some day the captain wishes to have his house to himself, but you can carry yourself and your two hundred and fifty pounds off somewhere else; if, indeed, I have not claimed you to come and keep house for me first. Then as to dress, and Dixon, and personal expenses, and confectionery (all young ladies eat confectionery till wisdom comes by age), I shall consult some lady of my acquaintance, and see how much you will have from your father before fixing this. Now, Margaret, have you flown out before you have read this far, and wondered what right the old man has to settle your affairs for you so cavalierly? I make no doubt you have. Yet the old man has a right. He has loved your father for five and thirty years; he stood beside him on his wedding-day; he closed his eyes in death. Moreover, he is your godfather; and as he cannot do you much good spiritually, having a hidden consciousness of your superiority in such things, he would fain do you the poor good of endowing you materially. And the old man has not a known relation on earth; 'who is there to mourn for Adam Bell?' and his whole heart is set and bent upon this one thing, and Margaret Hale is not the girl to say him nay. Write by return, if only two lines, to tell me your answer. But *no thanks*.

Margaret took up a pen and scrawled with trembling hand, 'Margaret Hale is not the girl to say him nay.' In her weak state she could not think of any other words, and yet she was vexed to use these. But she was so much fatigued even by this slight exertion, that if she could have thought of another form of acceptance, she could not have sate up to write a syllable of it. She was obliged to lie down again, and try not to think.

'My dearest child! Has that letter vexed or troubled you?'

'No!' said Margaret feebly. 'I shall be better when tomorrow is over.'

'I feel sure, darling, you won't be better till I get you out of this horrid air. How you can have borne it this two years I can't imagine.'

'Where could I go to? I could not leave papa and mamma.'

'Well! don't distress yourself, my dear. I dare say it was all for the best, only I had no conception of how you were living. Our butler's wife lives in a better house than this.'

'It is sometimes very pretty – in summer; you can't judge by what it is now. I have been very happy here,' and Margaret closed her eyes by way of stopping the conversation.

The house teemed with comfort now, compared to what it had done. The evenings were chilly, and by Mrs Shaw's directions fires were lighted in every bedroom. She petted Margaret in every possible way, and bought every delicacy, or soft luxury in which she herself would have burrowed and sought comfort. But Margaret was indifferent to all these things; or, if they forced themselves upon her attention, it was simply as causes for gratitude to her aunt, who was putting herself so much out of her way to think of her. She was restless, though so weak. All the day long, she kept herself from thinking of the ceremony which was going on at Oxford, by wandering from room to room, and languidly setting aside such articles as she wished to retain. Dixon followed her by Mrs Shaw's desire, ostensibly to receive instructions, but with a private injunction to soothe her into repose as soon as might be.

'These books, Dixon, I will keep. All the rest will you send to Mr Bell? They are of a kind that he will value for themselves, as well as for papa's sake. This – I should like you to take this to Mr Thornton, after I am gone. Stay; I will write a note with it.' And she sat down hastily, as if afraid of thinking, and wrote:

DEAR SIR, – The accompanying book I am sure will be valued by you for the sake of my father, to whom it belonged.

Yours sincerely,
MARGARET HALE

She set out again upon her travels through the house, turning over articles, known to her from her childhood, with a sort of caressing reluctance to leave them – old-fashioned, worn and shabby, as they might be. But she hardly spoke again; and Dixon's report to Mrs Shaw was, that 'she doubted whether Miss Hale heard a word of what she said, though she talked the whole time, in order to divert her attention.' The consequence of being on her feet all day was excessive bodily weariness in the evening, and a better night's rest than she had had since she had heard of Mr Hale's death.

At breakfast time the next day, she expressed her wish to go and bid one or two friends good-bye. Mrs Shaw objected:

'I am sure, my dear, you can have no friends here with whom you are sufficiently intimate to justify you in calling upon them so soon; before you have been at church.'

'But today is my only day; if Captain Lennox comes this afternoon, and if we must – if I must really go tomorrow –'

'Oh, yes; we shall go tomorrow. I am more and more convinced that this air is bad for you, and makes you look so pale and ill; besides, Edith expects us; and she may be waiting me; and you cannot be left alone my dear, at your age. No; if you must pay these calls, I will go with you. Dixon can get us a coach, I suppose?'

So Mrs Shaw went to take care of Margaret, and took her maid with her to take care of the shawls and air-cushions. Margaret's face was too sad to lighten up into a smile at all this preparation for paying two visits, that she had often made by herself at all hours of the day. She was half afraid of owning that one place to which she was going was Nicholas Higgins'; all she could do was to hope her aunt would be indisposed to get out of the coach, and walk up the court, and at every breath of wind have her face slapped by wet clothes, hanging out to dry on ropes stretched from house to house.[2]

There was a little battle in Mrs Shaw's mind between ease and a sense of matronly propriety; but the former gained the day; and with many an injunction to Margaret to be careful of herself, and not to catch any fever, such as was always lurking in such places, her aunt permitted her to go where she had often been before without taking any precaution or requiring any permission.

Nicholas was out; only Mary and one or two of the Boucher children at home. Margaret was vexed with herself for not having timed her visit better. Mary had a very blunt intellect, although her feelings were warm and kind; and the instant she understood what Margaret's purpose was in coming to see them, she began to cry and sob with so little restraint that Margaret found it useless to say any of the thousand little things which had suggested themselves to her as she was coming along in the coach. She could only try to comfort her a little by suggesting the vague chance of their meeting again, at some possible time, in some possible place, and bid her tell her father how much she wished, if he could manage it, that he should come to see her when he had done his work in the evening.

As she was leaving the place, she stopped and looked round; then hesitated a little before she said:

'I should like to have some little thing to remind me of Bessy.'

Instantly Mary's generosity was keenly alive. What could they give? And on Margaret's singling out a little common drinking-cup, which she remembered as the one always standing by Bessy's side with drink for her feverish lips, Mary said:

'Oh, take summut better; that only cost fourpence!'

'That will do, thank you,' said Margaret; and she went quickly away, while the light caused by the pleasure of having something to give yet lingered on Mary's face.

'Now to Mrs Thornton's,' thought she to herself. 'It must be done.' But she looked rather rigid and pale at the thoughts of it, and had hard work to find the exact words in which to explain to her aunt who Mrs Thornton was, and why she should go to bid her farewell.

They (for Mrs Shaw alighted here) were shown into the drawing-room, in which a fire had only just been kindled. Mrs Shaw huddled herself up in her shawl, and shivered.

'What an icy room!' she said.

They had to wait for some time before Mrs Thornton entered. There was some softening in her heart towards Margaret, now that she was going away out of her sight. She remembered her spirit, as shown at various times and places, even more than the patience with which she had endured long and wearing cares. Her countenance was blander than usual, as she greeted her; there was even a shade of tenderness in her manner, as she noticed the white, tear-swollen face, and the quiver in the voice which Margaret tried to make so steady.

'Allow me to introduce my aunt, Mrs Shaw. I am going away from Milton tomorrow; I do not know if you are aware of it; but I wanted to see you once again, Mrs Thornton, to – to apologize for my manner the last time I saw you; and to say that I am sure you meant kindly – however much we may have misunderstood each other.'

Mrs Shaw looked extremely perplexed by what Margaret had said. Thanks for kindness! and apologies for failure in good manners! But Mrs Thornton replied:

'Miss Hale, I am glad you do me justice. I did no more than I believed to be my duty in remonstrating with you as I did. I have always desired to act the part of a friend to you. I am glad you do me justice.'

'And,' said Margaret, blushing excessively as she spoke, 'will you do me justice, and believe that though I cannot – I do not choose – to give explanations of my conduct, I have not acted in the unbecoming way you apprehended?'

Margaret's voice was so soft, and her eyes so pleading, that Mrs Thornton was for once affected by the charm of manner to which she had hitherto proved herself invulnerable.

'Yes, I do believe you. Let us say no more about it. Where are you going to reside, Miss Hale? I understood from Mr Bell that you were going to leave Milton. You never liked Milton, you know,' said Mrs Thornton, with a sort of grim smile; 'but for all that, you must not expect me to congratulate you on quitting it. Where shall you live?'

'With my aunt,' replied Margaret, turning towards Mrs Shaw.

'My niece will reside with me in Harley Street. She is almost like a daughter to me,' said Mrs Shaw, looking fondly at Margaret; 'and I am glad to acknowledge my own obligation for any kindness that has been shown to her. If you and your husband ever come to town, my son and daughter, Captain and Mrs Lennox, will, I am sure, join with me in wishing to do anything in our power to show you attention.'

Mrs Thornton thought in her own mind, that Margaret had not taken much care to enlighten her aunt as to the relationship between the Mr and Mrs Thornton, towards whom the fine-lady aunt was extending her soft patronage; so she answered shortly,

'My husband is dead. Mr Thornton is my son. I never go to London; so I am not likely to be able to avail myself of your polite offers.'

At this instant Mr Thornton entered the room; he had only just returned from Oxford. His mourning suit spoke of the reason that had called him there.

'John,' said his mother, 'this lady is Mrs Shaw, Miss Hale's aunt. I am sorry to say, that Miss Hale's call is to wish us good-bye.'

'You are going then!' said he, in a low voice.

'Yes,' said Margaret. 'We leave tomorrow.'

'My son-in-law comes this evening to escort us,' said Mrs Shaw.

Mr Thornton turned away. He had not sat down, and now he seemed to be examining something on the table, almost as if he had discovered an unopened letter, which had made him forget the present company. He did not even seem to be aware when they got up to take leave. He started forwards, however, to hand Mrs Shaw down to the carriage. As it drove up, he and Margaret stood close together on the door-step, and it was impossible but that the recollection of the day of the riot should force itself into both their minds. Into his it came associated with the speeches of the following day; her passionate declaration that there was not a man in all that violent and desperate crowd, for whom she did not care as much as for him. And at the remembrance of her taunting words, his brow grew stern, though his heart beat thick with longing love. 'No!' said he, 'I put it to the touch once, and I lost it all. Let her go, – with her stony heart, and her beauty; – how set and terrible her look is now, for all her loveliness of feature! She is afraid I shall speak what will require some stern repression. Let her go. Beauty and heiress as she may be, she will find it hard to meet with a truer heart than mine. Let her go!'

And there was no tone of regret, or emotion of any kind in the voice with which he said good-bye; and the offered hand was taken with a resolute calmness, and dropped as carelessly as if it had been a dead and withered flower. But none in his household saw Mr Thornton again that day. He was busily engaged; or so he said.

Margaret's strength was so utterly exhausted by these visits, that she had to submit to much watching, and petting, and sighing 'I-told-you-so's,' from her aunt. Dixon said she was quite as bad as she had been on the first day she heard of her father's death; and she and Mrs Shaw consulted as to the desirableness of delaying the morrow's journey. But when her aunt reluctantly proposed a few days' delay to Margaret, the latter writhed her body as if in acute suffering, and said:

'Oh! let us go. I cannot be patient here. I shall not get well here. I want to forget.'

So the arrangements went on; and Captain Lennox came, and with him news of Edith and the little boy; and Margaret found that the indifferent, careless conversation of one who, however kind, was not too warm and anxious a sympathizer, did her good. She roused up; and by the time that she knew she might expect Higgins, she was able to leave the room quietly, and await in her own chamber the expected summons.

'Eh!' said he, as she came in, 'to think of th' oud gentleman dropping off as he did! Yo' might ha' knocked me down wi' a straw when they told me. "Mr Hale?" said I; "him as was th' parson?" "Ay," said they. "Then," said I, "there's as good a man gone as ever lived on this earth, let who will be t' other!" And I came to see yo', and tell yo' how grieved I were, but them women in th' kitchen wouldn't tell yo' I were there. They said yo' were ill, – and butter me, but yo' dunnot look like th' same wench. And yo're going to be a grand lady up i' Lunnon, aren't yo'?'

'Not a grand lady,' said Margaret, half smiling.

'Well! Thornton said – says he, a day or two ago, "Higgins, have yo' seen Miss Hale?" "No," says I; "there's a pack o' women who won't let me at her. But I can bide my time, if she's ill. She and I knows each other pretty well; and hoo'l not go doubting that I'm main sorry for th' oud gentleman's death, just because I can't get at her and tell her so." And says he, "Yo'll not have much time for to try and see her, my fine chap. She's not for staying with us a day longer nor she can help. She's got grand relations, and they're carrying her off; and we sha'n't see her no more." "Meester," said I, "if I dunnot see her afore hoo goes, I'll strive to get up to Lunnon next Whissuntide, that I will. I'll not be baulked of saying her good-bye by any relations whatsomdever." But, bless yo', I knowed yo'd come. It were only for to humour the meester, I let on as if I thought yo'd mappen leave Milton without seeing me.'

'You're quite right,' said Margaret. 'You only do me justice. And you'll not forget me, I'm sure. If no one else in Milton remembers me, I'm certain you will; and papa too. You know how good and how tender he was. Look, Higgins! here is his bible. I have kept it for you. I can ill spare it; but I know he would have liked you to have it. I'm sure you'll care for it, and study what is in it, for his sake.'

'Yo' may say that. If it were the deuce's own scribble, and yo' axed me to read in it for yo'r sake, and th' oud gentleman's, I'd do it. Whatten's this, wench? I'm not going for to take yo'r brass, so dunnot think it. We've been great friends, 'bout the sound o' money passing between us.'

'For the children – for Boucher's children,' said Margaret, hurriedly. 'They may need it. You've no right to refuse it for them. I would not give you a penny,' she said, smiling; 'don't think there's any of it for you.'

'Well, wench! I can nobbut say, Bless yo'! and bless yo'! – and amen.'

CHAPTER XLIV

Ease Not Peace

A dull rotation, never at a stay,[1]
Yesterday's face twin image of today.

COWPER

Of what each one should be, he sees the form and rule,[2]
And till he reach to that, his joy can ne'er be full.

RÜCKERT

It was very well for Margaret that the extreme quiet of the Harley
Street house, during Edith's recovery from her confinement, gave her
the natural rest which she needed. It gave her time to comprehend
the sudden change which had taken place in her circumstances
within the last two months. She found herself at once an inmate of a
luxurious house, where the bare knowledge of the existence of every
trouble or care seemed scarcely to have penetrated. The wheels of
the machinery of daily life were well oiled, and went along with
delicious smoothness. Mrs Shaw and Edith could hardly make
enough of Margaret, on her return to what they persisted in calling
her home. And she felt that it was almost ungrateful in her to have a
secret feeling that the Helstone vicarage – nay, even the poor little
house at Milton, with her anxious father and her invalid mother,
and all the small household cares of comparative poverty, composed
her idea of home. Edith was impatient to get well, in order to fill
Margaret's bed-room with all the soft comforts, and pretty knick-
knacks, with which her own abounded. Mrs Shaw and her maid
found plenty of occupation in restoring Margaret's wardrobe to a
state of elegant variety. Captain Lennox was easy, kind, and gentlemanly; sate with his wife in her dressing-room an hour or two every
day; played with his little boy for another hour, and lounged away
the rest of his time at his club, when he was not engaged out to
dinner. Just before Margaret had recovered from her necessity for
quiet and repose – before she had begun to feel her life wanting and
dull – Edith came down-stairs and resumed her usual part in the
household; and Margaret fell into the old habit of watching, and
admiring, and ministering to her cousin. She gladly took all charge
of the semblances of duties off Edith's hands; answered notes,

reminded her of engagements, tended her when no gaiety was in prospect, and she was consequently rather inclined to fancy herself ill. But all the rest of the family were in the full business of the London season, and Margaret was often left alone. Then her thoughts went back to Milton, with a strange sense of the contrast between the life there, and here. She was getting surfeited of the eventless ease in which no struggle or endeavour was required. She was afraid lest she should even become sleepily deadened into forgetfulness of anything beyond the life which was lapping her round with luxury. There might be toilers and moilers there in London, but she never saw them; the very servants lived in an underground world of their own, of which she knew neither the hopes nor the fears; they only seemed to start into existence when some want or whim of their master and mistress needed them. There was a strange unsatisfied vacuum in Margaret's heart and mode of life; and, once when she had dimly hinted this to Edith, the latter, wearied with dancing the night before, languidly stroked Margaret's cheek as she sat by her in the old attitude, – she on a footstool by the sofa where Edith lay.

'Poor child!' said Edith. 'It is a little sad for you to be left, night after night, just at this time when all the world is so gay. But we shall be having our dinner-parties soon – as soon as Henry comes back from circuit – and then there will be a little pleasant variety for you. No wonder it is moped, poor darling!'[3]

Margaret did not feel as if the dinner-parties would be a panacea. But Edith piqued herself on her dinner-parties; 'so different,' as she said, 'from the old dowager dinners under mamma's régime;' and Mrs Shaw herself seemed to take exactly the same kind of pleasure in the very different arrangements and circle of acquaintances which were to Captain and Mrs Lennox's taste, as she did in the more formal and ponderous entertainments which she herself used to give. Captain Lennox was always extremely kind and brotherly to Margaret. She was really very fond of him, excepting when he was anxiously attentive to Edith's dress and appearance, with a view to her beauty making a sufficient impression on the world. Then all the latent Vashti[4] in Margaret was roused, and she could hardly keep herself from expressing her feelings.

The course of Margaret's day was this; a quiet hour or two before a late breakfast; an unpunctual meal, lazily eaten by weary and half-awake people, but yet at which, in all its dragged-out length, she was expected to be present, because, directly afterwards, came a discussion of plans, at which, although they none of them concerned her, she was expected to give her sympathy, if she could not assist with her advice: an endless number of notes to write, which Edith invariably left to her, with many caressing compliments as to her eloquence du billet; a little play with Sholto as he returned from his morning's walk; besides the care of the children during the servants' dinner; a drive or callers; and some dinner or morning engagement for her aunt and cousins, which left Margaret free, it is true, but rather wearied with the inactivity of the day, coming upon depressed spirits and delicate health.

She looked forward with longing, though unspoken interest to the homely object of Dixon's return from Milton; where, until now, the old servant had been busily engaged in winding up all the affairs of the Hale family. It had appeared a sudden famine to her heart, this entire cessation of any news respecting the people amongst whom she had lived so long. It was true, that Dixon, in her business-letters, quoted, every now and then, an opinion of Mr Thornton's as to what she had better do about the furniture, or how act in regard to the landlord of the Crampton Terrace house. But it was only here and there that the name came in, or any Milton name, indeed; and Margaret was sitting one evening, all alone in the Lennox's drawing-room, not reading Dixon's letters, which yet she held in her hand, but thinking over them, and recalling the days which had been, and picturing the busy life out of which her own had been taken and never missed; wondering if all went on in that whirl just as if she and her father had never been; questioning within herself, if no one in all the crowd missed her, (not Higgins, she was not thinking of him,) when, suddenly, Mr Bell was announced; and Margaret hurried the letters into her work-basket, and started up, blushing as if she had been doing some guilty thing.

'Oh, Mr Bell! I never thought of seeing you!'

'But you give me a welcome, I hope, as well as that very pretty start of surprise.'

'Have you dined? How did you come? Let me order you some dinner.'

'If you're going to have any. Otherwise, you know, there is no one who cares less for eating than I do. But where are the others? Gone out to dinner? Left you alone?'

'Oh yes! and it is such a rest. I was just thinking – But will you run the risk of dinner? I don't know if there is anything in the house.'

'Why, to tell you the truth, I dined at my club. Only they don't cook as well as they did, so I thought, if you were going to dine, I might try and make out my dinner. But never mind, never mind! There aren't ten cooks in England to be trusted at impromptu dinners. If their skill and their fires will stand it, their tempers won't. You shall make me some tea, Margaret. And now, what were you thinking of? you were going to tell me. Whose letters were those, god-daughter, that you hid away so speedily?'

'Only Dixon's,' replied Margaret, growing very red.

'Whew! is that all? Who do you think came up in the train with me?'

'I don't know,' said Margaret, resolved against making a guess.

'Your what d'ye call him? What's the right name for a cousin-in-law's brother?'

'Mr Henry Lennox?' asked Margaret.

'Yes,' replied Mr Bell. 'You knew him formerly, didn't you? What sort of a person is he, Margaret?'

'I liked him long ago,' said Margaret, glancing down for a moment. And then she looked straight up and went on in her natural manner. 'You know we have been corresponding about Frederick since; but I have not seen him for nearly three years, and he may be changed. What did you think of him?'

'I don't know. He was so busy trying to find out who I was, in the first instance, and what I was in the second, that he never let out what he was; unless indeed that veiled curiosity of his as to what manner of man he had to talk to was not a good piece, and a fair indication of his character. Do you call him good-looking, Margaret?'

'No! certainly not. Do you?'

'Not I. But I thought, perhaps, you might. Is he a great deal here?'

'I fancy he is when he is in town. He has been on circuit now since I came. But — Mr Bell — have you come from Oxford or from Milton?'

'From Milton. Don't you see I'm smoke-dried?'

'Certainly. But I thought that it might be the effect of the antiquities of Oxford.'

'Come now, be a sensible woman! In Oxford, I could have managed all the landlords in the place, and had my own way, with half the trouble your Milton landlord has given me, and defeated me after all. He won't take the house off our hands till next June twelvemonth. Luckily, Mr Thornton found a tenant for it. Why don't you ask after Mr Thornton, Margaret? He has proved himself a very active friend of yours, I can tell you. Taken more than half the trouble off my hands.'

'And how is he? How is Mrs Thornton?' asked Margaret hurriedly and below her breath, though she tried to speak out.

'I suppose they're well. I've been staying at their house till I was driven out of it by the perpetual clack about that Thornton girl's marriage. It was too much for Thornton himself, though she was his sister. He used to go and sit in his own room perpetually. He's getting past the age for caring for such things, either as principal or accessory. I was surprised to find the old lady falling into the current, and carried away by her daughter's enthusiasm for orange-blossoms and lace. I thought Mrs Thornton had been made of sterner stuff.'

'She would put on any assumption of feeling to veil her daughter's weakness,' said Margaret in a low voice.

'Perhaps so. You've studied her, have you? She doesn't seem over fond of you, Margaret.'

'I know it,' said Margaret. 'Oh, here is tea at last!' exclaimed she, as if relieved. And with tea came Mr Henry Lennox, who had walked up to Harley Street after a late dinner, and had evidently expected to find his brother and sister-in-law at home. Margaret suspected him of being as thankful as she was at the presence of a third party, on this their first meeting since the memorable day of his offer, and her refusal at Helstone. She could hardly tell what to say at first, and was thankful for all the tea-table occupations, which gave her an excuse for keeping silence, and him an opportunity of recovering himself. For, to tell the truth, he had rather forced himself up to Harley Street this evening, with a view of getting over an awkward meeting, awkward even in the presence of Captain Lennox and Edith, and doubly awkward now that he found her the only lady there, and the person to whom he must naturally and perforce address a great part of his conversation. She was the first to recover her self-possession. She began to talk on the subject which came uppermost in her mind, after the first flush of awkward shyness.

'Mr Lennox, I have been so much obliged to you for all you have done about Frederick.'

'I am only sorry it has been so unsuccessful,' replied he, with a quick glance towards Mr Bell, as if reconnoitring how much he might say before him. Margaret, as if she read his thought, addressed herself to Mr Bell, both including him in the conversation, and implying that he was perfectly aware of the endeavours that had been made to clear Frederick.

'That Horrocks – that very last witness of all, has proved as unavailing as all the others. Mr Lennox has discovered that he sailed for Australia only last August; only two months before Frederick was in England, and gave us the names of –'

'Frederick in England! you never told me that!' exclaimed Mr Bell in surprise.

'I thought you knew. I never doubted you had been told. Of course, it was a great secret, and perhaps I should not have named it now,' said Margaret, a little dismayed.

'I have never named it to either my brother or your cousin,' said Mr Lennox, with a little professional dryness of implied reproach.

'Never mind, Margaret. I am not living in a talking, babbling world, nor yet among people who are trying to worm facts out of me; you needn't look so frightened because you have let the cat out of the bag to a faithful old hermit like me. I shall never name his having been in England; I shall be out of temptation, for no one will ask me. Stay!' (interrupting himself rather abruptly) 'was it at your mother's funeral?'

'He was with mamma when she died,' said Margaret, softly.

'To be sure! To be sure! Why, some one asked me if he had not been over then, and I denied it stoutly – not many weeks ago – who could it have been? Oh! I recollect!'

But he did not say the name; and although Margaret would have given much to know if her suspicions were right, and it had been Mr Thornton who had made the enquiry, she could not ask the question of Mr Bell, much as she longed to do so.

There was a pause for a moment or two. Then Mr Lennox said, addressing himself to Margaret, 'I suppose as Mr Bell is now acquainted with all the circumstances attending your brother's unfortunate dilemma, I cannot do better than inform him exactly how the research into the evidence we once hoped to produce in his favour stands at present. So, if he will do me the honour to breakfast with me tomorrow, we will go over the names of these missing gentry.'

'I should like to hear all the particulars, if I may. Cannot you come here? I dare not ask you both to breakfast, though I am sure you would be welcome. But let me know all I can about Frederick, even though there may be no hope at present.'

'I have an engagement at half-past eleven. But I will certainly come if you wish it,' replied Mr Lennox, with a little after-thought of extreme willingness, which made Margaret shrink into herself, and almost wish that she had not proposed her natural request. Mr Bell got up and looked around him for his hat, which had been removed to make room for tea.

'Well!' said he, 'I don't know what Mr Lennox is inclined to do, but I'm disposed to be moving off homewards. I've been a journey today, and journeys begin to tell upon my sixty and odd years.'

'I believe I shall stay and see my brother and sister,' said Mr Lennox, making no movement of departure. Margaret was seized with a shy awkward dread of being left alone with him. The scene on the little terrace in the Helstone garden was so present to her, that she could hardly help believing it was so with him.

'Don't go yet, please, Mr Bell,' said she, hastily. 'I want you to see Edith; and I want Edith to know you. Please!' said she, laying a light but determined hand on his arm. He looked at her, and saw the confusion stirring in her countenance; he sate down again, as if her little touch had been possessed of resistless strength.

'You see how she overpowers me, Mr Lennox,' said he. 'And I hope you noticed the happy choice of her expressions; she wants me to "see" this cousin Edith, who, I am told, is a great beauty; but she has the honesty to change her word when she comes to me – Mrs Lennox is to "know" me. I suppose I am not much to "see," eh, Margaret?'

He joked, to give her time to recover from the slight flutter which he had detected in her manner on his proposal to leave; and she caught the tone, and threw the ball back. Mr Lennox wondered how his brother, the Captain, could have reported her as having lost all her good looks. To be sure, in her quiet black dress, she was a contrast to Edith, dancing in her white crape mourning, and long floating golden hair, all softness and glitter. She dimpled and blushed most becomingly when introduced to Mr Bell, conscious that she had her reputation as a beauty to keep up, and that it would not do to have a Mordecai[5] refusing to worship and admire, even in the shape of an old Fellow of a College, which nobody had ever heard of. Mrs Shaw and Captain Lennox, each in their separate way, gave Mr Bell a kind and sincere welcome, winning him over to like them almost in spite of himself, especially when he saw how naturally Margaret took her place as sister and daughter of the house.

'What a shame that we were not at home to receive you,' said Edith. 'You, too, Henry! though I don't know that we should have stayed at home for you. And for Mr Bell! for Margaret's Mr Bell −'

'There is no knowing what sacrifices you would not have made,' said her brother-in-law. 'Even a dinner-party! and the delight of wearing this very becoming dress.'

Edith did not know whether to frown or to smile. But it did not suit Mr Lennox to drive her to the first of these alternatives; so he went on.

'Will you show your readiness to make sacrifices tomorrow morning, first by asking me to breakfast, to meet Mr Bell, and secondly, by being so kind as to order it at half-past nine, instead of ten o'clock? I have some letters and papers that I want to show to Miss Hale and Mr Bell.'

'I hope Mr Bell will make our house his own during his stay in London,' said Captain Lennox. 'I am only so sorry we cannot offer him a bed-room.'

'Thank you. I am much obliged to you. You would only think me a churl if you had, for I should decline it, I believe, in spite of all the temptations of such agreeable company,' said Mr Bell, bowing all round, and secretly congratulating himself on the neat turn he had given to his sentence, which, if put into plain language, would have been more to this effect: 'I couldn't stand the restraints of such a proper-behaved and civil-spoken set of people as these are: it would be like meat without salt. I'm thankful they haven't a bed. And how well I rounded my sentence! I am absolutely catching the trick of good manners.'

His self-satisfaction lasted him till he was fairly out in the streets, walking side by side with Henry Lennox. Here he suddenly remembered Margaret's little look of entreaty as she urged him to stay longer, and he also recollected a few hints given him long ago by an acquaintance of Mr Lennox's, as to his admiration of Margaret. It gave a new direction to his thoughts. 'You have known Miss Hale for a long time, I believe. How do you think her looking? She strikes me as pale and ill.'

'I thought her looking remarkably well. Perhaps not when I first came in − now I think of it. But certainly, when she grew animated, she looked as well as ever I saw her do.'

'She has had a great deal to go through,' said Mr Bell.

'Yes! I have been sorry to hear of all she has had to bear; not merely the common and universal sorrow arising from death, but all the annoyance which her father's conduct must have caused her, and then –'

'Her father's conduct!' said Mr Bell, in an accent of surprise. 'You must have heard some wrong statement. He behaved in the most conscientious manner. He showed more resolute strength than I should ever have given him credit for formerly.'

'Perhaps I have been wrongly informed. But I have been told, by his successor in the living – a clever, sensible man, and a thoroughly active clergyman – that there was no call upon Mr Hale to do what he did, relinquish the living, and throw himself and his family on the tender mercies of private teaching in a manufacturing town; the bishop had offered him another living, it is true, but if he had come to entertain certain doubts, he could have remained where he was, and so had no occasion to resign. But the truth is, these country clergymen live such isolated lives – isolated, I mean, from all inter-course with men of equal cultivation with themselves, by whose minds they might regulate their own, and discover when they were going either too fast or too slow – that they are very apt to disturb themselves with imaginary doubts as to the articles of faith, and throw up certain opportunities of doing good for very uncertain fancies of their own.'

'I differ from you. I do not think they are very apt to do as my poor friend Hale did.' Mr Bell was inwardly chafing.

'Perhaps I used too general an expression, in saying "very apt." But certainly, their lives are such as very often to produce either inordinate self-sufficiency, or a morbid state of conscience,' replied Mr Lennox with perfect coolness.

'You don't meet with any self-sufficiency among the lawyers, for instance?' asked Mr Bell. 'And seldom, I imagine, any cases of morbid conscience.' He was becoming more and more vexed, and forgetting his lately-caught trick of good manners, Mr Lennox saw now that he had annoyed his companion; and as he had talked pretty much for the sake of saying something, and so passing the time while their road lay together, he was very indifferent as to the exact side he took upon the question, and quietly came round by saying: 'To be sure, there is something fine in a man of Mr Hale's age leaving his home of twenty years, and giving up all settled

371

habits, for an idea which was probably erroneous – but that does not matter – an untangible thought. One cannot help admiring him, with a mixture of pity in one's admiration, something like what one feels for Don Quixote. Such a gentleman as he was too! I shall never forget the refined and simple hospitality he showed to me that last day at Helstone.'

Only half mollified, and yet anxious, in order to lull certain qualms of his own conscience, to believe that Mr Hale's conduct had a tinge of Quixotism in it, Mr Bell growled out – 'Aye! And you don't know Milton. Such a change from Helstone! It is years since I have been at Helstone – but I'll answer for it, it is standing there yet – every stick and every stone as it has done for the last century, while Milton! I go there every four or five years – and I was born there – yet I do assure you, I often lose my way – aye, among the very piles of warehouses that are built upon my father's orchard. Do we part here? Well, good night, sir; I suppose we shall meet in Harley Street tomorrow morning.'

CHAPTER XLV

Not All a Dream

Where are the sounds that swam along[1]
The buoyant air when I was young?
The last vibration now is o'er,
And they who listened are no more;
Ah! let me close my eyes and dream.
W. S. LANDOR

The idea of Helstone had been suggested to Mr Bell's waking mind by his conversation with Mr Lennox, and all night long it ran riot through his dreams. He was again the tutor in the college where he now held the rank of Fellow; it was again a long vacation, and he was staying with his newly married friend, the proud husband, and happy Vicar of Helstone. Over babbling brooks they took impossible leaps, which seemed to keep them whole days suspended in the air. Time and space were not, though all other things seemed real. Every event was measured by the emotions of the mind, not by its actual existence, for existence it had none. But the trees were gorgeous in their autumnal leafiness – the warm odours of flower and herb came sweet upon the sense – the young wife moved about her house with just that mixture of annoyance at her position, as regarded wealth, with pride in her handsome and devoted husband, which Mr Bell had noticed in real life a quarter of a century ago. The dream was so like life that, when he awoke, his present life seemed like a dream. Where was he? In the close, handsomely furnished room of a London hotel! Where were those who spoke to him, moved around him, touched him, not an instant ago? Dead! buried! lost for evermore, as far as earth's for evermore would extend. He was an old man, so lately exultant in the full strength of manhood. The utter loneliness of his life was insupportable to think about. He got up hastily, and tried to forget what never more might be, in a hurried dressing for the breakfast in Harley Street.

He could not attend to all the lawyer's details, which, as he saw, made Margaret's eyes dilate, and her lips grow pale, as one by one fate decreed, or so it seemed, every morsel of evidence which would exonerate Frederick, should fall from beneath her feet and disappear. Even Mr Lennox's well-regulated professional voice took a softer, tenderer tone, as he drew near to the extinction of the last hope. It was not that Margaret had not been perfectly aware of the result before. It was only that the details of each successive disappointment came with such relentless minuteness to quench all hope, that she at last fairly gave way to tears. Mr Lennox stopped reading.

'I had better not go on,' said he, in a concerned voice. 'It was a foolish proposal of mine. Lieutenant Hale,' and even this giving him the title of the service from which he had so harshly been expelled, was soothing to Margaret. 'Lieutenant Hale is happy now; more secure in fortune and future prospects than he could ever have been in the navy; and has, doubtless, adopted his wife's country as his own.'

'That is it,' said Margaret. 'It seems so selfish in me to regret it,' trying to smile, 'and yet he is lost to me, and I am so lonely.' Mr Lennox turned over his papers, and wished that he were as rich and prosperous as he believed he should be some day. Mr Bell blew his nose, but, otherwise, he also kept silence; and Margaret, in a minute or two, had apparently recovered her usual composure. She thanked Mr Lennox very courteously for his trouble; all the more courteously and graciously because she was conscious that, by her behaviour, he might have probably been led to imagine that he had given her needless pain. Yet it was pain she would not have been without.

Mr Bell came up to wish her good-bye.

'Margaret!' said he, as he fumbled with his gloves. 'I am going down to Helstone tomorrow, to look at the old place. Would you like to come with me? Or would it give you too much pain? Speak out, don't be afraid.'

'Oh, Mr Bell,' said she – and could say no more. But she took his old gouty hand, and kissed it.

'Come, come; that's enough,' said he, reddening with awkwardness. 'I suppose your aunt Shaw will trust you with me. We'll go tomorrow morning, and we shall get there about two o'clock, I fancy. We'll take a snack, and order dinner at the little inn – the Lennard Arms, it used to be, – and go and get an appetite in the forest. Can you stand it, Margaret? It will be a trial, I know, to both of us, but it will be a pleasure to me, at least. And there we'll dine – it will be but doe-vension, if we can get it at all – and then I'll take my nap while you go out and see old friends. I'll give you back safe and sound, barring railway accidents, and I'll insure your life for a thousand pounds before starting, which may be some comfort to your relations; but otherwise, I'll bring you back to Mrs Shaw by lunch-time on Friday. So, if you say yes, I'll just go up-stairs and propose it.'

'It's no use my trying to say how much I shall like it,' said Margaret, through her tears.

'Well, then, prove your gratitude by keeping those fountains of yours dry for the next two days. If you don't, I shall feel queer myself about the lachrymal ducts, and I don't like that.'

'I won't cry a drop,' said Margaret, winking her eyes to shake the tears off her eye-lashes, and forcing a smile.

'There's my good girl. Then we'll go up-stairs and settle it all.' Margaret was in a state of almost trembling eagerness, while Mr Bell discussed his plan with her aunt Shaw, who was first startled, then doubtful and perplexed, and in the end, yielding rather to the rough force of Mr Bell's words than to her own conviction; for to the last, whether it was right or wrong, proper or improper, she could not settle to her own satisfaction, till Margaret's safe return, the happy fulfilment of the project, gave her decision enough to say, 'she was sure it had been a very kind thought of Mr Bell's, and just what she herself had been wishing for Margaret, as giving her the very change which she required, after all the anxious time she had had.'

CHAPTER XLVI

Once and Now

So on those happy days of yore[1]
Oft as I dare to dwell once more,
Still must I miss the friends so tried,
Whom Death has severed from my side.

But ever when true friendship binds,
Spirit it is that spirit finds;
In spirit then our bliss we found,
In spirit yet to them I'm bound.

UHLAND

Margaret was ready long before the appointed time, and had leisure enough to cry a little, quietly, when unobserved, and to smile brightly when any one looked at her. Her last alarm was lest they should be too late and miss the train; but no! they were all in time; and she breathed freely and happily at length, seated in the carriage opposite to Mr Bell, and whirling away past the well-known stations; seeing the old south country-towns and hamlets sleeping in the warm light of the pure sun, which gave a yet ruddier colour to their tiled roofs, so different to the cold slates of the north. Broods of pigeons hovered around these peaked quaint gables, slowly settling here and there, and ruffling their soft, shiny feathers, as if exposing every fibre to the delicious warmth. There were few people about at the stations, it almost seemed as if they were too lazily content to wish to travel; none of the bustle and stir that Margaret had noticed in her two journeys on the London and North-Western line. Later on in the year, this line of railway should be stirring and alive with rich pleasure-seekers; but as to the constant going to and fro of busy trades-people it would always be widely different from the northern lines. Here a spectator or two stood lounging at nearly every station, with his hands in his pockets, so absorbed in the simple act of watching, that it made the travellers wonder what he could find to do when the train whirled away, and only the blank of a railway, some sheds, and a distant field or two were left for him to gaze upon. The hot air danced over the golden stillness of the land, farm after farm was left behind, each reminding Margaret of German Idyls – of

Herman and Dorothea[2] – of Evangeline.[3] From this waking dream she was roused. It was the place to leave the train and take the fly to Helstone. And now sharper feelings came shooting through her heart, whether pain or pleasure she could hardly tell. Every mile was redolent of associations, which she would not have missed for the world, but each of which made her cry upon 'the days that are no more,'[4] with ineffable longing. The last time she had passed along this road was when she had left it with her father and mother – the day, the season, had been gloomy, and she herself hopeless, but they were there with her. Now she was alone, an orphan, and they, strangely, had gone away from her, and vanished from the face of the earth. It hurt her to see the Helstone road so flooded in the sun-light, and every turn and every familiar tree so precisely the same in its summer glory as it had been in former years. Nature felt no change, and was ever young.

Mr Bell knew something of what would be passing through her mind, and wisely and kindly held his tongue. They drove up to the Lennard Arms; half farm-house, half inn, standing a little apart from the road, as much as to say, that the host did not so depend on the custom of travellers, as to have to court it by any obtrusiveness; they, rather, must seek him out. The house fronted the village green; and right before it stood an immemorial lime-tree benched all round, in some hidden recesses of whose leafy wealth hung the grim escutcheon of the Lennards. The door of the inn stood wide open, but there was no hospitable hurry to receive the travellers. When the landlady did appear – and they might have abstracted many an article first – she gave them a kind welcome, almost as if they had been invited guests, and apologized for her coming having been so delayed, by saying, that it was hay-time, and the provisions for the men had to be sent a-field, and she had been too busy packing up the baskets to hear the noise of wheels over the road, which, since they had left the highway, ran over soft short turf.

'Why, bless me!' exclaimed she, as at the end of her apology, a glint of sunlight showed her Margaret's face, hitherto unobserved in that shady parlour. 'It's Miss Hale, Jenny,' said she, running to the door, and calling to her daughter. 'Come here, come directly, it's Miss Hale!' And then she went up to Margaret, and shook her hands with motherly fondness.

'And how are you all? How's the Vicar and Miss Dixon? The Vicar above all! God bless him! We've never ceased to be sorry that he left.'

Margaret tried to speak and tell her of her father's death; of her mother's it was evident that Mrs Purkis was aware, from her omission of her name. But she choked in the effort, and could only touch her deep mourning, and say the one word, 'Papa.'

'Surely, sir, it's never so!' said Mrs Purkis, turning to Mr Bell for confirmation of the sad suspicion that now entered her mind. 'There was a gentleman here in the spring – it might have been as long ago as last winter – who told us a deal of Mr Hale and Miss Margaret; and he said Mrs Hale was gone, poor lady. But never a word of the Vicar's being ailing!'

'It is so, however,' said Mr Bell. 'He died quite suddenly, when on a visit to me at Oxford. He was a good man, Mrs Purkis, and there's many of us that might be thankful to have as calm an end as his. Come, Margaret, my dear! Her father was my oldest friend, and she's my god-daughter, so I thought we would just come down together and see the old place; and I know of old you can give us comfortable rooms and a capital dinner. You don't remember me I see, but my name is Bell, and once or twice when the parsonage has been full, I've slept here, and tasted your good ale.'

'To be sure; I ask your pardon; but you see I was taken up with Miss Hale. Let me show you to a room, Miss Margaret, where you can take off your bonnet, and wash your face. It's only this very morning I plunged some fresh-gathered roses head downward in the water-jug, for, thought I, perhaps some one will be coming, and there's nothing so sweet as spring-water scented by a musk rose or two. To think of the Vicar being dead! Well, to be sure, we must all die; only that gentleman said, he was quite picking up after his trouble about Mrs Hale's death.'

'Come down to me, Mrs Purkis, after you have attended to Miss Hale. I want to have a consultation with you about dinner.'

The little casement window in Margaret's bed-chamber was almost filled up with rose and vine branches; but pushing them aside, and stretching a little out, she could see the tops of the parsonage chimneys above the trees; and distinguish many a well-known line through the leaves.

'Aye!' said Mrs Purkis, smoothing down the bed, and despatching Jenny for an armful of lavender-scented towels, 'times is changed, miss; our new Vicar has seven children, and is building a nursery ready for more, just out where the arbour and tool-house used to be in old times. And he has had new grates put in, and a plate-glass window in the drawing-room. He and his wife are stirring people, and have done a deal of good; at least they say it's doing good; if it were not, I should call it turning things upside down for very little purpose. The new Vicar is a teetotaller, miss, and a magistrate, and his wife has a deal of receipts for economical cooking, and is for making bread without yeast; and they both talk so much, and both at a time, that they knock one down as it were, and it's not till they're gone, and one's a little at peace, that one can think that there were things one might have said on one's own side of the question. He'll be after the men's cans in the hay-field, and peeping in; and then there'll be an ado because it's not ginger beer, but I can't help it. My mother and my grandmother before me sent good malt liquor to haymakers, and took salts and senna when anything ailed them; and I must e'en go on in their ways, though Mrs Hepworth does want to give me comfits instead of medicine, which, as she says, is a deal pleasanter, only I've no faith in it. But I must go, miss, though I'm wanting to hear many a thing; I'll come back to you before long.'

Mr Bell had strawberries and cream, a loaf of brown bread, and a jug of milk, (together with a Stilton cheese and a bottle of port for his own private refreshment,) ready for Margaret on her coming down stairs; and after this rustic luncheon they set out to walk, hardly knowing in what direction to turn, so many old familiar inducements were there in each.

'Shall we go past the vicarage?' asked Mr Bell.

'No, not yet. We will go this way, and make a round so as to come back by it,' replied Margaret.

Here and there old trees had been felled the autumn before; or a squatter's roughly-built and decaying cottage had disappeared. Margaret missed them each and all, and grieved over them like old friends. They came past the spot where she and Mr Lennox had sketched. The white, lightning-scarred trunk of the venerable beech, among whose roots they had sate down was there no more; the old man, the inhabitant of the ruinous cottage, was dead; the cottage had been pulled down, and a new one, tidy and respectable, had been built in its stead. There was a small garden on the place where the beech-tree had been.

'I did not think I had been so old,' said Margaret after a pause of silence; and she turned away sighing.

'Yes!' said Mr Bell. 'It is the first changes among familiar things that make such a mystery of time to the young, afterwards we lose the sense of the mysterious. I take changes in all I see as a matter of course. The instability of all human things is familiar to me, to you it is new and oppressive.'

'Let us go on to see little Susan,' said Margaret, drawing her companion up a grassy road-way, leading under the shadow of a forest glade.

'With all my heart, though I have not an idea who little Susan may be. But I have a kindness for all Susans, for simple Susan's sake.'[5]

'My little Susan was disappointed when I left without wishing her goodbye; and it has been on my conscience ever since, that I gave her pain which a little more exertion on my part might have prevented. But it is a long way. Are you sure you will not be tired?'

'Quite sure. That is, if you don't walk so fast. You see, here there are no views that can give one an excuse for stopping to take breath. You would think it romantic to be walking with a person "fat and scant o' breath" if I were Hamlet, Prince of Denmark. Have compassion on my infirmities for his sake.'

'I will walk slower for your own sake. I like you twenty times better than Hamlet.'

'On the principle that a living ass is better than a dead lion?'

'Perhaps so. I don't analyse my feelings.'

'I am content to take your liking me, without examining too curiously into the materials it is made of. Only we need not walk at a snail's pace.'

'Very well. Walk at your own pace, and I will follow. Or stop still and meditate, like the Hamlet you compare yourself to, if I go too fast.'

'Thank you. But as my mother has not murdered my father, and afterwards married my uncle, I shouldn't know what to think about, unless it were balancing the chances of our having a well-cooked dinner or not. What do you think?'

'I am in good hopes. She used to be considered a famous cook as far as Helstone opinion went.'

'But have you considered the distraction of mind produced by all this haymaking?'

Margaret felt all Mr Bell's kindness in trying to make cheerful talk about nothing, to endeavour to prevent her from thinking too curiously about the past. But she would rather have gone over these

dear-loved walks in silence, if indeed she were not ungrateful enough
to wish that she might have been alone.

They reached the cottage where Susan's widowed mother lived.
Susan was not there. She was gone to the parochial school. Margaret
was disappointed, and the poor woman saw it, and began to make a
kind of apology.

'Oh! it is quite right,' said Margaret. 'I am very glad to hear it. I
might have thought of it. Only she used to stop at home with you.'

'Yes, she did; and I miss her sadly. I used to teach her what little I
knew at nights. It were not much to be sure. But she were getting
such a handy girl, that I miss her sore. But she's a deal above me in
learning now.' And the mother sighed.

'I'm all wrong,' growled Mr Bell. 'Don't mind what I say. I'm a
hundred years behind the world. But I should say, that the child was
getting a better and simpler, and more natural education stopping at
home, and helping her mother, and learning to read a chapter in the
New Testament every night by her side, than from all the schooling
under the sun.'

Margaret did not want to encourage him to go on by replying to
him, and so prolonging the discussion before the mother. So she
turned to her and asked,

'How is old Betty Barnes?'

'I don't know,' said the woman rather shortly. 'We'se not friends.'

'Why not?' asked Margaret, who had formerly been the peace-
maker of the village.

'She stole my cat.'

'Did she know it was yours?'

'I don't know. I reckon not.'

'Well! could not you get it back again when you told her it was
yours?'

'No! for she'd burnt it.'[6]

'Burnt it!' exclaimed both Margaret and Mr Bell.

'Roasted it!' explained the woman.

It was no explanation. By dint of questioning, Margaret extracted
from her the horrible fact that Betty Barnes, having been induced by
a gypsy fortune-teller to lend the latter her husband's Sunday clothes,
on promise of having them faithfully returned on the Saturday night
before Goodman Barnes should have missed them, became alarmed
by their non-appearance, and her consequent dread of her husband's
anger, and as, according to one of the savage country superstitions,

the cries of a cat, in the agonies of being boiled or roasted alive, compelled (as it were) the powers of darkness to fulfil the wishes of the executioner, resort had been had to the charm. The poor woman evidently believed in its efficacy; her only feeling was indignation that her cat had been chosen out from all others for a sacrifice. Margaret listened in horror; and endeavoured in vain to enlighten the woman's mind; but she was obliged to give it up in despair. Step by step she got the woman to admit certain facts, of which the logical connexion and sequence was perfectly clear to Margaret; but at the end, the bewildered woman simply repeated her first assertion, namely, that 'it were very cruel for sure, and she should not like to do it; but that there were nothing like it for giving a person what they wished for; she had heard it all her life; but it were very cruel for all that.' Margaret gave it up in despair, and walked away sick at heart.

'You are a good girl not to triumph over me,' said Mr Bell.

'How? What do you mean?'

'I own, I am wrong about schooling. Anything rather than have that child brought up in such practical paganism.'

'Oh! I remember. Poor little Susan! I must go and see her; would you mind calling at the school?'

'Not a bit. I am curious to see something of the teaching she is to receive.'

They did not speak much more, but thridded their way through many a bosky dell, whose soft green influence could not charm away the shock and the pain in Margaret's heart, caused by the recital of such cruelty; a recital too, the manner of which betrayed such utter want of imagination, and therefore of any sympathy with the suffering animal.

The buzz of voices, like the murmur of a hive of busy human bees, made itself heard as soon as they emerged from the forest on the more open village-green on which the school was situated. The door was wide open, and they entered. A brisk lady in black, here, there, and everywhere, perceived them, and bade them welcome with somewhat of the hostess-air which, Margaret remembered, her mother was wont to assume, only in a more soft and languid manner, when any rare visitors strayed in to inspect the school. She knew at once it was the present Vicar's wife, her mother's successor; and she would have drawn back from the interview had it been possible; but in an instant she had conquered this feeling, and modestly advanced, meeting many a bright glance of recognition, and hearing many a half-suppressed murmur of 'It's Miss Hale.' The Vicar's lady heard the name, and her manner at once became more kindly. Margaret wished she could have helped feeling that it also became more patronizing. The lady held out a hand to Mr Bell, with –

'Your father, I presume, Miss Hale. I see it by the likeness. I am sure I am very glad to see you, sir, and so will the Vicar be.'

Margaret explained that it was not her father, and stammered out the fact of his death; wondering all the time how Mr Hale could have borne coming to revisit Helstone, if it had been as the Vicar's lady supposed. She did not hear what Mrs Hepworth was saying, and left it to Mr Bell to reply, looking round, meanwhile, for her old acquaintances.

'Ah! I see you would like to take a class, Miss Hale. I know it by myself. First class stand up for a parsing lesson with Miss Hale.'

Poor Margaret, whose visit was sentimental, not in any degree inspective, felt herself taken in; but as in some way bringing her in contact with little eager faces, once well-known, and who had received the solemn rite of baptism from her father, she sate down, half losing herself in tracing out the changing features of the girls, and holding Susan's hand for a minute or two, unobserved by all, while the first class sought for their books, and the Vicar's lady went as near as a lady could towards holding Mr Bell by the button, while she explained the Phonetic system to him, and gave him a conversation she had had with the Inspector about it.

Margaret bent over her book, and seeing nothing but that – hearing the buzz of children's voices, old times rose up, and she thought of them, and her eyes filled with tears, till all at once there was a pause – one of the girls was stumbling over the apparently simple word 'a,' uncertain what to call it.

'A, an indefinite article,' said Margaret, mildly.

'I beg your pardon,' said the Vicar's wife, all eyes and ears; 'but we are taught by Mr Milsome to call "a" an – who can remember?'

'An adjective absolute,' said half-a-dozen voices at once. And Margaret sate abashed. The children knew more than she did. Mr Bell turned away, and smiled.

Margaret spoke no more during the lesson. But after it was over, she went quietly round to one or two old favourites, and talked to them a little. They were growing out of children into great girls;

passing out of her recollection in their rapid development, as she, by her three years' absence, was vanishing from theirs. Still she was glad to have seen them all again, though a tinge of sadness mixed itself with her pleasure. When school was over for the day, it was yet early in the summer afternoon; and Mrs Hepworth proposed to Margaret that she and Mr Bell should accompany her to the parsonage, and see the – the word 'improvements' had half slipped out of her mouth, but she substituted the more cautious term 'alterations' which the present Vicar was making. Margaret did not care a straw about seeing the alterations, which jarred upon her fond recollection of what her home had been; but she longed to see the old place once more, even though she shivered away from the pain which she knew she should feel.

The parsonage was so altered, both inside and out, that the real pain was less than she had anticipated. It was not like the same place. The garden, the grass-plat, formerly so daintily trim that even a stray rose-leaf seemed like a fleck on its exquisite arrangement and propriety, was strewed with children's things; a bag of marbles here, a hoop there; a straw-hat forced down upon a rose-tree as on a peg, to the destruction of a long beautiful tender branch laden with flowers, which in former days would have been trained up tenderly, as if beloved. The little square matted hall was equally filled with signs of merry healthy rough childhood.

'Ah!' said Mrs Hepworth, 'you must excuse this untidiness, Miss Hale. When the nursery is finished, I shall insist upon a little order. We are building a nursery out of your room, I believe. How did you manage, Miss Hale, without a nursery?'

'We were but two,' said Margaret. 'You have many children, I presume?'

'Seven. Look here! we are throwing out a window to the road on this side. Mr Hepworth is spending an immense deal of money on this house; but really it was scarcely habitable when we came – for so large a family as ours I mean, of course.' Every room in the house was changed, besides the one of which Mrs Hepworth spoke, which had been Mr Hale's study formerly; and where the green gloom and delicious quiet of the place had conduced, as he had said, to a habit of meditation, but, perhaps, in some degree to the formation of a character more fitted for thought than action. The new window gave a view of the road, and had many advantages, as Mrs Hepworth pointed out. From it the wandering sheep of her husband's flock might be seen, who straggled to the tempting beer-house, unobserved as they might hope, but not unobserved in reality; for the active Vicar kept his eye on the road, even during the composition of his most orthodox sermons, and had a hat and stick hanging ready at hand to seize, before sallying out after his parishioners, who had need of quick legs if they could take refuge in the 'Jolly Forester' before the teetotal Vicar had arrested them. The whole family were quick, brisk, loud-talking, kind-hearted, and not troubled with much delicacy of perception. Margaret feared that Mrs Hepworth would find out that Mr Bell was playing upon her, in the admiration he thought fit to express for everything that especially grated on his taste. But no! she took it all literally, and with such good faith, that Margaret could not help remonstrating with him as they walked slowly away from the parsonage back to their inn.

'Don't scold, Margaret. It was all because of you. If she had not shown you every change with such evident exultation in their superior sense, in perceiving what an improvement this and that would be, I could have behaved well. But if you must go on preaching, keep it till after dinner, when it will send me to sleep, and help my digestion.'

They were both of them tired, and Margaret herself so much so, that she was unwilling to go out as she had proposed to do, and have another ramble among the woods and fields so close to the home of her childhood. And, somehow, this visit to Helstone had not been all – had not been exactly what she had expected. There was change everywhere; slight, yet pervading all. Households were changed by absence, or death, or marriage, or the natural mutations brought by days and months and years, which carry us on imperceptibly from childhood to youth, and thence through manhood to age, whence we drop like fruit, fully ripe, into the quiet mother earth. Places were changed – a tree gone here, a bough there, bringing in a long ray of light where no light was before – a road was trimmed and narrowed, and the green straggling pathway by its side enclosed and cultivated. A great improvement it was called; but Margaret sighed over the old picturesqueness, the old gloom, and the grassy wayside of former days. She sate by the window on the little settle, sadly gazing out upon the gathering shades of night, which harmonized well with her pensive thought. Mr Bell slept soundly, after his unusual exercise through the day. At last he was roused by the entrance of the tea-tray, brought in by a flushed-looking country-girl, who had evidently been finding some variety from her usual occupation of waiter, in assisting this day in the hay-field.

'Hallo! Who's there! Where are we? Who's that, – Margaret? Oh, now I remember all. I could not imagine what woman was sitting there in such a doleful attitude, with her hands clasped straight out upon her knees, and her face looking so steadfastly before her. What were you looking at?' asked Mr Bell, coming to the window, and standing behind Margaret.

'Nothing,' said she, rising up quickly, and speaking as cheerfully as she could at a moment's notice.

'Nothing indeed! A bleak back-ground of trees, some white linen hung out on the sweet-briar hedge, and a great waft of damp air. Shut the window, and come in and make tea.'

Margaret was silent for some time. She played with her teaspoon, and did not attend particularly to what Mr Bell said. He contradicted her, and she took the same sort of smiling notice of his opinion as if he had agreed with her. Then she sighed, and putting down her spoon, she began, apropos of nothing at all, and in the high-pitched voice which usually shows that the speaker has been thinking for some time on the subject that they wish to introduce – 'Mr Bell, you remember what we were saying about Frederick last night, don't you?'

'Last night. Where was I? Oh, I remember! Why it seems a week ago. Yes, to be sure, I recollect we talked about him, poor fellow.'

'Yes – and do you not remember that Mr Lennox spoke about his having been in England about the time of dear mamma's death?' asked Margaret, her voice now lower than usual.

'I recollect. I hadn't heard of it before.'

'And I thought – I always thought that papa had told you about it.'

'No! he never did. But what about it, Margaret?'

'I want to tell you of something I did that was very wrong, about that time,' said Margaret, suddenly looking up at him with her clear honest eyes. 'I told a lie;' and her face became scarlet.

'True, that was bad I own; not but what I have told a pretty round number in my life, not all in downright words, as I suppose you did, but in actions, or in some shabby circumlocutory way, leading people either to disbelieve the truth, or believe a falsehood. You know who is the father of lies, Margaret? Well! a great number of folk, thinking themselves very good, have odd sorts of connexion with lies, left-hand marriages, and second cousins-once-removed. The tainting blood of falsehood runs through us all. I should have guessed you as far from it as most people. What! crying, child? Nay, now we'll not talk of it, if it ends in this way. I dare say you have been sorry for it, and that you won't do it again, and it's long ago now, and in short I want you to be very cheerful, and not very sad, this evening.'

Margaret wiped her eyes, and tried to talk about something else, but suddenly she burst out afresh.

'Please, Mr Bell, let me tell you about it – you could perhaps help me a little; no, not help me, but if you knew the truth, perhaps you could put me to rights – that is not it, after all,' said she, in despair at not being able to express herself more exactly as she wished.

Mr Bell's whole manner changed. 'Tell me all about it, child,' said he.

'It's a long story; but when Fred came, mamma was very ill, and I was undone with anxiety, and afraid, too, that I might have drawn him into danger; and we had an alarm just after her death, for Dixon met some one in Milton – a man called Leonards – who had known Fred, and who seemed to owe him a grudge, or at any rate to be tempted by the recollection of the reward offered for his apprehension; and with this new fright, I thought I had better hurry off Fred to London, where, as you would understand from what we said the other night, he was to go to consult Mr Lennox as to his chances if he stood the trial. So we – that is, he and I, – went to the railway station; it was one evening, and it was just getting rather dusk, but still light enough to recognize and be recognized, and we were too early, and went out to walk in a field just close by; I was always in a panic about this Leonards, who was, I knew, somewhere in the neighbourhood; and then, when we were in the field, the low red sunlight just in my face, some one came by on horseback in the road just below the field-stile by which we stood. I saw him look at me, but I did not know who it was at first, the sun was so in my eyes, but in an instant the dazzle went off, and I saw it was Mr Thornton, and we bowed,' –

'And he saw Frederick of course,' said Mr Bell, helping her on with her story, as he thought.

'Yes; and then at the station a man came up – tipsy and reeling – and he tried to collar Fred, and over-balanced himself as Fred wrenched himself away, and fell over the edge of the platform; not far, not deep; not above three feet; but oh! Mr Bell, somehow that fall killed him!'

'How awkward. It was this Leonards, I suppose. And how did Fred get off?'

'Oh! he went off immediately after the fall, which we never thought could have done the poor fellow any harm, it seemed so slight an injury.'

'Then he did not die directly?'

'No! not for two or three days. And then – oh, Mr Bell! now comes the bad part,' said she, nervously twining her fingers together. 'A police inspector came and taxed me with having been the companion of the young man, whose push or blow had occasioned Leonards' death; that was a false accusation, you know, but we had not heard that Fred had sailed, he might still be in London and liable to be arrested on this false charge, and his identity with the Lieutenant Hale, accused of causing that mutiny, discovered, he might be shot; all this flashed through my mind, and I said it was not me. I was not at the railway station that night. I knew nothing about it. I had no conscience or thought but to save Frederick.'

'I say it was right. I should have done the same. You forgot yourself in thought for another. I hope I should have done the same.'

'No, you would not. It was wrong, disobedient, faithless. At that very time Fred was safely out of England, and in my blindness I forgot that there was another witness who could testify to my being there.'

'Who?'

'Mr Thornton. You know he had seen me close to the station; we had bowed to each other.'

'Well! he would know nothing of this riot about the drunken fellow's death. I suppose the inquiry never came to anything.'

'No! the proceedings they had begun to talk about on the inquest were stopped. Mr Thornton did know all about it. He was a magistrate, and he found out that it was not the fall that had caused the death. But not before he knew what I had said. Oh, Mr Bell!' She suddenly covered her face with her hands, as if wishing to hide herself from the presence of the recollection.

'Did you have any explanation with him? Did you ever tell him the strong, instinctive motive?'

'The instinctive want of faith, and clutching at a sin to keep myself from sinking,' said she bitterly. 'No! How could I? He knew nothing of Frederick. To put myself to rights in his good opinion, was I to tell him of the secrets of our family, involving, as they seemed to do, the chances of poor Frederick's entire exculpation? Fred's last words had been to enjoin me to keep his visit a secret from all. You see, papa never told, even you. No! I could bear the shame – I thought I could at least. I did bear it. Mr Thornton has never respected me since.'

'He respects you, I am sure,' said Mr Bell. 'To be sure, it accounts a little for –. But he always speaks of you with regard and esteem, though now I understand certain reservations in his manner.'

Margaret did not speak; did not attend to what Mr Bell went on to say; lost all sense of it. By-and-by she said:

'Will you tell me what you refer to about "reservations" in his manner of speaking of me?'

'Oh! simply he has annoyed me by not joining in my praises of you. Like an old fool, I thought that every one would have the same opinions as I had; and he evidently could not agree with me. I was puzzled at the time. But he must be perplexed, if the affair has never been in the least explained. There was first your walking out with a young man in the dark –'

'But it was my brother!' said Margaret, surprised.

'True. But how was he to know that?'

'I don't know. I never thought of anything of that kind,' said Margaret, reddening, and looking hurt and offended.

'And perhaps he never would, but for the lie, – which, under the circumstances, I maintain, was necessary.'

'It was not. I know it now. I bitterly repent it.'

There was a long pause of silence. Margaret was the first to speak.

'I am not likely ever to see Mr Thornton again,' – and there she stopped.

'There are many things more unlikely, I should say,' replied Mr Bell.

'But I believe I never shall. Still, somehow one does not like to have sunk so low in – in a friend's opinion as I have done in his.' Her eyes were full of tears, but her voice was steady, and Mr Bell was not looking at her. 'And now that Frederick has given up all hope, and almost all wish of ever clearing himself, and returning to England, it would be only doing myself justice to have all this explained. If you please, and if you can, if there is a good opportunity, (don't force an explanation upon him, pray,) but if you can, will you tell him the whole circumstances, and tell him also that I gave you leave to do so, because I felt that for papa's sake I should not like to lose his respect, though we may never be likely to meet again?'

'Certainly. I think he ought to know. I do not like you to rest even under the shadow of an impropriety; he would not know what to think of seeing you alone with a young man.'

'As for that,' said Margaret, rather haughtily, 'I hold it is "Honi soit qui mal y pense." Yet still I should choose to have it explained, if any natural opportunity for easy explanation occurs. But it is not to clear myself of any suspicion of improper conduct that I wish to have him told – if I thought that he had suspected me, I should not care for his good opinion – no! it is that he may learn how I was tempted, and how I fell into the snare; why I told that falsehood, in short.'

'Which I don't blame you for. It is no partiality of mine, I assure you.'

'What other people may think of the rightness or wrongness is nothing in comparison to my own deep knowledge, my innate conviction that it was wrong. But we will not talk of that any more, if you please. It is done – my sin is sinned. I have now to put it behind me, and be truthful for evermore, if I can.'

'Very well. If you like to be uncomfortable and morbid, be so. I always keep my conscience as tight shut up as a jack-in-a-box, for when it jumps into existence it surprises me by its size. So I coax it down again, as the fisherman coaxed the genie. "Wonderful," say I, "to think that you have been concealed so long, and in so small a compass, that I really did not know of your existence. Pray, sir, instead of growing larger and larger every instant, and bewildering me with your misty outlines, would you once more compress yourself into your former dimensions?" And when I've got him down, don't I clap the seal on the vase, and take good care how I open it again, and how I go against Solomon, wisest of men, who confined him there.'

But it was no smiling matter to Margaret. She hardly attended to what Mr Bell was saying. Her thoughts ran upon the idea, before entertained, but which now had assumed the strength of a conviction, that Mr Thornton no longer held his former good opinion of her – that he was disappointed in her. She did not feel as if any explanation could ever reinstate her – not in his love, for that and any return on her part she had resolved never to dwell upon, and she kept rigidly to her resolution – but in the respect and high regard which she had hoped would have ever made him willing, in the spirit of Gerald Griffin's beautiful lines,

> *To turn and look back when thou hearest*[7]
> *The sound of my name.*

She kept choking and swallowing all the time that she thought about it. She tried to comfort herself with the idea, that what he imagined her to be, did not alter the fact of what she was. But it was a truism, a phantom, and broke down under the weight of her regret. She had twenty questions on the tip of her tongue to ask Mr Bell, but not one of them did she utter. Mr Bell thought that she was tired, and sent her early to her room, where she sate long hours by the open window, gazing out on the purple dome above, where the stars arose, and twinkled and disappeared behind the great umbrageous trees before she went to bed. All night long too, there burnt a little light on earth; a candle in her old bedroom, which was the nursery with the present inhabitants of the parsonage, until the new one was built. A sense of change, of individual nothingness, of perplexity and disappointment, overpowered Margaret. Nothing had been the same; and this slight, all-pervading instability, had given her greater pain than if all had been too entirely changed for her to recognize it.

'I begin to understand now what heaven must be – and, oh! the grandeur and repose of the words – "The same yesterday, today, and for ever." Everlasting! "From everlasting to everlasting,[8] Thou art God." That sky above me looks as though it could not change, and yet it will. I am so tired – so tired of being whirled on through all these phases of my life, in which nothing abides by me, no creature, no place; it is like the circle in which the victims of earthly passion eddy[9] continually. I am in the mood in which women of another religion take the veil. I seek heavenly steadfastness in earthly monotony. If I were a Roman Catholic and could deaden my heart, stun it with some great blow, I might become a nun. But I should pine after my kind; no, not my kind, for love for my species could never fill my heart to the utter exclusion of love for individuals. Perhaps it ought to be so, perhaps not; I cannot decide tonight.'

Wearily she went to bed, wearily she arose in four or five hours' time. But with the morning came hope, and a brighter view of things.

'After all it is right,' said she, hearing the voices of children at play while she was dressing. 'If the world stood still, it would retrograde and become corrupt, if that is not Irish. Looking out of myself, and my own painful sense of change, the progress all around me is right and necessary. I must not think so much of how circumstances affect me myself, but how they affect others, if I wish to have a right judgment, or a hopeful trustful heart.' And with a smile ready in her eyes to quiver down to her lips, she went into the parlour and greeted Mr Bell.

'Ah, Missy! you were up late last night, and so you're late this morning. Now I've got a little piece of news for you. What do you think of an invitation to dinner? a morning call, literally in the dewy morning. Why, I've had the Vicar here already, on his way to the school. How much the desire of giving our hostess a teetotal lecture for the benefit of the haymakers, had to do with his earliness, I don't know; but here he was, when I came down just before nine; and we are asked to dine there today.'

'But Edith expects me back – I cannot go,' said Margaret, thankful to have so good an excuse.

'Yes! I know; so I told him. I thought you would not want to go. Still it is open, if you would like it.'

'Oh, no!' said Margaret. 'Let us keep to our plan. Let us start at twelve. It is very good and kind of them; but indeed I could not go.'

'Very well. Don't fidget yourself, and I'll arrange it all.'

Before they left Margaret stole round to the back of the Vicarage garden, and gathered a little straggling piece of honeysuckle. She would not take a flower the day before, for fear of being observed, and her motives and feelings commented upon. But as she returned across the common, the place was reinvested with the old enchanting atmosphere. The common sounds of life were more musical there than anywhere else in the whole world, the light more golden, the life more tranquil and full of dreamy delight. As Margaret remembered her feelings yesterday, she said to herself:

'And I too change perpetually – now this, now that – now disappointed and peevish because all is not exactly as I had pictured it, and now suddenly discovering that the reality is far more beautiful than I had imagined it. Oh, Helstone! I shall never love any place like you.'

A few days afterwards, she had found her level, and decided that she was very glad to have been there, and that she had seen it again, and that to her it would always be the prettiest spot in the world, but that it was so full of associations with former days, and especially with her father and mother, that if it were all to come over again, she should shrink back from such another visit as that which she had paid with Mr Bell.

CHAPTER XLVII

Something Wanting

Experience, like a pale musician, holds[1]
A dulcimer of patience in his hand;
Whence harmonies we cannot understand,
Of God's will in His worlds, the strain unfolds
In sad, perplexed minors.

MRS BROWNING

About this time Dixon returned from Milton, and assumed her post as Margaret's maid. She brought endless pieces of Milton gossip: How Martha had gone to live with Miss Thornton, on the latter's marriage; with an account of the bridesmaids, dresses and breakfasts, at that interesting ceremony; how people thought that Mr Thornton had made too grand a wedding of it, considering he had lost a deal by the strike, and had had to pay so much for the failure of his contracts; how little money articles of furniture – long cherished by Dixon – had fetched at the sale, which was a shame considering how rich folks were at Milton; how Mrs Thornton had come one day and got two or three good bargains, and Mr Thornton had come the next, and in his desire to obtain one or two things, had bid against himself, much to the enjoyment of the bystanders, so as Dixon observed, that made things even; if Mrs Thornton paid too little, Mr Thornton paid too much. Mr Bell had sent all sorts of orders about the books; there was no understanding him, he was so particular; if he had come himself it would have been all right, but letters always were and always will be more puzzling than they are worth. Dixon had not much to tell about the Higginses. Her memory had an aristocratic bias, and was very treacherous whenever she tried to recall any circumstance connected with those below her in life. Nicholas was very well she believed. He had been several times at the house asking for news of Miss Margaret – the only person who ever did ask, except once Mr Thornton. And Mary? oh! of course she was very well, a great, stout slatternly thing! She did hear, or perhaps it was only a dream of hers, though it would be strange if she had dreamt of such people as the Higginses, that Mary had gone to work at Mr Thornton's mill, because her father wished her to know how to cook; but what nonsense that could mean she didn't know. Margaret rather agreed with her that the story was incoherent enough to be like a dream. Still it was pleasant to have some one now with whom she could talk of Milton, and Milton people. Dixon was not over-fond of the subject, rather wishing to leave that part of her life in shadow. She liked much more to dwell upon speeches of Mr Bell's, which had suggested an idea to her of what was really his intention − making Margaret his heiress. But her young lady gave her no encouragement, nor in any way gratified her insinuating enquiries, however disguised in the form of suspicions or assertions.

All this time, Margaret had a strange undefined longing to hear that Mr Bell had gone to pay one of his business visits to Milton; for it had been well understood between them, at the time of their conversation at Helstone, that the explanation she had desired should only be given to Mr Thornton by word of mouth, and even in that manner should be in nowise forced upon him. Mr Bell was no great correspondent, but he wrote from time to time long or short letters, as the humour took him, and although Margaret was not conscious of any definite hope, on receiving them, yet she always put away his notes with a little feeling of disappointment. He was not going to Milton; he said nothing about it at any rate. Well! she must be patient. Sooner or later the mists would be cleared away. Mr Bell's letters were hardly like his usual self; they were short, and complaining, with every now and then a little touch of bitterness that was unusual. He did not look forward to the future; he rather seemed to regret the past, and be weary of the present. Margaret fancied that he could not be well; but in answer to some enquiry of hers as to his health, he sent her a short note, saying there was an old-fashioned complaint called the spleen; that he was suffering from that, and it was for her to decide if it was more mental or physical; but that he should like to indulge himself in grumbling, without being obliged to send a bulletin every time.

In consequence of this note, Margaret made no more enquiries about his health. One day Edith let out accidentally a fragment of a conversation which she had had with Mr Bell, when he was last in

London, which possessed Margaret with the idea that he had some notion of taking her to pay a visit to her brother and new sister-in-law, at Cadiz, in the autumn. She questioned and cross-questioned Edith, till the latter was weary, and declared that there was nothing more to remember; all he had said was that he half-thought he should go, and hear for himself what Frederick had to say about the mutiny; and that it would be a good opportunity for Margaret to become acquainted with her new sister-in-law; that he always went somewhere during the long vacation, and did not see why he should not go to Spain as well as anywhere else. That was all. Edith hoped Margaret did not want to leave them, that she was so anxious about all this. And then, having nothing else particular to do, she cried, and said that she knew she cared much more for Margaret than Margaret did for her. Margaret comforted her as well as she could, but she could hardly explain to her how this idea of Spain, mere Chateau en Espagne as it might be, charmed and delighted her. Edith was in the mood to think that any pleasure enjoyed away from her was a tacit affront, or at best a proof of indifference. So Margaret had to keep her pleasure to herself, and could only let it escape by the safety-valve of asking Dixon, when she dressed for dinner, if she would not like to see Master Frederick and his new wife very much indeed?

'She's a Papist, Miss, isn't she?'

'I believe – oh yes, certainly!' said Margaret, a little damped for an instant at this recollection.

'And they live in a Popish country?'

'Yes.'

'Then I'm afraid I must say, that my soul is dearer to me than even Master Frederick, his own dear self. I should be in a perpetual terror, Miss, lest I should be converted.'

'Oh,' said Margaret, 'I do not know that I am going; and if I go, I am not such a fine lady as to be unable to travel without you. No! dear old Dixon, you shall have a long holiday, if we go. But I'm afraid it is a long "if."'

Now Dixon did not like this speech. In the first place, she did not like Margaret's trick of calling her 'dear old Dixon' whenever she was particularly demonstrative. She knew that Miss Hale was apt to call all people that she liked 'old,' as a sort of term of endearment; but Dixon always winced away from the application of the word to herself, who, being not much past fifty, was, she thought, in the very prime of life. Secondly, she did not like being so easily taken at her word; she had, with all her terror, a lurking curiosity about Spain, the Inquisition, and Popish mysteries. So, after clearing her throat, as if to show her willingness to do away with difficulties, she asked Miss Hale, whether she thought if she took care never to see a priest, or enter into one of their churches, there would be so very much danger of her being converted? Master Frederick, to be sure, had gone over unaccountable.

'I fancy it was love that first predisposed him to conversion,' said Margaret, sighing.

'Indeed, Miss!' said Dixon; 'well! I can preserve myself from priests, and from churches; but love steals in unawares! I think it's as well I should not go.'

Margaret was afraid of letting her mind run too much upon this Spanish plan. But it took off her thoughts from too impatiently dwelling upon her desire to have all explained to Mr Thornton. Mr Bell appeared for the present to be stationary at Oxford, and to have no immediate purpose of going to Milton, and some secret restraint seemed to hang over Margaret, and prevent her from even asking, or alluding again to any probability of such a visit on his part. Nor did she feel at liberty to name what Edith had told her of the idea he had entertained, – it might be but for five minutes, – of going to Spain. He had never named it at Helstone, during all that sunny day of leisure; it was very probably but the fancy of a moment, – but if it were true, what a bright outlet it would be from the monotony of her present life, which was beginning to pall upon her.[2]

One of the great pleasures of Margaret's life at this time, was in Edith's boy. He was the pride and plaything of both father and mother, as long as he was good; but he had a strong will of his own, and as soon as he burst out into one of his stormy passions, Edith would throw herself back in despair and fatigue, and sigh out, 'Oh dear, what shall I do with him! Do, Margaret, please ring the bell for Hanley.'

But Margaret almost liked him better in these manifestations of character than in his good blue-sashed moods. She would carry him off into a room, where they two alone battled it out; she with a firm power which subdued him into peace, while every sudden charm and wile she possessed, was exerted on the side of right, until he would rub his little hot and tear-smeared face all over hers, kissing and caressing till he often fell asleep in her arms or on her shoulder.

Those were Margaret's sweetest moments. They gave her a taste of the feeling that she believed would be denied to her for ever.

Mr Henry Lennox added a new and not disagreeable element to the course of the household life by his frequent presence. Margaret thought him colder, if more brilliant than formerly; but there were strong intellectual tastes, and much and varied knowledge, which gave flavour to the otherwise rather insipid conversation. Margaret saw glimpses in him of a slight contempt for his brother and sister-in-law, and for their mode of life, which he seemed to consider as frivolous and purposeless. He once or twice spoke to his brother, in Margaret's presence, in a pretty sharp tone of enquiry, as to whether he meant entirely to relinquish his profession; and on Captain Lennox's reply, that he had quite enough to live upon, she had seen Mr Lennox's curl of the lip as he said, 'And is that all you live for?'

But the brothers were much attached to each other, in the way that any two persons are, when the one is cleverer and always leads the other, and this last is patiently content to be led. Mr Lennox was pushing on in his profession; cultivating, with profound calculation, all those connections that might eventually be of service to him; keen-sighted, far-seeing, intelligent, sarcastic, and proud. Since the one long conversation relating to Frederick's affairs, which she had with him the first evening in Mr Bell's presence, she had had no great intercourse with him, further than that which arose out of their close relations with the same household. But this was enough to wear off the shyness on her side, and any symptoms of mortified pride and vanity on his. They met continually, of course, but she thought that he rather avoided being alone with her; she fancied that he, as well as she, perceived that they had drifted strangely apart from their former anchorage, side by side, in many of their opinions, and all their tastes.

And yet, when he had spoken unusually well, or with remarkable epigrammatic point, she felt that his eye sought the expression of her countenance first of all, if but for an instant; and that, in the family intercourse which constantly threw them together, her opinion was the one to which he listened with a deference, – the more complete, because it was reluctantly paid, and concealed as much as possible.

CHAPTER XLVIII

'Ne'er to be Found Again'

My own, my father's friend!
I cannot part with thee!
I ne'er have shown, thou ne'er hast known,
How dear thou art to me.

ANON

The elements of the dinner-parties which Mrs Lennox gave, were these; her friends contributed the beauty, Captain Lennox the easy knowledge of the subjects of the day; and Mr Henry Lennox and the sprinkling of rising men who were received as his friends, brought the wit, the cleverness, the keen and extensive knowledge of which they knew well enough how to avail themselves without seeming pedantic, or burdening the rapid flow of conversation.

These dinners were delightful; but even here Margaret's dissatisfaction found her out. Every talent, every feeling, every acquirement; nay, even every tendency towards virtue, was used up as materials for fireworks; the hidden, sacred fire, exhausted itself in sparkle and crackle. They talked about art in a merely sensuous way, dwelling on outside effects, instead of allowing themselves to learn what it has to teach. They lashed themselves up into an enthusiasm about high subjects in company, and never thought about them when they were alone; they squandered their capabilities of appreciation into a mere flow of appropriate words. One day, after the gentlemen had come up into the drawing-room, Mr Lennox drew near to Margaret, and addressed her in almost the first voluntary words he had spoken to her since she had returned to live in Harley Street.

'You did not look pleased at what Shirley was saying at dinner.'

'Didn't I? My face must be very expressive,' replied Margaret.

'It always was. It has not lost the trick of being eloquent.'

'I did not like,' said Margaret, hastily, 'his way of advocating what he knew to be wrong – so glaringly wrong – even in jest.'

'But it was very clever. How every word told! Do you remember the happy epithets?'

'Yes.'

'And despise them, you would like to add. Pray don't scruple, though he is my friend.'

'There! that is the exact tone in you, that −' she stopped short.

He listened for a moment to see if she would finish her sentence; but she only reddened, and turned away; before she did so, however, she heard him say, in a very low, clear voice, −

'If my tones, or modes of thought, are what you dislike, will you do me the justice to tell me so, and so give me the chance of learning to please you?'

All these weeks there was no intelligence of Mr Bell's going to Milton. He had spoken of it at Helstone as of a journey which he might have to take in a very short time from then; but he must have transacted his business by writing, Margaret thought, ere now, and she knew that if he could, he would avoid going to a place which he disliked, and moreover would little understand the secret importance which she affixed to the explanation that could only be given by word of mouth. She knew that he would feel that it was necessary that it should be done; but whether in summer, autumn, or winter, it would signify very little. It was now August, and there had been no mention of the Spanish journey to which he had alluded to Edith, and Margaret tried to reconcile herself to the fading away of this illusion.

But one morning she received a letter, saying that next week he meant to come up to town; he wanted to see her about a plan which he had in his head; and, moreover, he intended to treat himself to a little doctoring, as he had begun to come round to her opinion, that it would be pleasanter to think that his health was more in fault than he, when he found himself irritable and cross. There was altogether a tone of forced cheerfulness in the letter, as Margaret noticed afterwards; but at the time her attention was taken up by Edith's exclamations.

'Coming up to town! Oh dear! and I am so worn out by the heat that I don't believe I have strength enough in me for another dinner. Besides, everybody has left but our dear stupid selves, who can't settle where to go to. There would be nobody to meet him.'

'I'm sure he would much rather come and dine with us quite alone than with the most agreeable strangers you could pick up. Besides, if he is not well he won't wish for invitations. I am glad he has owned it at last. I was sure he was ill from the whole tone of his letters, and yet he would not answer me when I asked him, and I had no third person to whom I could apply for news.'

'Oh! he is not very ill, or he would not think of Spain.'

'He never mentions Spain.'

'No! but his plan that is to be proposed evidently relates to that. But would you really go in such weather as this?'

'Oh! it will get cooler every day. Yes! Think of it! I am only afraid I have thought and wished too much – in that absorbing wilful way which is sure to be disappointed – or else gratified, to the letter, while in the spirit it gives no pleasure.'

'But that's superstitious, I'm sure, Margaret.'

'No, I don't think it is. Only it ought to warn me, and check me from giving way to such passionate wishes. It is a sort of "Give me children,[1] or else I die." I'm afraid my cry is, "Let me go to Cadiz, or else I die."'

'My dear Margaret! You'll be persuaded to stay there; and then what shall I do? Oh! I wish I could find somebody for you to marry here, that I could be sure of you!'

'I shall never marry.'

'Nonsense, and double nonsense! Why, as Sholto says, you're such an attraction to the house, that he knows ever so many men who will be glad to visit here next year for your sake.'

Margaret drew herself up haughtily. 'Do you know, Edith, I sometimes think your Corfu life has taught you –'

'Well!'

'Just a shade or two of coarseness.'

Edith began to sob so bitterly, and to declare so vehemently that Margaret had lost all love for her, and no longer looked upon her as a friend, that Margaret came to think that she had expressed too harsh an opinion for the relief of her own wounded pride, and ended by being Edith's slave for the rest of the day; while that little lady, overcome by wounded feeling, lay like a victim on the sofa, heaving occasionally a profound sigh, till at last she fell asleep.

Mr Bell did not make his appearance even on the day to which he had for a second time deferred his visit. The next morning there came a letter from Wallis, his servant, stating that his master had not been feeling well for some time, which had been the true reason of his putting off his journey; and that at the very time when he should have set out for London, he had been seized with an apoplectic fit; it was, indeed, Wallis added, the opinion of the medical men – that he could not survive the night; and more than probable, that by the time Miss Hale received this letter his poor master would be no more.

Margaret received this letter at breakfast-time, and turned very pale as she read it; then silently putting it into Edith's hands, she left the room.

Edith was terribly shocked as she read it, and cried in a sobbing, frightened, childish way, much to her husband's distress. Mrs Shaw was breakfasting in her own room, and upon him devolved the task of reconciling his wife to the near contact into which she seemed to be brought with death, for the first time that she could remember in her life. Here was a man who was to have dined with them today lying dead or dying[2] instead! It was some time before she could think of Margaret. Then she started up, and followed her upstairs into her room. Dixon was packing up a few toilette articles, and Margaret was hastily putting on her bonnet, shedding tears all the time, and her hands trembling so that she could hardly tie the strings.

'Oh, dear Margaret! how shocking! What are you doing? Are you going out? Sholto would telegraph or do anything you like.'

'I am going to Oxford. There is a train in half-an-hour. Dixon has offered to go with me, but I could have gone by myself. I must see him again. Besides, he may be better, and want some care. He has been like a father to me. Don't stop me, Edith.'

'But I must. Mamma won't like it at all. Come and ask her about it, Margaret. You don't know where you're going. I should not mind if he had a house of his own; but in his Fellow's rooms! Come to mamma, and do ask her before you go. It will not take a minute.'

Margaret yielded, and lost her train. In the suddenness of the event, Mrs Shaw became bewildered and hysterical, and so the precious time slipped by. But there was another train in a couple of hours; and after various discussions on propriety and impropriety, it was decided that Captain Lennox should accompany Margaret, as the one thing to which she was constant was her resolution to go, alone or otherwise, by the next train, whatever might be said of the propriety or impropriety of the step. Her father's friend, her own friend, was lying at the point of death; and the thought of this came upon her with such vividness, that she was surprised herself at the firmness with which she asserted something of her right to independence of action; and five minutes before the time for starting, she found herself sitting in a railway-carriage opposite to Captain Lennox.

It was always a comfort to her to think that she had gone, though it was only to hear that he had died in the night. She saw the rooms that he had occupied, and associated them ever after most fondly in her memory with the idea of her father, and his one cherished and faithful friend.

They had promised Edith before starting, that if all had ended as they feared, they would return to dinner; so that long, lingering look around the room in which her father had died, had to be interrupted, and a quiet farewell taken of the kind old face that had so often come out with pleasant words, and merry quips and cranks.

Captain Lennox fell asleep on their journey home; and Margaret could cry at leisure, and bethink her of this fatal year, and all the woes it had brought to her. No sooner was she fully aware of one loss than another came – not to supersede her grief for the one before, but to re-open wounds and feelings scarcely healed. But at the sound of the tender voices of her aunt and Edith, of merry little Sholto's glee at her arrival, and at the sight of the well-lighted rooms, with their mistress pretty in her paleness and her eager sorrowful interest, Margaret roused herself from her heavy trance of almost superstitious hopelessness, and began to feel that even around her joy and gladness might gather. She had Edith's place on the sofa; Sholto was taught to carry aunt Margaret's cup of tea very carefully to her; and by the time she went up to dress, she could thank God for having spared her dear old friend a long or a painful illness.

But when night came[3] – solemn night, and all the house was quiet, Margaret still sate watching the beauty of a London sky at such an hour, on such a summer evening; the faint pink reflection of earthly lights on the soft clouds that float tranquilly into the white moonlight, out of the warm gloom which lies motionless around the horizon. Margaret's room had been the day nursery of her childhood, just when it merged into girlhood, and when the feelings and conscience had been first awakened into full activity. On some such night as this she remembered promising to herself to live as brave and noble a life as any heroine she ever read or heard of in romance, a life sans peur et sans reproche; it had seemed to her then that she had only to will, and such a life would be accomplished. And now she had learnt that not only to will, but also to pray, was a necessary condition in the truly heroic. Trusting to herself, she had fallen. It was a just conse-quence of her sin, that all excuses for it, all temptation to it, should remain for ever unknown to the person in whose opinion it had sunk her lowest. She stood face to face at last with her sin. She knew it for what it was; Mr Bell's kindly sophistry that nearly all men were guilty of equivocal actions, and that the motive ennobled the evil, had never had much real weight with her. Her own first thought of how, if she had known all, she might have fearlessly told the truth, seemed low and poor. Nay, even now, her anxiety to have her character for truth partially excused in Mr Thornton's eyes, as Mr Bell had promised to do, was a very small and petty consideration, now that she was afresh taught by death what life should be. If all the world spoke, acted, or kept silence with intent to deceive, – if dearest interests were at stake, and dearest lives in peril, – if no one should ever know of her truth or her falsehood to measure out their honour or contempt for her by, straight alone where she stood, in the presence of God, she prayed that she might have strength to speak and act the truth for evermore.

CHAPTER XLIX

Breathing Tranquillity

And down the sunny beach she paces slowly,[1]
With many doubtful pauses by the way;
Grief hath an influence so hush'd and holy.

HOOD

'Is not Margaret the heiress?' whispered Edith to her husband, as they were in their room alone at night after the sad journey to Oxford. She had pulled his tall head down, and stood upon tiptoe, and implored him not to be shocked, before she had ventured to ask this question. Captain Lennox was, however, quite in the dark; if he had ever heard, he had forgotten; it could not be much that a Fellow of a small college had to leave; but he had never wanted her to pay for her board; and two hundred and fifty pounds a year[2] was something ridiculous, considering that she did not take wine. Edith came down upon her feet a little bit sadder; with a romance blown to pieces.

A week afterwards, she came prancing towards her husband, and made him a low curtsey:

'I am right, and you are wrong, most noble Captain. Margaret has had a lawyer's letter, and she is residuary legatee – the legacies being about two thousand pounds, and the remainder about forty thousand, at the present value of property in Milton.'

'Indeed! and how does she take her good fortune?'

'Oh, it seems she knew she was to have it all along; only she had no idea it was so much. She looks very white and pale, and says she's afraid of it; but that's nonsense, you know, and will soon go off. I left mamma pouring congratulations down her throat, and stole away to tell you.'

It seemed to be supposed, by general consent, that the most natural thing was to consider Mr Lennox henceforward as Margaret's legal adviser. She was so entirely ignorant of all forms of business that in nearly everything she had to refer to him. He chose out her attorney; he came to her with papers to be signed. He was never so happy as when teaching her of what all these mysteries of the law were the signs and types.

'Henry,' said Edith, one day, archly; 'do you know what I hope and expect all these long conversations with Margaret will end in?'

'No, I don't,' said he, reddening. 'And I desire you not to tell me.'

'Oh, very well; then I need not tell Sholto not to ask Mr Montagu so often to the house.'

'Just as you choose,' said he with forced coolness. 'What you are thinking of, may or may not happen; but this time, before I commit myself, I will see my ground clear. Ask whom you choose. It may not be very civil, Edith, but if you meddle in it you will mar it. She has been very farouche with me for a long time; and is only just beginning to thaw a little from her Zenobia ways.[3] She has the making of a Cleopatra in[4] her, if only she were a little more pagan.'

'For my part,' said Edith, a little maliciously, 'I am very glad she is a Christian. I know so very few!'

There was no Spain for Margaret that autumn; although to the last she hoped that some fortunate occasion would call Frederick to Paris, whither she could easily have met with a convoy. Instead of Cadiz, she had to content herself with Cromer. To that place her aunt Shaw and the Lennoxes were bound. They had all along wished her to accompany them, and, consequently, with their characters, they made but lazy efforts to forward her own separate wish. Perhaps Cromer was, in one sense of the expression, the best for her. She needed bodily strengthening and bracing as well as rest.

Among other hopes that had vanished, was the hope, the trust she had had, that Mr Bell would have given Mr Thornton the simple facts of the family circumstances which had preceded the unfortunate accident that led to Leonards' death. Whatever opinion – however changed it might be from what Mr Thornton had once entertained, she had wished it to be based upon a true understanding of what she had done; and why she had done it. It would have been a pleasure to her; would have given her rest on a point on which she should now all her life be restless, unless she could resolve not to think upon it. It was now so long after the time of these occurrences, that there was no possible way of explaining them save the one which she had lost by Mr Bell's death. She must just submit, like many another, to be misunderstood; but, though reasoning herself into the belief that in this hers was no uncommon lot, her heart did not ache the less with longing that some time – years and years hence – before he died at any rate, he might know how much she had been tempted. She thought that she did not want to hear that all was explained to him, if only she could be sure that he would know. But this wish was vain, like so many others; and when she had schooled herself into this conviction, she turned with all her heart and strength to the life that lay immediately before her, and resolved to strive and make the best of that.

She used to sit long hours upon the beach, gazing intently on the waves as they chafed with perpetual motion against the pebbly shore, – or she looked out upon the more distant heave, and sparkle against the sky, and heard, without being conscious of hearing, the eternal psalm, which went up continually. She was soothed without knowing how or why. Listlessly she sat there, on the ground, her hands clasped round her knees, while her aunt Shaw did small shoppings, and Edith and Captain Lennox rode far and wide on shore and inland. The nurses, sauntering on with their charges, would pass and repass her, and wonder in whispers what she could find to look at so long, day after day. And when the family gathered at dinner-time, Margaret was so silent and absorbed that Edith voted her moped, and hailed a proposal of her husband's with great satisfaction, that Mr Henry Lennox should be asked to take Cromer for a week, on his return from Scotland in October.

But all this time for thought enabled Margaret to put events in their right places, as to origin and significance, both as regarded her past life and her future. Those hours by the sea-side were not lost, as any one might have seen who had had the perception to read, or the care to understand, the look that Margaret's face was gradually acquiring. Mr Henry Lennox was excessively struck by the change.

'The sea has done Miss Hale an immense deal of good, I should fancy,' said he, when she first left the room after his arrival in their family circle. 'She looks ten years younger than she did in Harley Street.'

'That's the bonnet I got her!' said Edith, triumphantly. 'I knew it would suit her the moment I saw it.'

'I beg your pardon,' said Mr Lennox, in the half-contemptuous, half-indulgent tone he generally used to Edith. 'But I believe I know the difference between the charms of a dress and the charms of a woman. No mere bonnet would have made Miss Hale's eyes so lustrous and yet so soft, or her lips so ripe and red – and her face altogether so full of peace and light. – She is like, and yet more,' – he dropped his voice, – 'like the Margaret Hale of Helstone.'

From this time the clever and ambitious man bent all his powers to gaining Margaret. He loved her sweet beauty. He saw the latent sweep of her mind, which could easily (he thought) be led to embrace all the objects on which he had set his heart. He looked upon her fortune only as a part of the complete and superb character of herself and her position: yet he was fully aware of the rise which it would immediately enable him, the poor barrister, to take. Eventually he would earn such success, and such honours, as would enable him to pay her back, with interest, that first advance in wealth which he should owe to her. He had been to Milton on business connected with her property, on his return from Scotland; and with the quick eye of a skilled lawyer, ready ever to take in and weigh contingencies, he had seen that much additional value was yearly accruing to the lands and tenements which she owned in that prosperous and increasing town. He was glad to find that the present relationship between Margaret and himself, of client and legal adviser, was gradually superseding the recollection of that unlucky, mismanaged day at Helstone. He had thus unusual opportunities of intimate intercourse with her, besides those that arose from the connection between the families.

Margaret was only too willing to listen as long as he talked of Milton, though he had seen none of the people whom she more especially knew. It had been the tone with her aunt and cousin to speak of Milton with dislike and contempt; just such feelings as Margaret was ashamed to remember she had expressed and felt on first going to live there. But Mr Lennox almost exceeded Margaret in his appreciation of the character of Milton and its inhabitants.

Their energy, their power, their indomitable courage in struggling and fighting; their lurid vividness of existence, captivated and arrested his attention. He was never tired of talking about them; and had never perceived how selfish and material were too many of the ends they proposed to themselves as the result of all their mighty, untiring endeavour, till Margaret, even in the midst of her gratification, had the candour to point this out, as the tainting sin in so much that was noble, and to be admired. Still, when other subjects palled upon her, and she gave but short answers to many questions, Henry Lennox found out that an inquiry as to some Darkshire peculiarity of character, called back the light into her eye, the glow into her cheek.

When they returned to town, Margaret fulfilled one of her sea-side resolves, and took her life into her own hands. Before they went to Cromer, she had been as docile to her aunt's laws as if she were still the scared little stranger who cried herself to sleep that first night in the Harley Street nursery. But she had learnt, in those solemn hours of thought, that she herself must one day answer for her own life, and what she had done with it; and she tried to settle that most difficult problem for women,[5] how much was to be utterly merged in obedience to authority, and how much might be set apart for freedom in working. Mrs Shaw was as good-tempered as could be; and Edith had inherited this charming domestic quality; Margaret herself had probably the worst temper of the three, for her quick perceptions, and over-lively imagination made her hasty, and her early isolation from sympathy had made her proud; but she had an indescribable childlike sweetness of heart, which made her manners, even in her rarely wilful moods, irresistible of old; and now, chastened even by what the world called her good fortune, she charmed her reluctant aunt into acquiescence with her will. So Margaret gained the acknowledgment of her right to follow her own ideas of duty.

'Only don't be strong-minded,' pleaded Edith. 'Mamma wants you to have a footman of your own; and I'm sure you're very welcome, for they're great plagues. Only to please me, darling, don't go and have a strong mind; it's the only thing I ask. Footman or no footman, don't be strong-minded.'

'Don't be afraid, Edith. I'll faint on your hands at the servant's dinner-time, the very first opportunity; and then, what with Sholto playing with the fire, and the baby crying, you'll begin to wish for a strong-minded woman,[6] equal to any emergency.'

'And you'll not grow too good to joke and be merry?'

'Not I. I shall be merrier than I have ever been, now I have got my own way.'

'And you'll not go a figure, but let me buy your dresses for you?'

'Indeed I mean to buy them for myself. You shall come with me if you like; but no one can please me but myself.'

'Oh! I was afraid you'd dress in brown and dust-colour, not to show the dirt you'll pick up in all those places. I'm glad you're going to keep one or two vanities, just by way of specimens of the old Adam.'

'I'm going to be just the same, Edith, if you and my aunt could but fancy so. Only as I have neither husband nor child to give me natural duties, I must make myself some, in addition to ordering my gowns.'

In the family conclave, which was made up of Edith, her mother, and her husband, it was decided that perhaps all these plans of hers would only secure her the more for Henry Lennox. They kept her out of the way of other friends who might have eligible sons or brothers; and it was also agreed that she never seemed to take much pleasure in the society of any one but Henry, out of their own family. The other admirers, attracted by her appearance or the reputation of her fortune, were swept away, by her unconscious smiling disdain, into the paths frequented by other beauties less fastidious, or other heiresses with a larger amount of gold. Henry and she grew slowly into closer intimacy; but neither he nor she were people to brook the slightest notice of their proceedings.

CHAPTER L

Changes at Milton

Here we go up, up, up;
And here we go down, down, downee![1]
NURSERY SONG

Meanwhile, at Milton the chimneys smoked, the ceaseless roar and mighty beat, and dizzying whirl of machinery, struggled and strove perpetually. Senseless and purposeless were wood and iron and steam in their endless labours; but the persistence of their monotonous work was rivalled in tireless endurance by the strong crowds, who, with sense and with purpose, were busy and restless in seeking after – What? In the streets there were few loiterers, – none walking for mere pleasure; every man's face was set in lines of eagerness or anxiety; news was sought for with fierce avidity; and men jostled each other aside in the Mart and in the Exchange, as they did in life, in the deep selfishness of competition. There was gloom over the town. Few came to buy, and those who did were looked at suspiciously by the sellers; for credit was insecure, and the most stable might have their fortunes affected by the sweep in the great neighbouring port among the shipping houses. Hitherto there had been no failures in Milton; but, from the immense speculations that had come to light in making a bad end in America, and yet nearer home, it was known that some Milton houses of business must suffer so severely that every day men's faces asked, if their tongues did not, 'What news? Who is gone? How will it affect me?' And if two or three spoke together, they dwelt rather on the names of those who were safe than dared to hint at those likely, in their opinion, to go; for idle breath may, at such times, cause the downfall of some who might otherwise weather the storm; and one going down drags many after. 'Thornton is safe,' say they. 'His business is large – extending every year; but such a head as he has, and so prudent with all his daring!' Then one man draws another aside, and walks a little apart, and, with head inclined into his neighbour's ear, he says, 'Thornton's business is large; but he has spent his profits in extending it; he has no capital laid by; his machinery is new within these two years, and has cost him – we won't say what! – a word to the wise!' But that Mr Harrison was a croaker, – a man who had succeeded to his father's trade-made fortune, which he had feared to lose by altering his mode of business to any having a larger scope; yet he grudged every penny made by others more daring and far-sighted.

But the truth was, Mr Thornton was hard pressed. He felt it acutely in his vulnerable point – his pride in the commercial character which he had established for himself. Architect of his own fortunes, he attributed this to no special merit or qualities of his own, but to the power, which he believed that commerce gave to every brave, honest, and persevering man, to raise himself to a level from which he might see and read the great game of worldly success, and honestly, by such far-sightedness, command more power and influence than in any other mode of life. Far away, in the East and in the

West, where his person would never be known, his name was to be regarded, and his wishes to be fulfilled, and his word pass like gold. That was the idea of merchant-life with which Mr Thornton had started. 'Her merchants be like princes,'[2] said his mother, reading the text aloud, as if it were a trumpet-call to invite her boy to the struggle. He was but like many others – men, women, and children – alive to distant, and dead to near things. He sought to possess the influence of a name in foreign countries and far-away seas, – to become the head of a firm that should be known for generations; and it had taken him long silent years to come even to a glimmering of what he might be now, today, here in his own town, his own factory, among his own people. He and they had led parallel lives – very close, but never touching – till the accident (or so it seemed) of his acquaintance with Higgins. Once brought face to face, man to man, with an individual of the masses around him, and (take notice) out of the character of master and workman, in the first instance, they had each begun to recognize that 'we have all of us one human heart.'[3] It was the fine point of the wedge; and until now, when the apprehension of losing his connection with two or three of the workmen whom he had so lately begun to know as men, – of having a plan or two, which were experiments lying very close to his heart, roughly nipped off without trial, – gave a new poignancy to the subtle fear that came over him from time to time; until now, he had never recognized how much and how deep was the interest he had grown of late to feel in his position as manufacturer, simply because it led him into such close contact, and gave him the opportunity of so much power, among a race of people strange, shrewd, ignorant; but, above all, full of character and strong human feeling.

He reviewed his position as a Milton manufacturer. The strike a year and a half ago, – or more, for it was now untimely wintry weather, in a late spring, – that strike, when he was young, and he now was old – had prevented his completing some of the large orders he had then on hand. He had locked up a good deal of his capital in new and expensive machinery, and he had also bought cotton largely, for the fulfilment of these orders, taken under contract. That he had not been able to complete them, was owing in some degree to the utter want of skill on the part of the Irish hands whom he had imported; much of their work was damaged and unfit to be sent forth by a house which prided itself on turning out nothing but first-rate articles. For many months, the embarrassment caused by the strike had been an obstacle in Mr Thornton's way; and often, when his eye fell on Higgins, he could have spoken angrily to him without any present cause, just from feeling how serious was the injury that had arisen from this affair in which he was implicated. But when he became conscious of this sudden, quick resentment, he resolved to curb it. It would not satisfy him to avoid Higgins; he must convince himself that he was master over his own anger, by being particularly careful to allow Higgins access to him, whenever the strict rules of business, or Mr Thornton's leisure permitted. And by-and-by, he lost all sense of resentment in wonder how it was, or could be, that two men like himself and Higgins, living by the same trade, working in their different ways at the same object, could look upon each other's position and duties in so strangely different a way. And thence arose that intercourse, which though it might not have the effect of preventing all future clash of opinion and action, when the occasion arose, would, at any rate, enable both master and man to look upon each other with far more charity and sympathy, and bear with each other more patiently and kindly. Besides this improvement of feeling, both Mr Thornton and his workmen found out their ignorance as to positive matters of fact, known heretofore to one side, but not to the other.

But now had come one of those periods of bad trade, when the market falling brought down the value of all large stocks; Mr Thornton's fell to nearly half. No orders were coming in; so he lost the interest of the capital he had locked up in machinery; indeed, it was difficult to get payment for the orders completed; yet there was the constant drain of expenses for working the business. Then the bills became due for the cotton he had purchased; and money being scarce, he could only borrow at exorbitant interest, and yet he could not realize any of his property. But he did not despair; he exerted himself day and night to foresee and to provide for all emergencies; he was as calm and gentle to the women in his home as ever; to the workmen in his mill he spoke not many words, but they knew him by this time; and many a curt, decided answer was received by them rather with sympathy for the care they saw pressing upon him, than with the suppressed antagonism which had formerly been smouldering, and ready for hard words and hard judgments on all occasions. 'Th' measter's a deal to potter him,' said Higgins, one day, as he heard Mr Thornton's short, sharp inquiry, why such a command had not been obeyed; and caught the sound of the suppressed sigh which he heaved in going past the room where some of the men were working. Higgins and another man stopped over-hours that night, unknown to any one, to get the neglected piece of work done; and Mr Thornton never knew but that the overlooker, to whom he had given the command in the first instance, had done it himself.

'Eh! I reckon I know who'd ha' been sorry for to see our measter sitting so like a piece o' grey calico! Th' ou'd parson would ha' fretted his woman's heart[4] out, if he'd seen the woeful looks I have seen on our measter's face,' thought Higgins, one day, as he was approaching Mr Thornton in Marlborough Street.

'Measter,' said he, stopping his employer in his quick resolved walk, and causing that gentleman to look up with a sudden annoyed start, as if his thoughts had been far away.

'Have yo' heerd aught of Miss Marget lately?'

'Miss – who?' replied Mr Thornton.

'Miss Marget – Miss Hale – th' oud parson's daughter – yo' known who I mean well enough, if yo'll only think a bit –' (there was nothing disrespectful in the tone in which this was said).

'Oh yes!' and suddenly, the wintry frost-bound look of care had left Mr Thornton's face, as if some soft summer gale had blown all anxiety away from his mind; and though his mouth was as much compressed as before, his eyes smiled out benignly on his questioner.

'She's my landlord now, you know, Higgins. I hear of her through her agent here, every now and then. She's well and among friends – thank you, Higgins.' That 'thank you' that lingered after the other words, and yet came with so much warmth of feeling, let in a new light to the acute Higgins. It might be but a will-o'-th'-wisp, but he thought he would follow it and ascertain whither it would lead him.

'And she's not getten married, measter?'

'Not yet.' The face was cloudy once more. 'There is some talk of it, as I understand, with a connection of the family.'

'Then she'll not be for coming to Milton again, I reckon.'

'No!'

'Stop a minute, measter.' Then going up confidentially close, he said, 'Is th' young gentleman cleared?' He enforced the depth of his intelligence by a wink of the eye, which only made things more mysterious to Mr Thornton.

'Th' young gentleman, I mean – Master Frederick, they ca'ad him – her brother as was over here, yo' known.'

'Over here.'

'Ay, to be sure, at th' missus's death. Yo' need na be feared of my telling; for Mary and me, we knowed it all along, only we held our peace, for we got it through Mary working in th' house.'

'And he was over. It was her brother!'

'Sure enough, and I reckoned yo' knowed it, or I'd never ha' let on. Yo' knowed she had a brother?'

'Yes, I know all about him. And he was over at Mrs Hale's death?'

'Nay! I'm not going for to tell more. I've maybe getten them into mischief already, for they kept it very close. I nobbut wanted to know if they'd getten him cleared?'

'Not that I know of. I know nothing. I only hear of Miss Hale, now, as my landlord, and through her lawyer.'

He broke off from Higgins, to follow the business on which he had been bent when the latter first accosted him; leaving Higgins baffled in his endeavour.

'It was her brother,' said Mr Thornton to himself. 'I am glad. I may never see her again; but it is a comfort – a relief – to know that much. I knew she could not be unmaidenly; and yet I yearned for conviction. Now I am glad!'

It was a little golden thread running through the dark web of his present fortunes; which were growing ever gloomier and more gloomy. His agent had largely trusted a house in the American trade, which went down, along with several others, just at this time, like a pack of cards, the fall of one compelling other failures. What were Mr Thornton's engagements? Could he stand?

Night after night he took books and papers into his own private room, and sate up there long after the family were gone to bed. He thought that no one knew of this occupation of the hours he should have spent in sleep. One morning, when daylight was stealing in through the crevices of his shutters, and he had never been in bed, and, in hopeless indifference of mind, was thinking that he could do without the hour or two of rest, which was all that he should be able to take before the stir of daily labour began again, the door of his room opened, and his mother stood there, dressed as she had been the day before. She had never laid herself down to slumber any more than he. Their eyes met. Their faces were cold and rigid, and wan, from long watching.

'Mother! why are not you in bed?'

'Son John,' said she, 'do you think I can sleep with an easy mind, while you keep awake full of care? You have not told me what your trouble is; but sore trouble you have had these many days past.'

'Trade is bad.'

'And you dread –'

'I dread nothing,' replied he, drawing up his head, and holding it erect. 'I know now that no man will suffer by me. That was my anxiety.'

'But how do you stand? Shall you – will it be a failure?' her steady voice trembling in an unwonted manner.

'Not a failure. I must give up business, but I pay all men. I might redeem myself – I am sorely tempted –'

'How? Oh, John! keep up your name – try all risks for that. How redeem it?'

'By a speculation offered to me, full of risk; but, if successful, placing me high above water-mark, so that no one need ever know the strait I am in. Still, if it fails –'

'And if it fails,' said she, advancing, and laying her hand on his arm, her eyes full of eager light. She held her breath to hear the end of his speech.

'Honest men are ruined by a rogue,' said he gloomily. 'As I stand now, my creditors' money is safe – every farthing of it; but I don't know where to find my own – it may be all gone, and I penniless at this moment. Therefore, it is my creditors' money that I should risk.'

'But if it succeeded, they need never know. Is it so desperate a speculation? I am sure it is not, or you would never have thought of it. If it succeeded –'

'I should be a rich man, and my peace of conscience would be gone!'

'Why! You would have injured no one.'

'No; but I should have run the risk of ruining many for my own paltry aggrandisement. Mother, I have decided! You won't much grieve over our leaving this house, shall you, dear mother?'

'No! but to have you other than what you are will break my heart. What can you do?'

'Be always the same John Thornton in whatever circumstances; endeavouring to do right, and making great blunders; and then trying to be brave in setting to afresh. But it is hard, mother. I have so worked and planned. I have discovered new powers in my situation too late – and now all is over. I am too old to begin again with the same heart. It is hard, mother.'

He turned away from her, and covered his face with his hands.

'I can't think,' said she, with gloomy defiance in her tone, 'how it

413

comes about. Here is my boy – good son, just man, tender heart – and he fails in all he sets his mind upon: he finds a woman to love, and she cares no more for his affection than if he had been any common man; he labours, and his labour comes to nought. Other people prosper and grow rich, and hold their paltry names high and dry above shame.'

'Shame never touched me,' said he, in a low tone: but she went on.

'I sometimes have wondered where justice was gone to, and now I don't believe there is such a thing in the world, – now you are come to this; you, my own John Thornton, though you and I may be beggars together – my own dear son!'

She fell upon his neck, and kissed him through her tears.

'Mother!' said he, holding her gently in his arms. 'Who has sent me my lot in life, both of good and of evil?'

She shook her head. She would have nothing to do with religion just then.

'Mother,' he went on, seeing that she would not speak, 'I, too, have been rebellious; but I am striving to be so no longer. Help me, as you helped me when I was a child. Then you said many good words – when my father died, and we were sometimes sorely short of comforts – which we shall never be now; you said brave, noble, trustful words then, mother, which I have never forgotten, though they may have lain dormant. Speak to me again in the old way, mother. Do not let us have to think that the world has too much hardened our hearts. If you would say the old good words, it would make me feel something of the pious simplicity of my childhood. I say them to myself, but they would come differently from you, remembering all the cares and trials you have had to bear.'

'I have had a many,' said she, sobbing, 'but none so sore as this. To see you cast down from your rightful place! I could say it for myself, John, but not for you. Not for you! God has seen fit to be very hard on you, very.'

She shook with the sobs that come so convulsively when an old person weeps. The silence around her struck her at last; and she quieted herself to listen. No sound. She looked. Her son sate by the table, his arms thrown half across it, his head bent face downwards.

'Oh, John!' she said, and she lifted his face up. Such a strange, pallid look of gloom was on it, that for a moment it struck her that this look was the forerunner of death; but, as the rigidity melted out of the countenance and the natural colour returned, and she saw that he was himself once again, all worldly mortification sank to nothing before the consciousness of the great blessing that he himself by his simple existence was to her. She thanked God for this, and this alone, with a fervour that swept away all rebellious feelings from her mind.

He did not speak readily; but he went and opened the shutters, and let the ruddy light of dawn flood the room. But the wind was in the east; the weather was piercing cold, as it had been for weeks; there would be no demand for light summer goods this year. That hope for the revival of trade must utterly be given up.

It was a great comfort to have had this conversation with his mother; and to feel sure that, however they might henceforward keep silence on all these anxieties, they yet understood each other's feelings, and were, if not in harmony, at least not in discord with each other, in their way of viewing them. Fanny's husband was vexed at Thornton's refusal to take any share in the speculation which he had offered to him, and withdrew from any possibility of being supposed able to assist him with the ready money, which indeed the speculator needed for his own venture.

There was nothing for it at last, but that which Mr Thornton had dreaded for many weeks; he had to give up the business in which he had been so long engaged with so much honour and success; and look out for a subordinate situation. Marlborough Mills and the adjacent dwelling were held under a long lease; they must, if possible, be relet. There was an immediate choice of situations offered to Mr Thornton. Mr Hamper would have been only too glad to have secured him as a steady and experienced partner for his son, whom he was setting up with a large capital in a neighbouring town; but the young man was half-educated as regarded information, and wholly uneducated as regarded any other responsibility than that of getting money, and brutalized both as to his pleasures and his pains. Mr Thornton declined having any share in a partnership, which would frustrate what few plans he had that survived the wreck of his fortunes. He would sooner consent to be only a manager, where he could have a certain degree of power beyond the mere money-getting part, than have to fall in with the tyrannical humours of a moneyed partner with whom he felt sure that he should quarrel in a few months.

So he waited, and stood on one side with profound humility, as the news swept through the Exchange, of the enormous fortune which his brother-in-law had made by his daring speculation. It was a nine days' wonder. Success brought with it its worldly consequence of extreme admiration. No one was considered so wise and far-seeing as Mr Watson.

CHAPTER LI

Meeting Again

Bear up, brave heart! we will be calm and strong;
Sure, we can master eyes, or cheek, or tongue,
Nor let the smallest tell-tale sign appear
She ever was, and is, and will be dear.

RHYMING PLAY

It was a hot summer's evening. Edith came into Margaret's bedroom, the first time in her habit, the second ready dressed for dinner. No one was there at first; the next time Edith found Dixon laying out Margaret's dress on the bed; but no Margaret. Edith remained to fidget about.

'Oh, Dixon! not those horrid blue flowers to that dead gold-coloured gown. What taste! Wait a minute, and I will bring you some pomegranate blossoms.'

'It's not a dead gold-colour, ma'am. It's a straw-colour. And blue always goes with straw-colour.' But Edith had brought the brilliant scarlet flowers before Dixon had got half through her remonstrance.

'Where is Miss Hale?' asked Edith, as soon as she had tried the effect of the garniture. 'I can't think,' she went on, pettishly, 'how my aunt her to get into such rambling habits in Milton! I'm sure I'm always expecting to hear of her having met with something horrible among all those wretched places she pokes herself into. I should never dare to go down some of those streets without a servant. They're not fit for ladies.'

Dixon was still huffed about her despised taste; so she replied, rather shortly:

'It's no wonder to my mind, when I hear ladies talk such a deal about being ladies – and when they're such fearful, delicate, dainty ladies too – I say it's no wonder to me that there are no longer any saints on earth –'

'Oh, Margaret! here you are! I have been so wanting you. But how your cheeks are flushed with the heat, poor child! But only think what that tiresome Henry has done; really, he exceeds brother-in-law's limits. Just when my party was made up so beautifully – fitted in so precisely for Mr Colthurst – there has Henry come, with an apology it is true, and making use of your name for an excuse, and asked me if he may bring that Mr Thornton of Milton – your tenant, you know – who is in London about some law business. It will spoil my number, quite.'

'I don't mind dinner. I don't want any,' said Margaret, in a low voice. 'Dixon can get me a cup of tea here, and I will be in the drawing-room by the time you come up. I shall really be glad to lie down.'

'No, no! that will never do. You do look wretchedly white, to be sure; but that is just the heat, and we can't do without you possibly. (Those flowers a little lower, Dixon. They look glorious flames, Margaret, in your black hair.) You know we planned you to talk about Milton to Mr Colthurst. Oh! to be sure! and this man comes from Milton. I believe it will be capital, after all. Mr Colthurst can pump him well on all the subjects in which he is interested, and it will be great fun to trace out your experiences, and this Mr Thornton's wisdom, in Mr Colthurst's next speech in the House. Really, I think it is a happy hit of Henry's. I asked him if he was a man one would be ashamed of; and he replied, "Not if you've any sense in you, my little sister." So I suppose he is able to sound his h's, which is not a common Darkshire accomplishment – eh, Margaret?'

'Mr Lennox did not say why Mr Thornton was come up to town? Was it law business connected with the property?' asked Margaret, in a constrained voice.

'Oh! he's failed, or something of the kind, that Henry told you of that day you had such a headache, – what was it? (There, that's capital, Dixon. Miss Hale does us credit, does she not?) I wish I was as tall as a queen, and as brown as a gipsy, Margaret.'

'But about Mr Thornton?'

'Oh! I really have such a terrible head for law business. Henry will like nothing better than to tell you all about it. I know the impression he made upon me was, that Mr Thornton is very badly off, and a very respectable man, and that I'm to be very civil to him; and as I did not know how, I came to you to ask you to help me. And now come down with me, and rest on the sofa for a quarter of an hour.'

The privileged brother-in-law came early; and Margaret, reddening as she spoke, began to ask him the questions she wanted to hear answered about Mr Thornton.

'He came up about this sub-letting the property – Marlborough Mills, and the house and premises adjoining, I mean. He is unable to keep it on; and there are deeds and leases to be looked over, and agreements to be drawn up. I hope Edith will receive him properly; but she was rather put out, as I could see, by the liberty I had taken in begging for an invitation for him. But I thought you would like to have some attention shown him: and one would be particularly scrupulous in paying every respect to a man who is going down in the world.' He had dropped his voice to speak to Margaret, by whom he was sitting; but as he ended he sprang up, and introduced Mr Thornton, who had that moment entered, to Edith and Captain Lennox.

Margaret looked with an anxious eye at Mr Thornton while he was thus occupied. It was considerably more than a year since she had seen him; and events had occurred to change him much in that time. His fine figure yet bore him above the common height of men; and gave him a distinguished appearance, from the ease of motion which arose out of it, and was natural to him; but his face looked older and care-worn; yet a noble composure sate upon it, which impressed those who had just been hearing of his changed position, with a sense of inherent dignity and manly strength. He was aware, from the first glance he had given round the room, that Margaret was there; he had seen her intent look of occupation as she listened to Mr Henry Lennox; and he came up to her with the perfectly regulated manner of an old friend. With his first calm words a vivid colour flashed into her cheeks, which never left them again during the evening. She did not seem to have much to say to him. She disappointed him by the quiet way in which she asked what seemed to him to be the merely necessary questions respecting her old acquaintances, in Milton; but others came in – more intimate in the house than he – and he fell into the background, where he and Mr Lennox talked together from time to time.

'You think Miss Hale looking well,' said Mr Lennox, 'don't you? Milton didn't agree with her, I imagine; for when she first came to London, I thought I had never seen any one so much changed.

Tonight she is looking radiant. But she is much stronger. Last autumn she was fatigued with a walk of a couple of miles. On Friday evening we walked up to Hampstead and back. Yet on Saturday she looked as well as she does now.'

'We!' Who? They two alone?

Mr Colthurst was a very clever man, and a rising member of parliament. He had a quick eye at discerning character, and was struck by a remark which Mr Thornton made at dinner-time. He enquired from Edith who that gentleman was; and, rather to her surprise, she found, from the tone of his 'Indeed!' that Mr Thornton of Milton was not such an unknown name to him as she had imagined it would be. Her dinner was going off well. Henry was in good humour, and brought out his dry caustic wit admirably. Mr Thornton and Mr Colthurst found one or two mutual subjects of interest, which they could only touch upon then, reserving them for more private after-dinner talk. Margaret looked beautiful in the pomegranate flowers; and if she did lean back in her chair and speak but little, Edith was not annoyed, for the conversation flowed on smoothly without her. Margaret was watching Mr Thornton's face. He never looked at her; so she might study him unobserved, and note the changes which even this short time had wrought in him. Only at some unexpected mot of Mr Lennox's, his face flashed out into the old look of intense enjoyment; the merry brightness returned to his eyes, the lips just parted to suggest the brilliant smile of former days; and for an instant, his glance instinctively sought hers, as if he wanted her sympathy. But when their eyes met, his whole countenance changed; he was grave and anxious once more; and he resolutely avoided even looking near her again during dinner.

There were only two ladies besides their own party, and as these were occupied in conversation by her aunt and Edith, when they went up into the drawing-room, Margaret languidly employed herself about some work. Presently the gentlemen came up, Mr Colthurst and Mr Thornton in close conversation. Mr Lennox drew near to Margaret, and said in a low voice:

'I really think Edith owes me thanks for my contribution to her party. You've no idea what an agreeable, sensible fellow this tenant of yours is. He has been the very man to give Colthurst all the facts he wanted coaching in. I can't conceive how he contrived to mismanage his affairs.'

'With his powers and opportunities you would have succeeded,' said Margaret. He did not quite relish the tone in which she spoke, although the words but expressed a thought which had passed through his own mind. As he was silent, they caught a swell in the sound of conversation going on near the fire-place between Mr Colthurst and Mr Thornton.

'I assure you, I heard it spoken of with great interest – curiosity as to its result, perhaps I should rather say. I heard your name frequently mentioned during my short stay in the neighbourhood.' Then they lost some words; and when next they could hear Mr Thornton was speaking.

'I have not the elements for popularity – if they spoke of me in that way, they were mistaken. I fall slowly into new projects; and I find it difficult to let myself be known, even by those whom I desire to know, and with whom I would fain have no reserve. Yet, even with all these drawbacks, I felt that I was on the right path, and that, starting from a kind of friendship with one, I was becoming acquainted with many. The advantages were mutual: we were both unconsciously and consciously teaching each other.'

'You say "were." I trust you are intending to pursue the same course?'

'I must stop Colthurst,' said Henry Lennox, hastily. And by an abrupt, yet apropos question, he turned the current of the conversation, so as not to give Mr Thornton the mortification of acknowledging his want of success and consequent change of position. But as soon as the newly-started subject had come to a close, Mr Thornton resumed the conversation just where it had been interrupted, and gave Mr Colthurst the reply to his inquiry.

'I have been unsuccessful in business, and have had to give up my position as a master. I am on the look out for a situation in Milton, where I may meet with employment under some one who will be willing to let me go along my own way in such matters as these. I can depend upon myself for having no go-ahead theories that I would rashly bring into practice. My only wish is to have the opportunity of cultivating some intercourse with the hands beyond the mere "cash nexus."[1] But it might be the point Archimedes[2] sought from which to move the earth, to judge from the importance attached to it by some of our manufacturers, who shake their heads and look grave as soon as I name the one or two experiments that I should like to try.'

'You call them "experiments," I notice,' said Mr Colthurst, with a delicate increase of respect in his manner.

'Because I believe them to be such. I am not sure of the consequences that may result from them. But I am sure they ought to be tried. I have arrived at the conviction that no mere institutions, however wise, and however much thought may have been required to organize and arrange them, can attach class to class as they should be attached, unless the working out of such institutions bring the individuals of the different classes into actual personal contact. Such intercourse is the very breath of life. A working man can hardly be made to feel and know how much his employer may have laboured in his study at plans for the benefit of his workpeople. A complete plan emerges like a piece of machinery, apparently fitted for every emergency. But the hands accept it as they do machinery, without understanding the intense mental labour and forethought required to bring it to such perfection. But I would take an idea, the working out of which would necessitate personal intercourse; it might not go well at first, but at every hitch interest would be felt by an increasing number of men, and at last its success in working come to be desired by all, as all had borne a part in the formation of the plan; and even then I am sure that it would lose its vitality, cease to be living, as soon as it was no longer carried on by that sort of common interest which invariably makes people find means and ways of seeing each other, and becoming acquainted with each other's characters and persons, and even tricks of temper and modes of speech. We should understand each other better, and I'll venture to say we should like each other more.'

'And you think they may prevent the recurrence of strikes?'

'Not at all. My utmost expectation only goes so far as this – that they may render strikes not the bitter, venomous sources of hatred they have hitherto been. A more hopeful man might imagine that a closer and more genial intercourse between classes might do away with strikes. But I am not a hopeful man.'

Suddenly, as if a new idea had struck him, he crossed over to where Margaret was sitting, and began, without preface, as if he knew she had been listening to all that had passed:

'Miss Hale, I had a round-robin from some of my men – I suspect in Higgins' handwriting – stating their wish to work for me, if ever I was in a position to employ men again on my own behalf. That was good, wasn't it?'

'Yes. Just right. I am glad of it,' said Margaret, looking up straight into his face with her speaking eyes, and then dropping them

under his eloquent glance. He gazed back at her for a minute, as if
he did not know exactly what he was about. Then sighed; and
saying, 'I knew you would like it,' he turned away, and never spoke
to her again until he bid her a formal 'good night.'

As Mr Lennox took his departure, Margaret said, with a blush
that she could not repress, and with some hesitation,

'Can I speak to you tomorrow? I want your help about –
something.'

'Certainly. I will come at whatever time you name. You cannot
give me a greater pleasure than by making me of any use. At eleven?
Very well.'

His eye brightened with exultation. How she was learning to
depend upon him! It seemed as if any day now might give him the
certainty, without having which he had determined never to offer to
her again.

CHAPTER LII

'Pack Clouds Away'[1]

For joy or grief, for hope or fear,
For all hereafter, as for here,
In peace or strife, in storm or shine.

ANON

Edith went about on tip-toe, and checked Sholto in all loud speaking
that next morning, as if any sudden noise would interrupt the
conference that was taking place in the drawing-room. Two o'clock
came; and they still sate there with closed doors. Then there was a
man's footstep running down stairs; and Edith peeped out of the
drawing-room.

'Well, Henry?' said she, with a look of interrogation.

'Well!' said he, rather shortly.

'Come in to lunch!'

'No, thank you, I can't. I've lost too much time here already.'

'Then it's not all settled,' said Edith despondingly.

'No! not at all. It never will be settled, if the "it" is what I conjecture
you mean. That will never be, Edith, so give up thinking about it.'

'But it would be so nice for us all,' pleaded Edith. 'I should always feel comfortable about the children, if I had Margaret settled down near me. As it is, I am always afraid of her going off to Cadiz.'

'I will try, when I marry, to look out for a young lady who has a knowledge of the management of children. That is all I can do. Miss Hale would not have me. And I shall not ask her.'

'Then, what have you been talking about?'

'A thousand things you would not understand: investments, and leases, and value of land.'

'Oh, go away if that's all. You and she will be unbearably stupid, if you've been talking all this time about such weary things.'

'Very well. I'm coming again tomorrow, and bringing Mr Thornton with me, to have some more talk with Miss Hale.'

'Mr Thornton! What has he to do with it?'

'He is Miss Hale's tenant,' said Mr Lennox, turning away. 'And he wishes to give up his lease.'

'Oh! very well. I can't understand details, so don't give them me.'

'The only detail I want you to understand is, to let us have the back drawing-room undisturbed, as it was today. In general, the children and servants are so in and out, that I can never get any business satisfactorily explained; and the arrangements we have to make tomorrow are of importance.'

No one ever knew why Mr Lennox did not keep to his appointment on the following day. Mr Thornton came true to his time; and, after keeping him waiting for nearly an hour, Margaret came in looking very white and anxious.

She began hurriedly:

'I am so sorry Mr Lennox is not here, – he could have done it so much better than I can. He is my adviser in this –'

'I am sorry that I came, if it troubles you. Shall I go to Mr Lennox's chambers and try and find him?'

'No, thank you. I wanted to tell you, how grieved I was to find that I am to lose you as a tenant. But, Mr Lennox says, things are sure to brighten –'

'Mr Lennox knows little about it,' said Mr Thornton quietly. 'Happy and fortunate in all a man cares for, he does not understand what it is to find oneself no longer young – yet thrown back to the starting-point which requires the hopeful energy of youth – to feel one half of life gone, and nothing done – nothing remaining of wasted opportunity, but the bitter recollection that it has been. Miss

Hale, I would rather not hear Mr Lennox's opinion of my affairs. Those who are happy and successful themselves are too apt to make light of the misfortunes of others.'

'You are unjust,' said Margaret, gently. 'Mr Lennox has only spoken of the great probability which he believes there to be of your redeeming – your more than redeeming what you have lost – don't speak till I have ended – pray don't!' And collecting herself once more, she went on rapidly turning over some law papers, and statements of accounts in a trembling hurried manner. 'Oh! here it is! and – he drew me out a proposal – I wish he was here to explain it – showing that if you would take some money of mine, eighteen thousand and fifty-seven pounds, lying just at this moment unused in the bank, and bringing me in only two and a half per cent. – you could pay me much better interest, and might go on working Marlborough Mills.' Her voice had cleared itself and become more steady. Mr Thornton did not speak, and she went on looking for some paper on which were written down the proposals for security; for she was most anxious to have it all looked upon in the light of a mere business arrangement, in which the principal advantage would be on her side. While she sought for this paper, her very heart-pulse was arrested by the tone in which Mr Thornton spoke. His voice was hoarse, and trembling with tender passion, as he said: –

'Margaret!'

For an instant she looked up; and then sought to veil her luminous eyes by dropping her forehead on her hands. Again, stepping nearer, he besought her with another tremulous eager call upon her name.

'Margaret!'

Still lower went the head; more closely hidden was the face, almost resting on the table before her. He came close to her. He knelt by her side, to bring his face to a level with her ear; and whispered – panted out the words: –

'Take care. – If you do not speak – I shall claim you as my own in some strange presumptuous way. – Send me away at once, if I must go; – Margaret! –'

At that third call she turned her face, still covered with her small white hands, towards him, and laid it on his shoulder, hiding it even there; and it was too delicious to feel her soft cheek against his, for him to wish to see either deep blushes or loving eyes. He clasped her close. But they both kept silence. At length she murmured in a broken voice:

'Oh, Mr Thornton, I am not good enough!'[2]

'Not good enough! Don't mock my own deep feeling of unworthiness.'

After a minute or two, he gently disengaged her hands from her face, and laid her arms as they had once before been placed to protect him from the rioters.

'Do you remember, love?' he murmured. 'And how I requited you with my insolence the next day?'

'I remember how wrongly I spoke to you, – that is all.'

'Look here! Lift up your head. I have something to show you!' She slowly faced him, glowing with beautiful shame.

'Do you know these roses?' he said, drawing out his pocket-book, in which were treasured up some dead flowers.

'No!' she replied, with innocent curiosity. 'Did I give them to you?'

'No! Vanity; you did not. You may have worn sister roses very probably.'

She looked at them, wondering for a minute, then she smiled a little as she said –

'They are from Helstone, are they not? I know the deep indentations round the leaves. Oh! have you been there? When were you there?'

'I wanted to see the place where Margaret grew to what she is, even at the worst time of all, when I had no hope of ever calling her mine. I went there on my return from Havre.'

'You must give them to me,' she said, trying to take them out of his hand with gentle violence.

'Very well. Only you must pay me for them!'

'How shall I ever tell Aunt Shaw?' she whispered, after some time of delicious silence.

'Let me speak to her.'

'Oh, no! I owe it to her, – but what will she say?'

'I can guess. Her first exclamation will be, "That man!"'

'Hush!' said Margaret, 'or I shall try and show you your mother's indignant tones as she says, "That woman!"'

*New readers are advised that the Notes
make details of the plot explicit.*

CHAPTER I

1. ***Wooed and married and a'*** An ironic reference to a poem by Joanna Baillie (1762–1851) in which a bride laments that her husband is poor. Edith's is only very relatively so.

2. ***Titania*** Edith's 'Queen of the Fairies' prettiness contrasts with Margaret's more irregular beauty – an example of the increasing practice in nineteenth-century novels of pairing two women to the advantage of the unconventional looking one. See J. Fahnestock, 'The Heroine of Irregular Features', *Victorian Studies*, 24 (1981), 3, pp.325–40.

3. ***Corfu*** There was a garrison at Corfu, a British Protectorate from 1815 to 1864.

4. ***staid down stairs*** i.e. in the dining-room to drink – while the women gossiped in the first floor drawing-room.

5. ***Belgravia*** A rich and fashionable district, south of Knightsbridge and west of the Houses of Parliament.

6. ***laden with shawls*** The first of several instances culminating in her intervention in the strike when Margaret is on public display (see chapter III, Note 4; chapter VIII, Note 5; chapter XXII, Note 3). In an unpublished letter (1852) Gaskell describes such Indian shawls that formed part of a friend's trousseau: 'O dear, they were so soft and delicate and went into such beautiful folds' (*Biography*, pp.299–300).

7. ***are all these quite necessary troubles?*** The first sign of Margaret's scepticism over 'feminine' activities and projects thought proper to middle-class women.

8. *I am trying to describe Helstone as it really is* Lennox's remark draws attention to her over-idealized picture but he later (pp.29–30) does the same himself. She painfully revises her view on a return visit there (chapter XLVI) after her parents' death.

CHAPTER II

1. ***By the soft green light*** From 'The Spells of Home' which according to Felicia Dorothea Hemans (1793–1835) are never broken. The cliché proves untrue.

2. ***Helstone*** Taken from the name of Charlotte Brontë's heroine in *Shirley* (1849), Caroline Helstone. At first it serves as an idyllic contrast

to Milton but later is found by Margaret to have changed for the worse, or perhaps never have been as she perceived it.

3. *Figaro* As merely adoptive daughter, she is made use of by everyone, like Figaro in Rossini's opera, *The Barber of Seville*. The reference is to his complaint in 'Largo al Factotum' that everybody wants him at once.

4. *not beautiful at all* See chapter I, Note 2.

5. *shoppy people* *shoppy* – a pejorative term originating in the nineteenth century for those engaged in retail trade. In this first of many discussions of social class she relies on a conventional definition of gentleman depending on birth, property and appropriate (or no) occupation. Milton tests and changes this. See chapter IX, Note 3 and chapter XX, Note 6 for later discussions.

6. *Thomson's Seasons, Hayley's Cowper, Middleton's Cicero* James Thomson (1700–1748), *The Seasons*; William Hayley (1745–1820), *The Life of William Cowper*; Conyers Middleton (1683–1750), *The Life of Cicero*. The objection to these works is that they symbolize the absence of access to more recently published reading matter that Margaret had in her London life. Later in Milton-Northern the Hales' books are favourably compared with the Thorntons' by John Thornton himself (chapter X).

<h2>CHAPTER III</h2>

1. *Learn to win a lady's faith* From 'The Lady's Yes' by Elizabeth Barrett Browning (1806–61), a monologue contrasting a lightly won 'yes' (revoked the next day) with the one hard-won by a true lover. Lennox proposes in what he feels as a weak moment. His proposal serves as a foil to John Thornton's (chapter XXIV) which she also rejects.

2. *parler du soleil* To talk of the sun (like the devil) is to cause it to appear. Lennox's sun soon sets as Margaret's relief at a change in her life fades when he turns into a lover.

3. *Paradiso* The 'dull list of words' impresses Lennox because it shows that Margaret is really reading Dante, anticipating Thornton's lessons on the classics with her father. She thinks of herself later as a figure in the *Inferno* (see chapter XLVI, Note 9).

4. *Mr Lennox . . . introduced the two figures into his sketch* The sketch including Margaret, later shown to her father, is the second instance of her as a public spectacle (see chapter I, Note 6).

5. *'Mine be a cot' . . . and that sort of thing* Lennox's etcetera is apt. He quotes from 'A Wish' by Samuel Rogers (1763–1855), four stanzas of cliché about an idyllic country life. Lennox does not know the life and would not like it if he did.

6. *the story of the eastern king* The tale, put to telling use to express the effect of intense feeling on awareness of time, was a familiar folk motif. Also referred to in *Hard Times* (II ch. I) to indicate Mrs Sparsit's rapid power of observation. A possible source is Addison, *The Spectator*, 18 June 1711.

CHAPTER IV

1. *Cast me upon some naked shore* From 'Show me O Lord your paths', in *Castara, Third Part* by William Habington (1605–64). The poem's wish for exile rather than acceptance of sin in a familiar place relates to Hale's dilemma of conscience about keeping his Helstone living when he has religious doubts.

2. *Margaret felt guilty and ashamed* Guilt at finding herself a sexual being captures the Victorian model of the unmarried girl 'untainted' by sexual knowledge.

3. *you could not understand . . . my efforts to quench my smouldering doubts* He never fully explains these 'doubts'. A. Easson in 'Mr Hale's Doubt's' (*Review of English Studies* 31 (1980), pp.30–40) argues that they are about accepting the rigid doctrines of the Church of England embodied in the Thirty-Nine Articles – to which those who take Orders must subscribe. Gaskell herself was a Unitarian who did not accept a tripartite God, nor Christ as God, as the Articles required. This is hinted at as Hale's position. Uglow (1993) suggests that the model for Hale was J.A. Froude, whose doubts caused him to resign his fellowship at Oxford and settle for some time with his wife near Manchester (pp.228–9).

4. *the two thousand who were ejected* On St Bartholomew's Day 1662, many Anglican ministers were expelled from their livings because they could not accept everything in the Book of Common Prayer. Easson (1980) argues that similarly Hale finds the compulsion of conscience repugnant.

5. *the soliloquy . . . written by a Mr Oldfield* Hale supports his resignation by referring to John Oldfield (?1627–82), ejected from his living for rejecting Anglican doctrines. The soliloquy had been so used in 'The Apology of Theophilus Lindsey' (1774) when Lindsey left the Anglican church after a crisis of faith and became a Unitarian minister. This is presumably Gaskell's source and supports Easson's interpretation as to what Mr Hale's 'doubts' were. Dickens objected to this part of the novel as 'a difficult and dangerous subject' that should be cut (G. Storey, K. Tillotson and A. Easson, *The Letters of Charles Dickens,* vol. 7, p.356).

6. *Sodom apples* 'Dead sea fruit', something which looks fine but turns to ashes or smoke at the touch, according to Josephus, the Jewish historian (AD 37–?93).

7. *Milton-Northern* Manchester, where Gaskell lived from 1832. The

city was well established as a controversial symbol of northern industrialism. Fictions using it include Harriet Martineau's *A Manchester Strike* (1832), Elizabeth Wheeler Stone's *William Langshawe, the Cotton Lord* (1842), Gaskell's *Mary Barton* (1848). In 1844 Friedrich Engels based his German version of *The Condition of the Working Class in England* on his two-year stay there.

8. *a hundred and seventy pounds a year* The £100 that remains from this after Frederick's share may be compared with Mr Quiverful in Trollope's *The Warden* (1855), scraping a living for a wife and fourteen children on £400 per annum. Also see chapter XLIX, Note 2.

CHAPTER V

1. *I ask Thee* ... From 'Father I know that all my life' in *Hymns and Meditations* by Anna Laetitia Waring (1823–1910). It is a poem on the value of renunciation such as Margaret's here.

2. *and yet no sign of God!* Margaret's brief crisis of faith goes further than that of her father, who has no doubts on that score. This is one of the many instances when she becomes the crucible for every painful and disturbing experience in the narrative.

3. *Mr Lennox ... haunted her dreams* A rare use of the dream to reveal a disturbance of the unconscious mind. The significance of her feeling responsible for Lennox's death remains unclear. Perhaps the implication is that she knows she could have 'saved' him from a materialistic life. Mrs Hale's dreams (chapter XIV) are by contrast a transparent reliving of traumatic experience.

4. *'Church and King, and down with the Rump'* The 'loyal' toast alluding to the anti-monarchical anti-Anglican rump of the Long Parliament of 1648. Mrs Hale refers to it out of snobbish allegiance to her upper-class past, equating monarchy and church as typifying the group she belongs to.

5. *Heston* Perhaps a reshaping of the name Helstone; possibly based on the Lancashire seaside towns of Morecambe or Southport.

CHAPTER VI

1. *Unwatch'd the garden bough* ... From Tennyson's *In Memoriam* (1850), when the family leave home and countryside associated with the dead man. Anticipatory reference to the death of Margaret's parents.

2. *Temple Gardens* Lennox's real milieu, one of the Inns of Court.

3. *Margaret knew it was some poacher* Her identification with the outsider and lawbreaker looks forward to her role in Milton.

NOTES

4. Camilla   As well as being renowned for her speed, she is known (from the *Aeneid*) as a *warrior*-princess – an apt figure for the future Margaret.

5. London life is too whirling   Her London friends, unlike the friends of Job (Book of Job 2:13), would be too embarrassed to sympathize with distress.

CHAPTER VII

1. Mist clogs the sunshine   From 'Consolation' by Matthew Arnold (1822–88), which contrasts his own desolation with other scenes (even of joy) experienced simultaneously elsewhere – a recurrent idea in Gaskell (cf. chapter III, Note 6).

2. 'unparliamentary' smoke   The Town Improvement Act of 1847 decreed that every fireplace or furnace should 'consume the smoke arising from the combustibles used'. The law was often disregarded: Thornton expresses contempt for it (chapter X, Note 8) and Dickens refers to the outrage of Coketown manufacturers when 'it was hinted that they perhaps need not make quite so much smoke' (*Hard Times*, II, ch.1).

3. not quite a gentleman   Margaret still used her conventional yard-stick (see chapter II, Note 5).

CHAPTER VIII

1. And it's hame, hame, hame   From 'Hame, Hame, Hame', *Jacobite Relics* (printed in 1819) by James Hogg (1770–1835). The poem ends with a hope of return home – another ironic reference to Margaret's later disillusionment with Helstone (pp.377ff.).

2. most of the manufacturers placed their sons in sucking situations   To be suckled by industry and turned into manufacturers rather than 'gentlemen'.

3. Aristides ... the Just   An Athenian general so named for his rectitude, patriotism and moderation. Plutarch tells of an illiterate voter, who wished to vote for his exile though he did not know Aristides but was sick of hearing him called 'the Just'.

4. his courtiers shading their eyes   A story recounted by Gaskell in her *French Life* in *Works*, ed. A.W. Ward (1906), VII, p.630 (cf. chapter III, Note 2).

5. these outspoken men   Margaret is again a public figure here. See chapter I, Note 6.

6. amaranths   Everlasting flowers. Bessy's brand of religion is presented as escapist: the outcome of privation and disease. It relies almost entirely on the Book of Revelation, a fact which Margaret criticizes in chapter XVII.

430

CHAPTER IX

1. ***Let China's earth*** ... From 'The Groans of the Tankard' (1825) by Anna Letitia Barbauld (1743–1824), mildly mock heroic verses on its social downfall. A satirical dig at Mrs Hale's social pretensions.

2. ***Pythias to your Damon*** Damon, a philosopher proverbial for his friendship with Pythias, for whom he was prepared to surrender his life.

3. ***Mr Thornton's being in trade*** See chapter II, Note 5.

4. ***Matthew Henry's Bible Commentaries*** The only obvious reading matter at the Thorntons' is a non-conformist commentary on the Bible by Matthew Henry (1662–1714). A contrast is made with the Hales' books noticed by Thornton (chapter X).

CHAPTER X

1. ***We are the trees whom shaking fastens more*** From 'Affliction V' by George Herbert (1593–1633), in which God gives peace to those who trust Him in their affliction. The seriousness of the poem fits oddly with the Hales' tea party, even though it is their first attempt at a new social life.

2. ***all these graceful cares were ... of a piece with Margaret*** For the significance of this interior compared with that of the Thorntons', see Introduction, pp.ix–x.

3. ***a peculiar languid beauty ... almost feminine*** For other references to Mr Hale's femininity, see chapter XXV, Note 4; chapter XXX, Note 6; chapter XLI, Note 4; chapter L, Note 4; and Introduction, pp.x–xi.

4. ***her mother's worsted-work*** Needlework using fine coloured wool. Women's 'work', when unspecified, referred to sewing, always to hand in a middle-class house. It was already referred to in fiction as one among other domestic impositions e.g. Charlotte Brontë's *Shirley* (1849), chapter VII: 'she tried to sew – every stitch she put in was an ennui – the occupation was insufferably tedious.'

5. ***wonderful stories*** Thornton is unique among fictional manufacturers in his grandiose descriptions (echoed by his mother) of his class as merchant princes and of factories as magnificent. Such speeches are perhaps Gaskell's response to the criticism that her earlier novel *Mary Barton* took a one-sided and unfair view of employers. (See Introduction, p.viii.)

6. ***the old lines*** The lines quoted are words of defiance spoken in the 'Ballad of Chevy Chase' by King Henry on the death of Lord Percy.

7. ***in the South we have our poor, but there is not that terrible***

expression ... of a sullen sense of injustice She gives a more adverse picture of the southern poor later to Higgins when he thinks of seeking work there (chapter XXXVII).

8. *you had altered your chimneys* See chapter VII, Note 2.

9. *that rude model of Sir Richard Arkwright's* Arkwright (1732–93) patented the first mechanical spinning frame in July 1769.

10. *a working-man may raise himself into the ... position of a master* The familiar excuse of the capitalist that with self-help and self-reliance any man can rise to the top in most spheres. Famously expressed in Samuel Smiles's *Self-Help* (1859): 'Rising above the heads of the mass, there were always to be found a series of individuals distinguished beyond others' (chapter 1).

11. *I was even considered a pretty fair classic* This interest in learning facilitates Margaret's ultimate acceptance of him as a gentleman.

CHAPTER XI

1. *the land o' Beulah* The name to be given to Jerusalem when it is saved (Isaiah 62:4).

CHAPTER XII

1. *Well – I suppose we must* From *Prose Works* of Arthur Helps, author of *The Claims of Labour* (1844), in which he pressed for the kind of paternalist approach that Margaret Hale imposes on Thornton.

2. *'killed off'* Mrs Thornton's idea of social life is to repay hospitality by metaphorically 'killing off' her debt by large parties. Her perception is that the Hales belong to a lower social class than herself. The hierarchy to which the Hales see themselves belonging is not recognized in Milton. (See Introduction, pp.ix–x.)

3. *'Flimsy, useless work'* Mrs Thornton naturally judges Margaret by her 'work'. (See chapter X, Note 4.) She thinks it decorative, not useful, symptomatic of 'fine ladyism'.

4. *Tales of the Alhambra* Again the individual's reading or lack of it is to be decoded as character revealing (see chapter III, Note 3, chapter IX, Note 4, and chapter X, Note 11). *Legends of the Alhambra* (1832) by Washington Irving (1783–1859) intersperses tales of medieval Moorish Spain with anecdotes of contemporary life and architectural description.

CHAPTER XIII

1. *That doubt and trouble* ... From 'The Kingdom of God' by

Richard Chevenix Trench (1807–86). It ends with the assertion that, taking this view, life is a blessing. It may be a naïve statement about Bessy or, given the implicit criticism of her religion as escapism, a more ironic reference.

2. *the fluff . . . poisoned me*   A rare use in Gaskell of Blue Book detail to make a point. The disease *byssinosis* was first medically described in 1860.

CHAPTER XIV

1. *I was used To sleep at nights* . . .   From 'The Sailor's Mother' by Robert Southey (1774–1843). The 'little fault' in the original poem is not mutiny like Frederick's but 'wiring (snaring) hares', for which the poacher was deported and so drowned at sea.

2. *I dream of him*   cf. Margaret's dream and chapter V, Note 3. *Biography* (pp.53–4) connects this dream with Gaskell's elder sailor brother John, who was either lost at sea or disappeared after arriving in India in 1828.

3. *it is still finer to defy arbitrary power*   Some critics have related Margaret's defence of the workers to her feelings about her outcast brother. (See Introduction, pp.xi–xii.)

CHAPTER XV

1. *Thought fights with thought* . . .   From 'Epigram 23' in *The Last Fruit off an Old Tree* (1853) by Walter Savage Landor (1775–1864). A characteristically belligerent epigraph prefacing Margaret and Thornton's first discussion of class relations.

2. *Classics may do very well*   *Biography* (pp.9–10) points out that Gaskell's father wrote the forceful *Remarks on the Very Inferior Utility of Classical Learning* (1796).

3. *'the pride that apes humility'*   Possibly from 'The Devil's Thoughts' (1799) by Samuel Taylor Coleridge (1772–1834), where the devil views generic examples of sin with satisfaction. This instance illustrating pride is a 'cottage with a double coach-house', a reference to the Thorntons' lavish interior set close to the grime of the mill.

4. *Many a missy young lady*   *Missy* 'affected, prim' – Mrs Thornton discards her first illusion about Margaret.

5. *What are they going to strike for?*   The beginning of the lengthy controversy, central to the narrative, about the significance of a strike. (See Introduction, pp.xivff.) Harriet Martineau in *A Manchester Strike* (1832) had used it as a parable for the workers' folly.

6. *We see the storm on the horizon and draw in our sails . . . we*

don't explain our reason   This refusal on principle to be account-
able is offered as part of the description of entrepreneurial spirit. Cf. his
attitude to unparliamentary smoke in chapter VII, Note 2 and chapter
X, Note 8.

7. *I had better not talk to a political economist like you*   Gaskell,
in her Introduction to *Mary Barton*, disclaimed all knowledge of political
economy. A letter of 1851 (*Letters*, p.148) shows that she was *not* unin-
formed but had certainly read Adam Smith's *The Wealth of Nations*
(1776). Her father, William Stevenson, wrote articles on 'The Political
Economist' in *Blackwood's Magazine* 15–17 (1824–5). In popular forms
economic ideas had spread to most classes. See chapter XXVIII, where
Higgins speaks of an employer thrusting a book on the subject at him.

**8. *My theory is, that my interests are identical with those of my
workpeople***   Not what Engels, for example, thought. The idea was
often used by those who thought paternalism a remedy for industrial
unrest. A. Ure, in *The Philosophy of Manufacturers* (1835), claims that
British industry 'beset by the industry of rival nations … can only
maintain its place in the van of improvement by the hearty co-operation
among us of head and hand, of employers and employed' (p.363).

9. *the Platonic year*   A learned reference to the imaginary cycle in
which all heavenly bodies were supposed to pass through all possible
movements and return to their original positions. An ironic reference to
Margaret's view of class relations as Utopian.

**10. *the time is not come for the hands to have any independent
action during business hours … [but] I do not see that we have
any right to impose leading-strings upon them for the rest of
their time***   The contradiction in this argument was familiar. It is
countered by J.S. Mill's assertion that 'paternal authority' is connected at least to 'paternal care' (*Edinburgh Review* 80 (1845), p.507).

11. *he is a little ignorant of that spirit which suffereth long*   Charity (1 Cor. 13:4, 5).

12. *Rose-water [surgery]*   'Mild, gentle'; Carlyle uses the epithet to
describe a feeble revolution.

13. *Cromwell*   Uglow (1993), p.371, suggests an allusion here to Carlyle's *Oliver Cromwell's Letters and Speeches* (1845).

CHAPTER XVI

1. *the spirit of the Elder Brother*   If this is a reference to Luke
15:11ff. it means 'in a state of pique at having been ousted from a
rightful position', like the brother of the Prodigal Son.

CHAPTER XVII

1. **There are briars . . .**   Also from the poem referred to in chapter V, Note 1. It is again used to stress the value of renunciation.

2. **'Why do you strike?'**   Speaking as the South to the North, she continues the debate on the significance of the strike. See chapter XV, Note 5.

3. **none on 'em factory age**   In 1833 the minimum age for children to work in factories was fixed at nine. The Factory Act of 1844 laid down six and a half hours as the maximum working day for children under twelve.

4. **to go drink**   To get drunk. Compare John Barton's use of opium (*Mary Barton*, chapter 10). Both are unusually direct references to the few means of blotting out working-class privation. Carlyle speaks of the labourer in times of poverty as given 'to acrid unrest, recklessness, gin-drinking and gradual ruin' (*Chartism* (1839), chapter 2).

5. **the star is called Wormwood**   A burning star that falls from Heaven signalling disaster (Rev. 8:11). Margaret here criticizes Bessy's focus on the apocalyptic part of the Bible.

6. **the verses in the seventh chapter**   They refer to the white-clad elect (Rev. 7:1–17). Bessy now changes uncharacteristically to optimism.

7. **fustian-cutting**   The job of cutting the surface threads of a coarse cloth into a pile.

CHAPTER XVIII

1. **My heart revolts within me . . .**   From Schiller's *Wallenstein*, adapted into English (1800) by Samuel Taylor Coleridge (1772–1834). The speaker (2.9.11–12), Max, is divided between his love for Wallenstein's daughter and the wish of his father that he fight against Wallenstein. The divided thoughts may refer to Margaret's feeling about telling her father of Mrs Hale's illness; to Hale's refusal to take it in; to Thornton's ambivalence about Margaret; or to his mother's wish to please him, struggling with her dislike of the girl.

2. **Lyceum**   A literary institution of a type that grew up in towns in the early nineteenth century, offering a library and lectures.

3. **the Americans are getting their yarns so into the general market**   This was criticized as an example of Gaskell's ignorance by the *Leader* reviewer (14 April 1855), who claimed that American competition was 'altogether a bagatelle' (*CH*, pp.335–6). In fact Gaskell seems to be right.

4. **the old combination-laws**   These (1799–1800) forbade workers to combine for purposes such as fixing wages. They were repealed in 1824

but combination was again restricted by an Act of 1825. It generally met with disapproval whether legal or not.

CHAPTER XIX

1. *As angels in some brighter dreams* From the 'Ascension Hymn' – 'They are all gone into the world of light' by Henry Vaughan (1621–95). Bessy equates the next world's glory with what is to her Margaret's wondrous beauty.

2. *I never thought yo'd be dining with Thorntons* Like Mrs Thornton (chapter XII, Note 2), Bessy is unaware of the rank to which the Hales themselves feel they belong.

3. *Lazarus* A reference to the popular tale of the beggar and the rich man, Dives, found in contemporary ballads and in narratives, including *Mary Barton* (chapter 9). The source is Luke 16:21. See S. Smith, *The Other Nation* (1980), pp.15ff.

4. *th' great battle o' Armageddon* Again Bessy transposes her experience into terms of the Apocalypse (Rev. 16:16). Armageddon is the scene of the Day of Judgement.

5. *there must always be a waxing and waning of ... prosperity* Thornton's defence of manufacturers as caught up in a necessary 'struggle for existence' is common. This latter phrase is the title of the third chapter of Darwin's *Origin of Species* (1859). The idea provoked scorn from a few such as John Stuart Mill, who wrote: 'I confess I am not charmed with the ideal of life held out by those who think that the normal state of human beings is that of struggling to get on ... trampling, crushing, elbowing, and treading on each other's heels' (*Principles of Political Economy*, 4.6.1).

6. *isn't wise ... some one to love, and be loved by, just as good as Solomon* One of Bessy's few non-apocalyptic references. It means that, though not as wise as Solomon proverbially was (1 Kings 4:29), the poor show the love expressed in the Song of Solomon.

CHAPTER XX

1. *Old and young, boy, let 'em all eat ...* From *The Bloody Brother* (?1616), possibly by John Fletcher (1579–1625). The implication is that the Thorntons' 'feast' is vulgar and excessive.

2. *turn-out* A pejorative term for strikers.

3. *an Infirmary order* A paper giving access for the poor to hospital treatment. It had to be signed by either a Poor Law Guardian or a District Medical Officer.

4. *a weariness to the eye*   For other adverse comments on the Thorntons' ostentatious vulgarity, see the description in chapter XV.

5. *rascally set of paid delegates*   Thornton's view that trade union officials are political agitators is usual in industrial novels, e.g. H. Martineau's *A Manchester Strike* (1832), Charlotte Elizabeth Tonna's *Combination* (1844), Charles Dickens's *Hard Times* (1854).

6. *to decide on another's gentlemanliness*   This denial of any wish to define or to be a gentleman means Thornton knows that Margaret and others like her would not regard him as one. Like other rising men he wishes to substitute success and wealth for birth and property as a measure of status. For related discussions see chapter II, Note 5, and chapter IX, Note 3.

7. *Robinson Crusoe*   The castaway in Daniel Defoe's novel (1719). Significantly, Thornton chooses a hero now widely seen as a figure for the rising bourgeoisie.

8. *a saint in Patmos*   St John the Divine, who was on the Isle of Patmos in the Aegean when he saw the vision of the Apocalypse (Rev. 1: 9).

CHAPTER XXI

1. *On earth is known to none* ...   From 'The Exile' by Ebenezer Elliott, 'The Corn Law Rhymer' (1781–1849), a master founder in Sheffield who wrote simple popular poems on social injustice. See also epigraphs to chapters XXII and XLIII.

2. *like Leezie Lindsay's gown*   The ballad tells of the well-born Leezie's faithful love for a man below her in rank who turns out to be a great landowner. An anticipatory reference to Margaret and Thornton's marriage and to her changing perception of his class.

3. *he is my first olive*   Pithily put, but probably not an original comparison. See Emerson (1856): 'I found the sea life an acquired taste like that for tomatoes and olives.'

4. *a water-bed*   An early reference to a water-tight mattress partly filled with water, used for the comfort of invalids.

CHAPTER XXII

1. *But work grew scarce* ...   From 'The Death Feast' by Ebenezer Elliott. See chapter XXI, Note 1.

2. *has imported hands from Ireland*   Cheap Irish labour was a frequent resource for manufacturers faced with strikes, e.g. it is used by Robert Moore in Charlotte Brontë's *Shirley* (1849). The Irish were denigrated on all sides, even by Engels (1844): 'These Irishmen who migrate for fourpence to England ... insinuate themselves everywhere. The worst dwellings are good enough for them ... shoes they know not; their food consists of potatoes and potatoes only; whatever they earn beyond these needs they spend upon drink. What does such a race want with high wages?' (ed. V. Kiernan, *The Condition of the Working Classes in England* (1987), pp.124–5).

3. *in face of that angry sea of men* Margaret's climactic appearance as a public figure or on stage. See chapter 1, Note 6.

CHAPTER XXIII

1. *Which when his mother saw* ... From *The Faerie Queene* (4.12.21) by Edmund Spenser (?1552–99). Cymodoce is bewildered by her son Marinell's decline, which turns out to be caused by his love for the beautiful Florimell. The reference is to Mrs Thornton.

2. *'stiller than chiselled marble'* From a passage in 'A Dream of Fair Women' by Alfred Tennyson (1809–92) which describes Helen of Troy.

CHAPTER XXIV

1. *Your beauty was the first* ... The last lines of sonnet 9 in 'The Tarantula of Love' by William Fowler (1560–1612), summarizing Thornton's state of mind towards Margaret.

2. *We all feel the sanctity of our sex as a high privilege when we see danger* It was supposed unthinkable for a man to strike a middle-class woman. Consequently such acts have a powerful impact on their rare occurrences in Victorian novels (e.g. Dombey striking Florence in *Dombey and Son* (1847–8), chapter 47). Violence against working-class women is not similarly regarded (see the abuse of the brickmaker's wife in *Bleak House*, chapter 8).

CHAPTER XXV

1. *Revenge may have her own* From 'The Island' by Byron (1788–1824), a poem about the mutiny on HMS *Bounty*.

2. *To parody a line out of Fairfax's Tasso* Gaskell alters an original line from the translation (1600) of Tasso's *Gerusalemme Liberata* (1581) by Edward Fairfax: 'Her sweet idea wandred through his thought' (*Godfrey of Bulloigne or Jerusalem Delivered*, I.48.6). The beautiful image that haunts the mind of the Christian hero, Tancred, is that of a 'pagan damsell' with whom he has fallen in love. Gaskell again tries to capture the ambivalence of Margaret's feelings about Thornton by equating her with Tancred.

3. *New Heavens, and the New Earth* Bessy alludes again to Revelation (21:1), the final chapters of which predict a New Jerusalem.
4. *I durst not have done it myself* Another reference to Hale's feminine qualities. See chapter X, Note 3.

CHAPTER XXVI

1. *I have found that holy place* ... A reference to the mother's breast in 'The Bride's Farewell', from 'The Bride of the Greek Isle' by Felicia Dorothea Hemans (1793–1835).

CHAPTER XXVII

1. *For never any thing can be amiss* From Shakespeare's *Midsummer Night's Dream* (5.i.82–3), alluding to Thornton's kindness to Mrs Hale. The speaker in the play is Theseus, condescending to watch the artisans' play.
2. *the song of the miller* Oxford Dictionary of Nursery Rhymes (1962), p.308.
3. *Thornton had no general benevolence* Gaskell, in practice, found benevolence combined with the 'want of love for individuals' hard to take when she met it in Florence Nightingale. However, she convinced herself then that 'this want ... becomes a gift ... if one takes it in conjunction with the intense love for the *race*' (*Letters*, p.320).

CHAPTER XXVIII

1. *Through cross to crown!* ... From 'Via crucis, via lucis' by Ludwig Gotthard Rosegarten (1758–1818).
2. *Ay sooth, we feel too strong in weal* ... Part of the speech of the dying Onora to her mother and brother in 'The Lay of the Brown Rosary' (Fourth Part) by Elizabeth Barrett Browning (1806–61).
3. *beautiful scriptures* Rev. 14:13; Isaiah 28:12; Psalms 127:2.
4. *the gin-palace* Pejorative term for overdecorated public house.
5. *like Daniel O'Rourke* A popular folk hero. The story has been traced to R.H. Cunningham, *Amusing Prose Chapbooks* (1889, pp.150ff.). Its popular nature helps to associate Margaret and the narrator with the working class.
6. *'What shall I do to get hold on eternal life?'* A colloquial and satirical use of Matthew 19:16; Mark 10:17; and Luke 18:18.
7. *the fourteenth chapter of Job* Part of the Burial Service read at the graveside: 'Man born of woman is of few days/And full of trouble./He cometh forth as a flower and is cut down.'

8. *wages find their own level* The argument is that interference by legislation or by strikes for high wages cannot prevent the operation of economic laws which determine the prevailing wage level at a particular time.

9. *them's fined who speaks to him* In Dickens's *Hard Times* (II.14) Stephen Blackpool is ostracized in this way.

10. *'The fathers have eaten sour grapes and th' children's teeth are set on edge'* In Ezekiel 18:2 the saying is treated as an unjust proverb but Higgins accepts it as true.

CHAPTER XXIX

1. *Some wishes crossed my mind* From 'Notebook 2, Fragment 34' by Coleridge (1772–1834). Margaret's faint hopes seem to be focused on Edith and Corfu.

2. *Did not somebody burn his hand* Edith's trivializing allusion is to Thomas Cranmer, the Anglican martyr, who when burned at the stake put his hand into the flames because it had 'offended' by subscribing to the doctrines of Roman Catholicism (*Acts and Monuments* of John Foxe, martyrologist, first published in English in 1563).

3. *the Peace Society* A Christian society against war and violence founded in England (1816–1915). It wished to settle disputes by arbitration and published many tracts. Edith sees it merely as opposed to her husband's profession of soldiering.

4. *Cosmo* Later confusingly called Sholto in chapters XLII and XLVIII.

5. *descended from King Herod* A descendant of the man responsible for the Massacre of the Innocents (Matthew 2:16).

6. *I will put my arm in the bolt* To keep the door shut. A reference to the story of Catherine Douglas, who did this to try to prevent the assassination of James I (1394–1437).

7. *don't get to use these horrid Milton words* Margaret's defence of dialect aligns her firmly with the working class. She goes further later by claiming that such words are 'expressive'. (See Introduction, p.xiii.)

8. *Edith picked up all sorts of military slang* A deliberately provocative suggestion that posh, officers' slang can be equated with working-class dialect speech.

9. *I was very vulgar in the Forest* She implies that she used dialect words in Helstone but there is no evidence in the text that she did. Her espousing of such language starts in Milton.

CHAPTER XXX

1. *The saddest birds* ... From 'Tymes Goe By Turnes' by the Jesuit Robert Southwell (?1561–95), which suggests that sad times are designed by God to temper man.

2. *Never to fold the robe o'er secret pain* From 'The Two Voices' by Felicia Dorothea Hemans (1793–1835). One voice has the refrain 'Thou art gone hence', the other (speaking here) has 'Thou art gone home'.

3. *if I die – will you –* In December 1841 Gaskell made a similar request to her husband's sister, 'in case of my death ... would you promise, dearest Anne, to remember [Marianne's] peculiarity of character, and ... watch over her and cherish her' (*Letters*, p.46).

4. *to act the part of a Roman daughter* A reference to a familiar figure in Victorian art of the adult daughter who suckled her father in prison to save his life. She was usually called Roman Charity. Byron used the figure in 'Childe Harold's Pilgrimage' (1812–18), and Dickens in chapter 19 of *Little Dorrit* (1855–7).

5. *Poeta nascitur* ... A poet is born not made.

6. *like that of some mother-animal* Another reference to Mr Hale's feminine characteristics. See chapter X, Note 3.

7. *that chapter of unspeakable consolation* John 14, in which Christ comforts his disciples with the hope of heaven.

CHAPTER XXXI

1. *Show not that manner* ... From 'The Borough', Letter 14, by George Crabbe (1754–1832). Presumably a reference to the treacherous Leonards, though the poem is about a wealthy heir who goes to the bad.

2. *Frederick himself was Roman Catholic* A shocking thing for an Englishman at this date, though Margaret takes it mildly. The Catholic Emancipation Act was passed only in 1829.

CHAPTER XXXII

1. *'What! remain to be Denounced ...'* From the poetic drama *Werner* (1823) by Byron. It comes from a speech in which Ulric disowns his dishonoured father, Werner, whom he has hitherto attempted to protect. Its context is ignored by Gaskell, who is simply alluding to Frederick's danger.

2. *by some sleight of wrestling* Here Frederick does appear to cause the fatal fall though he is later presented as not guilty.

CHAPTER XXXIII

1. *Sleep on, my love* . . .   From 'An Exequy to his Matchless never to be forgotten Friend', written for his dead wife in 1624 by Henry King (1592–1669). Mr Hale, unlike King, does soon overtake his wife by dying.

2. *women do not generally go*   After Prince Albert died on 14 December 1861, the grieving Victoria left Windsor for Osborne on 18 December and Albert was buried later in her absence (see *Annual Register*, vol.103, pp.61ff.). Margaret's comment presumably vindicates the reason for such absences.

3. *It took a great moral effort to galvanize his trust*   Thornton's inability to believe any longer in her 'pure and exquisite maidenliness' because he has seen her at night on a railway station with a man indicates the Victorian honour culture for women where public reputation is definitive. To seem to lose honour is to do so. Compare Henry Knight's attitude to Elfride in Hardy's *A Pair of Blue Eyes* (1873).

4. *in the Charybdis of passion*   In Greek legend one of two whirlpools in the straits of Messina. The thought is presumably Thornton's own, gleaned from his classical reading: Homer pictured Charybdis as a female monster who sucked in sea water and spewed it out three times daily.

CHAPTER XXXIV

1. *Truth will fail thee never* . . .   From now on Margaret's guilt about publicly flinging herself on Thornton to shield him from the strikers is displaced into the lie she tells to protect her brother. Her guilt is quite disproportionate to the lie. (See Introduction, p.xix.)

2. *The Sunday post*   i.e. the absence of post on the Sabbath.

3. *'Cornish trick'*   Cornishmen were famous wrestlers and this is an allusion to a particular hold.

CHAPTER XXXV

1. *'E par che . . . sospira!'*   And through the expression of her face / A sweet spirit full of love / Speaks directly to the soul – 'sigh!' (Dante's *La Vita Nuova*, Sonnet 26).

2. *she had been as 'a dog, and done this thing'*   This occurs in 2 Kings 8:13. Hazael, in response to a prophecy that he will kill his master, asks: 'Is thy servant a dog that he should do this great thing?' but he does kill him. So the quotation suggests that rightly she feels the guilt of a murderer.

3. ***There will be no inquest*** As a magistrate, Thornton can make this decision, though it is clearly not impartial.

4. ***It seems strange*** *Dolores* is a Spanish word for 'sorrow'.

CHAPTER XXXVI

1. ***The steps of the bearers*** ... From 'The Sensitive Plant' (1820) by Shelley (1792–1822), when the plant hears the approach of the Lady's coffin.

CHAPTER XXXVII

1. ***A spade! ... school*** From 'The Lay of the Labourer' by Thomas Hood (1799–1845), which is about his desire to earn a living.

2. ***redding up*** Tidying up. Margaret uses the dialect word. See chapter XXIX, Note 7.

3. ***butcher's meat once a day*** Engels (1844) describes textile workers, in good times, eating 'meat and bacon daily ... Where wages are less, meat is used only two or three times a week' (ed. V. Kiernan, *The Condition of the Working Classes in England* (1987), p.107).

4. ***They labour on*** A different picture of the south from the idyllic one presented earlier. See chapter I, Note 8.

5. ***th' world is in a confusion*** cf. Blackpool's catchphrase in Dickens's *Hard Times* (1854) 'it's aw a muddle'.

CHAPTER XXXVIII

1. ***put out of his place by a Paddy*** Paddy from Patrick – 'Irishman'. Higgins shares the prejudice against the Irish. See chapter XXII, Note 2.

CHAPTER XXXIX

1. ***Nay, I have done*** ... From the sonnet 'Since there's no help, come let us kiss and part' by Michael Drayton (1563–1731), which ends unexpectedly with a plea for reconciliation, evidently anticipating the novel's end.

2. ***I am weary*** She rejects the Victorian ideal of feminine self-abnegation. See also her relief at her father's departure for Oxford in chapter XLI.

CHAPTER XL

1. ***I have no wrong*** ... 'Th'answere that ye made to me my dere' by

Thomas Wyatt (?1503–42); the answer from the woman is 'no', like Margaret's to Thornton.

2. *the Una from the Duessa*   True from false. These two characters in Book 1 of *The Faerie Queene* by Edmund Spenser (1552–99) look alike but the first represents true religion, the second Roman Catholicism.

3. *the Kilkenny cat's tail*   A cat reputed to fight until only claws and tail were left.

4. *I wonder when you Milton men intend to live*   Another ambiguous contrast between the North and the South (here Oxford, represented by Mr Bell, elsewhere Helstone or Harley Street).

5. *a different race from the Greeks*   Thornton meets Bell on his own (classical) ground.

6. *Heptarchy*   The decentralized government represented by the seven kingdoms of Anglo-Saxon England.

7. *Thor*   The Norse god of thunder, a symbol here of Milton's retrogressiveness. His weapon (appropriately) was a hammer.

8. *in the midst of 'her rocking it, and rating it'*   From 'In going to my naked bed' by Richard Edwards (1523–66), published in *The Paradise of Dainty Devices* (1576). Its refrain is 'The fallyng out of faithful friendes is the renuying of love.' Maternal love as a mixture of anger and tenderness is an unfamiliar one in a Victorian novel.

9. *the Arabian Nights*   In these tales Prince Caralmazan of the Isles and Princess Badoura of China are brought together by the genii, separated by them and finally reunited. Bell promises to act as benign magician to Margaret and Thornton.

10. *Pearl*   An affectionate translation of Margaret's christian name.

CHAPTER XLI

1. *I see my way ... good time!*   From *Paracelsus* Part I (1835) by Robert Browning (1812–89). The epigraph evidently refers to Mr Hale's imminent death.

2. *his renunciation of England*   Frederick is on a parallel course to his sister in moving away radically from his origins. He detaches himself from his country and religion; she to a large extent from the values of her class.

3. *Je ne voudrois ...*   'I would not wish to rebuke my heart in this way: "die of shame, insolent creature as you are treacherous and disloyal to your God" – and similar things; but I would like to correct it by means of compassion saying "Come then, my poor heart, we have fallen into a pit which we had resolved to escape. Ah! let us rise up and leave it forever, calling on the mercy of God and hoping that it well help us in future to be more resolute; and let us find again the path of humility.

Courage – let us henceforth be watchful with God's help"' (*Introduction à la vie dévote* (1608) III.9 by St Francis de Sales (1567–1622).

4. *which they would have shown to a woman* Another reference to Hale's femininity. See chapter X, Note 3.

5. *the angel with the grave and composed face* The angel of death, a decorative alternative to 'the grim reaper' which is found on Victorian tombs.

6. *the Odenwald* A wooded mountain area in Germany. From 1841 onwards, and particularly after 1853, Gaskell made trips to Germany.

CHAPTER XLII

1. *When some beloved voice* ... From the sonnet 'Substitution' by Elizabeth Barrett Browning (1806–61). She answers her own question by saying that Christ will 'fill this pause'. Gaskell chooses to leave this out.

2. *vis inertiae* Indolence. Gaskell wrote to a friend in 1831: 'I am writing near a window where puffs of wind come through ... you will ask why I don't move – I suppose it is my vis inertia (*sic*), and my being in a most comfortable armchair' (*Biography*, p.3).

3. *Sholto* Alias Cosmo, see chapter XXIX, Note 4.

4. *as the sparrow falls to the ground* Proverbially, the death of a sparrow goes unnoticed.

CHAPTER XLIII

1. *The meanest thing* ... From 'The Village Patriarch' by Ebenezer Elliott (see chapter XXI, Note 1). The next line, 'And long-neglected worth seems born anew', clearly refers to Margaret's perception of Milton.

2. *wet clothes ... stretched from house to house* Engels described this in the Manchester slums: 'the streets serve as drying grounds in fine weather; lines are stretched across from house to house, and hung with wet clothing' (ed. V. Kiernan, *The Condition of the Working Classes in England* (1987), p.71).

CHAPTER XLIV

1. *A dull rotation* ... From 'Hope' by William Cowper (1731–1800), a poem asserting that this virtue is the remedy for all kinds of sloth and despair. The quotation refers to Margaret's new distaste for the 'eventless' life of Harley Street.

2. *Of what each one should be* ... From 'Strung Pearls' in 'Pantheon' Part Five by Friedrich Rückert (1781–1866). Perhaps to be read as a comment on the Cowper lines above, indicating the necessity of struggling to achieve some virtuous end in order not to find life pointless.

3. poor darling!   The two following paragraphs were erroneously repeated in the first volume edition at a point in chapter XLVII. See Note 2 to that chapter.

4. the latent Vashti in ...   Margaret has a strangely modern reaction to Lennox treating his wife as a status symbol. Vashti (Esther 1) was the wife of King Ahasuerus who refused to come to his feast because he commanded her through chamberlains. She was in this period the symbol for a strong-minded woman. Charlotte Brontë, for instance, gives this name to the famous actress Rachel in *Villette* (1853), chapter 23.

5. Mordecai   The reference is to Mordecai (Esther 3) refusing to bow and reverence Haman, the favourite of King Ahasuerus, who then threatened to kill all Mordecai's race. Edith is here the favourite to Bell's Mordecai – an unflattering comparison.

CHAPTER XLV

1. Where are the sounds ...   From Epigram 24 in 'The Last Fruit off an Old Tree' by W.S. Landor (1775–1864). Only the last line is omitted: 'I see one imaged on the Leam.'

CHAPTER XLVI

This and chapter XLVII are not in *Household Words* but new in the book edition. Together they cover the visit to Helstone by Mr Bell and Margaret, expanding as Gaskell evidently originally intended on Margaret's reconsideration of her early life.

1. So on those happy days of yore ...   From 'On Crossing the Stream' by Johann Ludwig Uhland (1787–1862). Margaret is bound to the dead as Gaskell felt bound to her dead children: the German stanza from this same poem prefixed to *Mary Barton* (1848) asks for the speaker to be ferried to the land of the dead to join two others (see *Biography*, pp.154–5).

2. Herman and Dorothea   The title of a poem by Goethe about exiles from the French Revolution in Germany.

3. Evangeline   A sentimental narrative poem by Henry Longfellow (1807–82), set in the virgin forests of Nova Scotia where the outcast Evangeline searches for her lover Gabriel. She finds him only on his deathbed.

4. 'the days that are no more'   The refrain from 'Tears, Idle Tears' in 'The Princess' by Alfred Tennyson (1809–92).

5. for simple Susan's sake   Joking reference to the young village heroine of a children's story, who through her honesty, endurance and simplicity survives the machinations of an evil lawyer and his cronies (Maria Edgeworth, *The Parent's Assistant or Stories for Children in Six Volumes* (London, 1800), I, pp.43–207).

6. she'd burnt it This reveals that the apparently idyllic Helstone is a place of primitive superstition and cruelty. The practice originated in pagan sacrifices of human beings and animals. The burning of cats in particular, to bring good luck, survived into the seventeenth century in Paris on Midsummer (or St John's) Day. See J. Goudsblom, *Fire and Civilization* (Penguin, 1992, p.133).

7. 'To turn and look back' From 'A Place in Thy Memory, Dearest' by Gerald Griffin (1803–40). Such a place is all the speaker asks from his beloved, of whom he is unworthy.

8. From everlasting to everlasting Psalms 90:2.

9. the circle in which the victims of earthly passion eddy The circle in Dante's *Inferno* where illicit lovers are tossed in an incessant whirlwind (canto 5). A telling allusion, since it makes clear the sexual nature of her feelings of guilt which she attributes to her lie about not being at the railway station with her brother on the night of Leonards's death (chapter XXXIV).

CHAPTER XLVII

This chapter, like the previous one, is new in the volume edition and not found in *Household Words*.

1. Experience, like a pale musician From the sonnet 'Perplexed Music' by Elizabeth Barrett Browning (1806–61).

2. pall upon her At this point the second volume edition (on which this text is based) leaves out the two paragraphs repeated from chapter XLIV in the first volume edition. See Note 3 to that chapter.

CHAPTER XLVIII

1. Give me children The childless Rachel's words to Jacob when her sister Leah bore sons (Genesis 30:1). Gaskell herself lost three children: a stillborn daughter and two infant sons.

2. today lying dead or dying The suddenness of Bell's death was imposed on Gaskell by the constraints of serializing in *Household Words*. She wrote to Anna Jameson that 'at last the story is huddled and hurried up; especially in the rapidity with which the sudden death of Mr Bell, succeeds to the sudden death of Mr Hale. But what could I do? Every page was grudged me' (*Letters*, p.328).

3. But when night came From here to the end of the chapter is an addition to the second volume edition, further developing the emphasis in the changes in Margaret's feelings introduced into the first volume edition by adding chapters XLVI and XLVII.

CHAPTER XLIX

1. *And down the sunny beach* ...   From 'Hero and Leander' by Thomas Hood (1799–1845). It describes Hero after her lover Leander has drowned in the Hellespont: not quite apt for Margaret.

2. *two hundred and fifty pounds a year*   Compare this with £170 per annum which the Hales had to live on in Milton (see chapter IV, Note 8).

3. *her Zenobia ways*   Queen of Palmyra, soldier and autocrat. Presumably these are 'autocratic manners'.

4. *the making of a Cleopatra in her*   The Egyptian queen, seen as a type of voluptuary and seductress.

5. *that most difficult problem for women*   A central issue of this text and others like Charlotte Brontë's *Shirley* (1849). Gaskell wrote in a letter to Eliza Fox: 'that discovery of one's exact work in the world is the puzzle ... I am sometimes coward enough to wish that we were back in the darkness where obedience was the only seen duty of women' (*Letters*, p.109).

6. *a strong-minded woman*   Usually a disapproving term for a woman of advanced ideas about her role in life. See Bradden (1862): 'I don't want a strong-minded woman, who wears green spectacles and writes books.'

CHAPTER L

1. *Here we go, up, up* ...   An ironic nursery-rhyme reference to industrial competition from 'Hey, my kitten', *Oxford Dictionary of Nursery Rhymes* (1962), p.255.

2. *Her merchants be like princes*   If this refers to the merchants of Tyre whom the Lord decided to overthrow (Isaiah 23:8), Mrs Thornton is ignoring its import.

3. *'we have all of us one human heart'*   Paternalism such as Gaskell advocates has various roots as well as simplistic Christianity. They include the romantic poets who were violently opposed to the theories of political economists. Hence the reference to a part of 'The Old Cumberland Beggar' (line 153) by William Wordsworth (1770–1850), which urges communal kindness.

4. *his woman's heart*   A final posthumous reference to Hale's femininity. See chapter X, Note 3.

CHAPTER LI

1. *'cash nexus'* A frequently used phrase meaning 'the financial relationship', usually attributed to Carlyle, who spoke of it as Thornton does here: 'For, in one word, *Cash Payment* had not then grown to be the universal sole nexus of man to man' (*Chartism* (1839), chapter 6).

2. *the point Archimedes sought* In explaining the principle of the lever, Archimedes (287–212 BC) is supposed to have said, 'Give me where to stand and I will move the earth.'

CHAPTER LII

1. *Pack Clouds Away* From a morning song in 'The Rape of Lucrece' by Thomas Heywood (?1574–1641).

2. *I am not good enough* In the letter complaining of Dickens's restrictions on the 'quantity' she wrote for serialization, Gaskell indicates that this episode was curtailed though she adds, 'I am not sure if, when the barrier gives way between 2 such characters as Mr Thornton and Margaret it would not all go smash in a moment, – and I don't feel quite certain that I dislike the end as it now stands' (*Letters*, p.329).

GLOSSARY

Abbreviations

adj.	adjective	vb.	verb
neg.	negative	advb.	adverb
pa.t.	past tense	pr.p.	present participle
p.p.	past participle	pron.	pronoun
sb.	substantive	sb.pl.	substantive plural

ax, vb.	to ask	**dree**, adj.	wretched, hateful, cheerless
babby, sb.	baby		
bate, vb.	to reduce		
blench, vb.	to blanch, wince	**dunna**, vb.imp. + neg.	do not
bolus, sb.	pill (metaph.)		
brass, sb.	money	**dunno**, vb. + neg.	I do not know
brossen, p.p.	broken		
butty, sb.	slice of bread and butter	**dunnot**, vb. + neg.	do not
		dwam, sb.	faint, swoon
bug-a-boo, sb.	bogyman	**exoteric**, sb.	the uninitiated
childer, sb.pl.	children	**farred**, p.p.	*be farred*, be damned
clem, vb.	to starve		
cotched, pa.t.	caught		
cranching, adj.	crunching	**fettling**, sb.	putting in order
cranky, adj.	ill	**four-pounder**, sb.	four pound loaf
craddy, sb.	puzzle, mystery		
dang, vb.	to beat, overcome violently	**gait**, sb.	way
		gradely, adj.	fine, pleasing, handsome
dazed, pa.t.	stupefied, benumbed		
		his'n, pron.	his
		hissel', pron.	himself
deave, vb.	to deafen, bother	**hoo**, pron.	she
deaved, p.p.	deafened	**hou'd**, vb.	to hold
din, vb.	to deafen	**ill redd-up**, adj.	untidy, slovenly
doesna, vb. + neg.	does not	**knobstick**, sb.	strikebreaker, blackleg
dree, vb.	to suffer, endure	**larn**, vb.	to teach

450

liefer, advb. — rather
likely, adj. — capable
lile, adj. — little
lurry, sb. — four-wheeled wagon

main, advb. — very
m'appen, advb. — perhaps
methodie, sb. — Methodist
mithering, pr.p. — bothersome, worrying
moil, vb. — to toil
moped, p.p. — dejected
mun, vb. — must
nesh, adj. — squeamish, over-sensitive; feeble

nobbut, advb. — nothing but, only
nout, sb. — nothing
oss, vb. — to offer
oud, adj. — old
ourn, pron. — ours
peach, vb. — to inform
pottered, p.p. — disturbed, confused

purr, vb. — to kick
purring, sb. — kicking
rating, pr.p. — chiding, rebuking
redding up, sb. — tidying up, putting in order

redd-up, vb. — to tidy up, put in order
rough-stoning, sb. — scouring with a rubbing stone
rucks, sb.pl. — heaps
seed, pa.t. — saw
slack, adj. in phrase *slack of work*: — short of work

swound, vb. — to faint
thatens, advb. — in that way
tugged, vb. in phrase *tugged at*: — tussled with
turn-out, sb. — (1) striker, (2) a strike
turn-out, vb. — to go on strike
wait, vb. in phrase *wait him*: — wait for him
waur, adj. — worse
welly, advb. — almost
whatten, pron. — what
whist, vb. — to hush
whoam, sb. — home
wunnot, vb. + neg. — will not
yo, pron. — you
yourn, pron. — yours

PENGUIN ⟨🐧⟩ CLASSICS

The Classics Publisher

'Penguin Classics, one of the world's greatest series' JOHN KEEGAN

'I have never been disappointed with the Penguin Classics. All I have read is a model of academic seriousness and provides the essential information to fully enjoy the master works that appear in its catalogue' MARIO VARGAS LLOSA

'Penguin and Classics are words that go together like horse and carriage or Mercedes and Benz. When I was a university teacher I always prescribed Penguin editions of classic novels for my courses: they have the best introductions, the most reliable notes, and the most carefully edited texts' DAVID LODGE

'Growing up in Bombay, expensive hardback books were beyond my means, but I could indulge my passion for reading at the roadside bookstalls that were well stocked with all the Penguin paperbacks ... Sometimes I would choose a book just because I was attracted by the cover, but so reliable was the Penguin imprimatur that I was never once disappointed by the contents.

   Such access certainly broadened the scope of my reading, and perhaps it's no coincidence that so many Merchant Ivory films have been adapted from great novels, or that those novels are published by Penguin' ISMAIL MERCHANT

'You can't write, read, or live fully in the present without knowing the literature of the past. Penguin Classics opens the door to a treasure house of pure pleasure, books that have never been bettered, which are read again and again with increased delight' JOHN MORTIMER

CLICK ON A CLASSIC

www.penguinclassics.com

The world's greatest literature at your fingertips

Constantly updated information on over 1600 titles, from Icelandic sagas to ancient Indian epics, Russian drama to Italian romance, American greats to African masterpieces

•

The latest news on recent additions to the list, updated editions and specially commissioned translations

•

Original scholarly essays by leading writers: Elaine Showalter on Zola, Laurie R. King on Arthur Conan Doyle, Frank Kermode on Shakespeare, Lisa Appignanesi on Tolstoy

•

A wealth of background material, including biographies of every classic author from Aristotle to Zamyatin, plot synopses, readers' and teachers' guides, useful web links

•

Online desk and examination copy assistance for academics

•

Trivia quizzes, competitions, giveaways, news on forthcoming screen adaptations

•

eBooks available to download

READ MORE IN PENGUIN

In every corner of the world, on every subject under the sun, Penguin represents quality and variety – the very best in publishing today.

For complete information about books available from Penguin – including Puffins and Penguin Classics – and how to order them, write to us at the appropriate address below. Please note that for copyright reasons the selection of books varies from country to country.

In the United Kingdom: *Please write to* Dept EP, Penguin Books Ltd, Bath Road, Harmondsworth, West Drayton, Middlesex UB7 0DA

In the United States: *Please write to* Consumer Services, Penguin Putnam Inc., 405 Murray Hill Parkway, East Rutherford, New Jersey 07073-2136. *VISA and MasterCard holders call 1-800-631-8571 to order Penguin titles*

In Canada: *Please write to* Penguin Books Canada Ltd, 10 Alcorn Avenue, Suite 300, Toronto, Ontario M4V 3B2

In Australia: *Please write to* Penguin Books Australia Ltd, 487 Maroondah Highway, Ringwood, Victoria 3134

In New Zealand: *Please write to* Penguin Books (NZ) Ltd, Private Bag 102902, North Shore Mail Centre, Auckland 10

In India: *Please write to* Penguin Books India Pvt Ltd, 11, Community Centre, Panchsheel Park, New Delhi 110017

In the Netherlands: *Please write to* Penguin Books Netherlands bv, Postbus 3507, NL-1001 AH Amsterdam

In Germany: *Please write to* Penguin Books Deutschland GmbH, Metzlerstrasse 26, 60594 Frankfurt am Main

In Spain: *Please write to* Penguin Books S. A., Bravo Murillo 19, 1°B, 28015 Madrid

In Italy: *Please write to* Penguin Italia s.r.l., Via Vittoria Emanuele 451a, 20094 Corsico, Milano

In France: *Please write to* Penguin France, 12, Rue Prosper Ferradou, 31700 Blagnac

In Japan: *Please write to* Penguin Books Japan Ltd, Iidabashi KM-Bldg, 2-23-9 Koraku, Bunkyo-Ku, Tokyo 112-0004

In South Africa: *Please write to* Penguin Books South Africa (Pty) Ltd, P.O. Box 751093, Gardenview, 2047 Johannesburg

GEORGE ELIOT
Middlemarch

'People are almost always better than their neighbours think they are'

George Eliot's most ambitious novel is a masterly evocation of diverse lives and changing fortunes in a provincial community. Peopling its landscape are Dorothea Brooke, a young idealist whose search for intellectual fulfilment leads her into a disastrous marriage to the pedantic scholar Casaubon; the charming but tactless Dr Lydgate, whose pioneering medical methods, combined with an imprudent marriage to the spendthrift beauty Rosamond, threaten to undermine his career; and the religious hypocrite Bulstrode, hiding scandalous crimes from his past. As their stories entwine, George Eliot creates a richly nuanced and moving drama, hailed by Virginia Woolf as 'one of the few English novels written for grown-up people'.

This edition uses the text of the second edition of 1874. In her introduction, Rosemary Ashton, biographer of George Eliot, discusses themes of change in *Middlemarch*, and examines the novel as an imaginative embodiment of Eliot's humanist beliefs.

'The most profound, wise and absorbing of English novels ... and, above all, truthful and forgiving about human behaviour'
HERMIONE LEE

Edited with an introduction and notes by ROSEMARY ASHTON

GEORGE ELIOT
Silas Marner

*'God gave her to me because you turned your
back upon her, and He looks upon her as mine:
you've no right to her!'*

Wrongly accused of theft and exiled from a religious community many years before, the embittered weaver Silas Marner
lives alone in Raveloe, living only for work and his precious
hoard of money. But when his money is stolen and an orphaned
child finds her way into his house, Silas is given the chance to
transform his life. His fate, and that of the little girl he adopts,
is entwined with Godfrey Cass, son of the village Squire, who,
like Silas, is trapped by his past. *Silas Marner*, George Eliot's
favourite of her novels, combines humour, rich symbolism
and pointed social criticism to create an unsentimental but
affectionate portrait of rural life.

The text uses the Cabinet edition, revised by George Eliot in
1878. David Carroll's introduction is accompanied by the
original Penguin Classics introduction by Q. D. Leavis.

Edited with an introduction by DAVID CARROLL

ANTHONY TROLLOPE
Phineas Redux

*'He had given up everything in the world
with the view of getting into office; and now
that the opportunity had come . . . the prize
was to elude his grasp!'*

Phineas Finn is living quietly in Dublin, resigned to the fact that
his political career is over and coming to terms with the death
of his wife, when he receives an unexpected invitation to return
to Parliament. He jumps at the chance and old romances
and rivalries are revived. When his adversary Mr Bonteen is
murdered suspicion immediately falls on Finn, and even the
friends and lovers who formerly advanced him seem only to add
to his shame. The fourth novel in the Palliser series, *Phineas
Redux* stands alone as a compelling work of political intrigue,
personal crisis and romantic jealousy.

In his introduction, Gregg A. Hecimovich relates the political
and historical background of the time to the Phineas novels.
This edition also contains a detailed chronology, further reading and notes.

**'We have come to believe that his style of writing was certainly
the best (and probably the only) way of constructing a political
novel' ROY HATTERSLEY,** *Guardian*

Edited with an introduction and notes by
GREGG A. HECIMOVICH